THE TRIUMPH OF THE DWARVES

MARKUS HEITZ

Translated by Sheelagh Alabaster

Jo Fletcher
BOOKS

First published in English in Great Britain in 2018 by

Jo Fletcher Books
an imprint of
Quercus Editions Ltd
Carmelite House
50 Victoria Embankment
London EC4Y 0DZ

An Hachette UK company

A CIP catalogue record for this book is available from the British Library.

PB ISBN 978 1 78429 440 3
EBOOK ISBN 978 1 78429 439 7

10 9 8 7 6 5 4 3 2 1

Typeset by Jouve (UK), Milton Keynes

Printed and bound in Great Britain by Clays Ltd, St Ives plc

Dedicated to those patient souls
who hoped for more about the Dwarves.
The wait was not in vain.

'There are dwarves who seriously believe that the mountain barrier surrounding Girdlegard can be breached. In truth, I say, it is more likely that all the gates fall to beast attack than that a path through the mountain peaks be discovered.'

An anonymous dwarf

'Gold! What use is gold?

I strive for knowledge. With knowledge I can do anything. Gold makes only for envy.'

Kentaira the Invincible, former famula of Coïra

'Vraccas may have created us but what father gives more to one of his children than to the other four? Now you might say, "Can't you see? Vraccas gave you the gift of being the best warriors." But I would answer, "It was not his gift. We earned it."'

Rognor Mortalblow, Thirdling Chancellor

'I had a son. I thought of him, too, in Phondrasôn. I shall begin my search for him as soon as I can. After all those endless cycles where my mind was confused, I need certainty. I need certainty about so many things.'

Tungdil Goldhand

Prologue

Girdlegard
Elf realm of Ti Lesinteïl
(formerly the älfar realm of Dsôn Bhará)
6492nd solar cycle, early summer

Raikan Fieldwood reined in his horse at the edge of the barely perceptible old crater; this was where the realm of the hated älfar Triplets had been based. His escorts, two men and two women, rode up to him, fanning out to the right and left of Tabaîn's crown prince. Still in the saddle, all of them in rich clothing and light cloaks, the five surveyed the scene in amazement. They would never have believed such a transformation possible.

'Good thing I'm not a betting man.' Dark-haired and tall, Raikan was widely expected to take over as regent when his sickly, older brother Natenian gave up the throne as envisaged. Thus it fell to him to conduct negotiations with the elves who had settled here after their liberation from the älfar.

'I'd have lost that wager, too,' said his friend Tenkil Hoge, shielding his eyes and brushing strands of dark hair aside as he studied the scene. The warrior's chainmail had more than the usual number of metal rings to accommodate his powerful build. He had not wanted to leave his armour behind and had more weapons on his belt than the others, despite the fact this was supposed to be a peaceful neighbourly visit. 'How on earth . . . ?'

Lilia, Ketrin and Irtan gazed on, still speechless with astonishment.

*

Raikan thought back to the previous autumn, winter and spring, and the heroic deeds, deaths and victories recent orbits had brought.

Wave after wave of warriors had set out to destroy the Dsôn Aklán and the last of the black-eyes in Girdlegard's northern region. In the end their courageous fighters had won – but the losses had been horrific.

Afterwards they had begun to demolish the älfar buildings, to tear down the palace mount and to fill in the hole; the elf Ilahín and his wife Fiëa had overseen the works. Now, one sun cycle after the end of Lot-Ionan, the älfar, the dragon Lohasbrand, his orcs and the kordrion, Girdlegard was settling into peace. The human monarchs had been restored to power and chaos had given way to the rule of law.

Although there were still a few princelings and upstarts in the kingdom who needed seeing to, Raikan considered Tabaîn, the granary of the northwest, well on its way to establishing peace and prosperity. Together with his brother, he had been preparing for the planned abdication when Ilahín and Fiëa had invited them to Ti Lesinteïl.

To come to the *court*.

Raikan had not been aware that the elves, so few in number, had already chosen a king, or that enough of them had arrived to constitute a court. 'Let's go over and take a closer look at this marvel.'

The little group turned their horses to take the gentle slope of the broad highway.

You could only guess how deep the crater had previously been if you knew the old stories; this was where the northern älfar had ruled from. By filling in the crater, the elves had now managed to turn the place into a circular dip in the landscape, a good mile wide, but in Raikan's eyes the real miracle was the flourishing woodland.

The forest treetops formed a rich green, waving sea of foliage into which he and his companions plunged. They seemed to sink to an ocean floor as they rode between trees that were more than a hundred paces tall.

Raikan was enchanted by the interplay of light and shade, the various hues of leaf, bark and bud. The air smelled like honey, exotic spices and incense. His senses were aroused and entranced.

'I have never seen trees with blossom like this,' said Tenkil, sounding suspicious. 'Or ones that grow that fast.'

'I can't object – they hide the horror that lay beneath it all.' Raikan started to feel very positive about their coming visit to the elf court. He was sure he would return to Tabaîn with extremely advantageous agreements.

Secretly he was quite ready to make pacts with all three elf realms. It would put Tabaîn ahead of Gauragar and Idoslane.

It was true that a new era was being launched in Girdlegard, but Raikan did not trust the ruler of United Kingdom of Gauragar-Idoslane, Queen Mallenia. She might be a powerful and determined leader but he did not approve of her chosen lifestyle. *What kind of a monarch sets up with an actor, of all things – and one known to flaunt an open dalliance with a maga, at that?*

Raikan did not think Mallenia would attack him, but considered her moody and unpredictable. To have the elves on his side would make a good impression. His own people would be reassured, too. He wanted his country to be safe; that was all.

The Tabaîn delegation made their way along the winding road flanked by the mighty tree trunks.

The woodland was flooded with light; moss and ferns covered the floor but there was no dense undergrowth. From time to time, Raikan noticed animals watching the riders. The wildlife sensed it had nothing to fear from these humans.

'Over there on the right,' said Tenkil. 'Looks like the elves haven't been quite as thorough as we thought.'

Raikan turned to catch sight of an imposing sculpture of unmistakably älfar origin: it was composed entirely of bones. It portrayed the upper body of a powerful warrior, rising up to launch himself on enemies. Woodland creepers had almost covered the horrifying work of art, growing tight across the bone surface.

'The ivy will soon pull it down,' said Raikan, shuddering. *The älfar are being eliminated, together with everything they created.*

The five riders reached a wide clearing containing a dozen or so stone-built houses and a colossal tree at its centre, spreading its branches as a natural shelter over the settlement. Raikan tried to work out how deep the tree's root system must go to support the weight. The houses were grouped in the soft shade, each constructed like a small fortress but with playful decorative elements that stopped them looking like a giant's discarded building bricks. The carved blocks were painted in various shades of green and decorated with swirling ornamentation. Vegetation on the walls ensured the buildings blended perfectly with the surroundings.

Tenkil was already concerned. 'If you wanted to take this settlement you'd have to fight house to house.'

Raikan did not take the remark amiss. The warrior had long fought the enemies of Tabaîn; he always viewed any location from a strategic aspect rather than observing it with peaceful eyes.

There were elves, male and female, on the streets, smiling at the newcomers. Raikan reckoned there were at least forty of them walking around. He signalled to his escorts to stop. 'I thought only a handful of elves had come to Girdlegard.'

'More than that.' Tenkil exhaled sharply. 'Many more.'

'But they've no weapons.' Raikan smiled at his friend. 'They won't harm us.'

In the middle of the little settlement, at the root of the tree, stood a large house, a hundred paces square, with a curving roof a good fifty paces above their heads. Four long balconies, ten paces wide, were placed at intervals along the front.

The construction was mostly wood and the beams had been artfully carved; countless white lanterns decorated with red runes dangled in the light breeze. Two enormous black banners with glowing white designs hung all the way down to ground level where they framed a massive, bronze double door, inscribed with yet more runes.

'Elves are the fastest builders I've ever seen,' observed Tenkil, his tone implying that he did not believe things had been done in an honest and straightforward way.

That's enough of that. Raikan was about to reprimand his friend when the door opened and an elf in wide, dark green robes emerged, carrying a tray with a carafe and five goblets. His short black hair was combed back severely, showing his slightly pointed ears; the dagger in the belt around his slim hips was as long as his forearm.

He approached the delegation with steady steps.

Raikan did not consider it fitting to accept the refreshment while still in the saddle, so he dismounted. Tenkil, Lilia, Ketrin and Irtan followed suit.

A slight breeze travelled through the trees, setting off the gentle sound of bells fastened in the branches, giving the occasion a ceremonial atmosphere.

The elf bowed his head and proffered the drinks. 'Welcome, humans from Tabaîn. My master is delighted you have accepted his invitation.'

'We thank you.' The riders each took a goblet.

It was delicious from the first mouthful. The water tasted pure and more refreshing than anything the heir to the Tabaîn throne had ever drunk before. He could not place the faint aroma but it left a pleasant cooling after-effect in the throat.

When they had returned their empty goblets to the tray, the elf smiled at them. 'Step this way, please. My master awaits.'

Raikan followed the elf, keeping an arm's length or two behind. 'Ketrin, you stay with the horses.'

The blonde girl nodded and gathered the leading reins in her hand.

Tenkil looked up. 'Guards. Nine bowmen. They're standing in the shadow of the second balustrade.'

Raikan would have been surprised if this had not been the case. 'Let's assume they're there for our protection.'

So that meant yet more elves here in Ti Lesinteïl. *Where are they all from?*

Tenkil let out a coarse laugh. 'Oh, yes. Like the spies hidden in the woods, the ones aiming at us as we passed?'

Raikan did not answer. He had not noticed the elf-soldiers in the woods. His friend's remark ruined his cheerful mood.

They passed through the double doors into a large, bare hall that smelt of incense and flowers. On the walls there were symbols as well as stylised pictures of landscapes and birds. The colours shimmered as if liquefied metal had been used to varnish the images.

At the far end of the hall, an impressive figure of an elf with brown hair knelt back in an uncomfortable-looking posture on a platform with mats of plaited reeds. He wore an elegantly-cut robe of white fabric woven through with gold and silver threads. Rays of sunshine fell in from three directions from skylights, turning the elf into a figure of light. He kept his ringed hands open, resting on his thighs, as he directed his gaze to the visitors.

Raikan was surprised – he had only met Ilahín and his wife Fiëa, and thought that he was the king. But Ilahín was nowhere to be seen, nor was the sumptuous throne Raikan expected. The simplicity of the surroundings was as surprising as the unknown figure sitting in front of him. *Who is this?*

Their guide bowed and spoke in the elf tongue.

'Let us use human language,' the ruler interrupted in a sing-song voice, cutting the words sharply.

'It is impolite. Raikan might think we had something to hide.' The elf made an elegant gesture with his right hand, less inviting than commanding. Raikan nodded and moved to comply but Tenkil grabbed him by the arm.

'I'm not kneeling down for anybody,' he muttered; the emptiness of the room made his remark audible to all.

'The elf ruler is also kneeling.'

'He can do as he likes but I'll only bend the knee when I'm dead. I've fought enough battles in my time not to –'

That's enough. Raikan glared at him. 'Then go outside and wait with the horses.'

Tenkil opened his mouth to object but saw sense. He turned on his heel and left the hall.

He's been at war too long. Together with Lilia and Irtan, his remaining two companions, Raikan went over to the raised dais and knelt down at some distance from the elf, resting back on his heels in a similar posture. The ruler exuded an aura of power and self-assurance. The gaze from those bright grey-green eyes spoke of superiority.

There had not been much time for practising diplomacy in recent cycles and thus the young Tabaîner felt unsure of himself; he had no idea how he was supposed to conduct himself when faced with an elf ruler. There was nothing in the books. *I'll wait and see.*

The bronze door closed with a metallic clang as loud as a gong. The sound reverberated and then bells started to tinkle through the fading echo. Nothing happened for quite some time. They sat opposite each other and waited.

Raikan was forced to suppress a yawn. Because of the incense and the harmonious tones of the bells he found the atmosphere in the room increasingly relaxing. *Although sitting on my heels like this is getting less comfortable from heartbeat to heartbeat.* He felt the tension leave his body.

That was apparently what his host had been waiting for.

'I am Ataimînas, regent of Ti Lesinteïl and Naishïon of all elves. As I see it, Tabaîn has sent me its coming monarch.' He placed his hand on his breast at heart level. 'I am honoured.'

'The honour is mine.' Raikan felt flattered as he shifted uncomfortably; his feet and ankles were tingling. Before long this posture would make his legs go to sleep. 'You have created a miracle here.'

Ataimînas gave a grateful smile. 'Maga Coïra and our own humble gifts have worked together to ensure the horrors of the past are well and truly buried and forgotten.' He spread out his arms. 'Let us speak of the future, young king. That is the only thing that matters now.'

Raikan agreed. 'How can Tabaîn be of assistance?'

'By providing corn.' Ataimînas placed his hands in his lap,

where the jewelled rings sparkled and shone. 'The elf realms are in the process of re-forming and there has been little opportunity to pay attention to agriculture. During the course of the next ten cycles we intend to source the corn we need from the fields of Tabaîn. From what I hear, your harvests promise to be plentiful, as usual.'

This is going well. We're heading for an alliance. Raikan could not help smiling. 'We should be able to do without a few sacks of rye.'

'I speak of all the elf realms: Ti Âlandur, the Ti Singàlai you refer to as the Golden Plain, and Ti Lesinteïl. All in all we calculate our requirements to be eleven hundred twentners.' Raikan heard how Lilia next to him caught her breath in surprise.

'How many mouths do you need to feed, Regent Ataimînas?'

The elf seemed astonished at the question. 'I thought the Children of Vraccas knew all about our immigration campaign? We have made no secret of it.'

'The dwarves send regular briefings to the Council of Kings, but the last meeting was half a cycle ago,' Raikan explained. 'There has been a lot to do.'

'Of course. So you will learn that we have arrived from the south, the west and the east, responding to our Creator's sign that the threats to our people are now over.' Ataimînas pointed to the door. 'This is only one of our many settlements, King Raikan. We are re-forming our race and we shall not, in future, be cutting ourselves off from humans and dwarves as our ancestors were wont to do.' The elf straightened up, his robes brilliant in the light. 'I know what reputation goes before us in Girdlegard and I fear it was justified. But in less than a human generation that reputation will have changed.' He pointed to Raikan. 'Trade negotiations are the start. If you wish it.'

Of course I do. Raikan held back from confirming his willingness out loud. 'But you still have not said how many elves have come.'

'Up to the present orbit it will be about ten thousand.' Ataimînas registered the surprise on his visitors' faces and gave a friendly laugh. 'You should see yourselves, young king. We are not here as conquerors. We are merely returning to the place where our Creator formed us. And for that we shall be needing more corn.'

The chance of a business deal and an alliance was extremely tempting. Raikan ought to be excited. However, he felt undeniable unease about the sheer numbers involved. *That many elves in Girdlegard?* It was as if Tenkil had left his suspicious attitude behind when he marched out of the hall. *Annoying.*

'We will provide extra seed corn for Tabaîn to plant,' Ataimînas went on. 'It's a particular sort of wheat, very high quality. You will guard the crops for us. For that we will pay you handsomely.' He gave a condescending smile. 'I shall make you rich.'

He went on to specify these payments and the price for a twentner of corn.

Raikan did not even attempt to bargain with him. The amount of gold lay far beyond what he had expected.

Instead he replied, 'I am pleased to be able to assist the elf realms.' After an agreement of this kind it should be easier to put forward his suggestion of an alliance.

'Let us not waste any time.' Ataimînas made a sign and a hitherto hidden door in the wooden panelling opened to admit two elves.

They brought parchment and quill; the contract had already been drawn up and only the mutually acceptable details on price and volume needed to be inserted before both parties signed.

Raikan was aware that he was overstepping his authority here, as his brother had not yet abdicated, but he felt this was an opportunity that shouldn't be missed. Tabaîn's future was at stake.

'Many thanks,' he said to the elf, as he was handed the completed agreement. 'Might I use the occasion to . . .'

'Then that business is settled.' Ataimînas looked pleased. 'Now let us talk about something else: land.'

The royal heir was taken by surprise. 'I don't understand. Did you want to purchase the fields for your own type of crop . . . ?'

'The elf realm in which you and your friends currently find yourselves is to be merged with the other two. We are buying up the land that falls between the regions.' Reaching behind him, Ataimînas drew out a map and unrolled it. The new borders were already marked. 'We wish to acquire the part of Tabaîn that lies to the north of Âlandur and goes up to the mountains. The land does not strictly lie between our realms but it would complete our territory to perfection.'

Raikan realised that the elf was not expecting any objections. This was inevitably going to cause problems. An alliance with the elf kingdom ceased to be a suitable proposition: instead of security, it would only bring dispute. It seemed to Raikan that he had made the whole journey in vain. 'I expect you will put this idea to the Council of Kings? Queen Mallenia would be most affected by your plan.'

'That is so. I fear there will be petty objections. She has a relationship, of course, with the King of Urgon, which makes her a double monarch. This could mean there would be three votes against me.' Ataimînas looked Raikan up and down. 'You will be taking my side, I hope.'

Now the young man understood why the grain price had been set so generously. 'I will have to speak to my brother about this.' Raikan tried to avoid a direct answer. 'This is a matter of far greater implication than the decision concerning grain supply.' Tenkil's suspicions appeared to be well-founded. The next war was waiting in the wings, only one cycle after the liberation.

The elf's smile was non-committal; gold and silver light was reflected on his handsome face. 'Yes, do that, Raikan Fieldwood. I'm sure you will convince him. Who would not want to have the Naishïon as a friend?'

Raikan recalled that Ataimînas had used this term earlier in their talks. 'Forgive my ignorance, but for the last two hundred and fifty cycles there was no contact between our peoples. This title means . . . ?'

'It would translate in your language as ruler with unlimited powers.' The elf's manner continued to be friendly. 'Ruler over my own people, of course. Not over Girdlegard,' he added with a mischievous smile. 'We wouldn't want any misunderstandings.'

'Of course not.' Raikan was glad that Tenkil was outside with the horses. His warrior would have launched immediately into an argument. *There was a lot to consider on the journey home. An alliance would have to be thought about very carefully.*

'Have you heard about the child they found in the Grey Mountains?' Raikan asked, in an attempt to change the subject.

'The young girl?' Ataimînas became tight-lipped; he

stretched and leaned back slightly. 'If you ask me, I'd say Belogar Strifehammer should have killed her. The dwarf and I are of one mind here. I fear, as does he, that the child will prove to be anything but a blessing for our shared homeland.'

He'll have to explain what he means. Raikan was about to put forth another question when suddenly a loud shout was heard outside. A whoosh of arrows was followed by further shouts and the whinnying of terrified horses.

The man soon to be king of Tabaîn jumped to his feet, followed by Lilia and Irtan – but like him, they collapsed back onto the rush mats immediately. The circulation in their lower limbs had been badly affected by the unusual kneeling posture they had felt obliged to adopt. Sitting back on their heels like the elf meant that they had no feeling in their legs; they were essentially paralysed from the knees down. They lay there helpless: easy victims.

'Tenkil!' Raikan looked over to the closed door, then turned to face the elf ruler.

But Ataimînas was no longer there.

And so the times changed in Girdlegard.
From älfar hero to captive of the rulers and finally to being lapdog of the powerful – or so it seemed.
But my time will come, it will return.
For that is what I have learned from time.

Secret notes for
The Writings of Truth
written under duress by Carmondai

I

Girdlegard
United Kingdom of Gauragar-Idoslane
Freestone
6492nd solar cycle, early summer

'How quickly things change,' Boïndil 'Ireheart' Doubleblade of the clan of the Axe Swingers muttered into his splendid, carefully combed, black and silver beard.

Armoured, armed, and mounted on a black and white pony, he was riding into the little town of Freestone, where a cruel massacre had taken place less than two cycles previously. The älfar had taken a fancy to the bones of the local population and had driven the townspeople into the market square and killed them all. They had then used the bones they found suitable for their artworks.

The town had bled to death that day, but with the destruction of the black-eyes, the settlement had re-emerged as a source of life. The King of the Secondlings, and very recently also titled High King of all the Dwarf Tribes, proceeded slowly through the town's busy streets.

It was mostly young people who had come to settle here in the deserted houses. The fields were being cultivated again and had the makings of a rich harvest; the orchards promised a wonderful crop of fruit. The town was flourishing after decades of terror and darkness.

Ireheart was meeting with the Council of Kings here in the town that had come to stand for the transformation of

Girdlegard and the dawn of a new age. The elf Ilahín was also expected at the talks.

Half a cycle had passed since the last meeting and the ruler of all the Children of the Smith reckoned it was high time everyone got together and exchanged views. It was one thing sending messages, but nothing could replace a face-to-face discussion.

There were things that needed saying. Preferably over a tankard of black beer. He turned his pony off the road and through an entrance over which the banners of all the kingdoms fluttered. The name on the sign read proudly *House of Heroes.*

The sound of hooves clattering over the cobbles was magnified by the half-timbered walls of the inn yard.

Two human soldiers standing just inside the entrance noted the dwarf's emblem and saluted with their spears. The one on the right yelled out the name of the new arrival to inform those within.

'Is that really necessary?' Ireheart grumbled. 'Shouting right in my ear? Noiser here than on all the battlefields I've fought on. Enough to make a dwarf go deaf.' The soldier gave a shamefaced grin but did not dare respond.

The dwarf slid from the saddle in front of the barn, had a good stretch and patted the pony. 'You've done me proud. But I still don't like riding.'

Ireheart had decided not to come with a retinue. An experienced warrior like himself had no need of an escort; they just held you back. The journey from his kingdom in the Blue Mountains had been a long one but a single rider will always find fodder and stabling for the night as well as a good meal, black beer and a bed.

Ireheart tossed his black and silver plait back over his shoulder and reached for the crow's beak hammer that was fastened to the saddle. At that moment, the inn door flew open.

Out came Rodario the Incomparable, Urgon's king, new to the status of ruler. He was the descendant of the original and greatest actor in the land. He wore a dazzling white robe with brightly embroidered motifs and a black belt; draped round his shoulders hung a brown shawl with pictures of mountains stitched in green. His aristocratic features were enhanced by a short pointed beard and an audacious moustache and he wore his well-groomed brown hair in curls.

'O most glorious among the glorious,' he called out in an exaggerated manner, spreading his arms wide in welcome. 'Behold, here he is, small of stature but with the heart of a giant . . .'

Ireheart looked him up and down. 'What in the devil are you wearing?' He yanked the crow's beak out of its fixture and shouldered it with a grin, the rings on his chainmail clinking as he did so. 'A dressing gown?'

'This, you ignoramus, is the height of fashion in my country.' Rodario, king of Urgon and lover to both Mallenia and Coïra, twirled around theatrically, letting the skirts of the garment fly out. 'It's my own design.'

'Ho, has it slipped your mind? You're not on the stage any more. You sit on a *real* throne and you're supposed to *be* a ruler, not just *play the part* of one.' Ireheart stroked his beard. 'And you've put on weight. They'll have to make the throne wider.'

'There we have it, politeness personified in a dwarf.' Rodario put his hands on his hips and laughed. 'What a fine exchange of pleasantries!'

'You called me *small of stature*, didn't you? You were asking for it.' Ireheart went up to the one-time actor and held out his hand in greeting. 'But I'm still glad to see you, King Rodario the First.'

As their fingers touched, the man inclined his head, free now of any teasing expression. 'An honour to welcome you, my friend, High King Boïndil.'

Smiling at each other, they clasped hands warmly and then went inside together.

'When did you stop shaving the sides of your head? You look different.'

'There was never any time.' Ireheart did not indulge him. *He's an actor and he'll always be one. I'm not here to chat about hairstyles.*

The high-ceilinged hall had been decorated to host the coming meeting of the Kings' Council and black-haired Ilahín stood waiting. He was wearing a garment like Rodario's, but the white was less dazzling and without ornamental embroidery. Ireheart thought the elf looked much more dignified than Urgon's king.

Armed guards wearing the colours of the various rulers stood in the corners of the room. They were equipped with short shields and short swords; their task, to work together to protect the lives of the monarchs.

The innkeeper and his servants had gone to a great deal of effort and had even hung floral garlands at the windows; the whole place smelled faintly of the sugar soap used to scrub the floor. Add to the mix the fragrance of roasting meat – food was being provided – and the atmosphere was welcoming.

Ilahín nodded to the newcomer. 'Greetings, High King. It is good to see that you have arrived safely.'

Mallenia, in heavy armour as always, was already seated at the table studying news bulletins; she was concentrating so hard that she did not notice Ireheart come in. Rodario went over to interrupt her but the dwarf held him back. 'Time enough for that. Let her finish reading.'

Ireheart was handed a pitcher made of carved tusk ivory. He raised the black beer in toast to the assembled heads of state, all without removing his crow's beak from his shoulder. 'To Vraccas and the Council of Kings. May the road home be less dusty.'

He emptied the tankard in one go and called for the next, which Rodario obviously noted.

'Now then, Actor; we've got one of your women sat over there. Where's the other one?'

Mallenia's blonde head jerked up from her papers, her eyes narrowing.

'Don't make me think your mind has suffered from your many battles,' she said with a spiteful smile.

Ireheart swapped the empty mug for a full one. 'Am I wrong?'

He gazed at Ilahín with innocent eyes. 'Tell me I didn't say anything wrong?' He pointed his tankard at Rodario, slopping a little foam over the top as he did so. '*He* won't dare to. Her sword is bigger than his.'

The elf tried hard not to laugh.

Voices from the gate announced the arrival of Sangpûr's Queen Astirma and of King Natenian of Tabaîn. From the sound of hooves it seemed both of them had come with large retinues.

'Wonderful! Let's go and greet them.' Rodario was visibly relieved. He left the room.

What a little coward. Ireheart laughed into his beer. 'So the only ones missing now are Coïra and Isikor from Rân Ribastur.'

Ilahín shook his head. 'The maga won't be coming. She's

sent me a sealed letter giving her point of view in her own words.'

'Aha,' said the dwarf and went over to his seat at table. The banner of the High King hanging from the balcony above made it obvious where he was intended to sit. Ireheart put his crow's beak aside now and the heavy iron weapon with its curved prong crashed on to the floorboards. 'So why's she not coming?'

The elf took his seat next to Ireheart. 'She wants to continue investigating whether there are other magic sources. She has discovered our own has failed.'

Ireheart raised his eyebrows in surprise. 'Dried up?' That gave him enough of a shock to require more beer.

That meant the only known and accessible source was in his own realm, the Blue Mountains. It was guarded by his wife Goda and their three children.

He was worried less about security than about how difficult it would be for Coïra to get the energy she needed to draw on for her magic. Less of a problem in times of peace than it had been when Girdlegard was threatened with attack.

'There'll be new ones. There always have been,' said Ireheart, to reassure both of them.

Ilahín did not seem troubled. 'It is better this way. Anything that's been under älfar influence for such a long time may have changed nature. That's why Coïra is keen to find a new, pure source of previously untouched energy. Sitalia will help us find one.'

'True. Let's put our trust in your goddess. Vraccas wouldn't be any good. He hates magic.'

Queen Astirma and King Natenian came in, accompanied by Rodario and a number of guards and a few courtiers.

The queen was still quite young even by human reckoning,

and her tanned skin and bleached hair showed she spent much time in the open air in the desert. She wore the lightest of clothing with a transparent cloak of woven silk over the top.

Brown-haired Natenian, whose sweeping robe, the colour of corn, hid his fragile frame, had to be led in. He had difficulty staying upright in spite of his stick and the people guiding him. The man was coughing and spluttering and dragging his right foot, although he was hardly older than Astirma. It was no surprise to Ireheart that the king intended to abdicate in favour of his younger, healthier brother.

Mallenia collected her papers together and nodded to the new arrivals as if they were soldiers checking in for a campaign briefing. She had never been one for elaborate etiquette rituals among equals, as Ireheart recalled. *One of her better points.*

'We can make a start. Isikor has sent a message,' she said, showing a letter hung with several seals to demonstrate its authenticity. 'He writes that the weather prevents him from attending in person but says his vote, where needed, should go with the majority opinion. Always for the benefit of Girdlegard.'

'Hear, hear!' Ireheart looked happy. 'That will speed things up. And let's hear it for the man who brought the letter. He seems better able than his king to cope with bad weather.'

The assembled rulers laughed.

After a short welcome ceremony, everyone moved to their allotted places. Water, wine and beer were served and the courtiers retired to the back of the room. The Council of Kings could commence its business.

Mallenia was in charge of proceedings because the meeting was taking place in her land. 'I would like to bid all the rulers of Girdlegard welcome and I call on the gods in all our names to support our undertakings. May they protect us and give us the wisdom needed to make decisions in the interest of the welfare of our subjects and all who reside in Girdlegard.'

Ireheart mumbled his approval. *Vraccas can't object to any of that.*

'Ilahín, you've got a message from Coïra for us.' Mallenia indicated he should break the seal and read out what she had sent.

The elf opened the letter, explaining to the others before he read out her words that the maga was still exploring in the hope of locating new magic sources.

Most esteemed Council of Kings,

I send warm greetings from the unknown place in Girdlegard where I shall be when Ilahín reads out my words.

The source I use has lost its power and if I don't want to be exclusively beholden to my good friend Boïndil Doubleblade for access to his source in the Blue Mountains, I must explore and research. I am sure that Samusin will send me a better substitute for the source that has failed. Perhaps he has already done so.

Hear this: Weyurn matters of state are to be in Rodario's hands. He may vote for me in the assembly.

I shall not be away long from my duties.

I desire to emphasise that Ilahín, his wife and all the elves have treated me like a good friend.

May Palandiell and Sitalia sit at the table with you!

Coïra
Maga and ruler of Weyurn

Natenian closed his eyes and everyone could see that Astirma was displeased. This meant that the power to block any Council decision lay in the hands of just two humans. King Isikor's stated intention of having his vote go with the majority rendered it impossible to outvote Mallenia and Rodario.

This'll be interesting. Ireheart raised his nearly empty tankard and toasted the Incomparable. 'It seems we only have High Kings round this table now,' he called out in good humour and the elf laughed. 'We'll have to invent some new titles.' He drained his drink and was brought a replacement.

Nobody realised there was more behind his drinking than a general jovial conviviality. His straightforward manner seemed to make it acceptable.

'Reason prevails,' replied Rodario, with a pacifying glance towards the monarchs of Tabaîn and Sangpûr. 'Have no fear. The times are past when we expected each to strive only for his or her own advantage.'

Well, that sounded fairly majestic. Ireheart thumped the tankard down on the table to indicate his approval. 'Again: hear, hear!'

'I assume our objections will always get a hearing,' Natenian said, almost too weakly to be heard. 'And let me say this while I'm speaking, knowing I may be too frail to talk later: my orbits as king are numbered. I shall be abdicating in favour of my brother, who will be able to serve Tabaîn longer than I can.' He opened his grey-brown eyes and turned them on Ilahín, his chest heaving as if he had been running. 'As soon as he is back from Ti Lesinteïl, we will be effecting the change. Please regard me as his representative and my country's delegate.'

Mallenia was the first to applaud and then the others joined in. Ireheart banged the handle of his crow's beak against the edge of the table.

'Then let us discuss the state of our beloved Girdlegard,' Mallenia began. 'Everyone will know by now that Boïndil Doubleblade has been appointed as High King of the dwarves.'

Ireheart surveyed the assembled monarchs with a grim but amicable smile, hoping to forestall any questions.

'Why the change of mind?' Astirma threw in, to his consternation. 'Didn't you suggest yourself that the position should be left open for twenty cycles?'

He sighed to himself. 'Events,' he replied as lightly as he could. 'The tribes wanted a king and I couldn't refuse any longer. The will of Vraccas, if you like.'

He didn't tell them that it had been the condescending manner of the elf-woman Fiëa that had driven him to it. He had been keen that orbit to watch the demolition works in the älfar realm and had heard that there had been a crater collapse opening up a passage to Phondrasôn, where the worst of the monsters lived.

Like many in the dwarf tribes, Ireheart believed that Tungdil Goldhand, the true High King of the dwarves, was still alive and had disappeared in Phondrasôn. That was why he had immediately called up a search party, wanting to investigate. But Fiëa had refused him access. It had made him more convinced than ever that his friend was still alive – and that many elves were to be trusted at one's peril.

Ireheart had also wanted to unite the dwarves in case danger was looming. *With over ten thousand elves migrating here, it wasn't such a bad decision on my part.* He kept his thoughts to himself. It would only ruin the mood.

There was another thing that bothered him in lonely moments. The elixir he had tried . . .

He pushed those thoughts aside. *I can't be dwelling on that now.*

Astirma seemed happy enough with his explanation, but when she glanced down at his beer it was clear she disapproved. 'I can see that the Children of the Smith would want to have a leader to unite them in a time of need. A wise leader.' Ireheart chose not to rise to that. He merely flashed his eyes at her.

'Let's talk about Aiphatòn,' said Mallenia, getting back to the task in hand. 'He is still far outside Girdlegard, as you know. He has been following an älfar trail that took him through the Grey Mountains. That was at least one cycle ago. Has anyone had any more news?'

Everyone shook their heads, and Ireheart had some more to drink.

'I think it's good he's taking his task seriously.' Ilahín rose to his feet. 'We are also working on eradicating any evidence of the älfar. You would not recognise Dsôn Bhará now. The transformation is splendid.'

'It's not surprising; there's enough of you,' Ireheart said in a friendly tone. 'Did I mention it? More than ten thousand elves have entered Girdlegard in the past cycle, coming from the south, west and east. Our gate wardens have let them pass unhindered after checking that they were not älfar in disguise.'

A ripple of talk went through the council. Nobody had been expecting this news.

Ireheart noticed Mallenia looking suddenly thoughtful. The warrior queen was thinking of the possible threat this migration implied, and Rodario steepled his fingers and attempted to force an explanation from the elf by dint of staring at him pointedly.

'We are most grateful to the dwarves for this.' Ilahín did not hesitate. 'My people have had many different roles in the history of Girdlegard in recent cycles . . .' he began – and yet it was something else entirely that drew the dwarf's attention.

The elf's harmonious sing-song tones settled in Ireheart's ears as background noise while he focused on the entrance of a guard bearing the arms of Urgon.

Unlike his comrades, he walked with a perfectly upright posture. It was strange. And his armour did not appear to fit quite right: in some places it was too tight and in others too wide.

What's he carrying a spear for? Ireheart drained the wonderfully carved ivory beaker and turned so that the servants could see him. He noted how the guard was carefully tightening his grip; the leather gauntlet creaked slightly.

As if he were preparing to throw it.

Ireheart leaped up, jumped onto the chair and thence to the table, raising his crow's beak. 'Watch out!'

At that very moment the newcomer bent forward and launched his weapon in a single graceful movement. He took a step to one side in order to draw his short sword, and quick as lightning whirled round to attack the two guards closest to him.

Ireheart knocked the spear mid-flight with the crook of his weapon, sending it crashing into a wooden pillar.

The spear quivered, having missed the shocked elf by a narrow margin.

The assembled monarchs got to their feet, quickly grasping the fact that this was no beer-fuelled dwarf joke.

The bodyguards enclosed the would-be assassin, who had drawn his second short sword and was swinging it about.

'Ho, come on then! You wouldn't dare . . .' It suddenly grew dark round Ireheart. It was as if night had burst into the room, violating the daylight. The darkness revealed what kind of evil opponent they faced. 'Black-eyes!' Ireheart roared, and ducked, holding the long handle of the crow's beak in front of his body. The magic blackness was impenetrable. 'Fight in the daylight, you cowardly monster!'

There were metallic sounds nearby. Death screams echoed in the room and all around bodies in armour and dropped weapons were clattering to the floor of the inn. People were yelling, nailed boots scuttered on the stone and blades were slicing through the air, hopelessly off-target.

This headless chicken behaviour helped the älfar attacker no end.

Calm. Stay calm. I mustn't let the fury take over. Ireheart took cover and listened carefully for a sound that would betray the whereabouts of the assassin.

He could feel the heat of his internal furnace burning high as the zhadár elixir revived the terrible anger in him; he fought the great fury that would make him run amok. In such a state there was neither friend nor foe for Ireheart and this would have devastating consequences for Girdlegard's rulers.

He was often able to keep the anger in check by drinking alcohol, but in a case such as this there would be no restraint possible. He had almost been able to control it, before the fateful day he had slaked his thirst from the wrong flask.

There was a metallic smell of blood and of freshly-slit guts.

Ireheart pictured the älf slaughtering his way through their ranks with a supercilious grin, making his way towards the monarchs at the high table. This was likely the best opportunity in the whole cycle to launch an attack on the crowned houses of Girdlegard. *Mallenia should have had better security arrangements in place.*

A sudden draught brushed his wrinkled face and made his well-groomed beard sway.

Ireheart immediately jerked his right foot out – catching

something, and he heard a quiet älfar curse; he stood up and circled his crow's beak above his head to catch his swift attacker in the back.

The spike, as long as a forearm, found resistance and there was the sound of steel protesting. The spike tip got stuck and Ireheart had to yank at the handle to pull it away. 'Ha!' Hot sparks invaded his bloodstream, but he managed to control himself.

The light started to return to the darkened room. The blow seemed to have weakened the älf's powers of concentration. The light let the High King, now snorting with effort, see the enemy's back: a deep cut showed in armour and flesh.

But the älf stumbled on towards the frail figure of Natenian, bloodied swords in hand.

Ireheart had no hope of catching him so he hurled his crow's beak. 'Greetings from the smithy!'

Ilahín, too, made his way over with his weapon drawn to bring down the attacker. Two daggers came flying over from the right and whizzed past the assassin, barely missing the elf.

Ireheart clenched his teeth when he realised the crow's beak was going to hit the wrong pointy-ears target.

Ilahín vaulted over, ducked under the älf's sword swipe and stuck his long blade in the armpit from below. The end of the spike emerged at the shoulder, making the armour bulge and changing the direction of the assassin's attack. Then the crow's beak hurtled in and glanced off Ilahín's side. The elf was jerked round, pulling the opponent with him.

Together they flew off the table, pulling two of Natenian's companions over with them, and thumped to the ground next to Tabaîn's king.

Mallenia loomed. Her long blade flashed down, accompanied by a tremendous scream that told of all her hatred, cutting at the neck vertebrae before the älf came back on his feet; the sword swept down and plunged into the floorboards, sticking fast.

'Where there's one black-eyes there might be another one.' Ireheart drew both his short axes and turned round in an aggressive pose, his arms spread wide, as he watched out for other enemies. It was a huge effort not to erupt in fury. Hot blood roared in his ears and the red mist in front of his eyes did not bode well.

The room was transformed into a slaughterhouse.

The dwarf surveyed the scene: the guards were slit open or had deep stab wounds. Their armour would not have helped them against such a foe. The assassin had located and made use of the weak points in the armour.

Astirma's bodyguard lay around her, all of them dead, and the fair-haired queen herself had suffered a wound to the neck. Her breathing was laboured and her eyes wide. She was struggling to grasp what had happened. Two blood-smeared maids were attending to her. Ireheart noted that Rodario had a cut on his arm.

The fact that the älf had left it at that suggested that poison had been employed.

'Call the best healers,' Ireheart shouted, fighting down the urge to swing around and attack Mallenia. 'The blade was most likely treated with some noxious toxin.'

Mallenia, struggling to extract her sword from where it had stuck in the wooden floor, echoed his call.

Suddenly Rodario turned pale. 'By all the gods! The attacker was wearing the armour of the Urgon bodyguard! I must see to her!' He rushed out of the room.

'Who is this *her* he's talking about?' Ireheart looked puzzled. 'Have I missed something?' At last the red mist was starting to lift from his vision. *I need a beer, quickly.*

'We would have got to that eventually,' Mallenia did not give a direct answer. 'Let's move to another room. There is too much death here.'

They left the large saloon with the protection of new guards and a whole wall of shields, and went in to a smaller side room with its own fireplace.

The dwarf picked up his crow's beak and followed them. As he passed a table he grabbed a pitcher and emptied the contents down his throat. It seemed to him he heard a dull hissing sound as the fires of his rage were quenched.

Healers arrived to treat the injured, dosing them with a draught thought to counteract the effects of known älfar poisons. Wounds were bandaged and others were given wine against the shock.

Ilahín stretched out his hand to Ireheart. 'I owe you my life, Child of the Smith. We now live in times of true friendship between our peoples if a dwarf will save the life of an elf.'

'But I nearly finished you off myself,' he said with a grin. 'It wasn't you I was aiming at, though.'

'That does not detract from your heroism. Were it not for you, High King, the älf's spear would have pierced me through.' Ilahín bowed. 'I shall never forget this.'

'Let's get back to our debate,' Astirma said, though she was still staring blankly straight ahead and struggling to contain her terror. A maid handed her some wine, which she downed as swiftly as Ireheart had his black beer. 'The attack must not keep us from our purpose or it will mean that the älf has won.'

This made the young queen rise in Ireheart's estimation. 'Then I repeat my question. Where did the Incomparable Rodario rush off to?'

'To find my ward, a young girl.' Mallenia sat down and surveyed the others. 'We had been discussing the arrival of the elves in Girdlegard, possibly a cause of some consternation.'

'I would say – given the danger we face from älfar attack – we should be glad to have the elves here,' said Astirma calmly. 'You must hunt them down,' she said to Ilahín. 'Our own armies are not ready and you know the black-eyes better than we do.'

The elf gave a weak smile. 'I can promise you, Majesty, that we will be even more vigilant. But how does one hunt ghosts?'

'As far as I know, the last of the zhadár is after them,' Ireheart cut in. 'He set off to track them down and we mustn't forget that he's had some success.' He recalled the attempt on Mallenia's life that winter, on her visit to Oakenburgh. 'He's our best hope against the älfar.'

Mallenia agreed. 'There are only a handful of älfar still around. But we have seen what damage they can still do. Our security arrangements were comprehensive and yet they still managed to smuggle an assassin in.'

'If that is the price we have to pay for our liberation, I am happy to pay it if it means my people are no longer under the yoke of evil.' Natenian's voice came in a strained whisper, but he had the room's full attention. 'Tell us the älfar empires are a thing of the past, Ilahín.'

'Indeed they are. We have used Coïra's magic powers to turn Dsôn Bhará into a pleasant hollow in a landscape filled with trees. Their roots hold back the evil, preventing it from resurfacing. Both Ti Âlandur and Ti Singàlai – which is known to you as the Golden Plain – are being renewed. Sitalia called her children here in order to protect Girdlegard on the inside, just as the Children of the Smith protect it from outside threats.' He addressed Ireheart. 'A new era, my friend. We can live together peacefully without suspicion of each other.'

'I'll drink a toast to that.' Astirma raised her goblet of wine and the others followed suit.

'If we're talking about the new era, tell us where all these Outer Lands elves are coming from,' Ireheart wanted to know. 'Why were they living there in the first place?'

'You'll be able to ask them yourself soon. My king will attend the next Council of Kings and will outline his plans to you all. Not this time, but on another orbit not too far distant.'

Mallenia nodded carefully. 'We shall await that with interest.' She kept looking over to the door, anxiously, eager for Rodario to return.

Ireheart emptied the next tankard; he had forgotten how many he'd already drunk, but the alcohol had managed to suppress his dark burning rage. For now. He was counting on the iron will all dwarves shared, and he hoped to overcome his burden with Vraccas' help and his own effort. *No rages any more, no more unquenchable thirst, no more terrible dreams*. Until then he needed his mead. And his black beer.

'The young ward you mentioned,' he turned to Mallenia, 'she wouldn't be the girl they found in the abandoned settlement in the Grey Mountains, would she? What did they say her name was?'

All eyes were on the blonde woman from Idoslane. Word had gone round in Girdlegard about the foundling child, but no actual details were known.

'She is called Sha'taï,' Mallenia replied with a sweet smile. 'She's a good little girl.'

Everyone knew the story. A group consisting of human soldiers, dwarves and an elf had been searching for a deserted village in the Grey Mountains, after surprising descriptions found in älfar records. And they had indeed located the remains of a settlement where in the past, dwarves of the Fifthling tribe must have co-existed with elves.

Ireheart did not know what the purpose of the secret experiment had been or why it had only come to light via the älfar writings. The dwarves had searched their own archives in vain for a mention, and there were none of the original Fifthlings around they could ask.

While there, the group found a little girl from the Outer Lands, only able to speak in the älfar tongue. The dwarves had refused to take the child along, so in the end the human soldiers had brought her to Mallenia.

Since then nothing had been heard of Sha'taï.

'She's a bright child,' Mallenia told them proudly. 'I wanted to introduce her so she could tell us what she knows. There's a possible threat to Girdlegard from her homeland.' She looked from one to another in turn. 'That's why it's so important that we do away with suspicion and self-interest amongst us.'

Ireheart pricked up his ears. If the kid could speak the black-eyes' language, she must have lived with them.

Is that why the älf attacker went to her room first? To silence her? Or was it just for her guard's uniform? Ireheart would prefer to see the mysterious foundling safely stowed in a prison cell instead of sitting by the side of the queen who ruled two countries, but he was keen to see what the child was like nonetheless.

'So there are still some älfar on the other side of the mountains?' Ireheart muttered. 'I pray to Vraccas that Aiphatòn will find them and root them out.' *If he can't, then we'll be ready and waiting.*

He noticed how the blonde Ido woman bit her lip when he said that and decided she must know more than she was admitting.

'Let's wait till Rodario gets back. In the meantime, let's talk about some of the positives happening here in Girdlegard,' said Astirma. The wine was having its effect. She now seemed able to put aside the pain and the horror of the recent events. 'We mustn't neglect the good things.' The young queen gave Ireheart a friendly glance. 'High King, if you would tell us what's happening in the mountains.'

'With pleasure.' He slurped a mouthful of beer, drew breath and started his report of how the five dwarf tribes were progressing. Ireheart did not believe that Sha'taï had become a victim of the assassin, because Rodario would have come storming back already.

He was more puzzled that the actor king had not returned.

Girdlegard
Elf realm of Ti Lesinteïl
6492nd solar cycle, early summer

Lying on the floor of the large hall, Raikan Fieldwood heard curt elf commands coming from outside; the sound of arrows had not let up. His friend Tenkil was shouting desperately for Lilia.

We were sent into a trap. He still could not feel his legs. It was taking too long for his circulation to recover and his muscles work again; he could not fight. The elf ruler must have left by a concealed door. 'To the door!' he yelled to his two companions, and wriggled his way over the rush matting like a maggot. In his mind's eye he could see Ketrin and

Tenkil ambushed and shot full of arrows. 'I must know what's going on.'

Together, Raikan, Irtan and Lilia reached the large bronze door and used their weapons to prise it open far enough to see out. It was now clear that the arrows had not been intended for their friends.

Her clothing torn to rags, Ketrin lay on the ground, a deep gash in her chest and splintered bones sticking out. Something had dug furiously through her body to get to the soft innards.

What's happening? Raikan saw four mutilated elf corpses, attacked in the same way.

Tenkil was struggling out from under a fallen horse. His chainmail was torn full of holes; blood gushed from a shoulder wound. Arrows that had missed their targets were stuck in the ground on all sides.

So the guards on the balcony and skulking in the woods were not there because of us at all. Grabbing the door handle, Raikan pulled himself up. *They were watching out for whatever has cost Ketrin her life.*

Pins and needles took over from the numbness in his legs.

Without taking his eyes off the scene outside, the young king stamped his feet repeatedly to get the circulation going. He could feel his feet again. *Now we can fight.* 'Tenkil! Hang on! We're nearly there!'

'No!' Tenkil had freed himself from the weight of the horse cadaver and, crouching low, with sword and dagger drawn, he started moving towards the them. 'I'll come where you are. Whatever that is, there's no hope of confronting it in an open fight.'

Tenkil sprinted over.

Irtan and Lilia flanked the bronze door, weapons at the

ready. They, too, had been regaining the use of their lower limbs. *We should have been wearing armour.* 'Shut the door as soon as he's through.'

Tenkil flew across the ground he had to cover – and then the darkness behind him started to move.

A creature came storming forward, as steely black as night itself. It was like a huge, armoured wolf. Its eyes glowed white, its ears pricked up and the long snout gaped wide, displaying shining, sharp-pointed teeth too numerous to count.

Powerful jaws snapped at the man as he ran for his life, but he swerved instinctively. Raikan heard a loud clack as the jaws sprang shut. The creature snorted and roared.

Its armoured skin deflected swarms of arrows. Others missed their target as the animal zigzagged. One of the arrows hit its snout just as the creature launched another attack on Tenkil. It gave a furious barking sound.

'Run!' shouted Raikan. 'Or it'll have you.'

But the beast had ceased to care about Tenkil. It cast its shimmering eyes up to the balcony and sprang from its powerful hindquarters, disappearing from sight.

Tenkil made it into the hall and Irtan and Lilia slammed the bronze doors shut. The four friends from Tabaîn listened as the metallic echo died away.

They heard steps above their heads and then screams of terror. The archers were being killed one by one. Weapons clanked to the floor. It didn't seem there was any defence being put up.

'What do we do?' Irtan looked at the others.

'We get out of here while it's busy with the elves.' Lilia took a step back. 'Whatever it is.'

'I didn't even see it properly. I've battled enough monsters in my time, but . . .' Tenkil was shaking, looking at the dagger in his unsteady hands. 'It came out of nowhere, fangs glowing bright. It broke and tore anything in its path.'

Raikan forced down the panic clutching at his heart with an ice-cold hand.

A bold thought occurred to him suddenly, in spite of his fear: if he could manage to protect the elf ruler's life, there was bound to be something in it for him. Not only an advantage for Tabaîn, but something to benefit the whole of Girdlegard.

'Maybe something the älfar left behind?' Raikan moved towards the side door. 'Some creature conjured up by the blackest of arts?'

Tenkil grabbed his arm. 'Why didn't the elf warn us and take us with him?'

Irtan's face grew dark. 'We were the unwitting bait!'

Raikan was hoping against hope that there was more to the elf's behaviour than treachery. 'Let's see what we—'

All of a sudden, the beast burst through the wall and pounced at Lilia in a hail of splinters. The blade she jabbed at the wolf-like animal's shoulder shattered on impact. The beast's white fangs flared bright, gaped wide and slammed shut.

She fell with a scream, the beast flailing on top of her, as her severed arm flew up in the air still grasping the weapon. An arc of blood spurted out.

Raikan whirled round, wielding his long sword at its hind-quarters, hoping the plating might be less thick there.

But the creature sidestepped neatly, its front claws slashing Lilia's unprotected throat.

The woman gasped her last and was half-dragged and half-flung to one side, her corpse leaving red trails on the matting.

'Save yourself, my king,' Tenkil yelled, leaping in front of Raikan to protect him. 'Get word to Girdlegard—'

'He wouldn't get far,' came an elf voice from behind them. 'We've been trying to destroy the beast for over forty orbits.'

Ataimînas pushed past them, placing himself in front of Tenkil. He was now wearing close-fitting armour comprising a large number of tiny metal rods and he held a long, iron spike in his gauntleted hand. 'I was hoping it wouldn't get wind of your visit.'

The bronze doors opened and twenty warriors marched in, all equipped with lances and spears. Faced with a forest of sharp blades, the creature gave a throaty roar and bared its shining fangs threateningly.

Raikan and Tenkil exchanged swift glances. The elf had left them to put on defensive armour and fetch help; it had not been a trap after all. *We were victims of our own bad thoughts.* 'Kill it. Let's kill it together,' he said, a breath of guilt in his voice.

Ataimînas nodded. 'May we succeed.' He advanced with Tenkil and Raikan flanking him and Irtan covering them from the rear.

The warriors drove the beast back up against the wall.

The creature bared its teeth and stared at them all with luminous eyes, flaring its nostrils and snuffling. Their opponent seemed wily enough to know not to charge the wall of spikes; bright blood trickled from a wound on its snout where it must have broken off the arrow piercing the skin.

What is that? Raikan saw a fine chain round its neck with a capsule as big as a child's fist hanging from it. There was writing but the runes were unclear: strangely familiar but neither of elf nor älfar origin. *Could those be dwarf symbols?*

When Ataimînas gave the word, his soldiers stormed the beast.

Ten warriors directed their spear tips straight ahead; the others held theirs sloping upwards to prevent the animal leaping over the blades. The Naishïon himself was at the centre of the onslaught, his lance blade polished gold. Tenkil and Raikan were at his sides.

'Let's get that capsule off the beast,' cried the heir to Tabaîn. 'I want to know what's in it.'

'It won't be good,' Ataimînas said. 'This is bound to be something the älfar set up. They make a point of leaving vicious traps behind them.'

Any further words went unheard in the clash of blades.

The warriors stabbed and slashed at the creature, which was proving surprisingly agile. It jumped around and growled, bit spear shafts to pieces and crunched the metal parts seemingly without damaging its teeth. With its front paws, it made jabs at the row of soldiers: elves were flung injured to the matting. The beast's long claws cut through chainmail shirts and armour plate and blood streamed out, soaking into the rush matting and filling the air with its metallic scent.

Ataimînas ordered his elves back. 'Let's try and lure it outside. Our new archers should be in place,' he told Raikan.

'Didn't work just now,' Tenkil said.

'We've got some better arrows we can use. We'll see an end to the beast this night. Your friends' deaths will be avenged.' Ataimînas nodded at him. 'I swear it.'

They attacked the beast once more to provoke it and to distract it from the danger it would be facing outside, and then withdrew backwards through the bronze double doors.

The beast pursued them, now facing a reduced number of opponents. Raikan admired the nobility of the elf-soldiers and their readiness to sacrifice themselves, knowing they had very little chance of surviving the confrontation.

Outside the palace, the creature was challenged only by the Tabaîners, the Naishïon, and three elf-warriors. It crouched, ready to spring at the courageous band.

Ataimînas called out a command and a humming sound came from all sides.

'Get down!' he shouted, throwing himself to the ground.

Raikan and Tenkil immediately did the same, but Irtan was a shade too slow in reacting. There was a scream when he was hit. He and one of the elves who had not moved fast enough fell, their bodies stuck with arrows.

A wave of darkness flooded the scene as arrows and steel balls rained down on the beast.

Raikan saw how the missiles affected the wolf-like creature. The combination of sharp and blunt projectiles seemed to do the trick, with the slingshot pummelling the skin, making it easier for the arrowheads to puncture.

'It's working!' shouted Raikan excitedly. He got ready to jump up and attack the creature with his sword as soon as the deadly bombardment stopped. *I want that capsule.*

But the beast was not giving up.

It roared and barked in rage, leaped into the air and ravaged the two elf-warriors crouched under cover, unable to run away. It swung their bodies about like dolls, fangs tearing through their armour. Their corpses were hit by the arrows and steel balls in the air.

Then the creature turned on the Naishïon himself.

Its jaws gaped wide. It seemed nothing could halt its onrush, not even arrows and slingshots. But the thin wire the capsule hung from was not as tough and the mysterious metal object fell under one of the creature's blood-red clawed feet.

Before Raikan could leap into action to protect Ataimînas, braving the hail of arrows, Tenkil had rolled forward. The sturdy warrior grabbed one of the splintered lances and drove it into the beast's open maw.

The creature stopped, retching at the wooden lance lodged in its gullet. By now it had so many arrows sticking out of its hide that it looked like a porcupine. It dealt Tenkil a mighty blow with a foreleg, sending him spinning round to end up groaning on the ground. This slight delay served the elf bowmen. Eight arrows to the eyes and through the soft palate brought the animal down, burying the muscular Tabaîner under itself.

The elves abruptly ceased their fire.

'This is an orbit we will remember for a long time,' Ataimînas called out, getting to his feet. He proffered his hand to help Raikan up. 'The beast has been defeated. With your help.'

'Sure.' The young monarch sped over to the vanquished monster. 'But before we mourn the dead and celebrate our victory in honour of their sacrifice, give me a hand to free my friend. Otherwise he'll suffocate and add to their number.'

Ataimînas gave instructions Raikan could not understand. Elves emerged from their hiding places, hanging their bows on their backs. 'Take care. We might find there's still a spark of life in it.'

'Where did it come from?'

Ataimînas gestured. 'We assume that it dug itself out through the crater we filled in. There may be some narrow pipe or passageway leading up out of the cave system. At one time the Moon Pond used to be here, with the infamous realm of darkness underneath. Full of monsters and beasts.'

'Phondrasôn.' Raikan was aware of the älfar name for the

terrible place that reached all the way to the Black Abyss. It had been described in papers found after the fall of the Triplets, written about by an älf called Carmondai. 'Hang on, Tenkil. We're going to pull you out.' Raikan looked at the downed monster. 'I understood the underground had been fully sealed off?'

'Evil always finds a way.' Ataimînas gave another command and the warriors stood still. 'It is undoubtedly tragic that the young heir to Tabaîn should fall victim to this beast after he saved my life like a true hero.' With that he kicked the astonished Raikan's feet out from under him, making him fall at the creature's snout. 'A *dead* hero.'

'Have you gone mad?' Raikan attempted to raise his sword.

The Naishïon stepped back with a smile to allow four of the guards to march up.

The young man struggled and raged as they seized him and shoved his neck between the gaping fangs of the monster. The sharp teeth pierced his skin.

'Let me be,' he demanded. 'Ataimînas, what is this?' The elves held his arms fast, rendering him unable to defend himself. An overpowering stench came from the creature's open mouth and the blood of its victims was everywhere.

The Naishïon came close and placed his right boot on the creature's snout, increasing the pressure on Raikan's throat and neck. 'You should be pleased you managed to survive so long. We wanted you to die before you ever reached the palace, but the beast did not show in time.' The green eyes showed no sign of mercy.

Raikan was at a loss. 'What sort of game is . . .'

'Your brother and our new Elf Empire have come to an agreement. Your brother, my fine would-be King Raikan' – he bent close, strands of dark brown hair falling over his face – 'has no intention of abdicating. And now that you have met your death in this tragic accident, he will have to remain on the throne. That means we get our grain on much more favourable terms.'

'My brother?'

Ataimînas gave a spiteful laugh. 'He is devious, of course. So we will check the grain he supplies to see if it's poisoned. But on the other hand, he is also astute. It was his idea we make this contract; it bears your signature and proves that you went behind his back. Your name will be eradicated from the records, after some initial praise for saving my life.' The elf straightened up and swept back his hair. 'Everything has been thought of.'

Raikan uttered a cry of despair. 'No! It can't be true! Natenian would—'

Ataimînas pushed his foot down.

Two rows of razor sharp fangs pierced the young man's neck, turning Raikan's last words into an incomprehensible gurgle. He flailed wildly, aggravating the damage.

Ataimînas applied yet more pressure. Raikan hung there in the creature's jaws, groaning and choking. Blood ran from many wounds and dripped onto the ground.

The future ruler slowly bled to death and his limbs ceased to twitch as the life went out of him.

'*Palandiell*,' he prayed with his last breath. He did not know why he had to die – Natenian had only to say that he wanted to go on reigning and Raikan would have accepted it. *Palandiell, avenge me . . .*

Ataimînas stamped down, and the prince's neck broke.

The severed head fell, splashing down into a pool of blood before rolling aside in the dust.

Totally impassive, the Naishïon looked at the corpse. 'It's Sitalia who holds sway here,' he said coldly, 'not *your* goddess.' Striding back to the palace, he ordered the guards to pull out the other Tabaîner and arrange for the same injuries. 'Send the bodies back to Tabaîn. And the beast as well. The king will want to mourn his brother properly.'

Ataimînas was almost at the bronze door.

'Naishïon!'

He halted and looked back over his shoulder.

'The other one's disappeared.'

He frowned and turned round. They had concentrated on Raikan too much. 'Find him. Follow his tracks and bring him back alive so he can be killed here like his leader.'

'At once, Naishïon.'

Ataimînas pressed his lips together and went on back to the palace. 'And watch out for the other two beasts that are roaming around. Kill them. We don't need them any longer.'

He clenched his fists, furious at himself. A few heartbeats of inattention and his clever plan was in danger. It had been a real bonus when the narshân beast had turned up. Nobody would ever suspect anything untoward when there had been a heroic death like that.

He won't get far. Ataimînas had seen the wounds the man had received. Sure, he might be a veteran soldier, strongly built and with great stamina. But the fangs of a narshân beast were not only sharp but contaminated. *Wouldn't give him more than four miles.*

Ataimînas came to an abrupt stop. 'Where's that metal phial?' he said.

'It's not here, Naishïon. He . . . must have taken it.'

The ruler closed his eyes and silently begged Sitalia to use her powers to fell the man who had escaped. Any other outcome could put paid to his dream of a mighty elf empire.

If anyone finds him before we do . . .

If Vraccas had intended his children to be cut down with ease, he would have made them out of wood.

Dwarf saying

II

Girdlegard
United Kingdom of Gauragar-Idoslane
Freestone
6492nd solar cycle, early summer

Rodario hurried through the inn complex with a healer and three Urgon soldiers to reach the rooms where the young foundling girl had been waiting to be summoned to the assembly hall.

To the Incomparable Rodario, it seemed that the corridors extended for miles, and every step he and his companions took was tiny and laborious.

At last they were getting near.

The door to her chamber stood open and the all-too-familiar smell of blood hung in the air. He rushed in, terrified for the child – and found Sha'taï crouched in a corner of the room. Her nurse and a guard had both been butchered, their throats neatly cut. The soldier had not had time to go for his weapon.

Sha'taï's dark brown dress with bright yellow embroidery had black splashes on it. Blood ran from a small cut on her throat. *She's alive!*

'My little one!' Rodario knelt down, putting an arm round her. He beckoned the healer over with his other hand. The woman approached and carefully inspected the cut while the guards carried the bodies out.

'Night was falling,' said Sha'taï, her accent showing she was not from Girdlegard. 'Then the älf attacked us and he—'

She fought down the tears. 'I wanted to call for help but I was so afraid.' She burst into tears and clutched Rodario's arm.

'He can't hurt you now.' He stroked her dark hair to calm her. 'We've killed him.'

'I don't think poison has been used,' whispered the healer, giving the injured girl a dose of a calming essence from a dark blue phial. 'It's quite deep, though, and needs stitches. We need to ensure the wound closes up properly.'

Rodario nodded and rocked Sha'taï gently to and fro until he felt her body relax and fall into a restorative sleep.

Thank the gods! Lifting her, he stood up and carried her into an adjoining room. He laid her on the bed, ignoring the bloodstains on his exquisite robe.

The healer was at his side, pressing a cloth onto the wound. While the child slept, she took out needle and thread and swiftly sewed the edges of the cut together. *It could have ended quite differently.*

Rodario looked at Sha'taï, wondering at how quickly the young girl from the Outer Lands, probably not more than twelve cycles old, had acquired his language and adapted to the culture of Girdlegard. When she had first been found in the deserted village in the Grey Mountains, the dwarves were adamant that she should not be brought to Girdlegard; they were suspicious of the fact that she spoke only the älfar tongue. One of them had even tried to kill her.

But despite this opposition from the others, Rodîr Bannerman had brought the child to Mallenia, who had immediately taken her under her wing and made the girl her ward. Since the queen had no children of her own, Mallenia saw this as a gift from Samusin.

How little we know about the Outer Lands. Sha'taï had talked about being forced to flee from mighty cities plagued with family feuds. The girl had also mentioned älfar settlements that had been destroyed in a terrible war.

And she had spoken of Aiphatòn. The shintoìt seemed to have been involved in events, though the girl was not able to say whether or not he was still alive.

So he kept his vow to destroy his own people. Rodario twirled the end of his moustache and smiled down at the sleeping child. *She can tell us so much about the Outer Lands to the north.* And that was why she had been brought along to Freestone. Mallenia wanted her to give a report to the assembled heads of state and disperse any suspicions. The dwarves in particular seemed to view Sha'taï as evil incarnate, in the form of a child.

The healer applied an ointment to the stitches and then bandaged the wound before rising to her feet, bowing and making her way out of the room.

Once she addresses the crowned heads, everyone will see they've been mistaken about her. Rodario sat on the edge of her bed and held the girl's hand in his.

'Sleep,' he murmured into her dreams. 'You're safe here with us.'

'That's what you think,' she whispered back, to his surprise. Her eyelids were still shut. 'Not even *you* are safe. You rely too heavily on the dwarves and their gates.' She turned her head towards him and opened her eyes abruptly. 'But they've been defeated once before. It will happen again.'

Rodario noticed her frightened expression and how utterly convinced she was that her prophecy would come true. He shuddered at the thought. 'High King Boïndil and the Children of the Smith are well prepared. They have strengthened the fortresses.'

'There are powers no axe or stone or shield is effective against,' she contradicted him.

'Magic. I know,' he said with a smile. Her little hand was grasping his more tightly now. She must be afraid. 'But we have Coïra. She is clever and powerful and she has trained all the new magi and magae. And anyway, we've got more elves living here now than ever before. They are renowned for their military prowess.'

Sha'taï was not to be persuaded.

'You have no idea what kind of magic the nhatai are capable of,' she said softly, half-asleep again. 'The power they have can break through any gate, no matter how secure, and can defeat the strongest of armies.'

She swallowed hard and her eyelids fluttered. 'I saw . . .'

The girl fell back into slumber, her fragile little hand still tightly clasped round his fingers.

Rodario shuddered again. They had spoken of Girdlegard before but Sha'taï had never seemed this frightened.

'What are the nhatai?'

He jerked round at the sound of the deep voice behind him.

'Since when do dwarves creep around silently?' Rodario asked the High King, who was standing on the threshold.

'I knocked . . . Hard.' He showed how the head of his crow's beak had banged on the door frame. 'I was worried. I gave my little speech about the dwarf kingdoms and wanted to come along and see for myself where you'd got to.'

Rodario smiled. 'I was deep in thought, that's all.'

'Thinking about the nhatai?' Boïndil shouldered his weapon and grinned. 'Don't tell me it's the first time you've heard her mention the name?'

It had been. 'Maybe the sleeping draught has affected her mind.'

The High King pulled himself to his full height and looked deep into Rodario's eyes and then down at the child. 'If there's magic that can compromise the security of the fortresses at the pass, I need to know, Incomparable One,' he stressed, whirling the crow's beak, causing a draught that made his facial hair flutter. His beard had survived the fighting in top condition. 'We need to know what's what so we can be ready for it.'

'I'll ask her again.'

'It's *me* who should ask her,' Boïndil insisted, concerned and commanding.

'You forget that I'm as much of a king as you are.' Rodario forgave the High King the patronising way he had spoken, and placed his free hand on the dwarf's shoulder. 'You forget it when you're dealing with many of us.'

'Ho! You're forgetting you used to be a showman. Some thespian on a throne wants to tell me how best to look after Girdlegard's interests?' He gave a belly laugh. 'I hope for Urgon's sake the country made the right decision.'

Rodario's face darkened. *It must be the beer talking.* 'Now you're speaking out of turn.'

'I am High King and a Child of the Smith. I'm allowed to speak out of turn.' Boïndil pointed at Sha'taï. 'We've both made sacrifices for the liberation of our homeland. Liberating Girdlegard from all evil. But I still don't know what to make of this child. Her first words were in the älfar tongue.'

'She is innocent and good-hearted.'

'*I'll* be the judge of that.' The dwarf took a deep breath in and blew it out again. The smell of beer wafted over to Rodario. 'You and Mallenia brought her here so she could give an account of herself.'

'That's right.'

'Then wake her up and we'll start questioning her. If she satisfies the Council, then I'll be ready to change my tune.

Otherwise I say it would be better to send her back.' Boïndil made no attempt to conceal his distaste. 'And anyway, she could tell us anything she likes. We won't know if it's true.'

Rodario grinned. 'You mean to say you think she's made them up? These nhatai you're so scared of?'

'No, that sounded genuine enough. There was fear in her voice. And . . .' He stopped in surprise and glanced down. 'By Vraccas!'

Sha'taï's other hand had reached for his and appeared to be seeking his protection, too.

'There, look at that. She seems to like you.' Rodario tried not to laugh. 'She wants an alliance with the High King of the Dwarves.'

But Boïndil was not impressed. He took a step backward and extricated his hand from her fingers. 'Have you thought about why that black-eyes chose to come to her room first instead of attacking the Council straightaway?'

'He needed armour. As a disguise.'

'He could have seen to that on the way. As it is, he risked getting caught in a murder. If Sha'taï had screamed, his plan would have been scuppered.' Boïndil went over to the door, his steps heavy and slow. 'Maybe she was helping him.'

'Nonsense! He had her paralysed with fear,' Rodario disagreed hotly, not wanting to allow the dwarf's suspicions to raise doubts about the girl's innocence.

'A child that speaks älfar, comes from the Outer Lands and survives a visit by a black-eyes who goes on to butcher multiple experienced guards. Could work on the stage, of course,' said Boïndil, keeping his voice steady. 'But just have a little think as to why I might find this hard to believe.' And he left the room.

Rodario looked at the door, hearing the hobnailed dwarf

boots echo down the corridor. *Pig-headed and stubborn. Vraccas certainly did chisel you dwarves out of the mountains.*

'Why don't you have a High King?'

He looked down at Sha'taï, who was watching him intently with eyes blue as the sea.

'You're awake? Were you just pretending to be asleep?'

She avoided answering. 'If the dwarves have one to unite their tribes, surely Girdlegard should have one, too.' She sighed and stroked his arm before turning her head and closing her eyes again. Her dark blonde hair brushed his arm. 'You'd be the one to choose. I think I'll make you emperor, uncle.' She let go of his hand and curled up like a cat.

Rodario wondered if he had dreamt that last bit. The words seemed to have such conviction in her young mouth.

She had not hesitated or shown any doubt. It had sounded like a declaration of intent that would be followed through. Rodario gave her a kiss on the forehead, pulled the blanket up over her and got to his feet. *And how would you do that?* The one-time actor smiled to himself and smoothed his moustache. He stood tall and tried out his best heroic stance. *But it would be the biggest audience a showman could ever wish for.*

Girdlegard
United Kingdom of Gauragar-Idoslane
Gauragar
6492nd solar cycle, early summer

As his trusty black and white pony trotted along, Ireheart was only partially aware of the landscape: soft hills, interspersed with gentle hollows and meadows. Occasionally there would be the odd little patch of forest with pine, oak and beech trees predominating. The sun was high in the sky and it was a sweaty old ride.

And no sign of any cold beer.

Since leaving Freestone, he had not been able to stop thinking about what had happened. The pony kept steadily to the road to the north; they were approaching the Grey Mountains. All the while his thoughts were going round and round like cogwheels, making a great deal of noise but not actually connecting with each other.

His own homeland and Goda and the children, grown now, would have to wait. He needed to talk to Balyndis.

The queen of the Fifthlings was a friend and she was wise and she'd be sure to help him make sense of things. She was good at that. She could help him *brew a good steel*, as the dwarf adage went, or *grease the cogwheels*.

Following on from the attack, the Council had met again the next day to discuss the situation in Girdlegard.

If it had not been for the assassination attempt and the Outer Lands girl with the funny accent, Ireheart would have left the conference a happy High King.

But Rodario, King Rodario, of course, had to bring the child into it.

As soon as the girl entered the council chamber, Ireheart had felt thing change. Everyone seemed to fall for the creature, hanging on her every word, listening attentively and nodding agreement. Some of them took notes when she spoke. They asked her a few questions. She had answered politely and told them all about life in the north of the Outer Lands. The elves kept their distance, but were friendly.

And yet she's lying through her teeth, I'm convinced she is. Ireheart had questioned her on the nhatai.

Suddenly, it seemed, she had forgotten the name. She

claimed just to have made it up. She said the healer's sleeping draught had made her confused. Rodario said she had spoken of a threat, but tried to allay fears generally.

After that Sha'taï went from chair to chair, bowing prettily and having the kings and queens pat her on the head, stroke her hair or pinch her cheek.

So I'll have to see what I can do about it. Ireheart was angry, impatient, and, worse, thirsty.

Very thirsty.

The old rage he and his twin brother had so feared was still hovering in every fibre of his being, waiting to break out. The zhadár elixir had exacerbated it.

The fury made him crave the zhadár drink, however revolting it was. But the zhadár, a strange fighting unit of Thirdlings created by the älfar, were no more. There was only one of them still in existence in the Outer Lands.

So Ireheart would never lay his hands on the drink again, no matter how desperate he was for it. Even though he had noted a slight improvement over the previous cycle, it was still difficult to counteract the destructive rage bubbling up, or to quell his craving for the drink. As long as he had some alcohol in his blood, he could keep the rage at bay and cool the fury.

Is that an inn over there? Ireheart stood up in the stirrups, optimistic. He made out a farm on the horizon, next to a large field with horses. *That'll be the way-station for the couriers.*

He estimated he would arrive before the end of the orbit. So he would have a bed for the night and stabling for his valiant pony.

Ireheart sat back, his mood improving; he clapped the pony's neck, making dust rise. 'Looking good,' he told it.

'Let's give your poor back and my poor behind a little rest first. There'll be something good to eat later, you'll see. For both of us.'

He laughed as he led the pony over to the shade of a giant oak tree whose full, green roof of foliage would shelter them from the glaring sun.

The dwarf dismounted and sat down on the grass. The pony walked on a few steps to drink from the stream.

There was no undergrowth to speak of and thus no danger of attack, so Ireheart leaned back against the tree and closed his eyes. His warrior instincts would warn him if anyone approached.

He took his flask and drained what was left: honey beer that was far too warm. *That's the last of it till this evening.*

He rested his head on the trunk of the oak and hummed a typical dwarf ditty, trying to quieten the grinding cogs in his head. He made the words up as he went along:

Here I sit in my cellar
With a barrel of good dwarf beer
Happy as a hog with my black beer keg
Bring on your best beer, landlord
Hand me a tankard every time I wave
And I'll drink and I'll drink and I'll drink

I'm plagued by the demon thirst
So to see him off
I'll have a tankard in each hand first
Give us a try of your excellent mead
The whole world's looking honey-coloured
I could split the skull of the biggest orc
If I've got a drink, drink, drink

But the more I drink the greater my thirst
That's the snag, that's the worst
For a proper mead wine drinker
But I'll find good cheer
When I slip from my chair,
As long as there's a tankard in my hand
Steady, steady, stop! I won't spill a drop,
As long as I can drink, drink, drink

The sound of the insects buzzing and the leaves rustling on the branches would have lulled him to sleep had it not been for the penetrating smell of resin.

The dwarf lifted his head and inspected the tree trunk. He did not find anything untoward on the side next to him so he lay back on the grass to have a look at the other side – and was astounded at what he saw.

The bark had been almost completely scraped off by sharp claws making a zigzag pattern, and the wood underneath had been splintered. Curls of bark lay trampled into the ground and golden tree-blood was leaking from the trunk.

Must have been a bear! Ireheart sat up and saw his pony was still drinking from the stream. It didn't appear to have been spooked by the presence of a predator. *That's a relief.*

He started to search the ground for tracks to see whether his first assumption had been correct. *More like a dog's prints.* But a dog would never tear at the hard timber of an oak like that.

Ireheart put his head back and looked up to see if there was any reason an animal would climb the tree; perhaps it had just been sharpening its claws. If it had been hungry, a predator of this size would have had its choice of horses at the nearby way-station.

A gust of wind let lances of light stream down through the moving leaves, preventing any clear view of the upper branches.

Is that someone up there or is it a bunch of mistletoe? Ireheart took a few steps to the side to get out of the dazzling light.

At that moment there was a high-pitched whinny of fear as the stream erupted into a fountain of shimmering droplets. A huge black wolf-like creature thrust its way up out of the water and towards the pony. Its strong jaws gaped wide, fastened on the animal's neck and bit through.

The horse fell in the shallow waters of the stream, flailing about with its hooves as it tried in vain to scramble back up the bank. Ireheart's heavy crow's beak lay near where the pony finally lay still: it might have served him well in what was to come.

'By Vraccas!' He stared at the beast heading his way, pony blood dripping from its fangs. The two short axes on his belt found their way automatically to his hands. 'It's down to you that I'll have to walk all the way to the farm now!' He swerved out of the reach of the wildly snapping teeth. 'And how you stink!' The long claws shot past his face, missing his nose by the length of a beard.

Ireheart felt the accursed fury rising in him; this time he gave it free rein.

A red veil obscured his vision and his body became searing hot.

The beast snapped at the dwarf, growling, and received the blade of an axe in its glowing row of teeth. It shrieked with pain as its fangs splintered.

Using the momentum, Ireheart swivelled round and sank his second blade in the mysterious wolf's thick skin; its eyes glowed white. But the axe did not go deep enough.

'So how do I kill you?' he yelled at the beast, bursting its sensitive nose with a sharp blow from his armoured elbow. The blood streaming out was white in colour. 'Huzzah! You're not keen on that, are you?'

The predator leaped back and lowered its head, its ears erect. Its roar was like a bark: loud and full of spite; the dwarf's axe was lodged in the tough skin of its side.

'Get back here! You've stolen my axe!' Ireheart tossed the remaining blade from one hand to the other and jerked his long braid neatly over his shoulder. 'That's not going to save you, monster. No matter what nest of demons you've crawled out of, I'm going to split your belly!' He would have shouted *Oink, Oink*, his battle cry for orcs, but this beast would not have understood.

He noticed a wire with a long thin metal capsule fastened round its throat. *What's the significance of that?* He'd be able to investigate once he'd killed the creature.

Ireheart made a move to the side in order to get nearer to the pony's carcass where his crow's beak lay. The spike on that should be strong enough to pierce the creature's hide. A weapon that had brought night-mares to heel would surely put paid to this adversary – just as long as he could get his hands on it.

The monster seemed to guess his intention. It kept its distance, watching Ireheart and wearing the axe as if it were a trophy. Its ears were still erect, but its eyes narrowed to slits.

'What's the matter, you stinking dog?' The hot rage prevented Ireheart from taking the sensible option. 'Here you are, I'm bringing you my other axe!' He charged.

So did the beast, throwing up mud and bits of grass from under its talons.

Ireheart laughed and stretched out to land a thundering blow – but a shadow threw itself down from the oak to attack the back of the animal.

A blood-encrusted human in tattered chainmail drove his double-edged long sword into the creature's body with all the force from his leap.

But the monstrous wolf did not die.

It hurled the man off, snapped at him and then made for Ireheart, limping now.

Overcoming his shock, the dwarf ran over to the bank of the stream. *I must get my crow's beak.*

He could hear the beast approach and he quickened his own pace, laughing out loud. His armour clinked, a further taunt.

'Come on! Try a little bit harder!' he mocked, reaching the edge of the stream.

He slid feet-first down the bank past his dead pony.

He snatched the long handle of the crow's beak with one hand and hacked the spike in to the soft earth, abruptly curtailing his descent before he could fall into the water. He did not want to chance his luck with the goddess Elria.

'Got you!' Still lying on the ground, he grabbed the crow's beak with both hands and yanked it out of the earth; the beast was glowering down at him, drooling, jaws agape. 'Huzzah!'

The long steel spike went through the back of the creature's neck, piercing the spine at the base of the skull. Ireheart jerked the handle and the monster flew over him. This dislodged the weapon. The beast landed in the water and lay still.

'To Tion with you!' The dwarf sprang to his feet and crushed the creature's skull with hammer blows from the side of his weapon. Ireheart was in such a frenzy that he continued to belabour the battered head until he was boiling hot and exhausted. He stopped, gasping for air, and wiped the sweat from his brow. 'Filthy cur.'

His fury ebbed away, the thirst did not.

With great caution, not wanting to fall in, he bent down and scooped a handful of water from the stream. *What I wouldn't give for a long, cool honey beer.*

He went back to where the warrior had leaped from the tree. The black-haired man lay in the grass, gasping for breath. The beast had pulled half his arm out from the shoulder. There was a smell of rotten flesh. Older wounds had become infected and gangrene had set in. There was no helping this soldier. As he lay there, a pitiful spectacle, he had no fear in his eyes. He seemed clear that he was about to die and was not raving with fever.

'A Child of the Smith,' he murmured, attempting a smile. 'Vraccas must have known I would meet you.'

'He *did* know.' Ireheart took the man's hand. 'My thanks for your action. My name is—'

'There's something in my leather bag. Get it. A capsule with runes, dwarf runes. It was round the neck of a beast just like the one you killed. The monsters come from Phondrasôn and they've found a way through into the elf realm.' He spoke quickly, knowing death was upon him. 'Take them to your king. And know this: the elves murdered my young king. Their Naishïon is behind everything. They made a pact with Natenian – he wants to stay ruler of Tabaîn . . .' The man's bright eyes dimmed in the space of his final heartbeat.

Ireheart had listened intently to what the dying man had told him. *I'd better write it down before I forget.* He cut a large piece of bark from the oak and used the warrior's blood to note key words. *That'll have to do till I get to the courier station*. He could write it up properly on paper or parchment once he was there.

Ireheart found the small, matt-black metal container secured with a safety lock and inspected it closely.

The runes were certainly of dwarf origin, though exaggerated, as if to attract attention.

They formed a name.

'By Vraccas!' Ireheart leaped to his feet and ran back to the beast's cadaver, breaking the wire round its neck and looking at the second capsule.

He rinsed it in the stream, still taking care not to go too near. He did not trust the goddess.

The same runes. The two monsters had been sent as messengers.

The name of the intended recipient was clearly punched in.

'"For Ireheart",' he read, dumbfounded.

There was only one dwarf who had gone to Phondrasôn and would know him by that name.

Girdlegard
Kingdom of Tabaîn, Wheattown
6492nd solar cycle, early summer

King Natenian felt the sweat coming out from every pore, and it was staining his wide yellow robe, either as droplets or large patches. He limped along, flanked by two nurses, heading for the throne room of the simple palace building that was more a fortress than anything else. This was where the nobles of the land were meeting to determine who should be his successor.

On the face of it, at least.

The news of his younger brother dying a hero's death had spread like wildfire across the kingdom. The elves had packed the Tabaîn delegate's remains in ice and delivered it before decomposition could set in.

The body of the popular heir apparent had been embalmed and put on show for three days in the Palandiell temple, so that the citizens could pay their last respects. The unmistakable bite wounds on the other deep-chilled bodies that had been transported at the same time, together with the carcass of the beast itself, dispelled any doubts in people's minds. What the elves told them must indeed have been what happened.

Only one body was missing: Tenkil, the young king's best friend, was said to have been devoured completely. Skin and hair and all.

Natenian had summoned all the nobles to get to the bottom of why Raikan had ever gone to Lesinteïl in the first place.

The guards at the entrance to the throne room saluted and opened the double doors for their king.

Natenian stepped in, escorted by his carers. He walked slowly past all the courtiers in their finery and made his way to the top of the table. The sound of his laboured breath echoed back from the walls.

Portraits of earlier rulers hung from the walls; they stared down on the proceedings as if to ensure that everything was done properly. Antique tapestries covered the stone walls and dusty banners hanging from the ceiling beams showed the coats of arms of distinguished families.

Although the sun was still high, lamps and candles had been lit. No one knew how long the meeting would go on, and anyway, the windows were only narrow slits, which did not allow much light to come through. The kingdom suffered from frequent gales and storms so the traditional method of building eschewed extra storeys or wide windows. The palace itself was half-sunk in the earth, like a crouching animal.

His breath whistling, Natenian sat down in his special chair that gave the necessary support for him to sit upright. The nurses accompanying him both stepped back a little, remaining on hand if needed.

The seat to the king's right was empty and a black sheet covered the chair. Everyone knew who was missing.

'My brother,' Natenian began, 'was a traitor.'

Lightning hitting the centre of the table could not have made more impact. The assembled nobility stared at him; nobody spoke.

Natenian drew breath with a groan. 'You're thinking I have lost my mind. But I am just as horror-struck as yourselves.' When he made a gesture, a servant went to open a side door to admit a blond elf belonging to the delegation from Lesinteïl. He was wearing a white robe with a black sash draped around his hips as a sign of mourning. 'This is Phenîlas. He has the evidence with him.'

A murmur ran round the room as the elf approached the table, taking the contract out of its leather case.

'Honourable ladies and gentlemen,' he said, his voice as soft as velvet. 'Here you see the pact that Raikan wanted to make with my people. We pretended to go along with it, in order to then inform Natenian and the people of Tabaîn without delay.' He passed the parchment around. 'His conduct seemed strange, although he assured us he was about to be appointed king, irrevocably.'

'He was planning to go behind my back. Perhaps he was going to have me murdered, to make sure he would come to power! This is treachery of the highest order. Against me. Against you. Against Tabaîn.' He had the appearance of a man utterly shocked; his breath rasped with emotion. 'The shame he has thus brought on the whole family – no word of this may ever leave this room. I am counting on your discretion.'

The nobles swore an oath or nodded compliance.

'You will understand that under the present circumstances I can no longer remain in office as monarch,' he said, his voice breaking. 'The stigma of shame taints me, too. And I am growing weaker by the orbit.' Incensed voices were heard calling on him not to abdicate. Natenian raised his hand. 'My thanks. I understand your objections. However . . .'

'Your Majesty,' came an interruption from the red-haired Cledenia, friendly in tone but firm. Her high-collared black gown made her face appear hard. 'The people know you and hold you in high regard. Your brother has become a legend because of his heroic death. As no one will ever learn what he did in secret, nothing would reflect badly on yourself.'

'Ah, but *I* know about it.'

She pointed at the others. 'We all know about it. But it does not upset us.' Again, shouts of agreement were heard. 'Your family enjoys a good reputation and you emerged unscathed from all the confusion when Lohasbrand's reign crumbled. Your character is spotless and, combined with your stamina and determination to carry on despite your state of health, you provide a wonderful example for us all – from the highest to the lowest of the population.' Cledenia bowed. 'Remain as our king until the gods call you to join them.'

Natenian glanced at Phenîlas and the elf permitted the slightest of smiles to cross his face.

'Well, then.' He levered himself up out of the chair and indicated to the nurses that he wanted to try to stand by himself. The women stepped back once more. 'If no one speaks against me, then I swear by all the gods that I shall do everything in my power to eradicate the shame my brother has brought. I will be a wise ruler. Tabaîn shall blossom and my subjects shall flourish under my regency. This I swear by Palandiell' – he turned to Phenîlas – 'and by Sitalia. My thanks to your people, friend elf.'

Phenîlas sketched a bow. 'Girdlegard is not in need of more deceit and falsehood,' he replied. 'We fight together against injustice.'

Natenian seemed to grow a little taller at the uproar of applause from the nobility. He relished the attention and esteem he would not in normal circumstances have merited. *You're all pitiful.* He smiled at each of them in turn. *You won't be around for too long. You are not included in my plans.*

'Forgive me,' Cledenia said when the applause started to die away. 'Who have you selected as your heir in place of Raikan? Do let us know who you think is worthy of succeeding you. We're dying to know.'

Natenian lifted his crippled left hand and pointed a bony finger at Dirisa. *That'll set the cat among the pigeons and get them all jealous of each other. A good diversionary tactic.* 'Dirisa would be my choice. She is young and healthy and intelligent and a second cousin to Queen Astirma. Alliances among the kingdoms are all the rage nowadays,' he answered. His veiled reference to Mallenia and Rodario was met with laughter.

Dirisa got to her feet, adjusted her pink dress and bowed graciously. 'My gratitude.'

To Natenian's surprise, the beautiful ebony-haired woman with the slender figure of a young boy left her place and went to remove the black sheet on the seat to the king's right hand.

A sudden silence fell.

She gathered her skirts and sat down as slowly and carefully as if the seat were made of glass. 'I have been thinking about your words. I understand why you would want to abdicate after the shame your brother has brought on your family.' She shot him a devastating smile. 'You are wise, and I accept.'

Natenian was at a loss. His plan was crumbling away and he was finding it hard to breathe. His heart was pounding with rage against this usurper. He sat back with a groan, in a coughing fit. Then he choked and swallowed his tongue; it seemed he might suffocate. One of the nurses rushed up, took hold of his lower jaw and forced it down. She reached two fingers inside his mouth and saved his life with a skilful move. He had not intended to leave office in that way.

Natenian tried to catch his breath but was not able to speak. He choked back all recriminations and threats. It was obvious his chosen successor did not approve of his intentions. The successor he had selected and named himself. On a whim.

Nobody spoke.

Incredulous eyes were focused on the young woman who was already in place at the top of the table, standing tall and beaming. 'I accept your decision,' she said with the sweetest of smiles. 'It is better for Tabaîn. But I shall often come and ask for advice, should I need it. I would suggest that a few more privileges for the aristocracy would not go amiss. In honour of the occasion, of course. That is my first decree.'

Phenîlas turned into a statue whose expression could not be read. But with his eyes he promised Natenian support. The elves had absolutely no wish to enter a new round of negotiations.

This was a relief to the ruler. *Privileges. What a clever piece of work she is. As soon as I've got my breath back I'll send her straight back to where she's from and from there directly to her death.*

But Cledenia led the cheers, warmly and firm: 'Long live Dirisa the First!'

At that moment Natenian knew that at least two of the nobles had been prepared for this turn of events.

I was in a quandary.
To go into endingness?
To join the älfar resistance?
Or to stay calm and wait for my time to come?
It was hard to quash my pride.
Mallenia will never learn how often I stood secretly at her bedside at night with the metal quill in my hand ready to cut her throat.
I may be an old älf – but I can do more than my enemies and deriders fear I can.

Secret notes for
The Writings of Truth
written under duress by Carmondai

III

Girdlegard
United Kingdom of Gauragar-Idoslane
Gauragar
6492nd solar cycle, early summer

'Give us another.' Ireheart waved the empty mug that had been roughly carved out of a lump of wood.

The serving lad nodded. 'At once, Master Dwarf. It's the best from our ice cellar.'

Ireheart chose not to respond, as his opinion of long'un beer, after ten large beakers of it, was not favourable. It was the colour of piss, tasteless, and had so little effect on his head that he had to down two brandies with each tankard. Puzzlingly, the long'uns seemed to like it cold, as cold as if it came straight from a glacier. It froze his teeth and numbed his palate.

He sat at a long table in the smoky atmosphere of the main drinking room of Gauragar's courier way-station, located at the crossroads where a southern branch joined the main east–west route. Candles and soot-covered lamps gave the dimmest of light but this did not bother him.

The captain of the couriers had allowed the dwarf in to take a rest with no idea who he was. Ireheart did not let on. As long as he had coins in his pocket and could pay for his keep, they would leave him in peace.

The beer arrived and he mumbled a thank you to the skinny lad in charge of the bar.

You little so-and-so! Ireheart stared at the capsules he had collected. Absentmindedly he twisted his beard into two braids and fastened the ends together with a silver clasp. *How am I going to get you open?* For four orbits now he had been trying to open the casings, but they resisted every attempt; it made little difference whether he hit them with a hammer or fiddled patiently with the catch. He was starting to think it was a practical joke.

The inscription FOR IREHEART in large dwarf runes mocked him.

'What've you got there, Master Dwarf? A puzzle?' The dark-haired youth wearing his innkeeper's long leather apron had come back to the table. 'Sorry if I'm being nosy. But we've seen you working at it for quite a time. Everybody's wondering what it is.'

Ireheart threw his head back and laughed. 'Vraccas! I may be dim but I'm providing entertainment for the entire place.'

'That's true,' the boy grinned back at him.

'And who are you, you cheeky beggar?'

'I'm Heidor.'

Ireheart patted the seat next to him. 'Right, Heidor Big Mouth. These capsules – I can't get them open.'

'What's inside?' Heidor sat down, his eyes sparkling.

'Haven't got the foggiest.'

'And what's this writing say?'

'My name.' Ireheart crossed his arms and grinned. 'Alright, clever clogs, what do you make of it?'

Heidor weighed the capsules in his hands and spun them on the tabletop. 'Uneven. Either one part is thicker or there's something heavy inside,' he said enthusiastically.

'I'm way ahead of you on that.'

Heidor swept them off the table, observing how they fell.

They clinked and rolled around and ended up with the runes underneath.

'Hmm.' The youth picked them back up and looked closely at one. 'There are no scratches even though you banged it with the hammer.'

'It's an alloy with a high tionium content.' It appealed to Ireheart to have company as he tried to solve the puzzle. Reaching into his pocket, he took out his small travel pipe and filled it with honey tobacco. Heidor brought him a lighted spill. *Makes the beer taste better.*

'Some new couriers have arrived, yes? There's been a lot of coming and going recently, hasn't there?' He blew out the flame on the spill and put it down on the table. 'What's been happening in Girdlegard?'

Heidor filled him in without taking his eyes off the capsules. 'King Natenian's brother has been killed. A beast attacked him and his friends.' The boy was set on solving the puzzle. 'It's said one of them was devoured whole. Not a trace left.'

Swallowed whole, my foot. A lie spread about the fate of the brave soldier he had encountered. *He escaped, that's what.* Ireheart had buried the warrior next to the oak tree and had taken the signet ring as proof of having met him.

The dwarf had dismembered the monster and chucked the pieces into the stream. He didn't want word to get around there had been a fight. If what the injured Tabaîn soldier told him was true, it seemed the elves were playing their own treacherous game and involving some of the humans. It might be up to the dwarves to save the day.

Not again, Vraccas. It's only been a few cycles. First Tion sends that child from the Outer Lands and now the elves are playing false again. 'What was the king's brother doing at the time?'

'Courtesy visit of some kind.'

'Then Natenian's still king of Tabaîn?' Ireheart puffed at his pipe, sending a stream of smoke up to the blackened rafters where clothes hung to dry. They would carry a nice smell of smoked bacon, for sure.

'It seemed so, but then we heard there was a new successor, a woman.' Heidor was engrossed in his task. 'Why don't you ask the couriers? Over there. They'll know.'

Ireheart got up and clapped the youth on the shoulder with enough force to nearly knock him off his chair. He weaved his way over to the bar, where a couple of men, one blond, one dark, were helping themselves to beer from the new barrel, not wanting to wait for the landlord. The two men wore sweaty loose-fitting shirts and brown leather trousers and they had unlaced their boots for comfort. They had washed their faces but their clothes were covered in dust from the ride.

'Tell me the latest. What's the news in Tabaîn?' The dwarf placed a silver coin on the counter. 'Drinks on me. The king: he's been chucked out?'

'That's right, friend Short Leg.' The blond rider grinned. 'Thanks. Shan't forget it.' They raised their tankards. 'To the health of Girdlegard's protectors.'

Short Leg, eh? Ireheart seethed. 'So who's made a play for the throne?'

The dark-haired one mimed a feminine role. 'Her Graciousness Dirisa, a distant relative of Astirma's.'

'Good impression.'

'He can do a dwarf, too,' the blond one joked.

'If he walks on his knees,' Ireheart quipped. 'I can help out with my axe if he likes. We can give him the end of a cow's tail for a beard.' He gave a belly laugh and the others joined in. They seemed to have had more than the one beer.

The dark-haired courier began to speak again. 'Natenian was going to abdicate, people say, and he was looking for a suitable successor among the nobility.'

'Dirisa seized her chance,' the other continued. 'Nobody knows quite what the actual situation is.'

'Simple enough in my eyes: Natenian's on the throne and he's calling himself king. So he can have a usurper put to death,' Ireheart cut in. 'Hasn't anyone suggested that? You long'uns always take the long way round, don't you?'

The dark-haired one had a conspiratorial expression. He leaned in. 'There's said to be a secret about the royal family that's preventing Natenian from wielding power.' He spat into the fire. 'Else Dirisa would have been out on her ear.'

'Their family tree, perhaps?' Ireheart drank from his tankard, clamped his pipe between his teeth and got a refill, tipping the brandy in. 'It's been only one cycle since the last war. Nobody's going to be mad enough to start another one in the kingdoms,' he mumbled past his pipe stem. *Unless, of course, he'd something to gain.*

He was always keen to believe in the humans' power of reasoning, but found it hard. Mallenia and Rodario he was prepared to trust. To a point. But ever since that child had turned up at court in Grandcastle, they'd been less reliable.

'I expect someone will get rid of her,' the blond rider mooted. 'The nobles can't agree, I hear. They wonder if Dirisa might be better for Girdlegard in the end.' He raised his beer in a salute to the company. 'It's all up in the air over there with our neighbours. I'm sure to get some despatches to bring over soon.'

'I don't care who's in power as long as they give us some of their corn,' his friend laughed.

Grain! That'll be why the elves are interfering in Tabaîn

events. Ireheart stroked his beard braids thoughtfully. 'Thank you, gentlemen. That's got me up to date. Now go and get washed, the pair of you. You stink to high heaven, you do. Could easily have mistaken you for orcs. It might have ended badly.' He returned to his table with a smile on his face, wanting to see if Heidor had made any progress. 'Hey, stupid, how're you getting on?'

Taken by surprise at the deep dwarf voice, Heidor fell off his seat. He got up, ruefully rubbing his behind. 'I tried puzzling it out but then I resorted to brute force, like you did.'

'Best leave brute force to me.' Ireheart helped the boy to his feet and patted him on the shoulder. 'Get me another spill for my pipe.'

Heidor hobbled over to the fireplace.

The dwarf watched him. His mind was full of swirling thoughts: the capsules, the child, the dead warrior, the lies the elves were spreading. *I'm not getting anywhere with any of this.*

The dark-haired despatch rider chucked two logs on the fire, sending up sparks. There was a sizzling when the man sent a gout of saliva onto the embers.

Of course! He had a sudden inspiration and drained his tankard in one.

'Heidor,' he bellowed, startling the other drinkers and rattling the plates. 'I'll be in the blacksmith's. Bring me a sack of ice. And some beer.' He bent down to pick up the capsules then hurried out.

'And some brandy. And make it quick.'

At the back of the shed, the brazier still had glowing charcoal in it; the dwarf used his foot on the bellows to stoke up the heat. He laid his pipe aside.

Sparks shot up as Ireheart piled on more coals, spreading

them out with a poker. A chain device on the main bellows quickly helped bring the temperature up.

He placed the capsules in the fire and continued to blast air at the coals, which were now white-hot. They would have melted conventional iron and even good steel, but the two containers showed no sign of being affected by the heat. They did not change shape nor did any additional runes become visible.

But that was not what Ireheart had been hoping for.

Heidor came across the courtyard with a plump jute sack on his back. The contents crunched like fresh snow. 'Your ice, Master Dwarf.'

'In that tub over there.' Ireheart wiped salty drops from his brow before the sweat could run into his eyes. 'Now for the beer and the brandy, lad.'

The ice fragments floated in the horse trough.

'At once, Master Dwarf.'

Using tongs, Ireheart lifted the metal capsules from the glowing bed of coals and tossed them into the water, where they sank into the fragments of ice.

He fished them out, placed them on the anvil and hit them with the heaviest hammer the smithy afforded; he turned his face away to avoid injury from flying metal splinters. The sudden change in temperature had placed the metal under extreme stress and with a loud bang, the containers shattered into several pieces.

'Huzzah!' he crowed, looking at the two white-hot palladium discs on the anvil. They had absorbed the heat but had not melted inside their cocoon. *Evil protects the good.* Ireheart used the hammer to sweep the discs into the ice bath to cool off so he could study them. Clouds of steam rose up as the metal sank to the bottom. *That looks like the Scholar's work.*

It was clear to him that these were messages from Tungdil

even if reason dictated caution: the messages might have been sent on their way before the Scholar died.

Heidor came hurrying back with beer and brandy. He noticed the metal splinters on the anvil. 'You've done it!'

'I should have thought of it sooner.' Ireheart picked up his pipe and fished a piece of glowing coal out with the tongs to reignite the tobacco.

The youth hopped from one foot to the other impatiently. 'And? What was inside, then?'

Ireheart puffed out a cloud of smoke, hiding his face and making Heidor cough. 'Nothing.'

'Nothing?

'Just air.' He regretted having to lie to the youth who had been so helpful and eager, but it really wasn't any of his business. 'The secret was in working out how to open it.'

'Oh.' Heidor looked very disappointed. 'So I've lost my wager.'

'What wager?'

'They were betting on whether you'd be able to break it open, and, if so, what would be inside.'

Ireheart puffed away at his pipe and rewarded himself for his hard work with a mouthful of honey-flavoured beer. 'And what did you predict?'

'A magic diamond.'

The dwarf smiled broadly and put his tankard down on the anvil, gathered the various bits of the tionium alloy casing and pressed them into the boy's hands. 'It's not a diamond, but almost as valuable. Sell it to a swordsmith. He'll know its worth and will pay you for it.' He grabbed the boy by the collar. 'But not a word to the others. Or it'll be nicked before you know it.'

'Of course, Master Dwarf!' Heidor was profuse in his

thanks as he stowed the metal carefully in his apron pocket. 'May Vraccas heap blessings on you.' He took the tankard. 'I'll bring you another.' He hurried off to the main building.

Good lad. Ireheart smiled and pulled at the mouthpiece of the pipe, releasing grey-blue smoke. As soon as he had been given the promised refreshment, he sent Heidor off, claiming he wanted to stay in the forge for a while: perfectly natural behaviour for a dwarf.

Once he was alone he fished out the coin-sized palladium discs and took them into the depths of the shed. Meticulously-crafted dwarf runes covering the surface were just visible in the light of the forge.

What will you be telling me? Ireheart was afraid his dearest hopes would melt away like a wax mould in the flames.

He rubbed the thin metal with his thumb.

He had waited so long, had railed against fate, had given in to doubt – but this could be the proof he had longed for. Proof that the great hero of Girdlegard was still alive and that it had been *something else* that had died by the Black Abyss, killed by the axe Keenfire in Kiras' hand.

A *something* that had not been a true Child of the Smith.

Ireheart was convinced for a long time that he had been the reason the blade's diamonds had lit up. All because of the dreadful zhadár elixir he had tasted; it had been produced with the dark arts of the älfar using distilled älf blood. The magic blade had recognised the evil within him, not Tungdil. So he had thought. But in the cycles that followed, he had started to wonder. He put his hopes on Vraccas sending some miracle to save his lost friend, the Scholar.

Ireheart took a deep breath, put his pipe down and took a final draught of beer. 'Father of all the dwarves, I beseech you: restore him to me,' he whispered.

His chestnut brown eyes focused on the runes.

His heart thumping in his chest, he scanned the message by the light of the forge's glow.

Girdlegard
Black Mountains
Kingdom of the Thirdling dwarves
Eastern Gate
6492nd solar cycle, early summer

Grey-haired Rognor Mortalblow stood next to his friend and king and looked down from the battlements to where, one hundred paces away, the eastern gate to Girdlegard stood.

The fortress had been hewn out of the cliff in the shape of the helmeted head of a dwarf, through whose open mouth travellers would pass. If the upper half and the lower half of the gates closed, like a nutcracker, those outside would see the grim sharp teeth of sharp-edged steel.

All the arrow slits and the outlets for heated pitch, burning oil or other liquids were cunningly concealed about the stone face. When the fortress was constructed, iron and steel vertical and horizontal beams had been incorporated within the balustrades. No battering ram had been able to breach the walls in recent cycles and no bombardment had been able to inflict serious damage.

Behind the fortress a sheer cliff of glass-like basalt reared up: it looked as if Vraccas had tried to thrust the mountain peak up through the clouds to tower to the stars. Polished surfaces mirrored and focused the dazzling sunshine and reflected it back down on the open plain in front of the entrance like the light of the night constellations. Light could be a useful weapon. Now in the early afterzenith, the rows of granite-black teeth were wide open and the banners above the portal fluttered a welcome to all arriving with peaceful intent.

On the Black Abyss road there was a wagon train approaching, a few miles distant still. White pennants fluttered in the cold north wind. No one walking along the road would be aware of the numerous traps the Thirdlings had constructed. Pits were concealed under the road's surface that could be activated by a system of ropes and pulleys from inside the fortress. Every single patch of stone or earth around the entrance could bring instant death without the dwarves' having to employ their catapults, spear-slingers and crossbows.

'Elves,' said Hargorin Deathbringer of the clan of the Stone Crushers. He was ruler of the Thirdling dwarves – the best warriors among the Children of the Smith. In earlier times the Thirdlings had waged war against all the other dwarves but Hargorin had declared the feud ended. Rising to his full height, he stood broader than any other dwarf. 'They'll be here in less than an eighth of an orbit.'

'Do you know the High King's view?' Rognor turned to him, revealing the tattooed side of his face with its decorative black runes. His smartly-trimmed beard was dyed dark blue.

Both dwarves wore chainmail with reinforced shoulder pieces that had spikes attached. They had short blades in their forearm protectors and they wore the traditional Thirdling skirt of iron platelets to protect the hip and thigh area. A black cloak was a defence against the wind.

'Boïndil will have his reasons for the order.'

'I didn't mean that.'

Hargorin growled under his breath and did not answer immediately. He was struggling with conflicting arguments and emotions.

One cycle ago the whole of Girdlegard had Hargorin down as the worst possible traitor because he had collaborated with the älfar and collected taxes for them. And had killed for them.

But it turned out that he had been working in secret against the Thirdlings, planning their fall, in spite of all the horrific acts he and his Black Squadron had committed. When Tungdil Goldhand emerged from the Black Abyss, Hargorin was able to drop his mask and turn the hated Black Squadron into an indispensable unit for the fight against the älfar occupying force.

Hargorin kept his eyes fixed on the approaching wagons. He had never reproached himself over his previous deeds; he put up with the abuse and accusations heaped on him by the humans. He had paid his debt by riding against evil in the battle. *The Thirdlings, too, had to make sacrifices. Great sacrifices.*

The wind started to turn, bringing strains of music from drums and stringed instruments. The elves seemed to be in festive mood.

'They are coming to the land of their creator,' said Hargorin, the breeze playing with the red hair of his beard as if it were grass. 'Let's see what they do.' Then he reached into the folds of his black cloak.

To Rognor's surprise his hand came out again with a small vraccasium box etched with dwarf runes.

Each of the dwarf tribes, as well as the Freelings, had been given just such a precious casket; it contained some of Tungdil Goldhand's ashes. It was a relic of the last High King, the greatest hero Girdlegard had ever known.

'I saw him, Rognor.' Hargorin sounded thoughtful. 'He was there at my feet, cut down by the very weapon that once brought him victory.' He clapped his hand against his breast.

'Keenfire was here at my breast and the diamonds were glowing. That meant the axe sensed the presence of an evil that had to be destroyed.'

'Or at least that evil was nigh.' Rognor was well aware of the various versions doing the rounds about why Keenfire had turned on its previous owner. 'Are you saying you believe Boïndil?'

'I'm saying I can't with any certainty exclude the possibility that Goldhand is still alive.' The red-haired broad-shouldered dwarf opened up the lid of the box.

The wind caught the contents and wafted a breath of the ashes into the air. The small grey cloud rose and disappeared.

'We may be making a big mistake if we're not careful. Perhaps the hero needs *our* help to escape from the realm of demons where he's imprisoned.'

'Could be a trick, though. A trap for our best fighters.'

'I knew you'd throw that one in.'

Rognor gave a hollow laugh. 'I am your chancellor, advisor and friend. How can I hold my peace?'

'But what do you *really* believe?' Hargorin looked him in the eyes. 'What does your heart say, Rognor Mortalblow? *Could* it be true?'

The grey-haired dwarf sighed and did not answer.

'I can't rule out the possibility that it might be bogus,' the Thirdlings' king went on. 'So I've no choice in the circumstances: I must go myself to check it out.'

'You?' Rognor grasped his arm. 'Have you lost your mind?' Consternation caused the tattoos on his face to form dark islands. 'You are our ruler!'

Hargorin laughed. 'But they thought *you* were their king. For many cycles, at that.'

'Because in secret I was carrying out your orders.' Rognor

was incensed. 'Why not send Jarkalín Blackfist? He was with the Black Squadron and obeys . . .'

Hargorin removed his friend's hand gently. 'Tungdil is a Thirdling. A dwarf of our own tribe. And I have only been elected king because he is not here. There could be no better deed than to ride out and fetch our hero home in order that he may take my place.'

'So what was it that died at the Black Abyss?' Rognor was not giving in easily. 'If it wasn't Tungdil, who sent him to us to fight against evil?'

'Maybe it was Vraccas? Or perhaps even evil itself, to drag us to our ruin, but the demonic plan failed?' Hargorin clapped him on the chest. 'Be my deputy again, Rognor. You are my chancellor and will have all the authorities you need.'

'Get Boïndil to show you the message again . . .'

'The Thirdlings trust you. And that is why you will lead them while I'm searching for Goldhand.' This time Hargorin's interruption sounded sharper. 'Senseless to debate it further.'

'Yes, my king.' Rognor knew when it was time to keep silent.

'Officially, I shall be going on a visit to the Fourthlings. A friendly visit,' Hargorin continued. 'Nobody must find out where I'm really going.'

'What will you do if you're found out? I don't suppose the elves will let a handful of dwarves search for the entrance to the breeding-ground of darkness in their realm, when they've just filled it all in.' Rognor diverted his attention to the practicalities, seeing as how he was not going to change the king's mind about going in person. The tattoos on his face resumed their normal format.

'The elves won't stop me.' Hargorin said nothing more. But the words he spoke made clear how intent he was on this mission to help Tungdil.

'You'd risk a skirmish, risk even a war, with the pointy-ears?'

'It won't go that far.' Hargorin glanced at the wagon train as it made its way up the road; the music and singing were louder now. 'The elves have changed. I'm positive they'll let us pass. Maybe a few of them will come along with us. It's in their interest, too, to have the great hero back in Girdlegard. We are not safe yet, despite having swept the evil out of our lands.' He cast his eyes on the north for a number of heart-beats, dwelling on the mighty peaks where ice, snow and glaciers held sway. 'Something tells me we're not out of the woods yet, old friend. We'll be needing a true leader. One of a kind.'

He opened the casket lid to its full extent.

The mountain wind snatched the remaining ashes and scattered them to the cool air. Nothing was left but a grey veil on the battlement wall that resisted the wind. But it, too, surrendered at last.

Rognor clenched his jaw. Throwing away the ashes said more than words could have done.

Standing together, they waited until the elves' train had arrived within hailing distance of the entrance. The two dwarves were lowered down on the lift platform that was operated by a series of pulleys and counterweights.

Once on the ground, Hargorin warned the guards to be ready to close the gate at his signal. Then he and Rognor stepped out onto the open area in front of the fortress to greet the new arrivals and tell them what the High King had decreed.

There were about a hundred elves in the convoy. A third of them appeared to be soldiers and the rest were women and children of various ages. They drew nearer with their twenty wagons and thirty exquisite horses.

Their music was not to Rognor's taste. The high notes produced by the harp and the stringed instruments hurt his ears.

'Maybe they could be taught to play something different?' he grunted to Hargorin.

'They're not going to take to our drinking songs, are they?' Grinning, the king stepped forward, while from the other side, one rider galloped up.

The elf was wearing light leather armour dyed white, with a mantle over it that seemed to Rognor to be unnecessarily thick. *If they're feeling the cold now, what'll happen when winter kicks in here in the mountains? Freeze to death?*

The elf drew up in front of the dwarves and sprang from the saddle before his white stallion had even come to a complete halt. He bowed his head.

'My greetings, Lords of the Mountains,' he said with a soft lilt, using the common language of Girdlegard. 'We wish to enter, bringing peace and good intentions. Our destination is the elf realm of Âlandur.'

'To settle there, I assume,' Hargorin added. 'Just like the others who came through the gates before you.'

'Indeed.'

The elf smiled warmly at the two dwarves, a smile that was honest and free of arrogance. 'My name is Nafinîas and I have my friends and my family with me. We shall live here in Girdlegard and we shall live for Girdlegard, our home. Our goddess summoned us hither.'

An expression of regret spread over Hargorin's face. 'You

will have to wait until the sickness is passed, Nafinîas. Or you will enter endingness earlier than you wish.'

'Sickness?' The elf looked shocked. 'What is it?'

'Your people are still trying to find out exactly what nature the illness is, but it is thought to have been introduced by the älfar with the aim of wiping out the entire elf race,' Hargorin explained. It sounded true enough. 'They must have laid poison in their city of Dsôn Bhará before they abandoned it; they must have realised the elves would come.'

Rognor nodded silently to indicate the veracity of the story. He did not think the elves presented any danger, and thus he could remain relaxed. He kept his hands away from the grip of his war club.

Nafinîas turned to the convoy, calling them to a halt. Animated talk ensued.

Then the elf addressed Hargorin once more. 'My people and I are of one mind: let us pass regardless of this sickness. We are skilled healers and have much experience in diagnosing different illnesses and soothing symptoms.'

Rognor's lips narrowed to a line.

'There is an order in place for the protection of all. No further immigration is permitted until the source of the infection has been located and dealt with,' said Hargorin firmly.

'Who gave the order?' Nafinîas wanted to know.

'The order came from my High King.'

'He isn't *my* High King!'

'But this' – Hargorin indicated the impressive fortress – 'is definitely *my* gate. So I am afraid you will have to do as I say. It is the will of our High King. It is for your own good.'

'You'd like us to withdraw and wait for more of my people to die?' Nafinîas looked at him in outrage. 'What would you do if you knew dwarves were dying and that you had it in your power to help them?'

Rognor quite understood why the elf was indignant at being refused entry. It seemed they would not turn back on hearing about a fatal illness affecting elves. The ploy was not working.

Hargorin pointed to the road behind them. 'If you turn your convoy around you'll soon be . . .'

Nafinîas took a step towards the king. 'We shall only comply if my ruler commands us to turn back.'

'But entering a land where your lives are at risk? Doesn't sound like a sensible course of action,' Rognor interrupted impatiently. He realised he had been rude. 'Forgive the harshness of my words. It was not my intention to insult you.'

Nafinîas looked at him and then faced Hargorin once more. 'Let me pass, dwarf.'

The king shook his head and raised his hand in the air, pointing to the east. 'That way. Two orbits' journey. I can provide you with food if your rations are not sufficient.'

The elf studied the two dwarves. 'Since when does the High King of the dwarves show himself so considerate of us?'

'There is a new pact of friendship between the races,' Hargorin replied calmly. 'Every life counts. Especially a life that is supposed to be eternal.'

Nafinîas indicated the convoy. 'We are not the last ones. Over four thousand elves will be following us. They, too, will want to enter. They will arrive in half a cycle's time.'

'Pray to Sitalia that she may help Ilahín conquer the plague by then and we will be glad to welcome you through to Girdlegard.' The king's voice took on a more authoritative note. 'Turn around, Nafinîas, and do not cloak me with guilt for the plague that has struck your people.'

'I shall leave.' Nafinîas mounted his horse. 'I shall leave as soon as I have a letter from my king in my hands confirming what you say. If *he* sends me away, we shall withdraw from the gate without delay.' He called out a series of commands and the band of elves started to move the wagons and horses to the side of the road. 'Until then we wait here.'

Hargorin lowered his head. 'That is not possible, elf. The plain is of strategic importance for my fortress. If an attack were to come, I would need to react without compunction.'

'We will encamp here at our own risk,' the elf replied. 'Regard us as your spies, as your vanguard, the first line of defence. Send a messenger to Âlandur and ask for a letter from my ruler. Not from Ilahín.'

'I cannot permit that,' Hargorin was angry. 'You must—'

'We are both in an unenviable position,' said Nafinîas from the saddle. '*You* are under strict orders from your own High King and *I* am asking for a confirmation order from mine. This is only fair.'

'You are right,' Rognor agreed, trying to lift the tense atmosphere. 'We shall send a messenger. It will take some time.'

'We have plenty of time.' Nafinîas gave a forced smile. 'Meanwhile, enjoy the fact that your fortress now has its own crack unit of elf-warriors at the gate. This must be a first.' He gave a curt nod and returned to the wagon train, which was forming a defensive circle, preparing to set up camp.

'There's one problem with Boïndil's plan,' murmured Hargorin. 'It doesn't work.'

'In their place we would do the same.' Rognor looked at the defences, calculating probabilities. 'We wouldn't just go away. We'd try to get over or round the obstacle. Straightaway. Or when we'd had enough of all the waiting around.'

He looked his red-haired king straight in the eyes. 'What do you reckon? How long would an elf stay patient, thinking that his people are dying in droves on the other side of the mountains?'

Hargorin uttered an oath and turned to go back through the entrance. 'Boïndil must be told about the obstinacy of these pointy-ears.' Then he stopped short. 'Isn't Ilahín their king and his wife their queen?'

This was bothering Rognor, too. 'It seems there've been some changes for the elves.' He threw his head back to watch a flock of birds rounding the mountain peaks. 'How would Nafinîas know about that?'

'So how are we supposed to know what name to put on our fake letter, you mean?' Hargorin corrected him.

'Know anyone that can do elfish?' Rognor suppressed a laugh. Everything was a mess, perhaps, but the situation still had its funny side: a load of pointy-ears settling down to defend a dwarf fortress.

'We'll find someone.' Hargorin strode through the open gateway. 'Or Vraccas will send you inspiration while I'm gone.'

Rognor's mood plummeted. 'Send *me* inspiration?' *I'd prefer Lorimbur's help*. But he did not dare voice his thoughts. Hargorin had showed himself to be a true follower of the divine Smith, while his chancellor clung to the old ideas. Like most did.

'Exactly. *I'll* be busy. I've got a hero to rescue.' The king pointed out at the plain. 'Mind the pointy-ears don't start to pile up while I'm away.' He turned left into the courtyard where the tunnel entrance was. 'I have every confidence in you, Chancellor.'

'Of course, my king.' Rognor stayed put, his thumbs jammed in his belt.

Elf melodies reached his ear on the wind and the dwarf gave a shudder.

Can't put up with much more of that. They'll have to go.

There's good beer and there's bad beer. They're both good. You drink the good stuff and drown orcs in the bad stuff.

Dwarf saying

IV

Girdlegard
United Kingdom of Gauragar-Idoslane
Gauragar
6492nd solar cycle, summer

And I thought my travelling and waiting days were over. Ireheart sat under the way-station porch sweating away and cursing the sun that was doing its level best to get the crops ripe for harvest. He had placed a wet rag on his head. Occasionally he'd waft it around in the air to cool it before putting it back on his forehead. He was starting to appreciate the cold beer from the ice cellar.

He had been writing a letter to his family in the Blue Mountains so they would not be concerned at his prolonged absence. His return was long overdue. Goda would be coping splendidly with the day-to-day business of ruling the country – bringing about improvements and getting the repair work done on the fortresses – but he didn't want her distracted by worrying about him.

The tavern lad brought him a fresh beer.

'Thanks,' he said, noticing that the youth had a mounted capsule splinter on a leather thong hanging round his neck. 'So. You've found a use for it?'

Heidor nodded proudly. 'I hid the other pieces, Master Dwarf.'

'That's the way.' Ireheart winked at him. 'Have you heard the one about the orc that asked a dwarf for directions? And the dwarf says . . .'

'Riders!'

'No, not riders,' Ireheart mumbled, following the boy's glance to the south. 'That's a stupid answer.'

They saw a pony with a squat figure on its back. A cloud of dust thrown up by the galloping hooves showed the direction they had come from.

'And there's another dwarf!' Heidor said, pointing eastward. 'Do you think they've arranged to meet?'

'It'll be the wager I told you about.' Ireheart got up and raised the tankard to his lips. *Here we go*. 'Bring three more beers.'

Heidor hurried off to do his bidding.

Ireheart had invented the story with the wager. A dwarf far from home and making no effort to get back to his homeland was going, sooner or later, to arouse suspicion. The captain of the way-station had plenty of questions. Ireheart spun him a line about a wager he had lost: the task had been to get as many dwarves as possible to turn up in one place at the same time. It was a kind of test.

The captain had pretended to go along with it, because having Ireheart stay was providing a nice little earner. But he was probably curious.

Let him wonder. It would not cause trouble for Ireheart if the commander asked Mallenia what the dwarf was doing, and how he should deal with him. *Once they're all here, we can start and I shan't have to answer any more silly questions.* He remained in the shade, staring at the crossroads.

Ireheart reckoned that the rider from the south was Beligata; she called herself Hardblow or sometimes Deathstrike, whichever took her fancy. She used to live in the Black Mountains but now she belonged to the Freelings. Along with several other dwarves under his command, he had taken her to inspect the crater and to ask the elves how the work was progressing. Ireheart liked her and trusted her implicitly.

The other pony would probably be bringing Rognor Mortalblow. The one-time king of the Thirdlings was a warrior of renown and an experienced strategist who had turned the Black Mountains into an impregnable fortress.

Before long Ireheart could see that it was indeed Beligata. She waved, spurring the pony on. 'Welcome! You're the first.'

'I came as fast as I could,' she said, reining in her pony in front of the porch; she was wearing a blackened chainmail shirt under her grey mantle. Dusty and sweaty from the journey, she stepped into the shade, her double axe in her right hand. She bowed her head before going down on one knee to greet him. 'High King Boïndil, I am yours to command.'

'Get up,' he muttered. 'Nobody here knows who I am.'

He called out over his shoulder, 'Heidor, where's our beer?'

She got to her feet, light eyes full of questions. 'Why is that? They'd be honoured to have you as their guest.'

'Fine by me, but they'll have to wait until we're recounting our adventures in a couple of cycles' time.' As usual, he was fascinated by the fine line of scar on her right cheek. The damaged skin had a greenish sheen. She had never explained the injury. 'We're dwarves with a wager to win, that's all.'

'I see. A wager. Right.'

Heidor came over with the beers on a tray. He was astonished at how easily the dwarf girl shouldered her heavy double-headed axe. 'Here you are.' He held the tray out to them. 'The best our ice cellar can supply.'

'Take care, it's practically frozen solid. That's how they like it here,' Ireheart warned her.

An imposing red-haired dwarf arrived, almost as tall as a

human. He had a long-handled axe tucked into his belt and he wore a knee-length garment covered in metal plates for protection.

'Don't you start drinking without me!' he called out. 'I've earned one.' He slid out of the saddle and came over to join them in the shade. 'Give my pony a bucket of that water, lad, will you?' He grasped the third tankard and crashed it against the other two in a toast before draining the contents. 'My Vraccas, that's cold. My guts are turning to ice!'

Beligata and Ireheart laughed out loud; they all shook hands.

Heidor stared at the newcomer, whose broad stature was unusual for a dwarf. 'But you . . .' he said, terrified. 'You're . . . Hargorin Deathbringer!'

How does he know him? Ireheart noted the casual atmosphere change. The boy must have known the Thirdling king from back when he used to collect älfar taxes for the Triplets, at the head of the dreaded Black Squadron. The Desirers, these enforcers were called.

'You know, he only took on the role of collector of dues in order to deceive the älfar,' Ireheart told Heidor, placing his free hand on the boy's shoulder. 'Don't be frightened of him.'

'Don't know how I can stop being afraid,' the pale youth stammered, the tray shaking in his hands. 'I recall only too well how he came to our village. I remember the beatings. The punishments handed out.'

Hargorin's face showed his regret. 'I did what I did, my boy,' he said gently, 'but if I hadn't acted the part, you would not be standing before me now, a free man. I worked in the name of the black-eyes, but never with an easy heart.'

Heidor said nothing and scurried back into the house.

The initial good humour was poisoned and had died.

The dwarves drained their tankards in silence, as if they could wash down the past with the cooling drink.

After a while Ireheart cleared his throat to break the silence. 'Why have you come in person, Hargorin? I asked you to send your best warriors.'

The red-haired dwarf put down his beer and leaned against one of the porch supports. 'I am the best warrior my tribe has to offer. And if it's a case of seeking out the greatest hero of our race, who do you think I'd want to send?' He exchanged glances with Beligata.

'Can you show us the message Tungdil sent you?'

'Indeed I will. I'm just waiting for the others to turn up.' Ireheart wondered if he could call Heidor back or whether it was wiser not to make the boy confront Hargorin again. The dispatch riders would probably be gossiping by now about the former commander of the Black Squadron. There was always the danger they might want to get their revenge. 'I think we should be moving on.'

'We? Oh, no. You won't be going along.' Beligata laughed. 'That'd be ridiculous.'

'I am the best warrior of my tribe,' Ireheart protested.

'You are the High King,' she countered sharply. 'I told you last time we met that the tribes and their clans need the presence of a strong leader to give them stability and motivation. Your age, your experience and your history made it essential you become the High King and, what's more, stay High King. You won't be able to rule from Phondrasôn.'

'And if we didn't come back and you went to the Eternal Smithy, your loss would be more than Vraccas' Children could cope with,' Hargorin took over. 'And when Tungdil—'

'The *false* Tungdil,' Ireheart interjected.

'Who can say? The proof won't be evident until we bring back the true Scholar.' Beligata was in no doubt as to the eventual success of their mission. 'The tribes were unanimous, Ireheart. They have confidence in you.'

'And however things turn out in the next few orbits and cycles, they'll be glad to have you making the decisions.' Hargorin gazed out at the distance. 'That foundling child will cause no end of trouble, I'm sure. For us and for the elves.'

'I've ordered the gates to be closed. There won't be any more new elves coming in.' Ireheart felt the need to quench his thirst starting to get out of hand. The more he tried to ignore the craving, the stronger it became.

'These elves we've refused entry to – if even one of them contacts the Council of Kings, the humans will be in uproar, not to mention the elves already here in Girdlegard.' Hargorin put his right hand on to the head of his axe.

'By then the elves will have had to answer for another deed that'll cause outrage enough.' Ireheart told the others about the encounter with the fatally-injured Tabaîn warrior and his testimony. 'I can't make out what's afoot.'

'Nor can I. Which is all the more reason for you to stay here in Girdlegard. Convene the Council of Kings. It's vital the humans get to hear about this.' Beligata nodded, thoughtfully stroking the scar on her face. 'Is it true that Coïra has extended her search for a new magic source?'

Ireheart started to answer, 'That's what it said in the letter that Phenîlas . . .' but he stopped. *How do we know he was telling the truth? The elves could have forged the paper, or altered it.* At the same time, he resented how quickly these bad thoughts came rushing into his mind. It seemed the ancient feud between the two races was going to be hard to eradicate.

'We'd best ask one of her trainee famuli.' With a heavy heart he had to admit to himself that he could not go with them. 'You're right. I must see to things here in Girdlegard. There's too much at stake.'

Beligata pointed northward. 'Look! A couple of Fifthlings on ponies. I can see the symbol on their chainmail. This must be Balyndis' delegation.'

Ireheart came over to Hargorin's side. They watched the two newcomers ride up.

'I am glad you have found your way here,' he called to them in greeting.

'It is an honour for us to be here,' responded the girl dwarf with peat-coloured hair poking out from under her helmet. 'This stalwart Fifthling warrior here at my side is Belogar Strifehammer of the clan of the Boulder Heavers. And I am Gosalyn Landslip of the Fifthling clan of Tunnel Seekers. Our queen sent us to report to you that the gates have been duly closed, as ordered.'

The pair dismounted and were about to kneel in homage until Ireheart stopped them.

'So it was you two who found the abandoned settlement in the Grey Mountains? How do you feel about some more adventures?'

Belogar nodded; his brown beard had caught the dust of the journey. 'And this time I shan't hold back if I see something that seems odd. No matter what it is.' Ireheart knew that this was the Fifthling that had wanted to kill the girl Sha'taï when he first encountered her; he would not break his promise.

'Whatever seems odd to you,' Beligata contradicted him, 'is irrelevant. What you will do is what your High King commands. Or the leader of the expedition.'

Belogar flashed a scowl at her. 'So who are you to talk like that?'

She gave her credentials.

'Aha. You've quite a reputation as a warrior woman.' He took a tight hold on the handle of his club. 'But then so have I. So . . .'

'You're a warrior woman?' Beligata feigned astonishment. 'By Vraccas! One would never have guessed you were female.'

Hargorin burst out laughing. 'A sharp weapon and a sharp tongue.'

Belogar's expression changed from surprised to bad-tempered.

Gosalyn grabbed his arm before he could give vent to his fury. All Hargorin managed was a stifled grunt.

Ireheart was reminded of the time when his brother Boïndal was still alive. His twin had always been able to calm him down when he got angry and was threatening to erupt in a frenzy of rage.

'Let's wait till the warriors from the other dwarf tribes arrive,' he said, heading for the door to fetch his own beer. Heidor had looked too frightened.

He had taken three strides when he was suddenly blinded. The whole area was swamped in darkness.

It could not have been the beer. Ireheart stretched out his hands to feel his way. The others shouted out, obviously experiencing the same phenomenon.

So that means . . .

A vulgar chortle rang out. Then the sun reappeared and Ireheart could see his surroundings again.

Right next to him he saw a dwarf he knew very well indeed – unmistakable in his tionium-plated black leather armour with its reinforced skirt of steel discs. He had pushed up the visor of the black leather helmet, and the studs and ornamental silver-thread designs flashed in the sunlight; he was carrying a rucksack.

'Balodil!' Boïndil had gone through many an adventure with this bizarre zhadár. They had fought side by side for Girdlegard's sake. But this dwarf, who had been transformed by magic älfar potions, had not been invited to join them. 'What are you doing here?'

'That old name is now consigned to history. Now I'm known as Carâhnios. In the älfar tongue it means the *Exterminator.*' He bared his black teeth; his beard was cut close. 'And exterminating is what I do. Been doing it for a whole cycle now. Successfully, at that. Haven't you heard about me? All my heroic deeds?' He giggled. 'There's twenty-three älfar less than there were before. They keep sending them against me and I just take what I need.' His eyes sparkled with madness. A halo of darkness flared around the zhadár as if it emanated from inside him, eager to blot out the sun. 'Their blood is a vital ingredient for my new potion. Far superior to the other one,' he murmured. 'Can I interest you in a top-up, High King?'

'No.' Ireheart swiftly rejected the offer and moved sharply away from the new arrival, who now looked like a living shadow. The last of the zhadár – or Invisibles, as the elite fighting unit had been known until its destruction – spread a painful sense of unease. Ireheart's glance fell on the weapon Carâhnios wore at his side and felt a shiver up and down his spine.

'Where did you get that?' he croaked, unable to speak naturally.

'What? This?' the zhadár drew the night-dark weapon, its blade longer than a human's arm. It bore on one side a row of spikes arrayed like the teeth of a comb, while on the other side the metal was like a conventional sword. 'Got it off a blacksmith. Dead cheap.' He gave a braying laugh.

'Don't pretend to be stupid.' Ireheart had regained his composure. 'Who gave you Bloodthirster?'

'Told you. I bought it. Very recently. You'll like this: it was a Thirdling that sold it to me. After any battle, the commercially-minded trawl through the field looking for loot: weapons and other things the dead have no further use for but the living are happy to buy.' Carâhnios essayed a swipe in the air with the blade. 'I liked it. Only the gods will know if it's the genuine article – Tungdil's Bloodthirster. But if it is' – he giggled, drooling – 'then it's a bargain.' He stowed the weapon. 'Either way, it serves me well. Good for killing älfar.'

Ireheart stared at the weapon. *Is he entitled to use it?*

He could not remember where Bloodthirster had ended up after the battle at the Black Abyss. On that orbit he had been overwhelmed by the death of his friend.

Bloodthirster was the second most powerful weapon in the whole of Girdlegard. The Scholar had forged it himself from the sword of one of the Inextinguishables. The evil that lodged within the metal suited the zhadár, and now it was being deployed against the älfar.

The thought of the weapon being used against its original owners pleased Ireheart but he was deeply disturbed to know Carâhnios was in charge of it.

'Keep your talents under wraps, or you'll scare all the humans and provoke an attack,' Hargorin said. 'We know what you're capable of.'

Carâhnios harrumphed with disappointment. 'I only wanted to show you' – he lifted his right arm to display the swirls of darkness that floated from his gloved fingertips – 'how useful I can be to you. If you're travelling through elf territory, or if you're in Phondrasôn clandestinely. Believe me. You *will* need my arts.

Ireheart stared at him. 'How do you know about that?'

'The last älf I killed told me.' Carâhnios shrugged off his rucksack and extracted a bloodstained letter with the High King's seal broken. 'He was waiting about half an orbit's ride from here and shot the two dwarves you're waiting for out of the saddle with his arrows.' He pressed the rolled parchment into Ireheart's hand. 'I found him, killed him and saw the message. Thought to myself, I'd be an excellent substitute. And then of course it occurred to me that down there' – he stamped on the ground – 'there'll be a few more black-eyes I can do away with.' His terrible, distorted grin caused shudders of horror in the others.

Ireheart looked at the red-stained letter the zhadár had given him. *All the warriors and warrior women we were expecting – they're all dead.*

'Right,' he agreed, reluctantly. 'You can go with them. Otherwise it will take too long. Time is of the essence.' He gestured toward the entrance. 'Come on. I want to share the Scholar's message with you. It's vital you understand why I am convinced the real Tungdil is still alive.'

They followed the High King into the main building, where, apart from Heidor, there were also five despatch riders at table. They were riveted by the sight of the dwarves and when Carâhnios stepped in they froze, spoons halfway to their mouths. Soup dripped back into bowls. The zhadár's outward appearance and uncanny vibe sent them into a trance.

Ireheart led his group to the table that was farthest away and they sat and put their heads together. Only then did he take out the disc he had recovered from one of the capsules.

Placing it where the others could read it, he went over to Heidor to order beers.

Ireheart did not need to read Tungdil's words again. He knew them by heart.

Dear Ireheart, my cherished friend, much missed,

Tell the Children of the Smith: hold on to hope as I have been doing in this dark place.

I will soon return and I pray Vraccas permits me to see many old friends alive.

The search has begun for a way out of this place and I am sending messengers so you may know that I live and have never forgotten you.

Preserve Girdlegard at all costs, for thoughts of that dear land and of yourself, Ireheart, are what help me to survive.

Warmest greetings,
Your Scholar
Tungdil

Evading the dwarf's eyes, Heidor did not speak to Boïndil while he filled the tankards.

Ireheart could not catch what the couriers were saying. But he did not need a crystal ball to know the dwarves were the object of more than idle curiosity. The zhadár was the most remarkable figure and, like Hargorin, known in these parts.

I wonder what they think? Ireheart paid up and came back to the table with the beers. He expected the couriers' captain would have them evicted. *As long as he doesn't tell the elves, it doesn't matter.*

As he sat down and distributed the drinks, the look on Hargorin's face told him that the one-time leader of the Black Squadron was the most sceptical of the group. 'You were going to say you need more proof that this is from the genuine Tungdil.'

The others said nothing, taking hold of their tankards.

'Let me explain how the message fell into my hands.' Ireheart told them of the beast and the struggle, explained how the warrior who fell out of the tree had helped to save his life. He related the soldier's dying words.

'There's no doubt at all in my mind,' he summed up.

'My chancellor insisted I get shown the message before entering the dark depths and putting my life at risk. I have heard how the message reached you.' Hargorin picked up his beer, gesturing at the disc with the tankard. 'But where is the proof, High King?' The red-haired dwarf leaned back. 'Give me one clear piece of evidence and I'm with you. First in line.'

'I'll always be in front. Or maybe I'll be behind you,' Carâhnios tittered. 'You'll think I'm your very shadow, Hargorin Deathbringer.'

Ireheart had been expecting this.

He turned the palladium disc over and showed the golden inlay on the obverse. 'It's the exact dimension and shape of the gold mark in the flesh of Tungdil's hand that he got in the fight for the throne. No one else could know it so exactly and reproduce it in such detail.'

Hargorin muttered. 'What kind of proof is that?' He took a long draught of beer.

'But choosing to use those beasts?' objected Belogar. 'Couldn't he have sent friendlier messengers?'

Beligata spoke up, putting a fat tobacco roll between her lips: 'They don't do friendly down there. The savagery of the beasts was what guaranteed they would survive long enough to reach the surface.' She went over to the fireplace to rummage in the ashes for glowing embers. 'Sounds sensible to me.' Puffing her lit tobacco roll, she re-joined the others.

'How are we going to find our way through elf territory unnoticed, to seek out the entrance?' Belogar demanded. 'They have eyes and ears everywhere. Well nigh impossible, unless Vraccas sends us an invisible cloak.'

Ireheart sighed. He hadn't expected this much opposition. 'I am your High King and if you don't trust my instinct – powerful enough to lead me to search for the Phondrasôn entrance myself – then I'll have to command you to go.'

He was surprised to see Carâhnios reach for the disc, grasping it with his armoured gauntlet.

'I don't need your command,' he whispered. 'Phondrasôn doesn't hold any terrors for me. I'll bring back the one who calls himself Tungdil.' He stared at Ireheart as he drained his mug; then he belched and laughed. 'Then you can decide, High King, if it's the right one this time.'

Without waiting for a response the zhadár turned and made for the door, whistling.

Belogar raised his bushy eyebrows. 'Is he going without us?'

Beligata got to her feet and followed Carâhnios. 'Without *you*,' she corrected.

Gosalyn stood up, grinning. 'Some decisions are easy to make.'

Ireheart was relieved. 'As soon as you get back, send word to all the dwarf kingdoms,' he told Hargorin, who was slowly pushing himself up from his seat. 'I shall be taking care of Girdlegard and the concerns of our people.'

'I ask nothing more.' The red-haired dwarf warrior stomped out; the despatch riders watched him go.

'But you still haven't given me proper proof,' he called from outside.

I'll accept your apology. Just bring back my Scholar. Ireheart kept his response silent. He waved Heidor over. He was going to need more beer.

Girdlegard
Elf realm of Ti Lesinteïl, formerly known as
Dsôn Bhará under the älfar
6492nd solar cycle, summer

Phenîlas held his bow half-spanned diagonally, ready to fire off the specially-made hunting arrow.

He and ten companions were pursuing the third of the wolf-like beasts seen skulking in the vicinity of the palace before it suddenly took off towards the south, out of the area that was once the älfar crater of Dsôn Bhará.

It seemed to Phenîlas that the creature was on the trail of something. *But where was it headed?*

The troop moved slowly forward, step by step, through a black birch grove that had many thorn bushes and the occasional giant willow. *Just the right habitat for a creature like this.*

The hunters to his right and to his left faced the gentle breeze; five of them carried boar spears, while the other five had the short bows suited for shooting round or over impenetrable undergrowth.

The weapon smith had designed the arrows with particularly sharp tips for piercing the wolf beast's thick hide. They were unsuitable for long distance, but the additional weight would let them penetrate thin steel, releasing highly acidic poison from a glass tube that shattered on impact.

The elves kept their breathing steady and the leather soles of their shoes made no sound on the leafy woodland floor. Phenîlas could see from the older tracks that the second specimen had followed the injured Tabaîn warrior. He had probably been devoured by now. No need to worry about him. The brave folk in Gauragar would kill the beast.

Despite the initial rush of the hunt, Phenîlas had noted that this beast, too, had had a wire round its neck from which a black metal capsule dangled. He had not been able to decipher what was written on it.

Could it possibly contain some magic artefact? Something that would enable evil to regain entry to Girdlegard and, more to the point, to penetrate the elves' new territory?

Phenîlas caught a rustling sound from the bushes. *We'll find out, as soon as we've killed it.*

Learned elves had identified the creatures as narshân beasts, called night-biters by dwarves and humans. Hundreds of cycles ago they had found a way into Girdlegard through the Grey Range when the Stone Gateway fell, but they had all been swiftly exterminated because of the damage they caused.

So these ones must have come directly out of Phondrasôn. He gave a curt nod to two pike-bearers and they made their way forward, jabbing at the undergrowth with long lances that had forked tips and an extra retaining blade lower down the shaft. *Perhaps the creature is trying to get back there?*

Again there came the sound of twigs and breaking; a number of diamond pheasants took to the air, their plumage sparkling as they flapped off.

The elf next to Phenîlas laughed quietly. 'They'd be good to eat.'

With a mighty roar a shadow leaped out from the curtain of hanging branches of a particularly large willow tree. As it sprang it opened its jaws, taking the first pheasant with a single bite and using the claws on its front legs to drag two further birds out of the air.

Phenîlas and his crew stared at the beast – it was even larger than the one they had killed. White teeth agleam, it was intent on devouring its prey.

At that very moment the wind turned, bringing the hunters' scent to the creature.

It cocked its ears and gave a bloodcurdling growl.

'Loose your arrows!' Phenîlas shouted, firing first. 'Pike-bearers, beware! Don't let it through or none of us will survive.'

The narshân wolf launched itself upward, crushing the pheasants under its blood-drenched paws. The creature propelled itself straight up to disappear among the branches.

The first arrows missed it. *This one is bigger and faster than the others.* The beast used the hanging branches of the willow to get to a position directly overhead and hurled itself down on the elves like an eagle swooping down on a calf.

The pike-bearers had been watching and were prepared. They held their weapons vertically while the bowmen, notching their next arrows, knelt to take aim.

The animal realised its mistake too late and slammed head first onto the long blades.

The two pike-bearers who had been standing in the thicket threw their weapons, hitting the beast in the flank. The bowmen loosed more arrows and this time each one hit home.

The narshân slid down under its own weight, shattering the thick wooden poles. Fatally injured, it snapped and snarled, sending the elves on a hasty retreat.

Although Phenîlas felt the touch of the creature's fangs on his forearm guard he did not sustain a bite. But the screams, and the spurting fluids that splashed his face and throat – combined with the smell of blood – all told him that at least one of the hunters was critically injured.

Barking and roaring, the beast continued its attack despite its own death throes; it snapped at legs, arms and throats, leaving open wounds before Phenîlas boldly grabbed a handful of arrows from his quiver.

You must die! He hurled himself on to the narshân and rammed the arrow tips into the wound on the creature's neck.

This action came too late to save the screaming elf whose arm had been snatched into the animal's jaws, but the beast collapsed, its right hind leg still pounding the forest floor. It finally expired with a whimper and a snort.

'Look to the wounded!' Phenîlas ordered, as he cut through the wire round the giant wolf's neck to release the bloodied capsule. He got up.

Dwarf runes! he realised with a shock. *But the Children of the Smith would never breed and keep such animals, let alone set them to work.*

There remained the possibility that the zhadár might once have tried to use them as hunting dogs.

But in that case they'd have been seen at least once before now. Word would have got round. Phenîlas opened his water flask and washed away the blood and dirt from the chiselled runes.

For Ireheart.

The elf studied the runes several times to ensure he had got the correct meaning. They were shaped differently from the ones used by the five Girdlegard tribes.

There was something, surely, inside the black tionium casing. When he shook it he could hear a slight ringing. Could be palladium, he thought: an extremely valuable white metal the elves liked to use in their armour.

And every child in Girdlegard knew who was meant by the name Ireheart.

Who would be sending the High King a message by means of a narshân? Phenîlas looked round. They had lost four huntsmen to the beast. *It doesn't bear thinking about if the creature had taken us by surprise.*

'Unamîl, see about transport for the wounded and get the beast carried to the palace as evidence. I must report to our ruler at once,' he told his troop, as they looked after the injured.

Phenîlas held the matt black capsule tightly and ran back through the edge of the grove where they had left their horses.

He could not make any sense out of his discovery and prayed to Sitalia that the Naishïon would be able to solve the puzzle.

Don't run with your weapons drawn, except in battle.

Dwarf saying

V

Girdlegard
Grey Mountains
Kingdom of the Fifthlings
Stone Gateway
6492nd solar cycle, summer

Balyndar Steelfinger, of the clan of the Steel Fingers, from the Fifthling tribe, stood watching the Stone Gateway – or rather, stood staring into a wall of damp fog presently concealing the mighty gate. 'Vraccas is in his forge, I see, plunging hot blades into cold water,' he said. 'Must be getting ready for war.'

'As long as it's not our turn again when it all kicks off,' was the lacklustre comment from the duty watchman.

I can't remember this guard's name. I ought to spend more time here.

As they paced the walls together the watchman stopped to reprimand a solder for sloppy equipment. 'Let's hope the north is spared for a change. Time for someone else's turn.'

It had been raining continuously for orbit after orbit. The surrounding peaks of the Great Blade and the Dragon's Tongue were shrouded in heavy mist that appeared light grey, then white and then dark. Neither sun nor wind had managed to dispel the fog. 'We will do what is expected of us: our duty,' was Balyndar's response. The damp air had made his dark brown hair curlier than ever, despite the braids. His beard was trimmed short and under his thin mantle he wore armour that combined chainmail and linked metal discs.

Where he used to carry a double morningstar club, he now had the legendary Keenfire stuck in his belt. He was the son of Balyndis Steelfinger of the Firstlings, Queen of the Fifthling tribe, and following the battle at the Black Abyss he had been chosen to carry the celebrated weapon.

Balyndar was a warrior through and through.

He also possessed a marked similarity in appearance to Tungdil Goldhand. There was a reason for this: Balyndar's mother and the Scholar had once been partners. However, they had long gone their separate ways and Balyndis had left for the Grey Mountains, where she had entered the iron union with the king of the Fifthling tribe. A child was soon born, a son. Officially, Balyndar was accepted as the son of the ruler, whom his mother had succeeded. The Fifthlings had been re-established from various tribes to take on the legacy of the original protectors of the Stone Gateway, who no longer existed.

Balyndar stopped and looked at the inner courtyard between the gate and the entrance to the mountains. The sound of constant hammering could be heard. 'They're making good progress.'

Below, masons were chiselling away at blocks of stone, in readiness for repairs to the towers. Now the kordrion had been done away with and the old dangers no longer existed, the point was to reinforce the defences against whatever new peril might lurk in the wings.

'Very good progress.' The guard indicated the tower whose outline was looming up in front of them out of the fog. 'The foundations have been strengthened and the outer walls are now two paces wider than before, and they've used a straw and mortar mix on the joints to absorb the impact of bombardment. We've added stone buttresses and raised the granite gates, incorporating the defensive walkway.' He pointed down. 'Those bolts are new – we've installed ten now like your mother said, instead of the original five.'

Two bolts for each of the tribes. Balyndar could make out the scaffolding and the pulley systems for hauling building materials and the hefty beams up into place.

The dwarves were indefatigable, working all day and continuing through the evening by the light of the night stars. The battlement walkway had been widened to accommodate a larger class of catapult. The first of the giant slings was being erected.

'What with our improvements to the fortress and the new weaponry, there's no chance evil will get through.' Balyndar was proud of the new defences. He eyed the thirty-pace-wide road, the end of which disappeared into a foggy void half a bolt-flight away.

'I really hate this weather.' The watch stepped up to the edge of the battlements, peering into the mist to the right and to the left. 'Looks like Tion sent it. Don't think it was Vraccas.'

'Why do you say that?'

'It would be hot steam and carry the smell of glowing steel and burning coals. I'd prefer that.' The soldier placed a hand on the chest-high battlement wall. 'It's not a good orbit. I can sense it.' He cast a glance at the diamond-encrusted blade of Keenfire. 'I'm glad you're here.'

Balyndar had no idea why the sentry was being so gloomy. 'Things are looking up in Girdlegard,' he said. 'After the long period of austerity and suppression, the good times are coming. There are more dwarves than ever being born. Fifthling numbers are doing well.' The soldier said nothing. He stared into the fog.

'Remind me of your name,' Balyndar said.

'Goïmbar Gemfinder of the Opal Eyes clan,' the other dwarf answered briefly. 'I've only recently joined the squad here at the fortress.'

The curtains of mist whirled about; they made strange shapes that turned out to be real figures wearing long white mantles. They came stumbling out of the fog as if they had been spat out, their clothing torn, armour in disarray, cloaks and weapons splashed red.

'I knew it,' muttered Goïmbar. 'Bad orbit.'

A curt command from him had the catapult teams running from their quarters in well-practised moves to get the contraptions ready for action.

'You with your stupid talk. You were asking for it.' Balyndar stepped forward and looked at the tall strangers. 'By Vraccas! They're dressed like elves,' he said quietly. 'That's odd. That's the first time we've seen elves arrive from the north.'

'Mind, though – they could be black-eyes in disguise, coming to trick us,' Goïmbar pointed out. Extra torches were being hurriedly put in place. He tightened the belt of his chainmail jerkin and wiped the condensation from his axe.

Spear-throwing machines and bolt-launchers were pushed, rattling, to their stations. Cogs clunked into place, yanking on the sturdy ropes. Dwarves loaded lumps of rock ready to hurl death and destruction over the side of the battlements.

Balyndar felt the sentry was overreacting. It was only a handful of elves, after all. But he did not interfere. It was important to exercise the utmost caution, especially in the north where the beasts had always been most vehement in their attempts to storm the barrier and get into Girdlegard. 'Yes. You're right. It could be a trick.'

And even if it wasn't, it made no difference. The High King had decreed that no more elves be allowed to pass into

Girdlegard. It seemed Samusin was taking a perverse delight in sending some along now when entry would be refused.

Balyndar watched the figures approach and could now see the type of injuries the elves had sustained. *They've not been shot at. And it doesn't look like sword or axe cuts.* The ravaged armour looked as if claws had attacked them, tearing off great gobbets of metal, clothing and flesh. One elf was missing half a leg, two were lacking armour and another had lost part of a shoulder joint.

'Vicious starving ogres that wanted to dismember them alive?' Goïmbar wondered.

Balyndar saw the leading figure turn to look up at the battlements and gesticulate imploringly.

'He's asking us to let them in.' The catapult teams called over to the sentry that they were ready and after a final mechanical click, stillness descended on the fortress.

The torches spluttered quietly, sending the occasional spark to fizzle out in the damp mist.

'And so would I if I were injured and there was help at hand.' Balyndar laid one hand on Keenfire, a weapon whose magical properties had protected him from spells and sorcery in many a battle. He had a heavy burden of responsibility to bear. *I am not permitted to open the gates to elves. But I could go out there myself and see what's what.*

The pulley lift could be used to send food and tents and a healer down to help the elves until such time as the High King rescinded his decree. 'You don't want to go out, yourself, do you?' Goïmbar asked intuitively.

Balyndar said nothing.

'Hey, you down there,' he called out. 'Who are you and how did this happen?'

One of the elves at the back of the column stumbled and fell.

His companions tried in vain to get him back onto his feet. The others staggered onward towards the gate. The small band of newcomers was now a straggling group thirty paces long.

'Let us in, please, dwarves,' begged the elf in front, waving wildly as if afraid they would not see him. 'It's after us. It's on our heels. By all that's sacred to Sitalia and Vraccas, I beseech you to let us in. It will tear us to pieces!'

'It?' Balyndar glanced questioningly at Goïmbar.

'We're under orders from the High King,' he growled. 'I shan't let them in.'

Then we'll do this my way. The king's son gave the signal for one of the pulley-driven platforms to be winched up and made ready.

His dwarves responded quickly but the operation would take some time. And it was time, perhaps, that the newcomers were in most need of.

The elf that had waved for attention was by now at the impregnable double gate itself. Not even the smallest insect could have crawled through.

'Can you hear me, Children of the Smith?' he shouted in desperation. 'You must let us in. We're in mortal danger out here. There were a hundred of us and this is all that's left after . . .'

'Look!' Balyndar pointed to the wall of fog from which another figure was emerging.

It was quite different from the elves and seemed to be a brawny human warrior, well-protected against attack in an armoured leather tunic. His head was covered by a rune-engraved enclosed copper helmet; on the man's back there was a short pole bearing a white banner with green symbols.

He lifted and planted his leather-booted feet in a steady rhythm as he strode up to the far end of the column.

'By Vraccas,' Balyndar exclaimed. He saw blood dripping down the warrior's leather hose and from his arms. The drops splashing on to the flagstones were the colour of dark ink at this distance. 'He must be strong if he's able to pull arms and legs out of their sockets.'

Goïmbar was obsessed with staring at the human warrior. Surely this isn't the thing that attacked the elves? Using his bare hands? White steam clouds were forming at eye and mouth slits in the helmet. It must be his breath becoming visible in the cold air.

'Watch out!' Balyndar shouted to warn the elves. The group turned round; some were screaming in fear of death as they rushed to the gate.

'I beg you!' The elf sank onto one knee and stretched out both arms. 'Open the gates and save us from this creature. It can't be of this world.'

Balyndar drew Keenfire and waited impatiently for the platform. 'Stay calm,' he called out, not knowing what else to tell them.

By this time the martial figure had reached the two elves at the back of the group. The one who had fallen threw a dagger at him but the blade bounced off his leather armour. The silent warrior grabbed the prone elf by the foot with one hand and hurled him up and away to crash headfirst into the precipitous rock face. Balyndar could see by the unnatural position of the elf's body that the neck was broken.

The other elf attacked the man with his sword, stabbing down at his head, while at the same time he attempted to pierce the man's throat from underneath with his long knife. Balyndar stared in horror when he saw how the long, steel blade shattered like glass on meeting the copper helmet, which should, by all accounts, have been the softer metal.

The knife point slipped past the man's throat without purchase.

The man reacted by slamming both fists, right and left, against the elf's head. The elf's helmet was battered and bent as if it had been made of painted wax. Neither metal nor bone could withstand the force of the assault. Blood and grey matter shot out of mouth, eyes and nose and the originally fine features were transformed into a grotesque caricature.

The carcass fell on to the stone path and the attacker continued on his way, unconcerned and unaffected. It was as if he had killed a couple of bothersome flies.

'Ye gods,' exclaimed Goïmbar.

'Get an official artist. Tell him to copy all the runes he finds.' Balyndar sprang onto the platform that was now waiting to be let down on chains from the nearest of the battlements. 'Aim at the warrior with your catapults!' he shouted, giving the signal to let the platform down. Several dwarves joined him on the timber-framed lift and the chains rattled and clanked as they slowly descended.

Spears and bolts were being fired across over their heads. Because of the sheer numbers of projectiles, many broke up on the crag round the Stone Gateway, but just as many rained down on the attacker, who stood there, arms outstretched to take the impact.

The firing tower targeted the warrior and for a few blinks of the eye he disappeared in a cloud of flying metal, splintered wood and broken spear shafts. When the air cleared, Balyndar saw the unknown fighter rouse himself from the salvo of shots and start to march away. *Nothing but superficial scratches. No bleeding wounds.* And the grazed skin on the man's upper arms was already healing over.

'This foe has magic powers,' he said to himself while a

second wave of arrows and spears was launched overhead. But Balyndar knew what would happen. *He won't be stopped by conventional weapons.* He grasped Keenfire. *But this should do the trick.* 'Stay here,' he told the others.

This time the human evaded the hail of projectiles and made off at a run to pursue the elves that had taken to their heels.

Up on the battlements and towers the dwarves watched helpless with horror as elf after elf was brutally butchered, skulls crushed or limbs ripped off or fists punched through their very torsos so that the guts hung out. A red trail formed at the warrior's heels.

'Open the gate for us!' the elf cried, raising both arms in desperate pleading. But hope had left him. Balyndar could see the tears on his face. 'All we want is for you to protect us.'

'Hurry,' the dwarf bellowed at the team operating the lift. He was still too high up to risk jumping. He would have broken his legs.

Then with a jerk the platform came to a halt twenty paces above the ground where the last elf was.

'The chain has slipped off the drum,' Goïmbar called from the other side of the battlement wall.

'Then get us some ropes! But quickly!' Balyndar wrestled with the urge to leap down.

The human warrior had nearly reached the elf; hearing the pounding steps the elf slowly lowered his arms. There was no point now. There was no escaping this opponent.

The elf lifted his head and stared at Balyndar, eyes full of recrimination – and then the bloodied fist smashed his face to pulp. He died with a ghastly sound somewhere between a scream and a death rattle; the body fell to one side, leaving blood from the remains of the head forming a puddle on the threshold to the gate.

The uncanny being turned his visored head towards the lift platform. Fine white steam floated out from the eye slits. He seemed to be working out how best to reach the dwarves up on the platform.

'Stay where you are,' Balyndar raged, brandishing Keenfire. 'I am going to hack you into slices.' The diamonds on the cutting edge sparkled ominously as a ray of sunshine piercing the mist caught them.

The warrior lowered his head as if his curiosity were aroused by the strange weapon; his snorting breath could be heard from under the enclosed helmet.

Balyndar had never seen runes like his before. The Outer Lands were extensive and peopled by many different races, all with writing systems of their own. These symbols seemed to have the power to give the human warrior incredible strength. *Demonic strength. It has got to be destroyed.*

'Where are those ropes?' The platform shook. The chains they were suspended by juddered and all of a sudden they were jerked down. The dwarves were nearly thrown off balance.

For a few heartbeats the human warrior disappeared from Balyndar's field of vision, then the lift touched down.

The impact sent the queen's son tumbling to one side; he dived through under the railing and stepped out onto the bloodstained rock. 'Now it is your turn, cursed spawn of Tion!'

When he raised Keenfire and looked around for his target he saw the man disappearing into the wall of fog.

'You coward!' Balyndar yelled, and would have rushed after the man, but for his horrified companions calling him back.

There could be hundreds of bloodthirsty adversaries concealed in the mist, just waiting for a dwarf to approach.

Mother must be told. Perhaps she will be able to interpret the runes. Balyndar stopped and gave his brave troops instructions about retrieving the bodies and loading them on to the lift. The corpse of the elf leader was to be preserved in ice and packed with snow, and then sent to Lesinteïl. Ireheart had expressly forbidden further elves from entering the land but he could not object, surely, to letting in dead bodies.

He stood now at the foot of the mighty gates, hands on the head of his axe Keenfire. He thought he could still hear the echoing footsteps of the dread adversary and could still see the fluttering banner the man had been carrying. Balyndar's feeling of deep unease would only settle once the new equipment and the newly devised weapons were properly installed on the walls.

It would be sensible to get Coïra to examine this fog. Perhaps the very mist is magic. Balyndar looked at the patches of spattered elf blood and then watched as the elf corpses were loaded, one by one, on to the platform.

The elves, so desperate to enter Girdlegard, would finally get their wish. They would be allowed through. But as corpses to be buried.

Girdlegard
Elf realm of Ti Lesinteïl, formerly älfar Dsôn Bhará
6492nd solar cycle, summer

The band of dwarves made every effort to move swiftly and silently through the woods, but apart from the strange Carâhnios, it was as if they had some inner urge to be heard and confronted. Their steps cracked twigs and branches underfoot, crunched dry leaves, and dislodged pebbles.

'Are you sure you know the way to Bhará?' Beligata was amazed the elves had not yet noticed their presence.

Carâhnios gave an insane-sounding cackle. 'I know every hidey-hole the älfar used. How could I miss their crater?' He pointed up to the sun peeking through the foliage. 'Keep heading west. By sundown we'll get to the edge of the älfar Triplets' city. The elves have smoothed over the crater and planted trees as high as these ones here. A little miracle they put together with the maga's help.' He turned down a path on the right used by woodland creatures – and was lost to sight.

'Not again.' Belogar groaned. 'Does he have to keep doing that?'

'He's obsessed with playing games.' Gosalyn was walking directly behind him and gave him a push. 'Now be quiet, you, or the pointy-ears will hear us.'

'They'll certainly hear you. Your voice could cut diamonds,' he hissed, grinning.

Beligata glanced at Hargorin, who was making steady and silent progress along the narrow path. They all looked to him as their leader, while Carâhnios was merely a necessary evil. They could not deny the zhadár's presence might prove useful.

But could his story be trusted?

Beligata caught up with Hargorin. 'Tell me, do you believe what Carâhnios is telling us?'

'The fairy tale about the älf and the dwarves he says were shot and killed?' Red-haired Hargorin shook his helmeted head. 'I don't believe *anything* he says. He was bonkers even before his transformation. But the stuff he's taking now to boost his älfar abilities is making him much worse.' His expression was one of deep concern. 'Not even the älfar Triplets had that dark aura he has. And they were the most evil thing I could imagine.'

'But älfar are born with the ability to put out fire, to cast darkness and to paralyse any creature's heart with fear.'

'True.' Hargorin nodded. 'But they don't have the permanent shroud of dark he has. Carâhnios must have distilled some potion from their blood that gives him even greater power.' He looked worried. 'We need to get the maga to check him out.' He cleared his throat and went on in a lower tone. 'It would be best for Girdlegard if he were never to return from Phondrasôn. If he completely loses it and the last shred of reason goes, he'll be a danger that only magic could control.'

'But if Coïra's not around?'

Hargorin did not answer.

'I'm with you,' said Beligata. 'It's up to you to say when we action your plan.'

Hargorin nodded.

She returned to her usual place in the column. It was some time before she noticed that Carâhnios was walking right next to her, imitating her gait. *He's like a shadow!*

'Do you know what, pretty scar-face dwarf?' he whispered. 'You'd be just my kind of girl. Our children, and we'd have lots of them, would rule the whole of Girdlegard.'

'Yeah, right,' she said, playing down her disquiet. *I wonder if he heard what Hargorin and I were saying?*

But he did not accept the brush-off and inched even closer. 'I know all about scars like yours,' he whispered. 'What do you tell people when they ask? An accident with paint and a knife? A tattoo that went wrong?' He sneered. 'Hasn't anyone guessed yet?'

'No one is interested,' Beligata responded, uneasiness turning to anxiety. 'And keep your weird ideas to yourself.'

Carâhnios lost his frivolous artificial gaiety.

'Is that a threat?' he asked. 'Or are you making me an offer?' He let his eyes sweep over her figure. 'I imagine our offspring would be splendid. They'd have tremendous powers,' he enthused, clapping his hands. 'The two of us, my pretty scardwarf, will be getting to know each other very well, I think.' He jogged off to return to the front of the column.

For Beligata, it was now obvious that Carâhnios could not be allowed to survive the mission. His crazy theories aside, he might try to force himself on her and though she would fight him, she feared his strength was far superior to her own. *How does one kill a zhadár who's gone mad?*

'Riders ahead,' warned Hargorin, before diving into the undergrowth. 'Let them pass and then pray to Vraccas they don't see our tracks.'

The dwarves hid as best they could in the brambles. Beligata held her breath as the sound grew louder. A white stallion went past so swiftly that it had the air of a ghost. The hooves threw up clumps of mud that spattered the roof of her leafy hiding place. Then the sound of hoofbeats died away.

The dwarves emerged from the thicket, relieved not to have been discovered.

'There was only *one* of them.' Carâhnios was pensive as he studied the marks. 'He was in quite a hurry. A courier, perhaps. Good we escaped notice.'

'You did not escape notice,' came a refined and melodious male voice from overhead. 'And I am not a courier.'

Beligata and the others looked up and saw an elf in white armour standing on a sturdy branch. His expression was livid with anger and surprise.

'What are dwarves doing here in Lesinteïl trying to evade our eyes? And from a variety of tribes, I see. If this is a diplomatic mission, it's an odd way to behave, you'll agree.' He addressed Carâhnios. 'There are no älfar here to hunt. What are you after, zhadár?'

Beligata noticed that the elf was sweat-drenched and that he had bits of leaves clinging to his armour. He must have careered through the woods with no thought to his own safety. Since he had been surprised to find them it was unlikely his mission had concerned their arrival. *What message is he carrying, then?*

'It's Phenîlas,' whispered Gosalyn. 'We came across him in the abandoned settlement. In the Grey Mountains. He doesn't seem to recognise us.'

'What an arrogant pointy-ears. We all look alike to him. Shall I knock him off his perch?' muttered Belogar, whereupon the elf gave a scornful, ringing laugh.

'I want to do it now more than ever,' the dwarf grunted.

Hargorin approached the elf's tree. 'We were pursuing a wild animal,' he claimed boldly. Beligata was amused to hear him describe in detail the creature Ireheart had killed. 'We managed to prevent it attacking a lone farmstead but we were keen to finish the job.'

'We were hiding,' Beligata chipped in, 'because we were afraid your people would send us away.'

'I want to get my hunting trophy,' Belogar added, to round off the lie. 'I apologise for wanting to throw you off your branch. I would only have chucked a piece of wood at you. Quite a small one. Just enough to knock you out. We wouldn't have wanted your fragile skull to crack, lest your brains run out like yolk from an egg . . .'

Gosalyn elbowed him into silence.

The light-haired elf jumped nimbly down from his tree. He gave a whistle and his horse whinnied in answer and trotted up.

'Then forgive me for assuming you were plotting something bad.' He sketched a bow. 'My name is Phenîlas. My warriors and I have been hunting the very same beast.' He looked over at Gosalyn. 'And of course I recognised you both,' he said with a friendly smile. 'Our last encounter did not end amicably, did it?' He pointed at Belogar. 'Look at him. He wanted to topple me from that branch.' He laughed.

Beligata felt the tension lift slightly. She wondered how Hargorin was going to react.

The red-headed dwarf grinned. 'There you have it. Once again our races are united in pursuit of a common enemy. You killed it, then?'

'I was just riding to the palace to notify my Naishïon.' The elf thought for a moment. 'Do you require somewhere to stay the night? You won't get through Lesinteïl before nightfall on your way back to the mountains.'

'That's kind of you,' Hargorin said. 'We thought we'd make for the cave this beast must have used as a lair. There'll be more than two of them.'

'*More* than two?'

'One of them killed the Tabaîn heir apparent. Plus the one you found and killed. So if there's two, there could well be a whole pack.'

'I'm not leaving till I get my hunting trophy,' Belogar insisted.

Phenîlas looked disapproving as he drew himself up to his full height. 'I cannot allow that. My master would have to be consulted.'

'I quite understand.' Now it was Hargorin's turn to find a way out.

Beligata placed her hand over her heart. 'Our High King gave us further instructions because he is deeply committed to protecting the entire region from danger. And if there proves to be a tunnel from which these beasts are emerging from the evil depths, we are to go down and eradicate them.' She indicated Carâhnios. 'That's why we've got him with us.'

'Boïndil Doubleblade sends you?'

'I swear by Vraccas this is so.' Hargorin gave Beligata a look but she could not understand his meaning. 'He is concerned that there may still be a way through to Phondrasôn even though you have done so much to fill in and close up the crater. Elves are not adapted to working in tunnels and deep caverns; your element is nature and the forests. But we dwarves are at home in mines and underground. That's how Vraccas made us.'

'I owe Boïndil Doubleblade a good deal.' Phenîlas was lost in thought. 'I could only give you permission to remain right here. I'm off to see my master anyway and I'll ask him. Of course, if you're *gone* when I come back with his answer, there's not a lot I could do.'

All of them knew the elf ruler would never give his consent to the dwarves' plan for roaming the tunnels under Lesinteïl. There was too great a risk of evil escaping back into the upper world.

Hargorin nodded. 'Understood.'

'If you go further, I would have to hunt you down and force you to turn back. I shall follow your tracks, wherever they lead. Let this be my warning.'

'We understand.' Beligata suppressed a whoop. Whatever Ireheart might have done for this elf, it had certainly saved their mission, even if their task would hardly be made the easier with Phenîlas dogging their every footstep.

'One final thing: tell us where it was these beasts were first sighted.'

Phenîlas pointed to the east. 'My feeling is that they will

have surfaced near the edge of the crater, but our scouts have failed to come up with any evidence.' He looked at Carâhnios. 'But you've got a zhadár. He'll lead you to the best place. Evil always finds evil.' He swung himself up into the saddle. 'We are agreed. Give my thanks to Boïndil Doubleblade when you see him next. I hope that all of you will indeed see him again after your hunt.'

Before the dwarves could reply in a friendly vein, the elf had turned his horse and made off at a gallop.

Belogar breathed a sigh of relief. 'That was a near thing.'

'We've no time to lose.' Hargorin turned to Carâhnios. 'Do you think you'll be able to find where the beasts are crawling through?'

Reminding Beligata of a living shadow, the black dwarf gestured affirmatively and set off at a run. In single file they followed the zhadár at a jog that made their backpacks and armour jingle and rattle. Since this latest encounter there was no need to avoid discovery. Their task now was to find the entrance before Phenîlas came back to throw them out of the elf kingdom.

Beligata knew he would not come alone. And resistance would be hopeless. She was worried about having to fight off more of the beasts. It would be fatal to come across one in the confined space of a tunnel.

Lorimbur, I place my life in your hands. She scrutinised her surroundings in the grove watchfully. She did not want to be leaped on by some sharp-clawed creature.

And certainly not by Carâhnios, her new admirer.

But the zhadár seemed to know exactly where they should be going. He ran on ahead and no long pauses were taken. Their breathing was getting louder with the exertion and sweat poured off them despite the cool air of the shady woodland.

That evening, thoroughly exhausted, they reached the edge of the crater, which formed a gentle embankment at the spot.

Beligata watched with revulsion as Carâhnios sniffed the wind like an animal; she saw him take a sip from a small phial. He began to pant, and groan, then to utter cries of ecstasy and gales of laughter. He went down on his knees and threw his head back to stare at the stars.

'What's he doing?' Belogar tapped his war club, looking at Gosalyn. 'Has he gone completely mad? If so we could kill him now, because he'll be no further use to us.'

Beligata smiled at the Fifthling. She liked the straightforward way he thought.

Carâhnios suddenly got to his feet and rushed off.

'Follow him,' Hargorin ordered.

'I could really do with some food,' Belogar complained. 'My stomach is crying out for something to eat.'

'Mind it doesn't upset your guts,' whooped Carâhnios. 'They can easily get all tangled up. And then we'll have to cut you open, ha ha.' And off he went through the trees again.

The group had no option but to follow in his tracks; he had deliberately left signs, Beligata knew. The rest of the time the zhadár was quite capable of leaving no footsteps. *The uncanny power of his creators.*

The band of dwarves struggled through thickets of thorn bushes that tore at their leather and even the padded doublets they wore under their chainmail. Beligata's legs were badly scratched and all the dwarves got thorns through the soles of their boots. They had to stop and cut each other free when they become hopelessly ensnared in the brambles.

When the undergrowth thinned out they could see where earth had been thrown up in a heap. A shadow the size of a dwarf was waiting for them.

'This is where they came out.' Carâhnios bared his teeth and emitted a screeching laugh. 'And this is where we go in.'

And he hopped straight into the hole without further ado.

'Let's try our luck,' said Hargorin, shrugging off his rucksack. The dwarves all shook hands. 'May we find what has been so sorely missed.' He chucked his bag into the shaft and followed the zhadár.

Beligata looked up at the stars in farewell. *Let this not be in vain.* She was the last one to approach the opening.

'Psst,' she heard behind her.

She stopped dead and took her double axe in her left hand before turning round.

The thick brambles obstructed her view; she normally had excellent night vision.

Beligata said nothing, waiting to see if her senses had tricked her or whether there was indeed someone watching them all go into the shaft. *It'll have to show itself soon.*

She heard the faintest rustle to her left.

Now she was sure of it: someone was creeping forward. *Why would he first draw attention to himself if he's going to attack me?*

'Come over here,' came the whisper. Was it a man speaking or a woman? Either way she was not going to comply.

Gripping the double axe tight, she turned slightly without moving away from the spot. She wanted the option of jumping into the shaft to avoid trouble. It was her responsibility, as rear guard, to ensure they weren't attacked from behind.

No more rustling.

'Come this way if you want to go on living,' came the urgent whisper. 'The beast is about to spring.'

Not half a heartbeat after that warning she heard the roar.

A huge lupine head forced its way out of the hole and the

body followed so swiftly that she had no time to land a blow. Then the monster was directly in front of her, its sharp ears erect. Bits of earth and small pebbles rolled off its tough skin when it shook itself.

Beligata went cold: the gaping muzzle was dripping blood, black in the starlight. It had fresh meat fragments between its teeth. And some scraps of leather.

That's . . .

The beast launched itself at her.

If a mountain looks too high to climb, dig a tunnel under it.

Dwarf saying

VI

Girdlegard
Elf realm Ti Lesinteïl
6492nd solar cycle, summer

Phenîlas proffered the tionium capsule he had cut from the beast's neck. 'They were deployed as messengers. It is as I feared, Naishïon.'

Ataimînas was sitting back on his heels in the palace's large reception room, wearing wide, dark blue robes embroidered in gold thread and accentuated with a broad black sash. The sleeves had long silk cuffs from wrist to elbow and his hands were in white gloves.

He took the capsule with his left hand while the right rested on his thigh.

He read out the dwarf runes. ' "For Ireheart." Why hasn't it been opened?'

'It resisted every effort.'

Ataimînas laughed. 'Those dwarves and their metalwork.' He studied the symbols closely. 'There's a peculiar flourish to the characters. Whoever engraved it wanted to indicate he is not from Girdlegard.' He raised his green eyes to Phenîlas. 'There may be many explanations. But in combination with the beasts that brought them, not one is to my liking.' He placed the capsule down and called a servant to take it to the workshops.

'Find some way of opening it,' came the curt instruction. Turning to Phenîlas he said, 'After that we'll see if the contents mean danger for us.'

'I am curious.'

The Naishïon kept his gaze on the light-haired elf. 'Why do you think we've had no new arrivals recently?'

'Because the gates have been closed?' Phenîlas said, naming the most likely explanation. He could neither imagine their people had been attacked within Girdlegard, nor that the flow of migrants had dried up.

'I agree. I am sending out messengers at daybreak to the five dwarf kingdoms. I hope very much that the old feud has not broken out again. We thought that was all over.' Ataimînas turned his head to the portraits on the walls and then asked: 'Would you be able to sort out the confusion surrounding Tabaîn's throne?'

'I expect my influence will be helpful.'

'I don't want any further delay. Our subjects will need grain and I need to source it. Our reserves are almost gone and our neighbours are about to bring in the harvest. It's essential the king gives us access rights to fields where we can plant and tend our own corn. We had Natenian in the palm of our hands. What do we know about Dirisa?'

'Nothing,' admitted Phenîlas reluctantly. 'No one was expecting her to usurp the throne. None of Natenian's spies had any inkling of what she was planning. Like all the others in the council, she was not thought to be ambitious. But she must have been waiting for an opportunity like this.'

Ataimînas gave a mocking smile. 'Yet another unexpected turn of events. Like this foundling girl and Mallenia's new lapdog.' The ruler kept his eyes fixed on Phenîlas. 'Sort it. At once. Before they've stopped mourning Raikan. Otherwise Dirisa's support base will grow. Find out if anyone was behind the coup.'

'As you command, Naishïon.'

'After that we will have to consider how to get rid of the young girl. I share the dwarves' concern regarding her.' He exhaled sharply. 'A pity the älf didn't kill her.' Phenîlas recalled exactly how swiftly and surely the intruder had spread death amongst the guards at the inn. But an unarmed child had thwarted an attack?

'Come winter, something will have happened to the child.'

'That responsibility, too, I place in your hands.' Ataimînas smiled graciously. 'I intend to make you my deputy if you carry out these two tasks successfully.'

'That is most generous. But won't Ilahín object? He enjoys great popularity now that you've sent him to the Golden Plain; he attends to the people's needs and he is omnipresent. I am merely a warrior doing my duty in secret.'

'An empire needs both secret warriors and those who look after the subjects. He will also be rewarded.' The Naishïon raised his arm, pointing to the exit with his white-gloved hand. 'You know what needs doing.'

Phenîlas got to his feet. 'There's one more thing which may be significant. At the Lesinteïl border I encountered a small group of dwarves on the trail of the beast that escaped. They're determined to track it down and kill it.'

'Was there any mention of the missing Tabaîn soldier?'

'No.'

Ataimînas frowned. 'An obvious subterfuge. An excuse for sending a band of dwarves down to Phondrasôn to search for their missing hero. Send one of our crack units after them. Tell them to disguise themselves as älfar.'

As the Naishïon pointed to the door again the fabric of his robes rustled.

No further discussion was needed.

Girdlegard
United Kingdom of Gauragar-Idoslane
Freestone
6492nd solar cycle, summer

'It is an unusual way of proceeding but I can quite understand why the High King wants it urgently and without any public discussion.' Mallenia laid the invitation on the table: a summons to the Council of Kings convened by Boïndil in Freestone. She turned to Rodario. Compared to his extravagant get-up, she could, in her simple armour, have been one of her own bodyguards. 'It's the future of Girdlegard at stake.'

They had taken rooms again at the same guesthouse as a gesture of confidence; no one should think the älfar had intimidated them.

Together with Sha'taï they had the use of two large rooms and had not insisted on travelling with a large retinue. A few servants, a maid, a dozen soldiers: this would suffice.

The meeting was to be held without great ceremony. It was essential the rulers should come together to debate recent events at the Stone Gateway; no pageantry or spectacle was required. Rodario was the exception, given his penchant for showy attire.

'The monarchs will make their way here swiftly, as long as they can all read and have gathered what has happened at the Stone Gateway.' The former actor and chosen king of Urgon was perched on the window seat surrounded by documents.

Most of the papers were extracts from Carmondai's work. He was an älfar historian and story-teller who had witnessed many things in his long career and had kept records of events going back to before the evil invaded Girdlegard. Troops had found a fraction of his writings in Dsôn Bhará; much of the work had been destroyed during the attack.

'He wrote so much.' Rodario placed his hand on the next pile of papers. He wanted to find any mention of some similarly demonic foe, in the hope of coming up with a means of defeating it.

Certain humans were allowed sight of these papers, which portrayed events from the älfar point of view. Some critics warned that this was tantamount to glorifying evil. Simple souls might become fascinated and fanatical, taking sides with the enemy. This was why the papers were kept under lock and key. Rodario always kept them in a padlocked iron chest when he was not perusing them himself.

'Anything helpful?'

'I haven't found anything so far. You were quite right.' Rodario looked out of the window, having caught sight of some movement out in the courtyard. 'The proud flower of Sangpûr has arrived. So it's only Ireheart we're waiting for.'

'Natenian?'

'He arrived earlier and is resting. So he and' – Rodario had to think – 'what's her name again?'

Mallenia grinned. 'Dirisa. So she's come?'

'Yes. Until it's absolutely clear who's in charge she considers herself co-ruler. With equal status.' The ex-actor looked around. 'Where did I put my glass of water?'

'You drank it. But Sha'taï can go and fetch you some more.' Mallenia called her ward. The girl came in from the adjoining room wearing a pretty robe in light green and brown, her hair braided in a plait encircling her head. Mallenia was enchanted. 'Be a sweet thing and get us a jug of fresh water.'

'Of course,' replied the little one with a charming curtsey before hurrying off.

'How often have you told her she doesn't have to stand on ceremony?' Rodario levered himself up from the low window seat and crossed the room in a kind of obstacle race past the piles of papers.

Mallenia came over and embraced him in spite of her armour. 'She insists; she says it's only right. I wonder when the shadow of grief will fade from her eyes?'

'We must be grateful to the gods that she can feel any joy at all, after what she's been through.' Rodario kissed his consort gently on the mouth. 'Poor little thing. She's been driven out of her homeland, threatened by a dwarf, and she's lost her family. She has no real parents.'

'We're her substitute parents.' The blonde Idoslane queen stroked his brown hair. 'Or we should at least try to give her the stability she would have had in her previous life.' She looked intently at him. 'I want you to know that I am naming her as my heir and you as her guardian, should anything happen to me.'

Rodario looked concerned. 'How can you think that something . . .'

She laid a finger on his lips to silence him. 'It was a near thing during that attack. If it hadn't been for Ireheart there would have been many more victims. Especially among the rulers. That was what made me decide to put my affairs in order.'

Rodario gave a sigh and pulled her to him. Mallenia laid her head on his chest.

It was a rare moment for warrior queen and former actor. Standing close, they held each other in silence. Nightfall would bring time for caresses.

The sound of voices intruded on their tranquillity and from the main room they could hear the commotion of preparations for the coming meeting. Then they heard a dwarf's voice. With the arrival of the High King, council deliberations could commence.

Rodario laughed on hearing Ireheart shout. 'Never separate a dwarf from his tankard.' He slipped out of his companion's embrace. 'Read me the Stone Gateway report again before we head down.'

'But you just—'

'Yes, but it's better if I hear it read out loud. Easier to imagine.' He stretched his arms out and swivelled round, causing papers to flutter and dislodge. 'Like in the theatre.' Rodario paced up and down. 'Oh, if only I could get back to the boards from time to time. The stage for me is now the whole world. Though there I can be whatever I want!' He struck a dramatic pose. 'Dark älf, hero, villain, elf! Ah, I swear by the gods I'd be better than ever! I could do any part. My audience would adore me!'

'Stop play-acting. Leave it to those who are . . . free to perform,' Mallenia nudged him jokingly. 'Otherwise the people of Urgon would say their king should forget the throne and stick to the stage.'

She picked up the report and, more seriously now, started to read: ' "While the elves made for the gate, their pursuer loomed out of the unusually heavy and persistent fog. Before learning what happened next, listen to the description of the cruel murderer: a muscular bare-armed giant in human form, in boots, leather hose, brown leather armoured doublet and with a white flag marked in green. The runes were indecipherable. His head was completely covered in a copper helmet which had a light visor with white symbols . . ." '

A child's piercing scream tore into her words. It came from the threshold. Crockery crashed to the ground.

Mallenia and Rodario whirled round.

Sha'taï was at the open door, shrieking hysterically, gulping air and screaming again.

The Ido queen hurriedly replaced the paper on the table and went over to comfort the child; the screams subsided and turned to sobs.

'Ghaist!' the girl kept stammering, clutching Mallenia for protection. 'Ghaist!'

But Sha'taï was unable to say more.

Bodyguards with drawn swords came stomping up the stairs in heavy boots, but Mallenia dismissed them with a gesture. Her little charge would be even more frightened if they came in.

Rodario picked up the report and silently re-read the section that made the child scream so.

'It's the description,' he murmured. 'It must be that.' He looked at the girl, whose obvious distress was lessening. Both Sha'taï and the giant monstrosity of a warrior came from the Outer Lands. *Has she met him before?*

'I'll put her to bed,' Mallenia said quietly, taking her to the next room. 'You go down and explain to the others. I'll be with you soon. And don't forget to lock Carmondai's papers away.'

Rodario nodded and chucked the älfar report into the chest, turning the key in the lock. He left the room lost in thought. He went downstairs and sent the maid to sweep up the crockery shards.

He did not think Sha'taï would regain her courage any time soon to be able to give more details of what had caused her panic. *Good thing we have someone who might know more.*

The elf-slayer in the copper helmet now had a name: Ghaist.

If you could name your enemy you could defeat it; this was the commonly held view.

'But defeat it how?' he wondered.

The mighty catapults, able to deter any monster attack,

with arrows that could penetrate any known armour, and whose spears could pierce the hugest of bodies, would not work in this case.

This was going to cause him some sleepless nights.

Girdlegard
Elf realm of Ti Lesinteïl
6492nd solar cycle, summer

The creature launched itself at Beligata, its white fangs gleaming, each tooth sharper than the next. Just to be touched by one of them would slit her flesh open.

She suppressed her fear and the pain from the thorns. *Neither fear nor pain will help me here.* Lifting her double axe determinedly, she prepared to cut into the beasts' throat from below.

She forgot the voice from the thicket – until a sturdy figure appeared at her side, heading into her aim.

Beligata wanted to warn him, but felt him clutch her right arm firmly to divert the deadly blow. He let himself drop back, pulling her with him.

The beast realised too late that it was snapping empty air; its maw closed and the blades went through tongue and jaws. The axe crunched through the upper bone and split the creature's snout. Blood spurted out onto the two dwarves.

Beligata landed on something hard: it sounded like metal. Her unexpected rescuer was wearing armour. The howling beast was forced to follow them, hanging from the weapon like a fish on a hook. Beligata let go of the weapon to roll aside; she had to trust to the gods that the animal was already dying from the inflicted wounds. It hit the ground behind them with a terrible cry, its limbs jerking wildly.

She was kicked in the side by a flailing leg, sending her into the bushes where she hung upside down for a moment. Her arms and legs were caught in the unforgiving brambles; the vicious thorns stabbed through gaps in her armour, through her undergarments and into her flesh.

She groaned and looked round to see if the beast would try to attack her again, even in its death throes. But the animal lay quiet, the double axe still lodged in its snout. Beligata's unknown rescuer stood behind the creature and there was the clatter of metal on metal. His armour must have taken some punishment.

'Sheer luck we survived that,' he called over. His words sounded muted, as if he were talking through a helmet. He placed his foot on the lower part of the mouth and began to work the axe out. 'You should have listened to me.'

Beligata noted a particular accent to his dwarf language, as if he'd just learned it. There was blood dripping down her arms and legs and she was held fast by the thorns – while that dwarf was taking possession of her weapon. *He could simply kill me now.* 'Who are you?'

'Why did those fools go down the shaft?' he asked. 'They'll never survive.' He broke the axe free of the jawbone. The creature's mouth snapped shut. When the dwarf raised his left arm she saw a bloodied ring glint gold between his thumb and forefinger. 'They've already lost one of their number and I don't hold out much hope for the others.' He put the ring away and looked up at the night sky. 'The stars are still the same. But I don't know where we are.' He turned to her. 'Except it's Girdlegard.'

Beligata forced herself not to cry out. 'Get me out of these brambles.'

He nodded and came over, limping slightly on his right

leg. His armour squeaked and rattled. It had obviously been neglected and was in urgent need of a smith's attention to stop it from making more noise than an army of orcs. *No chance of the elves not hearing us.*

Now she could see him more clearly.

It must originally have been a splendid set of tionium armour. What remained – patched up and held together with leather thongs and chain links – showed deep cuts and scratches, and it was badly stained with unidentifiable substances that must have dried on.

The dwarf brought a hefty smell of dirt and blood. The doublet was filthy, and one boot sole was flapping free like a mouth. The helmet on his greasy brown shoulder-length hair was in a similar state – dented, battered and missing bits.

It made Beligata think he had forgotten to wash after the last battle he'd fought. *Or is he one of the undead who used to haunt Girdlegard?* She looked down at the narrow shaft. *He's come up out of the darkness, bringing new terror.*

He had reached her now and leaned forward to peer at her.

She shuddered at the sight of his misshapen features. He must have been terribly burned: there were horrible scars over one third of his face. Where his left eye should be there was an empty socket and an old cut ran down his face and neck, disappearing under his jerkin.

'You're a Thirdling,' he said, speaking through his half helmet. 'I can see by your weapon and your build. And you've got some unfinished tattoos on your chest.'

'I'm a Freeling,' she corrected him. 'My name is Beligata. Cut me free so I can follow my friends. They need my help.'

The unknown dwarf gave a short, hollow laugh. 'You'll only be able to bring back their corpses. But they can be buried.'

He lifted the double axe with ease and cut away the

brambles, liberating her from the thorny fetters. She slipped to the ground, and moaned softly as she straightened up.

'So you've come out of that hole?' The suspicion that had flickered on first seeing him – and had then died – rekindled now. *Missing left eye, brown hair, and the features . . . by Lorimbur . . . that means . . .*

He helped her pull off the rest of the tangled briars. 'I come from the underworld, pursued by that terrible beast. I had been lying in wait for it. You don't want them coming at you from behind. They never give up once they've picked up your smell.'

'Which tribe are you from? How did you end up down there? Did you find a way through to Phondrasôn? What happened to you?' Beligata took the double axe he was handing her with a smile.

'I did indeed get through to the realm of demons through a shaft,' he told her, amused by her questions. 'But what do you and your friends want down there? Looking for treasure?'

She swallowed, her mouth dry. She had to gulp down some water from her flask before she could speak. 'The High King sent us to look for someone.'

'Aha.' The sturdy dwarf had no other weapons, it seemed. 'So who rules the Children of the Smith?'

'Boïndil Doubleblade of the Secondlings,' she answered. 'We were to go down and . . .' She muttered an oath. *I have to know.* 'Are *you* Tungdil Goldhand?'

The remaining eye flashed under the crusted flesh and bushy brows. 'It took you some time to gain the courage to ask.' He showed her the gold inlay on his hand. Even though the skin was dark with filth the sun-gold metal glinted in the moonlight. 'Yes, I am. You've no idea how glad I am to hear that Ireheart is alive and on the throne!' He stretched out his hand for her flask. 'Now, tell me about this place. It's not the mountains, that's for sure.'

'It's Lesinteïl. The new Lesinteïl.' She gasped. 'But . . . if you . . .' She glanced back at the hole.

'Exactly. There was no point in their going down. To their deaths.' Tungdil placed the flask to his lips and gulped down the water. 'How is it only now you've started to search?'

Beligata was not in the mood to fill the dwarf in on the history of the last two hundred and fifty cycles. 'Only just got your message.'

'What message?'

'Tied round the beasts' necks.'

'By Vraccas! Good for them. My loyal night-biters.' Tungdil wiped the excess water off his beard with his arm. 'I sent them out forty cycles ago.' He laughed. 'They took as long as I did to find the way out. Samusin still enjoys a joke.' He tossed the empty flask back to her. 'Shall we go to the elves and let them know they've got a tunnel to Phondrasôn on their territory?'

'Not a good idea. We don't have permission from the pointy-ears to carry out our search.' Beligata went over to the edge of the gaping hole to be greeted by strange-smelling warm air. Impossible to miss the fact that blood had recently been spilt there. *I must get them back*. But it was probably more important to get this returned hero, unfriendly and ungrateful though he might be, safely to the High King and to report the success of the mission.

But she was not yet convinced that she was dealing with the genuine hero. As far as she knew, the other, the first Tungdil, had also shown the gold mark on his hand. Perhaps only the High King would be in a position to decide for sure. And even he had been mistaken in the past. *Hadn't he?*

Time was running away as she stared down into the dark. Beligata cursed her dilemma. *Lorimbur, send me another sign!*

Tungdil was running his calloused fingers along the bark of a tree trunk in wonder. 'There's nothing like this down below.' He was clearly emotional. 'So much you forget. So many little things that cannot thrive in the dark. But there are other things that you never stop missing: like how the air smells. Trees that grow in the open.'

Beligata turned around. She had come to a decision. 'If you are Tungdil Goldhand and not another copy, like the one from a cycle ago –'

'A *copy*?' he cut in, his disfigured face whirling round. His greasy brown hair stuck to his neck. 'A dwarf reached you claiming to be me? And Ireheart fell for it?' He came over to where she was. 'Tell me what happened.'

She pointed to the shaft. 'I must find the others and bring them back. It was for your sake that they endangered their lives. How are they supposed to know that you're already out? Their sacrifice would be pointless.'

'True.' Tungdil watched her and then turned his good eye to the entrance. 'A copy,' he repeated pensively. 'Then I was right.'

'You were right about what?'

Tungdil gave a faint smile. 'I'll tell you later, young dwarf-woman. I presume you were going to say: "If you're really Tungdil Goldhand, help me find the others – the ones that came to rescue you."'

Beligata nodded.

'Let's go and see what's left of them. Do exactly what I tell you, keep quiet unless I ask you something and don't attempt any more silly heroics. Samusin seldom helps out more than once.' Tungdil stepped forward and disappeared in the depths.

Without a weapon. Beligata sprang up to follow him. *Absolute madness.*

We never took the easy path
and we looked for others to blame
for everything that went wrong after the liberation.

We looked first in our own ranks
then we looked among our enemies.
We even looked to blame the gods.

Each of us was secretly convinced
that we alone were innocent
and had made no mistakes.

This will have been our greatest failing.

First draft for the foreword to
The Writings of Truth
written under duress by Carmondai

VII

Girdlegard
Underneath the elf realm of Ti Lesinteïl
6492nd solar cycle, summer

By the dim light of fluorescent moss in the narrow tunnel she was crawling through, Gosalyn saw the marks on the wall. 'Vraccas, no!'

It was the rune she herself had scratched. She had come this way before and had taken the wrong turning.

The innate orientation skills that she could usually rely on underground did not work in this part of Girdlegard, it seemed. Maybe elves and maga had put some kind of spell on the place, or perhaps it was a leftover from the time of the älfar.

She had lost all sense of time. It could have been ten orbits since she entered the tunnel shaft. Or even one hundred. Her food was running low and Phondrasôn had swallowed up her companions.

She took a left at the next junction, to get back to the small cavern she had explored previously.

She slipped in and kept her back to the wall so as not to be jumped from behind. She allowed herself a short rest to gather her strength. But sleep was difficult: her thoughts were circling wildly.

She thought most of the tunnels through which she was ceaselessly crawling must have been created by worm-like creatures. The walls told her that no tools had been employed; there was no evidence of force. The lupine beasts must have located the tunnels and used them to get out to the surface. But the dwarf-woman did not have the sophisticated sense of smell that would have allowed her to sniff her way through the maze as they did. The air smelt to her only of metal, slack and damp earth where the beasts had widened the tunnels to get through.

There was another worrying aspect: the elves had filled in the crater but the material they had used – rubble and sand – were not always as stable a layer as intended. If Gosalyn heard a slight movement of soil or pebbles in a particular tunnel or shaft, she picked a different path to be on the safe side.

She had no idea what the other dwarves were doing.

On first entering the sloping tunnel, they had come to a junction. Out of one of the tunnels came the roar of the beast. Belogar had hurled himself at the creature and pushed her down the other way.

Since then Gosalyn had been wandering aimlessly. At first she kept shouting their names, but when she never heard a tap on the wall in response, she gave up calling out. But she did not stop exploring.

Gosalyn's priority was to stay alive; the next most important thing was to find Tungdil Goldhand. Whether she ever came across her companions again was up to Vraccas. She put her life in the hands of the divine Smith.

'Follow my voice,' came the echoey tones of the zhadár. 'I know you can hear me, Gosalyn.'

Of course. It had to be him that would survive. She lifted her head. 'Call out again, Carâhnios.'

She then heard his exaggerated laugh right next to her.

'Just a little joke,' he giggled. 'I thought I'd drop by and collect you.'

Gosalyn's heart was beating fast. She had neither heard nor seen him coming.

'Thank you,' she replied. 'Where are the others?'

'The other *one*,' the zhadár corrected her, taking her hand, uninvited, and pulling her along after him. 'Deathbringer is waiting for us. The little scar-faced beauty stayed up on the surface and she's probably fallen victim to the beast. Pity, really.' He gave a hefty sigh but one heartbeat later he was laughing once more. 'We would have made a splendid couple. So attractive, both of us. We shared a secret, we did.' He chuckled.

She did not pursue the subject. It sounded so contrived. 'And Belogar?'

Carâhnios made a snapping sound with his black teeth. 'Gobbled up. Idiot.'

'He was no idiot!' Gosalyn wanted to hit him for denigrating her friend in that way. 'He sacrificed himself for my sake.'

'No, he didn't. He was just plain stupid.' Carâhnios seemed not to have the faintest trace of empathy. 'How on earth can anyone in a situation like this start a fight with a narshân beast? I told him to follow me but he tried to play the hero. Now he's turned into a meal. A nice snack.' He snapped with his teeth again and laughed. 'It's enough to make me hungry. Hung, hung, hungreee.'

Gosalyn had to hurry to keep up with the zhadár as he led her into a part of the labyrinth where the slope was steeper. She had to concentrate hard to stop herself slipping; it made memorising their path nearly impossible.

Two down already, and there might be further losses to their ranks before they found Tungdil Goldhand.

There was a greenish glow from the moss on the rock walls. They must be in a much older part of the underground maze, perhaps directly under the crater. The air was getting warmer and there was a smell of excrement and rubbish, together with smoke. There must be a fire somewhere.

Gosalyn's boot soles slithered over the slippery floor. She saw she was in a tiny cave that must once have collapsed on one side and had since been smoothed over. *Who would have constructed a ramp like that?*

There were several large holes out of which a mixture of solidified glass, clinker and metal had been poured, making columns that now supported the roof. Gosalyn supposed this was the result of the elves' attempts to seal off the whole area. The molten slack must have worked its way down through the crevices. *Those pillars look so strange. Bizarre but oddly beautiful.*

'We're nearly there.' Carâhnios dragged her onwards round a heap of stones, behind which they found Hargorin sitting by a small fire to which he was adding animal dung. 'Here we are,' Carâhnios whooped with glee, wrenching her arm up into the air. 'We've done it, little warrior! You have survived. So far. But who knows? Death lurks everywhere. Everywhere, everywhere!' Then he leaned back against the rock and closed his eyes, beginning to snore and giggle intermittently.

Gosalyn could hardly believe it. 'He's asleep,' she confirmed, shaking her head. 'By Vraccas! He's actually asleep!'

'Leave him to rest.' Hargorin, who had obviously lost weight, handed her his water flask. 'I hope Samusin will make up for our losses,' he said, his voice full of regret. 'Otherwise I'm afraid we'll never make it back alive.'

The dwarf-woman drank from the flask. 'The way Carâhnios found his way in the tunnels – he must have been here before.'

'I expect he has. He'll have got around quite a bit in

Girdlegard in his search for älfar.' Hargorin stared at the dancing flames. 'I shouldn't be at all surprised. What could the elves have done to stop him?' He looked at the sleeping Carâhnios. 'It's good we have him with us.'

Gosalyn felt the tension ebb from her. A feeling of emptiness started to spread, with the grief at her friend's loss bringing tears to her eyes. She gulped and took another drink of the water before returning the flask. There must be no doubt in her mind.

The map she knew well came to mind. There were several complex branching Phondrasôn tunnels below Girdlegard, reaching far to the east where the Black Abyss lay, and going underneath the Stone Gateway. Because of the distances involved, this mission of theirs could take cycles and cycles.

There was one faint hope: with great luck they might come upon the abandoned express tunnel system. There'd be no crew and no time to repair the rail and pulley connections between the various dwarf kingdoms, but in places there were exits to Girdlegard.

I wonder how often our ancestors travelled through Phondrasôn without knowing? She studied the red-haired dwarf critically. *Now there's only three of us. Hardly any supplies, and absolutely no idea where we should be looking. We've as much chance of success if I threw a pebble in the air expecting to hit a unicorn.*

Hargorin warmed his hands at the fire and started to sing quietly.

The earth conceals you in the land
Deep within the shaft
Vraccas holds you in his hand
And Vraccas' eye is watchful

So, brave dwarf, whate'er your plight
Your trusty axe befriends you
Your eye can see where there's no light
Your courage bold defends you

Dark may be the path you walk
And your steps may echo hollow
What if deadly terror stalk
And danger always follow?

So, brave dwarf, whate'er your plight
Your trusty axe befriends you
Your eye can see where there's no light
Your courage bold defends you

What slithers there? What whispers here?
What seems to mock and taunt?
Stay calm and don't give in to fear
The phantom flees – avaunt!

So, brave dwarf, whate'er your plight
Your trusty axe befriends you
Your eye can see where there's no light
Your courage bold defends you

If mountains fall and crumble
And floods of beasts o'erwhelm
Be bold and you'll not stumble:
Victorious to the end.

Gosalyn made an effort to pull herself together. The strength of her race was in their ceaseless determination in the face of adversity and perseverance at all costs, though others might see this as pig-headed obstinacy. Hargorin's song had reminded her of her heritage. *We'll cope. We'll do it.*

'Did he say which way to go?' she asked, indicating the sleeping zhadár. 'Has he any idea where we've landed?'

Hargorin shook his head. 'No. But by my calculations we must be somewhere under the city the Triplets ruled. Those columns of melted rock are a good clue. I know that Fiëa intended to fill up a hole with clinker and metal.'

'Sounds like the place.' In the dim light from the fire, Gosalyn looked up at the cave roof, noticing the cracks threading across it. From time to time there came the clatter of small fragments falling. 'There must be unbelievable pressure on these rocks.'

'I'm no expert on these matters but as soon as the zhadár has rested, I think we need to get on our way. The roof could come down any moment. I see new cracks every time I look up.'

'Maybe it's the heat from the fire? Why did you make camp here?'

'There's fresh water just behind that boulder. That seemed reason enough.' Hargorin got to his feet. 'Come on. Let's fill all the flasks and then we're ready.'

Gosalyn opened her flask and shook out the remaining stale drops. All of a sudden Carâhnios leaped at her and Hargorin, his arms outspread.

'You madman! What the—' Then she heard the hum and felt the rush of air and a touch on her shoulder. *Arrows!*

The three of them tumbled to the ground; the zhadár landed in the fire, sending up sparks. The flames went out.

The cascade of arrows did not stop but the dwarves were protected by the boulder and by the dark. They could hear the sound of wood or metal tips hitting stone as the arrows hit the rock or overshot the mark and disappeared down the tunnel.

'Stay down,' whispered the zhadár, his black eyes glinting merrily. He wasn't bothered by the fact that tiny flames were still licking at his armour. 'They're good. Good, good, good! Nearly didn't hear them coming because you were singing. Your song would have been the death of us, Deathbringer. That's a laugh.' Then he jumped to his feet and disappeared.

Älfar skills. Gosalyn and Hargorin crawled closer to the boulder's protection. Both dwarves drew their weapons and waited for an opportunity to risk a look over the top. They wanted to see where the enemy was that had used the cover of darkness to creep up on them.

Hargorin raised his long-handled axe with its polished metal head and used the reflection as a mirror. Dwarf vision was good in the dim light of the moss. 'They're over there in the tunnel you and the zhadár arrived through. They must be following your tracks.'

'Phenîlas?'

An arrow whirred and lodged in the wooden shaft of the axe. It was a long black arrow with dark feathering.

'Älfar,' exclaimed Gosalyn. 'But it can't be!'

'We're in Phondrasôn, remember. Tion alone knows what devilry is assembled here.' Hargorin lowered the axe, pulled out the arrow and broke it in half with one hand. 'The time of the älfar is long gone. We'll never let them take over again.'

'What shall we do?'

'The zhadár will have got to them by now . . .'

There came a scream that was not from a dwarf's mouth.

'Here we go!' Hargorin stormed out from behind the boulder and ran, doubled over, with Gosalyn at his heels.

They headed for the ramp, zigzagging across the empty

space and using the rock columns for cover where they could. The arrows were still coming but they were going wildly astray or falling short. They lacked the momentum to pierce armour now. Gosalyn gave thanks to Vraccas for his aid.

A number of figures were coming down the ramp, still shooting. Carâhnios, behind them, struck the head off one of the älfar with Bloodthirster and severed the archer's bow.

How did he get up there so quickly? Gosalyn threw herself behind one of the pillars, and the arrow aimed at her shattered on the hard surface of the fossilised column. Five älfar streamed across the cavern floor while two others remained on the ramp and confronted the zhadár. But they had to negotiate the obstacles of three decapitated älfar rolling towards them. And then the heads.

Their losses will mount. Gosalyn directed her anger towards the five adversaries who were trying to locate and surround the dark-haired dwarves. *But not ours!*

She somersaulted over to the next pillar and threw a handful of pebbles far to her right to lure her enemies into the open. Two älfar stepped into view and ran over, short swords in their hands. They wore leather armour and black leather hose with greaves attached; their heads were concealed in plain helmets.

That's not right. Gosalyn jumped to her feet, raising her short axe and her dagger. Fighting off two älfar at the same time was more of a challenge than she had wanted. She grinned. Ireheart was always the one for *challenges*, as he called any totally hopeless situation. *Pretend you're the High King. That'll be the way to deal with the black-eyes.* She heard the tune of the dwarf song in her head.

She lowered her head determinedly and made sure she kept the pillar at her back for protection. 'Over here!' she yelled, and then had to duck to avoid a thrown knife. The tip glanced off the column as the älfar reached her. 'I'll show you the quickest way to endingness.'

She parried the next lunge with her short axe. She forced her attacker's sword arm up and tried to stab him where he was unprotected, but the second älf went for her. She fended him off with her dagger and the blades clashed in mid-air without touching flesh.

Gosalyn saw the knee coming at her face. Instead of swerving sideways she put her head down to take the impact on her helmet. The impact was horribly loud, but her opponent screamed even louder and fell. Gosalyn immediately took her axe to the second foe, but he parried the blow and thrust at her in return.

A swift sword fight ensued between the dwarf-woman and the älf, taking them weaving between the pillars, using the columns in turn as cover; bits of the pillars were hacked off as the fight progressed.

The älf parried a mighty blow and Gosalyn's axe stuck fast in one of the pillars, producing an ominous crunching sound. The bottom half of the pillar collapsed and a cloud of dust rose up; her adversary was momentarily blinded.

Looking round she saw that Hargorin had felled one of the älfar and was striking another on the neck, forcing him to his knees. She couldn't see the fifth älf anywhere.

The zhadár pierced his last remaining opponent with his sword, laughing wildly. He made no effort to help either Hargorin or Gosalyn but bent down, doing something at the dead älf's throat.

Is that a flask he's found? It seemed to her the zhadár was collecting the blood.

Another cracking sound. She saw Hargorin heading at speed for the tunnel.

The unsupported broken pillar next to her crashed down. New cracks and holes appeared in the roof.

We've got to get out of here! Gosalyn saw the älf launching himself at her out of the cloud of dust and was about to crack him in the knees with her axe when he was struck on the head and shoulders by falling debris and crushed. This was the overture to a wholescale avalanche of rocks and stones.

Her first adversary got up, cursing, and limped off towards the ramp. The fight seemed to hold no more interest for him.

Was that oath in elvish? Gosalyn could hardly believe her ears. But when the fleeing figure shouted orders to his last, unseen companion, there was no doubt. *They are pointy-ears! They wanted us to think they were älfar!*

She sprinted through the hail of falling stones and overtook the limping elf, slicing through the tendon at the back of his sound leg, bringing him down. 'You're coming with me.'

Without listening to his screams, she grabbed him by the collar and dragged him to the tunnel that led out of the collapsing cavern. Hargorin and Carâhnios were waiting there. The three of them moved down the corridor, pulling their captive behind them.

'It's an elf,' announced Gosalyn furiously, landing a kick on the prisoner's side. She pulled off his helmet to expose fair hair. 'What have you got to say for yourself?'

He flashed a look at her.

The zhadár lifted up a slim phial where blood was bubbling away, smokily dissolving.

'He doesn't need to say anything. Here's the proof. They're not älfar. I collect älfar blood to distil. I put an alchemist preservative in the phial so the blood keeps.' He showed the clouded glass to the elf. 'The reaction is quite different.' He smashed the glass tube on the elf's forehead. 'Who sent you?'

Behind them the cave collapsed with a loud rumbling crash and small boulders rolled along the tunnel where they were. Clouds of reddish dust surged through. It smelt of metal and sand.

'Things aren't always what they seem,' the captive replied with much effort, grasping his wounded knee. He did not concern himself with the blood and glass splinters on his face. 'You don't know what . . .'

Another hum and a black arrow hit home with a clang, piercing the breast of the elf-warrior. He crumpled up. Gosalyn turned.

An elf stood in the tunnel veiled in dirt, about to notch a follow-up arrow.

Everything went black for the dwarf-woman. 'Carâhnios, don't do the dark thing now!'

'It's not me. That one's a *genuine* älf.'

Gosalyn's heart thudded.

Carâhnios' laugh was hysterical and high-pitched. 'Oh, now things are hotting up! Exciting!'

Girdlegard
United Kingdom of Gauragar-Idoslane
Freestone
6492nd solar cycle, summer

Dirisa was seated at her dressing-table in a small room lit by lamps to supplement the meagre dawn light. She was still wearing her night attire while her attendant examined her day-clothes for any imperfections. Looking at her reflection critically, she beckoned to her maid.

'Brush my hair again,' she ordered. 'It doesn't look right.'

'At once, mistress.' The young woman picked up the brush and devotedly drew the fine bristles through the black hair.

Phenîlas was standing at the window with a smile that concealed his impatience. He was dressed in a deep yellow flowing robe with black lacing at the waist; he wore a cape to enhance the appearance of his shoulders. He had brown gloves and his forearms were wound in silk protectors. 'You are taking your time.'

Dirisa frowned at him in the mirror. 'And *you* are wasting my time, friend.'

'You don't have anything to do.' The elf looked down at the courtyard, where Natenian, surrounded by his attendants, was returning from his outing.

The invalid king was having trouble breathing and it was obvious that he was bathed in sweat in his long garments. He had insisted on visiting the sights of the little town. Only a few orbits earlier such strenuous activity would have been out of the question and a litter needed.

He is rising to the challenge. 'You can listen to me just as well here.'

'What is there to discuss?'

'The future.'

Dirisa gave a scornful laugh. 'Since when is the future of interest to your people? Sitalia is no goddess of fate.'

'Sometimes we must take our fate into our own hands.' Phenîlas knew that he did not have much time to affect a change of heart. 'Send your maid out.'

'Are you going to brush my hair for me?' she snapped.

'I can try.'

Dirisa sent the young woman out.

'There are the combs,' she said. 'And mind you're careful.'

Phenîlas took up his stance behind her chair and picked up

the comb with sea whale tines; it went through her hair smoothly. The polished ivory slipped through like velvet, but her hair still looked rough and brittle compared with that of an elf-woman. 'Tell me why you are claiming the throne? You lead a comfortable life, you are rich and . . .'

'Tell me why Natenian has sent you instead of negotiating with me himself,' she retorted cuttingly.

'He did not send me.'

'Then you're his friend and you're acting on your own initiative?'

'I care about Girdlegard. It's only one cycle since the end of the terror; discord amongst our races must not be allowed to arise. A dispute such as the one between yourself and Natenian will only weaken the country internally, making it vulnerable.'

'A queen who is healthy and strong must be more to your liking than a man who has to thank the gods if he even wakes up alive in the morning.' Dirisa glanced at Phenîlas in the mirror with her nut brown eyes and held his gaze. 'You are aware who my relative and good friend is?'

'Everyone knows,' he replied with a smile.

She indicated where she wanted him to work with the comb. 'Wouldn't it be better if I were the all-out ruler? How else could we bring about closer collaboration between Tabaîn and Sangpûr?'

'I agree.'

'If you can't cite any definitive arguments in favour of Natenian,' she said, turning to face him directly, 'then tell me why you are continuing to support an invalid.'

'I never said I was continuing to support him.'

'I see.' She raised an eyebrow, a smile playing at a corner of her mouth.

'I'm not trying to get you to change your mind. I just want to find out how serious your intentions are,' said Phenîlas.

'And to find out whether you and I can make a deal?' She studied him carefully and then added, 'Grain.'

'How do you mean?'

'You wanted Natenian to give you access to grain. Probably a large quantity and at a favourable price.' Dirisa kept her dark eyes focused on his. 'We are, after all, Girdlegard's corn chamber. You will be in need of a good few sacks of corn if it's true what they say about your growing population. Haven't you had ten thousand elf-immigrants arriving?'

Phenîlas realised he was dealing with a clever woman who had thoroughly considered her prospects for the country following her attempt to take over the throne.

'Yes, indeed. We need corn. And we need land.'

'To grow your own crops or for purchase?'

'Both.' He silently complimented her on her straightforward and astute way of conducting negotiations. *She is shrewder than Natenian.*

Dirisa placed an arm over the back of the chair, a graceful pose. Almost as graceful as an elf. He had to admit she was almost pretty in her way. 'I must be grateful to the elves,' she said.

'Why is that?'

'If that beast in Lesinteïl had never . . . had never happened, by a weird set of coincidences, to kill the upcoming heir, I would never in my wildest imaginings have considered vying for the throne. To contest Raikan's claim would have ensured the hatred of the people.' She narrowed her eyes. 'How much grain?'

Phenîlas saw the princess was ready to bargain. 'One thousand twentner sacks.'

'How much land?'

'Eight hundred square miles to grow our own crops. You look after it for us. And then enough territory to take our borders over to the foothills of the Grey Mountains.'

'We can agree a price.' Dirisa turned back and adjusted her night-robe. 'I'll name the price and you'll pay it.'

Phenîlas had to laugh. 'You have a steely nerve, I must say.'

'Don't forget the tips,' she instructed. 'If there are split ends, snip them off.' She watched him at work with the comb.

'What will happen to Natenian? He has many supporters. Some members of Council are concerned about what privileges they might get. They'd have to be dealt with, too.'

Dirisa gave a twisted smile. 'How many of those beasts have you elves still got? Or what's your plan to keep Natenian quiet?'

Phenîlas was relieved to see a solution in the making. He would have preferred the invalid as a business partner – easier to manipulate because he had been promised treatment by elf healers – but Dirisa had a sound head on her shoulders and seemed to have few scruples. Land and corn, that was all that mattered.

'The gods will advise us,' was his rather vague answer. 'Sometimes events change overnight.'

'Simple as that, my friend?'

'Simple as that, princess.' Phenîlas put down the comb. 'Would it . . .'

'You think I'll overlook that your race did nothing to help when we were in need of every sword and every arrow?' she said, her voice cold. 'Now you fall on us in your thousands like locusts and you'd like to live in peace? A peace *we* fought for, after terrible suffering and adversity.'

'But we have changed.'

'Some things don't change. Some things have to be eradicated.' Dirisa got to her feet and the strands of black hair slipped out of his fingers. 'I have had eyes and ears in Tabaîn for over half a cycle and so I know what you and Natenian plotted. *That*,' she said, drawing nearer, 'is the reason why I want to rule my country. I am not selling you half our harvest while the rest of Girdlegard starves, *my friend*.'

Phenîlas' expression grew dark. 'You are mistaken.'

Dirisa laughed in his face. 'I know exactly what I'm saying. And everything we have discussed today only strengthens my opinion of your race: deceitful, cowardly and cunning. I would rather set fire to the entire harvest, and blame the gods, than supply the elves!'

'That was unwise.' His lips narrowed. *She tricked me.*

Dirisa grabbed the hairbrush and struck him across the face with the sharp bristles, leaving a deep scratch. 'No, *that* was unwise *of you*. I see no point in dissembling. You know where you are with me and you have revealed just what I should think of you.'

'You're risking civil war within the ranks of the nobility and within the general population if you pursue your plan.' Phenîlas checked the scratch in the mirror. The wound was bleeding freely, letting drops fall on his robe. He blotted the scratch with his silk sleeve.

'And risking my life?' she mocked. Dirisa pointed to the door with the bloodied hairbrush. 'I know what I am letting myself in for. Don't make the mistake of thinking I haven't considered the consequences of my actions.'

'Are you sure?' Phenîlas did not believe it for a blink of an eye. He strode past her to the corridor where the maid stared at him, open-mouthed.

He hurried back to his own chamber, grabbed a towel and pressed it against the wound on his face. *It is true. We both know where we stand.* If the trade deal with Dirisa for corn and land had fallen through, the elves would be supporting Natenian's candidacy. Phenîlas needed to investigate whether there might be a way to speed things up.

There could be no attempt on the princess's life, he decided. It would raise questions if yet another heir to the throne died in mysterious circumstances.

The remaining option was intimidation.

Dirisa had a weakness as every living creature does. Phenîlas vowed to find out where hers lay. Perhaps he could get her to withdraw her claim to the throne. Natenian would take more care in naming an heir next time.

I'll see to that. Phenîlas studied his reflection.

His face had stopped bleeding, so he laid aside the sullied garment, washed his chin and neck and put on a fresh robe. The council were meeting that evening and Natenian would receive a visit in advance of the session.

How do I explain the injury? He would have to think of an excuse.

Phenîlas opened the door and stepped out into the corridor and found himself face to face with a tall, thin älf in an obviously weakened state. He was unmistakable, however, due to his stature and black eyes. His head was covered in grey stubble and his features betrayed his advanced age. Brands on face and brow proclaimed him the property of Mallenia. A red-hot wire had marked his forehead with runes stating *If anyone harms this älf, the same fate shall befall him.* No one was permitted to lay a finger on him.

Phenîlas knew who this was: Carmondai, the only älf whose life had been spared. In earlier times he had kept records for the älfar and now the humans were forcing him to write up the history of the downfall of his own race. And he knew a great deal. About events in the past still affecting the present and the future, too.

He lived out his days in a fortress in Oakenburgh, Phenîlas knew. Mallenia must have summoned him. *Why? Is there something to report?*

Carmondai's glance showed a definite lack of interest. The branded älf made his way along the corridor towards the stairs down to the main hall. He wore only the simplest of clothing, marked with the emblem of Idoslane.

'They should have destroyed you and all your writings,' Phenîlas muttered.

Carmondai halted at the top of the stairs and placed a thin hand on the banister rail. 'I wish the same thing myself, elf,' he said with a broken voice.

'Wouldn't it be easy for you to put a stop to your unendingness?' The elf went over to him. 'Why do you poison Girdlegard with your lies and fabricated stories about the black-eyes?'

Carmondai smiled. 'You would be glad if the stories *were* made up. But there is truth in their core.'

Phenîlas sneered.

'Did the settlement in the Grey Mountains really exist, or did it not?' Carmondai cut through the elf's scornful laughter. 'Then you can imagine just how true my other tales are.'

'They are poison,' Phenîlas spat. 'Your words sit fast in people's minds and glorify your race. But there's nothing admirable about your people. Nothing at all.'

'It is the same with your own folk.' Carmondai regarded him without passion. 'There remains much to tell that has not yet been recorded. Mallenia likes to listen to me.'

If I were to push him now . . . Phenîlas came up behind

the älf to place his hand on the älf's back, but his fingers met no resistance.

Carmondai was somehow now standing at his side, still indifferent, but with a coldness in his eyes that engendered more fear in the beholder than any älfar power. The cold came from his innermost soul.

'If I ever consider wanting to die, elf, I'll do it myself,' he whispered. 'But try that one more time and I'll ensure you'll meet your end before I meet mine.' He turned and walked down the steps.

Phenîlas watched him descend, boiling with fury. *Bastard!* The lie-teller was next on the list after Dirisa of people to be dealt with.

Perhaps the easiest solution would be to raise a mob against him – to string him up, stone him or burn him alive. Some criminal act could be invented and blamed on him. Perhaps a dead child whose bones he had liked the look of.

Something like that. But one thing at a time. Phenîlas turned round and went along to Natenian's rooms.

Carmondai was unfortunately correct about one thing: his stories held a core of truth.

And there were plenty of stories where the elves had played a part.

We are hard as stone yet we are not stone. A stone never retaliates.

Dwarf saying
attributed to the warrior Chonglirabur

VIII

Girdlegard
Underneath the elf realm of Ti Lesinteïl
6492nd solar cycle, summer

The dwarves' eyes could not penetrate the darkness the älf had brought about in the tunnel. But Gosalyn had seen her adversary place an arrow to his bow and so she dropped to the floor.

'Get under cover,' she shouted. She did not know who the arrow had been aimed at. She could hear it hiss past but could not tell where it landed. There was no sound of a body falling so she hoped for the best.

Suddenly her vision cleared. She could still taste the fear swirling round her, making her heart like lead.

The älf, wearing the same kind of armour as the elf that lay dead, was standing over Hargorin, stabbing down at him with a long sword; he had thrown his bow aside. The dwarf fended off the attack with his axe and forced his opponent back.

The älf swerved to avoid him and kicked Hargorin in the head, delivering the blow over the top of a rock used as cover. The dwarf crashed against the tunnel wall, and slid down, stunned.

'I shall take your life, traitor,' the älf said with malice in his voice as he raised his blade. 'May Tion rob you of your soul.'

Gosalyn could not move a muscle. The fear the enemy had inflicted on her prevented her from coming to the Deathbringer's aid. *I must do something. I can't let fear be my master.* She put one foot forward and remembered the words of the song her leader had sung to her: *Be bold and you'll not stumble: Victorious to the end.*

'Over here! I challenge you,' she shouted to the älf.

He halted his strike in mid-air and stared at her with his bright black eyes. 'You're only delaying your end and that of this mountain maggot here,' he retorted, placing the tip of his blade at Hargorin's throat. 'And you won't stop me, anyway.' He pointed upwards. 'I shall drag your corpses to the Naishïon and I'll say I caught you spying for the High King.'

'Never. Phenîlas knows what we're . . .' Gosalyn bit her lip. *How did he fool the elves? Did they know they had an älf with them?*

'Phenîlas knew about you, of course. Everybody does.' The älf laughed. 'But I shall make a formal complaint to the Council of Kings in the name of my Naishïon and the star of the dwarves will start to fall.' He spat at Hargorin. 'It's enough to know the disputes will grow and bear fruit. Accusation alone will ensure that.'

Him? Addressing the council? Gosalyn was given fresh hope by the news and she managed to take another step. It felt as if she was walking on the thinnest of ice and any second she could be plunging into freezing water to drown. 'They'll kill you!'

'They'll take me for an elf.' The älf readied himself to strike, angling to cut off Hargorin's head. 'I would invite you to come as a witness but I fear I may need your ugly skull, you dirt-digger,' he sneered. Before his blade could touch the dwarf's neck, Carâhnios suddenly appeared at his side, emerging as if born of shadow, and stopped the vicious blow using Bloodthirster.

'Zhadár,' the älf hissed, kicking out. 'Another traitor!' Carâhnios used his armoured fist to stop the kick, forcing the älf violently backwards. The zhadár avoided the following stroke by swerving and retaliated for good measure.

Gosalyn lost all her fear. The älf was not able to maintain his magic power. He and Carâhnios were engaged now in a swift exchange of sword thrusts.

When the dwarf-woman tried to come to his aid he sent her back with a wave of his hand. 'Look after Hargorin,' he ordered, crowing with delight. 'I'm enjoying crossing swords with a black-eyes.'

Gosalyn hurried over to Deathbringer, who was crouched down, blood covering his face.

'It's only a scratch,' he growled, grasping his long axe. 'Let's hack him into little pieces.'

Gosalyn helped him to his feet and supported him with her arm.

He swayed a little because of the kick in the head. The dent in his helmet showed that the älf was wearing reinforced boots.

Carâhnios was now in trouble. His opponent had adjusted his attack and was employing a short sword. The intense speed and agility of the älf meant that the zhadár had to rely on parrying the attacker's sword thrusts. Gosalyn realised that there were no gaps left by the attacker, no opportunities for Carâhnios to sink his blade into the foe.

'Like it or not,' she called. 'Here I come.'

The zhadár seemed to lose his footing in the scree and his opponent took a side step, thrusting straight forward with his sword.

That was apparently just what Carâhnios had wanted to happen, Gosalyn realised; he dropped to the ground, letting the blade pass harmlessly in front of his face. And because the älf was at that moment at full stretch, he presented an increased target area.

Bloodthirster's blade swiped diagonally into the belly of the älf, who was now aware he had made a fatal mistake. But it was too late to recover: the weapon had pierced through his armour and cut his belly.

With a groan he sprang back, blood spurting from the wound. It had not been deep enough to put the dangerous opponent out of action.

'You shall die with me!' the älf shouted. Black lines of fury zigzagged across his face.

Darkness overwhelmed Gosalyn once more. She and Hargorin had almost reached the enemy.

There was a clink of metal and Deathbringer groaned and slipped out of her arms; she was hit on the shoulder, but she fended off the blow with her axe before it could touch her chainmail jerkin and slide to her neck.

Carâhnios was howling, too, but from rage more than anything else.

'Underhand coward!' he bellowed. 'I'll have your blood and I'll boil it. I'll let you bleed to death and you'll wish you'd never been born!'

Where is he? Gosalyn drew her dagger, turned round, feeling her way. The tunnel seemed wider now, in the dark.

The darkness ebbed away after a few blinks of an eye – and there was the älf, towering over her.

Gosalyn knew she had no time to do anything to prevent the sword plunging at her head.

'Move.' Suddenly a figure shoved hard against her, pushing her to one side.

She landed on the stone and saw Beligata somersaulting

off her, her double war axe in both hands. Hargorin crouched nearby, clutching a badly damaged right leg with a broken shin bone protruding from the flesh. Carâhnios got up, cursing; the opponent's sword had cut him on his right upper arm.

Two paces further away, a stranger in a battered suit of tionium armour pushed himself in front of the älf, hands balled to fists.

'I have met so many of your kind,' the newcomer dwarf said calmly. 'Very few of them went on living.'

The älf attacked.

The newcomer let the blade shatter on his right shoulder where the armour was still intact. Then he hurled the stones he held in his hands. First the right, then the left.

The sharp projectiles hit the surprised älf square in the face, leaving an open wound on the forehead. His nose was broken and impacted. He fell over backwards and lay still, blood oozing from the injuries, running over the ruined features and then dripping onto the ground.

Gosalyn got up and stood next to Beligata. 'Who is that?' She shuddered at the sight of his deformed face.

The new dwarf took the älf's own sword in his hands and decapitated him without further ado.

'My name is Tungdil Goldhand,' he replied. Gosalyn closed her mouth, which had been hanging open. 'I had already reached the outside world' – he pointed at Beligata with the sword – 'when she told me what you were all up to. We came back to reward you for your courage.'

It's him? Gosalyn didn't know what to say. She saw the gold inlay on the back of his hand. She had never met the hero of Girdlegard, being a full hundred cycles too young to have done so. But she knew the stories about him, the songs and the pictures and friezes depicting his exploits. There had been no mention of facial disfigurement, however. Except for the missing left eye, which was as described.

Is that proof enough? She was unsure of herself and looked at Beligata in the hope of confirmation.

'I don't know,' said the other girl, reading the unspoken question in her eyes. She went over to Deathbringer and pulled off her belt to bind round two long daggers as a makeshift splint for the shattered leg.

Carâhnios came over, his black eyes viewing the newcomer suspiciously. 'So you say you're the Scholar?'

'What are you doing with my weapon?' Tungdil frowned, seeing Bloodthirster in the zhadár's hand. 'How did that get here?'

'The other Tungdil was using it to free Girdlegard from evil when he lost his life,' Carâhnios answered, leaning on the weapon. 'Nobody else wanted it.'

Tungdil studied him closely. 'What are you? You're no Child of the Smith.'

'I used to be,' Carâhnios replied. 'I was a Thirdling. The black-eyes transformed me, taught me their skills. I'm the last of my kind.' He giggled. 'How many Tungdils are there altogether? Every so often we get sent another version, happy to be back. You could all get together and make a new tribe.'

No one joined in his thundering laughter. There was too much possible truth in what he had said.

'I am the only *genuine* Scholar,' Tungdil said, calmly and very quietly.

Carâhnios bent down, took a phial from his rucksack and held it to the neck stump of the dead älf. He pressed the chest area of the torso to pump out more blood. 'At least I've earned that,' he murmured. His night-dark eyes glittered happily as he watched the blood seep into the glass tube. Gosalyn observed his actions with a mixture of fascination and horror. 'New supply for my elixir. The elixir of the—'

The thrust was so swift that no one saw it coming. No one could have prevented it. Tungdil pierced the zhadár's nape from behind as he knelt and pushed it down with all his strength, straight through into the älf's torso. Carâhnios' face was pinned to the corpse.

Then Tungdil took Bloodthirster and stared at it pensively. 'You should never have been here. And never in the hands of one such as him.'

Long black strands wafted from the zhadár's body to swirl around Tungdil like snakes, as if intent on crushing him.

Darkness flared round Carâhnios' helmet and drowned out the light. Limbs jerking, he attempted to drag the blade out from his neck. The elixir gave him the power to resist death despite the horrendous injury. Gosalyn and the dwarves stared – until blackness obscured the scene once more. But it didn't last long: the artificial gloom flickered, faded and then retreated entirely.

'I know what you became, for I knew those who took you over and made you what you are,' said Tungdil, unaffected by the wreaths of black strands. 'Evil through and through.' Then he plunged Bloodthirster through Carâhnios' body with all his might. The zhadár gave a scream and arched his back but the teethed blade held him pinned fast to the body of the älf, which he dragged with him as he flailed about.

'Nothing evil shall torment my homeland. Even if it claims to be doing good. This is the vow I made Vraccas.' Tungdil picked up a large lump of rock.

Showing no emotion, he took off the zhadár's helmet, revealing black curls. He smashed the stone into the skull three, four times. The black halo lessened and dissolved into thin air.

Black blood flowed from the shattered head and down onto the älf's corpse. There was no more movement. The zhadár was dead.

'Let's go back.' Tungdil turned to the others with a relieved smile on his face as they overcame their shock and approached gingerly. He let the rock fall to the ground. 'Beligata and I have marked the path. As soon as we've found a way through the cave that collapsed, there shouldn't be a problem.'

'You'll have to explain everything to the High King.' Hargorin said, his wrinkled features distorted with pain, though he bore it with courage.

'I'll tell him everything. About the potions and elixirs the Triplets used, too, to turn dwarves into creatures like the one I just released. On the outside a dwarf, but on the inside an älf.' Tungdil was calm and relaxed.

'I want to take the heads of the pointy-ears and the black-eyes with us,' Hargorin announced. 'Proof that something is afoot in the elf realm.'

But Tungdil turned down this request. 'Our words are evidence enough for the dwarf tribes. The other races would never believe it whatever proof we gave them. Let's go. The tunnels are unstable and can collapse at any moment. I didn't climb back down here just to get buried.'

'Wait.' Beligata swiftly searched the bodies of elf and älf. In the älf's clothing she found two small glass bottles inscribed with älfar runes.

'What does that say?' She held one up.

'*Elf eyes*,' Hargorin translated. 'What on earth?'

Tungdil put himself in the lead and started walking slowly. 'I expect they use it to change the colour of their eyes so sunlight can't betray them.' With each step he took, he discarded a piece of his filthy, battered tionium armour. They clanged to the ground as he walked. 'Eyes like elves.'

That's how the älf managed to deceive the pointy-ears, Gosalyn realised. She could see the others were coming to the same conclusion.

This led to other questions that could not be answered down here underground.

Were the elves already being infiltrated by älfar?

Was their enemy from the tunnel a survivor of the Girdlegard älfar? Or had he ambushed an elf in Phondrasôn and stolen his armour?

Why did the elf ruler try to have us killed? Gosalyn walked along, supporting Deathbringer together with Beligata. They stepped carefully over the discarded tionium, each piece worth a small fortune.

She had the impression Tungdil wanted nothing to do with his past. In front of their very eyes he was forswearing the dark shell of tionium like a cocoon he would emerge from cleanly to climb towards the light.

Without a weapon. Without protection. There was little in common with the martial aspect of the other Tungdil, about whose intentions opinions had differed so strongly.

He's even left the mighty Bloodthirster behind. Gosalyn started to hope this was really the true Tungdil they had found – or rather, they had been found by.

'If his soul can adapt that easily to the darkness of the last two hundred and fifty cycles, Girdlegard is home and dry,' murmured Beligata, her scar more obvious than usual. 'But only then.'

Girdlegard
United Kingdom of Gauragar-Idoslane
Freestone
6492nd solar cycle, summer

The atmosphere in the Council of Kings had undergone a subtle change, Ireheart noticed, without needing any special insight or having access to more beer than usual. He surveyed the scene over the rim of the tankard of spiced stout he had requested.

Everyone was silent.

Some were consulting their notes, some simply staring at nothing in particular, or studying the behaviour of the flies on the ceiling.

What's happened? What's different?

The Council normally assembled to discuss necessary improvements but it had become a place where suspicion ruled the day.

King Isikor had sent his excuses again, citing heavy rainfall and floods. His vote was to be disposed of as before, he wrote.

I'm starting to have my doubts about Isikor. Could he have sent the first assassin, I wonder? Is he working with the älfar? Ireheart fingered the end of his silver beard braid. *Rubbish. I'm drinking too much. Or not enough.*

He was reluctant to let the humans' mutual mistrust infect him, and was glad he had convened the Council. Events in Tabaîn and the role of the elves had to be discussed as a matter of urgency.

There may be a simple explanation. He drank thirstily from his mug of aromatic black beer. *I certainly hope so. Indeed I pray this may be the case.*

The High King was afraid that the news of the mysterious,

demon-like warrior at the Stone Gateway would take over the agenda. A justified amendment, but the elves' conduct also needed clarification. *And we still don't know where Coïra is. Supposed to be out exploring for a new source of magic, but without update?*

Dirisa and Natenian were sitting together at the table, but they did not seem to be on good terms; it had not yet been decided which of them would represent the kingdom. Ilahín remained in the Golden Plains; Phenîlas would take his place as delegate.

An armour-clad Mallenia came in, the last to enter the council chamber. She led Sha'taï by the hand, her foundling ward from the abandoned settlement. The young girl, wearing an embroidered dress, took a seat on a stool at Mallenia's feet. Fair-haired Mallenia stood up and opened the session briskly by asking the High King to address the Council.

That was quick. I like her style. Ireheart nodded and got to his feet. 'Thank you for responding to my call. We know that in Tabaîn . . .' he began.

'Excuse me, High King, but I think we ought to start with the events at the Stone Gateway,' Mallenia said in a friendly tone. 'We can discuss the internal arrangements of individual kingdoms later. This touches Girdlegard as a whole.'

His sympathy for the Idoslane monarch shrivelled. 'What I need to tell everyone also touches Girdlegard as a whole,' he protested. He was annoyed by how the assembled kings and queens were beaming sweetly at the little girl. Dirisa seemed to be the only one not affected by the child. *She's not a cuddly pet.* 'It could be . . .'

'High King, I don't wish to seem rude but I must insist. We are concerned about the report from the Fifthlings. Do you have anything to add on that subject?'

All eyes turned to the High King of the dwarves.

'No,' he admitted slowly, and was about to raise his tankard to his lips before he remembered that it was to have been his reward for his little speech. 'There have been no further sightings or findings.'

'About the granite gates at the fortress of the Stone Gateway,' Phenîlas chipped in from the side, wearing an ostentatious robe but also sporting a conspicuously fresh wound on his cheek. 'They won't have been closed quickly when this strange figure appeared.'

Ireheart had no idea what he meant by this. 'I was not there at the time.' He indicated the elf's face. 'What happened to you? You didn't have that when you rode up.'

'Not important.' The elf made clear he did not want to discuss it.

'When I was reading out the report from Queen Balyndis,' Mallenia said, getting in before Ireheart could carry on, 'something strange happened.' She laid her right hand on the child's fair hair. 'Sha'taï started to scream in terror when she heard the description of the mysterious warrior with the copper helmet.'

'We heard her,' said Astirma, sounding alarmed. 'We thought the worst had happened.'

Everyone looked at Mallenia's protegée with concern – everyone except Dirisa and Ireheart, that is. Ireheart made a to-do of sitting down, and pulled his tankard noisily over the table surface. *You'll have to address your issue later.* He drained the beer and signalled for a refill.

Sha'taï got to her feet and stood straight-backed, but shy. 'I know these beings,' she stammered. 'They are called ghaists and they are nothing to do with what you call phantoms or ghosts. They are the forerunners of mighty armies and serve the generals as scouts. They are invincible, my father said.' She sat down again and Rodario handed her a glass of water from which she hastily drank.

The rulers clapped and made encouraging comments on her contribution.

'Didn't tell us much,' muttered Ireheart, scratching his head. He really didn't like having his hair long at the sides. Didn't feel right.

Mallenia smiled. 'Of course my little one couldn't sleep at all after that,' she added, patting the girl on the shoulder. 'But her reaction gave me a hint where to look for more information.' She nodded at one of the guards by the door. He went out and returned with Carmondai.

Ireheart stole a sideways look at Phenîlas, who was looking anything but pleased. The elf would have loved to kill the historian-poet but as long as Carmondai was Mallenia's captive and on her own territory, there was nothing to be done. *I like to see you angry.* He took another mouthful of beer.

People soon stopped murmuring amongst themselves.

'Tell us what you recall of the ghaists,' Mallenia ordered Carmondai, a figure now lacking the älfar arrogance of yore. The branding had robbed him of any dignity; the fire had extinguished his rebelliousness.

Ireheart knew the scribe was extremely old and that the Triplets had banished him to a dungeon. *Was his work so badly written?* He emptied his mug with a grin and waved for a new one. *They must be using really small tankards today.*

Carmondai inclined his head to the assembled Council members, but kept his black eyes on the middle of the table. This älf did not present any danger to anyone, because he knew his life would end the moment Mallenia was no more.

Ireheart had faced älfar too often in the field to experience any sympathy for the historian. *He is a symbol of the downfall of our greatest enemies. They keep him like a pet dog that can be put down as soon as he fails to do what's needed.*

'It will have been about the time Sinthoras and Caphalor were relieved of their duties as commanders,' he began. His voice was pleasing but a little croaky. *His voice is suffering from old age, like he is,* thought Ireheart as he settled in to listen to the älf's account.

'It occurred a little while after the groundlings' Stone Gateway had fallen and the homeland empire of my race had been destroyed.

'The älfar had closed the fortress because by that time we knew the secret password, and we occupied the gates.

'Then it happened that a group of humans approached, pursuing a ghaist: a giant warrior with a polished copper helmet inscribed with runes, very little in the way of armour, and carrying a flagstaff on his back bearing a banner with writing on it.

'The humans failed in their attempt to destroy him or even to slow his progress.

'Instead it was they who died.

'Caphalor was the commanding officer at the time in charge of the watch crews and he opened fire on what they thought was a human soldier.

'No matter what they fired at him, they could not harm or hurt him in any way. It is just as the groundlings have reported. Not until they dropped live coals on him, followed by a vast quantity of burning pitch and petroleum, was there any effect.

He expired in an enormous explosion that the fortress and the surrounding mountains only just withstood.'

Carmondai asked for something to drink before continuing.

'When they heard the description and deciphered what had been seen on the helmet, our experts then recalled what had been previously known about ghaists: that they are beings that consist of a powerful spell and many imprisoned souls. They can only be destroyed if the copper loses its shape in intense heat and the runes dissolve.

'Apart from that, they are absolutely invincible. None of the conventional weapons we deployed had the slightest effect.

'And so my advice would be this: you must have to hand sufficient quantities of blazing combustible material. Only then could you see off a ghaist attack successfully.'

While Carmondai was speaking, Ireheart had been taking surreptitious sips at his beer. The thirst he was plagued with was nigh on unquenchable. He was as quiet as possible, not wanting to interrupt the narration. *So this being has visited Girdlegard in the past.*

When the älf fell silent, Ireheart rose to his feet. 'All the time the Fifthlings have been in charge of the Gate I have never heard of such a foe. We have never found any reports or drawings mentioning anything similar,' he told Carmondai. 'Were the älfar fighting them while the Perished Land held sway?' The historian shook his shaved head.

'This is the only encounter I know about.'

'Can you recall what runes were displayed on the ghaist's banner?'

The älf went up to the table, poured some wine onto the top as if it were the most natural thing in the world and, without a second's hesitation, started to reproduce the runes by painting with his finger. 'This is how Caphalor described the writing to me.'

'Stand aside and let the girl see.' Ireheart pointed at Sha'taï. 'You. Can you read that?' He made no effort to be especially nice to her. *Why bother?*

The child started to shake violently as soon as she had sight of the runes.

'Nhatai,' she said, terrified, dropping her glass of water. She hugged her knees as if trying to escape from the writing.

People in the room chattered with amazement.

'The ghaist the elves killed had the same runes on his banner. It looks as if we are being revisited by an old adversary.' Ireheart glared at the älf.

'Come on, what are you going to tell us about nhatai?'

Carmondai straightened his shoulders. 'I would be guessing.'

'Not a good idea.' Ireheart grinned.

'There are various legends about the adventures Sinthoras and Caphalor had together. One of their missions had them going to the Outer Lands, as you call it. And there, apparently, they met with sorcerers able to create just such a creature in a complicated ritual.' He seemed secretly amused by the High King's attitude. 'These sorcerers created enormous armies. Their soldiers would obey any order, no matter how crass, ridiculous or downright dangerous. One of these families was known as' – he pointed to the writing he had done in wine – 'Nhatai.'

Astirma summed up for the council: 'And so one of their spies has found a way into Girdlegard again.'

'We can't discount the possibility that there's more in store for us than just a visit from the odd scout.' Mallenia shot

Ireheart a concerned glance. 'High King, you know what advice to send to Balyndis about how to handle this threat.'

In response, Ireheart raised his tankard to her. 'And we've got more than enough ammunition to eliminate the magicians' armies. If they are committed to losing their fighting forces, we'll be happy to help them out.' He saw how relieved everyone was. Until a few minutes ago it seemed they were facing the prospect of an unstoppable enemy, but this new knowledge meant that they would be in a position to destroy him. 'We, the Children of the Smith, will ensure the safety of all Girdlegard's peace-loving inhabitants, the duty that Vraccas laid at our door.'

'Is that right?' Phenîlas appeared to be implying something else.

His comment fell on fertile ground.

His breathing laboured, Natenian turned to stare. 'What do you mean, my good friend? Have the dwarves ever given us cause to doubt them? They threw themselves into battle for our sake, regardless of the cost to themselves, and have always kept the gates secure.'

'And they refuse my people entry.' Phenîlas stood up suddenly. 'I *have to* speak about it. For some time now the flow of elf immigration has been held up. When I sent out messengers to the mountains to find out what was happening, my delegates weren't allowed to pass. Even when they said they only wished to go to the other side of the gate, which is the right of each and every Girdlegard inhabitant. They were not permitted to pass.' He glared at Ireheart in challenge. 'Why don't you tell us what is happening in the mountains?'

I'm more than happy to take this up. Feeling the blood rush warm in his veins, Ireheart reached for his beer. 'Why don't you tell us what is happening in Tabaîn?' he countered, smooth as silk.

'You're asking the wrong person.'

'Perhaps I should summon your Naishïon for him to explain things to the Council of Kings?' The dwarf was relishing the elf's discomfiture. Phenîlas looked as if he wished the subject had never been broached. 'And while we're at it: what is a naishïon when it's at home?' Ireheart noticed how pale the elf had gone. It was as if he was shrinking into himself. *You realise that I know more than you thought.*

'Let's not confuse the two issues,' said Phenîlas, trying to bring the debate back as he awkwardly returned to his seat. 'This is about the refusal of the dwarves to admit elf-immigrants.'

'The two issues are closely connected in my view.' Ireheart reached into his pocket and fished out the bloodied ring he had taken from the dead warrior's hand. He held it high. 'This piece of jewellery used to belong to a Tabaîn warrior who helped save me from a night-biter's attack, even though he was half-dead himself. As far as we knew, night-biters had been exterminated in Girdlegard. He told me the creatures had come from Phondrasôn and had dug their way up through the earth into elf territory.' He placed the soiled ring in the middle of the table for all to see. *That's got everyone's attention.*

'That's . . . the seal of the royal house of Hoge. It must have been Tenkil's,' Dirisa exclaimed. 'He went to Lesinteïl along with Raikan, didn't he?' She picked up the ring.

Natenian's breath was coming in tortured gasps; one of his carers started to mix medicine to administer.

'I thought the beast had devoured him?' Dirisa looked at Phenîlas accusingly. 'Were you lying?'

Cries of indignation and disbelief sounded round the table.

Look at the pointy-ears now. He's really regretting ever

having opened his mouth. Ireheart got to his feet and looked from Natenian to Dirisa. He consciously suppressed the growing rage in his belly. The fact that he was winning the argument helped a great deal. 'More importantly: the dying warrior imparted to me the news that the elves had murdered the young king.' The hum of comment grew louder, but the dwarf's dark tones could be clearly heard above the tumult. 'The Naishïon is behind it all. He made a pact with Natenian. Natenian wanted to retain power.' When the noise got too loud, Ireheart slammed his fist down on the table for silence. 'And now, Phenîlas, you will understand why I gave the order that no elves were to be permitted to cross into Girdlegard until the circumstances surrounding Raikan's death had been investigated.'

The assembled nobles all stared at the blond-haired elf, who remained seated, his face ashen and expressionless.

The tension in the room was electric.

'Naishïon means *supreme ruler*.' Some of the audience reacted with a start when Carmondai made this pronouncement. 'It is a concept that goes back to the creation myth the elves tell of their gods.' He laughed quietly. 'I would never have thought I would live to see the day a Naishïon would be nominated. Even in the old days when the elves were at the height of their power, they never appointed a Naishïon. There must be a reason for this new development.'

Phenîlas shot up from his chair. 'You have no right to . . .'

'Let the black-eyes finish speaking,' thundered Ireheart. 'It's obvious from your reaction that he's telling the truth.'

Nonetheless, Carmondai waited until Mallenia told him to continue.

'The title of Naishïon may only be applied when the elf kingdoms are united into a great empire as envisaged by their goddess Sitalia in the scriptures.' He gave a faint smile. 'It seems someone couldn't wait. I would assume it's one of the new arrivals. Ilahín and his spouse Fiëa won't have been pleased about it. But that's the price cowards have to pay for hiding in the woods when there's trouble. The elves only joined forces with the humans against my race when . . .'

'That's quite enough,' Mallenia admonished.

Dirisa raised her arm and pointed accusingly at Phenîlas. 'And just now in my chamber you tried to get me to enter a pact with you. The elves want grain and they want to purchase land. The wound you all see on his cheek was my response.' She spat at Natenian. 'May the gods punish you more than they have done already! You had the elves murder your own brother. Back in Tabaîn you will be condemned to death for that.'

'It's a lie,' mumbled Natenian. He was dribbling and shaking now. 'It's not true.'

Although Ireheart kept his eyes on the elf, he still noticed Carmondai's malicious smile. The älf was enjoying this. *He was only telling the truth.* 'How do you answer these allegations, Phenîlas?'

The elf replied slowly. 'Please excuse me. I am not at liberty to disclose anything further. Only my . . . lord can pronounce on these matters. I shall report to him what has been said here in the Council of Kings. He will decide what must be done.'

'Once a Naishïon has been appointed,' Carmondai added coolly – and no one rebuked him for taking the stand once more – ' it is written that he must not rest until he has established the united elf empire.' The älf crossed his arms with the air of an official prosecutor. 'As far as I am aware, any means at all are considered legitimate in pursuit of this aim.

Do correct me, elf, should I have misremembered what is contained in the scriptures.'

Phenîlas said nothing, but his facial muscles were twitching. He was under tremendous strain.

Ireheart was beginning to doubt the wisdom of making his discovery so public. The important thing was to have all the kingdoms working together against the elves if the Naishïon was unable to dispel their concern. What was at stake – namely, the elves assuming supreme power in Girdlegard – was something nobody present could welcome.

We won't stand for that. Ireheart had to inform the dwarf kingdoms what had happened. In the north, in the Grey Mountains, Balyndis' throne would be in jeopardy. *They shan't overcome us.*

At that point the young Sha'taï, frightened, slipped off her stool and sought Mallenia's hand.

The blonde queen of Idoslane smiled reassuringly. 'Everything will be alright, my dear,' she said, standing to address the Council. 'It looks as if Girdlegard may be at a crossroads. It is time to demand answers, both from the elves and from Natenian. But before we reconvene, let us reach out to each other and pray in silence to our gods that they may help us find a way out of our difficulties.' She looked at each member of the Council resolutely. 'We must continue to stand united at this critical time, when an enemy may soon be at our gates. Let us ask Vraccas, Palandiell, Sitalia and Samusin to be our guides.'

Sha'taï reached for Natenian's hand, Rodario took Astirma's, and so on, round the table. The only one not included was the älf.

With great reluctance Ireheart forced himself to stand and hold his neighbours' hands.

His skin started to crawl and tingle, a most unpleasant sensation. *Am I the only one that can feel it? Has my hand gone to sleep?* When he looked at the others he noted an inexplicable peacefulness in their faces. All the previous fury, outrage and suspicion seemed to have vanished. All the rulers were standing together harmoniously, their eyes closed.

Ireheart was not prepared to consider the possibility of divine intervention. *Coïra might have an explanation for what's just occurred.*

But the maga remained unaccountably absent. Nobody else seemed concerned about that.

It'll be up to me and the dwarves to sort out this mess. Ireheart would have loved to grab himself a drink. There it was on the table, enticingly near. But he was stuck holding hands with the others. *It always falls to us to sort the mess out.*

Take cloves and cinnamon
and a pinch of pimento.
Add honey and spices
to taste,
according to your palate.

Boil up with water in a pot
until reduced to an essence.
Put a suitable amount in a tankard
and fill up with strong black beer.

Recipe for dwarf spiced beer (serve cold)

IX

Girdlegard
United Kingdom of Gauragar-Idoslane
Gauragar
6492nd solar cycle, late summer

It was a long time before Gosalyn, Hargorin and Beligata managed to make their way, under Tungdil's leadership, through the crevices and hollows of the collapsed cave system and then up through the narrow passages to the open air.

It was arduous. Dirt and sand combined with their sweat to form crusts on their skin and the dwarves all suffered discomfort: itching, grazes, blisters and rashes.

Deathbringer's leg injury was what held them back most, but the females also had various wounds that caused them to require frequent rest. They had little drinking water left and no food to speak of. All of these factors made the journey extremely difficult.

As they passed they noted more cracks in the walls, as Tungdil had already pointed out. Several times they heard worrying subterranean rumblings, when some tunnel further back gave way and collapsed. They were slowly but surely leaving evil behind them.

Vraccas took pity: when they finally emerged, at night, exhausted and emaciated, it was in a different place from where they had entered. There were no vicious thorn bushes awaiting them and no beasts ready to attack.

They crawled out through the root system of a giant tree and found themselves in a blue-apple grove. They sheltered from the light rain under the trees. They were too tired to even wash off the dirt in the drizzle.

Except for Tungdil. He seemed in better shape than the others. He lit a fire, gathered their drinking flasks and went off to collect the rainwater dripping from the foliage. He then brought the flasks back to the dwarves.

Gosalyn watched him, too tired to do anything but wonder: *Is it really him?* She thought of Belogar and suppressed her tears. *His death was so cruel and such a waste.*

By now the hero of Girdlegard was dressed only in a tattered linen tunic that exuded a pungent smell of sweat and various layers of dirt.

He stepped out into the rain once more to gaze at the night sky, entranced, even though no stars were visible. He did not mind getting wet. On the contrary, he was glad to catch enough water in his hands to wash his disfigured face.

Beligata undid Hargorin's bandage and drew in her breath. 'It's infected.'

'Who knows what that wretched black-eyes dosed his sword with,' growled the red-haired dwarf, squinting down at the wound. 'It looks really bad. There's a black line leading up from the injury.'

'We need to get help quickly.' Gosalyn washed her face with water from her flask. She had lost weight with all the tribulations of the journey, as they all had. 'I'm going to climb up and see where we are.' The others tried to talk her out of it but she was already halfway up the tree, despite the excruciating pain in her muscles. The branches and trunk were wet and slippery but she still managed to gain the top.

The sky was cloudy. There was nothing to be seen except for dark woodland. No sign of lights or even a clearing.

Without stars it was impossible for Gosalyn to get her bearings. They would have to wait till first light to decide which direction to take. But she did enjoy the feel of the rain on her skin, soaking the encrusted filth away.

Climbing down she picked a few blue-apples to share with the others. The sharp, fresh taste would do them all good.

She reached the ground just as Tungdil was distributing the water flasks he had refilled. The group perked up somewhat when she showed them the fruit she had gathered.

'I'll take first watch,' Tungdil announced, going to sit next to Hargorin. He no longer stank so badly, but his clothes were in urgent need of soap and a washboard. 'You understand we'll have to take your leg off if we can't get you to a healer?'

The veteran warrior nodded. 'If it comes to that I'll have a new leg made. Silver, I think. I might have to change my name, but I'd be able to kick a few skulls in successfully. Or at least take a door down,' he replied with black humour. The others laughed.

'Why do you want to keep watch?' Beligata asked as she checked out her battered armour. 'We should be safe from the elves and the beasts won't have been able to follow us out here. The only way out of the passage was through that cave.'

Tungdil smiled. Somehow that made his disfigured face look even worse. 'Maybe it's best if I just keep one eye open when everyone else has theirs shut.' He tapped the trunk. 'You never know: a tree might fall on us.' He brushed his wet hair back with his hands and squeezed the rain out of his beard.

He's so glad to be alive now he's out of Phondrasôn. Gosalyn was tired after climbing the tree. She could feel all her bones aching and her eyelids were heavy. But she still had so many questions she wanted to ask Tungdil. He, on the other hand, did not seem at all curious to know what had occurred during his long absence of two hundred and fifty cycles, wandering in the labyrinths of the underworld. He did not ask about the present state of affairs in Girdlegard.

'Why didn't you bring Bloodthirster with you?' she murmured sleepily.

Tungdil was feeding the fire with twigs he had gathered from round the base of the tree. The fire crackled away merrily. Beligata and Hargorin were already asleep.

'Because the weapon has no place in Girdlegard,' he replied with a smile. 'It carries the evil of an Inextinguishable älf. I deemed it a triumph when I forged his sword anew and made it my own. But evil was still embodied in the metal. The same was true of the tionium armour I wore. It had a hold over me.' His voice grew quieter. 'I am excluding everything that's bad.'

'What was the issue with the armour?'

'It served me well and protected me. But when it was made it was decorated with älfar runes and imbued with harmful magic I no longer wish to make any use of.' Tungdil pulled off his soiled tunic and threw it outside the shelter of the branches. He sat only in his loin cloth. 'I still stink as if I'd been swimming in the sewers.'

Gosalyn made a face. 'We're none of us too fragrant.' If her eyes did not deceive her, Tungdil's body was covered in scars: long ones from sword cuts, smaller ones from stab wounds or arrows. Some of the welts seemed be of an ornamental nature.

Tungdil picked up a blue-apple, closing his eye as he took a bite. His face relaxed and he chewed with great attention.

'Can't get these in the demon land I've just escaped from, you know,' he whispered. 'Delicious. It tastes amazing. One could almost want to die, knowing there'll never be anything better.'

'There are many better things still to come,' she assured him. 'What about the beer only the dwarves know how to brew?'

He laughed warmly. 'Oh, yes, that was one of the memories that helped to keep me alive.' He opened his eye. 'I'm so looking forward to drinking a toast with my old friend Ireheart. To his new high office.' He took another bite. 'The other Tungdil is dead, I understand?'

She nodded. 'He was killed with Keenfire.'

'Who struck the blow?'

'Kiras. A descendant of . . .' Gosalyn was finding it hard to keep her thoughts clear.

'Of Sirka,' he said, sadness in his voice. 'I have been away far too long. It was never my intention. My soul is tired and wants to find a place it can recuperate. Forgive my seemingly harsh attitude when we first met.' He saw she was fighting a yawn. 'Go to sleep. We must make swift progress tomorrow. We need to find a healer or Hargorin will be getting that silver leg he joked about.'

He raked the fire and watched the small branches crumple into the flames. The heat and the sound of the rain were sleep-inducing.

Tungdil placed some larger logs on the fire. 'I'll keep watch, Gosalyn. I'll watch over you and your friends. And soon, I hope, I'll be keeping our homeland safe again.'

'Will you do that?' she asked, hardly able to keep her eyes open. The fire crackled and sparks shot up towards the branches that were swaying gently in the rising heat.

'As soon as my soul has rested and recovered. I shall.'

Gosalyn slumped back against the apple tree trunk and fell into a deep slumber.

She was woken by a half-stifled scream. She bolted up, grabbing her short axe.

The sun was up but there was some early morning mist. Birds were singing and flying about. The fire was more or less out apart from glowing embers.

'What happened?'

Her eyes still gummy from sleep, she saw Tungdil pressing the blade of Beligata's axe to Hargorin's leg stump. Smoke rose and there was a smell of burning flesh. The dwarf-girl with the ever-more-noticeable greenish facial scar was holding Hargorin down. There was a loud hiss.

They couldn't wait any longer. Gosalyn got to her feet. 'Maybe I could have helped,' she said, grasping the strong warrior's other arm to assist Beligata.

Hargorin groaned. It started with a low rolling moan and then his breath came in tortured pants. A tourniquet had been applied below the knee and the amputation wound was cauterised by the hot steel.

Tungdil's tunic had been cleansed overnight by the rain. He wiped the sweat from his brow. 'We had to act quickly; the infection had spread. We were about to wake you to be our back-up in case of an attack.' He nodded at Hargorin. 'We've taken off the septic part and we've cleaned the wound. But we'll need to get you to a healer who can put a herbal bandage on to speed up the process.'

Hargorin shut his eyes and took deep breaths, in and out. 'Thank you,' he said, clearly enough though his red beard was wobbling. 'I could use some good brandy right now. Put the leg in the fire to burn. It was trying to kill me.' He slumped back and fell quiet.

'Vraccas has taken pity on him. He has lost consciousness.' Beligata came over to put more wood on the fire, which had been near to going out. 'We'll turn the limb to ashes.'

'He should do that himself when he wakes up. It's his leg, after all; he should be the one to cremate it.' Tungdil stood up. 'I'll start making a stretcher.' He gestured to the northeast. 'The Fifthling kingdom must lie in that direction. With Vraccas' help we'll find a healer soon.' He wiped his bloodstained hands on the grass. 'Beligata, stay with him. Gosalyn, you come with me. You've had more sleep.'

She nodded and followed him, finding branches that would be long enough while Tungdil cut sturdy ones to use for the frame. They gathered moss for a cushioning layer and tied the construction with saplings and reeds that were growing by a small pond.

They worked fast; now was not the time for chatting.

Gosalyn still had burning questions but held back. This dwarf might still prove an imposter, another version of Girdlegard's hero.

Cautious suspicion struggled with natural curiosity. She thought she had noticed a tear falling when the name Sirka had cropped up. That spoke in his favour. She made a private decision not to volunteer too much information herself. *Best avoid giving details, at least.*

They returned to their camp with the rough timber frame for a stretcher.

'What did you mean by having to let your soul recover?' it occurred to her to ask. It had been the last thing he'd said to her the previous night by the fire.

'I didn't suppose you'd forget I said that. I expect you saw all the scars I've collected?'

Indeed she had. 'There were . . . a lot of them.' *And they were unusual.*

'While I was in Phondrasôn it was a case of constant warfare. There was no relief. I was either defending myself or attacking others to forestall an assault. Down there, there's nothing good or beautiful.'

It didn't seem to Gosalyn as though an experience like that would be sorted by a few orbits' sleep and relaxation. 'How do you envisage this recovery happening?'

Tungdil gave a friendly laugh. 'By not having all of my senses in a constant state of alert. My soul needs space and quiet, so that I'm not always on edge, watching out for danger, wherever I am. I don't want to have to mistrust those around me simply to stay alive. That's what I want.'

'Couple of beers might help,' Gosalyn grinned.

He unleashed a peal of laughter. Gosalyn was convinced it was sincere.

They had reached the tree where Hargorin and Beligata were waiting.

There was a smell of burned flesh. Bones were charring among the branches that fed the fire. They were Deathbringer's foot and lower leg. The red-haired dwarf was watching them smoulder. His gaze was blank but tears were running down his cheeks. He made not a sound. Gosalyn and Tungdil sat down at his side without speaking. They waited until the flames had finished their work and the blackened remains were no longer recognisable for what they were.

They laid Hargorin gently on the stretcher and set off at a smart pace, with Tungdil and Beligata carrying the invalid out through the grove.

Gosalyn led the way, looking out for obstacles. From time to time she thought of Belogar and what he might have said. *You won't be forgotten. Your tribe is as proud of you as I am.* She forced herself not to give way to tears and concentrated on observing their surroundings carefully.

The important thing was to get Hargorin and Tungdil safely to the court of the High King.

Girdlegard
United Kingdom of Gauragar-Idoslane
Gauragar, Oakenburgh
6492nd solar cycle, early autumn

Carmondai was in his tower room at the fortress-like town hall. He always retreated up here when his services were not required elsewhere by the queen, who often wanted certain pages of his writings clarified or expanded. He felt relatively safe this high, overlooking Oakenburgh; here he was unlikely to be confronted by men and women desperate for revenge and ready to tear any älf limb from limb. Being a prisoner had saved him from that fate.

Mallenia found him useful enough to keep him alive. Following the surprisingly peaceful and amicable closing ceremony of the Council session, she and Sha'taï had gone down into the town and would soon be making their way south back to Idoslane.

After the northern älfar empire had fallen, Carmondai's library in Dsôn Bhará, the prison the Triplets had consigned him to, proved to contain valuable revelations for the peoples of Girdlegard. As the author of the numerous historical records, almanacs, tales and many other kinds of writing, it fell to him to fill in the gaps in people's knowledge and to continue with his record-keeping. But this time he was compelled to write from the standpoint of the victors: Girdlegard's present residents.

Mallenia had had him branded. The runes on his skin and the shaved head added to his humiliation. But she had saved him from entering endingness. These obviously punitive measures assuaged the populace's revengeful desire for his death. This was why the älf preferred to stay in his tower, even if the royal seal protected him from outright attack. *It wouldn't save me from a stone thrown from the back of the crowd.*

The encounter with Phenîlas could have turned out quite differently. The shove intended to send him flying headfirst down the stone steps? Carmondai had avoided that successfully, but he would have to be watchful.

The elf hoped I'd break my neck, or would have made sure I did. Carmondai was well aware that the elves wanted him dead.

Because he knew their secrets.

Because he knew the elves. The mere fact that he knew what a naishïon was made them uneasy. When he had announced in public that the elves were working towards a great empire and were determined to join forces with each other, it had worried both dwarves and humans. And Carmondai wanted to fan those flames.

Not from any fundamental malevolence, in the way his race was normally characterised: he wanted to warn Girdlegard.

I still have much to write. I intend to warn the humans about the pointy-ears. Carmondai took some tea and went over to the window. *Just because they dress in light-coloured robes doesn't mean their hearts are pure.*

The forest stretched out below, surrounding the town.

Timber was the foundation of its prosperity. Oak, first and foremost, but also mighty pine trees and other evergreens. From the far side of the Hulmen river, logs were floated downstream to be processed in the sawmills of Oakenburgh, or to be sold wholesale to dealers.

Wraiths of mist swirled round the tops of the tallest trees; everything was still in full foliage but the leaves were turning to their autumn colours. Soon they would die and fall; this was Nature's way. Cycle for cycle.

What a glorious spectacle of decay. The älf put on a dark grey mantle, opened the window and breathed in the cool autumnal air with its faint fragrance of woodland floor, moss and resin. In the skies he could see the raptors circling. Their cries indicated they were buzzards. Heavy clouds piled up at the horizon, threatening rain.

The tower did not merely offer safety but also commanded a wonderful view. It caught his imagination and inspired him to paint. Carmondai drank in these sensations. *I must draw this.*

He fancied using rich red tones. To his eyes, Nature was at her most beautiful when near death like this.

Selecting a large piece of paper and a board to rest it on, he went over to the broad window seat and made sketches of what he saw. He used compressed charcoal and made careful note of the various reds he would later apply. Most of them he would have to mix himself from the necessary basic pigments. Humans had no sophisticated appreciation for the subtleties of colour.

In earlier times he had enjoyed painting with the blood of other creatures, treated with various substances to keep it free-flowing until it was applied. But as a prisoner he could not take the risk of asking for pig's blood, let alone blood from a human. Oakenburgh's woodcutters were not known for their artistic bent. They would not have understood such a request.

They would make me use my own blood for my painting and happily slit my gizzard to get it. Carmondai's gaze travelled from the forest in the distance to the lines on the paper.

'What do you want?' he said, not looking round. He heard the sharp intake of breath. 'If you think you can creep up on an älf unnoticed, you've another think coming. Practise more.' Turning, his branded features confronted the secret visitor.

Sha'taï's presence had been swiftly detected. She froze motionless, less than two arm-lengths' away.

'I wanted to see how you were,' she said, pulling at the sleeves of her bright green dress with its black embroidery. She wore her hair in two fair plaits.

He stopped trying to draw and gave a faint smile. 'To see how I am?' he repeated. 'Don't worry. Your benefactor's guard looks after my needs, thank you.'

'I thought the elves might send an assassin to kill you,' she replied. 'Phenîlas calmed down in the end but they know you have access to their secrets.'

Carmondai showed her his sketch. 'It's the forest,' he explained. 'And the notations are the abbreviations for the red tones I want to use.'

She approached, her curiosity aroused. 'I've heard you like to paint with blood. Is that true?'

The älf's smile widened. 'Yes. In the old days. Nowadays it would have to be human blood and if I tried that, I'd lose my own life, whatever the runes on my forehead say. Even Samusin wouldn't be able to hold back the throng baying for my blood.'

The girl, who he judged to be about twelve, studied the picture then stood on tiptoe at the window to compare it with the view. 'It looks very realistic, even if I can't imagine what it'll look like in red when it's finished.'

'I can show you when I've completed it.' Carmondai was surprised no guard had yet put his head round the door to check on her. *She must have slipped away without asking permission.*

Sha'taï was delighted and took hold of his hand. 'That's so nice of you. And could you teach me to draw?' Her eyes were big and innocent in her small face, a little like a puppy or a kitten.

'You should speak to your aunt,' he said. 'She won't like the idea, and simple folk may suspect we are cooking up a plot together.'

'A plot?' Sha'taï looked bemused.

'Well, you speak fluent älfar and you are from the Outer Lands and, well, I am an älf. There could be all sorts of rumours.' Carmondai looked down at his hand, which was starting to tingle; pain shot up his arm as if he had been drawing too long. 'You can let go now.'

Her sweet expression disappeared when she released his hand. 'Just as I thought.'

'The humans see what they want to see and what suits their world picture.'

'That's not what I mean.' Sha'taï leaped forward, arms outstretched, and gave him a shove. Taken completely by surprise, he lost his balance and slipped. His hand clutched at empty air and he fell out through the open window, saving himself at the last moment by grabbing the frame with one hand. He was not prepared to drop his drawing board. The sketch had been too good to waste.

Before he could heave himself back into the room Sha'taï was standing over him, her eyes cold.

'I have no use for anyone who does not obey me,' she pronounced indifferently. Lifting her foot she stamped on his fingers. 'I don't want you spoiling things for me.'

Carmondai tried to understand her motives. It couldn't have anything to do with the drawing, which must have been an excuse to get near him without arousing suspicion. He looked down and saw there was no foothold that would help him. *I've got to get back inside, no matter how.*

He slung his sketchpad and drawing board at Sha'taï with all his strength. She ducked.

The paper landed safely in the room and Carmondai grabbed hold of the frame with his newly-freed hand. He yanked himself back in through the window, slamming into the child. She kicked him in the head and they both tumbled from the window seat to the carpet.

She touched me! he realised with a shock. *Of course! Samusin! I have been so blind. Those shooting pains – that was magic.* That explained the remarkably peaceable atmosphere at the close of proceedings in the Council session. *She has the power to influence people.*

Carmondai got to his feet.

'You're one of them,' he exclaimed. 'You're a botoican! And you've got them all under your spell.' He approached her. 'That's something they should all hear about.'

Sha'taï moved back away from him. One of her braids had come unplaited. 'Nobody will believe what an älf says. And anyway, it's not true.'

'Oh yes, it is.'

'You're making it all up.' Sha'taï saw the knife lying next to the fruit bowl on the table and snatched it up. 'Your whole race is a hateful nuisance. They killed my family.'

'How do you mean?'

'One of your warriors – he had armour plates sewn into his skin – came and waged war on the town where my ancestors had always lived. He didn't have many soldiers but they were unstoppable under the älf's command.' Tears rolled down the young girl's cheeks. 'I had to run away with my uncle. There was snow everywhere, blinding me. And then he died. He died although he thought he had got us to safety.' She raised the knife and her voice lost any childish tinge. 'I hate the älfar. Every single one of them. None of them must be allowed to live. And that means you.'

It must have been Aiphatòn. Carmondai made a placatory gesture. 'That was nothing to do with me.'

'The others may not have noticed but I saw how you tried to turn the Council against the elves. You stood by that crazy dwarf who can only see malice and deceitfulness in those glorious creatures.'

'They seem to have interfered in the internal affairs of Tabaîn. That could be seen as deceitfulness,' Carmondai countered, hardly questioning why Sha'taï suddenly sounded so grown up. *She has been playing a double hand ever since she was found in the abandoned settlement and taken to Mallenia.* She was far from any childlike innocence. Carmondai was intent on knowing more about her background.

But it was more important still to work out her intentions. If she managed to get the rulers to obey her – what would she do with them? Where would the girl lead them?

'You have to disappear, älf.' Sha'taï took a step nearer.

This made Carmondai laugh. 'You know I was a trained warrior. I may be many times your age but I am agile enough not to let you stab me in the belly with that silly little knife.'

'Of course I know that. And I know Mallenia thinks a great deal of you. So much so that neither elves nor humans can demand your death.' She lifted the sketch board with the picture of the forest. 'You won't want to believe it, but Samusin is on my side.'

'No, he's not. If he were, I should be lying smashed to pieces at the foot of the tower.'

'Can still happen.' Sha'taï took the picture in her hand. 'You noted the tones of red you wanted and you've written them, as you are used to, in the old älfar way.' A malicious, calculating smile played round her lips and her eyes narrowed. 'That's very convenient.'

She uttered a long, shrill scream that must have been audible at a considerable distance through the open window.

No! Carmondai leaped forward and tried to grab the knife.

She expected this and avoided his grasp. She made a slit in the artery on her wrist and made a small cut at her throat. It was not deep but bled profusely. She threw herself at him.

The door flew open. The history-teller's armed guards stormed in, weapons drawn.

Carmondai knew exactly the picture that was presenting itself to their eyes: an älf, an injured child, and a sketch done in his own hand bearing the names of various reds – one of them called 'Blood of Young Barbarian.'

'Get away from her,' the captain roared.

'He wanted my blood,' Sha'taï whimpered, pretending to pull herself away from him, subtly dropping the knife as she did so to make it look as if he had been the one wielding it. 'He wanted my blood for his picture!' She stumbled and fell, sliding away from him, fear in her wide, childish eyes. 'I fought back and . . .' Her words were lost in loud sobbing.

'How dare you?' yelled one of the guards, rushing forwards,

brandishing his sword. 'Paint with your own wretched blood, you black-eyed bastard.'

It was clear. Sha'taï had achieved exactly what she had wanted.

There was no point in Carmondai's trying to deny anything. *Nobody's going to believe me.*

Carmondai was confronted by the four strong guards that were usually posted outside his room for protection in case the Oakenburghers or the elves decided to do away with him. Now they were ready to be his executioners.

And I thought I would spend my days safely in the tower. Carmondai dodged a sword thrust and a stabbing dagger, kicked the second guard in the groin, and punched the third in the face, hurling the soldier at his captain so that both fell to the floor.

The älf jumped over them and made for the door.

'Help!' Sha'taï shouted out of the window. 'By all the gods! We're being attacked by the älf! He's trying to kill us all!'

How gladly I would wring her neck. Carmondai saw the soldiers struggling to their feet to set after him.

If he didn't get down the stairs and out through the town swiftly enough, he would end his long life on an improvised gallows. An attack against the child and then violence against the queen's soldiers? His powers of producing darkness and instilling fear would not protect him from a furious mob.

'Stay here and face your punishment!' The captain was at his heels.

Carmondai turned and delivered a sharp uppercut to the captain's chin, lifting the man off his feet before he crumpled to the ground. Carmondai rushed down the spiral staircase.

He could hear the shouts of his pursuers and, each time he

passed a window, Sha'taï's accusations as she begged and cried out to the townspeople for help.

Inàste, if I survive this, I'll sacrifice whatever you desire. Carmondai did not waste time looking round to see what was happening but ran as fast as he could away from the council building, taking a left turn down an alley.

People were pointing and starting to run after him. The queen's brand on his face would not protect him now.

And if you'd like that scheming child as a sacrificial offering, I'll be happy to oblige! Carmondai was now panting with effort, dodging down alleyways and side streets wherever he could. Having studied the layout of Oakenburgh from his overhead vantage point for some time now, he knew exactly which direction offered the best chance of escape.

Inquisitive eyes followed his progress and busy mouths passed the news along, keeping the hunt on his trail. The curious, and those too cowardly to join the pursuit, popped their heads out of their windows to watch from above, throwing objects and excrement down at his head.

He reached the river and dived in, his heart beating wildly.

The water of the Hulmen was cold; the shock of it took his breath. The current carried him off and he was able to use some of the free-floating logs for cover. He feared it would not be long before he was shot at. Several people appeared on the bank, among them soldiers with crossbows. He ducked his head down between the timbers floating downstream. He picked up a few splinters when the bolts were loosed, but nothing significant.

Carmondai knew Mallenia would not be able to protect him any longer, even if she wanted to. *There will be so many different versions by now of what actually occurred. And I'm sure there are such awful stories about my alleged cruelty that as a story-teller myself, I'd have to bow in admiration.*

He drank some of the river water as he pondered what to do. All that running had made him thirsty.

Even if the blonde queen of Idoslane issued the command, she could not realistically expect the älf to be delivered to her alive.

Sha'taï is clever and has no scruples. Carmondai was carried along by the current and left Oakenburgh behind. He planned to leave the river as soon as possible given that the town had plenty of small boats in which to pursue him. He would make his way on foot. He would have to abandon his treasures: all his work had been stored in the tower. All his records about the past and the present.

I'll get them back somehow. It would be unforgivable to leave them in barbarian hands. Carmondai registered the smell of damp bark and timber resin.

His heart rate had settled. The flight had awoken the old fire inside him. For a whole cycle he had been a humiliated figure – the broken älf, the captive, a predator whose teeth had been forcibly removed. Tamed. Subordinate. The animal had shaken off its chains, albeit not of its own volition. Now he had to rely on his own instincts to stay alive. He had his natural powers and the skills life had taught him.

Presumably neither Mallenia nor Sha'taï had any idea that there was more to him than being a mere story-teller, record-keeper and artist, able to entertain his audience. The barbarians knew that Carmondai had assisted in the construction, planning and design of Dsôn Bhará, from whence the Inextinguishables had once ruled the whole of Girdlegard.

But nobody knew he was an experienced warrior and tactician and that he used to be one of the few lance-bearers who was privileged to ride a night-mare. And it was unlikely anyone would ever learn about this side of him.

I'm taking up the gauntlet, Sha'taï.

He had to think of somewhere to go that no one would expect.

Think it through, make a plan and execute it.

He could only think of one place that would do. But the words *insane* and *deadly dangerous* came to mind.

He heard dogs barking in the distance. They had been set on his trail.

They're going to a lot of trouble. The älf left his cover where the bank was less steep, keen to reach land before the river took him past the sawmills.

Their efforts will get them nowhere.

Avalanches are the winter tears of the mountains.

Dwarf saying

X

Girdlegard
United Kingdom of Gauragar-Idoslane
6492nd solar cycle, early autumn

Ireheart made quickly for the courier station from whence he had sent out the search party to find his friend. The drumming of his mount's hooves merged with the sounds of the other animals.

This time the High King was accompanied by thirty soldiers, male and female. It was possible that powers were at work in Girdlegard that would not welcome the return of the homeland's greatest hero and he was taking no chances. After the mysterious way the proceedings at the Council of Kings had ended, he was prepared for more surprises. Only this time he preferred to rely on the weapons and shields of his dwarves.

Ireheart had been astonished to get the message about the search party's return. He had only just arrived in the Blue Mountains when the news reached him. He barely had time to let to his wife, Goda, bring him up to date with a report on defence improvements before saddling a fresh pony and heading north once more. As the rapid tunnel connections were not in operation, there was nothing for it but to ride, no matter how little he liked the idea.

He passed the oak where he had buried Tenkil and he said a brief prayer to Vraccas for the brave warrior's sake. *If it hadn't been for him, we'd never have heard about the Scholar.* His destination appeared on the horizon and he could see only two horses in the paddock. There must be a great deal of news making the rounds if all the despatch riders were out. This worried him, although he had no specific reason for his concern.

The group of riders headed for the courier station, signalling their approach with a rolling cloud of dust from their cavalcade, together with the sounds of clinking weapons and armour. The station captain appeared at the threshold to check out the unexpected visitors. He held his sword drawn until he recognised the High King.

'Well, well,' he called out above the noise of their arrival. The group came to a halt and their cloud of dust swept over the man. 'Here you are again. I don't know if our cellar can cope with the likes of you for long.'

Ireheart laughed and dismounted. 'We shan't be staying long. You ice-cold brew is safe.' He gestured for ten of his soldiers to dismount and follow him. The others kept watch. He went up to the captain. 'It is time to introduce myself properly: my name is Boïndil Doubleblade from the Secondling tribe clan of the Axe Swingers, High King of the dwarf tribes.'

'I knew who you were. I could tell from your stature, your weapon, the emblems and insignia. You are well known throughout Girdlegard. I'd have to have been blind not to see it was you.' The captain inclined his head respectfully. 'Your friends await you within. We have looked after them well.'

Ireheart could not contain his excitement. *I wonder what he looks like. Will he look different from that other Tungdil?* His thoughts were tumbling over each other as he approached the door to the inn, mouth dry, blood pounding in his ears.

Beligata, Gosalyn and Hargorin were seated round one of the tables, still looking the worse for wear after their exhausting ordeal. The red-haired dwarf was missing a lower leg; the stump was padded, ready for a wooden limb. His crutches were propped against the edge of the table. They were all wearing their chainmail as if about to plunge into a new adventure.

The three stood when the High King entered the room, Beligata assisting Deathbringer to his feet. 'No. Don't get up,' he said, going over to them. 'And Belogar's body?' he asked, as he shook each of them by the hand, all the while glancing round.

'We had to . . . there wasn't much . . .' Gosalyn started to explain and then stopped. She put the ring on the table. 'This is what we are bringing home for his clan.' Her voice broke.

Ireheart laid a comforting hand on her shoulder and she gave a brave smile. 'He will always be remembered and celebrated for his deeds.' Looking at Hargorin's leg, he promised, 'You shall have the best artificial limb that can be produced.'

'Someone's already at work on that.' Deathbringer pointed behind him. 'He's out in the smithy. I don't think he'll have seen you arrive.'

'Is he alone?'

'Yes.'

'And the zhadár? Is he still roaming the land hunting down black-eyes?'

'Tungdil killed him and left his body back in the tunnels,' Beligata answered. 'Together with one of the black-eyes disguised as an elf.' She stepped forward to hand him the phial on which the älfar runes read *Elf eyes*. 'The elves were out to get us, High King. They may have disguised themselves as älfar but we saw through their trickery.'

An älf pretending to be an elf, and elves pretending to be älfar? What the blazes is happening out there in the forest? 'We'll talk more very soon.' Ireheart straightened up. 'You will all be receiving generous rewards for your courage. You shall never have to worry about earning your bread.'

He went past them and over to the side door that led to the stables and the smithy. He told his guards to remain in the main room. He did not want witnesses when he met his friend. *This time it must be him. Vraccas, let it be him. No more disappointments.*

He could hear the bellows working and the coals hissing as they were made red hot. Ireheart opened the intervening door and felt a blast of heat from the forge. Then there came a rhythmic clanging as hammer blows fell repeatedly on iron. Sparks flew up.

There he is!

A sturdy dwarf in a dark red, knee-length tunic stood with his back turned, a leather apron knotted firmly. He had rolled his sleeves all the way up to his muscular shoulders.

Numerous old cuts and incisions showed as scars in the red glow from the fire, and there were dwarf runes tattooed on his skin. The long brown hair was tied back in a braid.

Or perhaps it isn't him after all? Ireheart stole round to see the profile while the other dwarf worked away at the anvil.

No question: the face was that of his Scholar. But a good deal of it was badly burned and the scar that ran in a straight line from his right temple to under his tunic must have received bad treatment. The left eye was hidden by a white leather patch.

The hammer at the anvil was getting faster, dancing around on a hinge he was fixing bolts to and welding to the fitting. He was working on a metal leg.

'Scholar,' Ireheart murmured, not really intending to speak so low.

The raised hammer paused in mid-air.

Tungdil turned his head slowly and he lowered his arm. 'Isn't it odd?' he said, his voice thick with emotion as he laid the hammer down. 'I've been longing for this moment for two hundred and fifty cycles, but now it's arrived, I'm afraid.'

'Afraid? How?' Ireheart's throat was constricted and his mouth dry. So dry he would even have downed the beer they served ice-cold from their cellars here.

'Because you might not believe me when I say I am the real Tungdil Goldhand. I understand another one turned up from Phondrasôn and did heroic deeds.' He took off his leather apron. 'I have nothing in the way of proof. Only my memories of every orbit I was lucky enough to spend in Girdlegard. Every detail. Every word you and I spoke to each other. Balyndis. Sirka. I remember everything.' He displayed his scarred and calloused hands. 'Test me. Put any question you like. Keep interrogating me until you are positive it's really Tungdil Goldhand you've got standing before you. Then send me to Balyndis and any of the dwarves who'll still remember me. Get them to test me, too.' A long exhalation. He rubbed the sweat from his brow with the back of his hand. 'But let's do it over some good black beer.'

He is quite different from the Scholar who emerged from the abyss a cycle ago. Ireheart's mouth was already opening with the first question.

'But for pity's sake, not the wretched orc-meets-dwarf joke. And if you try to tease me with mention of dwarf girls and smelly cheese, I shall consider it an insult.'

Ireheart burst out laughing. 'So it really hurt your feelings, that time?'

'It was intolerably inappropriate, given that I was the heir apparent to the High King.' He grinned. 'And now *you* rule over all the dwarf tribes. How times change. Did they make you do ordeals? Did you have to copy a page of writing? Or lead an expedition?'

'They voted. Simple as that.' Ireheart smiled at Tungdil. 'Forgive me for not seizing you in my embrace and rejoicing as the moment demands. But the last time I met a Tungdil I was . . .' He had to swallow. 'I thought he was the real one. I believed it so strongly, with my heart and with my head. You . . . he performed heroic deeds, he saved us, as the Scholar . . . as you would have done, and then he was killed, and . . .' Ireheart took a lungful of the smoky air and fell silent, to compose himself. 'It was not easy for me or the dwarves or indeed Girdlegard as a whole. And after your . . . after the first Tungdil's death, I was convinced I had lost you for ever. It was only gradually that certain doubts crept in. Then more doubts. Then a flicker of hope. And suspicion.'

'I understand. I truly do.' Tungdil nodded. 'Beligata, Gosalyn and Hargorin have spent from sunup to sundown filling me in on all the events of the cycles while I was away. All the tragedies that happened in my absence. And after the false Tungdil died. You have all gone through so much.' He picked up the artificial limb formed from metal sheets. 'And hardly do I emerge from the shadows when one dwarf dies and another loses a leg. Far from a glorious return.'

'We have much to speak of. Like why you killed the zhadár.'

Ireheart listened to his own inner feelings, which yearned to believe. But his head insisted he hold back and not commit. As this Tungdil had just said himself: no proof. *Except for the memories of their shared adventures.*

'But let's start by finding out if you're just another doppelgänger – or whether I can nurture a hope that my Scholar has come back to me.'

Tungdil smiled and then became serious. 'Since you ask: the zhadár embodied and dispensed cruelty, treachery, and danger. Down in Phondrasôn, only demons and the deadliest of evil creatures emit an aura of the kind he had. Something of that order must not be allowed to live.' He checked the metal leg for smoothness. 'He would soon have noticed that I had seen through him and he would have attacked me. I had to get in first.'

Ireheart had been told about the change that Carâhnios had undergone in the last cycle. He remembered finding him deeply repugnant the last time they had met.

'Hmm,' Ireheart grunted. 'I'll need to know more.'

'Of course. And I can tell you how my doppelgänger came to be formed.' He pointed to the public room of the tavern. 'Let's talk back there. I'm thirsty from working at the forge and Hargorin'll be keen to see his new leg. He's desperate to try it out, though he ought to wait for the wound to heal over completely first.'

'Let me warn you. The beer is appalling. The long'uns can't brew for toffee.' He stood back to let Tungdil pass.

When they were eye to eye, Tungdil searched Ireheart's face.

'What are you looking for, Scholar?'

'There's something I recognise. And it surprises me.'

Ireheart felt himself freeze. 'What do you mean?'

'Your rages. Your pupils have the red flecks in them again. But that's not all.'

'Ho, you must be imagining it.'

Tungdil gave a faint smile. 'I acquired new skills I would gladly have eschewed because they were from the älfar. But I cannot unlearn what I know. And that's what makes what you call "imagining" so difficult.'

He can tell I drank some of the zhadár's elixir! 'Let's talk about that some other time,' Ireheart said quickly. 'Hargorin needs his new leg.'

They walked over to the bar together.

Ireheart observed him closely and saw that he did not hesitate when approaching the armed soldiers. He greeted them warmly and wished them Vraccas' blessing, which they muttered in return. *They're the same as me. They don't know what to believe. They don't want to open their hearts to a counterfeit version.*

'Tell the others to dismount and find quarters in the barn,' Ireheart told one of his retinue. 'We're staying overnight.' He called over to the bar where the captain of the way-station was still scratching his head about the new arrivals. 'I'll pay for everything.'

'Make yourselves at home if you can,' the man replied.

Tungdil was kneeling in front of Hargorin fixing the new leg into the special harness. 'It fits.' He looked up at the red-haired dwarf. 'This is only for now. Till I get you the silver one we talked about.'

Supported by Beligata, Deathbringer got up, putting one hand on Tungdil's shoulder, too. Gingerly he tried putting weight on the tin leg. 'Bit uncomfortable, but it'll be alright.'

'Except it's the left,' said Ireheart with a grin, crossing his arms. 'We'll soon have you back in battle.'

'Of course, my king,' Hargorin replied, taking cautious steps across the room to accustom himself to the feel of the new limb. 'I shall deliver only the most deadly of kicks.' He asked Tungdil: 'Can you fit a blade on the end?'

The Scholar stood up with a laugh. 'Sure.'

'I can already see him in the front line,' joked Beligata. 'He won't need his axe at all.'

Heidor brought full tankards and put them on the table before turning swiftly back to his bar. Ireheart noted with regret that the boy obviously no longer felt at ease with the dwarves, ever since first recognising Deathbringer.

They took hold of their tankards and the ten guards took off their helmets and went over to order for themselves. The ponies' hooves clattered on the cobbles outside as they were led to their stabling.

'It's that easy to get outranked,' said the way-station captain, but he did not sound annoyed. His curiosity was blatant. Presumably no one had thought to tell him who the dwarf with the burned face was.

And let's leave it that way.

'You'll get back your status soon enough,' Ireheart called, raising his beer in a toast. 'Thank you for your hospitality.'

'Anything in the cause of friendship between our peoples,' the officer replied, raising his glass of spirits.

Ireheart tugged Tungdil's sleeve and led him over to a small table in the corner. 'Let's start the inquisition.' He was trying not to yawn.

Hargorin, Beligata and Gosalyn were talking together and admiring the new leg. Other dwarves came over to join them bit by bit. The room filled up.

'Shall we leave it till the morning?' the Scholar suggested. 'You've a long ride still in your bones.'

Ireheart secretly thought this a great idea but he was reluctant to waste any time. There were many Girdlegard matters he wanted to discuss with his friend. *But first I have to be sure it is him.* He laughed, earning a curious look from Tungdil. *Any surer than you were a cycle ago?*

'Let's start with the obvious ones,' he began. 'You bear no weapon, you wear no armour. You haven't even got a dagger, as far as I can see.'

'I don't need those things now. I am home.' Tungdil seemed calm and relaxed. 'I made a vow to the Divine Smith: if I ever managed to get back to Girdlegard alive, I would never bear arms again, or wear armour.' He indicated his clothing. 'This is all I need. That and ' – he reached under his collar and took out a pendant with the Vraccas rune – 'this.'

Ireheart's eyes widened. 'You're joking? Hero, warrior, and . . .'

'Scholar and smith,' he cut in. 'That's the way my life originally started. And that's what I want to get back to. Let my soul breathe for a time. After that, we shall see what Vraccas holds in store for me.'

'How long will that take?'

'It'll take as long as it takes. But I'm already feeling better. One cycle, perhaps ten. Who knows?'

'But . . .' The High King was lost for words.

One Tungdil had turned up bristling with tionium, furious and eager to fight, and full of new talents he'd learned from the älfar. This one wanted only a quiet life, it seemed: a bit of smithing, a bit of sitting with dusty, boring old books. Or maybe a bit of consulting work.

I don't have to ask if he wants to be High King. Ireheart was starting to yawn again. 'Tell me how the doppelgänger came about,' he said. 'Perhaps I'll try it.'

'You'd need a miracle.'

'Why do you say that?'

'I saw it happening but I don't understand it.' Tungdil grinned, and it was a grin Ireheart knew through and through.

But the High King held back. It was too soon to celebrate. The other Scholar had been equally convincing.

'It was like this: I was in the middle of a battle against a great number of foes in an endless underground realm and we were suddenly all swamped by a wave of magic. It filled the entire cave we were in and randomly created doubles of anything it touched: bits of buildings, objects, älfar, living creatures. There was no rhyme or reason to it. In the midst of this confusion I saw myself. The magic wave had created a copy of me. It escaped from the cave and went on living its own existence. From then on there were two of me.' Tungdil looked at his friend. 'I hear the forgery died with Keenfire in his breast at the Black Abyss. The original version is sitting opposite you now.' He took a mouthful of beer. 'Now let's have your questions.'

Girdlegard
Elf realm of Ti Lesinteïl
6492nd solar cycle, early autumn

'It had not been on the agenda that the älf would speak at the Council session.' Phenîlas addressed the Naishïon in the minimalist but impressive reception hall of his palace; as was appropriate, he was kneeling, wearing his light travel outfit with a red mantle over it. He had to admit to a defeat and was acutely embarrassed. 'It made a mockery of all my careful planning. I tried to silence him but he evaded my attack.'

'You are not to blame. Sitalia sometimes shatters things with the intention that we put it all back together differently.' Ataimînas remained on the dais, attired in a close-fitting black tunic and a flowing white cloak. The rays of sunlight that shone down on him through the overhead windows were less powerful now autumn had come. He surveyed the empty room, studying the painted walls where the reflected sparkle from his rings danced merrily. 'However, our plans are no secret any longer.'

'Indeed they are not, Naishïon.'

'Then there is no need to wait. The warriors will move out in the course of the next orbits. I shall expedite arrangements. Ti Âlandur, Ti Singàlai and Ti Lesinteïl will unite to form one over-arching state: Ti Lesîndur.' Ataimînas looked at Phenîlas. 'The foreign-held lands between us will be occupied and isolated. Subsequent to that, we will conduct negotiations with Tabaîn and Mallenia.'

'The queen of Idoslane isn't likely to agree, even if she was civil to me when I left and assured me she would study the purchase terms.' Phenîlas recalled her words. 'We should not risk losing her goodwill with a premature land grab.'

Ataimînas inhaled sharply, his nostrils narrowing. 'I think you underestimate me. We shall tell the humans that we are still hunting the dangerous beasts that are after them. If we do that, we'll be able to shift camp and get our soldiers in position before they realise what's happening.'

Phenîlas bowed his head. 'Forgive me. *That* argument would be a winner with Mallenia.'

'Exactly.' Ataimînas stood up and indicated that the other should accompany him. 'I have received a message from the Gauragar way-station near our border, saying that a group of military dwarves has arrived. And one of the dwarves is being addressed by the name of Tungdil.'

'Yes, I heard.' Phenîlas followed him to the bronze door.

'And did you hear what happened to our hunting party?' Ataimînas' voice grew hard.

'It was the first piece of news to reach me after my return. It seems the circumstances have yet to be investigated.'

'They had found the entrance the dwarves used to enter the caves. From the tracks, it is clear they went in and did not come back out. I have occasioned the hole to be filled in with rubble. The fact we have experienced some subsidence locally indicates that other parts may have caved in. There is no hope for our soldiers.'

'I would never have thought they would find him so quickly.'

'The carcass of a beast was found near the entrance. Tungdil must have defeated the creature and then returned to the tunnels to find the dwarves. Otherwise our soldiers would surely have triumphed.' Ataimînas reached under his sash. 'This was also found.'

Phenîlas took the small bottle and studied the älfar inscription.

'*Elf eyes*,' he read out. 'Is this what Tungdil had on him?'

'I fear trouble is brewing.'

In front of the imposing palace, preparations were underway for the festival in honour of the Creating Spirit. It was scheduled to take place in ten orbits' time, when the moon would be high. Grandstands were being erected around three giant, spanned drums, each four paces across. They were the size of huge wine barrels and the drumskins were decorated with the goddess's symbols. They would be beaten by the best elf drummers in the land and there would be a sung accompaniment. The Naishïon would open the ceremony of unification against the sound of drumrolls. From then on, there would be but the one empire.

'What is the trouble you fear?'

Ataimînas watched the preparations without a word and then held out his hand for the phial. 'Let's assume the älfar have found a way to prevent their eyes reacting to daylight – how could anyone tell us and them apart?' He pointed to the square where the artisans and the public were going about their legitimate business. 'How many älfar might we have there, in the local population?'

Phenîlas found the idea deeply disturbing. He handed the phial back. 'If that's true, the swine may already be infiltrating our towns and we'd have no idea.'

'They could have come up through the same passage the dwarves used. Perhaps they followed this Tungdil. Or they smuggled themselves in to Girdlegard with the new wave of immigrants. The border guards would not be able to identify them. There could have been a traitor within our own search party.' Ataimînas tossed back his mane of black hair and clasped his gloved hands behind his back. 'It's essential we find out the numbers involved.'

'But there are over ten thousand new arrivals.' Phenîlas was at a loss to know how they could be tested.

'The elf-eyes mixture won't stop anger lines forming when they're injured or insulted.' Ataimînas turned to head to face the warrior. 'That will be your task. Form a unit and traverse all the elf territories. Every elf, male or female, must be checked, no matter what their age is. You and your people will interrogate them comprehensively. If you find any älfar, send them here to me. They are not to be executed in situ.'

Phenîlas considered the size of the various elf territories. 'Word will get round that we're hunting disguised älfar. The ones we're looking for will go into hiding and won't come out till we've moved on to a different town.'

'The neighbours would see.' Ataimînas gave him a hard stare. 'This task I'm entrusting you with is the most important one of our new empire, Phenîlas. The enemy within is far more dangerous than any foe threatening Girdlegard from outside. We have to be able to trust our fellow elves in battle.

If we're busy worrying about whether our comrade is a black-eyes about to fall on us, we'll never be safe.'

'I shall do what needs to be done, Naishïon.' Phenîlas bowed. 'I will honour my duty.'

'It's a good thing they're not letting any more elves in. Let's hope it stays like that till we can be sure there are no black-eyes in our midst.' Ataimînas nodded and went on watching the workers. 'But first, you must finish what you started in Freestone. You have an opportunity to put things right. And when you come back, you'll be appointed sorânïon with special rights.'

Phenîlas heard the implied reproach. 'I will make haste to Tabaîn and see to the matter.'

'That's the spirit.' The Naishïon looked up at the brilliant blue sky. 'The harvest is in; the barns and the grain sacks will be full. Make sure we get as much of it as we possibly can. We know the king of Tabaîn; he'll provide for us together with the purchase of land we want. That rival of his, on the other hand, is no good to anyone.'

Phenîlas bowed. 'I'll leave at once.' The blond elf hurried down the steps and went to the stables to collect his horse.

Don't fail this time. My patience has its limits. Ataimînas turned and went back inside the palace. Once the food supply for his empire was assured, other concerns would disappear.

His steps took him over reed matting across the main room and out through a side door in the panelling, leading to a corridor. Going up a series of steps, he headed for a steel-framed chamber. The huge palace was, apart from this one room, constructed entirely of timber, making it comparatively easy to dismantle and move to a new location.

He was worried about the existence of the älfar medicinal

drops that changed the properties of light-sensitive eyes. *We have misread the Creating Spirit's scriptures on this point. Many of her prophecies regarding Girdlegard seem to mirror actual events.*

The investigations must not on any account arouse disquiet in the populace. It would be vital in the coming orbits and cycles to stress the need for unity. But with the potential of treacherous death lurking in the elf ranks, this would be difficult. He would have to rely on Phenîlas. *But only if he can finally sort out the situation in Tabaîn.*

Phenîlas was unaware of the Naishïon's plan to get rid of him if he fell short. He was a popular figure but this was no proof against punishment if he were to fail again.

Ataimînas had reached the steel door that secured the chamber. He pulled out a key from his sash and placed it in the lock, giving it four turns to the right and two to the left. He touched a combination of elf runes on the door.

Only then did the lock click and release the key. The door opened.

The Naishïon stepped inside the palace treasure house, which contained a number of lockable drawers for the safekeeping of valuable papers, works of art, and gems or relics from the old elf kingdoms that the new arrivals had brought him. The door closed behind him. Fragrant oil lamps shed enough light and the air supply was good. That was important.

A naked, black-haired älf formed part of the collection. He was kept tethered and chained on the hard metal floor with only a mat to lie on. He had been captured quite some time ago when he had made an attempt on Ataimînas' life. A conventional prison cell had not been thought secure enough.

'What a good thing we showed mercy.'

'I don't call torture showing mercy,' the älf replied. He had refused to give his name. His mouth was bruised and his white torso showed wounds that had been stitched, together with fresh scars; many of the marks shimmered red or violet.

Ataimînas crouched down and took out the phial. 'We have been more merciful to you than you deserve. Humans are much more brutal to your kind than we are.' He examined the injuries. 'You seem to have recovered well.'

The älf gave a contemptuous laugh and spat at the Naishïon.

Ataimînas grasped the älf's face and forced the eyelids apart, dropping some of the phial's contents into each eye.

'What's that?' the älf fumed. 'Another attempt to drive the evil out of me?' He yanked on his chains and lines of fury started up on his visage. 'I was made by Inàste and none of your preparations will work on me. I shall never worship Sitalia! You cannot change my mind-set.'

Ataimînas observed how tears and surplus medication trickled out of the corner of the eyes. 'We shall see. The prophecies demand we try, at the very least.' He stood up and activated the door mechanism by touching certain runes. '"*In the new empire, my untainted children will live in harmony with their purified brother-killers,*"' he said, reciting a prophecy from the times in exile. '"*And behold, a new era shall dawn.*"'

Sunlight flooded in to the chamber, and onto the disdainful captive.

Ataimînas ignored the älf's gestures and watched the effect on his eyes: the part of the eye round the iris did not turn black. *Not a trace of colour change.*

Noticing how quiet the elf was, the prisoner stopped laughing. 'What are you staring at?' He turned his head to face the light and realised the familiar tugging at the corners of his eyes had not occurred. 'To Tion with you! You may have made my eyes white but you can never make me one of you!' He caught a glimpse of the phial in the Naishïon's hand although the elf tried to hide it. 'Wait. That's not an elf remedy?' Then he laughed. 'Praise be to Inàste! My people have found a way to circumvent the eye change.' His eyes sparkled with delight. 'Now we can infiltrate your population. No one will be able to tell the difference and the elves will all start mistrusting and fearing each other!'

Ataimînas raised his foot and stamped down hard on the captive's hand, making him cry out in pain; dark lines zigzagged across his face until it looked about to shatter into pieces.

'That's how we'll recognise you.' He put the remedy away and left the chamber. The door closed and locked itself automatically. *I'll find a way to bring Inàste's creations down.*

Pain would be the best way to differentiate between elves and imposters, though he hoped Phenîlas would not have to go so far in order to determine who he had before him. It would make a bad impression if his own folk were subjected to a regime of torture right at the beginning of his rule. The most lavish of moon festivals would not alter that.

Girdlegard
Kingdom of Tabaîn
6492nd solar cycle, early autumn

Phenîlas doubted his own senses when Dirisa came over with a broad smile to welcome him. *Has she dosed herself with some friendship potion?*

He was on the princess's estate where she was taking part in the grape harvest. She swore her presence there always made for a fine vintage. One of her curious whims, as the elf had learned.

She had been responsible for the construction of the artificial hill on which the vineyards were planted, because Tabaîn was too flat otherwise for successful viticulture. Phenîlas had ridden across miles and miles of harvested grain fields where the first ploughing was going ahead. The straw stalks were turned over under the soil to make the ground fertile for the next sowing. This broad, terraced mound was around three hundred paces in height and it rose up like the stump remaining after a mountain top had been sliced off. It faced south to ensure optimum sunshine for the grapes.

The estate house was at the base of the hill, and this was where Phenîlas had reined in his horse. The dust of his arrival had hardly settled before Dirisa strode out to welcome him. Like all of Tabaîn's buildings, it was a stone construction, made to withstand the vicious winds the region was prone to. Whirlwinds were the curse of a flat country.

'How nice to see you again,' the princess called, smiling. She was wearing a grape-stained apron over her warm woollen dress. 'May Sitalia's blessing be upon you.' Phenîlas swung himself down from the saddle and bowed to her. Now that times were less safe than expected, he was wearing light body armour and over it a cloak to protect him from the dust and from the weather. *She must be drunk.* This explanation seemed more plausible as the conversation progressed. *Or maybe it's fumes from the wine cellar.* The last time they'd met she had threatened him, but now it seemed she wanted to be the best of friends. 'My thanks.'

Dirisa took off her apron, arranged her black hair and came over to his side, grasping his arm. 'Come with me. What a pleasant surprise. You couldn't have picked a better moment.' She escorted him along the front of the grey estate building with its decorative murals. It had been painted to look like a rural half-timbered house.

In the distance, singing could be heard: call and response in chorus, with guitars, flutes and bagpipes accompanying the voices.

They stepped into the busy courtyard, still arm in arm. Maids were barefoot, pressing the grapes in huge tubs, and there was an intoxicating smell of sweet fresh juice. In other tubs young children were stamping happily away and further on, men were doing the same. The music was helping them keep the rhythm with their feet.

'As you see, part of the basis for my wines comes from the pressure of different sets of feet.' Dirisa explained. 'That accounts for the nuances that can be tasted later, when the wine is ready. It's to do with the weight applied to the fruit at the time of pressing.'

The workers acknowledged them with nods without breaking step. The juice ran free from the exit runnels in the sides of the tubs, where it was then filtered through linen sheeting and carried down to the cellar by the bucketful. The air was full of the sweet aroma.

'This is interesting.' Phenîlas already knew humans had this revolting practice of pressing the fruit with their feet. He did not want to think where those feet had been before. *And the hairs and the dirt under the nails and the nails themselves . . .* 'We employ different methods, ourselves.'

'You don't necessarily make better wine, though.' Dirisa winked at him. 'I was about to fill a small cask as a gift for your Naishïon. This will be the first vintage in the era of peace and friendship between all the peoples in Girdlegard.'

Phenîlas thought he must have misheard. 'Forgive me for

speaking frankly, but what you said in Freestone did not lead me to expect . . .'

To his surprise, Dirisa burst out laughing and pulled him to her. He noted how thin she was and that she didn't smell of wine at all. 'My dear Phenîlas. The gods have told me how foolish my attitude was towards your race and towards Natenian. Please forgive me.'

'Of course I accept your apology,' he replied, not knowing what else to say. In his mind he was searching for some explanation for her change of heart.

'I really hope you will. Please be my guest at the coronation in two orbits' time. It is to be held in Wheattown. It won't be anything fancy. No pomp.' *So that's where this is leading. She wants me on her side.*

'If you are crowned, Natenian will contest it. There could be unrest among the people if there are two rulers.'

Dirisa stared at him with her nut brown eyes. 'So you haven't heard?'

'Apparently not. What is there to know?'

'Natenian and I are reconciled. It happened on the ride back from the Council. He's handing the throne over to me. He's proclaimed his abdication with a country-wide announcement using despatch riders and posters.'

The fool! 'And what were his reasons?'

'The same as ever: his failing health.' The princess pulled the elf slightly to one side so that a laden cart could pass. 'He told me all about the business deal he had made with you,' she added, her voice low. 'All the details.' She fished a cluster of grapes from the cart and offered it to him. 'Try these.'

Phenîlas took some grapes, which burst on his palate at the slightest pressure. 'Absolutely delicious,' he said, not needing to dissemble in the slightest. As long as they hadn't yet been touched by a human foot he had no objection to eating grapes.

'Then perhaps you can work out how good the wine will be.' Dirisa ate a handful herself. 'We shall never mention the contract you made with Natenian,' she said firmly. 'That's all in the past and it won't bring Raikan back to life. It's a shame the High King spoke to Tenkil, but our people won't be told what he said. As far as Tabaîn's concerned, the warrior died defending his master and was devoured by a beast.'

'I like what I hear.' *But I shan't believe it straightaway.*

Dirisa turned towards him and placed a grape provocatively between her lips. She played with the fruit in her mouth. The elf did not find this attractive. 'You'll like this even more: we've agreed to stick with the terms and conditions of the original deal,' she said. 'As soon as the coronation's over, I shall supply the Naishïon with all the grain he wants. And I'll sell you the land you asked for. And I'll let you have several square miles to cultivate your own varieties. My best soldiers will guard the fields.' She pulled another grape off the stalk.

'I am . . . overcome. In the best of all possible senses,' he admitted. *But where is the catch?*

'Thanks be to the gods that they sent me the wisdom to see what is best for Tabaîn. Friendship with the Naishïon will bring us great prosperity.' Dirisa laughed gaily, thrilled her surprise had worked so well. 'Friendship leads to unity, my dear Phenîlas. And after what the High King reported about events at the Stone Gateway, it looks as if we might have urgent need of it.'

'You speak the truth.' The elf had no idea what was happening here. In the cuff of his long gloves he had concealed a small bottle of poison with which he had intended to kill her.

But that seemed unnecessary now. *Unless she's playing a trick.*

But he wouldn't find out until after the coronation. And after that, it would be well nigh impossible to get close to her again and poison her drink.

Had she guessed the purpose of his visit? Was this welcome an attempt to avoid an assassination?

I should get rid of her anyway. She's too unpredictable to be a reliable ally. He gave a forced smile. 'You shame me with your invitation to the coronation. I have no gift for you. As ambassador for my country, I should have some precious metalwork or an elf speciality to give you to mark the day.'

'You, my good friend, are welcome, even if you turned up naked in the Palandiell temple.' Dirisa burst out laughing. 'May I ask you for something?'

'Of course, Princess.'

'Pretend you don't know anything about the coronation if word reaches you in public.'

'I swear.' Phenîlas looked at the fruit in his hand. 'Or may this grape be the death of me.' He placed the grape in his mouth.

Dirisa grinned. 'Mallenia will also let you have land in recognition of your promise to be here for us if Girdlegard is ever faced with danger.' She clapped her hands. 'Isn't this great? You elves can start building your empire now.'

Phenîlas had seen many things and gone through a great deal. But this was nothing to what was awaiting him in the courtyard. He was so surprised that the grape went down the wrong way and he choked. He would have entered endingness had Dirisa not banged him on the back between the shoulder blades.

And so he had no choice but to keep his promise.

He gasped, filling his lungs with the autumn air, his face bright red. In this case staying silent and waiting to see what would happen would not be a problem. *This is going to be quite a moon festival.*

A dwarf who likes to fight with a sword probably likes his beer watered down.

Dwarf saying

XI

Girdlegard
United Kingdom of Gauragar-Idoslane
6492nd solar cycle, early autumn

Ireheart sat by himself nursing his beer at the fireside in the main room. There were maybe two dozen dwarves sitting around. This was probably his fourth or fifth tankard of the evening.

He had drawn aside from the others on purpose to give himself a chance to think. Staring at the flames, he went over the events of the past few orbits and in particular the words he had heard from his friend's mouth.

Tungdil had vouchsafed to him some of the adventures he had had in Phondrasôn, where one met with death, pain, cruelty, demons and beasts, warlords and death queens, passionate torturers, slave-abusers, and unimaginable creatures. There strange alliances were entered into with the object of strengthening evil powers.

The Scholar told of his own part, doing things that vied with the worst of deeds, purely in order to survive. But there was neither pride nor pleasure in the telling – only repugnance. *Repugnance at his own behaviour.* Ireheart was aware of stark contrasts between this Tungdil and the first version to arrive back.

He had none of the instability and mysterious nature of the other one. His body bore witness with numerous scars to the wars he had fought in. Though there was a powerful aura around him, there was no air of evil or treachery. Whatever the älfar Triplets had done to him, he had shaken off their influence completely. The fact that he had taken off the tionium armour that had manipulated him, and had left Bloodthirster behind, all proved to Ireheart that Tungdil had changed.

The High King did not allow his heart to have the upper hand. His head was too afraid he might make the wrong decision and it would cause a catastrophe. A catastrophe that had not occurred with the first Tungdil.

What if it's a well-rehearsed masquerade? What if it's a shape-shifter that's come back to us, dead set on playing a game with the whole of Girdlegard? Ireheart wiped his furrowed brow and stroked his silver beard as if trying to calm and placate the individual hairs. *I've been presented with yet another Scholar and I've no idea if it was Tion or Vraccas who delivered him.*

His uncertainty was made worse by the fact that Tungdil was making no attempt to assume any power, as a true hero would. He did not demand the office of High King nor the throne of the Thirdlings tribe, as Hargorin had suggested he do.

Rest. That's all he wants. Ireheart grunted crossly and emptied his mug of beer. *I can see why he'd like to put his feet up for a bit. But his soul needs rest? What does that mean? How long does that take?*

But this attitude had good sense behind it. It was probably better if the Scholar kept out of dwarf affairs at first. Everyone in Girdlegard would regard him with suspicion because they'd gone through all this before: a long-lost Tungdil coming up from the dark underworld, and an Ireheart convinced of his authenticity.

There was a bitter irony to the genuine hero being viewed

with suspicion whereas the magically-conceived version had been followed without hesitation.

That's if he is the genuine article, Ireheart added, pulling at his hair. *Enough to drive you mad. Vraccas, it's time for you to do something!*

A commotion started in the room: it was the dwarves changing guard duty teams. When the soldiers came in from outside they brought with them the smell of rain. Autumn brought misty rain and fog to show the Girdlegarders that the nights had lost their warmth.

Someone approached the High King. Judging by the sound of the footsteps, it was Beligata.

The dark-haired dwarf-woman came up and bowed. She wasn't carrying her usual double axe but something longish wrapped in a cloth. 'Have you got a moment?'

'Sure.' Ireheart was glad of the interruption. His thoughts were going nowhere sensible, so they might as well stop.

He noticed her leggings and boots were soaked. 'I didn't know they'd put you on guard duty.'

'I've been wandering around.' Beligata cast a quick glance round the room before she took a seat and undid the fabric wrapping. A black blade appeared, one side of it adorned with long spikes.

'In case we ever need it,' she mouthed, looking at him expectantly.

Ireheart stared at the weapon then at the girl, whose facial scar was glowing. 'The Scholar told me he had left it behind.'

'He did.' Beligata covered it over again. 'In the general confusion, nobody noticed when I went back for it.' She placed her hand on it carefully and as she did so, her sleeve fell back, revealing a tattoo. 'Bloodthirster is powerful. It is the only weapon that could rival Keenfire. It would not only suit a returned hero but also a High King.'

Young and inexperienced. Ireheart wiped his beard. It needed combing.

'You joined the Freelings,' he replied, in calm and fatherly tones. 'But you think like a Thirdling. You want to be well-prepared for combat.' He placed his hand, too, on the shrouded weapon. 'But this weapon is not suited for those wanting to do good. Tungdil left it behind on purpose.'

Beligata shifted uneasily on her chair. 'It wasn't easy keeping Bloodthirster hidden from the others. I expected praise, not a scolding.' Her expression was dark.

'I have given you an explanation. And I cannot let you keep the weapon.' Ireheart gave her a smile. 'But I will arrange for it to disappear. For ever.' He took hold of it.

But Beligata did not release her grip, staring at Ireheart open-mouthed. There came a flash of animosity in her eyes. 'I brought it back and so . . .' She bit her lip.

She needs someone to lead her. He maintained his friendly manner. 'I think you are forgetting you are talking to your High King.'

'I'm a Freeling!'

'And you are clever. And you will sit at the same table when the dwarf kings deliberate. You can't use that as an excuse.' He applied more pressure and felt rage begin to rise within him. Her disobedience was provoking him. His face felt hot and flushed. 'You should never have gone to look for the weapon once its original owner had discarded it. Believe me: Tungdil knew why he wanted to leave it in the realm of demons.' He thought Beligata's scar was starting to glow in the dull firelight, not unlike the illuminating moss underground. *I wonder what that's all about?*

Beligata swallowed – and let go of Bloodthirster. 'Then hide it somewhere I can't find it,' she advised him, standing up briskly. 'Or I'll take it and do heroic deeds.'

'You've got a perfectly good double axe,' retorted Boïndil. He quickly took a swig of his drink. *I mustn't lose my temper.* 'It will bring you renown. But this weapon here,' he said, tapping the cloth, 'would cost part of your soul.'

The girl turned on her heel and left the room.

'She's a bold one,' came a voice out of the darkness at his ear. 'But crazy.'

Tungdil stepped out of the shadows and sat down on a stool opposite his friend. He was wearing his usual red garment with its embroidered Vraccas rune over his heart. 'Sometimes she reminds me of you.' He grinned. 'I mean when you were younger, and launched yourself with a wild *oink, oink* against the orcs, as if they couldn't possibly hurt you.'

'Well, they couldn't, could they?' Ireheart had recovered from his surprise. 'You steal around like a black-eyes.'

'I was half a black-eyes.' Tungdil laughed and tapped the white eye patch. 'See this?'

'That's a good one.'

'But I no longer use those powers. The zhadár would have had the better of me in many ways. That älf blood elixir that gave him fuel must have been tremendously strong.'

'Let's hope he didn't have any apprentices.' It occurred to Ireheart that Tungdil had the same grounding in alchemy. The firelight softened the otherwise alarming aspect of his disfigurement. Ireheart pointed at Bloodthirster. 'I'll have it destroyed.'

'It can withstand Keenfire. What could destroy a sword that used to belong to one of the Indestructibles? Magic?'

Tungdil did not sound convinced. 'All I could do was to reshape it. If you want my advice, stick it in a catapult on one of the dwarf fortresses and hurl it out into the Outer Lands as far as it will go. It shouldn't stay here.' He watched the flames. 'Do you know what I long for?'

'A beer?'

'A book.'

Ireheart had to grin. 'That's my Scholar.'

Tungdil made a sound somewhere between laughter and melancholy. 'An empire that doesn't respect book-learning is a lost empire. I intend to rest and to read. To read a lot. A great deal of new writing will have mounted up in the last two hundred and fifty cycles. I hear that an älf has made extensive records.'

'Indeed, there's that and a whole range of other new works.' Ireheart placed Bloodthirster under his chair; he was delighted that his friend was not even attempting to steal a glance at it. 'In the last few orbits you've been telling me about your life, terrible things.'

'And you had to soften the effect with beer,' Tungdil cut in, laughing. 'Mind you don't drink too much. You'll recall I used to. Someone who drinks excessively won't be able to make sensible decisions, and he'll go downhill, always seeking to deal with his own needs first.' He put his hand on Ireheart's shoulder. 'I'd like to see you drinking less, old friend. Or can I guess the reason? It has something to do with the alteration.'

He can actually tell. The High King busied himself putting extra logs on the fire and got ready to reveal the truth about the zhadár potion. It was a tremendous effort but he forced himself to relate the story in detail.

'And ever since I tasted it, I've been addicted to it. It brings back the madness. It's only when I have enough beer or spirits that I can keep the fury in check.' He struck himself on the chest. 'It's the old anger. If I hadn't had a skinful, I'd have shouted at Beligata till her ears rang.'

Tungdil was thoughtful. 'Do you know where the zhadár's laboratory was?'

'I expect . . . I can find out,' Ireheart said cautiously. 'Why?'

'If I can work out what ingredients he and the älfar used to distil the älf blood and alter its composition, I can make an antidote.' The scholar gave a slight nod. 'It shouldn't be difficult. I've learned a lot. Perhaps I can use it to help free you from that burden.'

Ireheart's joy was short-lived and suspicion surged in to take its place. *How do I know I can trust him? He could give me anything he likes.*

'I'll look into it,' was his non-committal response.

'I'm at your service. Thank you for confiding in me.' He pointed at the weapon lying under the chair. 'And get rid of that. Once and for all.'

'While we're dispensing advice: tell me what you think about the elves.'

'I'd need to know more.' Tungdil bent forward, elbows on knees, folding his scar-ravaged hands with their faded tattoos. 'I assume there's a specific issue?'

Ireheart nodded and related what he had learned about events in Tabaîn, explaining that the elves were in the process of forming a united empire from their three previously separate realms. 'Their ruler is pushing the idea with vigour and there are several camps of pointy-eared would-be immigrants outside Girdlegard's gates, begging to be admitted.'

'How many?'

'There are ten thousand already in with us and about four thousand waiting outside for admittance. I've sent a messenger to Ataimînas to inform him about the phial with eye-white.'

'Good. Until the eye business has been investigated, I would suggest keeping the gates closed and avoiding any contact,' he said after due reflection. 'The tincture you describe sounds like älfar work, true enough. It will cause unrest among the elves. Their supreme ruler must at all costs establish how many disguised mortal enemies he has in his ranks. He would never admit it but I expect he is secretly relieved that you are refusing entry to newcomers.'

Ireheart scratched his initials into the surface of the table with his nail. 'And what they're up to in Tabaîn?'

'Let them sort it out for themselves. Remember how strong the dwarves are: we hold the gates and we'll take up arms if Girdlegard is in danger.' Tungdil adjusted his eye patch. 'You might find all this commotion blows over quickly.'

Ireheart gazed at him in astonishment. 'Killing the heir to the throne . . . you call that a *commotion*?'

'These events don't impinge on Girdlegard as a whole, do they? Hold back. See what happens and don't get involved.' He sat up. 'Pay heed to the gates. The elves on the outside, if they're forced to wait, will move heaven and earth to find a way to get in. And any disguised älfar will be the first to try it.' He got up wearily. 'My bed is calling, if you can save your other questions for tomorrow. And Hargorin wants me to make some improvements to his new leg.'

'You'll think of something, Scholar.'

He smiled. 'Has our wild young thing of a Beligata ever told you how she got her scar?'

'Never.'

'I see.' Tungdil turned and went over to the stairs. They had given him a room in the attic so that he wouldn't be in close contact with the other dwarves in the barn, seeing that his background had not been verified.

I see. Is that all? Ireheart was about to follow him but forced himself not to. It was vital not to leave Bloodthirster unsupervised. He would not put it past Beligata to snatch it back if an opportunity arose.

The flames crackled and flickered in the fireplace and attracted Ireheart's attention again. There was much he had heard that needed thinking through, from the zhadár's laboratory to the scar and the advice to steer clear of events in Tabaîn.

If only there were someone I could ask about the Scholar's magical powers.

He got Heidor to bring him another beer. He wasn't going to stop drinking as long as alcohol reliably held his wild rages in check. It might be harmful in the long term but it was essential for now.

He urgently needed to speak to Coïra, but nobody knew where the maga currently was. There had been no signs of life apart from the letter Ilahín had read out to the assembled monarchs.

Ireheart raised his head and saw Hargorin talking to Gosalyn and Beligata. *They have all been part of a small miracle, even if the Scholar did find his own way to the surface.* He drank some more of the ice-cold beer; no matter how much he drank, it never tasted any better. He got to his feet and walked over to their table. *A small miracle. I could do with one of them.*

Girdlegard
Grey Mountains
Kingdom of the Fifthling dwarves
Stone Gateway
6492nd solar cycle, autumn

Balyndar muttered a curse as he paced along the broad battlements of the right-hand section of the gate. He peered into the grey. It was coming closer and closer to the gate, which was now securely shut. *Vraccas, use your divine bellows and blow this fog away.*

He was accompanied by the silent figure of Girgandor Summitstormer, his second in command. The two dwarves were similar in stature but Girgandor had shaved his head and had a long blond beard reaching to his middle; with its occasional black strands and woven braids, it was a work of art.

The heavy mist had not budged, despite the wind and the sun above the fortress walls peeking through the grey cloud like a yellow ball.

Every five paces he encountered the next guard posted on the walls. They were all listening out for trouble. Great caution was the order of the day but there was no panic or fear.

Balyndis had taken the unusual step of issuing a command to bring wild ravine wolves to the fortress. These animals with their thick, brown pelts had a fantastic sense of smell; they could catch the scent of any enemy ages before the soldiers spied anything untoward. They would not miss a thing.

The wolves lay in their cages, gnawing at bits of bone.

With the beginning of autumn, temperatures in the Grey Mountains fell sharply, so guards and commander wore thick coats and animal furs over their chainmail. The fog settled on the armour, collecting in transparent droplets.

Now Balyndar cast his eyes over the rows of defensive equipment standing ready for use. 'Wonderful machines,' Girgandor commented. 'It's difficult not to give in to the desire to let off a trial shot or a flare.'

The catapults had been loaded with petrol bombs, as the High King had commanded. The thin leather skins could be filled in seconds from the open barrels, then set on fire and sent off. Since they now knew how to defeat the ghaist, the crew on duty were not particularly apprehensive about the possibility of it turning up again.

'Not a bad idea.' Balyndar was less enthusiastic about the thick curtain of fog filling the ravine and spreading to nearly fifty paces from the gate itself. It was not just that the eye couldn't penetrate the mist; it also deadened the sound of any noise an enemy might give off.

Fifty paces was also too short a distance for the powerful catapults with their petrol-bomb projectiles. The dwarf craftsmen and researchers had already created some weapons that could send fire in a straight line for this eventuality; they had come up with a throwing device that used earthenware pots. It was similar to a catapult sending shot, but the items to be hurled at the enemy were burning porous containers that would burst on impact, letting the petrol spread and ignite. The weapon with its eight-pace-long adjustable barrel was specially designed to be able to shoot downwards.

Balyndar came to a standstill, running his hands over the machine and pointing it towards the Gateway. *I have no objections to the quiet. All we need now is for the fog to disappear.* 'Let's load one up. We'll see if we can drive away fog with fire.'

Girgandor was thrilled and shouted for the team to come over.

Questions had cropped up after Queen Balyndis' report was read out in Council, particularly from the elves. A few orbits previously a delegate from Lesinteïl had turned up but after they had shown him that there were no elves there, he disappeared, to report back to his ruler. None of the Fifthlings had told him the elves had not been allowed through in their greatest need. *There would have been no point.*

Girgandor and Balyndar watched the automated pulley load the catapult's counterweight system with an earthenware vessel the size of a dwarf's torso. There was a soaked lint wick at the top and the whole pot had a coating of flammable seeds to ensure it would catch even if the fuse were lost. The speed of trajectory flight would never manage to extinguish both sources. A whole magazine of these projectiles waited at the foot of the catapult, so it was possible to keep up a near constant barrage.

'What about the "dragons"?' asked Balyndar. 'Are their wings mature enough?'

'Not yet. But they're being well-looked-after and they're coming along splendidly,' Girgandor replied. 'They'll be a majestic sight when they take off in our defence.'

Balyndar tucked his hands into his belt. 'Magnificent.'

From the right-hand tower a lightly armoured dwarf came running up with a leather roll in his hand. 'A message from the queen,' he panted, hand outstretched as if running a relay race along the ramparts.

'Must be important, if you're in such a rush.' Balyndar opened the container and extracted a paper bearing his mother's handwriting. A brief scan of the contents was enough to explain the urgency.

'Hold your fire,' Girgandor told the catapult crew. 'I want you to enjoy the spectacle, Balyndar. Has the queen sent new orders?'

'It's new information.' Balyndar was at a loss to understand what had got into the powers that be. What was happening in Girdlegard? 'Imagine! Mallenia has handed over parts of Gauragar to the elves!'

'Handed over as in given away?'

'I think so.'

Balyndar took out a second sheet with a sketch map depicting the new borders. 'Under the Naishïon's rule, the elves' grand empire stretches right up to our Grey Mountains.'

Girgandor studied the map and grimaced. 'Looks like Tabaîn's done the same.' Parting the decorative curtain of his blond beard, he scratched his chin. 'If I've got this right, the queen of Idoslane has voluntarily given away half of Gauragar. Her people won't be best pleased.'

Balyndar scanned the letter for any mention of what was to happen to the human residents of these territories now they were to live under an elf regime. 'They'll have to pay levies or else they'll have to go.'

'If I know the pointy-ears, they'll want exclusive rights to the land.' Girgandor shook his head, unable to understand. 'And Council allowed it?'

'Apparently the monarchs are all of one mind. I suppose it oughtn't to affect us if they choose to give their land away.'

'What can have been the price? Even a gift has some kind of a price. An invisible one that everyone will come to feel.'

'If you have the elves for allies you have nothing to fear. That's what Mallenia and Dirisa will have thought.' Balyndar rolled up the papers and replaced them. 'But old friends would surely be more important.'

'We can't really call ourselves their *friends*.' Girgandor raised his head, noticing a change in the wind. It was switching from south to north. 'We stayed true to our god Vraccas and fulfilled the task he gave us.'

'And don't we live in peace and harmony with the humans as a result?' Balyndar thought his deputy was being simplistic. 'Let's wait and see what these changes will involve. Perhaps Girdlegard will benefit from them and flourish as never before.'

'I still see this as a cleverly-disguised occupation. What the Perished Land, the älfar, the monsters and demons couldn't do, the pointy-ears have managed: they've inveigled their way in under the blanket of friendship.' Girgandor gave the signal to light the fuse in the amphora. 'Vraccas seems to have turned his bellows on that damned fog, so let's see what kind of a range our new catapults have got.'

Balyndar dismissed the messenger. There was no need to send an acknowledgement. 'I really hope this takeover of land in Tabaîn and Gauragar can be effected without some kind of revolt from the settled inhabitants.'

'The elves are clever. They'll be handing out glass beads and wine; the natives will grin and leave the fields their ancestors ploughed, thinking they've done well out of it.' Girgandor had the barrel set almost perpendicular, as if the projectile was intended to send a new small sun into the firmament. 'Ready when you are, Balyndar.'

He trained his brown eyes on the retreating strands of fog which were being driven back by the gusts of wind. Now you could see for seventy paces. 'Fire.'

The catch was released and the tensed wire propelled the sledge with its fiery cargo through the iron tunnel and up and out. The earthenware vessel hissed and sparked on its way, flying into the mist and beyond.

Balyndar and Girgandor listened out for the impact, waiting for a burst of flames. Nothing.

Disappointing.

'Maybe it broke up in mid-air,' suggested Balyndar, but one of the crew vehemently dismissed the possibility. They had calculated the strength of the wind exactly.

Girgandor reacted pragmatically. 'Reload. Fire when ready. And I want absolute silence.'

In a few blinks of an eye the second projectile was underway, flying between the parapet's crenellations above the great gate, to pierce the fog that was now eighty paces away.

The guards were stock still, listening intently for the impact.

Again, nothing. No crash, no shattered pottery, no burst of flame.

'Is it the fog?' Balyndar leaned over the battlements, turning his head right and left to pick up any sound. 'Come on, Vraccas, send us a wind straight from your forge. Get rid of this mist for us,' he muttered, extremely concerned by now.

'Look!' Girgandor pointed down.

Balyndar looked over at the Stone Gateway.

Two lights were floating across at head height in the swirling fog. Then the outline appeared of two naked, muscular arms, carrying the two amphorae. The next thing to emerge was the torso in a brown leather reinforced doublet, then the booted legs, and finally the white runes on the polished copper helmet that covered head and face.

He's caught them! Balyndar screamed out the order to stand by all the catapults. Alarm bugles sounded and bells clanged. From all sides came the sound of running feet and the clanking of chains.

Girgandor went round urging his troops to their stations and encouraging them to work more swiftly.

Balyndar looked at the ghaist, which was standing motionless, flaming earthenware vessels in its hands. As a magic being, composed of banned souls and a powerful spell, no pain could reach it.

'Don't shoot,' Balyndar called. 'Not till I say.'

'Why not?' Girgandor came over to his side, not understanding. 'We won't get a better sighting of the target.'

'It's going to hurl those fire pots and I want to know how far it can throw.' Balyndar wanted to know as much as possible about their adversary before destroying it with tremendous heat. 'It's clearly not afraid of fire.'

'As long as the copper helmet doesn't melt it can stand there for orbit after orbit like a lighthouse at our gates,' Girgandor laughed. 'Not a bad addition to the overall look of the fortress, don't you think? We should keep it there.'

'It's not just standing there.' Balyndar suddenly realised what was happening. 'It's signalling!'

The wind blew the remains of the fog further back – to reveal legs, bodies and heads belonging to the most incredible mixture of creatures. Like a curtain, the mist drew back from the army that had assembled on the thirty-pace-broad approach road.

The majority of the throng on the gateway path seemed to be humans but there were also beasts that would normally have eaten them. Orcs of various builds, two ogres and other monsters from Tion's realm all waited silently, eyes fixed on the fortifications.

'Only a few thousand.' He heard Girgandor's confident guess. 'A random collection of fighters. We'll soon see them off. It'll be a quick blood bath.'

They don't have any battering rams or siege ladders and they're not carrying ropes. Balyndar wondered what their intention could be. They would never climb the smooth surface of the granite gates with hands and feet alone. Very few of them seemed to be armoured and armed. *What've they got up their sleeves?* He stared into the lifting mist with great concentration. *Are they waiting for siege towers to arrive?* Even then he was at a loss to work out how they planned to attack. The Children of Vraccas here at the fortress had never been faced by so ill-prepared an onslaught.

Are they undead, perhaps? Balyndar couldn't work it out, but he felt that his people had all the right equipment to repel the attack. He did not, however, want to count his chickens before they were hatched.

As the mist drew away from the army, it was clear that the column stretched back along the road between the mountains.

And back.

And back.

Several thousand, standing densely packed on the road. Not moving. Silent.

The breeze played with the flags on the battlements, making the fabric rustle. That was all you could hear.

In spite of himself, Balyndar felt a shudder go down his spine when he confronted those impassive faces. *I shall have to recalculate.* 'They're packed in so tightly. Every time a fire bomb or a catapulted boulder hits home, it'll kill hundreds of them,' he said to Girgandor.

The sun shone down on the poorly assorted throng, showing the dwarves they had no reason to be worried. Not even the sheer weight of numbers ought to be a problem.

'That should save us ammunition,' the dwarf replied drily. 'And we –'

Without any discernible signal from the ghaist, the mass of soldiers started to move. They stormed along in silence, skirting round their copper-helmeted leader. If anyone collided with the magic being by mistake, he was thrown back or squashed against it by the rest of the crowd, then trampled mercilessly under the boots of his fellow-fighters.

The stream of attackers surged onward like a mighty river; all eyes were on the battlements. That was their target. That was where they were headed.

'What are they up to?' Girgandor's expression was one of disbelief. 'Have they got invisible ladders?'

The ghaist was motionless in the middle of the army's flow, still holding the burning vessels. Then it hurled them towards the fortress.

It did not surprise Balyndar that the burning amphorae made it all the way to the base of the gates, but they broke at the foot and their blazing fire spread over the stone.

As soon as the petroleum and small amount of pitch had burned away, the flames went out. There was never any danger of the granite being affected. Granite was used to higher temperatures than that. The black smoke drifted away north with the remains of the fog.

'Exterminate the scum!' Balyndar commanded and the catapults released their deadly barrage as soon as Girgandor gave the signal. *I wish we had our 'dragons'.*

Just as Balyndar had envisaged it, the liquid fire burned holes and corridors through the throng. At one stroke, a catapulted projectile could fell dozens of them, before rolling on and crushing countless others. The grey of the rocks gradually turned red or black or green, depending on what kind of blood had flowed in the veins of the fallen. Fragments and lumps of victims were tossed high into the air.

'They don't scream,' Girgandor shouted against the noise of the catapults that were being constantly reloaded to send out more death and destruction. 'What are they on? What've they been dosed with to make them walk into annihilation as if they had no will of their own? How can they not react?'

They are out of their minds. Balyndar had no explanation. Even dwarves yelled and bellowed when they were burned. Or they shouted the name of Vraccas to give each other courage to face and defeat the enemy. 'They don't seem to care what happens to them.' An old saying had it that these were the most dangerous of opponents – the ones who didn't care. 'Open up the sluices and get the clinker and hot water ready.'

Balyndar climbed up onto the wall, holding on with one hand so as not to be blown off by the wind. He could see the horde was pressing closer together. The pressure was breaking the bones of those forced together at the front. There was a smell of blood. Soldiers were dying at his feet although not under direct attack from the fort. The catapults were aimed further back at the great mass of the army advancing towards the gates.

'It's not stopping,' Girgandor called. 'The more the fog retreats, the more of them there seem to be.'

What kind of general wastes soldiers in such a senseless way, even if they do seem so unsuited for battle? It occurred to Balyndar that this was no more than a rehearsal for the main attack. The true adversary had not yet emerged and might well be watching proceedings through a telescope in safety far away from the fatalities. *He'll be gathering knowledge about our defences and our weaponry.*

They had never made a secret of the weapons they deployed. The information was of little use to an attacker. The dwarves reloaded swiftly and there was practically no end to their stock of ammunition. It would be many an orbit of a siege before the fortress began to run out of arrows, spears and petroleum.

Is that the intention? They want us to waste our resources? Standing on the wall, Balyndar looked along the approach road to the north. *Is that where a more dangerous army is waiting?*

'They're making a ramp out of their own bodies,' Girgandor observed. 'Look! They're scrambling over each other to get over the top, like red-handed cave crabs.'

In Balyndar's opinion this was not a technique promising any success. The battlements were a good hundred paces above ground level. *We will have swept them away long before they get near.* He realised the ragged bunch of monsters, starving humans and miscellaneous creatures were heaping themselves up with extraordinary rapidity and the peak of the wobbling tower was near the middle of the gates. It seemed like a living forest creeper or the arm of an octopus, jerking its way ever upwards.

'I've not been served crabs for some time,' was his response to Girgandor's comment. 'You know, there are far fewer of them in the mill ponds nowadays.' He gave the signal for the liquid slack to be released onto the attackers.

A bugle sounded.

The huge cauldron was ten paces in diameter and kept heated on the next level down from where Balyndar stood. It was now slowly tipped by means of pulleys and chains and the contents were poured into various distribution channels.

The bubbling, melted slack, the waste-product of iron making, surged down through the openings, swamping the growing mound of assailants as if they were troublesome vermin. The trembling tower of bodies collapsed and disintegrated, falling at the same rate as the burning slack. Steam and smoke rose up, making it impossible for the dwarves to see what was happening. There was a terrible smell of burning flesh.

Balyndar expected screams but still heard nothing apart from the hiss of the falling slack, the sound of the chains unrolling and the constant hum of arrows flying to their targets. *I still wish we had the 'dragons'. They have a far greater range than our catapults.*

He turned his eyes to the gateway road and was amazed at what he saw.

The army had gathered all the boulders and stones the fortress had bombarded them with and they were using these to form a more stable ramp; it looked like the beginnings of a bridge. It was already forty paces high and ten in length, but it was too far distant to be any threat.

'Concentrate the heavy catapults on this attempt of theirs to build a ramp,' Girgandor ordered, laughing. 'They're not doing badly, given the conditions. But they're too far off. Bad planning.'

But this time Balyndar was convinced the whole thing was a trial run. The army was working out its techniques, and seeing how quickly the fallen projectiles could be transformed into a construction. They were not concerned about aesthetics. It had to be high. It had to be fast.

'Forget the bridge,' he countermanded. 'Let's get these monsters burned to cinders. Then we can send out troops later to demolish their work. I'm not leaving all that material in their hands.' Balyndar was determined to completely wipe out the attackers.

There was something happening underneath the bridge. The creatures were working together to construct a kind of seesaw affair out of planks tied together. One end was pointing upward underneath the bridge.

And on the other end . . .

'By Vraccas, don't tell me there's *two* of them!' Girgandor had seen the two copper-helmeted figures on the lower end of the seesaw. 'Give it all you've got!' Balyndar shouted, narrowing his eyes. 'Drown them in petroleum and send them a sea of burning pitch!'

The long steel barrels swung round, and even the largest of the heavy-duty catapult platforms moved quickly thanks to ball bearings. The crews swiftly accommodated their new targets.

The attackers had not been idle: the front half of the bridge-ramp was broken off by a band of beasts and the rubble that ensued fell directly on to the higher end of the seesaw, forcing it abruptly downwards and sending the two magic ghaists hurtling into the air as projectiles. Half an eye's blink later and both ramp and seesaw contraption had disappeared in the devastating storm of fire and rock. *Too late*. Balyndar gauged the trajectory of the two giant figures. 'Their momentum will be sufficient,' he muttered. Jumping down from the parapet wall, he drew Keenfire.

'Watch out,' he called to the guards, alerting them to the attack. 'They're coming down now!'

'They'll smash themselves to smithereens when they hit the deck,' said Girgandor. 'Idiots.'

'No, they know exactly what they're doing.' Balyndar lifted the axe. 'They can only be destroyed through great heat. Had you forgotten?'

'They're flying . . . nearly one hundred . . .' the other dwarf started to reply.

Then the first of the ghaists landed feet-first onto one of the catapults, splitting the heavy hurling-arm beam. The half with the counterweight plummeted down and the half with the basket attached crashed on to the fortifications, crushing several dwarves.

The gigantic warrior landed on the walkway with a dull snort, some thirty paces from Balyndar.

The other ghaist flew right over the parapet wall.

The steel barrels followed his arc and long tails of light from the burning earthenware pots painted the sky, but none of them hit their target. Whether or not it was intentional, the creature managed not to hit any obstruction and landed behind the massive portal. As it landed, the impact caused the granite to splinter, and cracks spread throughout the courtyard. The figure itself had sustained no damage to legs or spine.

'By Vraccas!' Girgandor yelled out commands but the catapult crew had to stop firing because their own forces were now crowding the area.

The ghaist in the yard stood up and – not even looking back to the parapet – raced for the entrance to the Grey Mountains and the Fifthling realm. It thrust attacking dwarves aside and was unaffected by the barrage of axes, morningstars and war clubs.

'Close the inner gate!' But Balyndar's order came too late. The ghaist had already dived into the tunnels, disappearing from sight.

With a curse, Balyndar turned his attention to the other ghaist. 'I shan't let you through!' He ignored the fact that his opponent could just leap down.

With his axe raised, Balyndar rushed forward, ready to deliver a mighty stroke. 'Let's see whether Keenfire has fire enough to strip the runes off your helmet,' he shouted. 'I bet it will have.'

It looked as though the ghaist was up for the challenge.

There was a white glow behind the copper mask's eye slits. The being did not waver or step aside.

Balyndar had nearly reached the foe. He uttered an ear-splitting battle cry, swung round and struck hard at the copper helmet. The diamonds on the axe's blade awoke with a blaze of light.

Note to self:

- *Use thimin root extract to write up parts of the Shameful Script. That way only älfar eyes will be able to read my true opinion and the real facts.*
- *Find some thimin root. Very little of it around in Idoslane.*
- *Source some needles, too fine to be noticed when they enter the flesh. Mallenia and all the others who deserve to die will carry the mark so any älf will know who to aim at first.*

Secret notes for
The Writings of Truth
written under duress by Carmondai

XII

Girdlegard
Kingdom of Tabaîn
6492nd solar cycle, late autumn

On the estate belonging to Tabaîn's abdicated ruler, Phenîlas was seated on the generously proportioned roof terrace of the square stone building, where he had a good view over the surrounding fields and the low-growing fruit trees. A canvas canopy protected him from the strong heat of the autumn sun.

The upholstered armchair was comfortable, and the silk garment he wore under his leather armour kept him pleasantly cool. His host was taking his time, it seemed: the platform lift that had taken the elf to the roof terrace was still waiting at ground level. Servants proffered fresh fruit, tea and various sweetmeats.

With the taste of the wonderful fire apples still on his tongue, Phenîlas tried to make sense of the sensational changes that Girdlegard had recently undergone, not least the now widely-publicised gift of land that Mallenia had mystifyingly agreed to make. He had attended Dirisa's coronation celebrations in Wheattown and had somehow been appointed the official representative for the Naishïon and the whole elf race.

Natenian and Dirisa had put on a stupendous spectacle for the occasion, first at the temple and then on the steps of the public square where thousands of well-wishers had gathered. In their speeches they made reference to the heroism shown by Raikan and his troops. At this, Phenîlas expressed deep regret and sympathy.

After that Natenian explained how fragile his health had become and how he could never hope to fill the gap left by his brother. Therefore, he was thus choosing to abdicate, and no one was more suitable to replace him on the throne than Dirisa.

Then the incredible happened: the crowd was *ecstatic*.

What Phenîlas had feared did not come to pass. There was no unruly behaviour, no rebellious rumbling, no defiant insults, and nobody chucked eggs or rotten fruit at the new monarch. One or two aristocratic faces showed incomprehension at Natenian's choice, but as long as the people were so taken with the new queen, there was little point in objecting.

In the council session that followed, Phenîlas made it clear that the Naishïon endorsed the new appointment and offered Dirisa the hand of friendship – this was intended as a warning to anyone planning to withhold cooperation. By then Natenian had withdrawn; he didn't appear again until after the coronation.

So it was all the more surprising, Phenîlas found, that he had been invited to Natenian's estate. There was nothing to discuss. Natenian no longer had any say in events touching Girdlegard.

What does he want? Sheer curiosity had brought Phenîlas here to the terrace, where he waited with his tea, fruit and biscuits.

The sound of cogwheels clanking announced the arrival of the lift.

Phenîlas replaced the apple he had been about to eat and stood up to greet the man who was now simply one of the nobles of the land, a noble born of a line of kings. Historians would mention his name only briefly and then he would be forgotten. *And no one would know that he had his own brother murdered.*

Phenîlas bowed slightly as the crooked man in the wheaten yellow robe approached, gasping.

The invalid made his own way over on two crutches without help, then let his misshapen body fall into the specially-designed chair. He was brought pieces of fruit and juice in a precious goblet. He dismissed the servants.

'Go downstairs,' he ordered them.

Phenîlas saw them exchange surprised glances and hesitate.

'But, sire,' one of them started to object. 'We . . .'

'Go. Even if I am no longer king, you owe me obedience,' Natenian berated them, brushing sweaty locks from his brow.

The servants retreated to the platform lift. Again, the cogs and chains clanked.

At first Natenian took no notice of the elf. He used his crutch to bring certain dishes closer and bits of food fell on the table or the floor. He tried all the dishes with obvious enjoyment, then closed his eyes, giving little moans of delight.

Phenîlas cleared his throat and drank some water. *My time is too precious to waste watching him guzzle.* He was carrying the contract between Tabaîn and the elf realm that the Naishïon was so keen to receive; another reason for haste was the weather. Dark clouds were gathering in the east. As the warm air rose from the harvested fields, thunderstorms and tornados were always likely. This was why Tabaîn's citizens built their houses out of heavy blocks of stone. A lone elf on horseback would be swept away by the high winds. *I should set off now.*

'You're wondering why you are here.' Natenian's mouth and chin were covered in juice and smothered in crumbs.

'Exactly.'

The nobleman pointed at the plates and dishes. 'My physicians have been forbidding me all these delicacies. Apparently they weaken me. And I was supposed to stay alive for a long time to rule over Tabaîn.' He placed a reddish-hued gooseberry in his mouth, spurting out juice as he bit into it. 'I was a good monarch and would have been a better one than Raikan or Dirisa.'

'All the more reason for my Naishïon to appreciate how you have abdicated to ensure peace for your land.'

Natenian laughed out loud. 'I still don't understand what I was thinking of. I can hardly believe it, and yet strangely, it feels somehow right. Unreal but right.' He belched and selected another piece of cake.

'And now you can enjoy these things without worrying about how they will affect your lifespan,' Phenîlas continued the train of thought. *This is a known trait of human behaviour.*

'I was your ally once, elf,' Natenian went on, licking his fingers clean. 'I entered into a pre-contractual agreement and sacrificed my own brother and his companions for the welfare of my kingdom. What am I left with?' He indicated the stubble in the harvested fields. 'Grain that doesn't belong to me.' His saliva-damp finger pointed at the fruit trees. 'And fruit that will kill me if I eat it. A fantastic life, isn't it?' He slapped himself on the chest with his right hand. 'What a good thing I am healthy and in excellent physical shape. Otherwise I'd have nothing,' he said with a bitter laugh.

'I am certain my master will compensate you for your losses.'

'How can he? My actions would only have been worthwhile if I were continuing to rule Tabaîn,' Natenian whispered sharply. 'I've got a heap of rubbish, that's all. No, I've got a heap of shit.' He grabbed the bowl of gooseberries and hurled it over the edge of the terrace in a fit of temper. 'Shit!' Cakes, apples and flagons of juice followed in the wake of the gooseberries, while the demented monarch kept swearing.

Phenîlas got up. He did not want to risk getting fruit juice stains on his expensive silk garments. 'You can shout and swear and throw your food around just as well without my help.' He nodded, taking his leave. 'I must go. My Naishïon is waiting for me.'

With immense effort, Natenian forced himself up onto his crooked legs, supporting himself by holding on to the corner of the table.

'You were my downfall. *You* were the death of my brother,' he said darkly. 'And I can see not even the faintest gleam of remorse in your eyes and on your arrogant face. You have perfected this game of intrigue at others' cost.'

'It's about something more important than merely the life of kings,' Phenîlas countered. 'I would have gone further than that to secure my own people's survival.'

'Blood wheat!' Natenian shouted in his outrage. 'It is blood wheat your elves will be eating. May it distend their stomachs and may their guts explode. May they all die.' He staggered along the length of the table, gripping the wood for support. 'This is my curse.'

'That would be the end for more than just my own people.' Phenîlas moved slowly back towards the lift platform.

'Stay here and listen to my accusations!' the former regent lunged at Phenîlas, but the latter turned adeptly, so that Natenian's sticky fingers only brushed the elf's silken collar.

Damn! He's ruined my shirt. 'If you live to see it, you'll understand my words. We shall make the writings of the Creator public when the due time comes. I am not at liberty to tell you when that will be.' He pointed at the half-demolished piles of fruit and fragments of cake. 'Although by then maybe you'll have stuffed yourself with everything that is bad for you and you'll be dead.' With an impatient gesture he tugged at his own collar and frowned at the obvious marks.

Natenian lowered his head and the strands of his brown hair now looked black. 'I don't know how you can live with it.' He looked down at his fingers with their juice stains from the berries.

The elf smiled blandly. 'Find yourself a drug that'll give you sweet dreams. Let my master know what you have in mind as compensation for the throne you have given up.' He turned and went to the lift. *What a pointless meeting. I still don't know why he wanted to see me.*

'Tell your Naishïon that his betrayal will cost him dear,' the old man called after his retreating figure.

Phenîlas was tempted to stop and advise him not to threaten the elf realm, but after a short hesitation, he continued on his way. The disempowered king needed to vent his anger and hurt and feelings that he had been the victim of treachery. *He would understand if he knew Sitalia's writings.* 'Have some more berries if they're so bad for you. And eat them fast.'

There was no response.

When Phenîlas had reached the lift shaft with its heavy stone-flagged cover, he touched the activator with his foot. This alerted staff inside the house and the grinding of cogs and gears began. The next sound, however, was a dull thud from behind him.

The elf turned back to Natenian.

But the man had disappeared; shouts of dismay were heard. Natenian had thrown himself over the edge of the terrace. *It seems he thought it would take too long for the fruit to kill him.*

A bell rang, the shaft cover opened and two servants arrived with the platform. They stared at him aghast. Their eyes travelled down to the marks on his collar tabs. *The fingermark stains.* The elf realised just what picture the scene presented: the broken crockery, the shouts, the crutches leaning against the table, and the nobleman himself lying in a heap in the courtyard – everything pointed to a violent struggle.

And murder.

Girdlegard
United Kingdom of Gauragar-Idoslane
Gauragar
6492nd solar cycle, early winter

'How far still to go?'

Gosalyn drew in her breath in exasperation on hearing Beligata's nervous question. It must have been the fourth time that orbit.

'We'll be there soon,' she threw back the answer over her shoulder, getting a mouthful of snowflakes for her pains. 'Tomorrow at the latest.'

Hargorin grunted agreement and silence fell once more as the little band of dwarves continued on their way through Girdlegard on the secret mission directed by the High King.

Their first destination lay to the south, in the Blue Mountains.

To get there they had to get through Gauragar and then attempt the crossing of the desert kingdom of Sangpûr. They were all three dreading that. The soft hills of sand often shifted position and one could sink down and disappear in the dunes. Forbidding stretches of bare hot scree where nothing grew offered no shelter from the pitiless sun. Nights would be cold and there would be no fuel for a fire to warm them.

But for now they were still riding through Gauragar.

Winters here in the southern region adjoining the Sangpûr border were milder and kinder than those the mountain dwarves were accustomed to. So Hargorin, Beligata and Gosalyn had not bothered with cumbersome furs and had made do with lined cloaks worn over their doublets and chainmail. They were too hot more often than they were cold. But they presented an odd picture to the locals in their flimsy get-up as they passed through the towns and villages, trotting southward-bound on their ponies.

And they call this cold. Gosalyn was tickled at the thought. *Not even an infant dwarf would be shivering in this weather.* Anyone who had ever stood keeping watch at a dwarf festival knew the biting winds that put icicles in your beard; they made you feel like your eyeballs were freezing over or your limbs were about to shatter.

What the Gauragarian winter was offering was more like late autumn. Hargorin, riding out in front, headed for a thatched farmhouse a little way back from the road. The border town of Blackground was only four miles away but the dwarf seemed to have a reason for diverting from the main route.

'What's the matter?' asked Gosalyn. 'You hungry?'

'The pony's going lame. I think he needs shoeing. Talek's done well so far and I don't want to overdo it with him. We've a long journey ahead of us and he has to know I appreciate him.' Hargorin and Gosalyn heard the clearly audible groan.

The two Fifthlings declined to comment on Beligata's attitude. She had been complaining ever since they set out. She did not like the pace of progress, she did not like the route chosen and she did not agree with decisions about when and where to stop for rests. *If she makes one more remark, I'll confront her.*

They reached the farm.

Hargorin indicated that Gosalyn should dismount and knock. Though they were far enough south that there was less likelihood any of the locals would recognise the red-bearded one-time delegate of the Black Squadron, a female dwarf face would ensure a better reception. Gosalyn stomped through the mounds of heavy, wet snow. This was not a bit like the soft flakes that fell in the mountains.

A couple of loud knocks on the wooden door brought a response. The door opened a crack and a wrinkled, stubbly masculine face appeared. He looked out at the wrong level at first, over Gosalyn's head.

'Oh, so there you are,' the old man giggled, looking down. His teeth were yellow and misaligned and his breath smelt of food and red wine. 'Three Children of Vraccas. Looking for somewhere to stay the night.' Sulphur-coloured hair hung thin across his pate.

Gosalyn nodded. 'Would you have somewhere for us?'

A gouty finger emerged and pointed at the barn. 'Over there. You can sleep in the barn. It's warm there. I'll send you over some food.' And the door slammed shut.

Hospitality of sorts. The long'uns are full of surprises.

'I suppose that was a no?' Beligata called. She was already turning her pony.

'No.' Gosalyn jogged over. 'He said we could stay in the barn.'

The scar-faced dwarf-woman corrected her pony's direction and headed for the attached stables.

'Well done,' Hargorin said. 'Do you think he'd let me use his forge?'

Oh dear. Gosalyn knocked once more.

The door opened again, just a little. 'What is it?'

'Can we use your forge? We need to fix a horseshoe.' She couldn't see the man through the slit. *Strange behaviour.*

'Since when do dwarves wear horseshoes?' croaked the old man, opening the door a little wider and handing out a tray with black bread, some cheese and smoked meat. 'Here you are. Sure, you can use it but don't burn the place down.'

And the door slammed shut again.

Wonder what'd happen if I knocked again. She grinned. *Best not try. Or I might have to give the food back.*

'That's a nice welcome,' Hargorin said with a grimace. He took the reins of Gosalyn's pony and led it over to the barn while the dwarf-woman carried the food.

Beligata had already opened up the stable door and ridden in. There was a loud moo and the smell of cattle steamed out into the air. The vicinity of the animals would warm them in the hayloft.

Gosalyn quickly lit the petroleum lamp that hung on one of the pillars. The three tethered their ponies at the back of the stable, keeping them apart from the poorly-tended cows with their dangerously long horns. It was not a given that herd animals would be friendly to other beasts.

A cow would be no substitute for a pony. Gosalyn tried to picture Beligata riding a long-horned cow, bouncing up and down on its curved back. The thought made her laugh.

The cattle were starting to settle and the ponies fed on the dried grass. Gosalyn unsaddled them and rubbed them down, while Hargorin made for the little forge.

Beligata sat up in the hayloft, letting her legs dangle over the edge, melted snow dripping from her boots, as she watched what Gosalyn was doing. 'Do you think we'll find anything at all in the magus' writings?' She sounded doubtful as to the outcome of their mission.

This put Gosalyn into a bad mood. 'Why else would the High King have sent us out?'

'Because he doesn't know what else to do?' Beligata stared at the roof supports. 'Bad construction, this. He'll lose his thatch the next time there's a big storm. The wires are loose.'

'Why not mend it? It could be our way of thanking him.'

'Do I look like an artisan?'

'You're a Freeling, aren't you? You people can do anything,' was Gosalyn's acid reply, referencing the fact that the warrior woman actually belonged to the Thirdling tribe.

'I can do more than you can, that's for sure,' said Beligata, taking up the gauntlet. 'It wouldn't be hard to beat you.'

Gosalyn raised her head slowly. 'Beat me? At what?'

Acting innocent, the dark-haired dwarf-woman swung her legs faster, making some of the hay fall down; the light of challenge shone in her light-coloured eyes. 'It doesn't matter. Anything. You choose and I'll win. I'll wipe the floor with you.'

Gosalyn laughed and went on grooming the ponies. 'Sure.'

'Are you waiting to be told what to do?'

'I'm not playing your game. The High King told us our mission is to get to the Blue Mountains and give his wife a message. We also have to look at Lot-Ionan's sketches and plans to see if there are any indications of other magic sources in Girdlegard.'

'I was stood right next to you when he said that,' Beligata crowed, sticking a dried flower stem between her teeth and flicking it up and down, sending petals everywhere. 'But we'd need an expert to understand the books. Or are you any good with magic formulae and the secret language of a magus? That is, *if* the writings still actually exist and haven't been destroyed ages ago by the Secondlings.'

The Secondling dwarves had been obliged to cleanse their homeland from the influence of the magus. It was extremely unlikely they would have treated the books with care if that was where all the evil had started.

Then she pointed out, 'Can you see the Scholar anywhere?'

'No,' said Gosalyn, controlling her anger.

Beligata spat the flower out. 'He should have come with us.'

'Tungdil needs rest. Have you seen how many scars he has?' Gosalyn went to the next pony and took a couple of handfuls of fresh straw to rub it down with. 'He must have gone through appalling experiences in the last two hundred and fifty cycles.' She thought back to that night under the shelter of the tree when she'd seen his upper body naked as they sat together at the fireside. *Plenty of pain for body and soul.*

'Exactly the same as the other Tungdil.' Beligata gave a harsh laugh. 'There's probably a mould in some smithy back in Phondrasôn for turning out Tungdils. New one each cycle, I shouldn't wonder. Wake them up, breathe magic into them and send them to us.' She stopped swinging her legs. 'But he would still be useful.' Gosalyn had been thinking during the journey along much the same lines.

'I agree with you.' The brown-haired Fifthling rubbed the pony's back. 'We could do with having him along.'

'If we don't find the books and we don't find any clues – or even any records and sketches' – Beligata went on – 'what then?'

'Then we carry on searching.'

'What for? Searching for the source or for Coïra?'

'Both.' Gosalyn was wishing Hargorin would come back. The veteran soldier would know better than she would and could explain things. *He could make Beligata shut up*. 'If you don't think we can succeed, I don't see why you came.' She looked up at the Freeling.

'I obey the High King. Well, almost.' Beligata grinned and reached between the hay bales at her side. To Gosalyn's surprise, she drew out and brandished Bloodthirster. 'And anyway, I want a chance to try out this beauty.'

'Where did you get that?'

The scar-faced dwarf-woman laughed at her. 'I took it, showed it to the High King and he . . . let me have it.'

'I don't believe you!'

'He did express it slightly differently, I admit,' Beligata said. 'But he can't really object.' She laid the weapon across her knees. 'Finders-keepers. And I'm looking forward to slicing some beast in half with it. Bloodthirster's said to be able to do that.'

What recklessness. Vraccas must have hewn her ancestors from particularly rebellious stone. Gosalyn exhaled sharply. 'Does Hargorin have any idea that you're doing your own thing here?'

'No. And it makes no difference. I'm keeping it.' Beligata laid the weapon lovingly onto the ground at her side. 'I wonder if there are still any monsters in the Blue Mountains? Do you think the Secondlings eliminated them all? People say the gate was open for quite a time when Lot-Ionan was in charge. Perhaps there'll be one of those nice little freaks mooching around in the valleys for me to kill.'

Gosalyn moved to tend the last of the ponies. 'There are hardly any more beasts. You won't need that terrible blade.'

'What if the elves attack?'

Gosalyn rolled her blue-brown eyes. 'The elves are glad we're keeping the gates closed.'

'That's not what I mean.' Beligata cut herself a slice of cheese the farmer had given them. 'They could have captured the maga. Maybe they're lying to us. As soon as they hear we're looking for Coïra, they might think they need to get rid of us.'

'If you could give me *one*' – Gosalyn held up one straw – 'very, very good reason why and how the elves would have put a maga in chains, then you'll have won.'

Beligata grinned and bit into her cheese. 'I'll have a think.' She chewed. 'There's that elf they're holding in Wheattown for murdering Natenian.'

'What's that got to do with the maga?' The dwarves had picked up the news about the events following the coronation on their journey. Dirisa had to keep the suspect in prison until investigations were complete. This was infuriating both the Tabaîn population and the elves' supreme leader. 'That's only just happened and Coïra's been missing for ages.'

'Hang on! I've got something better.' Beligata waved her free hand to and fro. 'The united elf state must not be endangered in any way. Who could stop them? Human soldiers? Hardly.' She lifted one finger. 'Here's your answer: Coïra. She is the only one powerful enough to oppose Ataimînas. If they eliminate *her,* the elves can do anything they want. Apart from here in our dwarf regions.' She wiggled her finger triumphantly. 'And who's won the argument, do you think?'

'Coïra went to Ilahín and his spouse Fiëa as a friend and ally,' Gosalyn objected, only to earn raucous laughter.

'You know how quickly things can change.' Now her voice lost its mocking tone. 'Combat comrades can become enemies.'

She lifted Bloodthirster again, pointing its tip to the roof. 'That can happen in the very midst of battle.' Her features took on a cruel tinge. 'Take Hargorin and me: we're both Thirdlings. Known as the *dwarf-haters*, heirs to Lorimbur,' she hissed. 'And you, Gosalyn? What are you?'

'Your king declared the feud was over. And anyway, you call yourself a Freeling.'

'My tribal designation doesn't have anything to do with how I feel.' Beligata frowned down at Gosalyn. 'Perhaps I left the tribe so I wouldn't have to renounce the feud.' She was speaking quietly, her voice merciless. 'Quite a few Thirdlings did the same.' At this the scar on Beligata's face opened, releasing deep red blood that trickled down her cheek like a stream of dark tears.

Gosalyn swallowed hard. She wasn't afraid for her own safety, being a hardened fighter who knew how to defend herself, but Beligata's words sounded plausible. *Our own unity is at stake.*

Noticing the trickle of blood, Beligata wiped it away and pressed her hand on the scar. 'We call ourselves . . .' she began, bending forward, but then the stable door slammed shut with a crash.

Both the dwarf women were startled, eyes turned to the doorway.

Good thing he's come back, thought Gosalyn.

But there was no sign of Hargorin. It must have been the wind. The girls looked at each other questioningly. Without voicing their concerns, both of them were worried that their leader had been out so long.

'I'll go and check on him,' Gosalyn said. 'Perhaps he's having trouble with his leg.'

'And a warrior like him wouldn't be able to sort himself

out or call for help?' Beligata slid over to the edge of the hayloft platform and got ready to jump down. Her scar had stopped bleeding. 'I'll come with you. We don't know who else might be in the house with the old fellow.'

This was fine by Gosalyn. She turned to go out, loosening the fastening of her short axe. 'I didn't hear any voices, but you're right.' *And it'll divert her attention from this stupid challenge she thinks she's won.*

When she reached the door she still hadn't heard the sound of Beligata landing in the soft straw.

'What's the matter? Scared?' She looked back over her shoulder.

There was no dwarf-woman up in the hayloft and there was no sign that anyone had jumped into the pile of straw on the floor.

Gosalyn drew her weapon and moved cautiously sideways, her back to the brick wall, the better to look up at the loft and roof beams. *If this is some kind of a joke . . .*

From nowhere a long, shadowy shape sprang down from one of the horizontal beams, landing silently in front of her. The figure brandished Bloodthirster and slowly pointed its tip at her. Everyone in Girdlegard knew the face – old for an älf – with the branding marks on the cheeks.

It must be that Carmondai person. Gosalyn raised her weapon determinedly. 'I don't care if you're the queen's pet lapdog, black-eyes. I'm going to hammer you to shreds if you've hurt my friends.'

The älf directed a superior smile at her. 'I am no longer the property of the Ido queen. I freed myself.'

He sprang overhead to the side wall and launched himself off, landing on one of the beams and merging back into the shadows. The lamp went out and the stable was pitch black.

'You're welcome to kill me,' came a disembodied voice; then Gosalyn received a sharp push to the back of the knees, sending her face first to the straw-covered ground. A foot was placed on her wrist, preventing her from using her axe. 'That's if you can, of course.' The voice was at her ear now. A cold blade touched the nape of her neck. 'But I think I've won. Wouldn't you say so?'

Girdlegard
Grey Mountains
Kingdom of the Fifthling dwarves
Stone Gateway
6492nd solar cycle, autumn

Balyndar aimed the glowing diamond blade of Keenfire at the copper helmet in which the banned souls lay magically imprisoned, keeping the freakish being alive.

The ghaist shot up an arm in self-defence. Instead of attempting to block the blow by grabbing the axe handle, the creature seemed to be relying on its own indestructible nature. It was futile – the weapon swept through the limb, meeting no resistance. The giant creature recognised its mistake too late and tried to step back, bending its neck to keep the helmet out of the range of the diamond-encrusted axe blade.

'You shan't escape!' Balyndar had aimed with skill, having included this possible reaction in his calculations. *Perish as all evil perishes when struck by this weapon.*

The glowing gem-encrusted edge crashed into the polished amber metal, making a dent and creating several individual holes that merged into a single cut. There was a noise like steam escaping from a pressurised boiler. With a screaming hiss, a dazzling white stream gushed straight up into the air.

The air smelt of melting metal and burning stone as the ghaist staggered around. The souls that had been so abruptly freed shot upwards in a surge of fiery sparks.

Balyndar raised Keenfire once more. *Was one blow sufficient?*

He made sure he did not come into contact with the stream of escaping souls. The myths about the weapon held that it would protect whoever wielded it against any spell – this he knew from the battlefield – but what he was confronting here was an entirely new form of energy born of the Outer Lands. He would take no chances.

The shrill whistling sound grew stronger as the pressure increased.

The giant creature laid a hand over the opening in the helmet, but its fingers were torn off by the strength of the light-stream. The helmet started to glow and the white spell runes melted together.

If it was good enough against a demon, it should be good enough for this thing! Balyndar leaped forward, intending to slice the helmet through with a powerful horizontal blow, allowing the banned souls a swifter departure. 'For Vraccas!'

But before the blade even touched the magic creature, there was an explosion that burst the helmet wide open, sending shrapnel in all directions; the ear-splitting bang was followed by a pressure wave that swept over all the dwarves on the battlements.

Balyndar felt several metal splinters hit his helmet and chainmail. Keenfire could not shield him from the force of the detonation: it was only effective against magic and this was pure energy.

The fortress captain was lifted up like a leaf in the wind and whirled through the air. Many of his soldiers were also caught up in the tornado, and ownerless weapons, shields and parts of the catapults were flying around. All he could hear was the echo of the explosion. Balyndar stumbled and blundered in a spiralling cloud of debris. Now it was the stronghold beneath him, now the sky, and finally the fortress walkway again. He crashed down onto the battlements. Landing on his back, all the breath thumped out of him, he dropped Keenfire. He heard a crack and hot pain raced up his back. He had broken something.

Before he could assess the damage or grab his weapon, there was a bolt of lightning. He threw himself onto his front and instinctively jammed his helmet on tight, just as a wave of heat rolled over him. It was as if a god had tipped a huge furnace crucible over the fortress walls. Holding his breath to stop his lungs from burning, he prayed to Vraccas that his clothing wouldn't catch fire. He could already smell his hair singeing. And he seemed to have gone deaf.

As soon as the heat let up, he raised his head to see what had happened and to gauge the extent of the damage.

He was now lying at the other end of the walkway, close to the tower by the gate hinges. Where the ghaist had been, the granite-block wall had been blasted away, leaving an opening two paces deep and ten paces long. The battlements had been demolished in that section and none of the machines were intact.

Many dwarves must have been hurled off the top of the gates; Balyndar could only see a few guards. Some lay under rubble or had been fatally injured by flying debris. It would look no different on the western side.

The metal wolf-cages had withstood the blast but they

were glowing. What remained of the animals was grotesquely deformed, their bones broken and sticking out through burned fur. No survivors.

The ghaist has been exterminated.

As the pain from his injuries hit, Balyndar uttered a loud cry that to his own ears was almost inaudible. With a great effort and the last of his strength, he pulled his axe over and used it to help him get to his feet. He leaned against the wall to look over and see what had happened to the attacking army.

It seemed catapults and spear-throwing machines had done their work well before the devastating explosion had occurred. The road up to the gates was ablaze, and with it, the remains of the tattered rag-tag army had burned to ashes. The ramp they had erected had collapsed.

Balyndar sent a prayer of thanks up to Vraccas. He looked straight down at the outer gates, seeing nothing but smouldering flesh, bones and clothing.

He cried out in pain again, then bit down on his lower lip. He knew he was bleeding from several small, but deep, wounds where the copper fragments had torn into his body. He was about to lose consciousness and his vision blurred.

'Over there! There he is! Quick, get the healers up here!' He could just hear Girgandor's voice, but it was indistinct. 'You're alive! Vraccas be praised!' A hazy outline of a figure approached.

Before Balyndar collapsed he thought he had seen something marked where the gates met. It could have been the point the man at the topmost point of the living ramp had reached before being crushed by the scalding pitch.

'They've . . . marked it,' he whispered to Girgandor, tasting blood on his burnt lips. 'On the outside . . . they've marked how high they got.'

'I'll go and check,' his deputy promised. 'You killed it! A miracle! We've sent scouts to hunt down the other ghaist.'

Balyndar gave a sigh of near despair as his senses started to leave him. He had forgotten about the second ghaist.

Nobody will be able to stop it without Keenfire. Evil was making its way through the Grey Mountains into the heart of Girdlegard. *And I'm just lying here.* In confusion he tried to struggle up but Girgandor restrained him. 'Get the dragons. We need them. We . . .'

It was no use. Everything had gone black.

Girdlegard
United Kingdom of Gauragar-Idoslane
Gauragar
6492nd solar cycle, early winter

Gosalyn knew which blade it was that she could feel pressing against the nape of her bare neck.

All she could think about was the fact that this sword was being deployed once again by an älf against a dwarf, for the first time in many cycles. And that she had Beligata to thank for it. She was about to die by a stroke from Bloodthirster.

Face down in the straw, she waited for the fatal blow that would extinguish the fire in her life-forge and send her to the Eternal Smithy to be reunited with friends and forebears.

'Your two companions are still alive,' Carmondai whispered in her ear. 'I have merely put them out of action so you don't all attack me at once when I have shown myself.'

'You're going to let us live?'

'Of course. What use are your crooked bones to me?' He

laughed and removed the tip of the weapon from her skin. 'Just a joke. I'm not in the mood for bone-sculpting.'

Gosalyn reviewed the situation. Since he hadn't killed her he must have some other aim. *Taking hostages?* Surely not. They weren't important enough.

The letter to Boïndil's wife? Hardly.

The knowledge from Lot-Ionan's books? Gosalyn pushed herself up to sitting among the straw. 'Where are my friends?' She looked at the älf who was wearing a long black mantle over simple dark-coloured clothing. Although his skull bore only stubble and his thin face had lost much of its beauty due to the branding, he still had an impressive aura of distinction. It had nothing to do with fear.

The lamp regained its brightness.

'I've tied Hargorin to the anvil. Beligata will wake up sooner or later with her mouth full of hay.' Carmondai held Bloodthirster like a seasoned warrior. She could tell the älf was capable of more than merely writing. Not only had he retained his agility, it was obvious he knew how to wield the blade.

'How do you know our names?'

He gave a friendly smile. 'I have been listening to you for some time. You all seem quite at ease in spite of being on a secret mission for your High King. There could be assassins lurking.'

'Ones like you, black-eyes?'

He sat down cross-legged in the straw so they could look each other comfortably in the eye. 'That's better.' He seemed alert but not on edge. 'I'll talk to you first since you're the most sensible one.'

'I know what is said of you. You can charm anyone with your flattery.'

'No, that's Rodario you mean,' he said with a smile. 'I prefer to use my intellect rather than dazzle. Same as you.' The älf pointed north. 'I had to flee from Oakenburgh because that little girl from the Outer Lands accused me of a deed I did not commit.'

'Well, of course.' Gosalyn made a dismissive gesture. 'We all know your race is famous for being peace-loving.'

'Did I spare your life or didn't I?'

'Only because you want to lull me in a false sense of security and then use me for your own ends.'

Carmondai sighed. 'The celebrated stubbornness of the groundlings.' He sat up straight and rubbed his back. 'I used to find it easy to jump like that.'

The dwarf-woman grinned maliciously. 'You should be glad that you're getting older.'

'I'm not glad yet. Maybe one day.' He looked her over. 'That Outer Lands child has magic powers,' he continued. 'I know what she is and that she has used spells to subject all of Girdlegard's heads of state to her will. Mallenia has given all that land away to the elves, and then there's the weird reconciliation between Dirisa and Natenian. And that's only the beginning. By the time she's older and more powerful, she'll have entire regions under her thumb.' Carmondai inclined his head a little. 'She belonged to the magician families from the Outer Lands who send out the ghaists as scouts.'

'Rubbish!' Gosalyn tried to contradict the älf's words, spoken with such calm clarity. But she remembered what the High King had said about the assassin who had broken in to the council meeting. *He couldn't understand how the älf missed his mark with the child.*

'Ask your ruler. He was in that session recently when sworn enemies were suddenly all hand in hand and best friends.' Carmondai looked at her. 'You will have talked about it. I can see it in your face.'

Gosalyn did not tell him she had been part of the troop that had originally found Sha'taï in the abandoned settlement.

'Can the girl influence an älf, too?' She told Carmondai what had happened during and after the attack at the first Council meeting in Freestone – and was horrified when she saw him nod.

'We do possess an inherent degree of magic that can protect us to a certain extent, but we're not wholly immune,' he said thoughtfully.

'How come she didn't get you under her spell?'

Carmondai nodded again. 'Good question. I think it was because she's not strong enough yet to break my will. I'm too experienced. Simply too old.'

'Like the High King, I suppose.' It slipped out.

'Did she try it with him?'

'He said he felt pins and needles when everyone was praying to the gods and they all held hands. And Sha'taï was standing right in the middle.' Gosalyn had stopped fighting against everything Carmondai was telling her. It all seemed to make sense when she compared it with what her own monarch had said. 'So she wants to take over as ruler.'

'She wants *power* in Girdlegard,' he corrected. 'She's clever enough not to launch a direct attempt. She will put a figure on the throne who thinks he is in charge, but in reality she'll be the one driving him. I think she's planning to use the kings and queens for her own ends until she's strong enough to do it herself.' He slid his hands along Bloodthirster's blade. 'Nobody listened to my warning.'

'Who's going to believe what an älf says?' said Gosalyn.

Carmondai tapped out a little applause on the weapon

with his free hand. 'I need someone people are going to trust, who can rip Sha'taï's mask of cute innocence off.'

'Us, of course!'

'I'm afraid it was the missing maga I was thinking of,' he replied politely. 'You and your friends are looking for her. I'll help you. And between us we'll make sure Girdlegard doesn't fall under yet another yoke of subjugation.'

Gosalyn had to laugh. 'Don't tell me there's such a thing as an *honourable* älf? Never. Inàste and Tion gave you black souls. There's something else you're working towards. Perhaps you're in cahoots with Sha'taï and you're making fools of us.'

'Or perhaps I'm telling the truth, little dwarf. And if so, you'd regret not believing me till the end of your days. And the end of your days would arrive soon enough if you confront that child.'

'What if we don't want to go along with your plan?'

'I'll carry on the search on my own and leave you to your fates. But in my view we'd have a better chance of success if we work together.'

'You'll get no thanks for it.'

'All I want is a pardon.' Carmondai seemed to have a sudden thought. 'Did I mention that I've got a good idea where there might be other magic sources in Girdlegard?' He placed both slender hands on Bloodthirster. 'I don't want to boast, but I've been here for a very long time. There are secrets that only I know.'

Gosalyn hated herself for it but she got up from the straw and headed for the door. 'I'll get Hargorin. I think we can talk him round.' Carmondai smiled at her; it made him look more dangerous than ever. Wielding the black weapon that used to belong to the Inextinguishables, he had tremendous presence. He looked authoritative and dynamic enough to found his own empire.

Gosalyn left to see how the red-haired dwarf was. She would not trust the älf. *No matter how he whispers and flatters.*

And anyway, Hargorin might come storming into the barn to cut the runaway history-teller's head right off.

A dwarf will always avoid long fights and long speeches. It simply takes too much effort.

Dwarf saying

XIII

Girdlegard
United Kingdom of Gauragar-Idoslane
Gauragar, Highstead
6492nd solar cycle, winter

Mallenia was truly delighted to see so many familiar faces in Highstead's temple to Palandiell. The only thing that made her uneasy was her own attire: she was wearing a dress rather than her normal warrior's garb and it made her feel somewhat weak and vulnerable. She noticed the men looking at her in a way they wouldn't have done if she had been wearing armour. *Why do women like to dress like this?*

On this sacred festival-orbit of the goddess, shortly after the winter full moon when night and day were equal, the United Kingdom of Gauragar-Idoslane's contract with the elf realm of Ti Lesîndur was to be finalised, relinquishing possession of a large number of square miles of land to the northeast.

The circular green and white marble form of the consecrated building was highly symbolic. There was a ten-pace tall statue of the goddess at the south side and the walls bore murals depicting the deeds of Palandiell. No benches or chairs were present. The floor was soft raked earth and since it was still warm, plants and flowers decorated the temple. Some wooden planks formed a pathway so that the nobles' shoes stayed clean.

The goddess was portrayed carrying an abundant sheaf of grain in her outstretched right hand and a cornucopia under her left arm. A wreath of grapes and vine leaves crowned her head and golden grass sprouted under her feet. The sculpture was in magnificent white marble left unpainted for the stone's warmth to be admired. She towered over the assembled throng.

Directly in front of Mallenia there were five steps leading to a long, steel altar heaped with gifts and offerings to be burned. The sacrificial stone for the killing of animals was off to one side. Mallenia had issued instructions to the priests that there was to be no blood sacrifice today; she did not consider it appropriate for a gift ceremony.

Apart from Rodario, those present for the ceremony included Dirisa, Astirma and even the oft-absent Isikor. Pomp and circumstance ruled the day and guards lined the walls behind the heads of state in case the älfar made a new assassination attempt.

Mallenia's young protégée Sha'taï was in the middle of the crowd, having chosen to remain with her maid.

The High King of the Dwarves had been invited but had not appeared. It was a shame but it would not spoil the day. It was the elves she was entering into a contract with, not the dwarves. The monarchs and notables stood together with their retainers in the front part of the temple, while three thousand other people gathered in the main body of the building, separated from the proceedings by a row of soldiers. Their reverent and respectful whisperings sounded like the breeze going through a field of corn.

'The temple's full to bursting,' Rodario murmured. He had arranged to have every imaginable colour incorporated in his ceremonial garments, which swamped the skilful tailoring. 'Your subjects are jostling each other out on the square. They're queuing all the way into Highstead's streets.'

'You don't sound very happy about everybody coming along to watch.' Mallenia looked up at the smiling face of the Palandiell statue. The air was full of incense and smouldering herbs; the temple glowed in the sunshine that streamed through the high windows to focus on the form of the goddess.

'There are enough malcontents, you know. Not everyone agrees with this new development,' Rodario said quietly. His beard had been freshly trimmed and his eyes were emphasised with a little make-up. He was not capable of neglecting his appearance, given an occasion. 'Before you transfer ownership, you ought to ask the elves – to be on the safe side – about what's to happen to the local populace in the areas you're giving away.'

'There are less than a million. There weren't many people living there because it's not particularly good agricultural land. Palandiell never blessed that region. We can easily make room for our people elsewhere in Gauragar and Idoslane,' she said with confidence. Her hair was heaped high on her head in a style that pulled slightly at the temples. 'People will grow to understand that this is all for the good.'

'That's one million disgruntled citizens, my queen,' he pointed out. 'Sparks of discontent can travel quickly and far.'

In spite of herself Mallenia spun round to face him. 'It's a bit late now. The Naishïon's delegation will be here soon.'

'Yes, but you could still put that question to them when they arrive. They must have a plan for the land they're acquiring.' He touched her hand gently. 'I just want to avoid the possibility that your own subjects might turn on you if they misinterpret your actions with this contract with the elves.'

Mallenia's good mood was on the verge of tipping, and she was uncomfortable with how revealing the seamstress had made her new dress. And it was not right to be sitting with her back to her people.

She was about to reply when the five priestesses and five priests emerged from a side door and moved in a slow procession towards the statue of the goddess.

It was too late to discuss anything now. The ceremony had begun.

The ten holy figures in their embroidered green robes were offering songs of praise to Palandiell. Everyone joined in.

Mallenia stopped feeling ill at ease and entered into the spirit of the moment, a shiver going down her spine when the choral voices resonated in the temple's high dome. *Girdlegard is becoming more united than ever. It has taken two hundred and fifty cycles of gloom to get us to this point.*

The fire on the altar was ignited with a holy spark from Vraccas' forge. One donation after another was burned in sacrifice to the goddess, sending fragrant smoke rising to the round dome, where it escaped through concealed openings.

Fanfares sounded outside the temple, announcing the elves' arrival. In they came, bowing low, wearing a preponderance of white and green, in honour of Palandiell.

The crowd drew respectfully apart and the new guests made their way to the wooden dais, strewing corn seeds on the earthen floor.

'Let's hope it's not weeds,' muttered Rodario, louder than he'd intended. One of the priests laughed.

'These are the seeds of the grain species that Sitalia blessed us with,' called the white-haired elf at the front of the procession in an authoritative voice. His appearance was spectacular and he had a golden strand of hair that reached almost down to his waist. 'May the corn bear rich fruit that can ripen in harmony with that of the humans. May we all eat bread made from the same flour.' The first to walk through the ranks of local citizens, soldiers and courtiers, he bowed his head to the statue. 'My name is Tehomín, I am here as my Naishïon's representative.' The other elves moved up close behind him in an arrowhead formation. 'The sun has never risen on an orbit more extraordinary and significant than this one, Queen Mallenia, ruler over Idoslane and Gauragar.'

'Let us give thanks to Palandiell for it,' she responded, gesturing to the elf to stand next to her. 'The terror-times are past. Friendship blossoms where once enmity held sway.' As she saw Rodario open his mouth – no doubt to ask about the fate of the displaced humans – she flashed him a warning with her eyes. *This is my business.*

Tehomín came over to stand at her side. 'I assure you that we shall care for the land that we are receiving from you and from Gauragar,' he said quietly. 'It will flourish under our guardianship and bring plentiful harvests. It will take time, but time is what we have in abundance.'

Mallenia indicated the priest should resume his rituals. New hymns were struck up and the ceremony continued until they thought that the goddess was satisfied and would give her blessing.

Two chairs were brought in and placed at the foot of the statue: one for the queen of Idoslane and one for the elf. Servants provided ink and quills and the documents, when signed, would formalise the previously-agreed oral contract.

She read out the text: 'I, Mallenia of Ido, ruler over the land and the peoples of Idoslane and Gauragar, hereby covenant in trust to the elves possession of the land that lies in the north of Gauragar as shown in the maps. No money or donations in kind are asked for in return. This settlement has immediate validity and is permanent and irrevocable.'

Leaning forward, she picked up the quill and dipped it into the inkwell, ready to write her signature.

'If any here wish to object, let them speak now or forever hold their peace.' A deep voice echoed through the temple.

Audible gasps were heard from the audience. For the second time, a gap opened up in the throng and the soldiers were thrust aside.

An armoured dwarf with a stylised crown on his helmet stepped up, his nail-studded boots clattering on the wooden planking, the dais creaking under his tread. In his right hand he bore the crow's beak, which was enough to tell even the most unworldly of the spectators exactly who it was that was threatening to disrupt the harmonious occasion.

No one dared challenge the High King of the dwarves who had achieved such a dramatic entrance.

Mallenia was at a loss. She glanced at Rodario, who made a gesture implying she should stay calm, then she turned to see how Tehomín was reacting. The elf raised his eyebrows, right up almost to his hairline.

'By Vraccas: *I* wish to object. And in the strongest terms,' Boïndil went on, coming to a stop three paces from the table and slamming the end of the crow's beak shaft down on the wooden planking, causing the sound to reverberate round the temple like distant thunder. 'That's if anyone were to ask my opinion.'

The blonde queen sighed. 'So you have taken up my invitation,' she said, speaking in formal tones. Friendship was not on the cards. 'However, you were asked to attend a ceremony and a celebration, not a debate. I must ask you,' she said, keeping her annoyance in check as far as possible, 'to take your place with the other Council members. Or to leave, of course, should you prefer to do that.'

Rodario nodded in her direction, as if he were directing from the wings at the theatre. He would not step in at this point.

'It may be your land, Queen. But the contract makes the Fifthlings close neighbours of the elves,' he said, choosing his words with care. 'That is why I consider it appropriate for my opinion to be taken into consideration. The Naishïon will doubtless want everything clarified before the elves move in.' He looked at Tehomín. 'Is that not the case?'

The elf beckoned one of his escort over and a swift murmured exchange in elvish flowed before he nodded.

'I should like to offer regrets in the name of our supreme ruler, the Naishïon,' Tehomín said. 'We would of course have spoken with you and the Fifthlings, High King Blindil.' He placed his hand solemnly over his heart. 'I beg you to accept our apologies, friend dwarf.'

'Ask the queen to tell you how to say my name correctly, or I'll be calling you Tüdelün.' Boïndil was not impressed. He nodded up at the statue. 'Palandiell and Vraccas fought side by side against Tion. They were allies. I want to make sure that we have true allies in our union.'

'His name is Boïndil,' Rodario prompted in a whisper, looking mortified. 'He is Boïndil Doubleblade of the clan of Axe Swingers, King of the Secondlings and High King of all the dwarf tribes.'

'But we *are* allies,' Tehomín insisted, the gold strand glowing in the sunlight as he looked at the dwarf. 'Are those your only . . .'

'What happens to the people living in the territories you're taking over?' the dwarf interrupted brusquely, placing his beringed hands ostentatiously on the head of the crow's beak. There seemed no need for urgency in his eyes, and he remained dignified and unruffled. 'All I have heard so far is about a gift of land but there is no mention of the population being given away. Or, for that matter, the people's assets, goods and chattels. Can you elucidate?' He gestured over his shoulder with his thumb. 'We're really keen to hear what you have to say on this issue.'

It could be his words. Mallenia glanced at Rodario and tried to work out whether he had had previous knowledge of the High King's sudden appearance.

Tehomín smiled at the dwarf more amicably and courteously than anyone in Girdlegard had ever seen an elf smile before. 'You're ruining my surprise.'

'Because you're going to throw everyone out?'

'No, because we intend to compensate all the inhabitants for the loss of their property, whether it is a simple farmer or an aristocrat with a large estate.'

'Very decent.' Boïndil gestured at the document. 'And that's included in the contract?'

'Of course, High King.' Tehomín placed two fingers on the paper. 'Third line down. Perhaps you'd like me to read it out?'

'Please do.' The dwarf took on a more relaxed posture. 'And don't forget the wage-earners with no land who depend on farm work for their livelihood.'

All he needs now is his tankard of beer. Mallenia was incensed by the way the High King was behaving. But at the same time, she wondered why it had not occurred to her to ask these same questions. And that is exactly what she read in the faces of so many of those gathered in the temple. The dwarf had showed her up horribly.

Tehomín had regained his composure. He was obviously enjoying the confrontation. He shot a look at Mallenia, a smile tugging at the corner of his mouth. 'The elves hereby swear that they will always prove true allies of the peoples of Girdlegard and will, with them, combat evil in all its forms. They will stand shoulder to shoulder with dwarves and humans and all those who serve what is good and right.' He slipped down to the next paragraph. 'We will cultivate and care for the land we are given by Queen Mallenia, from the smallest plant to the largest animal.' He looked at the dwarf. 'And here's the bit you were asking about: Every man, every woman, every child – anyone who depends on the land for their livelihood in the north of Gauragar – will receive compensation. The land is to be cleared of its inhabitants by spring of the coming cycle.' Tehomín sat upright. 'Are these terms acceptable to you, Queen Mallenia of Ido?'

She nodded.

'And to you, High King?'

'Write in that you'll contribute fifty barrels of black beer as a welcome gift for your new neighbours,' Boïndil said, pointing at the contract. 'And that's to make up for getting my name wrong.'

Rodario burst out laughing, and restrained hilarity broke the tension in the temple.

Mallenia twitched, her muscles tensing. As she saw it, the dwarf had upstaged her, threatening her authority. He was taking over the ceremony and behaving as if he could influence whether or not she chose to donate her own land.

Rodario moved quickly to her side and restrained her gently when she attempted to rise. Tehomín was laughing too. 'Boïndil Doubleblade of the clan of the Axe Swingers, King of the Secondlings and High King of all the dwarf tribes, you are a true ruler in all senses of the word and a unique character. It will be an honour for us to have the Fifthlings as neighbours and to contribute fifty barrels of black beer to the occasion.'

Boïndil nodded and shouldered the crow's beak. 'Fine. Then I've no more objections.' He didn't move away, waiting to watch her sign. When neither Mallenia nor the elf made a move, he motioned them to pick up their quills. The priests raised their voices in song while the parties to the contract signed their names. The ceremonial atmosphere returned.

Boïndil stayed to witness the signatures, his beard-clad face showing no emotion. Mallenia reckoned he was concerned about more than just the present issue of the fate of the humans in the new territories. She also knew better than to ask.

She and Tehomín stood up and shook hands. Then the elf walked along the row of monarchs and bowed to each in turn. To Boïndil as well, though he was met with only a grim-faced nod. Protocol dictated that Mallenia and Tehomín should appear in front of the temple to announce the beginning of this new era to the throng. They left the marble building together and waited on the topmost step.

Guards with long shields surrounded them, to protect them from any attack by a marksman. Before the ceremony, all the neighbouring houses had been thoroughly searched and soldiers had been posted on the roofs, to observe the crowd and note any strange behaviour. It was thus extremely unlikely that anyone would attempt an assassination. When the crowd recognised them the level of noise increased. Mallenia smiled – until she realised they weren't cheering, but booing. *Surely not?*

'I bet you wish you'd put those questions out here where the people could hear you,' Boïndil said, his watchful eyes roving over the crowd.

Rodario took her by the arm. 'You haven't got enough people to protect you. Let's get going.'

Tehomín had grasped the situation and raised his arms to address the mob.

'Listen to me,' he cried, waving the signed agreement in the air. 'Listen to what has been agreed to the benefit of Girdlegard!'

Boïndil jumped up onto the pedestal of one of the columns in order to be seen. He brandished his crow's beak.

'Will you quieten down, for Vraccas' sake!' he thundered over the heads of the crowd. 'Listen to what he's got to say before you bleat like silly sheep.'

And, amazingly, silence fell.

'We don't trust these elves,' a bold voice called out near the front. 'Why are they turning up now? Where were they in previous cycles when we could have done with their support?'

Mallenia recognised the protestor. 'Come here, you. Let everyone hear what you have to say.'

The man pushed his way to the dais and took two steps towards the queen before being stopped by one of the guards. He repeated his question and the spectators murmured in agreement.

'It's like the old tales,' he added. 'When the Eoîl Atár overran our land.'

Mallenia's lips narrowed. *I hadn't thought of that.* Another circumstance she found surprising.

At this point Tehomín did something that almost caused Boïndil to lose his grip on the pillar: he knelt down in front of the disaffected man, the strand of gold-wrapped hair clinking against the marble.

'I beg your forgiveness if the Eoîl Atár harmed your forebears. The Eoîl Atár were dazzled fanatics. They were mad.

They considered themselves purity incarnate, yet their inmost beings were darker than Tion.' Tehomín stretched out his arms. 'This will never happen again. *This* elf empire stands for integrity.'

The man cast a sceptical glance his way.

'That's only words,' he responded. 'We could believe them or we could not. They sound good, but elves have always had silver tongues.'

Mallenia felt a touch on her hand.

Sha'taï had crept up to her and was pressing herself against her. 'Don't be frightened. It will all come right.'

The queen noted the conviction in the girl's voice and looked at her young ward in astonishment. She realised the childish confidence was taking her over, too.

'Do you need proof?' Taking a dagger from one of the guards, Tehomín handed it hilt-first to the man. 'Kill me; I swear there will be no retribution from any elf.'

It had gone so quiet in the square that the wings of the doves overhead could be heard in flight.

The man looked bewildered. He slowly took hold of the dagger and kept his eyes on Tehomín. The elf remained kneeling.

'Today is a moment of history that will never be forgotten.' He spoke without fear. 'Test us.'

Mallenia did not dare move. Boïndil's gaze flicked to and fro from the elf to the man and back again.

The arm with the dagger reached out and the blade tip shot at the elf's heart, only to halt as the steel pierced the fabric. It had been enough to reach the skin, as was evident from the spreading stain.

The man dropped the dagger in shock and took several steps backwards down the stairs.

'I thought . . . he would dodge the blow,' he stammered.

Tehomín gritted his teeth. 'Thank you for sparing my life.' He got to his feet, paying no attention to the wound. 'Are you convinced now?'

The man nodded and slunk back into the crowd, as if he were expecting to be pursued. *What a gesture!* 'You have seen that the elves have become your friends. The gods have formed a new union between us, indestructible, no matter what Tion and Samusin plan against us,' cried Mallenia, inspired. She took Dirisa's hand. 'Let us all show solidarity!'

Each person on the dais took his neighbour's hand and even the soldiers joined in; the crowd followed suit. Boïndil was the only one to distance himself from it, needing one hand to hold on to the column and the other to hold his crow's beak.

'Long live Mallenia of Ido,' called Rodario. 'Long live friendship!'

The crowd took up his toast enthusiastically, and the people clamoured for the queen and the elf. Their voices grew ever louder and people held their clasped hands aloft before breaking into applause.

'Allow me also a symbolic gesture,' Dirisa stretched out her hand to Tehomín. What with all the noise and rejoicing, Mallenia could barely hear what was being said. 'I shall release Phenîlas as soon as I am back in Tabaîn. He was never a murderer. I shall say it was an intrigue set up by the servants.'

'Accept my gratitude,' the elf replied.

'I propose that Rodario bring him to your sovereign lord himself,' she said graciously.

Boïndil jumped off the pedestal, shouldering his weapon

now. It was obvious that he was dumbfounded by this rapid turn of events. 'What does Rodario the Incomparable have to do with anything?'

'As *Emperor* of Girdlegard he should meet with the Naishïon,' Dirisa said, as if she were stating a well-known fact. Boïndil burst out laughing. 'Of course. An actor as supreme leader! What a farcical idea. Look at him: his clothes would make a rainbow feel faint.'

Mallenia, on the other hand, was ecstatic about Dirisa's suggestion. *It would serve to counterbalance the elves' power.*

'Brilliant!' she cried. 'The dwarves have their High King and the elves have their Naishïon. We need an emperor.'

'I agree,' Astirma said with a nod.

'No better candidate,' confirmed Isikor, a colourless figure in simple clothing.

Mallenia laughed and gave Rodario a kiss. 'That's how quickly an emperor can be made.'

'We don't have Coïra's vote yet,' Boïndil objected, looking at the monarchs as if each and every one of them had lost their minds.

'I have her proxy vote,' Rodario said, glowing with excitement. 'And I'll vote for myself in the name of Urgon and of Weyurn.' He accepted congratulations from the other rulers and Tehomín. 'We must make an announcement to the people. What an orbit the gods have sent us today! Girdlegard will never be vanquished again.' He clapped Boïndil on the shoulder. 'We're both high kings now.'

Lost for words, the dwarf scratched his silver and black beard.

Mallenia was immensely proud. *A triumph like no other.*

Sha'taï moved away from Mallenia's side and went up to

the kings and queens, to be patted on the head by everyone in turn.

Mallenia came over to Rodario again. 'We must make more sacrifices to Palandiell. We want your regency to last a long time.' Out of the corner of her eye she saw her little ward take the dwarf's hand to study the High King's ring. Boïndil grunted and pulled his hand away, turning to leave. *Let's hope full of peace. Please, ye gods, please.*

Girdlegard
United Kingdom of Gauragar-Idoslane
Idoslane
6492nd solar cycle, winter

It'll cause a lot of trouble. Hargorin did not like this constant heavy rain. He didn't mind snow because you could always shake it off, but this icy wet soaked through your clothes, chilling you to the bone.

He had wanted to strike the älf's head off after Gosalyn had released him from his fetters in the smithy. He had no doubt he could have managed it, too. Carmondai was old and no comparison with the other black-eyes Hargorin had met in battle. *The Triplets would have sent him off to endingness with a couple of blows.* Only Gosalyn restrained him.

The dwarf turned his pony's head to the east. 'We should reach the foothills soon,' he called back to his companions.

'We have to keep going south, and turn east in two miles,' the älf said, walking beside them.

'Tell me how long you've been in captivity?' Beligata mocked.

'This region has hardly changed. I could find my way blindfolded.' Carmondai stayed calm, presumably used to snide remarks since his release from the Triplet's dungeons. The victors made the decisions. And the victors were not the älfar.

'Let's do as he says,' Gosalyn suggested, trying to shrink down in the saddle to escape the rain. In vain. 'What happened to this area when the Triplets were in charge?'

'I am afraid I don't know,' Carmondai said. 'I was . . . busy.'

Hargorin laughed. 'If you care to put it that way.' He reluctantly followed the route the älf had proposed. 'I came this far south only seldom. The Triplets had forbidden the pig-faced orcs to get anywhere near Toboribor. They didn't want another orc realm starting up after they'd finally cleared the beasts from the caves.'

'Then that means none of us knows the territory round here,' said Beligata. 'Hey, black-eyes!'

'Hush.' Hargorin knew exactly what was coming. '*He's* got the sword now. It's better with him than in the hands of a dwarf-woman.'

'I don't agree. It's me that crawled back in to Phondrasôn to rescue it.' Beligata urged her pony forward to come level with the älf. 'You're a thief.'

'No one protests louder than a thief who's been robbed.' Carmondai regarded her. 'Much truth in the old saying, wouldn't you agree?' He placed his hand on Bloodthirster's hilt. 'This sword and I have known each other for a long time. It is more secure with me. Should I be killed, feel free to take it back.'

Hargorin encouraged his pony to trot faster. Their arrangement with the älf would be clarified in Toboribor. If what the älf claimed proved false, they could forget about him and go off to the Blue Mountains to search for Lot-Ionan's archive.

I'll tie him up first and deliver him to Mallenia's troops. Hargorin disliked the thought of having an älf roaming round Girdlegard unsupervised, even if this one was ancient and only capable of carrying a sword rather than fighting with it.

He was doubtful about what Carmondai had told them about Sha'taï. But Gosalyn seemed to be taking the älf's side, so he was prepared to allow him some credit there.

Their path took them eastwards.

A fortified farm reared up round the next bend; it looked like a small castle and had the Idoslane flag flying. To the left a huge horizontal tree trunk studded with metal spikes served as a barrier across the road.

The man on watch in the five-paces-high tower was alert and spotted them immediately; he called out to those below.

'Great,' said Beligata. 'That's all we need.'

Carmondai slackened his pace and fell back. 'Better if these people don't see me. I'll find you in Toboribor,' he said, taking his leave. In the next instant he had disappeared into the torrential rain.

'However old he may be, he's good at that.' Gosalyn rode up next to Hargorin. 'What do we say when they ask us what we're doing in the old orc realm?'

'That we're looking for an älf,' he replied with a grin. 'There's a reward.'

'Not bad.' She laughed.

'Or we could say Hargorin lost his leg at the battle in the caves and wants to have it back,' Beligata chipped in, riding up to the other side of the leader. 'That way nobody'll want to come along for the ride.'

Gosalyn grinned. 'Two good ideas.'

The dwarves laughed.

Arriving at the barrier, they saw the iron spikes made it impossible for anyone to get over or under it. They looked up at the windows of the tower and caught sight of a man in a simple brown coat. Armour seemed not to be de rigueur in these parts. They must be relying on the thickness of their walls for protection.

'What brings Children of the Smith to the south?' he called, in a not unfriendly tone.

'We're looking for an älf on the run,' Hargorin replied.

'Oh, I see. That'll be the queen's pet lap dog.' The man laughed. 'He's not been through here.'

The party joined in the merriment, even if for different reasons.

If you had any idea what's afoot you'd go and put on your sturdiest armour. Gosalyn wiped the rain out of her eyes.

'Give us a chance to look around in Toboribor,' Hargorin requested. 'Those caves would be an ideal hiding place.'

'Indeed they would, my dwarf friend, but no one can get in there any more,' the man explained. 'Our sovereign got us to wall up all the entrances. And before that we demolished many of the tunnels. You can save yourselves the trouble.' He pointed down. 'Come on in and get dry. First round is on me. Let's drink to the health of the new emperor.'

'Oh! So Girdlegard has got itself a supreme ruler,' Beligata commented. 'Now we're all on the same level: humans, elves and dwarves.'

'That's right.' He gave the order and the gates swung open. 'We'll drink to Emperor Rodario the First.'

All three burst out laughing.

'Good joke,' Hargorin said. 'Thank you for the offer but we want to get going.'

'It's not a joke. The monarchs all decided on him, the day Mallenia and the elves signed their treaty. Never been closer. All agreed.' The soldier raised his right hand. 'I promise you it's true.'

The dwarves exchanged surprised glances.

'Then let us hope Palandiell knows what she's doing, letting them choose a showman to run the whole of Girdlegard. As long as it's not one of Samusin's dirty schemes, to set confusion in the ranks. May we pass through?'

'Please,' Gosalyn added.

'If that's what you want. But you'll quickly get bored and soaked through. We'll have a warm fire and some beer ready for you on your return.' The man called out an order and the barrier was lifted. 'Good hunting.'

'Is the bounty still the same or have they upped the reward?' Beligata pretended they knew the exact amount.

'Still one thousand gold pieces. Dead or alive.'

'It was a terrible crime he committed!' Gosalyn added.

'Between you and me,' the soldier said, 'he must be the most incompetent black-eyes ever seen. They're after him for the *attempted* killing of the queen's little foster child.' He laughed out loud. 'Let's thank Palandiell that nothing happened to the girl, but what sort of an älf could fail at something as easy as that?' He waved and closed the window.

'A very old one,' Beligata joked.

'And one who managed to overpower you and throttle you till you passed out,' Gosalyn gloated.

Hargorin looked at the others. 'You know, it occurs to me that's the second time an älf tried and wasn't able to kill that girl,' he said. 'There's something amiss here.'

'But nobody sees it,' said Beligata.

'Except for us,' added Gosalyn. 'I've been thinking about Belogar. He had wanted to send the girl back out over the border. He would have killed the child as soon as he heard it speak the älfar tongue, but the humans and the elf stopped him. Perhaps I was sorry for the wrong one?'

Her companions were at a loss as to what to say. They rode through under the opened barrier, each deep in thought. They trotted along the overgrown path that in recent times had seen no traffic.

Southern Idoslane's rainy winters ensured everything stayed green in the countryside, but as they drew nearer to the former orc realm, things started to gradually change and grow greyer. Hargorin had heard there were several entrances to the cave system and assumed there had been connections through to Phondrasôn in certain parts of the caves.

'Do you know about the battle that took place here?' Beligata squeezed the rain water out of her hair. She ran a finger along her scar to check whether it had opened again.

'Must have been . . . more than two hundred and fifty cycles ago. In the days when the Scholar did his heroic deeds.' Gosalyn noticed a mound in the distance, showing less green than the surrounding area. The remains of a ruined building could be seen on top. 'An orc stronghold, perhaps?'

Hargorin nodded, shedding thick drops from his beard. 'Prince Mallen of Ido led an army of thousands from all the kingdoms in Girdlegard and they stormed the caves. The quest was for a particular diamond with magic properties, if I remember rightly. Or was that the battle about the Inextinguishables and their incestuous bastard children? Or maybe both those things?' He shrugged his shoulders. 'I'm not really interested in the past.'

It was obvious there had been a pronged siege. The army must have dug a ditch all around the fortress. Some ramps were still visible in the dip. On the outside of this ring, neglected fruit trees had taken over, leafless now, and the grass grew high. But the place where the monsters had been based seemed as though it had never recovered from the harmful pollution of those distant times. Nothing wanted to grow there other than grass and weeds.

'Can you imagine what it must have looked like? The pennants flying for the different clans and the dwarf tribes' flags flapping in the wind right and left?' asked Gosalyn emotionally. She licked the rain water from her lips. 'We dwarves have always been on the side that opposed evil.'

'Who else?' Beligata pointed to a grove of trees. 'We can tether the ponies over there. They won't manage the steep bank.'

Gosalyn couldn't tear her eyes away from the ruins and the wide ditch, until . . .

'There's someone there, lying down!' she cried excitedly, pointing to the north. 'Over there by the heap of stones. Down there in the hollow.'

'A human, I think,' Beligata guessed. 'A woman. I can see her. Dark blue robe. No mantle.'

Gosalyn kicked her pony's side. 'It's Coïra!'

Perfect ambush setup. Hargorin tried to grab her bridle. 'Wait!'

But she'd galloped off. Straight into the thick growth of grass between her and the ditch.

Note to self: always remember

- *None of them deserved mercy.*
- *They did not treat me with the respect I merited, yet I never harmed one of them.*
- *Be nice. Until you have achieved your aim.*

Secret notes for
The Writings of Truth
written under duress by Carmondai

XIV

Girdlegard
Grey Mountains
Kingdom of the Fifthling dwarves
Stone Gateway
6492nd solar cycle, winter

'Get rid of it,' Balyndar ordered from where he stood on the right-hand tower, allowing himself no rest in spite of his injuries. His hauberk wouldn't fit over all the bandaging and he made do with lots of layers of clothes and a black wolf-fur mantle over the top. 'I don't want anyone able to use it as a guide.'

In the mountains, winter had struck with an icy fist, affecting every inhabitant, every plant and even the solid stone. Whole sections of rock had split open with the cold. The bitter frost made everything freeze where there was no heat source. Braziers and hot honey beer had been placed at intervals on the walkway for the dwarves on sentry duty to warm them.

Balyndar kept his eye on the artisans who had gone down on the platform outside the gate. They were looking for the mark he had noticed shortly before he passed out. *I'm sure I wasn't imagining it.*

'It's quite high up,' Girgandor said in a concerned tone. 'It must have been the highest point reached by the ramp of bodies. They hadn't sent any projectiles.' His gloved fingers drummed on the frosty wall. 'If they bring more people next time, they'll be able to reach even higher if we can't burn them and shoot them down.'

'So we must get the new machines in place as fast as possible.' Up to now Balyndar had been forced to rely on the small contingent of catapults they had erected as a first line of defence. 'Are the chests of ammunition in the supply chambers all full?'

'The master armourers told me they're at two-thirds of their potential capacity. Their workers are hard at it in the smithies and the watermill lathe operators are not letting up, either,' Girgandor detailed, hoping to allay any fears. 'They've nearly got sufficient wood for all the arrows and spear shafts. And the "dragons" are on their way over.'

This was a relief for Balyndar to hear, but it did not dispel his worries. *Not by a long chalk*. The Fifthlings had worked miracles, setting their inborn stubbornness against the rigours of the winter weather. 'It's vital we are fully prepared, even if the next attack won't be coming for some time.'

'How do you know?'

'It's too cold.' Balyndar reached behind him, resisting the urge to groan with the pain. He scooped a ladleful of hot honey beer from the steaming pot and hurled the contents over the battlements.

In spite of the heat and the alcohol, the liquid was instantly transformed into dark crystals, making a dense cloud. Some of the crystals hit the gate while the rest were carried away by the wind.

'The ragged army that attacked us had no warm clothing,' he said. 'And that was autumn. Take a look around. No one in their right mind starts a campaign in winter unless there's reliable protection from the cold.'

'Their soldiers weren't undead,' Girgandor confirmed.

'Even the undead would freeze.' Balyndar laughed, which was a mistake. His injured chest also hurt. 'Now what?' he called to the dwarves outside on the platform. 'That marker is still there.'

'Can't budge it,' one of them shouted back. 'It's become part of the stone.'

Girgandor tutted. 'Nonsense. Surely no material can do that?'

'It might be magic,' Balyndar surmised.

'Keep hammering till it falls off!' he instructed the troop.

'It's not working,' came the answer a while later. 'It's iron. And there are white runes engraved on it.'

'I'll get Keenfire,' he growled. 'That'll shift it. Send the platform up for me.'

Girgandor nodded and issued the order. There was little point in protesting. Only the commander was able to release the weapon's diamond-edged power. For all intents and purposes, no other Fifthling tribe member could wield it.

It'll be what I inherited from my own father.

Balyndar pulled his hood up. He had lost most of his originally-brown hair when the fire swept over him. His beard would have to regrow, too. He went over to the tower lift, travelled down on the open platform, then limped across the courtyard to his official quarters. While he was recovering from his wounds, the weight of the mythical axe had been too much for him so he had stored it under lock and key in his chambers. It was too important an item to use merely as a walking support.

His painful injuries forced him to move slowly and this gave him time to dwell on the news that was spreading like wildfire: the High King had apparently found Tungdil Goldhand. Balyndar tended to think of this as the discovery of 'yet another Tungdil Goldhand.' *How many of them can the earth spit out?*

It was said that this Tungdil's face was partially distorted by burn scars. And his demeanour was quite different. The other one had come back with a warlike bearing, sporting dark runes on his black tionium armour.

Balyndar thought back to the discussion with Ireheart. They had talked it all through a cycle ago: was that weirdly armoured figure the real Tungdil? No one could say for certain.

Not even me. Many chose not to speak of what most had guessed. Namely that Balyndar was the Scholar's own child, born in the Grey Mountains and accepted as the son of the king. *Would I be aware of a bond between us? He means nothing to me.*

Balyndar had lost his father once before – or could it be that this one was truly his father?

Best not to ponder too long on the whole thing.

It was a wonderful thought that the true lost dwarf hero of Girdlegard had returned, but the Children of the Smith had to deal with the task ahead without the benefit of their champion's help. Balyndar had got on with life for cycle after cycle without his father. He did not need him. Not in this orbit or any other.

My task is to hold the gates. He had reached his room now. He went over to the cupboard built into the stone wall and took Keenfire out of its fastening. *And that's exactly what I'm doing.*

Balyndar gripped the sigurdacia wood handle just below the axe head and went back into the open air. His mother's communication had warned him against getting too excited about the prospect of meeting his progenitor. The way he was feeling at the moment, there was little danger of that. And anyway, the new Tungdil seemed to have gone undercover again. He had apparently set off after a longish stay at the courier station in Gauragar, without even taking his leave of Ireheart. He'd left a note saying he was going to travel round Girdlegard for a time to let his soul rest and to enable him to gauge the extent of the damage his homeland had suffered.

The High King had sent soldiers out to track Tungdil down so that he would not be left without protection. *Protection or surveillance?* Balyndar had no idea whether or not this search had been successful. There was still doubt attached to Tungdil's return and his intentions. He might be another duplicate version from Phondrasôn on a spying mission for some army about to emerge out of the pernicious depths.

Samusin is having a little game with us. Balyndar had reached the tower and activated the lift. In his view the ghaist was a whole lot more of a danger at present than a Tungdil who was said to have foresworn the use of weapons.

Girgandor came straight over to his side and accompanied him along the parapet walk, offering an arm, which he was glad to accept. 'The piles of hardened slag are a problem. Difficult to clear away. Next time we should only use boiling water and burning petroleum,' he reported as they walked.

'As far as I know, we've often used molten slag in the past for our defences.'

'The composition must have been slightly different. Not the usual waste products from the forges. This time it baked itself onto the ground and fused with the enemy corpses.' Girgandor stopped to look out between the crenellations. 'The sharp frost has turned the result as hard as steel.' He indicated the road.

Dwarf workers were hacking at the layer with mattocks, hammers and axes, laboriously revealing small sections of road surface. Stone splinters, fragments of bone and lumps of flesh were being scattered. Shovel by shovel the refuse was carried away in wheelbarrows and carts to be burned in the furnaces. As they worked they were singing in chorus. The lyrics were hard to understand but it was not a song of praise.

'We can count our blessings it's not summer. It would stink to high heaven, worse than a putrefying orcish demon.' Girgandor led Balyndar over to the platform.

'You're right there.' The commander climbed over the wall with difficulty, helped by the masons and smiths on the work platform. 'Have we lost any more of the wounded?'

'We're still at a total of one hundred and eighty injured and seventy-four dead.' Girgandor wanted to come with him, but Balyndar motioned him away. 'Why can't I come?'

'If I die or fall, there's got to be someone to take over.' He grinned and signalled for the platform to be let down.

'Vraccas forbid.'

Balyndar took up a wide stance to be less vulnerable to the wind if the planks started to rock. He was not sure how strong the wooden railing was. The whole contraption moved slowly down towards the level of the granite gates until they reached the place where the strange object was. An engraved piece of iron the length of a finger had been rammed into the stone.

How did that happen? The gates of the Stone Gateway were of the hardest stone imaginable. Even the largest of boulders fired from afar could make no impression and would shatter into pieces. The ten bolts the dwarf smiths had fashioned on the other side ensured no one could open the gates or use spells to force them. Vraccas endowed his Children with the ability to produce true miracles with their mastery of stone and metal-working skills.

Balyndar could not believe his eyes.

'It's withstanding the hammers?' he asked his companions,

who were all dressed in the thickest of coats and wearing scarves and gloves to counteract the effects of the dangerous temperatures.

'Resisting every tool in the box, captain,' said a female worker.

He touched the small piece of iron but it did not feel in any way out of the ordinary. He could see it had penetrated the stone as if the granite had been soft at the time and had then hardened again around it.

'This is not normal,' Balyndar commented, taking Keenfire in his hands. 'Mind out. Make sure you don't fall.'

He took aim carefully and struck the diamond-encrusted edge against the thin iron peg from the side. He had expected resistance or a bang or a flash – but there was only a flicker from the gemstones and then the iron snapped off. A tiny segment remained on the surface, thin as a fingernail.

He would not be able to remove it from the gate using Keenfire. And if he made a gash in the granite, that would serve the enemy as a marker just as well as the original peg. Balyndar was pretty sure the last piece could not be removed. 'Let that bit stay till I've worked out how best to deal with it,' he told the dwarves. He picked up the snapped-off peg section. 'For now just paint over it so it doesn't show up.'

They nodded. He gave the signal for the platform to be hauled up.

Girgandor was waiting for him and Balyndar let him know the results. 'I'll send this piece to Coïra.'

'As soon as she's been found.' His deputy and two other guards assisted him along the parapet walkway. 'She's still out, trying to find a magic source in Girdlegard.'

Balyndar stowed the fragment in his coat pocket. 'I'll keep it till then. As soon as the maga . . .' He stopped. His brown eyes registered a tubular metal object lying next to the remains of a catapult. It did not look like it belonged with the mechanism. 'What's that thing?'

Girgandor sent a warrior over to bring back the object. The bronze casing had been singed and damaged. When it was handed to Balyndar, he was surprised to see runes similar to those on the helmets the ghaists were wearing.

A trap! His first instinct was to hurl it over the battlements, but he held back. *If it were a magic artefact meant to cause damage, surely it would have done so by now.*

'Well, well, a souvenir from our visitor. It must have come off when Keenfire destroyed him.' He tilted the tube this way and that. 'Either it's empty or what's inside is very light.'

'A message.' Girgandor studied the container carefully and motioned some shield-bearers over. 'Do you think that could have been their mission? To get a message to us?'

Balyndar shook his head. 'Hardly, or the ghaist would've handed it to me instead of fighting.'

The ghaist that had escaped remained at large. It must still be inside the mountains, making its way relentlessly to the destination named by its master. Or mistress. *Perhaps carrying the same message?*

Girgandor pulled his gauntlet tighter on to his right hand. 'For whom, then?'

Balyndar shook the container, turning it this way and that until it opened with a click.

A parchment scroll in an unfamiliar hand came to the fore. It was grey and smooth as glass, unsuitable for any ink, so the runes it bore had been scratched on to its surface.

Girgandor said, 'That's the common script of Girdlegard.'

Balyndar held the scroll so only he could read the contents. 'I'll read it out. So stop craning your necks,' he announced. *That way I can omit anything that may be only intended for my mother's eyes.*

> To the powerful masters of the land behind the gate,
>
> You have taken a demon to live amongst you. I have been trying for some time to destroy it but it has escaped my clutches.
>
> There are two options.
>
> The first is the easier: you throw the demon's dead body over the gate and nothing further will occur.
>
> The second path is hard, painful and involves many deaths on your side: I shall send my armies, constantly, by day and night, at will, until I have gained entrance to your land and can bring the demon down.
>
> If you force me to take the second path, I shall destroy your land when I have entered it. This I promise.

The message was signed with a rune Balyndar could not read.

For the space of a few eye-blinks there was silence on the parapet.

'The child.' Balyndar knew the others were already racking their brains to figure out how they could speed up the final arrangements for improving the defences to ready the fortress for the next onslaught. There was no reason not to believe what the message said. 'So now we know where the second one was heading.'

'I wonder,' Girgandor pondered, 'how the writer knows we *aren't* the powerful ones he wants to negotiate with. The ghaist headed straight for the tunnel as if it already knew the way into Girdlegard.'

Balyndar shared his comrade's view. 'Maybe it has some

magic way of knowing about events in Girdlegard, or maybe there are still spies in our midst, from back when evil ruled here.'

'Or it's just guessing,' objected someone else.

'The queen and the High King must be told immediately.' Balyndar pressed the message and its container into the hands of the nearest guard. 'Take this to a courier. Everyone has to be warned: Girdlegard and all the dwarf kingdoms.'

'We shall stand guard,' Girgandor said proudly. 'We shan't run out of ammunition, just as he won't run out of low-grade battle-fodder. Let him send the next hundred thousand – we'll greet them with our firestorm.'

'The attacks might happen at any of the gates.' Balyndar admitted this was unlikely, given the amount of time it would take for such numbers to make their way round the mountains. *But anyone who can drum up armies of this size, well, who's to say.* 'And they should all be warned about the girl. Belogar was right all along.'

'But that might be a falsehood,' said one of the others. 'Evil may be trying to force a wedge between our peoples and break our friendship pact.'

Balyndar nodded at the dwarf who had spoken. 'That could be true, my friend.' He turned and hobbled off along the walkway. 'Or else the child might indeed be a demon and we should chuck its dead body over the wall and save our land from further threats.' *Where will the second ghaist turn up?* 'Hurry the "dragon"-masters along. I want them here.'

He was diverted by the thought of his newest development for the defence of the Stone Gateway. The enemy would be terrified. The cunning Fifthlings had devised a weapon based on a child's toy that could be deployed if the wind was in the right direction: a kite.

Normally kites would fly along in the breeze on a string,

but the dwarves had adapted them and increased their size tenfold, to be able to take a heavy payload. Made from a combination of silk and willow wands, they could take off, their silken tails fluttering, and remain held up in the sky by ropes and a winding mechanism.

By means of a second string and a contraption with a brass ring, leather sacks of Vraccas fire could be placed over the heads of the enemy. Then either the line could be cut, causing the sack to plummet down, or a burning fuse could work its way along the bag's seam and the contents would spew out after a carefully calculated time. They flew high enough to be safe from shots from the enemy and they could drop unquenchable fire anywhere along the approach road to the gates. The dragon-kites needed wind but there was plenty of that in the mountains.

I want them here. Even if Balyndar had put his dark thoughts about the abandoned child of the Outer Lands into words, he would not be able to kill Sha'taï just like that. *The monarchs must take her captive and interrogate her.*

'Girgandor!'

His deputy hurried over. 'Sir! New orders?'

'Only one: *at the double.*' Balyndar clapped him on the shoulder. 'Everything. At the double.'

Girdlegard
Black Mountains
Kingdom of the Thirdling dwarves
Eastern Gate
6492nd solar cycle, winter

Winter doesn't get them down. They're still here. Rognor Mortalblow could not believe it. 'With each new orbit I think: I'll get up and look over the wall and they'll be gone. But not a bit of it.' He looked around. 'I would have lost the wager. There's four new tents now.'

The temporary elf settlement at the gates to the Black Mountains now housed two thousand souls, young and old. Despite the snow lying on their roofs, the semi-circular tents were holding up; smoke rose through the openings from the numerous fires with which they heated their accommodation.

Bolîngor Bladecatcher of the Iron Fists clan came over, well wrapped up in mantle and furs. He brushed the breakfast crumbs out of his chestnut-coloured beard. He was in charge of the archers on the north side of the stronghold and was regarded as a warrior with exceptional eyesight. He had a broad stripe tattooed across his face in recognition of his skill.

'Five.' Bolîngor pointed south. 'There on the ledge.'

'I don't know what I should hope for: that Lorimbur's spirit chases them away or that it protects them.'

Rognor sheltered by the wall. The gusts tore right through his face mask, the scarf he wore underneath it and his dark blue beard, biting into his very skin. He was used to the cold but this winter seemed to be breaking all records. 'The frost wants them gone. It's a miracle that none of them has frozen to death so far.'

Bolîngor took his telescope and observed the road leading to the stronghold from the east. 'And here come the next ones. Four . . . no, five sledges. That'll be around thirty extra mouths to feed, I'd say.'

Rognor groaned. This meant the elves would send Chynêa to the gate begging to be allowed through. Whenever there were new arrivals, she would stand in front of the fortress and make the usual speech, appealing to their sense of friendship. 'I know it all by heart now.'

Bolîngor put down the optical device. 'Another fifty of them and they'll block the gate, Chancellor.'

'I know, but we can't just wipe them out.'

'What if we just pretended?' He could tell by the tone that this wasn't meant seriously. Or at least not very seriously.

'How would they know the difference?'

'We could cover them in flour and say next time it would be fire we chuck at them. Or water. That'd be good. In these temperatures we'd have perfect little elf statues.

Both of them shared the joke, laughing without malice.

The dwarves hated having to refuse the elves entry, but conditions had changed. At first it had been a vague idea of the High King's that something wasn't quite right. But since the bottle of eye-whitener had been found, the policy was vindicated.

'How many älfar do you think there are out there?' Rognor saw Chynêa approaching the stronghold gate, in her white cap, scarf and fur coat with its turned up collar. *Here she comes.*

'If only I knew. Vraccas should let the traitors freeze to death or burn in the tents.' Bolîngor pointed the elf-woman out. 'Punctual as ever. Shall we go down?'

Rognor could see her gesturing in his direction. 'By Vraccas. She must know exactly where I am without being able to see me.' He got up. 'This has got to stop.'

He stepped out towards the steps down to ground level in order to talk to her through the grating. 'In the next few orbits.'

'I'll send out for the flour,' Bolîngor called.

Rognor stomped down the steps.

He was annoyed that the elves were proving so obstinate, defying all orders and persisting through fair weather and foul. *It's almost as if Vraccas had given them a touch of our tenacity. They're as stubborn as we are.* It made him grin. *Almost as stubborn.*

He and Chynêa arrived at the grating at the same time. The wind was howling through the apertures and making her clothing swirl about. The elf-woman had lost weight. Her slender face looked emaciated and her eyes, normally brilliant, were dull. Overwintering outside was taking its toll; all the others were probably suffering in the same way.

'Greetings, Chancellor.'

Her voice betrayed how weak she had become. 'May Sitalia be with you,' he responded courteously. 'I'll have some food brought down, if you'd like.'

'Very kind. But we will manage with what we have.'

'We have not been tasked with standing idly by, watching you all starve.' Rognor pushed up his face-protection, revealing his tattoos. 'But I am still not permitted to let you enter.'

'I shall save my breath and not try the usual pleading.' Chynêa tilted her head slightly forward. 'It's not just a childish whim that we want to get to Girdlegard. It is our *duty*,' she explained, her voice breaking. 'The Creator called us and we are following her lead.'

'I understand. But I have no powers to change anything.'

'It is our sacred *duty*, Chancellor.' She looked at him seriously. 'The number of those wanting to follow the call of the goddess is increasing all the time.'

This caught Rognor's attention. 'We have our own duty, decreed by Vraccas and Lorimbur.'

'I know.' She bit her lips. 'But I shan't be able to hold them back for long. The atmosphere is very tense. The constant privation is causing friction.'

I can't do more than offer food. 'Then turn around and go

back,' he urged. 'Three orbits' march from here. You wouldn't have to go further than that. Wait there until there is better news from Girdlegard. I promise to send a messenger straight to where you are to keep you in touch with events here.'

Chynêa gave a grateful smile. 'It is wonderful to find we have your sympathy. We had been told that the old enmity between elves and dwarves had perhaps not, in fact, ceased to be.'

'If the elves had taken more part in the freedom struggles of the recent past, I'm sure no trace of enmity would remain.' Rognor smiled. 'It will work out in time.'

Chynêa looked less convinced. 'I am afraid of the nights,' she confessed.

'You are safe here, at our gates.'

'I'm not troubled about any danger that might befall *us*.' The elf placed her thinly gloved hand against the grating. 'The rebellious ones amongst us could use the cover of darkness to force their way into your fortress. Only the gods know what would happen then.' Her voice took on a resigned fragility. 'Say ten of them try – and maybe they attack, or injure or even kill one of your guards in the attempt – what would the response be? I know about the boulder-throwing machines and the arsenal of deadly weapons you have.' Chynêa pushed her arm through the grating. 'May I ask for your word, Chancellor? That you would not punish those that are innocent?'

Rognor saw the fear in her big, sunken eyes. 'I promise your camp will not be destroyed if some of you manage to cross the walls,' he said with ceremony, taking hold of her hand. *It feels like a dry branch.* 'No innocent elf shall be made to suffer for the failings and mistakes of the guilty.' He was reluctant to press her hand too hard, thinking he might fracture some bones.

Chynêa was relieved. 'You are an honest Child of the Smith,' she said. 'I will try my hardest to prevent such an attempt being undertaken.' She bowed. 'I hope we shall meet again.' She turned and walked back to camp with graceful and yet unsteady steps.

Rognor was thoughtful watching her go. *She was giving me a warning, wasn't she? She was warning me about an attack.*

He looked up. 'Bolîngor!'

'Sir? Shall I send the first payload of flour?'

'Double the guard. And call the section commanders and the artillery masters to a briefing.' He stamped through deep snow across to the other side of the fortress where the main quarters and the assembly halls were.

Rognor could not take it amiss that the elves would attempt to scale the walls. But for all he knew, the attackers would not show the same mercy to the defenders. Would they be pitiless in their quest for admittance?

It won't be us spilling the first blood. He intended to issue orders that would limit the killing. On both sides.

Carrying a lidded mug of hot chicken broth, Bolîngor went to the look-out post on the tip of the dwarf stronghold's helmet. He relished the salty taste and the warmth and fullness in his stomach as he stood surveying the Black Mountains. The chancellor had forbidden the watch to drink any hot beer, which might give rise to unwise actions.

It had been seven orbits since Rognor had summoned the section commander and the artillery master of the fortress to give them his orders: no elves were to be killed if they managed to scale the walls. Wounded perhaps, but not killed.

Bolîngor entered the guards' shelter with its observation windows. They afforded good views to the east round the ramparts and also vertically, to ground level. To stop the icy draught coming through the floor gratings, there were iron covers that could be fastened shut. Straw was stuffed into any gaps to keep out the cold, otherwise there would be a constant whistling that would rob the guards of their sleep.

The five guards, male and female, saluted him.

'Nothing to report,' said one. 'The moon is bright. We can see everything that's happening in the Black Mountains. And it's exactly nothing.' He grinned.

'Let's hope it stays that way.' Bolîngor went over to the right, walking past the narrow windows to get a look at the mountain peaks, shimmering magically in the silvery light.

He liked snow and he liked winter. The air was clearer and you could see further than in the heat of summer. He flipped the lid of his mug open with his thumb and drank a mouthful of soup, while staring meditatively at the landscape. 'Anything else in the watch book?'

He gazed at the peak named Stone Fir. Wind and weather had shaped the rock like a fir tree. As a child he had once climbed it for a dare. Legend had it that Lorimbur would reward such bravery. *That was a long time ago*.

'Nothing to report,' came the answer again. 'Though one of their tents got blown away.'

'Where?' Bolîngor scanned the camp.

'Over on the right, on the very edge. See that ledge?'

He could not see from his window so he asked them to open the shutters on the floor on the right-hand side. They really ought to have reported that to the main watch. If a shelter had been lost, it meant there had been no one living in it, otherwise the tent would have been rescued and secured.

Two guards wrestled with the shutters but could not open them.

'Frozen shut?' Bolîngor took another swig of hot soup.

'Looks like it.'

Bolîngor tried a different window. But this one was equally impossible to open, as if an invisible force was resisting.

'Get it open.'

They tried with their axes, using them as levers.

The iron plate screeched in protest as it was forced, the dwarves grunting with effort. Something snapped off and the shutter plate flew open, allowing cold air to surge in.

Bolîngor leaned forward, screwing up his eyes to peer through the icy covering that had formed on the grating.

He dropped his soup with surprise. It clanged onto the criss-cross iron bars, sending the contents cascading down through the freezing night air to form crystals.

The tiny droplets showered past figures scaling the wall on ropes; small grappling irons secured the flimsy-looking ropes to the grating itself.

'Sound the alarm,' Bolîngor ordered, going down on one knee and pulling out his dagger to sever the ropes.

But the elves had been warned by the shower of crystallised soup particles. One of them glanced up and gave a signal to those below. Four of the climbers swung themselves on to different parts of the fortress walls and disappeared from view.

The sharp blade sliced through the finger-thick rope and the two elves that had been left with no safe place to cling to plunged fifty paces deep to the snows beneath. *If Sitalia loves them, they will survive.*

Alarm bugles rang out and in the distance gongs were sounded. The whole of the stronghold jumped into life and the hunt began for the intruders.

I hope the guards remember Rognor's orders.

'Open up the other shutters,' Bolîngor commanded,

running to the stairwell. 'Tell the chancellor if any elves turn up at the gates. The noise may arouse their curiosity and they'll want to help their comrades.'

He raced down the stairs, holding his club at the ready. It was easier to control the strength of a blow from a club. You did not have the same control using an axe or a morningstar. This was the reason Rognor had decreed the watch bear only blunted weapons.

In no time at all, the fortress was ablaze with light. Groups of four hurried past him, sticks and shields in their hands. Bolîngor made his way down to the right eye of the fortress's dwarf-face. Two elves had swung themselves in through this opening. He wanted to deal with them personally. All this running about was getting him warm.

Best replace those gratings with a different solution. He assumed the elves had shot the grappling irons up with arrows or maybe a small catapult. In the case of a siege, these methods would not have succeeded, but it was important to iron out these loopholes in the defences.

An elf jumped out in front of him, wearing a grey and white spotted leather doublet and breeches, which afforded excellent camouflage in the wintry conditions. However, in the dark corridors of the fortress he stood out boldly.

Bolîngor raised his club.

'We have no quarrel with you or the elves,' he said, speaking clearly. 'And we know that it is important for you all to enter Girdlegard. But this can only happen with our permission.' He pointed east with his club. 'If you go now of your own accord, nothing will happen to you. If not, I am afraid you'll be suffering a few broken bones.'

The elf listened and retreated a few paces; he had a short sword hanging from his weapons belt. He did not try to draw it.

'We are going to open the gates,' the elf replied. 'Once we are in your territory, you'll have no option but to let us all through.'

Bolîngor shook his head firmly. Calling out loudly, 'I've got one of them here,' he moved to attack, deliberately aiming not at the head but at the legs, to topple him.

'Forgive me for taking this shortcut.' The elf swerved to avoid the blow, then leaped up onto a roof beam, making his way along overhead.

That's not the way it's supposed to be. The dwarf threw his weapon and hit the elf in the side.

This was enough to make the elf lose his balance. First the club and then the elf crashed to the ground.

Dwarves came running up the corridor from both directions.

'Block the exits!' called Bolîngor, pouncing on the elf to bring him down. 'Two of you. Over here, now. Let's get him tied up.'

The intruder managed to struggle free but was soon outnumbered. They cornered him and he raised his arms in surrender.

Bolîngor was impressed the elf had not attempted to use his short sword. 'Tie him up and take him down to the gate. Wait there till the others are caught.' He turned to the right-hand doorway.

'That's not going to happen,' came the voice of a second elf that was standing over four felled guards, his long sword bloodied. 'Your ugly fortress will go up in flames before that.'

What nerve! This idiot has actually dared to hurt my guards! Bolîngor picked up his club. 'You're forgetting. Stone doesn't burn.' He stomped over to the elf without another word.

If this elf had deliberately ambushed and killed four of his men, there was no mercy to be shown. The Chancellor would have to see there was no other way.

Bolîngor pressed a catch on the shaft of his club and long spikes snapped out from the metal.

The notches on a blade tell us much about the owner.

Dwarf saying

XV

Girdlegard
Elf realm of Ti Lesîndur
Barrenbrig
6492nd solar cycle, winter

Ireheart and his companions rode ever deeper into the newly-formed united empire of the elves. This time he was accompanied by a larger contingent, and not only because it suited his status. And not only because of possible älfar ambush.

He felt ill at ease in the presence of the small girl from the Outer Lands. He had noted at the temple how quickly she had been able to change people's minds as soon as she appeared on the scene. Surrounded as he was by his best warriors, male and female, he was protected should the mood go against him.

Perhaps he was wrong, but he was convinced that the rapid changes taking place in Girdlegard all stemmed from Sha'taï's influence. He had to admit that she had – to her credit – brought about a sense of harmony and peace when things had been critical with the elves in Highstead, but there was a weird aspect to her good work: the inexplicable, sudden friendliness of all present.

Since the coronation of Rodario, a mysterious cheerfulness had spread abroad, as Boïndil had noticed as he travelled. Friendliness was stretching its tendrils out, wrapping itself round people and changing the way they thought. Except for a few critical voices in remote parts of Girdlegard, there was no dissent at the naming of Rodario the First as Emperor. It seemed that at long last the humans considered themselves equal to the elves and the dwarves. Everyone seemed euphoric. Ireheart was not bothered by the all-pervading good humour but he was sure it was not a natural phenomenon.

He looked ahead to the front of their cavalcade. The vanguard had entered a small village and sounded a bugle signal indicating No Danger. Further on there was a small pine forest, and beyond that still was the meeting-place.

'Yet another abandoned settlement,' said Aurogar Broadhand of the clan of Silver Seekers, a fine figure of a warrior from the Fourthling tribe. 'Mallenia's subjects are leaving fast.'

'Who would want to stay here if your pockets are full of gold?' Ireheart sat tall in the saddle and put his hands on his lower back. His buttocks were painful as well. *We need to get the fast tunnel system up and running.* All the riding he had had to do in the last few orbits was wearing him out. He was not used to it. 'If I had no conscience and no scruples, I'd get a bunch of blokes together and roam around robbing the humans.'

Aurogar nodded. 'Good thing we dwarves are always so honest. Though we do like gold, of course.' The High King joined him in the laughter.

The military cavalcade wound its way across the snow-covered landscape that had until so recently belonged to Gauragar. Even the unprecedented gift of territory seemed to provoke no objection. Elves and humans were growing closer, making Girdlegard stronger than ever. That was what everyone was saying.

Ireheart could not stop sighing about the present state of affairs. He was lost in thought. The fact that Tungdil had disappeared did not make anything easier. *They'll be asking me about him. They all will.*

Towards evening they reached the town of Barrenbrig, abandoned by its previous inhabitants. The elf standard was flying above its walls and in spite of the icy conditions, craftsmen had started to remove the sharp corners, replacing them with softer, rounder contours; painters were decorating the walls in red, purple, gold and black.

'Not bad progress,' Aurogar conceded. 'But they're trying to put curved lines into solid rock. That's not going to work. And they're using the wrong sort of tools.'

'They're not from here, are they?' Ireheart grinned. 'You should go and point out their mistakes. I expect your remarks will fall on deaf . . . I mean, pointed ears.'

The dwarves nearby all roared with laughter at the joke.

The elf-soldiers at the gate saluted and let them through.

'Never thought I'd see the day,' Aurogar commented, returning the salute with respect.

Like all the others he remained on his guard. The matter of the white eyes treatment meant that any elf could be an älf in disguise. *If we forget that, we could lose our life-spark quicker than a badly-secured axe head can fly.*

The sound of hammering resounded out of every street and alleyway as they passed. The town was being transformed by its new residents to comply with their own elf-aesthetic and to make their newcomers feel at home. Occasionally there would be a crash as part of a wall was demolished or roof tiles fell off, throwing up clouds of snow.

The dwarves arrived at the market place. Several of the surrounding buildings had been replaced by circular gateways, linked one to another. A tall house took pride of place in the middle. It was made entirely of wood and was several storeys high, with overlapping curved roof elements, small bells on the jutting beams and statues on top.

Gargoyles in the form of beasts had been fashioned to sit at the end of the roof gutters. The mighty roof beams were painted white and decorated with runes in red and gold. Long black banners with white flower runes hung from the highest storey, fluttering in the wind.

On examination of the construction, Ireheart could see that despite its impressive size, the building had been pieced together in kit form. *Quick to put up and take down.* The Naishïon seemed to prefer to sleep in his own palace, wherever he went.

'We should try prefabricating a dwarf stronghold,' he mused with a grin.

'I don't like it.'

'I don't mean the design itself. I meant it is clever to have a portable fortress you can put together quickly.' He was keen on the idea, but he knew it would not work for them because of the weight involved.

Aurogar smiled. 'Great idea. We could put up a dwarf refuge wherever we were. We should have thought of that earlier. It would have been a help in battle.'

Ireheart halted his party and told his companions to dismount. They formed an escort around him on foot and they made their way over to the building, which had a row of elves guarding it. 'What good is all that if they've got black-eyes lurking in their midst?' wondered Aurogar.

Shortly before they arrived at the stairway leading up to the broad, bronze entrance gates, half of the dwarves held back. The rest marched forward, up the steps. The gates swung open.

An elf in elaborate clothing confronted them, arms outstretched to prevent their progress. Then he folded his arms and bowed. 'In the name of my lord and master, I bid you welcome, High King Boïndil. Please ask all but three of your best people to wait here in this anteroom, after the precedent set by Rodario the First.'

Ireheart had no intention of doing without his bodyguards. 'My warriors are all *best* ones. How could I possibly choose?'

'Then take the cleverest ones.'

'But they're all clever,' he growled. 'You see? We're not going to agree on this.'

'The cleverest,' the elf replied, 'will be the ones who stand back and let the best ones forward.'

'Elf sophistry,' Aurogar sighed in exasperation, using his own language. 'They could talk even an orc into committing suicide. Just imagine if the pig-faces had asked an elf for directions . . .'

The dwarves laughed.

'This is getting us nowhere.' Ireheart quickly rattled out three names without further ado. He took his mantle off, revealing his armour. 'Aurogar, you stay here and listen out.' He handed over his cloak. 'When I give the signal, do what we've agreed.' He kept his right hand on the head of his crow's beak.

The elf's features narrowed but he said nothing as he led them through the anteroom.

There were soldiers standing around in small groups, the emblem of Urgon on their armour. They nodded at the dwarves. Elves circulated offering tea and refreshments.

Ireheart and his three companions were led through a corridor to another round entrance with a bronze door. Four elves were standing guard outside. They only opened it after their escort had spoken an incredibly complicated password.

This is getting interesting. Ireheart was lost after the first three syllables.

The room inside was full of the fragrance of incense and flower essences. It was all a bit heavy and it made Ireheart sneeze. He noticed there were three elf-soldiers and three humans standing behind Rodario and the Naishïon, who were both seated.

And that wretched child!

Sha'taï was sitting next to the Emperor of Girdlegard, prettily dolled up, looking harmless enough with her large eyes and shy smile. Ireheart exhaled heavily, a more honest comment than any words. *By Vraccas, this could get nasty.* 'Keep your eyes on me,' he whispered to the dwarf closest to him. 'If I start behaving strangely, knock me unconscious and carry me out.' This was met with an astonished look.

Ireheart waved his hand dismissively and made his way to the armchair provided for him. The extra height of the seat brought him eye to eye with the other two. He appreciated the thoughtfulness.

'Well, here we all are,' he said. 'The Mighty Three are gathered together.' He spoke respectfully. 'And perhaps the most powerful of all,' he added after a short pause, glancing at Sha'taï. He leaned his weapon against the table.

'How do you mean?' Rodario's costume was more flamboyant than a kingfisher's plumage. His hair was freshly arranged and his beard and moustache were waxed.

'Children can affect the hardest of hearts,' he said, covering up the implication of his words. Sha'taï had not reacted as he had expected she would. She did not seem startled and she did not send a malevolent glance his way. The injuries at her throat were now only visible as faint scratches. That must be where the history-teller's blade had touched her. 'Unless it's an älf wanting her blood and bones.'

Ataimînas smiled politely. He wore a cloak of white silk

embroidered with gold and silver thread over a slim-fitting black robe, with a black sash around his hips. 'Welcome to Ti Lesîndur, High King Boïndil.'

'I thank you. And may Vraccas' blessings be on us all.' He looked around ostentatiously. 'Where are the others?' *And where's the beer?*

'What others?' Rodario was puzzled.

'Girdlegard has other rulers – not only you.'

'Likewise, there are other dwarf kings, but you came on your own,' he answered with a mischievous wink.

'Cut out the winks! That might go down well with your women, but . . .'

Ataimînas stepped in. 'Today is a unique occasion. We three, rulers over the peoples of Girdlegard, will be discussing, and agreeing on, the overall strategy and way forward for our homeland in the coming cycles. Then we shall debate the details affecting what we will ask of the various kingdoms.'

'Each of us should contribute what he is best at and what he has the most of,' continued Rodario.

'Well, we dwarves have got an awful lot of stones.' Ireheart crossed his arms. 'So this means the others are turning up tomorrow?'

The elf and the human nodded.

'I find that remarkable.'

'Why so hostile, dear friend? Did you have an uncomfortable ride?' Rodario spread his arms in a patronising gesture. 'Look, we're all of us equal here.'

'You'll get my opinion on that,' Ireheart replied, his blood starting to boil. His last beer had been quite some time ago. 'I want *everyone* round the table when we discuss Girdlegard's future.'

'Then summon all the dwarf kings and queens to

Barrenbrig,' Rodario said, stroking Sha'taï's hair as if she were a lucky talisman.

'We don't need them. It's obvious what my race will contribute in the coming cycles.' He tapped the grip of his crow's beak. 'As long as there is a spark in the life-forge of a single dwarf, we will protect all humans and elves. You'd have to weigh that in the balance. And we can make steel. The best there is.'

Ataimînas relaxed slightly. 'I am glad.'

He is glad. His uneasiness increasing, Ireheart's words came thick and fast. 'I assume you are also grateful to me for keeping the newcomers out until such time as you've developed a method for neutralising the eye-whitener,' he hurtled on. 'That's also our way of protecting Girdlegard.' He bit his tongue. 'Is there any beer?' he asked, rather embarrassed at himself. 'A dark beer would be nice?'

Rodario placed both hands on the table, stretching out his arms in a somewhat grandiose manner. His training on the stage had combined with an exaggerated self-worth now that he was emperor.

'I would ask you, Ireheart, to be more measured,' he said snootily. 'We know that . . .'

'Forgive me for interrupting, Rodario the First, but High King Boïndil is absolutely correct.' Ataimînas looked gloomy. 'Ever since the hatred began between the elves and the älfar, they have been unable to avoid the curse. The greatest weapon they can wield against us is lack of trust. My race will not be able to develop fully until we can be sure that we have found and unmasked every single älf. This will take some time. Until then, High King, I beg you: keep the gates closed. Do not let any elf pass through unless they have been tested.'

This surprised Ireheart in spite of his unease. 'Are you working on a method of recognising the black-eyes?'

'We have not completed our research yet but we are optimistic we can speed up the process.' Ataimînas steepled his fingers, drawing attention to the many rings he wore over his delicate leather gloves. 'So far we have vetted four hundred – warriors and healers alike – and there is no doubt at all that they belong to our race. Ten of each profession will proceed to the dwarf regions to examine the new arrivals at the gates. Meanwhile, the rest will thoroughly check all the elves already here.'

Ireheart gazed at the elf, whose green eyes were shimmering as though he were holding back tears. *I want to know.* 'And what about you?'

'Ireheart!' Rodario was appalled. 'He is the Naishïon!'

'And an elf.' The dwarf stared at him intensely. 'Or could he be an älf? What proof have we got?' *Damn this passion! I need a beer to dampen my fire.*

Ataimînas got to his feet. Ireheart thought initially that the elf was about to leave and sabotage the meeting, but Ataimînas slipped the clothing from his upper body and showed them his back. There was a symbol that looked like a tattoo across the expanse of it. On closer inspection it proved to be a brand, together with small scars, making up a complex pattern. It could be interpreted as decorative but it was obvious the pain would have been atrocious.

'This is the seal of Sitalia,' he explained. 'A healer seals it into the flesh together with an elf spell. If one of my race were to touch it or if certain syllables are spoken, it will start to glow, demonstrating that the bearer is a true elf.'

'And what happens with an älf?' Ireheart wanted to know.

'Nothing at all. They'd only be able to paint on a copy.'

Ireheart was impressed. 'That's what I call a proper test.'

'May I see it from close up?' This was Sha'taï's polite request.

'No,' shushed Rodario. 'You can't . . .'

'Let her.' Ataimînas turned his back towards her and Ireheart held his breath. 'Take a good look.'

Sha'taï got up and gingerly went closer, climbing up on to the Naishïon's chair to admire the seal. 'How beautiful,' she breathed. 'How long do your artists need to do that, High Lord of the Elves?'

'It feels like an eternity while they're doing it,' he answered with honesty. 'The torture constitutes the actual test. The brand is the seal of approval. The evidence and the blessing the Creator gives.'

Ireheart's hands gripped the table edge as Sha'taï, all innocence, stretched out a finger to touch the Naishïon's skin. For a heartbeat the lines in his skin appeared to flash. But the dwarf could have been mistaken.

'Sha'taï!' Rodario was shocked and called the child to order.

The dark blonde-haired girl jumped down off the chair in shock and threw herself on the floor. 'Pardon me, O High Lord of the Elves! But I . . .'

Ataimînas slipped his robes back up over his shoulders and smiled, reaching a gloved hand out to her. 'Do not worry. What did it feel like?'

'Like soft tree bark,' Sha'taï replied as she was helped to her feet. 'High Lord of the Elves, please pardon my curiosity.'

By Vraccas. What hope have I got if she's wound him round her little finger? Ireheart swallowed. His throat was terribly dry. 'I'm thirsty,' he managed to croak.

Ataimînas called one of the guards over. 'Of course, High King. I'll have some refreshments brought. Your voice sounds as if you had been working at the furnace without a break. Black beer, then?' The dwarf nodded. 'And water and wine. I'm sure when we have all had something to drink we'll be better able to discuss the way forward.'

'Here's to us and all the gods! Girdlegard grows ever stronger!' Rodario was overdoing the jubilant tone. 'Oh, and do tell us: where's the new Tungdil? Is he coming?'

Ireheart asked for a second beer. *A very big tankard of very strong beer.* 'He's taking a break. May be some time,' he replied. And his answer was not far from the truth.

Girdlegard
Black Mountains
Kingdom of the Thirdling dwarves
Eastern Gate
6492nd solar cycle, winter

Bolîngor threw down the mantle and wasted no further words. He attacked the murderous elf who had treacherously slain four of the guards without giving them any chance to defend themselves. He did not even shout a warning.

As the elf parried his blows, his own club met metal with a thump and a clang. Bolîngor knew he must pursue the enemy and keep him busy. He struck deliberately high, aiming the spikes at throat and head. At such close quarters, the elf was in trouble and could not ward off the dwarf's attacks using his long sword.

You will kill no more dwarves. Bolîngor pulled a dagger out of the harness on his back and rammed it up to the hilt into his enemy's left thigh, yanking the blade sideways to the right, severing muscle and tendons. The injured leg shook and the elf collapsed with a shout. As he fell he struck out at the dwarf, who parried the blow with his bloody dagger and hammered the long spikes of his war club into the elf's face.

The elf was hurled back by the impact to land at the feet

of the reinforcements as they arrived on the scene. The dwarves stared at the dead elf's disfigured face. Alarm gongs and bugles were still sounding – the hunt was on.

'I was right to kill him. He killed four of my guards,' Bolîngor panted out his explanation, pointing at the pile of corpses. 'Take care when you find the other two.'

'Three,' came a pain-filled voice behind him. 'It's three again, Captain.'

Bolîngor turned around.

The dwarves who had captured the first elf lay groaning on the ground. The elf had used the confusion to overcome them and escape. But none of these guards had, it seemed, been killed.

'We'll get him,' Bolîngor vowed. Grabbing his cloak, he slung it on and went out through the door the first elf had fled through. *Not all of them are murderers*. It required some mental effort for him to press the catch on his club, making the spikes retreat. 'We will get each and every one of them!'

The steel and granite gates for the second and third lines of defence inside the mountain had been automatically and instantly closed at the first sounding of the alarm. The remaining three elves could not have got through into the tunnels, nor would any future intruders be able to. The search would be restricted to the foremost fortress.

'It's the advance party. They want to open the portcullis.' Bolîngor gave orders to double the guard at the controls for the massive iron grating. Then he took a quick look out of the window to see what was happening back at the camp.

The elves had been roused by the noise and lights in the stronghold. A large group of them had gathered in the middle of the camp, clearly debating what to do. Then around fifty broke away, led by Chynêa. They bore lanterns to light their path.

'I'll go down and calm her fears,' he announced. 'Get the Chancellor over here.' Bolîngor hurried down to the main gate, buttoning his coat. 'Leave the heavy screen open,' he commanded, as the procession of lights approached. 'Let the elves see we Thirdlings have nothing to hide.'

Chynêa was at the head of the band and her escort carried weapons and shields. 'What's happened?' she called out impatiently at the grating. 'Can we be of any assistance? How have the beasts got in to the fortress?'

This surprised Bolîngor. 'We have not been attacked.' Either the elves were putting on an excellent show of innocence or they were really unaware. It would be a clever trick to arrive fully armed claiming to want to help their allies in battle. 'Four of your people broke in. Two others must be lying in the snow by the outer wall.'

Chynêa noted the blood spatters on his face, hands and club. 'Are they still alive?' she asked quietly, indicating he should reply in a concealed gesture, not words. When he showed three fingers, she paled, turned to two of her escort and sent them over to where the elves who had fallen must be lying. 'Take care of them.'

'We will not harm any of your people if they don't harm us,' Bolîngor reassured. 'Otherwise we must respond in kind with the same degree of severity.'

Chynêa was about to reply but the murmuring behind her grew in intensity. She had to turn and speak to the crowd to settle them, but they were being joined by many more armed figures from the camp. Now some of the feared longbow archers were emerging. One of these marksmen might easily aim a shot through the portcullis grating.

A low cry, not from a dwarf throat, sounded in the passage. The elves pricked up their ears. Bolîngor turned to see what was happening behind him.

Four of his guards were pursuing an injured elf who was lurching rather than running. Blood spurted from a wound on his thigh and yet he continued to try to make his escape. Someone threw an axe that narrowly missed him. At that, the elves watching through the iron grating raised their voices in outrage and dismay.

The elf had no weapon to hand. This did not mean he had behaved peaceably up till then. But Bolîngor realised exactly how things must look to the others. He was especially concerned about the longbows. He wished Rognor were here. *Should I get this gate shut now . . . ?*

A war club came sailing through the air and hit the injured elf on the lower leg, tripping him up.

The dwarves were on him in a flash.

If I don't stop them, they'll kill him and there will be uproar here at the gates. 'Don't touch him!' Bolîngor yelled, seeing one of them circling his morningstar over his head ready to strike.

'He killed one of us,' the guard objected. 'And you . . .'

'Let him live,' Bolîngor roared, turning and stomping over to them. 'We will give him to his peers. They will judge his actions.'

The dwarves kept their hold on the elf, turning him over onto his front and forcing his arms behind his back to tie him up.

'Thank you,' Chynêa cried. 'We shall ask him what happened and we will give our verdict accordingly.'

'I shall see to it personally.' Bolîngor had covered a short distance when a shadow launched itself down at him. His right shoulder cracked and his arm went dead. Because he could not move his arm, he was unable to save himself as he fell; he crashed against the icy granite, snorting with fury. While he was still trying to swivel round, the elf ran over him towards the portcullis which now clattered its way up. He too had been injured and red life-juice was dripping from his side. 'Don't believe a word the mountain maggots say!' he yelled, incensed. 'They chased us and they killed Jorinîl. They slaughtered him in front of my eyes!'

Bolîngor forced himself up to sitting. *How did he get into the guardroom to turn the lever for the gate?* There were half a dozen warriors stationed in there to prevent exactly that happening. *He must have killed them all!*

The sounds of protest grew louder.

'Semhîlas, what have you done?' Chynêa asked reproachfully. 'What possessed you and your friends to break in to the fortress?'

'We did it because it is our sacred duty!' Semhîlas was close to the iron gate, which was steadily rising and would soon present an opening the crowd outside could storm through.

Some dwarves came marching up behind Bolîngor, holding shields and weapons. They formed a living defence wall and moved forward to protect him. Then came what Bolîngor had feared: the archers spanned their bowstrings to protect themselves and Semhîlas. At such close quarters, an arrow would go straight through a shield and possibly through a mail shirt as well.

A dwarf shout was heard, coming from above. The openings for the spear catapults showed the barrels pointing down at the elves gathered there. There were more shouted commands on the battlements, indicating that soldiers were ready to bombard the tented settlement.

The portcullis had completely opened by this time, clearing the way for a thousand angry elves. 'Stop!' thundered Bolîngor, struggling up with his one working arm and going to the middle of the gate archway. He stood between the two battle lines. *Where is Rognor?* 'Nobody is to fire a shot,' he shouted, clearly and with authority. 'We will go and find the last of the elf intruders. We will catch him and we will hand him over to you.'

'He killed Jorinîl!' Semhîlas shouted. 'And he was unarmed, just like me!'

'That's a lie,' bellowed the phalanx of dwarves in unison. Axes, clubs and morningstars were brandished. 'He killed four of us before Bolîngor struck him down.'

Chynêa, for her part, spread out her arms in an attempt to calm her people down and to stop her vengeance-crazed elves storming through, heaping disaster on them all. 'Semhîlas, I must ask you again: what right did you have?'

'It is the will of our goddess,' came the swift response. He pointed accusingly at Bolîngor. 'He is a murderer!'

'Your goddess holds no sway in a dwarf stronghold. And anyway, you weren't there to see it,' the dwarf thundered, clutching his broken shoulder. 'Tell us – did you harm any of my people?'

'I was defending myself.' Semhîlas spoke defiantly.

Chynêa flashed her eyes at the elf in anger. 'You have not acted as an ally or a future friend,' she admonished him sharply. 'Neither you nor the others that went with you.'

'We have to get into Girdlegard. Nothing must be allowed to hold us back. Not this fortress, not these mountains' – he raised his hand – 'not even the loss of a few of our people. And if we have to fight our way in,' he said, glancing at Bolîngor, 'then so be it. We are needed.' A few voices echoed his view, but Semhîlas did not seem to have much support.

The danger is not over. Bolîngor ordered the dwarves to lower their weapons and shields, even though the archers' arrows were still firmly aimed in their direction. 'We shall demand compensation from your Naishïon for those we have lost,' he made clear. 'We shall hand over our captives and the body of the elf we have . . .'

'A lie remains a lie,' Semhîlas howled, going to stand in front of Chynêa. 'Follow me!' he demanded, stretching up. 'Follow me through. They will be forced to let us pass.'

'We have been defending Girdlegard for thousands of cycles. You are not the first to fail in an attempt to break through.' Bolîngor had to stop soon; the pain was overwhelming. 'Don't force us to use our catapults . . .'

The spear-throwing machines clanked into action and a cloud of destruction pounded the ranks of the elves. The first spear pierced Semhîlas from the back, penetrating right through to stab Chynêa. The two of them staggered, bound together, and fell.

The first arrows flew in response and the dense lines of the defenders showed gaps. Bolîngor was hit in the left side and he stumbled away to the edge, avoiding further shots. The elves stormed in, covered by their archers' fire. The spear catapults in the passage were silent, as if there had been no time to reload.

No. Bolîngor slipped down the wall. Elf-warriors raced past him, swinging spears and long swords. Loud crashing and clattering ensued as the battle lines met.

Bolîngor was too weak to issue commands. Oblivion called, flattered, and enticed him. *It is so pointless,* he thought. *Both sides will be wiped out and no one will win.*

'Prepare the throwing machines,' boomed an angry, stentorian dwarf voice. 'Send burning pitch out onto the pointy-ears in front of the stronghold and burn them alive! Burn them all!'

'No,' whispered Bolîngor, stretching his arm out in appeal to the elves pushing past him to hurl themselves into battle against the defenders of the Black Mountains. 'No. Don't shoot. This must not happen. Take me up to the battlements. Let me stop it.' One of the elves noticed him and halted in his tracks while others raced past. Amid much shouting, death stalked through the ranks of elf and dwarf alike.

'You shan't be spared,' the elf said, speaking with clarity and fury. He jabbed with his spear – but at that moment an intricately engraved blade intervened.

Bolîngor saw the long spear point miss his throat by mere inches and heard it clang against the wall.

The elf whirled round, furious. 'Who—'

Bolîngor followed the elf's gaze even though by now his vision was blurring. He was nearing his end.

Next to him stood an elf in white armour of an elaborate and robust style bearing unfamiliar runes: identical symbols were visible on the blood-groove in the middle of the blade which had just saved Bolîngor's life. 'I am Phenîlas and my rank is that of a sorânïon. In the name of Ataimînas, Naishïon of the Grand Empire of Ti Lesîndur, I order you to lay down your weapon and go back to the far side of the metal gate.' His tone was cold and threatening. 'Otherwise you forfeit your infinitude.'

The elf-warrior laughed and reclaimed his spear. 'How can you . . .'

Bolîngor was not able to follow what happened next, so swiftly did the blow fall, but at the next troubled beat of his heart, the elf-warrior's head was severed from the shoulders to fall together with sheared-off hair and a bloodied neck chain. The torso and jerking limbs landed next to Bolîngor.

The white-armoured elf nodded at him. 'I can see you are dying, brave dwarf. But Vraccas will give you a worthy welcome and Sitalia's grace will accompany you. My people will cite your name in prayer as the one who tried to prevent this slaughter.'

Bolîngor realised the battle alarms had ceased. He saw the invaders withdrawing at great speed through the arched passage. Five armoured elves then followed, also wearing white emblazoned with the Naishïon's runic device. Bolîngor was too weak to question any of it. Only a slight breath left his lips. His eyelids were heavy.

His rescuer explained himself courteously. 'Our leader has sent us to support you. It is vital no black-eyes gain access to Girdlegard. We are here to ensure this.' He proffered his hand. 'This I promise you.'

Bolîngor nodded feebly. Just as the corners of his mouth twitched into a smile, his life-spark went out.

Rognor and Phenîlas stood side by side in the interior courtyard. The portcullis had been lowered and secured once more.

The bodies of eight warriors lay on a pile of petroleum-soaked wood. With them were heaped their weapons, their chainmail and their decorations. A layer of flammable cracklestone coals was ready under the pyre. Thirdling warriors of both sexes lined the high walls and walkways and gathered on the square and on the towers, ready to pay their last respects to the fallen. It would be Rognor's office to apply the torch and thus send the souls up to the Eternal Smithy with the flying sparks.

The five elves in their palladium armour who had arrived with Phenîlas stayed in the background and kept watch at the portcullis. Their presence served as a warning to the tent city inhabitants never again to attempt to storm the ramparts or to use guile to force an entrance.

A torch was passed to Rognor. 'Tonight we bid farewell to the brave souls who defended our fortress,' he said, his voice carrying. 'Älfar infiltrated the elf settlement and tricked them into the assault. Their deviousness bore bloody fruit. May they never succeed.' He held the blazing torch to the soaked logs and flames shot up. 'May Vraccas bid our brave ones welcome. And may their forebears receive them with open arms.'

Fire crackled and hissed its way under the bodies and through the woodpile, destroying everything it touched. A bass trumpet played the *Hymn to the Heroes*. The bystanders joined in with the words of the song and the sound of the dwarf chorus was heard far and wide, echoing back from the mountains in a carpet of sound.

Rognor felt shivers up and down his spine. He threw the torch onto the pyre. 'No one will hear of this,' he mouthed, without taking his eyes off the pyre.

'I thank you,' Phenîlas replied. 'I had the bodies thrown into the ravine without funeral rites. *Älfar* deserve no better.'

Rognor responded with a barely perceptible nod. The two of them had come to a secret agreement that all six of the assailants who had attempted to open the way for their compatriots should be designated älfar in disguise. Phenîlas would take an oath to that effect, with the aim of turning the anger in the camp to deep shame that they had fallen for the lies of their sworn enemies, thus bringing about the deaths of innocents.

The elves that had met their deaths in the battle of the passageway, on the other hand, were given every official recognition, and were seen as victims of the älfar.

No one should ever learn that the four elves who had forced their way into the stronghold had lied. Or that one of them had fired the catapult aimed at Chynêa and Semhîlas, sparking off the battle. Or that murder had been their motive.

Rognor kept his eyes fixed on the flames. Apart from himself and Phenîlas, nobody knew the awful truth. *It has to stay that way for peace.*

'I'll start tomorrow with the interrogation and vetting process. Don't worry about any screams coming from the tent city.'

Rognor was pretty sure many of the dwarves, on the contrary, would enjoy what they heard.

I am of the opinion that there could be no other crowned head better than my own.

Why is that?

I have already acted every conceivable role on stage, so it should be easy for me to portray a ruler.

As you see: all my time in the theatre was spent rehearsing for my true role in life and for my own regency. What other monarch could claim that?

From: *Rodario – King, Emperor and Showman*

XVI

Girdlegard
United Kingdom of Gauragar-Idoslane
Idoslane
6492nd solar cycle, winter

Hargorin saw the clouds of icy moisture sent up by Gosalyn's pony as it traversed the long grass, a dangerous terrain. Anything could be lurking there. Where there was a body lying face down in the middle of nowhere, an ambush was probably not far off. *Foolish girl.*

'And then she'll wonder why she got hit by an arrow,' Beligata muttered. She looked at Hargorin. 'What do we do?'

Gosalyn had dismounted by now and jumped over the bank. 'We make sure she doesn't get killed.' He urged his pony on and followed the tracks left by Gosalyn's mount. The two of them saw her running when they had reached the place where she had left her small horse. She was less than thirty paces from where the woman was lying.

'She hasn't even drawn her weapon.' Beligata was audibly critical. She dismounted and took hold of her double axe.

'Go, run,' Hargorin commanded as he got down from the saddle. 'I'll follow.' What with his metal leg, fast progress was beyond him. Beligata raced down the slope.

Hargorin gathered the reins from both ponies and fastened leather loops round their front feet to stop them straying. He set off, constantly vigilant, and held his long-handled axe diagonally across his body.

The rain refused to stop, making it difficult to hear noises that might indicate danger. The ditch offered no protection from any marksman who might be standing on the top with a bow or a crossbow.

Hargorin limped forwards to where the two dwarf women were attending to the figure on the ground.

'She's dead,' Beligata called out. She, too, was keeping her eyes skimming the surrounding area. She displayed a broken arrow. 'This was lying next to her. The rest is in her heart.'

An älfar war arrow. Instinctively he got down onto one knee, not an easy performance with his artificial leg. He used his axe to steady himself.

Hargorin stared at the dead woman. Gosalyn had turned her on her back. It was not Coïra but dressed to resemble her. She looked about sixteen cycles old. 'It'll be one of Coïra's famula, I expect.'

'A diversionary tactic.' Beligata showed them the pale face that had no marks of decomposition because of the cold.

'The maga did not have enough magic in her for a spell, so they had to make do with disguising her,' Gosalyn surmised, looking over to the ruins of the orc fortress that housed the entrance to the caves. 'We must find out whether they went in.' She got up. 'Let us cover the body with stones. And then we'll go and investigate.'

Hargorin was glad to see Gosalyn so eager for action, but this unrestrained wildness might make it hard to get all of them back home safe. 'In future you wait for my orders.'

She was about to answer back, but then nodded, realising she had been at fault. 'I was sure there was no danger.'

'I expect that's what she thought, too,' Hargorin replied as he closed the dead woman's eyes. 'And now she's dead.'

'If there's an älf on their trail, we'll have to hurry up,' said

Beligata. 'Leave her where she is. It'll take too much time and effort to get stones to cover her.'

Hargorin agreed; he wanted to get out of the ditch. They presented a very easy target there. He got to his feet and climbed up the other side of the trench. The two dwarf women followed his lead.

There was nothing left of the original fortress save for a few ineptly-hewn stones. Here and there sparse tufts of grass grew on the poor soil, and seemed half-drowned in the rain and sleet. The presence of the beasts had ruined the earth hereabouts, even though there were no longer any orcs to be seen. *It suits the area.* Hargorin saw the recently walled-up entrances. The blocks were as big as a man and impossible to shift. Elsewhere there were piles of debris that he thought had probably been intended for filling in the tunnels. The captain they had spoken to had not lied: Mallenia had ensured no one could get into the caves.

'We'll split up, but stay vigilant. Look for anywhere there's a crack in the ground,' he instructed them. 'It may prove easier to dig through a crack than to try to move those blocks of stone or shift the rubble.'

The others nodded and raced off. Hargorin limped on, stamping his mechanical leg down hard to gauge from the sound what the subsoil was like.

The rain was getting colder and there were now ice crystals mixed with it. His breath appeared as a white cloud in front of his face. His clothes were sodden and heavy. He would take up the captain's offer of the fireside if they didn't come up with something soon.

I wonder where the history-teller is? He was worried by the nagging thought that Carmondai might be working hand in glove with the älf that was roaming loose.

He kept stomping through the winter rain. He could not

see through it and it drenched right through to his skin. No shelter far and wide. *Looks like Elria wants to drown us from above.* He kept his eyes fixed on the ground, where the water made puddles or flowed downhill. He hoped the water would show him where there might be a crack in the stone they could use to force an entrance.

Suddenly the puddles were red.

Blood! Hargorin looked around to find the source of the colour change. It seemed to be flowing out from behind two weather-eroded rock columns.

He made his way over cautiously, axe in hand. He did not want to call for help unless he actually saw an enemy. There were two more blue-robed women lying on the rock, with long black arrow shafts sticking out of them. They had been shot from behind; they had clearly taken cover in the wrong direction. Crows hopped around near the bodies, squawking furiously at the dwarf as he approached. He could see there was no point in trying to help.

His caution turned to astonishment when he saw that the blood did not stem from the dead famulae. It came from an älf lying on his back ten paces away, half-hanging over one edge of the rock. The blood was pouring out of a cut in his neck and dripping down over the anger lines on his face and drenching his blond hair.

Still alive? Hargorin raised his axe. He felt he was being watched. The sound of the rain had altered, as if now it were falling on canvas.

'I went ahead. Hope that's all right,' said a friendly voice. And there was Carmondai, holding a kind of tarpaulin on a stick to keep the rain off. 'Otherwise you'd have been the next victims. Though I know you would have liked to deal with the assassin yourself.'

He may be old – Hargorin looked at the älf with the cut throat, the fury lines now fading – *but he's good. Unbelievably good.*

Carmondai smiled and held his hand out in the rain. 'Horrid weather for our trip. You should go back to the guardhouse and rest. We can follow the trail in the morning.'

'What trail?'

The älf pointed north. 'I found dwarf boot prints. One pair. A male dwarf. Carrying a fairly heavy burden, I'd say. And the blood I found among the trees is human. Probably a woman.'

'How do you know?'

'I can read tracks.'

'No, I mean the blood type.'

Carmondai's smile grew demonic. 'I am a master of word and image. Guess what I used to paint with?'

Hargorin could have kicked himself. 'Ugh. I'll call the others and you can show us the tracks.' He took his horn and sounded a few notes.

Carmondai nodded and relaxed his stance as they waited for the two dwarf women to join them.

'What's this canopy on a stick thing you've got there?'

'I made it on the way. Quite useful.'

'Only if you don't have to fight,' replied Hargorin.

'If you know enough about the art of killing,' said Carmondai, 'you only need one hand.'

The two dwarf women arrived from different directions, amazed at the tableau before them. The älf and Hargorin quickly caught them up. The story-weaver led them away from the ruin towards an overgrown copse where they did indeed see blood and trampled grass.

The small boot marks indisputably led northwards.

'Get the ponies.' Hargorin turned around. 'We can rest when we've caught up with this dwarf.'

Girdlegard
Elf realm of Ti Lesîndur
6492nd solar cycle, winter

Ireheart would have had every reason to be content following the meeting of the high kings. Elves, humans and dwarves were at last on the same page. They had unity, save for a few details. It was so complete that the dwarf wondered how there had been discord and strife for so many tens and hundreds of cycles in the past. But he was still unsettled. *If only that brat weren't involved.*

Ireheart was sitting in front of the ruler's palace wrapped in a warm coat, inhaling the sharp cold air. He had finished the pipe he had been smoking.

This orbit the other crowned heads were due to arrive in Barrenbrig to discuss what contribution each kingdom should make. *And all this hammering, sawing and banging. I could do without it.* The elves were hard at work: masons, carpenters, and painters were transforming the town to their own taste. *How about a bit of peace and quiet? I need to think.*

He picked up his crow's beak and went back inside the wooden building, strolling through the corridors to find a place that was less noisy. *And a beer would be nice.*

There were no guards to stop him exploring. If he met any servants, they unfailingly asked if he needed any help. The whole place smelled of incense. There were pots of sand in the niches with fragrant sticks burning. As the smoke drifted it seemed to form runes in the air like a constant blessing. Chimes tinkled.

But he could still hear the construction noises: thud, crash, bang.

I wonder if they've put in a cellar? He walked to where he thought the stairs might be. *I'm sure to find a beer down there.*

But the stairs led up, not down. All the steps in the entire place went up, not down. He took them anyway. A short while later he arrived at the entrance to a steel chamber with a complicated lock. He was filled with curiosity. The runes engraved on the doors did not help him at all.

I didn't know elves stored treasure. Ireheart took a look around him. There were no guards and he could not hear any footsteps. *Vraccas, would you like me to have a look?*

He placed his calloused hand on the door. *Steel. Cold.* No alarm sounded.

It may turn out to be the Naishïon's privy. Ireheart laughed to himself. *If so, I'm sure as High King I've every right to put my fat behind on it.* It would not make a very good excuse should he be found, but he was not going to miss this opportunity.

He looked at the lock and tapped the walls and door, examining the hinges. Ireheart was full of admiration for the metalwork but thought it badly mounted. He found the weak places in the joins and the closing mechanism. His people were better than anyone else at this sort of thing. He knew Freeling dwarves would occasionally work for outlaw bands, using their knowledge, instincts and specialised tools to break open the locks of rich humans' safes and treasure boxes. Ireheart himself punished any Freeling caught at such an activity.

But right now I could use one of those guys. He thought Beligata might be able to help, but she was away on a mission. *I'll have a go myself.* He took a metal fastening and bent it to shape; he used this and his dagger. *Here I am, High King of all the Children of the Smith. Steel will obey me.* He poked around in the lock mechanism, sweating with effort and cursing under his breath, but persisting with his endeavours. Suddenly there was a loud clunk.

'Aha!' he exclaimed.

A series of clicks ensued and then a low grinding sound set in. Bolts snapped back and the metal door started to open before him. In the nick of time he caught an elf's voice through the opening crack.

Someone's coming out. He looked at the piece of bent metal with a grin. *And there was I thinking I'd had a brainwave and cracked it.*

He moved swiftly behind the angle of the opening door where he would not be seen.

Ataimînas stormed out of the chamber, wiping his hands on a linen cloth that he discarded; the door began to close automatically behind him.

Thanks, Vraccas. You will have known what you were doing just now. Ireheart forced himself into the narrow aperture, slipping off his coat to get through. Otherwise he would have stuck fast, squashed like a grape.

He found himself in a dimly lit room whose walls were lined with small drawers and lockers. It looked at first glance like a huge reinforced safe, but then Ireheart realised it was a prison cell. A naked elf was chained to the floor, his body covered with cuts, some of which were freshly inflicted and bleeding.

But when Ireheart saw the fury lines on the face, he knew he was wrong. This was in fact an älf, even though the eyes were white. *An älf, of course.*

The captive looked up in astonishment. 'A rock-grubber,' he said, settling into a less uncomfortable position, the chains clanking as he moved. 'So you are working with the elves nowadays? Ataimînas bored of torturing and he's sent you in his place?' Then it dawned on the shackled älf. 'Or have you broken in? Thought you'd find elf treasure, did you, you greedy mountain maggot?'

The door slammed shut and the bolts closed.

Ireheart would have to put his mind to finding how to get out later. For the present he was too intrigued by what he had found. 'Don't expect any sympathy from me.'

'Then give me a swift death!' The älf proffered his bared throat. 'Go on, strike me.'

The High King laughed at him. 'As far as I'm concerned, you can go on being tortured for all eternity.' He looked at the little drawers as if their contents were of more interest to him than the prisoner, which was understandably not true.

The Naishïon had never mentioned the existence of this älf. There must be a reason for keeping it quiet and it couldn't merely be the pleasure of clandestine torturing. The fact there was a secret room at all spoke volumes.

Do the black-eyes have an aristocracy? But even that was no reason for keeping him hostage. There was no point negotiating with älfar.

'Kill me,' whispered the älf.

'What would I get from that?'

'I can tell you secrets first.'

'Of course you could.' Ireheart snorted with disgust. 'A black-eyes who wants to die and who speaks the truth.'

The älf hissed furiously and laid his head on the ground, staring at the ceiling. 'Then in that case I shan't tell you about the prophecy.'

Now Ireheart had to laugh. 'That's a cheap trick you're trying.'

'Let's make a deal where neither of us will lose or win.' The älf's voice was quiet but insistent. 'I'll tell you about the prophecy and you can challenge Ataimînas on it. He won't like it one jot.' He smiled. 'A secret as well-guarded as everything else in this room.'

'But I'm in here.'

'That's true.' The älf grinned. 'I'd love the door to open now for the Naishïon to come in.'

'So he can enjoy looking at your face.'

'Yes. Because then he'd have to kill you to keep his secret safe.' He drew a rattling breath. 'Whoever you are, mountain maggot, he'd kill you. Then war would break out between the grubbers and the pointy-ears and that would be a joy to me.' He gave a pained laugh. 'Go on, off you go and ask Ataimînas. I'd ask you to draw a picture of the face he makes so I can see it, but with your fat dwarf fingers you'd never be able to do it.'

Malice is one of the strongest weapons in the black-eyes' arsenal. But then again, there might be something to it.

Ireheart checked the rows of drawer handles and lockers but could not read the labels. 'What's in them?'

The älf shrugged. 'Ask Ataimînas. He brought the chamber with him.' The älf seemed to be thinking. 'You don't believe me, do you?'

'And why should I? Lies do more damage than any weapon.'

'The truth is deadlier than any lie.' The älf laughed, with difficulty. 'The truth, and this might sound strange, kills trust. Try it yourself. Always speak the truth and people will hate you for it.' His breath was shallow and quick. He was not in good health. 'Will you swear to ask Ataimînas about the prophecy?'

Ireheart laughed and shouldered the crow's beak.

The älf looked at him. 'Do you know how to get out of here?'

Ireheart had already observed that there were no handles or knobs or signs for operating the door mechanism. 'I'll find a way.'

'Ataimînas will find you first. And then you'll never be seen again.' The älf shut his eyes. 'But *I* know what to do,' he said with a joyless smile. 'That means I hold the key to your life. Isn't that ironic? Here I am, in chains and your sworn enemy. But you need me.'

Ireheart chose to ignore him. He tapped the walls but the sounds gave him no clues. He did not like the situation at all. And he suddenly felt thirsty.

Extremely thirsty.

His heart started pounding and the blood rushed through his arteries. With every breath he took, the steel chamber seemed to shrink in size and with it the amount of available air.

'Do let me know when I can help you. Despite the chains,' the prisoner mocked.

Ireheart intensified his search for the opening mechanism, his movements clumsier now and more frantic. He was exhausting his reserves of strength and getting nowhere. The feeling of unease was overwhelming and the onset of a raging fury announced itself.

He tightened his hold on the handle of the crow's beak. *It's no use to me. The steel is too thick. But maybe there'll be something in one of the strongboxes that'll help me get out.*

'I'm starting to feel sorry for you,' said the älf with a laugh.

'I'll tell you the place you have to press to open the door. But first' – he looked him in the eye – 'listen to part of the prophecy.'

'No.'

But the captive was already speaking:

In the new empire
My untainted children
Will live in harmony
With their purified brother-killers
And behold,
A new era shall dawn

Ireheart was too late in putting his fingers in his ears and then felt foolish, so he stopped.

'And that's supposed to be important?' He would have liked to smash the älf's head in for making him listen to those lines. *I'm not going to do him that favour.* In exasperation, he ran his hands through his hair where his scalp was itching. *I've got to get out of here! At once!*

'Second symbol on the left in front of you. Looks like a tripartite moon over a pond.' The älf shut his eyes.

Ireheart could not take the confined space any longer. He tried the symbol. The heavy door slid open to let the dwarf out. He stepped outside, drawing a deep breath and looked at the prisoner, motionless now on the floor.

Freedom!

The door swung shut and the bolts snapped into place again. Ireheart would have loved to know how the whole thing was constructed.

Prophecy. He exhaled, picked up his coat and left. *He just made that all up, to . . .* But as he marched through the palace, he could not think of any reason at all why the älf would have made it up.

At last Ireheart located a door from which an enticing smell of food came. Beer would not be far away. *When I've a mug or three I'll be able to think more clearly.*

Ireheart had found more than four mugs and then settled down for a little nap to help him think about things. As soon as he woke up he found a courier standing in front of him. He was from the Grey Mountains and must have ridden like a demon to reach Barrenbrig.

He had with him a report from Balyndar about progress on the fortifications and the new weaponry at the Stone Gateway. And there was also a message from whoever was sending the ghaists out. The threatening lines demanding Sha'taï be handed over were enough to sober the High King instantly.

I knew she was trouble! Ireheart was more concerned about how the letter's author in the Outer Lands knew what was happening in Girdlegard. *A ghaist loose in the Fifthling kingdom. That will mean losses for the tribe before Balyndar manages to destroy it.*

He ordered a generous portion of goulash but did not ask for an extra beer. He choose instead a stimulating herbal mixture to help shake off the mists in his mind before the forthcoming talks. There was nothing for it: he would have to broach the matter in the hope of averting harm to Girdlegard. Even though the humans would reject out of hand the demand for the girl or her dead body to be surrendered and the elves would probably do the same.

And what about me? Ireheart found he was leaning toward sacrificing Sha'taï, though there was no certainty the anonymous threat would be followed up.

It might be that the author of the message wanted to gain more magic power. Perhaps he needed the girl for a ritual or a special spell, or maybe there were difficult inheritance squabbles that would be laid to rest if she were dead.

Well then. Ireheart took the last mouthful and scraped his bowl. *It's going to be some picnic, these talks.*

Wiping his beard and combing his hair in front of the mirror, he considered his appearance. *Worrying is giving me wrinkles. Wish I could shave the sides of my hair and be a simple warrior again. Like before.* The office of High King made huge demands. 'Oink, oink,' he murmured. 'What a long time ago.'

Ireheart gave himself a shake and turned back towards the assembly hall, taking three of his own warriors with him as usual. With the exception of Rodario, all the powerful figures of Girdlegard were already gathered there. Dirisa and Ataimînas were talking and Isikor was reading through a pile of papers and making notes that he then handed to Astirma to skim through. Today Astirma was wearing simple clothing; there was nobody that needed impressing.

Mallenia, in armour, beckoned Ireheart to her side. 'Any news of Coïra?'

Ireheart kept his face immobile. 'She's not been seen in our kingdoms searching for magic sources. Why do you ask?'

'Since leaving elf territory she hasn't been heard of. I got a message from home.' The blonde Idoslane leader turned away from the others and lowered her voice. 'The captain of a unit that patrols the Toboribor area reported finding bodies in the ruins of an old orc fortress: three women, all slain by älfar arrows, and an älf whose throat had been slit.'

'Oh.' Ireheart had to suppress a desire to belch. It would have been unseemly to cover the queen of the double state in a cloud of goulash and beer fumes.

'A group of dwarves had previously entered the area saying they were on the lookout for Carmondai. They wanted the bounty money.' Mallenia gave him a stony stare. 'One of the group was recognised: Hargorin Deathbringer. Can you tell me, High King, what the ruler of the Thirdlings was doing in Idoslane? I am sure you know the answer.'

Why bother to lie? 'I sent him and a trusty band out to search for the maga.'

'So why didn't they say that was why they were there?'

'They didn't want any rumours going round.'

Mallenia fell silent for a few heartbeats. 'Why did the murderer get his throat cut?'

'To kill him, perhaps?' Ireheart suggested with a grin.

'Your dwarves would have hacked him to pieces. This injury was carried out with sophistication.' Mallenia's stare became even more intense. 'It sounds like the work of Carmondai.'

This genuinely surprised Ireheart. 'You think he's travelling with them?'

'Yes, I do.'

Ireheart did not know what to make of this.

In the meantime, Rodario and Sha'taï had arrived. The former actor had not wanted to miss an opportunity for flamboyant dress: his colourful robes would have put a summer flower meadow to shame. The girl, on the other hand, was wearing a simple, deep pink dress.

The assembled members of the council seemed to be waiting for Mallenia and Ireheart to stop chattering so that the talks could begin.

Look at that showman too long and it'll make your eyes go all funny. Ireheart shook himself. 'Take an älf with them? I can't imagine they'd do that. And why would he have killed an assassin of his own race? Wouldn't it have been more likely that they'd have got together and wiped my dwarves out?'

'The old älf knows many Girdlegard secrets. Tion and Samusin alone know what he's up to.' Mallenia bent down to speak quietly. 'If something happens to Coïra and your dwarves are involved in any way, Rodario will go crazy. He won't be answerable for his actions. Make sure things don't get to that point.' She placed her hand on his shoulder, before sweeping past him to take her seat.

But Rodario's always doing stupid things. How's it going to get any worse? Ireheart was still amazed at what he had heard. He went over to his special chair, so lost in thought that he missed the start of the Naishïon's opening speech. He was wondering if Mallenia could be right.

The assembly first addressed the question of which kingdom would take on what responsibility in the interests of the community as a whole in order to strengthen Girdlegard. There were a few intelligent proposals: in case of outside threat, new strongholds and fortified towns should be run jointly with multi-racial garrisons on standby. More famuli, male and female, should be trained and troops held in reserve.

Families should be settled in remote, underpopulated areas, to work on clearing the land and preparing it for agriculture, in the expectation that they would no longer be forced to rely on Tabaîn as their sole source of grain. A large project was mooted for Urgon, and in Sangpûr the plan was to double the number of irrigation channels.

Ireheart only half-followed the enthusiastic debate. His own people had enough of a task protecting the place. No time left to go off clearing forests or levelling hills. And then there was this news from the Grey Mountains. The message was burning a hole in his pocket.

'How much can the dwarf mines supply in the way of ore?' This was Ataimînas' question to Ireheart.

'Ore? What for?' Ireheart forced himself to bring his mind back to the discussion.

'For weapons, for the fortresses we'll be manning together, of course,' said the elf, with an air of having had to repeat himself.

'And we'll need your ideas about possible sites,' Astirma interjected. 'You dwarves know everything there is to know about minerals and geology.'

'Of course.' Ireheart felt bad about having to dampen everyone's spirits. The Council debate was going so well, their talk overflowing with confidence and eagerness. It was obvious everyone was counting on the peace lasting at least one hundred cycles. 'There are one . . . or two things I must bring to your attention.'

'Surely not the price of metal ore?' Rodario was enjoying his little joke. 'Even if the Children of the Smith are well known for their love of gold.'

Ireheart plunged in. 'It's about Queen Mallenia's ward. And about a prophecy.'

Rodario interrupted again. 'Oh, no, High King: please don't! Not some new ghost story about evil in the form of an innocent young child. Or that a creature from the Outer Lands is threatening war. We've been listening to this garbage for nearly a cycle now.' He emphasised his displeasure with grand gestures, using his stage experience to drum up amusement in his audience. 'Come on, we've got so much to discuss without your pessimism and catastrophising'

'The prophecy is not about Sha'taï, although that would not have surprised me.' Ireheart turned to Ataimînas, fixing his eyes on him. 'It's a question of the elves and Sitalia's predictions, brought to Girdlegard in a steel-clad chamber. This palace carries a steel cell, under thorough lock and key. It's full of lockers and drawers such as we use for our treasure hoards.'

Rodario blinked in astonishment. 'That does indeed . . . sound strange.'

All eyes focused on the Naishïon, who seemed to have been transformed into a statue.

So the black-eyes was right. Ireheart was not pleased about that. It was not a good feeling. It felt even more worrying to know he had come across secrets affecting his homeland. 'What do you say to this, Ataimînas?'

Sha'taï grasped Rodario's hand. He smiled down at her and touched Mallenia. The High King noted the movement run round the table. This did not include himself. Many of the monarchs, he saw, were touching feet under the table.

What's going on here? 'I can quote from the prophecy, if you like,' Ireheart went on.

Ataimînas raised his hand. 'It is too soon for that.'

The dwarf retorted: 'It can never be too soon, when the future of Girdlegard is at stake. Tell us the prophecies.'

'It is too soon,' repeated the Naishïon. His tone was friendly but he had gone very pale. He knew now that the High King must have been inside the steel chamber.

I wonder if he will try to have me killed, like the black-eyes predicted? Ireheart could not read any expression in the elf's frozen features.

'What do you mean by *too soon*?' Ireheart was relieved to hear Astirma enter the debate. 'Why don't we know about it or why are we not supposed to hear it?'

Outside, in the corridor, loud noises were heard: angry shouts, alarm horns, blades clanging, shields clashing. The guards in the hall turned towards the entrance, ready to defend their masters.

There followed the sound of several heavy objects crashing into the double doors. The bolts groaned under the strain.

The doors suddenly gave way, bursting open. They were forced off their hinges and floored several soldiers who had been standing near. Ireheart saw blood on the outside of the doors and twisted corpses in a heap on the threshold. Someone had hurled the warriors from a distance against the hall doors to force an entry.

Above them the huge form of a ghaist loomed up, instantly recognisable with the copper helmet and leather armour though it had lost its flagpole. It was covered in blood that was streaming down its muscular arms to drip on to the light-coloured floor matting.

Did it come through the mountains? Ireheart grabbed his crow's beak. *I should have started my speech earlier.*

The guards in the council chamber formed a defensive barricade round the crowned heads. This would be a suicidal endeavour. Two elves jumped from right and left to attack the ghaist from behind: one swung a long sword to the nape while the other wielded his weapon against the back of the creature's knees. One of these warriors had the sword ripped out of his hands, while the other found his blade snapped in two, as if the ghaist had skin of iron. It whirled around, fists clenched, striking the brave elves in their faces with a crack loud enough to be heard at the back of the room. Bones splintered as if fragile glass, fragments protruded through the flesh. The victims were thrown bodily against a far wall.

The ghaist stood up straight, arms stretched out to the sides, white steam leaking from the eyeholes in the full-face copper helmet. A high-pitched sound pierced the room but it did not come from the magic being – it was Sha'taï, screaming for all she was worth. The ghaist vaulted over the sprawled bodies to hurl itself feet first against the ring of soldiers. It threw five warriors aside as if they weighed no more than straw dolls. Spear shafts shattered under the impact and ineffective blades clattered to the ground, shields splintered or bent.

Standing in the middle of the group of brave bodyguards, the ghaist reached behind itself and took out a small metal container, such as Ireheart had heard described previously, casting it on to the table with an unexpectedly deliberate action: the very table where the powerful reigning heads of Girdlegard's people had been in council.

Before anyone could try to grab hold of the ghaist, it took another leap and landed behind Rodario, felling the young emperor with a blow. It used its other arm to ward off a sword strike from the queen of Idoslane; the steel sang out and vibrated, but remained intact.

Then the magic being grabbed hold of Sha'taï and clamped the shrieking child to its side before sprinting through the bank of soldiers and out of the room.

'Nobody shoot!' yelled Mallenia, rushing off. 'We must bring it down. I want my little girl back!'

Rodario lay unconscious on the floor. Astirma hurried over to see to him. All the guards streamed out in Mallenia's wake. Ataimînas looked at the metal capsule on the table, then glanced at Ireheart. To Ireheart's astonishment, he gave a smile. 'The prophecy,' he mouthed, 'has come true.' He picked up a spear and followed Mallenia.

Ireheart set off after the others as quickly as he was able. *I shouldn't have eaten so much goulash.*

Not that he wanted to help Sha'taï. But he was keen to see if the others would manage to fell the ghaist. Perhaps Sitalia's wisdom had something appropriate to hand that might come in useful in the Grey Mountains.

I talked with him a great deal.
A very great deal.
We had enough time, when we were incarcerated, and now I know his story.

I know there were doubts about whether he was genuine.
But I am absolutely positive that he is the one true Tungdil. I witnessed magic effects and waves in Phondrasôn. It would have been possible to create a copy. Realistically possible. It happened.

The question Girdlegard must ask: what else was affected by those mysterious eruptions of magic?
Did they perhaps change the original when they made the copy?
It would be prudent to remain watchful, even if no one else is vigilant.

Secret notes for
The Writings of Truth
written under duress by Carmondai

XVII

Girdlegard
United Kingdom of Gauragar-Idoslane
Idoslane
6492nd solar cycle, winter

Tungdil watched the sleeping, naked figure of the maga floating in the energy field, surrounded by scintillating sparks and the occasional lightning flash. Her long black hair fanned out as if she were swimming in water.

He had crouched down nearby to be on hand to see to her injuries if it should prove necessary. In the few moments he had spent asleep, he had had a dream. About Balyndis and about Sirka, the women who meant a great deal to him. Sirka had died a long time ago, and he had no idea if there was any way back for him and Balyndis. He could only hope there might be a chance. He was sure of his feelings for her. Phondrasôn had given him time enough to process his thoughts and emotions.

It's vital the maga survives this. Girdlegard needs her. Who else is capable of training the next generation of young magi and magae?

He had been able to close up the deep wound in her side long enough to keep her alive. But it had been a matter of a few heartbeats, trying to get her here in time. Tungdil had covered the whole way at a trot, not stopping for rest.

Her right arm seemed to have been subjected to a different sort of injury. Tungdil assumed it was from a spell that had gone wrong. Below the elbow, the arm looked made of glass, while in other places, muscles, arteries and tendons were visible under a transparent skin. But this magic source would mend that, too.

He had almost forgotten about this place where, in his time as a young smith, he and all others had been forbidden to go. The time in the empire of darkness had subjected his mind to harsh ordeals, stealing knowledge from him, substituting new material and changing familiar memories – sometimes for the better, sometimes not. But as he made his way through the land, letting his soul become acquainted once more with the peaceful surroundings, the memories began to come back. Even those he believed lost forever.

For Tungdil this magic wellspring was experienced as a prickling on his skin; the magic stretched feelers out in his direction and swiftly withdrew them. It did not wish to touch him or bind him to itself.

Tungdil saw the pearls of sweat on the maga's forehead. The wound fever had not completely receded. This was due to the poison the älf had put on his arrow tips and sword blade, as was their assassins' custom. A scratch would be enough to kill the victim.

But not her. Tungdil tried to find a comfortable position on the cold, damp ground, but here the earth gave no warmth such as he was used to in the mines and tunnels. His dark red robe with its Vraccas runes and the dark grey mantle he wore over it were clammy. Only the magic field gave protection – and it was a curse at the same time.

He kept remembering the story, as he had done during his captivity in Phondrasôn when he cast his thoughts to his homeland in an attempt not to lose his mind. But he never thought the legend would be of significance. This energy was something special: one of Lot-Ionan's famuli had conducted a clandestine experiment, trying to influence the magic field in which their tunnel was situated. He had wanted to see if the field could be made flexible and elongated, so as to have threads of energy like slow-flowing honey or caramelised sugar.

The basic idea behind the young wizard apprentice's proposal was excellent: one would be able to move away from the actual field while still remaining in contact with its magical power. But the experiment failed. As a result, a small part of the field changed its nature. To protect others, Lot-Ionan had it fenced off and walled up, so that no famulus or famula would have access – except for the one who had got caught there. Tungdil believed he had seen the bones of the unlucky apprentice lying in the dirt. Punishment for having acted without authority.

People had forgotten about the place. Apart from Tungdil, nobody that would have known about it was still alive.

The maga Coïra would now have a price to pay for her life. *But at least this way she will be in a position to pay that price. I hope she sees the situation like I do.* Tungdil observed the healing taking place, leaving out nowhere on her body. Whatever diseases she might have carried until this moment would be dissolved away.

The fact that this place still existed was gift from Samusin. The fields could have shifted and the new location might have closed off the source. *I thank you, Vraccas.* The dwarf had had a long search to find the entrance. The tunnel had for the most part collapsed and the roof had fallen in. Looters had left tracks, looking for plunder.

Tungdil temporarily wondered if he should light a fire, but thought too much smoke in the confined space might suffocate him. He also did not want to leave his present position, as he needed to watch over the sleeping maga.

Tungdil was undecided. He needed to find warmer, dry clothing. He would not be able to do that until he got to a village a few miles away. He had seen one that had been erected on the ruins of Goodmeadow, devastated hundreds of cycles previously by the orcs.

He remembered his time with the magus, the goodhearted old man, who, according to Ireheart, had turned into one of the most dangerous opponents of dwarves and humans alike. *I find that hard to believe.* It had been difficult for him to take in much of what he had read in recent orbits, turning the pages of history book after history book. What cruel ordeals Girdlegard had been subjected to since he had left to enter the Black Abyss. In Tungdil's view, it was Tion who was behind events. *But that will end now.*

He was astonished to find his own history and had just lapped it up. Apparently his magic doppelgänger had arrived, armoured in black tionium and equipped with älfar capabilities, full of mystery and puzzles and yet untiring in his efforts for Girdlegard. He was rewarded by receiving the sharp end of Keenfire.

It must have been that magic explosion. Tungdil stared at the golden mark on his hand. *Back then, in the cave in Phondrasôn.* Was that the reason the magic field was retreating from him? *Or could it be that I, too, am but a counterfeit version, a doppelgänger?* He was worried by this thought but found it funny, too. A replica, neurotic about being a fake – nice idea.

'You brought me here,' came the voice of the woman.

She's woken up at last. Tungdil looked over at her and bowed. 'My name is Tungdil Goldhand.' He indicated her dirtied clothing lying next to the field. 'I'm sorry I had to undress you. Your garments were filthy with dirt and blood.'

He admired the way she showed no disgust at his own disfigurements.

Coïra's bright, blue eyes explored her own body and her hands. 'This . . . how did this . . . ?' she stuttered in amazement, tears forming in her eyes. 'Where are we? What is this field?'

Tungdil explained. 'I saw your right arm was damaged, but as soon as I surrendered you to the energy, the change set in. I hope you are not dismayed?'

Coïra rubbed the salt drops away. 'It's wonderful! It was more than a blemish . . .' She laughed with relief. 'Thank you, thank you so much!' she called, much moved. 'You have done more than merely save my life.' She attempted to float down to ground level, putting her naked feet on the earth, toes gripping determinedly. 'To be able to see my arm as it always used to be . . .' She touched it. 'It was a spell that went wrong; the magic went off in my hand and stayed there,' she told him. 'That is why I could never heal the wound completely. I could only use the magic force in me, and the less magic I had, the more the wound would hurt and break open.'

'I expect the source has done away with the spell that was caught inside you.' Tungdil admired the immaculate skin, so different from his own scarred and tortured covering. *Now we have to talk about the price.*

'Where are my apprentices?'

'Dead. Victims of the älf. He must have been tracking you for some time, waiting for his opportunity. There was nothing and nobody in Toboribor that could have helped you.'

'Except for you.'

Tungdil nodded. 'But it was still only enough to save you from the black-eyes.'

She was silent for a while, swallowing down her distress. Tears ran down anew. 'My famulae were trying to divert the älf's attention away from me. They were good people that died there.' She looked at him. 'You say your name is Tungdil Goldhand?'

'Yes, and I know there's been another dwarf from the Black Abyss everyone thought was me.'

'Not everybody thought that. There were doubters.'

'Were you one of them?'

Coïra laughed. 'I was too busy defending Girdlegard. The other Tungdil was a great help. That's all we needed.' She gazed at him. 'You have collected serious injuries in your time.'

'They healed and don't bother me much. Unless there's a turn in the weather. Then the scars hurt.'

Coïra did not seem bothered by the fact that she was naked in front of the dwarf. She kept admiring her right hand and arm, which now mirrored her left. 'How did you come to be in Toboribor? Were you looking for anything in particular? It's a marvellous coincidence.'

'Not really. I was looking for you. I had got bored with just wandering about.' He did not tell her he had looked in another place first; Ireheart had given him a description of her likely route. 'People said you were looking for a magic source and I came along, wanting to tell you about the existence of this one. At first I thought you might be in Porista, then I tried the Blue Mountains where the Secondlings live, because I knew they had a magic wellspring. But on the way there a trader told me about one of your famuli that had bought supplies from him. I followed his trail and found you.' He made a regretful face. 'I'm sorry I got there too late.'

'That accursed älf!' Coïra exhaled sharply. 'It's wonderful to bathe in this energy and be full of magic again, but we must be on our way. I need clothing.' She walked a few paces, getting slower and slower. Then she tensed, digging in with her feet. She was being dragged irresistibly backwards, her heels making marks in the soft ground.

She looked at Tungdil. 'What's happening?'

'The field is unwilling to release any magic being that steps in.' Tungdil looked at her apologetically. 'I had no choice. I knew you would die if I didn't bring you here.'

The maga's pretty features lost all their colour. 'I have to stay here?' she whispered, staring at the saltpetre-stained brick walls. 'That must be one of your famous dwarf jokes. I'm sure Lot-Ionan would have known how to . . .'

The dwarf shook his head.

Coïra swallowed. 'How far does it go?'

'He always told me it's restricted to this chamber,' he said. 'We're in the remains of a side tunnel where the apprentices used to receive their training. I know a way out, hidden among a group of rocks. That's the way I got you in.'

Coïra looked around in horror. 'It's such a . . . hole! An abandoned mine. It's got . . . nothing.'

She gave a desperate laugh.

'Should I have left you to die with your famuli? You are the last maga of Girdlegard.' Tungdil was aware of the utter despair overwhelming the young woman. Her joy at the change in her damaged hand would never make up for this. 'I'm sure we can make it nice for you.'

She gave another joyless burst of laughter. 'I was supposed to reign over Weyurn, I wanted to find magic fields, and what have I got? A hole! A dungeon to share with worms and maggots!'

'What you *got* was an älf's poisoned arrow, gangrene and high fever,' he corrected her sharply. 'And then you *got* your life returned to you. And your arm like it used to be.'

Coïra uttered a furious scream and conjured up a spell.

Dark blue rays shot out from her fingers, shooting into the

roof above her head, then streaming out. Bits of the ceiling fell away, missing Tungdil by a beard-hair's breadth. The rock chamber filled up with more and more rubble. Rain washed down over him, rinsing the dirt off his face.

'I can't stay here!' Coïra launched herself vertically upwards within the field. 'I can't!'

Tungdil watched her go until she was a black spot against the sky, eventually disappearing into the grey clouds. He scrambled onto the surrounding stones and worked his way up the hill of collapsed rocks, without taking his eyes off the firmament. *Has she done it? Or has she fallen?*

Suddenly Coïra plunged down through the low-hanging wisps of cloud. Waving her arms about, she formed a symbol in the air with her hands. The air around her took flame and the maga became a dark blue comet, the tail a good fifty paces long behind her. Accompanied by growling thunder, she whirled down.

No, she has not managed to get away. Tungdil made his way onto the wet grass, ready to take defensive action.

Coïra sent a blazing ray vertically down into the middle of the magic source and a detonation followed like a volcano erupting. The ground surged under Tungdil's feet. He was hurled through the air with magic energy playing around him, tearing at him painfully, as if the field which was under attack wanted to avenge itself on him.

The world was spinning around him. He stretched out his arms to slow the whirling movement. The earth came up to meet him and he aimed for a hedge, which broke his fall. The flexible twigs worked like springs, saving him from any fractures. But his face was on fire and his remaining eye was flickering; he had to close the lid quickly to not feel giddy. *She has attacked the source.* He rolled himself out of his springy bed in the bushes, sat up carefully and tried to breathe away the pain in his head.

Coïra's long, tortured scream out of the depths told him her risky plan had failed and that the source had refused to release her.

Opening his eye, Tungdil saw his surroundings doubled and hazy. Not until he had blinked several times was his vision clear. *Something's not right. My sight has changed.* He put his hand to his sound eye to check, then made to adjust the patch over the other socket. It had gone.

Vraccas! Can it be true? He ran a shaking hand over smooth, rain-wet features. *The burn scars have gone! And . . .* he swallowed and nearly choked. He could not believe it. *I have both my eyes!*

He leaped to his feet with a whoop and ran over to the vast hole in the ground caused by the explosion. He called Coïra's name as he leaned over the edge. 'Look what your magic has done for me! It's amazing!'

The black-haired maga was seated on a stone. She raised her head and her expression brightened somewhat. 'That's great that it's helped you to health, too,' she said, generously glad for him. 'But I fear I can't get free. Lot-Ionan knew what he was doing when he fenced off the access to the field.'

'I'll get some clothes for you in the next village,' he promised, worrying, however, that the healing he had undergone would reverse itself as soon as he moved away from the source. The incessant rain made the fabric of his mantle heavier than ever.

Coïra waved her arm implying this was not necessary and formed a magic symbol in the air. Suddenly she was attired in a dark grey dress with light blue embroidery. 'The energy surrounding me lets me do more than any other magic source.

It's as if it reads my mind and then grants my wishes. Except for my desire for freedom.'

Her next trick was to get the boulders to float up and form a cliff. Together with the bricks from the collapsed tunnel wall, she erected a roof over the hollow in the ground, to protect herself from the rain.

'I shall spend my time making it . . . *nice* for myself,' she said in dismal tones. 'Go, and tell the Council of Kings what has happened to me. The way things look, I'll have to train Girdlegard's next generation of magae and magi from in here.'

'I will go now.' Tungdil raised his hand in farewell. 'Is there anything else I can do? I'll have food sent to you.'

Coïra did another spell and in an instant a table with all sorts of fine dishes appeared. Roasts and stews, bread, fruit and sweetmeats, a banquet fit for a king.

'Nice,' she repeated. 'I shall find out what this magic will let me have.'

'And I'll go and inform the Council.' Tungdil left the edge of the crater and set off, noticing three dots approaching on the horizon.

He could soon clearly see that the dots were dwarves and ponies. *My eyes are doing excellent service.* He halted and waited. Tungdil had no objection to a bit of company.

Girdlegard
Elf realm of Ti Lesîndur
6492nd solar cycle, winter

Fast as possible, keep going, no matter what the ground is like. Ireheart was riding next to Ataimînas' white stallion, not letting the ghaist out of their sight. *Pernicious being.*

Mallenia was there with her escort and Rodario had joined the column of over a hundred warriors, moving along about twenty paces behind the leading party. The ghaist was maintaining a steady jog through the landscape, be it forest, meadow, snowfields, or streams. Nothing slowed it down.

'The horses won't make it,' Ireheart called to the Naishïon.

'I'm more worried about the fate of the child,' said the elf in a tense voice. 'The ghaist won't stop to let her rest or drink.'

'It has no reason to want to.' *It's about the corpse, not the living child.* Ireheart knew that the other leaders were already aware of the deadly message in the second capsule. 'It wants to get Sha'taï over to the other side of the wall. Dead or alive is immaterial.'

'I shan't allow that to happen,' Ataimînas shouted. 'None of us will. She has to be saved, even if my own life is forfeit in the attempt.'

None of us will allow it except for me, Ireheart thought. Apart from the dwarves he led, he was alone in this. At the same time he did not assume the unknown message-writer would keep to his side of the bargain. *If he's already assembled his army, he will fall on Girdlegard. Again and again.*

He and Ataimînas saw the ghaist jumping over fallen tree trunks and launching itself over obstacles, the child in its arms bouncing up and down like a rag doll, her clothing in tatters, scratches on her thigh, one shoe missing. Ireheart could not exclude the possibility that her neck had already snapped during one of the leaps followed by a hard landing. *That might not be the worst idea.*

The ghaist changed course and raced down a snowy slope. The cavalcade followed.

Too steep! Ireheart managed to hang on in the saddle. *I really hate riding!* Some of the horses lost their footing and fell and several warriors were unseated and were trampled. By this time their quarry had already reached the plain and was making its way north once more. The company in pursuit was reduced to a tangled avalanche made up of snow, rubble, dwarves, elves, humans and animals.

But still Ataimînas would not stop. He raced on in pursuit accompanied by the handful of warriors still mounted. Mallenia came up to ride at Ireheart's side. 'We have to make it stop!' she called out to him and the Naishïon. 'Else Sha'taï will die.'

'I agree,' said Ataimînas, 'but I can't work out how. We must come up with a plan where she won't be harmed.'

Ireheart had been racking his brain for miles now but had had no inspiration, either. It wasn't that he wanted to save the child; he just did not want her falling into dubious hands. Arrows and spears were out of the question, and ropes across its path or hurled projectiles from catapults would endanger the girl as much as the ghaist. And he did not know which route the ghaist would choose, so it would be impossible to prepare a trap in advance of its progress.

Maybe we should turn the tables. 'Is there a passage or a narrow way we can drive the creature down?' he asked. The elf at his side called a scout over who knew the country well.

'Eight miles ahead, to the east of our road,' the warrior volunteered. 'There's a dry riverbed, a ravine which reduces to four paces wide. It's that narrow for about a mile before it widens out again.'

'How deep is it?'

'I'd say about ninety paces from the ground up to the top of the cliff wall.'

'What have you got in mind, Ireheart?' Mallenia looked at him quizzically.

'The chasm is perfect for our needs. We have to drive the

ghaist in there. One group should forge ahead and set a trap,' he said, thinking fast.

Ataimînas was enthusiastic. 'A net, spread out on the ground, well-concealed. And we pull it up when the ghaist steps on it.'

'We'll need several traps,' the dwarf advised. 'We must assume the ghaist will escape or evade at least one of them.'

'Good point,' conceded Ataimînas. 'I'll send a contingent off straightaway. They can drum up more support on the way and get supplies. It should work.'

'We've got to put the ghaist under pressure from one side. Let's see if it reacts when we get too close,' suggested Mallenia, drawing her sword. 'Give us two of your people so we can drive it where we want it to go, Naishïon. You can steer its direction from the other side.'

'Let's try that. But we don't want to force the pace or the traps won't be ready in time. And it might guess our plan, if we make it too obvious.' Ataimînas issued more orders and a group of elf-warriors fell back in order to change direction. Mallenia set off to the right with ten riders, while the Naishïon continued to follow the ghaist.

Typical! Why do I have to be the one to come up with a plan to save the wretched child's life? Ireheart observed the execution of his plan with mixed feelings. *Vraccas, I hope this means I can avoid a worse outcome for Girdlegard.*

The pursuit went on through the whole of the sharp cold orbit. The girl clutched under the muscular arm of the magic creature opened her eyes from time to time and tried to make a weak movement to show she was alive. Her strength was obviously dwindling.

Ireheart's plan worked; the ghaist was diverted in its path into the ravine.

Mallenia played her part in the undertaking cleverly so the ghaist did not notice what was happening. The magic being did not seem keen on a fight of any kind and it kept its head start on its pursuers. It was not clear at first what the dried riverbed was until it had eaten its way deeper and deeper through the forest floor.

Ireheart stayed close to the Naishïon. *I think it's going to work.*

Soon the walls of the ravine were getting higher and higher. The ghaist appeared to slow down. He was uneasy about the narrow path and was looking for a way out. But he had troops to the right and to the left of him. He lowered his copper-helmeted head and ploughed on at speed again.

'Let us hope they've got the traps prepared,' Ireheart called, urging his pony on to catch up with the others.

'I pray Sitalia will ensure this,' replied Ataimînas.

The ravine walls were almost vertical at this point. Mallenia was making her way along higher up and was soon out of sight of the pursuers, with only the occasional fall of pebbles indicating her presence. As the ghaist increased its pace, Sha'taï's limbs bounced all over the place and the child was whimpering and crying. The rock walls grew closer and forced the pursuers to go fewer abreast, the noise of their hoof beats, clanking weapons and armour echoing loud in the ravine.

Ireheart moved up to where Ataimînas was riding. 'Tell me about that prophecy,' he demanded, without others overhearing.

'I will tell you and the others what the creator goddess wrote,' replied the Naishïon. 'Her predictions affect all of us. With the appearance of the ghaist, the prophecy has reached the next level and shows me that Sitalia knows exactly what has to be done to prevent Girdlegard from being destroyed.' He pointed forwards. 'But let's save Sha'taï first.'

They were coming to the narrowest point in the gorge.

The ghaist unexpectedly made a leap – but the ground came up to meet him. The net missed the creature and its hostage by the length of an arm and flew up empty into the air in front of the pursuers. The elves appearing in niches at the sides of the ravine pulled the net up high enough not to ensnare their own riders. *As I thought.* Ireheart muttered to himself. 'We've only got half a mile. Or we'll have to come up with something else.'

'It *has* to work. The ghaist won't let itself be diverted so easily again.' Ataimînas' disappointment was audible. 'It's been warned now.'

There was a second and a third attempt with the nets, but the ghaist always seemed to sense where this would occur. The fourth time it jumped to avoid a net – only just skirting it – lassoes were thrown from the top of the cliffs. Three looped around the head and were pulled tight, pulling the ghaist off its feet.

Sha'taï moaned with fright when she saw the ground so far beneath her.

'Catch her!' Ataimînas ordered, coming up under where the ghaist hung suspended, snatching at the ropes with its free hand. It grabbed one and yanked it hard, causing four elves to plunge down the cliffside out of their niche in the rock. They had failed to tie the end securely.

The ghaist reached for the second rope.

'Make it fast!' Ireheart roared his command. The party had reached the narrowest spot now. Ponies and horses were snorting, shouldering each other out of the way, forming a moving carpet under her even though it would not cushion Sha'taï's fall if she were dropped.

Ireheart kept watching the ghaist. If it fell on them there would be any number of casualties. But the ropes held. As the ghaist could only use one hand to attempt to free itself, it grabbed Sha'taï by the nape of the neck and pressed hard; the girl screamed in anguish. Then it hurled its hostage against the cliff.

The crowd shouted out as the girl bounced lifelessly off the cliff wall to fall to the ground. With great presence of mind, two elves dropped their weapons and jumped up onto their saddles to link their arms and break her fall. This bold move succeeded but the way the girl's head was hanging was not a hopeful sign.

Ireheart concealed his relief. *But what do we do with the ghaist? It's not going to give up.*

The creature took the two ropes around his neck, one in each hand, and pulled. The fibres spanned and tensed – until one of the ropes suddenly snapped with a whip crack. This made the ghaist lurch down to the right, colliding with the rock wall. It quickly climbed up the rope and got to the ledge where three elves stood. In an instant they were overwhelmed and ripped to pieces by their opponent. They fell into the ravine, blood spreading out on to the warriors beneath them.

Ireheart looked up at the enemy, who stood motionless, staring out of the slit in its copper helmet. But there seemed to be neither eyes nor head in the helmet. Blood from its victims dripped off its fingers, splashing armour and legs. *Is it thinking?*

Spears and arrows bounced off it without it taking any notice. But then filled pig-bladders landed on the creature from above, covering it with a viscous substance. Ireheart's nose recognised the smell of pitch, oil, sulphur, burnt calcium and saltpetre. Archers with firebrand arrows stood waiting at the top of the cliff.

This was what the dwarves called *Vraccas fire,* used to defend their strongholds against aggressors; the elves, too, were versed in its use. *I hope they don't call it Sitalia's fire.*

Ataimînas gave a command in his own tongue and the elf-warrior holding Sha'taï in his arms raced off out of the gorge. 'Now the rest of you,' he ordered in their common language. 'Get back. Get out of range. The ghaist is going to go up in flames!'

Human-, dwarf- and elf-soldiers urged their mounts to a trot, the ravine being too narrow to allow a gallop.

Ireheart stayed behind to watch the ghaist, which stood as if rooted to the spot, its helmet slits directed at where the elf with the girl had raced ahead to get out of the riverbed. *It wants to get the child back!*

The first of the burning brands was loosed from an archer's bow, releasing a comet shower of sparks hailing down on the ghaist. Hissing brands shattered on its hard skin and on the armour. The enemy was soon covered in a burst of sparks until the flammable gel on its body caught and wrapped him in blazing fire.

The ghaist launched itself into the air, springing seven or eight paces over the top of the High King's head along the gorge – to land, aflame, in the middle of the horses, which pushed away to one side, rearing up away from the searing heat.

The fire-clad foe forced a path through the panicking animals, thrusting them aside if they impeded its progress. It reached the front of the group of riders – and suddenly turned round. With deliberate head-butting, it felled the first row of horses. In such a narrow spot, the fallen beasts became a dangerous obstacle for the others in their wake. It was preventing them following.

The flame-wrapped ghaist then threw itself around once more and sprinted through the ravine, following the elf carrying Sha'taï's body.

It can't be overcome. Ireheart dismounted and climbed a few paces up the side wall to be able to see down the riverbed. It looked as if a living flame were chasing its victim, driven to destroy its quarry by a higher power or by a wizard. The burning soles left marks on the rock, showing which way it had gone.

Midway between the small army and the speeding elf-warrior, the ghaist stumbled, grabbing its helmet in both hands, trying to press the copper together. 'Everyone under cover!' Ireheart bellowed, dropping like a stone in the midst of the ponies. He was less worried about their flying hooves than about what was going to happen. He remembered what Balyndar's report had said. *And that in a narrow ravine!*

The initial detonation and the ensuing down-draught were less powerful than the dwarf had feared. But this was only the overture to the explosion that would follow: a blinding flash of light and a burst of heat surged through the gorge, followed by a terrible gust of wind.

Burning soldiers were tossed about over Ireheart's head, mostly elves that had been in the first rows of the group. There followed horses, aflame, turning to ash while still airborne. Red hot metal parts and armour rained down. He shook a burning shard off the cuff of his glove before the leather could ignite.

The pressure wave hammered against soldiers and horses alike, hurling them against the rock face into so much bloody paste. Ireheart was hit several times by flying objects and his vision failed. He saw only a succession of whirling fiery circles.

The wind dropped as quickly as it had come.

The dwarf lay wedged under a dead pony. Using his crow's beak as a lever, panting with the effort, he gradually forced his way free, inch by inch. His ears were ringing with the effects of the blast. Small boulders and stones kept falling from the sides of the gorge, but they missed him. The ravine itself had been damaged. A shadow fell on him. He was grabbed under the armpits and pulled out from under the dead animal.

'Can't leave you alone for a second.' It was Tungdil's voice.

Ireheart wiped the dust out of his eyes and saw the Scholar in front of him. He could hardly believe his eyes. The disfiguring burn scars had gone and his friend had two eyes now. The brown hair on his head and chin looked as they had done when the pair had first met. Only the wrinkles and a melancholy turn to his mouth betrayed the fact that two hundred and fifty cycles had passed and much had occurred in that time.

'By Vraccas! Is that really you or is it Tungdil Number Three?' He saw the red robe and the mark of the Divine Smith at heart-height. 'What has happened?'

'I found Coïra. I'll explain later.' Tungdil surveyed the carnage. 'The survivors come first.'

In the background, Beligata, Gosalyn and Hargorin were assisting where they were needed.

Ireheart nodded and cast his eyes over the scene. Death and disaster everywhere he looked but his thoughts were occupied with the miraculous healing the Scholar had undergone. But then the cries of the injured caught his attention.

Together with the other humans, elves and dwarves, they carried the wounded to safety and laid the dead bodies to one side. Mallenia was bleeding from a deep gash on her cheek. Rodario's ribs had suffered. Ataimînas had broken his right arm but was otherwise unscathed.

'What tremendous force,' said the elf, flabbergasted. 'These creatures are more dangerous when they die than when they attack.'

'That depends,' responded Ireheart, staring at the crater in the floor of the ravine. Where the ghaist had ended its existence, there were extensive burn marks on the stone and great boulders had been torn away, causing additional casualties to their troops. There was absolutely nothing left of their enemy. 'If it storms through an army, it'll cause more havoc and destruction.'

Ataimînas gazed at Tungdil in surprise. 'You are healed? How did that miracle occur?'

'It was the maga's doing. I took her to a magic source.' Tungdil quickly filled them in on his recent excursion and how it had ended. 'Her life was saved. She will have to remain where she is for now, until she can work out how to break the prison-like quality of the energy's effect.'

'So our last maga is effectively banished, and when we need her help so urgently,' muttered the elf, turning his head on hearing hooves approach.

The warrior who had been sent on ahead returned with Sha'taï's body, holding her tenderly pressed against his chest.

'Naishïon!' the elf called out, ecstatic. 'She's still alive! Her neck was not severed. But she's hardly breathing. Death is near.'

Tungdil and Ireheart exchanged covert glances. How strange and yet how marvellous to be able to look the Scholar directly in both eyes. But in the new eye, too, there was nothing to be read but alarm and concern. *I think he too would have preferred to know the girl was safely dead.* Ireheart thought his friend's appearance now rang true. He looked so much more like the Tungdil he had missed for so long.

Ataimînas sighed with relief. 'Sitalia's predictions! They're coming true!' he said. His troops joined in with the rejoicing.

Mallenia ordered the remaining few unhurt human warriors to mount up. 'We'll bring Sha'taï to where the maga is,' she announced. 'Coïra will be able to help her.'

'That's just what I'm afraid of,' muttered Ireheart to Tungdil.

'Right,' said the Naishïon. 'We rendezvous with the maga. There is much to discuss.'

'It looks like you got here in the nick of time, Scholar,' said Ireheart.

'We'll see.' He grinned. 'You know, I was actually trying to give my soul time to recuperate.'

Being king?
Let me tell you, if you think a king's life is one of glory and pomp:
It means getting up every morning and having a good breakfast.
And if you eat slowly enough you can stay sitting till it's time for the noonday meal. And then there's afternoon tea.
And straight into supper and a nice bottle of wine and with any luck you can drop straight into bed again.
How's anyone going to get work started with all that to do?

From: *Rodario – King, Emperor and Showman*

XVIII

Girdlegard
Black Mountains
Kingdom of the Thirdling dwarves
Eastern Gate
6492nd solar cycle, winter

Rognor peered out through the grating into the raging storm whistling and howling round the corners of the fortress. The thin tents of the elf camp were filling with air like sails and flapping outward, shaking the snow off and letting all the warmth escape.

This new cold snap was presenting a problem for the chancellor. He wasn't worried about the castle – their fireplaces had plenty of wood – but rather the elves' makeshift canvas city. *They'll be running out of fuel. They'll die of cold in their sleep, freeze to death.*

Phenîlas had recently started the vetting procedure to allow those who proved indisputably to be of Sitalia's creation to make their way through the gate into the Black Mountains. Lots were drawn, to make the process fair. Those who passed the examination were stamped with a magic seal on their forearms to prove that they were true elves.

Rognor had expected more protest about the testing. But the report about älfar in disguise did not seem to outrage those waiting outside the walls. They continued to wait. *Admirable patience.* Presumably the elves would eye newcomers up carefully when they came drifting into camp. There would be plenty of suspicious looks.

Conducting the examinations and awarding the guarantee seal was hard work for the sorânïons. They could not process more than ten candidates in any one orbit. A certain amount of magic was needed for the stamp and as soon as they had used up their own store, they had to go find an energy-giving source. The best known wellspring lay in the Blue Mountains and took some time to reach.

Ten per orbit. He did his calculations. *At this rate, it will take a whole cycle to get them all tested.* The merciless winter conditions would reduce elf numbers faster than the sorânïons could.

No älf had yet been unmasked and this fact did not make the elaborate and harsh testing process any more popular.

He heard a loud scream from over in the tents. High-pitched and tortured. You heard ten of those every day: men, women and children. Phenîlas and his assistants in their white palladium armour made no exceptions. Age had nothing to do with it, though the dwarf could not understand the necessity for processing newborn infants.

Rognor was aware these sorânïon contingents had turned up in all the dwarf kingdoms to test the elves waiting at the gates and they were carrying out their investigations in ways that were tantamount to torture.

Several heavily burdened figures appeared out of the snowstorm, faces swathed in scarves. The icy winds would attack any exposed flesh and freeze it in the blink of an eye. The newcomers were accompanied by Phenîlas and his troops, all looking as exhausted as those they were escorting.

The chancellor counted eleven immigrants waiting to

come through the heavy iron grating when it was raised. The sorânïons would stay the night in the fortress as well. 'Pull the grating up,' he called to the sentries on guard at the portcullis. The grating was raised to let the elves reach the shelter of the entrance.

'The chancellor himself.' Phenîlas ordered his men to go to their quarters to rest. 'To what do I owe the honour?'

'I was wondering whether we should provide more coal for their stoves. In this weather the warmth is quickly lost.'

'Another fourteen froze to death last night,' said the sorânïon captain. 'And that was *in spite* of the heaters. The stoves *were* burning.' He looked at the sheltered inner courtyard.

'I know what you're thinking. But I can't give permission. I have my orders.' Rognor knew more would survive if they were allowed to camp here on the inside of the first wall.

Phenîlas watched as the portcullis was let down once more to meet the fixtures in the ground. 'I've noticed a couple of extra sections you could wall off in the corridor. You could easily still guarantee Girdlegard's security and keep the Black Mountains safe, as long as the inner gates are closed. There's plenty of room.'

Rognor nodded pensively. 'But the opposite might happen. It might encourage the more impatient of the migrants to try to force their way through from the courtyard. Like the six we dealt with recently.' He lowered his voice. 'Even if we said those ones were älfar, we should not underestimate the degree of desperation the others are under.'

For this reason he had tripled the guard and issued orders that any elf attempting to come closer than twenty paces was to be shot. He had done this with express approval from Phenîlas.

'They'd be more desperate outside in the camp than they

would be if you let them in,' the elf put forward, but he did not want to start an argument. 'You are in charge of the fort, of course. It's up to you to decide.'

Rognor signalled to the sentries guarding the inner gate to the mountain. The next passage was about to open for the elves who had undergone their painful trials. 'I am not the commander here. I am his representative. And I shall keep to my orders.' *And I'm certainly not about to take the risk of allowing älfar in disguise into our fortress. The only ones to be granted entry will be those who have been interrogated.*

The vast gate started to move after the sound of bolts shooting back. The construction was of such thick steel that no enemy would stand a chance of breaking it down with a battering ram, even if they had managed to break through the first line of defence. But heavy though the gate was, the special design of its mechanisms allowed it to swing open as smoothly as a knife would cut through butter.

Phenîlas made a gesture to indicate that he had understood. 'How many are waiting outside the gates?'

'If I subtract the number of those that died last night, it's around three thousand. Two of my people will be leaving for the source to refresh their magic powers. We can't afford any delays. Not with numbers like that.' The elf was about to add something but as he was watching the group, he saw something that disturbed him. 'Is that eleven, going through?'

Rognor was quite clear on that. 'Yes, eleven.'

Drawing his sword, Phenîlas set off after them. 'Tell them to wait. Don't open it yet.'

'One too many?'

The elf nodded and called out in his own language to the figures passing through. 'Someone has taken advantage of the storm and of how tired I am.'

Rognor followed him but did not draw his sword. He considered this an internal matter for the sorânïon to sort out. But he did alert the sentries with a gesture.

The gate-opening manoeuvre was interrupted.

Phenîlas issued more commands and the elves turned towards him. Then one of them ran off towards the gate, which was only open a hand's width. This seemed to give him hope he might get through to the passageway beyond.

As if he could escape like that. 'Stop! No further!' Rognor called. 'The corridor is locked. You won't get through.'

Phenîlas looked distressed. 'It's not enough that we have discovered älfar in disguise. Now I shall be forced to put this miserable specimen to death.'

'What for?'

'I told them anyone who tried to get into the fortress on his own initiative would forfeit his claim to eternity.' He pointed his sword at the cloaked form. 'No point making a threat and then not carrying out the penalty.'

The dwarf said nothing. *They're not my people.*

They had reached the figure, who was gasping for breath at the narrow gap in the gate. On turning, it proved to be a female elf. She was distraught, knowing what fate awaited her. The sword Phenîlas bore would end her life.

Rognor was astonished when she appealed to him for mercy. 'Lord of the fortress, have pity!' she begged, sinking to her knees. Her voice carried well and everyone heard what she said. She must have been hoping to make it difficult for the sorânïon to carry out his threat. 'I beg you, grant me asylum. Let me stay. Throw me in your dungeons or put me in chains, but don't let me be killed!'

'You have no right to apply to him for anything.' Phenîlas laid his blade on her shoulder and the lamplight reflected in its polished surface. 'You have not been tested and you do not display Sitalia's mark. Why risk your eternal life in this way?'

'I would not have lived through another night in the cold.' She placed her hand on her belly. 'I had to make the attempt. I am with child. The baby must not die, and I want it to be born in our new homeland.'

'But now it will have to die.' Phenîlas gazed at her pityingly. 'How could you have done this?'

She's carrying a child? Rognor placed his hand restrainingly on the sorânïon's sword arm. 'Why not subject her to the examination here on the spot?'

'Because she has forfeited her rights. She was not one of those chosen in the draw.'

'Nobody would know,' the dwarf responded. 'And she would keep silent.'

'Of course! I'll tell no one,' she cried. 'And I'll call my child after you! To thank you for your mercy!'

'But will the others keep silent? And what if your guard is down? You might blab. Or your child – one day he might ask why you chose that name for him.' Phenîlas raised his weapon ready to strike and put his other hand on the hilt of his dagger. 'You can take comfort in the fact that you will both die in the same instant.'

The elf-woman tried to avoid the sharpened blade but the sorânïon had expected this. Before Rognor could speak the words granting her asylum, the thin blade pierced her belly. She opened her mouth to scream but the dagger cut through her throat. She sank to the floor with a gurgling groan.

Phenîlas grimaced. 'What a senseless waste of two lives,' he said solemnly, wiping his sword on the dying woman's cloak.

He shouldered his weapon and turned around, going straight through the group of ten who had already undergone the examination and received the mark. Nobody criticised him for his action.

'Let the others through, Chancellor,' the sorânïon said as he passed. 'I must get her back to the camp to make an example of her. It's vital we deter any such attempts in future.'

The portcullis was opened for Phenîlas and he strode out with her body into the snow and the storm to spread the word about disobedience and the penalty for it.

Rognor stared at the pool of blood the dead woman had left behind. It had already frozen over. 'Open the gate,' he called to the sentries.

The mechanical noises started up once more and the heavy gate swung open for the elves, male and female alike, who struggled past the dwarf to get into the shelter of the passage.

One of them halted by the chancellor and gave him a grateful look. 'Accept my thanks for trying to stop the sorânïon doing his duty. She knew what she was doing. Neither you nor the sorânïon bear any guilt in her death.' The elf proceeded past. 'It's the älfar who are at fault. They're to blame for all this. They are evil. Were it not for them, this would never have happened.'

Rognor swallowed hard. *If I had granted her permission to stay it would not have happened.* He watched them go, then looked out through the portcullis. *It's not the älfar who are responsible for that double killing. It's to be laid at the door of the sorânïon and of the one who gave him his orders.*

With a heavy heart and dragging steps he returned to his quarters in search of a hot spiced beer.

He would never have believed that the elves would slay a pregnant woman merely because she had not respected the regulations. *I wonder what else they're capable of if they show no mercy to their own kind?*

Girdlegard
United Kingdom of Gauragar-Idoslane
Idoslane
6492nd solar cycle, winter

Tungdil was amazed, when he arrived at the source with the rest of the company, to see what Coïra had accomplished in his absence. There was an attractive half-timbered farm with two barns and a substantial main building in which presumably the maga herself resided. 'Not bad at all.'

Craftspeople – even a hundred carpenters working together – would take an eighth of a cycle to accomplish anywhere near what had been achieved here in a very short time. They would never have been able to complete three buildings, quite apart from the time needed to source and transport the materials.

'Is that all part of the original tunnel?' Boïndil strode into the courtyard with the rest of the band. Doors opened and servants emerged to see to their mounts.

'When I left here, it was nothing more than a hole in the ground with brick walls and a stone roof above her head.' Tungdil sensed that the magic field had it in itself to do more than simply provide the maga with the energy she needed. He doubted that any spell was able to conjure up a whole farm and outhouses from nothing. *Maybe Lot-Ionan had more reason than he let on for isolating this area?*

Mallenia and her soldiers had arrived some time before them. For the sake of the badly injured young girl, the company had split up to let those go first who could make swifter progress. The one hundred dwarves came along last because the terrain had done no favours to their short-legged ponies.

Tungdil and Boïndil dismounted and went over to the mansion by themselves. They walked up the flight of steps to the double doors where servants were waiting to receive them. The two dwarves were given water to drink and then taken straight through to the palatial interior of the building. Each room was different in style to the last. There was no hint of cosy half-timbered tradition in here. In one area there were domed glass ceilings, in another everything was marble; elsewhere there was even a little beach with real water lapping at it.

'Oh dear, bad sign: Elria's element inside a house.' Boïndil moved to the other end of the room, edging along the wall and eyeing the wavelets with deep suspicion. 'How do they do that, Scholar?'

'If I knew that, I'd be a magus, wouldn't I?'

They reached a room decorated like a small temple where the powerful human leaders of Girdlegard were assembled on benches, armchairs and sofas. There were chandeliers above their heads, paintings on the walls, thick carpets on the floor. In the corner a fountain gurgled and there was a scent of summertime and cornfields.

Dirisa and Astirma were seated side by side. Mallenia and Rodario were chatting quietly while Coïra spoke to Ataimînas. Isikor, goblet in hand, was admiring the décor.

In the centre of the room Tungdil could see Sha'taï floating in mid-air dressed in white, her eyes closed. 'That's just how Coïra was floating when I brought her to the source,' he told Boïndil.

'So the child is a maga, too?'

Tungdil could not rule out that possibility. 'Or maybe she

was born with magic powers. As are the älfar, of course.' He had heard from his friend about how the child had been able to captivate everyone. Only the dwarves had been able to resist her charm. *Our skulls are made of sterner stuff: steel and stone, that's us. Otherwise I'd never have made it out of Phondrasôn alive.*

'There you are,' Coïra called, coming over to them. Even though she was smiling there was a shadow on her face. She was inclined forward slightly as she walked, as if she was pulling against ropes that restrained her.

The source's own little doll. The magic field allows her no freedom to move.

'How is the child doing?' Tungdil nodded to everyone and was acknowledged, a good sign. He had been treated with caginess and even open suspicion since his return. But he could not blame them for that.

'She is in a death coma. Her mind cannot find the way out, it seems,' Mallenia told them, obviously extremely concerned.

'My spells have mended her broken bones and dealt with the fever. All the cuts and grazes have healed without leaving a single scar,' Coïra was reporting. 'But as to her spirit, I am powerless.' Rodario came over and embraced her. 'We shall have to wait and see. I shall continue to flood her with magic energy and I hope this will help.'

'I am sure it will,' her lover comforted her. He was delighted at their reunion but he controlled himself and did not over-indulge in kisses. 'Without you, Sha'taï would certainly have died.'

'But this is no life at all,' Mallenia objected. 'We'll do anything it takes to get her to wake up.'

'Why don't we just put her outside the fortress at the Stone Gateway?' growled Boïndil, leaning on his crow's beak.

Everyone's eyes swivelled round to focus on the High King of the dwarves. It was only Tungdil who did not have murderous accusation in his visage.

'Stop staring at me like that,' Boïndil snapped, tossing his braid back over his shoulder and pointing at the child. 'It's well known what was written in the message we were sent: she is a demon, it said. And I know she spoke the älfar tongue, nothing but älfar, before she was given lessons.' Tungdil tried in vain to restrain him. He had said enough. But his friend was on a roll. 'Don't pretend to yourselves this is a mad theory. We could well have taken a demon from the Outer Lands into our midst and you've all fallen under its spell. Because it's cute.'

'Boïndil, you're talking nonsense,' Mallenia cut him short. 'My young ward is definitely not a creature of evil.'

'I would never allow her to be left in the clutches of an unknown figure who wants nothing more than to know her dead.' Coïra's blue eyes sparked with passionate fury. 'How can you possibly suggest that, High King? Or is that supposed to be one of the famous dwarf jokes?'

'No, it's not that,' Rodario leaped in to the debate. 'Ireheart was not thinking when he said that.'

Tungdil followed the exchange and observed the assembled throng closely. They were all displaying violent, protective behaviour, as if Sha'taï had been their very own child. *Taken into everyone's hearts so soon? In only one cycle? Either she is incredibly charming and delightful or . . .* He studied the sleeping girl's features as she floated there, bathed in magic.

Tungdil had been speaking with Beligata, Gosalyn and Hargorin these past few orbits. They were all convinced the girl had influenced the minds of elves and humans. She came from the sorcerer families in the Outer Lands that used ghaists as scouts and messengers. They had learned this from Carmondai when they had met up en route.

A demon, a cunning sorceress or a pure soul who is only trying to stay alive. Who knows?

'The ghaist creatures were sent by someone who knows Girdlegard,' Coïra summed up.

'There are plenty of those. The gates were open long enough, and not only in the Grey Mountains,' Mallenia contributed. 'And in the south, too, it was possible to get in unnoticed and then disappear.'

'We must not underestimate the gravity of the situation. Anyone capable of creating creatures that are composed of magic and souls, and who can muster an army of the size reported, will not give up easily.' Astirma folded her arms across her chest. 'What do we do if a hundred ghaists turn up and more are catapulted over the defences? They can only be stopped with extreme difficulty.'

'I don't know,' Boïndil grunted crossly. 'Thousands of enemies turning up with siege towers and storming engines, well, we can get rid of them simply enough, by Vraccas. We simply beat them back, cut them to pieces and burn them. But these copper-helmets are a mystery. Keenfire is effective but Balyndar was nearly killed when he used it.' He ran his hand over his black and silver beard, then across the sides of his head. 'That's why I thought it might be better to surrender the child at the gates. Or maybe just pretend to, and then wait and see what happens.'

Tungdil watched Ataimînas, who had so far not said anything. *It's his turn. He certainly knows something.* 'Your prophecies might help us understand, Naishïon,' he said, addressing the lord of the elves in a friendly tone. 'Have I understood you correctly, that events so far have all been predicted?'

'I did promise to make the secret public.' Ataimînas stepped up and called a servant over to bring him a bag from which he extracted a book as thick as a fist, wrapped in waxed paper. It measured two by three human hands in size and the binding was in gold leaf with elf runes engraved on it. The pages appeared to have been dusted with black powder. 'I'll explain.'

Ataimînas carried the book to a table and pronounced certain formulae to open it up.

The pages, as thin as breath, glowed silver and released ruby red symbols that Tungdil understood. 'An unusual type of dialect. Your people do not use it anymore,' he told the Naishïon. 'It is very old.'

The elf ruler could not disguise his astonishment. 'It is not for nothing that you are called the Scholar.'

Tungdil sketched a bow in acknowledgement. 'But it should be you reading out what we can all see.'

Ataimînas agreed to this. 'First let me explain why we have come to Girdlegard in such numbers.' He smiled at the dwarves. 'In the old days there was always trouble between our races. Our creator Sitalia recognised that it would be better for our homeland if we went and remained in hiding as far away as possible. War between elves and dwarves would have meant the end of Girdlegard.'

'We'd have won,' Boïndil mouthed to Tungdil.

'But the goddess also foresaw that one orbit there would be a possibility for true peace amongst all the inhabitants and said we should return,' Ataimînas went on, ignoring the whisper. 'She wrote down her instructions and presented them to those who sought their fortunes outside the homeland.

Only when the life-star of the elves was shining brightly could she guide our steps into Girdlegard. Not until then.' He looked solemnly at everyone. 'This all happened a cycle ago. The wave of elves arriving will continue to increase until the very last elf returns from abroad.'

'I presume that means the first prophecy is fulfilled,' Tungdil guessed.

'That's correct.' Ataimînas turned the page. This time the symbols shone out in emerald green to make themselves legible. 'Here it says:

A child will be sent to you
charming all with its delightful nature
and who has greater value than salt or water.

The child's arrival will change everything.

Let my people form their own united realm
and focus their powers
since dark forces will seek to harm the child and
take it away.

Heed this warning: they will send their vanguard:
in their thousands in rags and tatters
and twice in copper.'

Boïndil banged his crow's beak down. 'That does indeed cover events in the Grey Mountains,' he said crossly. 'But with . . .'

'These are Sitalia's prophecies,' Ataimînas interrupted. 'There is no room for interpretation.' He turned more pages. 'Even Tungdil's return was foreseen by the goddess, though I originally thought she meant the first one.'

'Did he fit better?' Tungdil enquired with a considerate smile.

'Doubt is not appropriate when it comes to the writings of the goddess. They told me about the turmoil in Tabaîn and the attack on Sha'taï made by the ghaist.' Ataimînas pointed to the book. 'And her writings tell us what to do next. What we all have to do next.'

Boïndil laughed incredulously. 'If you knew she was going to be abducted, why didn't you prevent it?'

'It did not say when it would take place.' The elf remained friendly. He wanted to see what the effect on Tungdil would be. 'The wording is as follows:

The childlike jewel may get lost
through the copper hands of the bad ones.

If it dies
then so will the new home
together with every living thing
and every stone
and every drop of water.

If the jewel is kept safe,
answer must be given to the bad one
with hammer and anvil.

These are the only things
that cannot be bent out of shape.

Only these things are rigid and powerful, destructive enough and will resist storm, fire and steel.
Only hammer and anvil.'

Ataimînas looked at the dwarves. 'Hammer and anvil. That means your people.'

Tungdil found the words not unsuited but it was equally possible to include a different meaning.

'The Children of the Smith are flattered that Sitalia gives them this new role,' he replied before Boïndil could say anything untoward that might sound like an insult. 'What is the significance of the word *answer*?'

The elf turned the page. 'The goddess writes:

Send hammer and anvil out
to the north, always to the north
so they may find the bad thing, and break it up.

None but they
Stand a chance.'

Boïndil laughed out loud. 'To the north?'

'Translated, it means that all the dwarves, male and female, must leave their mountain fortresses and go on a journey together.' Ataimînas focused his intense gaze on the High King. 'And before you ask: we will keep the gates while you are gone.'

Tungdil grabbed Boïndil's shoulder to prevent him from storming forward. 'The dwarf rulers have been informed and will soon arrive. Your suggestion and your predictions can be discussed then.'

Ataimînas looked surprised. 'What is there to discuss?' He pointed at Boïndil. 'He is your High King. He will command them and we shall fulfil the prophecy.'

Rodario, Mallenia, Dirisa and Isikor stared at the dwarves in silence. The powerful monarchs made no effort to hide their expectations. Coïra's glance even held something of a threat.

'You see, we . . .' Tungdil began.

'Vraccas has not sent us any wise words demanding we do anything nonsensical like that,' Boïndil burst out, unable to restrain himself any longer. 'In past cycles we often went wandering. We wandered as far as the Black Abyss, leaving the gates vulnerable. We also marched against Toboribor. But then we lost the mountains.'

'But it ended in an eventual victory,' Rodario cut in, calmly.

'Because there were so many of us, Moustache-Man!' Boïndil drew himself up to his full height. 'It cost us many of our good people to liberate Girdlegard.'

'The same goes for us,' Mallenia said bitterly. 'We paid in blood as well.'

'Except there're more humans than there are dwarves,' Boïndil responded. 'By Vraccas, there are even more elves than there are dwarves, now. And that is why I know the kings and queens of the dwarf realms will never agree to this.'

Tungdil saw horror on many faces. Anger and disbelief were mixed in their features. 'We will put it to them and we will discuss it,' he stressed, so as not to stoke the fires of disagreement. 'We shall prepare for their arrival and we shall let you know how the talks proceed.' He led Boïndil out of the chamber.

Send hammer and anvil out
to the north, always to the north
so they may find the bad thing, and break it up.

None but they
stand a chance.

Ataimînas' words echoed behind them as they left. 'It all lies in your hands. Neither the humans nor the elves. The dwarves will make it possible to preserve Girdlegard.'

Boïndil made as if to halt, but Tungdil insisted he leave the huge hall, pushing him gently towards the exit. 'There is no point,' he whispered. 'They all think the same in there.' He cast a glance over his shoulder.

The humans and the elf were standing together like a solid wall, staring at the departing dwarves with malice. Behind them the sleeping girl floated like a haunting spirit. The distance made it look as if she were flying over their heads.

'They can talk prophecies till the cows come home,' Boïndil muttered, leaving the ornate council chamber. 'Who's to say who wrote all that?'

A good point. Tungdil was keen to take a closer look at the elf's book. 'Where is the älf?'

'The one I found in the elf's palace?'

'No, the one who was travelling with Hargorin and his band. Carmondai.'

'What do you want him for?' Ireheart wondered.

'He's old. Extremely old. And he will have heard many stories in his time.' Boïndil and Tungdil strode through the stately mansion side by side.

'He's written a lot of stories, but I don't know how much he actually knows,' said Ireheart doubtfully.

'Let's ask him. We've got a little time before our monarchs arrive.' Tungdil slapped his friend on the back. 'Well, how does it feel, being High King?'

'Terribly thirsty,' Boïndil growled into his beard. 'It's only bearable if you have limitless amounts of beer.'

'Let me buy you one.' The two of them made their way out

into the courtyard. 'Then go and fetch the älf for me.' *He may provide the answer to many things.*

'Quite the old Scholar, aren't you?' Ireheart replied with a grin. 'Not a bit like the version that turned up in the tionium armour.'

Tungdil's eyes flashed and a shadow passed over his features, taking the High King by surprise. 'Who knows?' He took a bottle out of his red robes and pressed it in to Boïndil's hand. 'Anyway, take this.'

'What's is it?'

'Don't drop it. It's the antidote to your thirst. You should down it in one.'

At first, Boïndil stared at the flask then he looked at Tungdil. 'You're having a laugh.'

'You mentioned where I might find the zhadár's laboratory and I paid the place a visit. I had a little time on my hands while I was away.' Tungdil smiled. 'You got your Scholar back and I want my Ireheart returned to me.'

Boïndil thanked him and stowed the offering away.

Girdlegard
United Kingdom of Gauragar-Idoslane
Idoslane
6492nd solar cycle, winter

Carmondai observed the farmhouse from a safe distance. More and more humans were arriving each passing orbit. The maga seemed to exert a special attraction on the surrounding villages; people were giving up their homes and farmsteads in order to seek a new abode near her. It was expected that a whole town would soon arise.

As the älf had heard, Coïra had no choice but to remain in this very spot, even though she was Weyurn's ruler. *A new magic realm where Lot-Ionan used to be.* He had known quite a few of the magae and magi now long gone. He had recorded their names in his histories. So much of his work – thousands of pages, drawings and even paintings – had got lost.

The älf had settled down in a broad hollow tree for warmth and shelter from the wind. He had arranged with Hargorin that he would remain nearby. He saw the Thirdling king as an ally he could make use of; after all, he would owe him since Carmondai had saved his life, as well as those of Beligata and Gosalyn. These had not been entirely selfless actions. Carmondai was still outlawed and if Mallenia's troops found him, he would have to fight to defend himself; he could use all the support he could get. And the älf was counting on Hargorin taking him to the Black Mountains. *From there I can escape into the Outer Lands.*

But for now there was something he wanted to do, as soon as night fell.

Carmondai was aware of the message the ghaists had delivered so obediently. Now there was no doubt about a power threatening Girdlegard.

The älf had learned in earlier times about the botoicans. He wrote about their dynasties, based on what Caphalor and Sinthoras had told him. The exact circumstances of their meeting had been kept vague but this kind of magic to influence and manipulate masses of people had impressed him. *If the Inextinguishables had known the extent of the botoicans' power they would have gone out on campaign against them.*

Apart from one small episode, those magicians had played no role at all in the fate of Girdlegard. The belt of mighty mountains, deep ravines and steep unclimbable slopes formed an effective protective barrier. *But now there's a reason to try to conquer the land.* Carmondai had seen how charming the child could be – it was as if she exuded a perfume that affected hearts and minds. *She is one of them.*

The älf was not concerned about whether Girdlegard was going to be destroyed. His own race was no longer in power; humans had disfigured and continually humiliated him. It would give a certain amount of satisfaction to describe the fall of Girdlegard, even though he might be the only reader. He had been compliant for too long.

But he owed Sha'taï something for her attempt back in Oakenburgh to have the mob kill him. Before following Hargorin to the Black Mountains, there was a task to carry out.

When the sun went down over the snowfields that night, the älf left his hiding place.

The fact that a group of dwarf riders arrived at the farmstead at the same time was convenient. It would divert any unwelcome attention from him. This would make it easier for Carmondai to carry out his mission.

He told me about his deeds – his feats in battle, his black moments and his glorious victories.
Folk in Girdlegard had no idea what their hero had suffered.
Or what he had done.
How he subjugated a large part of Phondrasôn and then awoke from the dream without being able to escape the terror. A horrifying intoxication.

Secret notes for
The Writings of Truth
written under duress by Carmondai

XIX

Girdlegard
United Kingdom of Gauragar-Idoslane
Idoslane
6492nd solar cycle, winter

They came and are saying nothing. Tungdil let his gaze roam round the dwarf faces gathered at the table. At the beginning of the session here on the maga's estate, he had filled them in on what they needed to know about his experiences in Phondrasôn and how his doppelgänger had come about, only to die at the Black Abyss at a blow from Keenfire.

After he had spoken, the High King took over. He told them about the prophecy, about the hammer and the anvil and how it was interpreted to mean the dwarves must take to the trail to combat and smash the evil.

From that point on silence had reigned. It was an uneasy silence, much as if something valuable had crashed to the floor or a favourite pet had died in full view of everyone.

Xamtor Boldface from the clan of the Bold Faces, King of the Firstlings, sipped at his glass of water, evaluating what he had heard, as the others were also doing. His armour was characterised by ornate steel and iron decoration, while the rings on his gauntlets and the clips in his rust-brown beard were made of vraccasium.

Balyndis Steelfinger of the clan of the Steel Fingers was looking at her hands as if she could see the future there. The queen was clad in black leather breeches, a white fur cloak and a simple mail shirt with her own device on it. Her long, dark brown hair she had piled high, held in place with a heavy, twisted gold ring.

It was not easy for Tungdil to look at Balyndis. Even after such a long time, he felt something stir inside. *Two hundred and fifty cycles*. Deep under the earth, hemmed in by evil, he had often thought about her – mostly with warm emotion, sometimes with melancholy and regret. Vraccas and Samusin had given them fates that drove them both apart. *What will happen now I have returned?* One thing he knew for certain: *I want her back*. But first she would have to forgive him.

Balyndis looked at him in the same way as she looked at all the others present: kind, but with no hint of anything more in her heart for him than friendship and a memory of good times in the past. *Is she faking the friendly attitude?* Tungdil was unsure. He glanced at her and away again, forcing himself to direct his thoughts to the assembly.

Frandibar Gemholder of the clan of the Gold Beaters, ruler of the Fourthlings, seemed lost in the engravings on his goblet. His silver armour with its polished gold inlay shone like the gemstones embedded in it. He wore his shoulder-length blond hair in ringlets; his side-whiskers grew down to his chest and his chin was decorated by a fine braided beard. The rest of his head hair was shorn short.

Brown-haired Gordislan the Younger from Trovegold, the underground city of the Freelings, seemed to be mulling things over, his expression blank. He was the only one to have eschewed armour, as if he wanted to challenge the traditions of his people. He wore a simple garment of red and brown leather.

Hargorin was the only one watching the High King. He was not surprised at the prophecy, having been close to events during the recent orbits.

'I may be King of the Thirdlings – and perhaps I really ought to be the last to speak – but if everyone's still lost in thought, I'm happy to start.' He tapped his metal leg. 'There has been much in the past in the way of measures to save Girdlegard. I never doubted what I was doing. I occasionally regretted having to make a show of carrying out the wishes of the Triplets, but I always knew where we were heading: to their downfall.' He got to his feet. 'When it comes to the subject presently under discussion, I have no idea. Neither where to go with our warriors nor what we might have to contend with – nor even whether there might be any prospect of success.' He pointed to Boïndil. 'I know that your word binds us all, High King, but if you let us choose, I would be against a campaign that is executed just for the sake of it.'

Frandibar tapped his goblet with be-ringed fingers, to indicate he wanted to speak. Xamtor interrupted by banging his gauntlet on the table surface. This was what Tungdil had feared. He would wait until the queen and all the kings had had their say.

Frandibar stood up, his armour shining. 'Never, in the history of our race, has an anvil gone out to collect the iron that its hammer was asked to beat into shape. The horseshoe always comes to the smith, to the anvil and the hammer.' He waved his chin in the general direction of the map they had spread out on the table and his beard braid swung hither and thither. 'We don't know even how many of us are still alive.'

'We have enough,' said Boïndil.

'Enough to man the ramparts and deter a larger number from attacking us,' the Fourthling king said.

'And even then it's touch and go with numbers.' Balyndis raised her hand, apologising for the interruption. 'The ragged army demanded everything our defences had to offer.

Our supplies of petroleum and Vraccas fire have been restocked but without our walls to protect us, they would have overwhelmed us in open field.' She indicated to Frandibar that he could continue.

'I have nothing more to add,' said the blond king, taking his seat.

'I'm against it, too.' Xamtor stuck by what had already been said. 'Enough talk. The reasons are obvious.'

'But if anvil and hammer do not take to the campaign trail,' Boïndil stressed, 'our homeland might be lost.'

'Whose prophecy are you going by? The one made by the elf goddess?' Xamtor shook his head, his salt and pepper locks flying. 'And to cap it all, we're supposed to hand over our strongholds to the elves to run things? They know nothing about the tunnels and have no idea how to use our catapults.'

The others agreed with him.

'There's no way of knowing whether or not the whole thing is a trick.' Frandibar looked at the map. 'Ever since the Eoîl Atár, the elves have given us problems. We've never been able to trust them. Now there are thousands of them here in Girdlegard and there are thousands more at the gates. If they are in charge of controlling admission, they'll have taken over completely. I'd be surprised if they let us back in.'

'Exactly.' Balyndis looked at Boïndil. 'Before you give us your command to follow Sitalia's predictions, please realise that I shall be resisting your orders.'

'Have we got anyone able to check the prophecy for authenticity?' Xamtor's gaze fell on Tungdil. 'They used to call you the Scholar. Any of that stuff left?'

Tungdil smiled and got to his feet. 'I saw the book where the words of the goddess are recorded. It's written in an ancient dialect and there were a few symbols I'd never seen before.' He shrugged. 'These are predictions that someone has written down. We weren't there at the time and we cannot guarantee they are authentic. Ataimînas and his subjects, on the other hand, are all totally convinced the words are beyond doubt.'

'That was an answer, of sorts, I suppose,' said Frandibar. 'But it's left us none the wiser.'

'Nothing I can say throws any light on the subject.' Tungdil was at pains not to mislead them.

'We have an old document. That much is known. For anything else, as concerns content and interpretation, we are dependent on the Naishïon.'

'That means we have nothing.' Xamtor leaned back in his seat. 'I'm with Balyndis. My Firstlings won't be shifting out of the fortress, High King. No self-respecting Child of the Smith is going to trust an elf goddess.'

Hargorin gave a tut of approval. 'Same here for the Black Mountains. My Thirdlings love a campaign, but against a foe they can see. To take off into the wild blue yonder? No. No way.' His expression was apologetic. 'The worst that could happen is they'd lose their confidence in me and in the High King, and that would be the end of our alliance. Going to war based on Sitalia's prophecy would cause more harm than the loss of some of our warriors.'

I think I know where he's coming from. Tungdil knew that there were a number of Thirdlings who did not hold with being allies with the other tribes. This was the legacy that Lorimbur had left them: keeping up the ancient feuds. It was only Hargorin's strict regime holding them all together.

Boïndil kept stroking his black and silver beard. 'This is just what I was expecting. The timing is bad, too – only one cycle after the last great battle.' He indicated the map. 'Our place is here, as hundreds of cycles have shown.'

'Until the orbit the battle at the Black Abyss broke out,' Tungdil contradicted. 'I have only heard about it, of course, but without the dwarf contingents, it could have ended very differently.' Before others could argue on this point he raised his hand. 'I am aware the aim was to protect Girdlegard. But I still think,' he said, pointing north, 'that this is an important undertaking.'

Balyndis frowned. Her round face was older now and the fuzz on her cheeks more pronounced. The burdens of high office had hardened her features. 'Do I understand correctly? That you are in favour of this campaign?'

His pulse quickened, feeling her eyes on him. 'I would consider it wrong to set out blind with a mighty army in tow,' he began, cautiously. 'But the thought intrigues me: how about sending out an advance party to investigate? To find out where the ghaists are from? Who sent them? And what's the story with this girl-child the humans and elves are so devoted to?'

'No! Don't do it! No way,' thundered Boïndil, horrified. 'We have not just welcomed back Girdlegard's greatest hero merely to have him head straight back out for the wilderness.'

'Wouldn't that be just what a hero does?' Tungdil laughed quietly and clapped his friend on the shoulder.

'I forbid it, Scholar! I'm the High King and you have to obey me!'

'Calm yourself, old friend. I'll go and I'll come back, trusting in Vraccas. He did keep me safe in Phondrasôn for two hundred and fifty cycles, after all.'

'And you'll have me at your side,' volunteered Hargorin swiftly. 'Rognor is an excellent chancellor and possibly even a better king than I am for the Thirdlings. I see myself cut out for other tasks. Beligata and Gosalyn will want to be there, too. Strictly speaking, we didn't actually find you the first time. You found us. We've got to make up for that.'

'Then my orders are that every tribe send a warrior, male or female, to accompany you,' said Boïndil, cleverly. 'Perhaps that might even fulfil the goddess' prophecy: a united army, on the campaign trail to confront the enemy.'

'You could be a scholar yourself, Ireheart,' Tungdil laughed. 'The handful of us against hundreds of thousands? But then you always did like a challenge.'

'Oink, oink,' Boïndil honked his battle cry with a glint in his eye, even though he was anything but joyful.

'Then we should focus our attention on two things,' Xamtor chimed in, satisfied with the new arrangements. 'First, how do we interpret the predictions Sitalia made? Second, what do we know about the land to the north our great hero is heading for?'

'Do you mean what do *we* know, ourselves, or do you want to ask someone who's been there before?' Hargorin inquired with a conspiratorial air.

Girdlegard
United Kingdom of Gauragar-Idoslane
Idoslane
6492nd solar cycle, winter

Carmondai had to admit the mission was more stressful than he originally expected. The time spent in Mallenia's custody, more or less restricted to the tower, victim to a mixture of self-pity, melancholy and defiance, had not improved his physical condition. He had made a gradual start with exercise – as he had done in a previous era when imprisoned by the Triplets – so as not to lose muscle or agility, but this was another thing entirely, creeping up unnoticed and quickly to a heavily guarded estate building. This was no gentle wander through Girdlegard at his ease.

Wearing black clothing that he had stolen off unsuspecting washerwomen at work by a stream, he was hard to spot in the dark as long as he was not forced to move across an open snowfield. He held Bloodthirster in his left hand, and darted from cover to cover, passing the sentries and reaching the outbuilding on the left-hand side. He had been aware for some time that there was a slight magical vibe radiating out from the source field.

Breathing too loud for his own comfort, he spied round the corner. The inner yard was brightly lit and armoured dwarves, humans and elves were gathered, talking as they stood round braziers, drinking together in a relaxed atmosphere. Nobody would be expecting trouble, given the number of people present.

That, at any rate, was what Carmondai devoutly hoped.

On the other hand, he remembered there had been an attack in Freetown. It had been quite some time ago but presumably it might have led to there being additional security measures in the interior of the building. Perhaps even magic ones.

In spite of all that, Carmondai was not willing to give up his self-appointed task. *But I'll never get past all these people without being seen.* He looked up to the roof. The distance between the main building and the outhouses he calculated to be around eight paces. As an älf, this could be done if you took a run at it. Though the roof tiles were covered in damp snow, which would make take-off and landing difficult. Any bits of snow falling from the roof would also alert the sentries or the crowd in the courtyard.

I'll have a go anyway. Carmondai fastened Bloodthirster to his back and climbed the rear wall of the adjoining building. It took some time and much effort on his part.

Once on the roof, he stayed lying in the wet snow, taking deep breaths and sending clouds of frozen white into the night air, before flipping over and making his way carefully up to the ridge. Below, the dwarves, humans and elves were still talking away to each other, laughing and joking. The alcohol in the spiced wine and beer seemed to be having its effect.

In the main building there were silhouettes to be seen at the brightly lit windows. The number of guests and serving personnel must be considerable. Carmondai tried not to think about that too much; he tied his weapons strap more securely round his body and started his run-up. *Inàste, stay by me!*

After a powerful sprint, pushing against the crunch of the snow, he launched himself into the air.

He did not land on the other side as he had intended; instead he crashed right below the roof ridge. He had miscalculated, underestimating the extra weight of Bloodthirster and his winter apparel. He slithered down the roof, coming to a stop at an attic dormer.

He made himself small so as not to be obvious from the yard. Stayed motionless. A window was opened.

'. . . heard something, I thought . . .' came a female voice. 'I'll tell the guards.'

That's Mallenia's voice! Carmondai shut his eyes for several heartbeats. The very monarch who had put a price on his head. And she was less than two paces beneath where he clung.

'Probably a really big snowflake.' This was Rodario speaking. 'What else could it have been? Come back over here.'

'Let's go and check on the little one,' the Ido queen said, concerned. 'Then I'll be able to sleep.'

'But I'm not going to let you sleep,' he teased.

Mallenia laughed. 'So the king is paying court to the queen?'

'Something like that.'

Carmondai heard them both leaving the room. *She's left the window open.*

He wriggled down on to the ledge below the window and slipped into a room that was as elaborately furnished as befitted two crowned heads, from the generously-sized bed to the luxurious carpets and tapestries.

That magic prickling feeling increased. Carmondai suspected this meant that much of the furniture and furnishings had been created with a spell, or that perhaps the magic source had spread. If so, this would make it hard to detect any traps based on magic.

Crossing quickly through the royal quarters, he spied out through the keyhole, encountering no hint that any guard was stationed there. Taking his courage in both hands, he opened the door and stepped out into the lamplight of the corridor, crouching down underneath a small table for cover. There was an unpleasant-looking sculpture on the pedestal. Not at all to his refined taste.

A bedroom door opened and out came Mallenia and Rodario, dressed in wide-fitting, comfortable mantles; they said their goodbyes to someone in the room and wished sweet dreams. Then they passed the place Carmondai was hiding and went back into their own room.

No guards on duty in the house itself. The älf stood up and listened out carefully. *How can they all be so sure that nothing can happen?*

He had a nasty feeling he was walking into a trap.

This was why he did not go in through the doorway the king and queen had just come out of. He went further down the corridor, looking for a stairwell. He wanted to explore the building; he would need to know the best way out soon. Finding the steps, he made his way down to the next floor, when possible stealing glances through keyholes and gaps under doors. Occasionally he was forced to take avoiding action if servants appeared, sometimes wreathing himself in shadow. The servants were all carrying trays with food and drink, which suggested the whole mansion was one big party.

He finally took advantage of an opportunity: grabbing one of the serving men, he knocked him out and stole his clothes, concealing Bloodthirster as well as he could in the folds of the garments he put on. His tall physique helped him in this endeavour. His slightly pointed ears were now hidden under a cap. He cut off the man's long hair and tucked it under the rim to fall as his own, masking his features to some extent.

Thus disguised, he strolled at his ease through the other floors of the building. Visitors were everywhere, celebrating and carousing. Odd snatches of conversation he caught made reference to Sitalia's prophecies and how to interpret them.

He reached a large hall where loud music was being played. The musicians were a mixed company of dwarves, humans and elves, somehow managing to harmonise, to the delight of all. A groundling sang one of the old mocking ballads, which ended with an orc dying in all sorts of extravagant ways.

A dwarf espied an orclet small
Orclet on the heathland;
So fat and asking for it.
He went to get a better look
And relished what he saw.

At this the assembled dwarves chucked their tankards in the air and thundered in with the chorus:

Orclet, orclet, orclet small,
Fat and fit for slicing.

Dwarfy spake: I'll hack you, orc,
Into little pieces.
Orky oinked: I'll stab you back
So you don't forget me.
I find you quite enticing.

With the dwarves taking over the main tune, humans joined boisterously in the refrain:

Orclet, orclet, orclet small,
Fat and fit for slicing.

The lusty dwarf now biffs him hard
And cuts him up in pieces.
Orky has a blunt-edged axe
Moans in a pool of juices
Like the others of his species.

Now in response, the whole assembled company joined in:

Orclet, orclet, orclet small,
Fat and fit for slicing.

The hall resounded with cheers as the final stanzas died away.

How utterly appalling. Then Carmondai caught a movement out of the corner of his eye: a child's figure carried on the shoulders of a soldier, who was hopping around merrily. Rhythmic applause broke out and her name was shouted: 'Sha'taï, Sha'taï!'

She must have escaped from her bedroom. The älf went over to where the buffet was laid and made as if adjusting the piles of plates for the banquet. From here he was able to observe how people were behaving round the young girl, who was laughing with delight and clapping in time with the music. *She made even the elves sing that ghastly dwarf song.*

At this point Mallenia came storming down the stairs, her night robe sweeping behind her. She must have been very worried indeed, if she was coming down in this attire.

'So that's where you've got to!' she yelled, loud enough to be heard over the voices, applause and the music. 'Up to bed immediately!'

The soldier let the girl slip down to the floor. The music stopped. Mallenia came over to Sha'taï, took her by the hand and dragged her away. 'Tomorrow will be a tiring day,' she explained. Turning to the party-goers she said, 'Time to quieten down here. There's no reason for celebrating as yet. The dwarf leaders are still deliberating. They have not marched off at the head of their armies.'

One or two tankards clattered. Guests got up, shamefacedly. Mallenia and the child hurried up the steps and the company dispersed.

That shouldn't hold me back. Taking a long napkin from one of the tables, Carmondai hung it over his shoulder, picked up a tray of food and went upstairs. It would appear he was taking refreshments to one of the guests. He kept his gaze firmly fixed on the queen and her ward. The girl was taken into the room Mallenia and Rodario had been seen coming out of earlier. *She sleeps on her own.*

When the queen came out into the corridor again to head for her own stateroom, Carmondai slipped into the girl's chamber.

His älfar sight allowed him to see in the dark. The girl lay in bed, face turned to the window.

This is too easy. Everything in the älf told him not to approach. On top of that, there was an increase in the magic prickling sensation. Perhaps he had triggered some defence trap. But how often would he be presented with an opportunity such as this?

He put the tray down carefully and put the cloth on the floor. He took out Bloodthirster and moved silently to the bed. He raised the weapon to deliver a cut, pointing the tip at the nape of the sleeping girl's neck. *She is an evil influence waiting to bring destruction to Girdlegard and many other worlds. She tried to kill me because I saw through her.* The älf took aim.

'Your death bears the name Carmondai,' he whispered. 'I shall take your life and your soul shall be ripped to pieces by Tion.'

He stabbed down at her neck.

The blade met an astonishing degree of resistance from the vertebrae of such a young creature. Blood gushed out of the open mouth and the child's body slackened – only to assume the form, in front of the älf's very eyes, of a guard, lying in the sheets. Bloodthirster had pierced the upper edge of his armour.

A trick. A trap. They were expecting me. Carmondai extracted the blade and whirled round at the sound of the door behind him opening. The prickling he had felt had come from a spell of deception. *I knew it was too good to be true.*

Lantern light fell on his face and a crossbow bolt whirred towards him, but he dodged it. Instead of resorting to flight, he went on the attack and struck right in the middle of the light. Several lamps clattered and broke in the hands of whoever was carrying them. Shouts were heard. The petroleum caught fire and spread.

Bloodthirster flared out and wielded death in Carmondai's cunning hands.

Wearing a quilted garment in the quarters assigned him by Coïra, Hargorin was content.

On the upholstered bench next to him stood the tin leg the Scholar had fitted for him. He kept useful items in the hollow receptacle of the artificial limb, in particular a slim knife for emergencies. His mail shirt with its reinforced shoulder armour and iron spikes hung on the stand and the short blades for the forearm protectors were on the table next to the axe awaiting sharpening. He had just finished oiling the protective skirt made up of iron plates. Everything was prepared for whatever the future held.

He picked up an engraving tool and did a few more decorations on the artificial leg, something that went well with runes and blessings. This was to be his talisman on the journey into the unknown.

The talk with the High King had ended with agreement for Tungdil's endeavour and both Beligata and Gosalyn were keen to go along. Together with him. Hargorin. It would be easy to select the best warriors the five tribes and the Freelings could provide. Then the adventure could begin.

Boïndil had been keen on accompanying them but they had turned the offer down. He was the second greatest dwarf hero. He must remain behind and provide stability and support for his people. They knew that Girdlegard would be reacting with incredulity to the dwarves' decision not to send a vast army. But the Children of the Smith would not shift from the spot until the prophecies were proved true and Tungdil's group of spies reported finding an enemy in the Outer Lands.

The enemy that's so desperate to get at the child. The Thirdling king blew the filings away and rubbed the surface of his metal leg. It was cold and felt like a part of himself that had turned to steel.

Thoughts were still whirling around in his brain, even after the meeting.

He had served the älfar; or had pretended to serve them, rather. He was guilty in this respect. But there had been no other way. His task now was to make suitable amends for any harm inflicted on others; that is what he hoped this expedition would allow him to do. Hargorin was not seeking his own death. He intended to go on living for many more cycles, should Vraccas be willing to keep his life-fire blazing. From this orbit onward, however, he would search the Outer Lands with a view to locating the all-powerful adversary.

The report Balyndis had sent from the Stone Gateway was terrifying; it showed with what degree of obsession and self-sacrifice thousands upon thousands had thrown themselves at the fortifications.

No beast would settle for destruction in the way that ragged army did. Hargorin agreed that the sorcerer responsible for them, perhaps known by Carmondai, must be found. Or at the very least, the race the enemy came from. Carmondai had been living in the Outer Lands for many cycles. *We should have a thorough talk about our strategy.*

They had also wanted to discuss what should happen with Sha'taï. But on account of where they were, where the walls undoubtedly had ears, they had skipped that question. Though a glance around the assembled leaders made it likely that all of them would gladly have seen the back of her.

But how? Hargorin did not believe that there was a demon in the little body. He had urged that the axe Keenfire, to be on the safe side, be brought in the vicinity of the child. If the diamonds lit up as they had done when the false Tungdil had come close, then they would know that there was evil in her. That would make even the elves and the humans think twice.

It would be simplest to incarcerate her. *She won't be able to cause any trouble once she's safely locked up.* However badly one might feel about treating a child in that way, the security of Girdlegard was at stake. They had narrowly escaped having the Stone Gateway overwhelmed by alien forces.

Hargorin realised he was both tired and hungry. The dwarf leaders' discussions had gone on for a long time and they had missed the party and with that, the banquet.

I expect I can still find something to nibble. He stowed away his tools, strapped his leg on and got up.

He walked over to the door with scarcely a trace of a limp, opened it – and came face to face with Carmondai, covered in blood. 'What the . . . ?'

The dark-clad älf pushed him back into the room and closed the door as quietly as possible. 'It's not my blood,' he explained. 'And it wasn't my fault.' He put his ear to the door and listened out.

'What are you doing here, black-eyes?' Hargorin growled threateningly. 'We agreed you should wait outside.'

'You told me to wait. But I did not agree.' Carmondai had Bloodthirster in his hand. Red drops trickled down onto the floor.

The red-bearded dwarf picked up his long-handled axe. 'Who've you killed?'

'I reckon it will have been around a dozen guards. At least half of them were magic.' He indicated Hargorin should not speak, because shouts and the sound of thudding feet could be heard outside. Hargorin would not keep silent. 'Why did you kill them?'

'By Samusin and Inàste,' whispered Carmondai. 'Hold your tongue!'

'Or what?' Hargorin raised his weapon, keen for a fight. 'I'll show you who's the better warrior.'

'The girl,' hissed the älf. 'The child needed to be killed. She wanted me dead. I would have been doing Girdlegard a favour.'

Hargorin grimaced. 'Well, shatter my iron when I hammer it.'

'Fine, as long as it happens quietly,' Carmondai snapped impatiently.

The hammering, however, was happening at the door.

'Hargorin Deathbringer, are you in there?' Mallenia called through the closed door.

'I am,' he answered, and then turned to speak to Carmondai. 'If I save your life, will you do me a favour?'

The älf's lips narrowed.

'Are you alone?' Mallenia wanted to know.

'Who else do you expect I might have with me? I've just gone to bed. If you want to know about the outcome of our session, go and ask Ireheart. I'm tired.'

'We're looking for an älf. He tried to kill Sha'taï,' Mallenia spoke through the door. 'It was that Carmondai, the älf whose life I was stupid enough to spare.'

'I remember exactly. I can picture him. Clear as if he were standing right here.' Hargorin stuck out his strong right hand

and whispered, 'Swear by your goddess and swear on your life, black-eyes.'

'I swear,' replied Carmondai and they shook hands.

The dwarf shoved him aside and then opened the door. There stood Mallenia in full armour and accompanied by several elf and dwarf soldiers. 'Can I help?'

'You go to bed dressed like that?'

'I like to keep my axe near. Makes me feel secure.' He stepped out into the corridor. 'Where was he seen?'

'We lost him.' Mallenia looked furious. 'I can't let him escape a second time. He would have stabbed Sha'taï in her sleep, the scum.'

'By Vraccas!' Hargorin raised his weapon. 'Then I'll come with you and help you look.' Taking the room key out of his pocket, he locked the door behind him. 'With my blade I can cut him in pieces!'

'You are welcome to join us.' The queen hurried off.

Hargorin slipped into the throng, allowing himself to drop back somewhat each time the search party came to a turning. He arrived at the kitchen.

Making as if he were checking out the pantry for hidden älfar, he helped himself to smoked sausage, cheese and bread. He drank a beer, toasting his own cleverness. Now the älf was bound to him.

Not that I trust him an inch. But I'll make him obey me. He downed his beer and refilled his mug.

But on his return to the room, he found Carmondai had disappeared.

After the meeting, Tungdil followed Balyndis through the corridors of the main building, not daring to attract her attention. *How shall I begin?*

The Fifthling queen was chatting with her retinue as they walked, seemingly giving orders to the clan leaders, who acknowledged her and turned to issue commands to their colleagues. Preparations were underway for an eventual military campaign starting from the Stone Gateway. Spies and scouts were being sent out to verify the safety of conditions in the first few miles, checking for traps or unexpected dangers. This at least is what he gathered from overhearing snatches of talk.

One of Balyndis' companions drew her attention to Tungdil's presence. She halted and turned around, dismissing her entourage to their quarters. His heartbeat quickened as she approached. *I don't have to take the first step. She's taking it for me.*

'You're testing me,' she said mysteriously. 'This is hard. Will Phondrasôn keep sending us one Tungdil after another?'

'I think not. There was only one doppelgänger that I saw formed.' His hands were sweaty and a thousand thoughts crammed themselves into his head. Phrases exploded in his mind. 'I was away a long time,' he said finally, 'and now I'll be going away again.'

'Yes.'

I'll have to take another tack. 'There was darkness in Phondrasôn. Darkness, pain and hatred. A bottomless pit of everything bad, stewing, fermenting, giving rise to yet more evil.' He looked her straight in the eyes. 'I have no right to ask you for anything or to demand anything from you. But should I return safely from my mission, would you allow me to visit you? I want to talk with you. Talk about the past and about what is to come.'

'What is there to come, Tungdil Goldhand? The past we have in common, it unites us, but I see nothing that could unite us in the future, apart from our common endeavours to ensure the welfare of Girdlegard.' Balyndis looked him deep in the eyes and her gaze was cool. 'Nothing apart from that.'

This answer inflicted more pain than any wound or blow received in Phondrasôn, although he should have expected it. 'I had many, many cycles in which to think about my feelings . . .'

'And so did I. Two hundred and fifty, to be exact.' There was no harshness in her tone but no softness, either. 'We thought you had died. And I never trusted the other Tungdil. So for me you *stayed* dead.' She pointed to him. 'And now another Tungdil turns up, with something of the one I knew, albeit changed. You have come back from the dead, but my heart buried you a long time ago.'

He felt a lump in his throat and his emotions were in upheaval. He was faced with a brick wall that Balyndis had constructed round herself. 'I know we have a son,' he said quietly. 'Permit me to see him and to spend time with him.'

Her smile was amicable but rejecting. 'He is a veteran warrior in his own right, commanding troops at the Stone Gateway. He bears the Keenfire weapon and so continues your work. He is no longer in need of a guiding hand from you.'

Tungdil was at a loss. The clever words he had prepared dissolved in the chaos swirling in his soul. But the certainty remained: he loved Balyndis. Sincerely loved her. *It must be too soon to tell her.* The dwarf-woman looked at one of the rings she wore on both hands. She pulled the largest of them off her finger and held it in front of his face. It was made of vraccasium and bore the symbol of the Divine Smith.

'Take this ring as a talisman. Bring it back to me and I shall allow you one visit to me in the Grey Mountains. We will have a meal together and I will invite Balyndar to be there.' She dropped the ring and he caught it adroitly. Balyndis turned aside and her white fur coat swung round with her.

Tungdil clasped the ring tight in his fist and watched her walk away. *That was more than I could have hoped for.* He tried it and found it would fit on the little finger of his right hand. It was still warm from hers.

He had deliberately not referred to the orders she had given. The whole of Girdlegard should believe that he and a small troop were to leave via the Grey Mountains, even though Tungdil and Hargorin had made a different plan that they thought was more promising.

Gosalyn still had the notes her friend Belogar had made about the abandoned settlement where Sha'taï had hidden from her Outer Land pursuers. Belogar had overseen the subsequent demolition work to destroy any trace of the tracks the girl had used to get to Girdlegard. These maps and notes were exactly what Tungdil intended to employ when the retinue departed the homeland.

We'll be taking almost the identical route that Sha'taï came in by. He thought it probable that in this way, they might find their evil enemy or hints to its whereabouts and be able to destroy it. *A bold and hazardous undertaking.* He turned his brown-eyed gaze to the window and the snowflakes falling outside. *Travelling in winter through a desert of ice, rock and snow.*

He caressed the ring. There could be no greater incentive to survive the expedition. The gods would decide what happened at the promised meal. He knew what he wanted. He made his way through the various corridors and stairwells to his own quarters and went to bed. He half-heard the uproar elsewhere in the building but paid no heed. Others would have to deal with whatever it was.

A hero once more? he wondered.

This time, he hoped, it would not be another two hundred and fifty cycles before he returned.

The Triplets had placed him under their perfidious protection but not in order to keep him safe in the Black Abyss.

They played the game the älfar are best at: they exerted influence on him, shaped him according to their will.

They possessed knowledge of potions and magic known otherwise to none.

Not even in the Outer Lands.

The Triplets were able to guide the will of the Hero, just as a rider controls his night-mare.

Secret notes for
The Writings of Truth
written under duress by Carmondai

XX

Somewhere in the Grey Mountains
6492nd solar cycle, winter

'What did you say?' Tungdil shouted against the wind. Gosalyn's words were impossible to understand from beneath the layers of material covering her mouth. And he, Tungdil, had a thick fur hood pulled up over his head to protect against frostbite.

The two of them were followed by a select band of bold warriors representing the Freelings and each of the dwarf tribes. They were roped together in case one should slip and take a disastrous fall. The lead soldier fastened a metal staple into the rock and the last man removed it to ensure they left no obvious trace.

'I said, Belogar was thorough!' she said, speaking as loudly as she could, indicating the map in her hands and then pointing ahead. 'It's all gone.'

Tungdil saw the artificially formed fissures. If there had ever been a track here, or a path, it had been torn away and demolished with pickaxe and crowbar, hammer and chisel, leaving in its place smooth slopes that only a bird could traverse.

'No chance. We'll never get through,' he yelled back.

'No.' Gosalyn pointed east to a wide expanse of snow leading to one of the peaks. Immediately below there was a sheltered ledge. 'That way.'

'What makes you so sure?'

'It's marked as a maintenance area,' she shouted back, her

finger on a dotted line on the chart. 'Good for spying from. But to get there we have to cross a bridge as narrow as a dagger blade. Follow my footsteps.'

They secured the rope anew, then Gosalyn changed direction, eyes firmly fixed on the ground at her feet. Tungdil followed hard on her heels and they moved off to the right, this time without setting pitons – they would not have been possible in the snow.

The last snow had fallen long ago but the wind was merciless, freezing even objects that contained no moisture. The cloudless skies helped temperatures plunge. Their fur coats were as stiff as frozen boards and the rope joining them together was like a wire. If anything metal touched rock, pieces of iron would break off or fracture – material that normally withstood tremendous impacts in battle.

Even without direct sunshine, the old snow was dazzling in its intensity, which was why the dwarves were wearing masks with narrow slits for the eyes. This did not make the climb any easier.

We'd have made little progress without Gosalyn's help. Tungdil was grateful Vraccas had sent her, along with her dead friend's detailed notes. From time to time he gave a backward glance to see if anyone was struggling. *I'd rather take more rest breaks than lose anyone to exhaustion.*

The column of dwarves trudged on, determined and silent, saving their breath for the climb. The altitude was challenging. Not all the dwarves were mountain-bred, used to breathing thin air. Tungdil was one of those having difficulty breathing. Occasionally he felt faint and his vision would blur. He was plagued with a constant headache. He grabbed a handful of snow, pushed his scarf up and sucked at the icy lump.

'How far?' he bellowed at Gosalyn's back.

She stretched out one finger but did not raise her head. *One mile. An eternity.* Tungdil had done longer marches in the chasms of Phondrasôn but heat and humidity were as nothing compared with this deadly chill and depleted air.

They had made good progress since their departure thirty orbits previously. They had passed the deserted settlement where the Fifthlings had set up a fort in case an army of beasts should attempt attack. *The orcs can't take this climate. The paths are dangerous. Not even mountain goats like it up here.*

Feeling giddy, Tungdil forced himself to concentrate on each step he took, but he still managed to miss Gosalyn's footprints.

Nothing untoward happened at first. The snow under his left foot crunched just like before – but there was an additional sound. Like ice breaking. Gosalyn stopped and looked back to the column. 'Stop where you are!' she yelled in warning. 'Nobody move!'

The sheet of snow to their left started to show long cracks, reaching as far as Tungdil could see through his snow-blindness protection, and then it plummeted down. A flurry of snow enveloped them in a glittering cloud of crystals that bit into their very eyeballs. A gust of wind occasioned by the snow-slip shook Tungdil so that he was forced to take a steadying step to the right, even though there was nothing but a sheer drop down the mountain waiting there as well.

A low growl increased in volume as if they had awakened a thunderstorm directly below them. He could hear shouts behind him and then there was a jerk on the safety rope. Tungdil tried to keep his balance as he glanced back to see what was happening.

The second-to-last figure of their column had fallen and was dangling over the edge, supported by the dwarves immediately behind and in front. But then the weight pulled the last one over, too, and there were two of them hanging in mid-air, swinging over the white abyss.

The rest of the troop shoved their feet as firmly as they could into the snow and held on to their comrades, hoping to save both the hapless victims and the lives of the whole team. Tungdil grabbed hold of the rope and applied his weight to pull on it.

'Pull!' screamed Gosalyn. 'But make sure you keep to my footprints! Don't slide to the right, whatever you do!'

Referring constantly to the chart and checking her route, she moved cautiously forward while the others tried to haul their comrades up. Tungdil could see where she was headed: they were nearly at the narrow rock bridge spanning the ravine, at the bottom of which a mountain torrent ran. Tungdil was surprised the river wasn't frozen over. White spray rose up in clouds from a waterfall that was partially concealed under a curtain of ice that covered the bridge like a roof. The spray turned to tiny beads of ice cascading down as soon as they found the freezing open air.

He took in all of this within the space of a couple of heartbeats, while still pulling on the rope with all his might. Gosalyn made it to the bridge and he and the rest of team were tugged along behind her.

At that moment one of the rescue team put a foot wrong and missed the safe path. A spectacle of destruction was unleashed. Tungdil stumbled to the right and only a stupendous effort on the part of Hargorin halted his fall. Four dwarves now hung to the right and two to the left of the narrow rock arch.

The King of the Thirdlings felt his arms nearly pulled from their sockets but the artificial limb had twice the strength of a normal leg and he was able to stand his ground. Beligata, standing in front of the red-haired dwarf, paid out more rope and fixed a piton hook into the rock bridge before Tungdil could call out a warning.

The metal clip sat fast and she was able to thread the cord through, but the rock itself reacted with a high-pitched clang. Fracture cracks immediately formed, running along and across. Tungdil could see catastrophe was inevitable, even if the bridge did not collapse with all of them on it. *Our mission must not end like this.*

'You keep going,' the first of the dwarves to fall called out, his axe at the ready. 'Vraccas awaits us.'

'No!' thundered Hargorin, seeing what the consequence would be. 'That is the wrong thing to do.'

But it was too late: the fibres of the rope had been severed. The last two in their company plunged into the deep, hitting the water after a long descent.

Elria, have mercy on their souls. Tungdil's arms were killing him.

But however high-minded the gesture had been, it meant that now there was no counterweight for the four figures dangling on the other side of the bridge. The anchoring hook was slowly being forced out of the stone and the fissures in the bridge grew more threatening.

Groaning, Hargorin threw back his head and then emitted a roar. He was leaning back, almost suspended over the far side of the rock bridge. He was holding the rope with super-dwarf strength, but his leg and the artificial limb were being dragged imperceptibly inch-by-inch closer to the edge.

The four dwarves called up to him but their words were

hard to understand. They seemed to be imploring him to cut them free and let them fall.

The pressure was now so great that Beligata, Tungdil and Hargorin all pulled at the same time.

'We've got to get everyone off the bridge!' Gosalyn shouted. 'It's going to collapse. The rock won't hold.'

'I'm not going without these four,' Hargorin replied. 'We've already lost two. They're our finest fighters.'

'Cut the rope through or we'll all die!' Gosalyn called. She had some freedom of movement but could not overtake the three dwarves in order to cut through the rope herself.

'If we reduce the traction, we'll overbalance and fall with them,' Beligata hissed.

'Throw your axe,' Tungdil demanded, hearing stones break off under his feet. 'And quickly!'

Gosalyn took aim and hurled her weapon – but a gust of wind took her by surprise and it was the handle, not the blade of the axe that hit the rope.

Tungdil was about to give the order that his own axe be used, but he recalled that he was alone in not being armed. It had been his intention never to fight again after two hundred and fifty cycles of blood-letting. *But my whittling knife.* 'Attached to my belt, look . . .'

He fell speechless, then, when he looked ahead and saw a dark-clad älf – unmistakeable in full sun as Inàste's creature because of his black eyes – rushing over the bridge towards them. He wielded Bloodthirster in his right hand.

How could that be? Ireheart had it last.

'Hargorin, mind out!' Tungdil bellowed.

The dwarves were unable to defend themselves and it was in the älf's power to destroy them all at one stroke.

The älf delivered the blow.

His blade severed the rope from which the four warriors dangled over the abyss. They fell, screaming, to disappear into the river like the previous two.

Hargorin overbalanced and the älf struck again.

Hargorin was hit on the back with the flat of the blade, sending him back onto the precarious bridge. The attacker grabbed him by the collar and held him fast. 'Off you go!' he yelled, pointing the way with Bloodthirster. 'This way. Get off the bridge if you want to live!'

Tungdil hesitated – but he was alone in doing so. Hargorin was not bothered that he was faced with an älf; Beligata turned her back on her mortal enemy, as well.

Gosalyn grasped Tungdil by the arm and hauled him along with her. 'Come on! You're blocking their path!' He moved forward, balancing rather than walking, keeping his eyes on safety.

Gosalyn reached solid rock and immediately placed an anchoring hook while Tungdil jumped past her, turning then to see who he could offer a helping hand to.

The bridge crumbled under Beligata's feet and she and Hargorin were thrown down towards the depths.

Tungdil hurled himself flat and grabbed her arm. 'I've got you. Hang on!'

She nodded, hiding the terror in her eyes. She seemed convinced she would not have to die. 'I'm quite comfortable like this,' she joked.

The älf leaped off the edge, his fingers fastening tight around Deathbringer's coat. He hauled the dwarf up on to the ledge before sinking down.

'I've made the rope fast,' Gosalyn reported, gasping with effort. 'We can pull her up.'

Together they heaved Beligata on to the ledge below the

towering peak. The wind relented somewhat as soon as the group was reunited on the safe side.

Samusin has got it in for us. Tungdil felt like he was about to pass out, his vision blurring and his breath rasping and rattling as if there were bits of metal in his lungs. 'Is that,' he gasped, 'is that . . . ?' He was fighting for air.

'It's Carmondai,' Beligata told him.

'I always wanted to have him along on our expedition,' Hargorin blustered, lying on his back. 'But . . .'

'Not necessary,' said the älf, with a little bow. His face was hidden behind a mask he had constructed to protect his skin from the dazzling light and the intense cold. 'I've been following you ever since I learned what you were up to. You're my only chance of getting out of Girdlegard. I've no place there any more, since that child turned up.'

It's the tale-weaver Mallenia was holding captive. I never thought I'd meet him.

Gosalyn nodded at him. 'He has helped us often.'

'And I for my part am indebted to Hargorin Deathbringer. He saved my life in Barrenbrig.' Carmondai's voice was pleasantly modulated and reflected his age and experience in its tones. 'It is an honour to meet you face to face, Tungdil Goldhand. I have written about you without knowing you.'

Tungdil pointed at Bloodthirster. 'Where did you . . . ?'

Carmondai indicated Beligata. 'She had it. But I thought the famous weapon would do better in an älf's hands so I took it back the first time I knocked her out. Now it's back to its roots.' He showed his right cheek. 'Not to mention Beligata has a penchant for . . .'

'You have sent four of our dwarves to meet their maker,' Tungdil said. 'We would have . . .'

'You know there was no other way. They would have

dragged you all with them. You yourself gave the order to throw the axe.' Carmondai watched the clouds of spray in the yawning chasm turn to pellets of ice and gradually start to form a new transparent cover. 'This way you can absolve yourselves of any blame regarding their deaths. Place the blame on the black-eyes.' He gave a quiet laugh. 'That way everyone profits.'

For a while they were silent. The dwarves, exhausted, were fighting for breath. The deaths of their comrades had placed a shadow over their mission it would be hard to shift.

'We can't fulfil the prophecy now,' said Gosalyn, deep in thought. 'We needed dwarves from each of the tribes.'

'If it's predictions you want, I can write you a new one,' Carmondai offered. 'It'll be good. Genuine Sitalia. No one could tell the difference.'

It seems everything's conspiring against us. Tungdil was more determined than ever to carry on and find out what was happening in the Outer Lands. They would deal later with the question of how to get back. The ring he wore on his little finger made their return essential.

Tungdil watched Carmondai warming his hands at the fire and working his fingers to get them supple. He had spread out several pages covered with sketches and notes from his travels. He used a compressed charcoal pencil; it was unaffected by the vicious cold, whereas ink would have frozen solid by now.

The remaining dwarves sat round in silence, leaning against their rucksacks. They had made the fire with petroleum and coal in the shelter of an overhang and they were holding bits of sausage to the flames to thaw them out and make them edible. Sucking fresh snow stilled their thirst.

The mountains were hidden under thick cloud. The world around them consisted only of the colour white. *We have many miles to travel still over ice and snow.* Tungdil's gaze switched from the älf's hands down to Bloodthirster, which Carmondai was sitting on.

'You're wondering how to get it back, aren't you?' Carmondai was amused. He took out his charcoal and notebook. 'You'll have to be quick. Beligata is wondering the same thing.'

'I would hurl the weapon over into the ravine so it disappears for ever,' Tungdil admitted. 'My hands will never wield Bloodthirster again. I have sworn an oath.'

'Then I vow that I shall look after it extremely well.' He started sketching the group as they sat warming themselves at the fire. 'It saved your lives, after all.'

'I could have cut the rope with my axe,' said Gosalyn, objecting.

'Of course, if you had actually hit it.' Carmondai was working swiftly, perhaps concerned his hands would get too cold to draw.

'Which brings me to the question of why you didn't warn us how dangerous this was,' Beligata reproached Gosalyn. 'If we had guessed there was only the thinnest of ice to each side of the path we would have been more careful. The others could still be alive.'

'There was nothing about it in Belogar's description,' Gosalyn defended herself. 'I just had very precise instructions where to place my feet. Nobody should have deviated from that path.'

'Perhaps he intended for any enemies using his notes to fall to their deaths,' Tungdil suggested, not wanting his team arguing.

The young Thirdling seemed to him to have a temper as fiery as Ireheart's. The scar on her cheek the älf had alluded to and which he had previously noticed glowing green was now concealed under layers of scarf. But he had not forgotten it.

Gosalyn felt the accusations were a slur on her honour. She fished out the notes. 'Read for yourself, if you don't trust me,' she demanded, thrusting the papers at Beligata. 'I would never have wilfully put you all in danger.'

The dark-haired dwarf-woman refused to look and concentrated on eating. She had nothing more to say on the matter. Gosalyn put the papers away and began to eat as well.

With Beligata's face more exposed now, Tungdil could see the shimmering green scar on the right-hand side. The edges of the wound had not healed. A drop of blood squeezed its way out and trickled down her face. She wiped it away with an oath and pressed her hand against the open sore.

'If you were all wondering whether I'd be sticking with you,' said the älf, 'let me put your minds at rest.'

'You owe me your life, remember,' Hargorin growled.

'And I've just saved yours, together with your friends here. I would say we were quits, wouldn't you? Not to mention this is the second time I've saved you all, so if anything, the balance is tipped in my favour. But this is the kind of adventure I've been missing – the unpleasant events of recent cycles notwithstanding – and I'm very keen to know how it ends.'

'Perhaps you will *end* before the mission does,' Beligata mocked.

'I'm sure, if we help each other, I shall survive to see the task completed.' Carmondai put down his drawing instruments. 'You'll be needing my knowledge. More than you think.'

Beligata snorted in scorn. Taking a handful of snow, she pressed it against her face to stop the bleeding. 'A storyteller's not going to be any use to us.'

'But a very old one? With countless cycles of experience?' Tungdil interrupted. 'Remember, he knew Sinthoras and Caphalor when they were in charge of the war against Girdlegard. He was there when our history happened.'

'But in the Outer Lands we're all on the same footing.' Gosalyn chucked another piece of coal on the fire to keep it going. It was not giving enough warmth to melt the snow on their coats.

Tungdil looked at the älf and his disfigured features. 'Tell us why the young girl wanted to kill you. Didn't she accuse you of lusting after her blood and bones for your artwork?'

Hargorin laughed grimly. 'Not difficult to believe.'

'She planned it impeccably.' Carmondai nodded. 'All because I dared to resist her. I have since thought it through carefully and collated a number of facts about her. I have come to the conclusion she belongs to the sorcerers known as botoicans.'

The dwarves raised their eyebrows. They had never heard the term before.

Even Tungdil was unaware of it. 'We don't have them in Phondrasôn.'

'Sinthoras and Caphalor came across them soon after the victory over Girdlegard. Caphalor told me many cycles later about the expedition the two of them had been on and how they came across these sorcerers, capable of influencing the minds of any creature . . . of *nearly* any creature, manipulating them so that they would do anything the botoicans wanted.'

Hargorin speared another slice of sausage and held it to the flames. 'So who is able to resist?'

'It seems the Children of the Smith are less susceptible to their wiles.' Carmondai gave a friendly smile. 'That would be due to their stubborn and pig-headed natures, I expect.'

'Vraccas knew what he was doing when he created us.' Gosalyn sighed. 'My dear good Belogar. You always knew it.'

Tungdil studied the tale-weaver's face. 'Are your people immune in the same way?'

Carmondai nodded. 'I assume so – or rather, let's say I hope so. Perhaps due to the magic power we're born with.'

'So why hasn't she tried to take over, if she's capable of subjugating the will of humans and elves?' Beligata chucked the red-stained snowball aside. The bleeding had stopped.

'She has not yet grown into her full powers, I think.' The älf held his fingers very close to the fire. 'She won't have completed her training. She had to flee, running away from a rival family of botoicans, and there won't have been time or opportunity to study. She told us her uncle died in that deserted village. She was very clever. She didn't arouse any suspicions. With the elves and humans manipulated into appointing Rodario as emperor, she's got everything her own way already.'

'And she'll be going from strength to strength.' Tungdil could see the problems this would give rise to. 'She will drop her mask of sweetness at some stage but people will be past caring.'

'We can't just kill her.' Hargorin was still eating his simple fare and had grease dripping on his red beard. 'Not now. She's wary of us.'

'And she knows she's got no power over dwarves,' Carmondai added. 'She'll be hatching a scheme to attack you but she'll get the others to implement it.' He opened and closed his fists. 'Be on your guard.'

'We already are.' It seemed strange to Tungdil to regard an älf as an ally. *He won't be above playing games with us.* 'Let's find out first who is sending the ghaists.'

'Can't we make common cause with whoever that turns out to be?' Beligata suggested.

'Against Sha'taï?' Hargorin looked at Tungdil. 'A pact with a demon?'

'Could go badly wrong,' Carmondai pointed out laconically. 'We älfar could tell you a thing or two about that.'

'Does the botoican influence end with the victim's death?' Tungdil wanted to know.

'As far as I know,' said Carmondai, picking up his drawing implements. 'The concept of a pact is a dangerous one. The botoican trying to get at Sha'taï will be far more powerful than she is. The reports from the Stone Gateway impressed me. And I've seen epic battles in my time.'

'Caution is needed, then.' Tungdil scratched his brown beard, brushing off the small lumps of ice that had formed. 'If that sorcerer were to get through our defences, Girdlegard would fall.'

'No pact, then.' Hargorin was calm. 'A major evil to drive out a minor evil is a pretty silly way to proceed.'

'Let's take things slowly here. I wouldn't want to dismiss the idea of an alliance.' Beligata was trying to win the others round. 'Perhaps we'll need the other botoican to help us get rid of the child and the elves, too.'

'What's it got to do with the elves?' Gosalyn shook her head. 'We're working with them.'

'They do nothing but blather about some prophecy that you can interpret this way or that. That prophecy book is thick. There'll be a lot of other stuff in there. Maybe it's all just to cover an attack on the dwarf tribes as soon as things quieten down?' Beligata looked at Hargorin, expecting him to agree with her.

'One step at a time is my advice,' said Gosalyn.

'Like back there on the ice, you mean?' Beligata said nastily. 'And then we wonder why the bad things happen to us?'

Gosalyn jumped to her feet. 'I've told you already . . .'

'Quiet, the both of you,' Tungdil bellowed. The wildest thoughts were spinning round in his head. *Nothing makes sense. Not yet.* 'We're here to reconnoitre. We're going to find out who's been sending the messages. And after that we'll make our decision.'

Gosalyn sat down abruptly and Beligata kicked at the snow crossly. Carmondai finished his sketch and put it down. 'Follow.'

Hargorin frowned. 'Tungdil doesn't need your say-so, black-eyes.'

The älf's laugh was arrogant. '*Follow.*' He pointed his charcoal over their heads to the overhang.

Tungdil turned to look.

Almost imperceptible symbols were visible on the rock face.

Hargorin got to his feet to examine the inscription, then he squatted down and felt around in the snow. 'It's been rubbed away. There's fragments of stone here. Someone didn't want the symbol to be seen.'

'Perhaps it was an älf spy looking for a path thorough the Grey Mountains.' Carmondai looked at the fragments Hargorin had sticking to his glove. 'It's got paint on it. Only we can see it,' he said, indicating his black eyes.

'The path the child used to get to Girdlegard had previously been used by älfar. But someone who recognised the paint has removed it,' Tungdil summed up. 'I think we're on

Aiphatòn's trail. It will be him that scratched it off.' Tungdil looked up at the clouds. 'As soon as the mist clears we're setting off.'

'There's a cave over there.' They had been travelling now for many orbits and the whole journey was, for Tungdil, merging into a single emotion. 'We could camp here overnight. Looks like there's a storm coming.'

Gosalyn, walking ahead with the älf, raised her arm to signal she had understood, and turned west. Tungdil could not say how long they had been marching. Their journey had provided a never-ending succession of paths, ravines, steep slopes, snowfields, ice sheets, mountain passes, fantastic views and heavy white mist. All-pervading: bitter cold and utter exhaustion.

After all the cycles in the caves of Phondrasôn, Tungdil was not used to an environment where the elements so conspired against one. Sunshine and wind were often of frightening intensity and the view past the peaks to the never-ending distance made his heart beat faster. *There is no relief in sight.*

The älf came across other instances of rune paint being scratched off. During their frequent rests to regain stamina he would tell them about the group of ten who had been sent out by the Triplets to explore the deserted settlement and to kill the elves who were also headed in that direction. All in all it was starting to look as if one of that original group had managed to make his way over the Grey Range, evading all the deadly traps the mountains held in store. This proved an added incentive to the dwarves.

Gosalyn, who lived with the Fifthlings, had more endurance than the rest and saw the exercise as a memorial to

Belogar. But then they came to the end of her friend's notes. This was as far as he had got. From that point on, they had to rely on the almost illegible runes and their own instincts.

The group was about half a mile from the entrance to the cave, with the setting sun drenching the slopes in a red glow. The snow had turned to frozen blood, as if a battle of immense proportions had taken place. *Or maybe the battle is up in the clouds and the rain drops down as blood.* Tungdil had to keep reminding himself to use both eyes. This was his gift from the magic source. *Will Coïra ever find out how to free herself from its power?*

Approaching now to within two hundred paces, Carmondai came to sudden halt and knelt down by Gosalyn's side, eyes fixed on the cave entrance. 'Over here!'

'Well, well. We seem to have a new leader!' Beligata mocked.

'No, just someone with better eyesight than you lot.' Carmondai pointed out the tracks where the snow had been trampled. 'We don't seem to be the only ones wanting to set up camp.'

'Mountain goats?' was Hargorin's theory. 'They'll have felt the thunderstorm coming on.' He turned to the southern sky where black clouds were threatening to extinguish the sunset. There was the occasional flash within the dark mass.

'No. The tracks weren't made by narrow hooves.' Carmondai sounded sincere. 'But who else would be roaming around in these parts?'

'Aiphatòn,' said Tungdil, wondering whether the älf would have left traces in the snow, given that he could not have taken off his armour. Carmondai did not seem to leave much in the way of tracks, himself. The extra weight of furs, cloak and armour made it impossible for the älfar trick of invisible footsteps to work, but his prints were noticeably fainter than those the dwarves made.

'Or monsters,' Beligata contributed helpfully.

'Or a ghaist,' Gosalyn added.

'A nice selection of nasty surprises,' Hargorin said. The storm was piling in, and the first rumbles of thunder could be heard. 'But we don't have a choice. We won't survive out in the open.'

Tungdil nodded in agreement. 'Let's find out who we'll have to share our shelter with.'

The group stamped their way through the snow over to the hole in the rock. The wind was growing stronger and sending blasts of ice crystals into their faces as if trying to prevent them from reaching the shelter. The icy needles penetrated their face masks and stung their eyes. They had to hold their hands in front of them or to walk with their heads down.

The sun went down and took with it its crimson colour, apart from the spot just in front of the cave. The red was at its deepest here and made long stripes in the snow.

It's real blood! It looked like a blood wave had run out of the cave, staining everything it touched. Hargorin uttered a curse and grabbed his axe with both hands. Carmondai drew his own weapon and Gosalyn was ready with her hand-axe. They split up, going to each side of the opening, trying to look inside.

The darkness gave forth the reek of cold blood and ripped intestines. There must have been a terrible slaughter here, and recently at that.

But where are the bodies? Tungdil could not see anything but blocks of stone. One of them had red prints on it that could have come from orcs and the ground was covered in a crusted sheet of blood that was partially frozen.

He stepped gingerly into the cave. The walls were uneven and sported deep niches and recesses where enemies might be hiding. Carmondai and the other dwarves followed cautiously. The thin veneer of ice crackled under the soles of their boots.

With great vigilance they stepped through the blood; they could taste it in the air they breathed. It left a hint of copper on the tongue.

Suddenly Tungdil heard a noise. Something cracked. He signalled to the others to stop. From further on in the cave came the sounds of bones being snapped and raw flesh being ripped.

The hunter enjoying the spoils. Tungdil expected to see a horde of orcs with their booty of mountain goats. These beasts would devour their prey cold. And anyway, there was no wood up here to provide fuel. He waved Beligata over, assuming she was the strongest of them. 'Go and take a look. Tell me how many green-skins there are,' he whispered. 'Note exactly where . . .'

'I know what to do,' she said, slipping her rucksack off and disappearing silently round the corner.

'Get ready, everyone,' he ordered. 'Hargorin first, then Carmondai. Gosalyn and I will bring up the rear.'

'Without a weapon?' Hargorin made to hand him a dagger.

'I'll come up with something.'

The dwarf and the älf nodded, tensely.

The snapping of bones continued, with the sound of more flesh being torn off and chewed. The echo made it impossible to guess how many were involved.

A thunder-clap came from the mouth of the cave and a lightning flash illuminated the walls for a split heartbeat. The storm was at its height, with gusts of wind howling round the cave in a shrill whistle. This unlooked-for concert drowned out the sounds they made; their enemies would not notice danger approaching.

If we hadn't made it to the cave, that wind would have swept us off the mountain by now. Tungdil peered past Hargorin and Carmondai into the depths of the cave.

The darkness did not permit a view of anything except for the vaulted tunnel into which Beligata had vanished. Her boots had left prints on the frozen surface of the blood-covered floor.

How high is the cave? Tungdil looked up.

At the same moment a shadow of imposing size dropped from the six-pace-high roof to land with a crash in front of Carmondai. It then unfolded to its full height.

A flash of lightning illuminated the walls. The light fell on the figure, nearly three paces tall, in an artistically engraved and embossed set of armour. The helmet was closed and formed in the shape of a skull, with three horns sticking out of the forehead.

'Dorón Ashont!' Carmondai shouted, moving back. 'Get back! He . . .'

A steel fist the size of a head zoomed out of the dark, hitting the tale-weaver full in the face, lifting him off his feet and sending him flying into the air to slam down onto the rock by the cave opening; Bloodthirster clattered down beside him.

A creature like Djerůn. 'No, don't! It won't hurt us!' Tungdil shouted, seeing Hargorin punched by the armoured gauntlet and thumped back against the wall.

'I am made of stone.' The red-bearded dwarf picked up his long-handled axe with a growl and answered the attack. 'Try my steel!'

Gosalyn jumped to his side.

Beligata appeared in the corridor behind him, her double axe raised to strike against the armoured figure's knees. 'And mine!'

Their adversary kicked back, hitting the dark-haired dwarf-woman in the chest, face and neck. She was hurled backwards into the tunnel, then, half-stunned, she turned over on to her front to clamber back on to her feet, pulling herself up with the help of a boulder.

Parried with a steel war-club, Hargorin's wood-handled axe snapped off under the impact.

Gosalyn's hand axe met the foe's armour-clad hip, making a dent in the metal. The creature snorted and replied with a kick the dwarf-woman managed to dodge – only for her to fall victim to the end of the war club. The blunt end struck her on the left shoulder, causing her to collide with Tungdil, who had been about to thrust himself between the combatants with arms outstretched.

'The acront is not our enemy,' he shouted to Hargorin urgently. 'He's jumping to the wrong conclusion because we have an älf with us.'

'I know that.' The red-bearded dwarf ducked under his opponent's weapon which then struck the wall, breaking a piece of rock off as easily as if it were constructed of plaster. 'But how's he going to get the picture? They don't speak our language.'

A deep rumbling sound ensued that had nothing to do with the raging storm. The beam of purple light from the helmet eye-slits seemed to want to root the dwarves to the very spot they stood on. Tungdil recalled the same effect the Djerůn had had on monsters, and remembered how they had fled in terror.

Even though the main motive of an acront was to hound

and destroy evil, it would clear any hindrance from its path. In the present situation that unfortunately meant the dwarves.

Beligata had got unsteadily to her feet and bent down to get her double axe. She cast her cloak aside because it was hampering her movements. 'Enough is enough,' she said, speaking with difficulty because of her split lip. She drew a rasping breath and held her side; ribs appeared to be fractured. 'I'll get him out of that armour.'

'What else?' Hargorin took a hand axe from his belt. Compared to the war-club the giant adversary was wielding, which was the size and weight of a full-grown dwarf, this seemed faintly ridiculous.

Before Tungdil could answer, steel fingers had grabbed Gosalyn's skull in a headlock.

She yelled and hacked at the arm but the only effect was that her blade was damaged. Her helmet was squashed out of shape and the inlaid pattern pieces fell onto fur and floor.

'Let go of her!' Beligata shouted, reeling towards them.

The acront whirled round, going down on one knee and sweeping his club at her sideways; there was a faint sound of his flexible metal armour creaking. Beligata managed to fend off the blow but was sent flying backwards. The enemy held her pinned against the wall; she was powerless to move or to harm the acront.

I have no choice. 'Get down!' Tungdil ordered Hargorin, who was about to launch a senseless attack.

Without questioning, Hargorin dropped to his knees. Tungdil took a run, used the crouching dwarf as a ramp and flew through the air, short knife in his hand.

He landed on the back of the acront, placed one hand round its visor and with the other hand inserted the sharp point between the giant's helmet and the throat.

But he did not press the blade home, leaving it as a deadly threat. *Let's hope he gets the message.*

The acront froze into the statue of a warrior, snarling; the purple light dimmed and died.

Increasing the pressure on the knife-blade, Tungdil could not help a silent laugh. *So I've brought him down with an apple-peeler.*

The steel-gauntleted fingers slowly released Gosalyn's head.

She fell half a pace to the floor, wrenched the twisted helmet off her peat-brown hair and collapsed to the ground, blood oozing out of cuts on her head caused by the broken metal.

Hargorin hurried over to see to her injuries.

Then the acront took away the war-club that had held Beligata against the rock wall. The young dwarf-woman dropped her double axe; she slipped to the ground, holding her side. Her shuddering breath came like that of someone drowning. She kept pointing at the acront but forming words was beyond her.

'He won't hurt us now.' Tungdil wracked his brain for a means of practical communication. The languages he had picked up in Phondrasôn would be of little use and if he fell back on the älfar tongue he feared it would only inspire more violence. *Shall I try in elvish?*

Their adversary put down his club and seemed to be waiting to see what the dwarf on his shoulder would do next.

'She's in a bad way,' he heard a worried Hargorin say. 'I think her skull is fractured.'

Tungdil looked over at Beligata whose arm was still raised. 'Acronta,' she gasped, coughing.

Violet light fell on Tungdil from behind. The rumblings

behind him made the hairs on the back of his neck stand up in fear. *Acronta. That was the plural form.*

The hard sideways swipe came from diagonally above him, meeting and snapping his collarbone. He felt the blood run warm. His arm and fingers became useless. He was brushed off the acront's back as easily as a fly might be swatted.

With his good arm he attempted to grab hold of something but he slid down the armour and came crashing face-first to the stony floor of the cave.

He could taste blood and his teeth were in bad shape. He sank down, all the strength gone out of him. He lost consciousness.

After the Triplets had left, handing him a recipe for the potion that was supposed to endow him with great strength, he began the search for an empire of his own.

For he thought he belonged to these regions and he intended to subjugate the place.

He looked for mercenaries, gave them riches in abundance and bound them to himself with threats. They in their turn made plans. They conspired to kill him.

They stayed loyal to each other as long as things went well.

One cave after another fell to Tungdil, who had forgotten his origins: he had forgotten that he was a Child of the Smith.

Secret notes for
The Writings of Truth
written under duress by Carmondai

XXI

Somewhere in the Outer Lands

Tungdil awoke to the sensation of the ground moving beneath him. With his senses not fully functioning yet, he assumed he was imagining it.

He had more certainty about the condition of his hands, which were tied together behind his back. They were tethered to his right ankle somehow. A blindfold cut into the bridge of his nose.

He concentrated on taking deep breaths and waited to feel pain. *Surely my shoulder should be hurting?* He remembered being struck and hearing the collarbone go. But, strangely, he found he could wriggle arm and shoulder joint without any soreness. It was only the fetters restricting his movements.

Odd. Either he had been dosed with a pain-deadener or magic treatment had been given – but it was the first he had heard of acronta using the magic arts. *Andôkai the Tempestuous would never have kept Djerůn as a bodyguard if that had been the case.*

Tungdil felt around on the ground. It felt cold. Cold and metallic.

Sitting up as well as he could, he swivelled round on the seat of his breeches to stretch his legs out. It must be a relatively large space.

The slight rolling motion had not ceased. The ground wobbled from time to time, but it did not feel like being on a boat. *Is it a sledge of some kind?* With his eyes bound he had no idea of his surroundings except for the sensation of clean, warm air. There was rough fabric covering him instead of the furs and cloak he had been wearing. 'Where am I?' he whispered.

'Here.' This was Hargorin's voice, coming from nearby. 'We're in some kind of a shed on a sledge, I think.'

'How long have we been here?'

'I've only just woken up myself.'

They were interrupted by a groan. Gosalyn, sounding bewildered, asked, 'Where are you both? I've got a blindfold on.'

'So've we,' Tungdil replied, trying to sound reassuring. 'The good thing is, we're still alive.'

'The three of us, at least,' Hargorin corrected.

'Four.' This was more a groan than a voice from Beligata. 'Why do I feel as heavy as lead?'

We've all woken up at the same time. Can't be coincidence. 'Anyone hurt?' All of them said no. 'Why have they taken us with them and why have they seen to our injuries?'

'Maybe they understood they made a mistake,' Hargorin attempted an explanation. 'Do you think the black-eyes is still alive?'

'Yes, it is,' said Carmondai, drowsily. 'If it had been a Dorón Ashont mistake, then you'd be free and I'd be dead. My thanks go to Inàste for ensuring I might wake.'

'Don't count your blessings too soon,' Beligata warned. 'We're all tied up, right?' They all agreed. 'We should all try to get rid of the blindfolds and describe where we are.'

'Each of us is in a cage and we've got a tarpaulin over us. There are two metal braziers between our prison cells,' Carmondai reported. 'And if I'm not mistaken we're being pulled along on a giant sleigh. But I can't smell any horses or other animals so it must be the Dorón Ashont themselves pulling us.' He cleared his throat. 'And we're wearing garments made of unbleached linen. Flax.'

He's damned clever. Tungdil tried to dislodge his blindfold by rubbing the side of his face on the floor. Despite these efforts he only succeeded in getting the bandage to slip a little, but it afforded him a view of the surroundings. The älf had not lied: Tungdil saw exactly what Carmondai had reported. Beligata, Hargorin and Gosalyn were still working at their own blindfolds.

The vehicle appears to have been constructed for the purpose of transporting captives and with thought given to minimising weight. The cages were made of twisted metal wire that would need an axe or pliers to cut through. 'Where could they be taking us?'

'And what are acronta doing in the mountains?' Hargorin wanted to know.

'I presume,' said Carmondai in measured tones, 'that the älfar runes are behind this. The Dorón Ashont are bitter enemies of my people. They defeated us once and destroyed the old empire of the Unslayables when we had attempted to eradicate them with poison. Poison, because we were not able to overcome them in battle.' He made the sign in the air. '*Follow!* I will wager that the älf who wrote that did not expect the Ashont would be the ones to find and read the message hundreds of cycles later.'

Tungdil thought back to the adventure he had had with the maga Andôkai and her bodyguard. 'It's a struggle without end.' He realised with a jolt that Carmondai was not manacled.

Carmondai showed his arms were free. 'I found a sharp bit of wire that was just right to pick the padlock with. But how to get out of the cage is another matter entirely. So far

I've not come up with anything.' He smiled. 'An älf with a load of dwarves. That'll have aroused their curiosity. That's why they're taking us with them.'

'Did the älfar know more about the acronta?'

'The Towers That Walk, we called them. A mystery to us. They would turn up out of the blue, bringing carefully calculated death, sometimes with the orcs as their targets, then the fflecx and other monsters Tion and Samusin had invented.' Carmondai tried to spy out through the tarpaulin but it was too thick. Impossible to say, with that canvas and the glow from the brazier, whether it was light outside.

'*Carefully calculated*. You mean deliberate planning of the strength of their attacks?'

'They always homed in on exactly the race they felt was the most dangerous at any one time. They eliminated those who outnumbered them or those who were subjugating others by means of technical supremacy or tricks.' Carmondai seemed to be sorting through his memories, as if he had a set of meticulously filed records concerning every event he had lived through. 'Except they would attack us whenever the opportunity arose. Because of the eternal feud.'

'Did you know how their armies were led?' Hargorin asked, finally ridding himself of the blindfold.

'No. If we had known that it would have made things easier for the Inextinguishables. We knew there were several different specimens, but apart from that, no details really. Only that they are clever and full of tricks.' He laughed. 'So full of tricks that they were able to inflict a sickness on us that killed us in our hundreds, destroying the old Dsôn.'

'All the more reason for wondering why they've left you alive.' Beligata had, by now, also freed herself from the bindings over her eyes.

Tungdil frowned when he looked at her face. The green scar had lengthened and forced itself further out from her skin. It did not look inflamed and did not appear to have suffered a recent cut. The green glow from the scar was getting longer, forming a straight line.

A glance at Carmondai told him the älf had also noticed this change. The älf's expression was one of surprise but also of satisfaction. This was never a good sign in an älf.

'We will learn why we have been spared,' the historian said, tapping a finger against his lower lip as he wrestled with his thoughts.

'Perhaps because we put up a brave fight?' Hargorin knelt down. 'That ploy with the fruit knife was splendid.'

Carmondai felt along the cage side. 'Fruit knives won't be much help if you are faced with more than one adversary.'

'Still better than lying about in a faint,' retorted the red-bearded dwarf with a cackle.

'I am old. Forgive me, groundling.' The älf took the jibe with humour. 'I confess I have no idea how much time has passed. But my wounds have healed and I can't find any bruises. There would have been a cracker of a bruise after I was punched with that gauntleted fist. I would say, working on the size of an acront and how strong the blow was, we might have been underway for at least ten or fourteen orbits.'

Tungdil judged the period must have been three times that long. After all, his collarbone had healed while they were out. 'They've kept us drugged for longer.'

'And they'd planned for us all to come round at the same time.' Agile as an acrobat, Beligata managed to pass her bound hands beneath her and over her legs in order to have her fingers in front of her. 'So we would appear to be near our destination?'

'How fast can an acront run?' Gosalyn looked at Carmondai expectantly.

'They could doubtless cover eighty miles in an orbit. If the going is easy then probably a hundred,' he reckoned. 'But if there's snow, and the acront's own weight and that of his armour taken into consideration, plus pulling a sledge, let's say, no more than thirty.'

'More than a thousand miles.' Tungdil gave a grunt of admiration. On taking a deep breath he was aware that he had no difficulties. *So we are no longer at altitude.* 'That's quite a stretch they've carried us.'

'And they never even asked us first.' Beligata was testing the wire for weakness, but she did not look hopeful. 'And knowing our luck, they'll have brought us in totally the wrong direction. It'll take ages to catch up again.'

Hargorin laughed good-naturedly. 'The optimism of youth. She already knows we're going to escape.'

'Well, we'll have to, one way or another.' Tungdil suppressed the fear his calculations had aroused in his mind. 'Their plans will be different from ours.'

'Of course.' Carmondai listened carefully and placed his hand flat on the floor of the cage. 'It's not shaking so much. We're slowing down.'

He was right. The rocking movement had stopped.

Nothing else happened.

'Shame I can't get to the hollow compartment in my metal leg. I could use that knife right now.' Hargorin glanced at the round metal braziers that were keeping them warm. 'Maybe the coals are hot enough to melt the wire. What do you say, Scholar?'

It was strange being addressed by that name, unless it was Ireheart talking. 'That should work.' Tungdil looked around.

'But if the sparks touch the tarpaulin, which is not unlikely, it'll catch fire and we'll be roasted alive.'

'They'll be even happier with an älf in that state.' Beligata passed her hand over her face, touching the scar with her fingertips. She hesitated when she reached the place, but said nothing.

'In my experience they prefer raw meat,' Carmondai said laconically.

'We'll wait and see what happens,' decided Tungdil. 'If they're merely taking a rest they'll have placed a guard and he'd hear what we were up to.' *Particularly since they've planned for us to be awake by now.*

They fell silent and concentrated on what they could pick up from outside. They heard only muffled sounds that gave them no clues as to what the acronta were doing.

At that moment the vehicle gave a jolt and tipped slowly forward, making them slide against the walls of their cages. Then the sledge picked up speed.

Tungdil hoped this was intentional and that they had not torn loose. 'Stand up against the wire with your backs to the direction of travel,' he called to the others. If there were an impact this should reduce the likelihood of serious injury.

The journey went at high speed, with many a curve. And then they came to a stop. Through the covering they could hear a continuous rushing sound.

The tarpaulin was pulled back and they could see where they had been taken. They were in a dome-shaped hall constructed of simple stones, nothing overly sophisticated. Light fell through a ring of holes in the roof. There was a smell of excrement and sweat.

That rushing sound proved to be a low murmuring and muttering from about a hundred prisoners in similar cages placed in niches in the circular walls. Turning his head, Tungdil saw he would have to amend his calculation: there were seven layers, one on top of the next. They were the only dwarves among the captives, it seemed. And he did not catch sight of any other älfar, either.

'Do you think this is their collection of curiosities?' Hargorin stared at the other inmates.

Beligata looked down. 'No. This is some kind of arena. I can see some teeth that have been knocked out. And bits of armour. A broken blade over here. It must be for gladiators.'

'They're going to make us fight.' Gosalyn was furious. 'For their entertainment.'

Tungdil had a different idea but kept quiet.

Nobody came for them. The tarpaulin was suspended from a hook and removed by a system of pulleys. Some curved metal arms descended from the primitively-built ceiling, clicked into place on their cages and lifted them into the air. After a short distance they were placed in adjoining niches. The hooks disengaged and were drawn up again.

The floor of the arena was some ten paces below them. Tungdil was at the outer edge on the right. The unfamiliar monster next to him seemed to be a composite of human and wolf, which growled at the dwarf, putting its ears back threateningly. A snake-like tongue slithered out.

'Can you understand me?'

The beast rumbled something, barked and sat down.

'It's not a proper theatre or the cellar of an actual arena.' Carmondai's cage was in the middle. The älf look around carefully. In front of the cages there were ledges for guards to stand, but there was no sign of any soldiers. Carmondai pointed up at the light openings in the roof. 'Mirrors. They can illuminate the whole area if need be.'

'So they can observe what's happening.' Gosalyn had, like Beligata, managed to get her arms round in front of her.

An armoured acront stepped out of the shadows, helmet-slits directed at the newcomers. He raised one arm, holding an iron staff as long as a man is tall. The stick was tapered to a sharp point.

This sharp end of the staff was pointing at Hargorin's cage. Hooks dropped down, catching on to the wire and manoeuvring it out of the niche.

'Vraccas is with you!' Tungdil shouted to him.

'Show them what it means to be a Child of the Smith,' Gosalyn yelled in encouragement.

The cage had hardly arrived on the floor before the acront used a floor-mounted trigger to activate a spring that lifted the cage lid off. Hargorin was free.

Now the acront threw Hargorin a key and then tossed the iron staff at his feet, taking a step back and drawing its sword.

Tungdil had noticed smaller figures taking their seats four ledges higher up where the view would be best. They were dressed in armour but also had paper, inkwells and quills with them. *They're going to be observing and making notes. Awarding points, perhaps? Referees? Judges?*

A low whistle sounded from up there. Preparations were complete.

'They're not getting the creatures to fight each other,' said Tungdil. 'I think *they're* fighting us. They will be observing forms of combat and noting the moves.'

The position of the mirrors was abruptly adjusted, directing the sun's rays so that there were no shadows anywhere for Hargorin to conceal himself in.

The noises died away. Tension was high.

'Do you think I won't be able to do it?' The muscular

dwarf surveyed the three-pace-tall opponent, looked at the staff and bent to pick up the key. 'I'll show you . . .'

'No!' shouted Tungdil. 'Don't touch it.'

'What? Shall I let myself be beaten?' Hargorin was still in a half-crouching position. 'It might save trouble but it goes against the grain.'

'Don't touch the key,' Tungdil insisted. 'I want them to know we're not going along with their game.'

'Is that wise?' Gosalyn looked worried. 'They could just kill him for not obeying.'

'That result would not give them any satisfaction,' was Carmondai's contribution. 'Tungdil is right. They want to watch and learn.'

Hargorin straightened up and folded his arms across his chest. This was a universally recognised gesture. The acront would understand.

The armed creature pointed at the iron staff. Purple light glowed behind the eye slits and there was a dull roar that made Tungdil's stomach churn even at this distance. Some of the other creatures shrieked in fright. 'Keep steadfast!'

'I shall,' Hargorin returned, looking at the large opponent with derision. 'Even if my fingers are itching to pick up the staff to show him what a Child of the Smith is made of.'

The acront made a sudden step towards the dwarf, grabbed him by the right arm and hauled him up into the air, to drop him crashing to the ground. Then he kicked Hargorin's motionless body so that it flew back into the cage. He slammed the lid shut. The fastening clicked into place.

'No!' groaned Gosalyn.

'He's not dead,' Carmondai reassured her. 'They need him. That was punishment for disobedience. But it was . . . a bit sudden.'

'They've still got *three* others. Why would they bother to spare one of us?' Beligata looked down, furious, watching the acront move towards a passageway.

The mirrors were folded back and shadows flooded the arena. The strange being vanished into the dark.

Hargorin's cage was fished up with a large hook and replaced in the wall niche. Blood trickled from his mouth into the red beard and his arms were twisted painfully. At least one of them seemed broken.

'By Lorimbur!' Beligata slammed her wrist chains against the wire. 'I'll kill that monster for that. Did you hear me? I'll kill it for doing that!'

'Be quiet, or else . . .' Gosalyn began.

The mirrors suddenly moved, re-filling the floor with light; the acront stood in the centre.

The hook that had moved Hargorin's cage now shifted to Beligata's, attaching itself and dragging her prison cell out of the hollowed-out space, taking it down to the combat arena.

'I swear I'll drag that helmet off your head,' the dark-haired dwarf-girl raged. 'And I'll take your skull with it.'

She won't, though. Tungdil looked up to the theatre boxes and saw quills dipped into inkpots.

'There's one good thing about her impending death: we know now that they can understand what we say,' Carmondai said. 'If life is a currency, we'll soon be running out of it.' He leaned against the side of his cage and turned his black gaze to what the fighters were doing.

'I wish it was *you* paying the bill,' hissed Gosalyn.

'Oh, I'll be down there soon enough.' Carmondai flashed his eyes at Tungdil. 'But *after* you, of course.' He pointed to the boxes in the gallery. 'What do you think? Will you be able to convince them to stop?'

Girdlegard
Black Mountains
Kingdom of the Thirdling dwarves
Eastern Gate
6492nd/6493rd solar cycles, winter

Rognor and Phenîlas were seated at their evening meal in the sparsely furnished inn. The only decoration was a Thirdling banner overhead and a picture of Lorimbur on the west wall.

The dwarf was surprised how quietly the blond elf was eating; he made no noise when chewing. In comparison Rognor was convinced that he was producing sounds like trees being felled. They were feasting on cooked vegetables, cereal broth and pickled meat that had been smoked slowly, resulting in what the dwarf found a most pleasant taste. He drank dark beer with his meal.

Phenîlas was concentrating on the vegetable dishes, trying a little porridge out of courtesy. He preferred not to touch the meat. 'Thank you again for your hospitality,' he said. He drank some of the water that he had been served.

'It is a pleasure to have you and the sorânïons staying with us. We share a common concern for the security of the homeland,' he replied in faltering elvish.

Phenîlas smiled in appreciation. 'You are making progress with your lessons.'

'Thank you.' Rognor had taken advantage of the opportunity to pick up some basic expressions in recent orbits, as he could not expect the new arrivals to speak the general tongue of Girdlegard. 'It is important to be able to communicate.'

'For this, too, my thanks.' Looking through the frost patterns on the window, Phenîlas looked over at the tent city.

'And for your donations. The extra heaters and coal have saved many lives.' He sighed and went on. 'It stopped the mood getting ugly.'

Rognor stopped eating and reached for his tankard. 'The mood, you say?'

'I don't mean their despair.' Phenîlas cleared his throat and placed a hand on the hilt of his sword. Rognor recognised the gesture. He had been noticing recently that the elf often sought reassurance from his weapon. To start with Phenîlas had been friendly, but his attitude had become colder and wary. Occasionally the Chancellor even detected outright disdain when the elf spoke of his compatriots waiting in the camp outside the walls. They were risking all in their zeal to enter Girdlegard.

The sentries told Rognor that the screams of the elves being tortured were longer than previously. Even the mountains themselves would soon surely take pity on hearing the cries of innocents.

Rognor drank a mouthful of beer and kept his eyes trained on the elf. 'You are hated,' he said, the black tattoos on his face moving as he grimaced. 'They don't like you or the sorânïons.'

Phenîlas ran his thumb over the decorations on the highly polished grip of his sword. 'I am only carrying out the Naishïon's wishes.'

Rognor put down his drink. The white of the elf's armour contrasted sharply with the sooty walls, and his own dark armour and his blue-dyed beard. 'You may do well to carry out your task with less cruelty.'

'I have to be thorough.'

'Your thoroughness causes resentment and scarred souls, Sorânïon.'

'Would you prefer me to be more lenient and risk letting

an älf through into Girdlegard?' His tone was cutting. 'I would rather have expected you to urge me to be more exacting. It is your empire that the new arrivals will be travelling through. Any black-eyes would be delighted to take a little trip around your fortress. You would never notice.'

'Indeed we would. And we would track it down.' Rognor regarded Phenîlas carefully. 'How many älfar have you brought to light?'

'None.'

'How many do you think there are among the . . .'

'Three thousand.'

'. . . among the three thousand, if you haven't even come across one so far?'

Phenîlas pushed his plate away and leaned back in his chair, keeping the other hand still on his sword. 'It's not a question of what I think, friend dwarf. There is no place here for believing or not believing. It's certainty we're after. We need absolute certainty.'

'I did not intend to criticise, merely to draw your attention to the fact that the waiting elves may start protesting about these strict interrogations you and your sorânïons are carrying out.' Rognor was suddenly aware of the hostile atmosphere.

'You refer to the possibility of rebellion?' He inhaled sharply, narrowing his nostrils. 'I am conscious of such a danger. But my request to the Naishïon for more officers has not been responded to. I presume there must be too many to check at the other gates. They won't have any other sorânïons available.' He looked the chancellor directly in the eyes. 'Would you do me a favour?'

Rognor guessed what was going to be asked. 'The interrogations are entirely an elf matter.'

Phenîlas leaned forward, one elbow on the table. 'On the contrary: it is a Girdlegard matter. What if you were to collaborate with me on this?'

'No.'

'I would only need fifty of your warriors,' the elf continued, in euphoric vein. 'They would not have to do anything apart from inflict pain on the newcomers and watch their faces. As soon as anger lines are observed' – here he pointed to his own taut features – 'they can execute the black-eyes.'

'In the light of the past animosity between our two races,' Rognor began, immutable in his refusal, 'I would consider such a thing extremely unwise.'

'The dwarf soldiers would merely be following orders,' Phenîlas wheedled. 'Exactly like the sorânïons.'

'That might be the case initially. But then voices would be raised in protest. They would accuse us Thirdlings of harsh and unfeeling conduct.' There was no way Rognor was prepared to allocate any of his soldiers for duty of this kind. 'The newcomers would spread the word about the way we had treated them and the old hatred would take hold again.'

But the elf in his white armour brushed this objection aside with a dismissive gesture. 'The Naishïon would make a covering announcement, and then . . .'

'I repeat. The answer is no.' Rognor pulled his tankard across to him. 'I have very cogent and clear reasons. I think you have lost sight of how cruel your procedures are.'

'The cruelty is to be ascribed to the älfar. I am doing my utmost to prevent them gaining any access to Girdlegard.' Phenîlas sat back in his seat, his displeasure and regret obvious. 'Your refusal merely prolongs the agony of freezing conditions for those waiting for admittance. Now *that* is what I call cruelty.'

Rognor snorted in disbelief. 'Don't try to pin the blame on me for the fact you don't have enough sorânïons.'

'Of course not.' Phenîlas got slowly to his feet. 'I shall make my request to the High King himself.'

Rognor, positive Boïndil would never agree to the allocation of dwarf troops, remained composed. 'Go ahead.' There was more he could have said, but he bit his tongue. No point in pouring oil on to a smoking anvil.

There was a knock at the door. A black-haired elf-woman was ushered in. Her hair was short at the sides and dyed a greyish white; Rognor could see she had a black braid hanging down her back. She wore white palladium armour emblazoned with the emblem of a sorânïan and the rune of the elf ruler. Her features, to a dwarf's eyes, were disturbingly even, as if the work of an obsessive sculptor striving to portray divine perfection. Rognor had no time for beauty of that kind.

The sentry and she approached the table together. Rognor and Phenîlas both realised who it was at the same time.

'May I present Ocâstia?' the sentry asked. 'She wishes to speak to the sorânïon commander.'

'There you are, you see. Your reinforcements.' Rognor's tone was friendly. He wanted to eliminate the ill-feeling between them. *With any luck he will forget about wanting our soldiers to join in.* He felt much more at ease now and played with the end of his long blue beard. 'Your rulers did not turn down your request for assistance after all.'

Phenîlas turned half-aside to see her better. 'Show me your Sitalia sign,' he demanded harshly before uttering any words of welcome. His hand was firmly on the grip of his weapon.

Bowing her head, Ocâstia walked past the guard, knelt in front of Phenîlas and took off her forearm protectors. She rolled up her sleeve. The symbol on her pure white skin denoted that she was a true elf. 'Look here, Sorânïon.'

Phenîlas ran his fingers over the place but his eyes were engaged with her beauty, Rognor was pleased to note. *If she distracts him . . . Maybe he'll fall for her and that'll make him less fanatic.*

Ocâstia kept her eyes cast down. 'I bring you a message from the Naishïon.' She took a leather wallet from her belt. It showed the supreme ruler's seal. 'He regrets that he is not able to send you any support. There is a situation of some urgency at the other gates, with many demanding admittance.'

Phenîlas accepted the wallet with a nod, broke the wax seal and extracted the parchment roll. Telling her to get up, he read the message.

'What news of Girdlegard?' Rognor asked the elf-woman courteously. 'And can I offer you some refreshment? Water, beer? Some food? There is plenty.' He noticed the curved hilt of her sword.

Ocâstia smiled and opened her mouth to reply.

'She needs nothing,' Phenîlas interrupted, still reading.

Ocâstia got to her feet and helped herself to black beer from the jug. 'My thanks, Chancellor. Most civil of you.' She raised her glass to him before drinking.

Phenîlas blinked as if he had misheard. He lifted his head and stared at her severely, but she was untroubled by his reproving glare.

'Your beer is extremely good.' Ocâstia looked at the array of food. 'And I am indeed somewhat hungry. The meat smells delicious.'

'You can have something later in our quarters,' Phenîlas grunted.

'If you can eat here, I don't see why I shouldn't,' she

retorted. Turning to Rognor, she went on, 'I'm afraid I don't have any Girdlegard news. I was in Ti Singàlai for some time waiting to be examined. I had to prove my worth as a warrior before I could join the sorânïons. I did not gather much about my surroundings on the journey to the Black Mountains. Apart from the fact that your hero Tungdil has set off with a band of dwarves, not going through the Stone Gateway as expected, but taking the route that leads from the abandoned settlement.'

Rognor laughed. 'He'll be looking for the path the little one used to reach us. The girl.' He liked Ocâstia already and was impressed that she had stood up to Phenîlas with his bad mood and reprimands. 'Please help yourself.'

The fact that she actually selected some of the meat pleased him even more.

Phenîlas put the letter away and got up to leave. 'We have work to do,' he said. 'Come with me.'

Ocâstia stayed where she was and had some more beer.

'Sorânïan!'

'You will have read that we both have exactly the same rank,' she responded calmly and continued to eat. 'I know what has to be done.' She flashed a smile at the dwarf with her carnelian-coloured eyes, before taking her last bite and following Phenîlas, who was simmering in the doorway. 'I'd love to have the recipe, Chancellor. Quite delicious. So tasty.'

Rognor grinned as he watched them both leave.

Something told him that conditions for the elves waiting outside in their makeshift shelters would improve. The arrival of Ocâstia might be a blessing to all and sundry.

Except for Phenîlas. But this thought pleased Rognor more than it troubled him. Phenîlas had met his match there.

Take red wine
and simmer with honey, cinnamon and cloves,
aniseed and citrus fruits
until the mixture starts to thicken.

Stir in some clear brandy
and place in a tankard,
then top it up with strong black bitter beer.

Recipe for dwarf spiced beer (serve cold)

XXII

Somewhere in the Outer Lands

The cage door had hardly opened over Beligata before she sprang out, picked up the key and unlocked the cuffs on her wrists and ankles. Then she picked up the iron staff. 'You'll suffer just like my friend has suffered! Don't trust your armour to protect you.'

The acront pointed at her with his sword to indicate he accepted the challenge. He did not move otherwise; it seemed he wanted her to have the first strike.

Tungdil looked up at the box where the judges were sitting. 'Gosalyn, keep your eye on the acront and watch how he fights. Whatever he can do, we can match.'

'Did she just refer to Deathbringer as her *friend*?' Carmondai mimed applause. 'We will learn from this. Beligata will be paying the same price as Hargorin here.'

'He needs help!' Gosalyn found it difficult to tear her eyes away from the Thirdling king; a pool of blood was collecting round his head. From time to time one of his limbs would jerk but it was not a conscious movement.

'Observe the combat,' Tungdil repeated, still looking up at the box. Notes were being taken.

Beligata feigned a strike against the hip, making the acront parry the blow he expected from the iron baton, whereas she had turned and changed her attack. The pointed tip pierced the acront's instep, taking him completely by surprise.

Beligata pulled her weapon out and jumped back behind the metal cover to avoid a counter attack and look for her next opportunity. The acront gave a roar and looked at the hole in his armoured boot, seeing the bright yellow fluid seeping out.

Carmondai was following the combat more acutely than Gosalyn, who was dividing her attention between Hargorin and what was happening. 'I wonder how the ashont will respond.'

Tungdil noticed that the fight was being discussed up in the box, and there was furious scribbling. *They had not been expecting her to score a single hit.*

The opponent hobbled over to Beligata, where in her linen shift she was dodging between the cage and her adversary. The half-hearted blows being launched at her got stuck in the grating of the metal cage. The acront pulled the blade out again each time.

Tungdil called out to get the attention of the people up in the box. Then he went back to watching the progress of the contest. *Let's learn about the enemy from watching how he fights.* Sooner or later he might find himself confronting one of them.

Beligata suddenly jumped out from behind the open cage and launched a blow with the spear-length staff against the acront. He fended it off and stabbed at her in his turn, but the bars of the cage stopped his blade. Beligata used the opportunity to force her sharp end through the acront's armour and then to withdraw it again sharply.

The adversary roared louder than ever and stumbled. Beligata darted round the acront and ducked under a sword swipe that might have sliced her in two. She stabbed through the calf of the acront's injured leg and then punched another hole in his armour.

With a growl the acront swung round but the dwarf-woman

kept behind him and ventured another blow, this time attacking the heel of his left leg. There was the sound of a whip cracking when the tendon snapped and the acront slumped down. He turned and kept his dogged opponent at a distance by waving his sword.

'You've nearly got him!' Gosalyn yelled excitedly. 'Kill him!'

'Don't kill him!' Tungdil commanded. 'We've got to show we're different from the beasts they usually deploy.'

'No way is this a trained ashont.' This was Carmondai's considered opinion of events. 'The movements he's using are uncoordinated. He's not accustomed to wearing armour and he's got no tricks up his sleeve. He stands no chance against Beligata.'

'She's very good.'

The älf laughed out loud. 'An ashont defeated several of our warriors. Nothing against the dwarf-woman, but if this had been an experienced fighter she'd have been finished off twice over.'

'Is that true?' Tungdil had an inkling what was going to happen next in the arena; he had gone through something similar in the past.

'I'd need to know more about the ashont as such, but if I put together everything I can see, this must be a very young Walking Tower. They must want to know if he has potential in the field. They're keen to see if he'd be any use against monsters.' Carmondai nodded up towards the box. 'This contest is less about how *we* fight; they want to see how this guy shapes up.'

Using her staff, Beligata took a run-up and vaulted feet first against the acront, hitting him from the side before he could strike her.

Together they fell in a heap, but the dwarf-woman was

uppermost, swinging her weapon around and slamming the tip between the acront's helmet and armour. 'Look: can be done without a fruit knife!' she shouted up to Tungdil, her voice exuberant.

'Indeed it can,' he confirmed.

The acront felt the metal against his throat and did not struggle, emitting only a roar that was echoed from the box above them.

She remained where she was, atop the giant, not letting the iron staff budge a jot. She waited nervously. 'What should I do now?'

Her adversary's left arm shot up, and, before Beligata could pull her weapon away, the acront had grabbed it and plunged it into his own throat. Glowing yellow blood flowed right and left to soak the sand on the arena floor.

'By Lorimbur!' Beligata hopped down. 'What was that in aid of?'

'They gave him an order from the box.' Carmondai pushed himself away from the bars of the cage and sat down on the floor. 'He had demonstrated lack of competence. He failed as a warrior and they can't tolerate weakness.'

'Get back in the cage!' Tungdil called out to Beligata. 'We'll show them that we have understood what they wanted.'

He expected a loud protest on her part, but Beligata stepped back into her cell.

The mirrors travelled to their original positions, leaving the dwarves in darkness.

Tungdil's eyes needed a little time to adjust but then he saw that an acront had entered the hall to lock the lid of Beligata's cage.

The hook came down from the roof, grabbed the cage and brought her back to the niche. Above them the scribes were getting up to leave their observation box. Meanwhile a soldier thrust one hand under the breastplate of the corpse and dragged the victim out.

Only when the gate closed behind the last acront did the other prisoners set to yelling defiance and jubilation. The beasts celebrated Beligata's victory: she had humiliated one of the enemy and driven it to take its own life.

'I don't suppose that happens often,' Carmondai commented, holding his hands over his ears. 'Appalling noise.'

'We don't seem to be at risk of vengeance.' Tungdil looked to see how Hargorin was doing. He was no better. 'How can we help him?'

Beligata pulled at the cage bars and managed to bend several sections. 'There was more than *one* reason for using the cell as cover,' she announced, forcing the bars apart wide enough to slip through. 'The acront's sword was a tremendous help, even if it didn't help him much.'

She hurried over to where Tungdil was and examined the mechanism. She looked around for some kind of tool. 'I can only break the lock with a sharp blow on the pin, but . . .'

'What about Hargorin's leg?' Gosalyn suggested. 'That could work. Or the little knife he keeps in it.'

Beligata scurried over to Hargorin's cell and put her arm through the bars but was unable to reach the metal limb.

The dark-haired dwarf-woman stripped off her linen shift and tossed it through the bars to fall like a net over the artificial leg. At the fourth attempt she was successful: the fabric caught on the metal. She dragged Hargorin by the limb over to the bars until his leg was close enough to unfasten.

Smart work. Tungdil and Gosalyn kept lookout, but the noise the beasts were making had not yet brought sentries in. *All the better.*

After Beligata had pulled the garment back out and dressed again, she yanked the leg through the bars. She extracted the knife from the cavity and put it on the ground. 'Too delicate. I'll try something else.' She went back to Tungdil's cage and inserted the thinnest section of the metal leg in the cage door. Then she lay down, took aim and kicked hard, attempting to sever the latch.

Tungdil noticed the beasts had calmed down. They had gathered what was happening. More and more eyes were focused on the dwarves. *Will they betray us now?*

'I wonder if they'll let us get away?' Carmondai was also on his feet. 'And where do we go? The ashont will be onto us immediately.'

'We'll stand no chance of succeeding if we stay here.' Tungdil saw Beligata try a second kick.

With a click the catch opened and the spring caused the lid to lift.

Noise broke out again: loud shouts, insistent voices. Words were not needed. It was clear the inmates were demanding their own release. The guards were sure to notice the change in tone.

'Shut up, the lot of you,' Beligata shouted furiously, but her voice was swamped by their cries.

'Quick! Hargorin first,' Tungdil ordered, getting out of his prison.

Together they knelt by the cage of the badly injured dwarf and Tungdil tried to open the cage using the same method to activate the catch.

'Look out,' murmured Carmondai. 'On your left.'

A door was opening on one side of the corridor and the silhouette of an acront became visible. As soon as he appeared the volume of noise increased and the beasts started throwing pebbles to alert the guard. They wanted to bring attention to what the captive dwarves were doing, just as Carmondai had feared.

They resent our break for freedom. Tungdil's first kick failed. It was not enough to budge the catch. *Tion take them all!*

The guard roared out when he saw them and started to run in their direction.

'Get away now!' Gosalyn urged. 'Make good your escape and save the mission!'

'Come back and rescue us,' Carmondai insisted. 'Don't forget: you'll be needing me if you are going to survive in the Outer Lands.'

'As if you've been any help so far,' Beligata grunted.

Tungdil gave another kick and the lid lifted. But the acront had almost reached them. If they tried to carry the unconscious form of Hargorin they would never get away. 'Run! Now!' He jumped up and sprinted along the balcony rail.

'Wretched beasts,' Beligata cursed, hurrying after him. 'I'd like to split their stupid skulls for them.'

'We'll come back for you,' Tungdil yelled to the abandoned älf and the dwarf-woman.

Because the door would not open, Tungdil and Beligata jumped down from cage roof to cage roof aiming for the dimly lit arena floor, toward the light coming through an opening on the right-hand side.

Better a slim hope than none at all. Tungdil was the first to reach the arena. He spied out through the doorway. 'No one in sight,' he called to Beligata, then he glanced up to the balustrade.

Up there the acront was like a monumental statue. Purple light streamed out of his visor and in his right arm he held the seemingly lifeless form of Hargorin Deathbringer as if it were no more than a large doll. Tungdil could see tubing that led over the acront's shoulders into his helmet near the mouthpiece.

What is that contraption? Dwarves at work among toxic gases in the mines used breathing devices made of leather sacks or animals bladders. *Is that what that is?*

There was an audible hissing.

Suddenly the cries of the beasts ebbed away. Beginning at the topmost rows the captives started to slump down in their cages. One level after another was silenced in this way. Gosalyn and Carmondai passed out.

'Get out!' Tungdil yelled to Beligata, already feeling light-headed. Some vapour heavier than air and with no detectable smell was being fed into the chamber. It reminded him of the death pits in the mountains where the dwarves mined, where gas would collect. Any creature that strayed in would succumb. *The acronta seem to be using a modified form of the death pit gas to keep their captives quiet.*

The two of them had to cling to the wall for support, feeling their knees go weak. With iron will they made themselves carry on and leave the arena. They reached a high-ceilinged corridor with suspended lights in wide dishes. Whatever was burning caused neither soot nor smell.

'Which way?' Beligata asked quietly. Staggering, she was held up by Tungdil. 'I . . . the gas . . .'

'Breathe deeply in and out. Expel it from your lungs like that,' he counselled, struggling to breathe just as he had on the highest peak of the Grey Mountains. 'The further away we get, the better we'll feel.'

He was surprised the acront had not overtaken them. Perhaps pursuing escapees was less important than supervising the captives and looking to Hargorin.

The two dwarves, vision blurring, stumbled on as best they

could, taking side passages without any notion of where they might lead.

Keep going. Tungdil hardly recognised his surroundings. The sedative effects of the gas seemed to stick in his airways, or maybe they had already seeped into his bloodstream. The fire-dishes above their heads appeared like floating moons, and the corridor itself a never-ending ravine with no possibility of escape.

'Let's keep going,' he encouraged, reaching behind him for Beligata's hand. 'We need somewhere to hide until we have recovered.'

But his fingers met empty air.

Tungdil turned round and leaned against the wall, exhausted. The dwarf-woman was slumped over a few paces back, hands on her thighs, retching.

In the same instant the acront appeared next to her, dragging Hargorin along. The outsized warrior still had the tubes attached to its helmet, but now it also had its sword drawn. Its intentions were deadly.

'Be with you soon,' she said faintly, not noticing their adversary. She vomited.

Vraccas! No! 'Behind you!' Tungdil just managed to say but the long sword blade pierced her back from above, pinning her to the ground.

The dark-haired dwarf-woman's body jerked and twitched and then was still. It was obvious that captives who tried to escape were not shown the mercy accorded to victorious combatants. A shadow crossed her face and her scar glowed and throbbed, only to fade and dim.

Oh Vraccas. What have I done to you that you must make me watch the good ones die? Tungdil had no strength left to shout in protest. He turned and tried to run away from the guard, knowing that the penalty for attempted escape, if he were caught, would be death.

His legs moved automatically but the movement caused him great pain. His lungs felt as small as a pea and he could not catch his breath. Tungdil forced himself not to give in, but to keep going, chopping and changing between identical-looking passages, stumbling through doors whose shape he could see only vaguely.

All of a sudden the ground gave way under his feet and he plummeted down.

As he fell he lost consciousness. It was thus a matter of indifference to him where he landed.

Girdlegard
Black Mountains
Kingdom of the Thirdling dwarves
Eastern Gate
6492nd/6493rd solar cycles, springtime

Rognor stood on the walkway watching as Ocâstia held out her hand to one of the tortured elves in the camp and made the sign of a blessing over his head. She smiled graciously as if she were a ruler, granting her subjects a boon.

The elf in front of her – who had received severe pain at Ocâstia's hands in order to prove that he was no älf – bowed his head in gratitude and moved over to join the group. Then the next small band marched up to the gate of the fortress to be admitted to the dwarf kingdom of the Thirdlings and thence through to Girdlegard. As they left they waved to Ocâstia.

'Quite a difference,' the blue-bearded dwarf murmured,

enjoying the warm breeze with its hint of snow melt and new greenery. 'They seem to love this sorânïan.'

Phenîlas, on the other hand, had become more brutal and rigid since Ocâstia's arrival; he now tended to prolong the painful testing procedures. It had happened twice that examinees had died at his hands. They were then declared to have been älfar, in order to prevent any unrest in the camp. But the troop leader was still the object of grumblings and resentment, whereas the remaining sorânïons took Ocâstia's side.

The watch should be kept at double strength. Rognor observed the procedures carefully. The left side of his face throbbed with the new tattoos decorating temple and forehead. He had asked for a rune showing him to be an admirer of Lorimbur. The feud with the four tribes might be at an end, but he was never going to betray his ancestors. *With any luck the plain outside our gates will soon be empty.*

Ocâstia's methods were gentler, but still thorough, and she created a better rotation for the elves' journeys to get magic for the stamps. In recent orbits the numbers being interrogated and processed in this way had been greater than expected. Phenîlas had complained that she was being too lax, but people liked her so there was little he could do.

From time to time desperate elves would make clandestine attempts to scale the walls, knowing that their families were already in Girdlegard, but both Thirdlings and the female sorânïan put a stop to such endeavours. Whereas Phenîlas would have declared these reckless elves black-eyes and executed them on the spot, Ocâstia preferred a different approach: she had an artist record their faces and had them sent back if they ever won a place by lot. In this way, they lost their chance to leave the tent city until the very end.

Ocâstia's system has worked as an effective deterrent

without bloodshed. Rognor watched her and she waved at him like Chynêa had done. *She is clever.*

Ocâstia approached the fortress, surrounded by other sorânïons in white mantles and white armour, with fur caps on their heads. They all congratulated each other on a successful orbit: they had carried out testing on sixty individuals. At a distance and with an expression usually reserved for terrifying an enemy on the field of battle, Phenîlas followed them, a hand cramping on the hilt of his sword.

Samusin was being kind to Rognor: the wind turned so that he could overhear what the elves were saying. The mountains made a kind of funnel, bringing the conversations up to him.

'Ocâstia!' Phenîlas called.

The group round her halted and dispersed but did not go to his side as they might have done a few orbits ago. Phenîlas still was regarded as the commander of all of the sorânïons, but Rognor, as an experienced fighter, was able to read the scene.

'What can I do for you?' she enquired.

'I need to talk to you. Alone.'

'The sorânïons can hear what you have to say, if it's about the interrogations. Or was it something else you had in mind?'

'Both.' Phenîlas signalled for the others to withdraw. But only when Ocâstia nodded to them did they leave the open square in front of the gate.

Rognor kept listening.

'I know what game you're playing,' Phenîlas said, his tone aggressive.

'I'm not playing any kind of game. I'm keeping a hold on what you have kicked away,' Ocâstia responded calmly.

'You are under my command even if we both have the

same rank. You should be supporting me, not undermining me, Ocâstia!' Phenîlas took a step towards her. 'How dare you?'

'You are too slow and you are inconsiderate to others,' she retorted, with no trace of fear in her voice. 'The other sorânïons have been unhappy with your command for some time. They don't like the way you do things. If it weren't for me, the new arrivals would have chucked you off the cliff, just like you've done with so many innocent victims. The sorânïons are aware of this. And so are the dwarves. And the new arrivals can work it out for themselves.'

Phenîlas drew himself up to his full height. 'I am not going to argue with you.'

'Indeed. We are not arguing. You are talking at me.'

'Listen. These are my orders: you are to cease working against me!'

'You are working against yourself, Phenîlas.' Ocâstia turned away. 'And you've just done it again.'

He grabbed her by the arm and pulled her back. 'How dare you turn your back on me when I'm giving you orders?'

'That's exactly what I mean.' She nodded to the tents. 'Everything we do outside the fortress is being watched. What you've just done, for example. How do you think your actions are being interpreted at the moment?'

Rognor saw the elf's sword hand grip the hilt and pull the weapon half out of the scabbard. *Don't do anything stupid.*

'I shall request that the Naishïon recall you and send me a different sorânïon,' he said, quivering with anger, his words as cold as winter ice.

'I have already sent a similar request. Ten orbits ago,' she replied, smiling serenely. 'You should be given other duties. In my view you would be best employed in battle, using your cruel nature against our enemies rather than against our own race. If you are lucky, the Naishïon will find another position for you.'

'You scheming, treacherous . . .' The sword emerged more fully.

'I am a sorânïan. I am trying to protect my people by inflicting only the minimum necessary pain,' she countered.

Rognor noticed she was speaking deliberately loudly, keen that the people in the tents should hear.

'You, on the other hand, enjoy causing pain.' She pulled herself free and strode to the gate, her black hair flying in the wind. 'The supreme ruler will already know about you, I'm sure. The newcomers won't be singing your praises.' She paid no attention to his angry shouts.

So that makes it clear whose orders she's under here. Rognor did not know if it had been wise of Ocâstia to bring things to the open directly in front of the tents. This was a humiliating insult to Phenîlas and robbed him of his authority. Anyone challenging him now faced severe consequences. *He will be making the examinations even more cruel as a result.*

The chancellor moved to the other side of the walkway and waved down to where Ocâstia was crossing the yard and looking round. She waved back, smiling.

I think she knows I was listening. Rognor followed her with his eyes. *I shan't play along with her scheme.* Being a Child of the Smith, he was not susceptible to the elf-woman's carnelian-coloured eyes and graceful demeanour.

But the elf officers were.

Rognor left the walkway and crossed the yard to his quarters. Islands of melting snow dotted the granite at his feet, remnants of the harsh winter that was now receding. At night the puddles of melt water froze over again and sand and salt were spread to remove the ice. It was vital that soldiers did not slip if the alarm were sounded.

The chancellor was used to hearing the ice crackle beneath his feet – but the crunch he heard now caught his attention. He stopped and lifted his foot to reveal a small phial that had shattered when he trod on it.

Rognor bent down. He immediately recognised the älfar lettering. *Elf eyes.* He turned to the gate that a group of the tested elves had just marched through. Could there have been an älf amongst them who had managed to fool the sorânïons? *Which one of them dropped this?*

Suddenly the recriminations Phenîlas had directed at Ocâstia did not seem so far-fetched. An oversight like this would have serious consequences.

He picked up the fragments, questions whizzing through his brain. How would an älf from the Outer Lands get his hands on this eye-whitener?

He called a messenger over and ordered the most recent group of elves to be apprehended. *The sorânïons must subject all of them to a new set of tests.*

Then he hurried to the quarters where Phenîlas and his troops were at table. He saw at once that the officers were clustered around Ocâstia, leaving their commander sitting on his own.

Hesitating for a heartbeat, Rognor decided he must let them all know what he had found. 'May I have a word?' He told them quickly where he had found the broken bottle.

'You'll have to test that whole group again,' he said in conclusion.

Phenîlas had already sprung to his feet and was buckling his weapons belt. 'Exactly what I've been saying all along,' he snapped, with a sharp look at the officers and Ocâstia. 'Vigilance! Extreme vigilance is needed. Or the black-eyes will make fools of us all.' He took the remains of the phial from Rognor's hand and put the fragments in his pocket. 'Let's go.'

The sorânïons followed him in silence.

Ocâstia brought up the rear and stayed back with Rognor, as if she wanted to admit her negligent attitude had allowed this infiltration to occur. 'That group had plenty of elves he tested. They weren't all mine, you know,' she said as they left together. 'We'll see who's at fault.'

'Who would ever be able to stand up to his interrogations?' he replied, his voice doubtful. 'As far as I know, he's the more thorough of the two of you with the tests.'

'It's just that he inflicts more pain.' Ocâstia's expression had darkened. 'I don't know what to make of all this.'

Rognor was unsure what she was getting at. 'We'll find out soon enough.'

They raced through into the realm of the Thirdling dwarves. The passages were laid out in such a way as to confuse any attackers who had managed to get through the fortifications. Certain segments could be sealed off with heavy steel gates.

The group of sixty elves was run to ground in just such a passage and they were being held waiting until the sorânïons arrived.

Rognor, with fifty guards who had joined them en route, reached the group of tested elves at the same time as Phenîlas' unit. The elves displayed fear, concern, outrage and helplessness. They had assumed themselves to be safe now, and under the protection of the Naishïon here in Girdlegard. A large cart with two horses spanned in front of it was loaded with heavy chests and boxes. The elves were carrying the rest of their baggage themselves.

Watchful eyes appeared in the arrow slits above their heads. Rognor knew there were enough of his troops concealed up there, with their catapults hidden behind metal flaps, to shoot at all sixty of the elves if they offered any resistance.

Phenîlas took a stance in front of the group of sixty. 'I am sorry we have had to stop you. But there has come to light a suspicion that there is an älf among you who has tricked us by means of this treatment' – he held up the broken phial for all to see – 'that stops the eyes going dark.'

'So what does that mean, Sorânïon?' an ash-blonde elf-woman asked tersely, swinging her rucksack from her back and plonking it down at her feet. The fur robe and the costly adornments she wore indicated that she was not one of the poorest elves.

'It means we will have to examine each of you again.' Phenîlas pointed at Ocâstia. 'We will divide you into two groups. I will take the ones originally tested by her and she will re-examine mine.' The elves exchanged glances, many of them now extremely frightened. 'Let's start . . .'

'No,' the elf-woman insisted, pushing up her sleeve to show Sitalia's seal on her forearm. 'Look. I have already been examined. There is no way I am going to submit to that procedure a second time. I suffered to acquire this sign. That should be enough.' The people behind her muttered their agreement. 'The fault does not lie with me.'

'Silence!' Phenîlas had not lowered the hand with the phial. 'There is an älf in the group and we are going to . . .'

'And who's to say it was one of our group that dropped the phial?' the ash-blonde elf-woman argued. 'Where was it found?'

'That's of no consequence.' He looked at her sceptically, one hand on the hilt of his sword. 'And if you are so vehemently opposed to a new examination, I must say I find it suspicious. What is your name?'

She drew herself up, her features dignified in the extreme. 'I am Vilêana, the daughter of Vilêonos, and mother of eighteen children. I am returning to where Sitalia created us. Where I come from, I was a princess, ruling over elves and humans alike. I have reigned over thousands; everyone knew my name and my ancestry.' She looked at Phenîlas with disdain. 'And you have the nerve to call *me* untrustworthy?' she snapped.

'I have the nerve to have you shot or beheaded.' Phenîlas had not been impressed by her pedigree. 'You have no status here. For me you are nothing but an elf I am examining at the request of the Naishïon. Who you have been in the past and what you may become in the future is of no interest to me.' He lowered his arm with the bottle. 'Step forward.'

'Or what?' Vilêana stuck her chin out defiantly, her ash-blonde hair spreading out over her fur robe.

'Or die.' Phenîlas swiftly drew his sword, the blade flashing. 'This is the task allotted to me. And as I was the one who interrogated you initially, you must now go to Ocâstia and answer to her.'

'No.' Vilêana did not shift her imperious gaze. 'I refuse to be subjected to a second round of torture. You will have to think of something else.'

Rognor was holding his breath as he followed the exchange. Ocâstia was keeping in the background, allowing Phenîlas to get himself into a situation that might end in a bloodbath. Three or four of the new arrivals had placed their hands on their weapons – either because they had previously served Vilêana or because they shared her point of view.

'There is bound to be another way of enticing the älf to throw off his masquerade.'

'Tell me what.' Phenîlas did not turn round, but kept staring at the princess as if he were determined to take her head off at any moment.

'The so-called eye whitener leaves traces on the eyelids, as I am sure you will know,' said Ocâstia, stepping forward. 'We realised that when we discovered the others.'

Rognor raised his eyebrows. *She's making that up.* For the life of him he could not remember having heard this story before.

'It's quite sufficient to scrutinise the eyes closely from very near to,' she went on. 'It won't be easy but it can be done, I am convinced. That way we can spare the innocent any further pain.' She gestured to the other sorânïons to come over. 'Shall we make a start?'

Phenîlas studied her face to see what her intentions were. He seemed fearful that she would challenge him further.

'I will get my soldiers to stand by,' said Rognor, who saw what the elf-woman was doing. Her idea was brilliant – any älf who believed her would lose his nerve and betray himself. If that were to happen, the ranks of dwarf marksmen were in place to bring him down. 'We are ready.' He reinforced this by bringing out his bladed morningstar and removing the protective covers for the sharp edges.

'Then let's start.' Phenîlas seemed willing to go along with the ruse in order to prevent any kind of uprising. This time, Rognor felt, Phenîlas was showing good judgement.

They had the new arrivals step up in two groups, one of which was to be retested by Ocâstia, the other by the sorânïon commander.

The staring began. The rims of the eyelids were studied closely. The officers were murmuring and examining the eyes, touching the lids and then smelling their fingers.

Did we make a mistake? As Vilêana had implied: the phial found in the yard might have been dropped several orbits previously by a different group.

Rognor played with the tip of his blue beard. *They would have reached Girdlegard a long time ago*. He had deliberately ignored this possibility. It was an appalling thought that somehow an älf might have escaped notice and got through to Girdlegard. *I would have failed in the same way.*

He noticed how a young elf at Ocâstia's side was clenching his fists. He was four back in the queue to be retested by the female sorânïan. He was rubbing his eyes, yawning expansively and then rubbing his eyes again. This was followed by a sneezing fit. He was struggling to breathe and there were tears streaming down his face.

I know what you are doing. 'That one!' Rognor pointed to him. 'He's been sneezing and coughing on purpose to make his eyes water. He is trying to wash away the evidence.'

'Rubbish!' the young elf called out, wiping his eyes on his sleeve.

Ocâstia came up to him, grasping his head with both hands and holding him fast. 'Look at me,' she commanded. 'And now show me Sitalia's mark.'

'His name is Rahîlas,' Phenîlas said, very sure of himself. 'His father was one of the last group to leave the tents. But there's some mistake, he . . .'

Ocâstia turned her head in his direction. 'You said I should be more thorough. Now I'm being more thorough and you don't like it.' She stared at Rahîlas with her carnelian-coloured eyes. 'Why is that?'

Rognor noted how Rahîlas grew tense. *He's going to . . .* 'Watch out!'

The elf on whom suspicion had now fallen kicked the sorânïan in the belly. She was taken by surprise. The young elf stabbed at the sorânïon next to him with his dagger. The blade failed to connect with the targeted armpit and slid ineffectively off the white breastplate.

At that moment the first bolt hit Rahîlas, making him lurch backwards. As soon as the dwarf marksmen had a clear view, he was bombarded by arrow after arrow.

Rahîlas collapsed, bringing up blood, then made to throw his dagger. Fury lines snaked across his face.

You shan't hurt anyone! Rognor leaped over and before the dagger could take flight, he hacked his hand off with his bladed morningstar. A fountain of blood spurted out, drenching the elves nearest to the dying victim. The catapults ceased their work.

'Phenîlas!' Rahîlas shrieked in agony, his body convulsing. Red blood sprayed over his darkened face and in his eyes there was a clear reproach aimed at the sorânïon commander. 'Why? Why did you . . . ?' The voice died away. As did the light in his eyes.

Ocâstia glared down at the corpse in disgust. 'There's your black-eyes.' She spat at the body. 'Throw him in the ravine where the others are.' She gave a signal to the unit at the gate. 'The rest of you: on your way into Girdlegard.'

'Halt!' ordered Phenîlas. 'There could be more than one of them.'

I think so too. Rognor nodded in agreement. 'Carry on with your examinations until there is no more doubt left. The passageway won't be opened up until then. And it will open on *my* order. Not on yours, Ocâstia.' The elf-woman sorânïan made a gesture of apology and went over to the line of previously tested immigrants. 'Let's continue the search.'

Phenîlas followed suit.

There were, however, no further anomalies. The would-be settlers showed obvious signs of relief. They picked up their luggage and made ready to march on. Vilêana swung her rucksack onto her back.

Just the one. Rognor was left with the question: *What did he want from the sorânïon commander as he was about to die?* He cleaned the bloodied blades of his morningstar, replaced the sheath and stowed it away. It was all a mystery and gave the impression that Phenîlas and Rahîlas had known each other – or maybe that they had had an agreement. An älf on his way to endingness would have no reason to lie. *Or did he do it to cause trouble?*

There were all sorts of possible explanations, some of them relatively harmless and some of them deeply worrying. The fact Rognor was mulling it over in his mind showed the effect.

Phenîlas, who was staring at the arrows and bolts piercing the body, was equally mystified. 'But I never tested him in the first place.'

'What?' The chancellor thought he must have misheard. 'He was standing in Ocâstia's line.'

'I know. But I didn't test him. As I said, it was a mistake.'

'He knew you and you knew him.' Rognor was at a loss.

'We'd often come across each other in the camp, yes.' Phenîlas turned his gaze on Ocâstia. 'You should have realised he was standing in the wrong group.'

'No! He was one of yours,' she replied in surprise. 'I didn't know him. Otherwise I'd have sent him over to you. I'm quite alert enough to have noticed.'

None of the other sorânïons said a word. It was one officer's word against another's. They were the leaders. And they could not abide each other.

Rognor had the gate opened. 'We found our älf. That's what counts,' he said, trying to break the ice. 'That ruse about the tell-tale traces round the eyelids worked really well. And all without using any violence at all.'

'Thank you, Chancellor,' Ocâstia bowed her head in acknowledgement.

'I still say he wasn't one of the ones I interrogated,' Phenîlas repeated, sheathing his sword. 'I would have known.' He dropped the shattered phial on to the body, turned on his heel and went back to the fortress.

The other officers looked at each other meaningfully, then followed their commander.

The new settlers passed through, moving more quickly than before, keen to leave the horror behind them; the cart wheels clattered as they left.

Ocâstia stared at the älf corpse as it was lifted and carried away by the dwarves. The body would be flung into the ravine for the ravens to devour. The bones would bleach in the sun.

'They knew each other,' she said, lost in thought. 'And he was definitely not one of the ones I examined. I swear by all that is sacred to me as a sorânïan.'

'But why would Phenîlas have a pact with a black-eyes? What would he have to gain from letting an älf through?' Rognor tried to work out a reason. He had a sudden idea. *Could it have been intended as justification for continuing the harsh regime of interrogations?*

'It would mean he had discovered an älf and let him through on purpose.' Ocâstia's visage darkened. 'Calculated treachery in order to strengthen his own position here. In order to continue his cruel procedures with the next new arrivals,' she said, coming to the same conclusion as Rognor. She shook her head in disbelief. 'No. It's not possible. There must be another reason.'

Like what? 'Let's not overthink it. Let's just be glad we unmasked a black-eyes.' The two of them walked back together through the passageways, past the bloodstains on the floor.

The chancellor still nursed a silent hope that Phenîlas would swiftly be recalled. *We have to get rid of this tent city.* He wanted nothing more to do with it. *And with Phenîlas still less. Before something terrible happens.*

Girdlegard knew nothing of what its hero was doing.
That he was hunting down his own kind as the Thirdlings had once done in Girdlegard.
For there were dwarves in Phondrasôn, those lost when excavating mines in the depths or those dragged out of their tunnels by beasts.
The Triplets' potion influenced the hero's mind and he felt invincible – a creature born to rule over others.
But as soon as he saw a dwarf he turned into a veritable monster and did all he could to kill or capture him. And he did terrible things to those he took prisoner.
Whether there are still dwarves down in Phondrasôn?
He did not know.

Secret notes for
The Writings of Truth
written under duress by Carmondai

XXIII

Somewhere in the Outer Lands

Tungdil gradually regained consciousness to find himself in darkness. But he was neither chained nor tied up. Wherever he was, it seemed the acronta had not found him.

Vraccas, I owe you some prayers. Tungdil got to his feet and felt around.

The walls of the narrow vertical shaft he was in were of roughly hewn sandstone; no care had been taken in their construction. Rubble and fallen stones crunched under his boots. It was a wonder he wasn't hurt when he fell.

'Beligata?' he whispered, hoping against hope that she would answer. *Nothing.*

He encountered symbols in several places on the walls but apparently further excavations had been abandoned.

It's a dead end. With caution, Tungdil started to climb, hoping to escape from his hiding-place. It was only a question of time before his pursuers looked for him here.

His strong fingers grasped the walls and he pushed his feet into the smallest of cracks. He continued his ascent in this manner until finally catching sight of light above his head; he levered himself onto a narrow ledge.

During the course of his escape, he must have found a passageway abandoned by the acronta because it led nowhere. He snaked his way cautiously to the next corner. Not twenty paces in front of him there was a corridor that had been properly shored up and was illuminated by the familiar ceiling-hung fire dishes.

The flames gave only a dim light, showing the bare sandstone walls where further symbols were visible. It seemed the constructors had marked places for subsequent planned excavations, but there was no attempt at decoration of any kind. *Sandstone. That means we are in the Grey Mountains.* Tungdil got up and made his way stealthily to the opening, peering round the corner. No one. They must all be searching elsewhere. He probed around, listened and sniffed the air, hoping for some clue.

He could not remember taking this route. The gas had wiped him out. He must have found his way here like some drunkard. He grinned. It didn't matter. He had managed to give the acronta the slip. Tungdil kissed the ring Balyndis had given him.

The air in the corridor was cool and clear and there was no sign of any rubble or refuse. Walls and ceiling were timber-lined and the floor was soft sand, making progress pleasant and silent. Occasionally he heard distant roars but not one of the acronta was to be seen.

He returned his thoughts to Beligata and Hargorin. *It was not right that they had had to die. With no chance to defend themselves.*

The passages were slightly curved. Did acronta not like straight lines? The huge doorways to the right and to the left were oval and always firmly locked. The dwarf had no tools with which he might have broken them open so he had to keep walking. He had been hungry and thirsty for some time now.

At long last he came to an entrance that stood open; he could hear familiar acronta sounds coming from inside. Tungdil decided to dare it.

He peered round the corner – and was astonished to find

something he would never have guessed. *The acronta had a library!*

The room he came across was a series of little cells like a beehive. He found himself on the topmost gallery of a hall that was eight storeys high: thirty paces in all. Each gallery was full of shelves and glass-fronted cabinets. Rolls of paper, parchments, books and large volumes were stacked everywhere; symbols and marks on the storage units denoted, he thought, the various categories of subject matter.

The acronta had taken more trouble here than they had in their tunnels. The painted shelves were ornate, with decorative inlay work. The floor was of black and white tiles and there were desks at which armoured acronta could be seen writing. It presented a strange contrast. They had light from glass-shaded lamps and mirrors on the sides of the galleries. Diagonally below Tungdil stood two of the warrior creatures studying a document together. They seemed to be discussing its contents in heated tones, but in an unintelligible language.

It all reminded Tungdil of the time in his youth he had spent with Lot-Ionan, but the archives the acronta had were immeasurably greater in size. *I must find out what they have stored here.*

It might be records taken from races they had subjugated or it could be their own writings. The challenge was to get to grips as soon as possible with the language these giants used.

One of the two nearest acronta suddenly looked up and spotted the dwarf. He gave a roar and the second one rolled up the parchment and ran to the stairs.

Curses! Tungdil backed into the corridor and started running.

He had ruined his chances of grabbing one of the library

volumes, even if his warrior soul was furious with him for having wasted time and effort here. His priority must be to locate and liberate his friends and then to escape from this mountain. *Or whatever this is.*

He raced along, up slopes and down steps. His made a note of the different kinds of timbers used to line the walls; he hoped to have the opportunity at some time in the future to find his way back to the fascinating library. He could hear his pursuers' heavy steps. They would not give up easily. *How can I escape?*

The smell that met his nostrils was familiar: fire, hot iron, steam, soot. There must be a forge in the immediate vicinity. He turned towards where the smell was most intense and found himself in a searingly hot workshop that would have done any dwarf tribe proud.

Iron ore was being processed in cauldrons and molten iron ran through channels in the sandy floor into moulds; in other places huge rolls as big as mill wheels were pressing metal flat; acronta were standing at anvils forming weapons and armour with hefty hammer blows. They were not wearing metal coats themselves because of the overwhelming heat.

Tungdil could see their human-like bony skulls with broad jaws and a row of needle-sharp protruding teeth; instead of a nose they had three breathing holes. The skin stretched over their muscular bodies was pale, with veins standing out in bright yellow. Light from the furnace flames played on their bodies as if on a canvas screen.

The forges had braziers as big as a tabletop, with flames licking round the side of the basic lumps of metal, bellows fanning to increase the heat; sparks flew up to the ceiling and water in buckets and pails hissed and bubbled when the hot metal was plunged to cool it.

Tungdil did a hasty calculation and came up with altogether about one hundred leather-aproned acronta working in the forge, intent on their tasks and with no eye for the silent observer. If their attention slipped for a moment, it would result in faulty workmanship – a blade with imperfections or pieces of armour with defects. *And we thought there were only a few of these creatures.*

Nearby there were tables where engravers were hard at work, chiselling or etching the metal. The master craftsmen sat in rows decorating suits of armour with ornate lines and inlays. Others were fabricating hinge joints, springs, pins, hooks and other tiny parts that would ensure a warrior's suit of armour showed no gaps and was flexible enough to allow the optimum range of movement in combat.

Vraccas, I thank you for letting me see this. Hearing his pursuers hard behind him, Tungdil gave a last look around the forge. He knew it would need a ventilation shaft to take away the exhaust fumes and steam and extreme heat. *That would be my quickest escape route.*

Instead of one big chimney, he noted several metal-lined shafts in the roof. They would be just wide enough to admit him. *Excellent! They won't be able to follow me up there.*

He hurried along the wall, keeping behind forges, stacks of coal and huge bellows for cover and thence to a chain he could climb. Clouds of water vapour meant he was temporarily shrouded from view.

The chain he ascended led to a pulley on the ceiling. It was an arm's length away from one of the ventilation shafts. With consummate skill and strength, he managed to launch himself off and catch hold of the edge of the copper hood. Hanging there, he blinked while the smoke and fumes attacked his eyes and airways, and tried to make out what kind of shaft this was.

The interior was smooth, offering no purchase for fingers or shoes. He would have to work his way up by pressing his shoulders and feet against the walls. It would take an enormous amount of effort to climb. Several acronta were gathering below. His presence had been discovered. Now the guards who had been pursuing him joined them, realising his intentions.

They fetched spears with tips red-hot from the smithy.

Out of here! And fast! Tungdil swung himself into the ventilation duct and squirmed upwards, his shoulders and feet pressed against the walls. He must avoid at all costs falling on to the floor of the forge. He had underestimated the temperature of the walls. He would have to move quickly before the heat got through the thin-lined garment he was wearing. And he must not make the mistake of pressing the back of his neck against the sides.

The red-hot tip of the first spear came sailing past. It threw light on the inside of the duct before it lost momentum and started to clatter back down. Even though the tip was now pointing away from him, it would be painful when it hit. Then it surprisingly got stuck half way.

So there's a shaft that goes off to the side! Good news! Panting, he forced his way up the smooth walls, coughing and retching from the fumes. Two more spears came at him and both just missed, getting tangled up with the first one on their descent, forming a wooden framework he would soon be able to hang on to.

The hot copper had burned his skin in several places already and blisters were starting to form on his hands and his neck.

The volume of smoke suddenly increased, making it impossible to breathe. The acronta were planning to smoke him out.

With his last ounce of strength and senses reeling, he grabbed the first spear and pulled himself up. Just as the wood broke under his weight, he got hold of the second one and heaved himself around into the side passage, dragging himself along on his stomach.

Fighting for breath, he rolled over on to his back and gasped for air. Breathe! Breathe!

And now, get on! he urged himself. *They know where I am and they'll think of something to bring me down.*

It was more than just his own life at stake. The whole of Girdlegard was counting on him, as were his friends. He kissed the ring once more. *And it's about her.* The talisman seemed to be working.

With this in mind he pushed himself up, took hold of two of the spears and wrenched off one tip, now cooled, to use as a short sword if need be. He concealed it in his clothing. Grasping the other spear he stumbled off, still finding it difficult to breathe. Tungdil knew he could not rest despite pain from the burn blisters and the retching and coughing – if he stayed he would suffocate.

He jumped over smoking outlets and after what seemed an eternity, he reached a narrow passageway the acronta had constructed for extra ventilation. Fresh air entered the shaft from here, causing a draught.

He soon realised he was in a complex system of air ducts similar to those the dwarves would engineer to ensure access to fresh air in deep mines and remote galleries. He could walk erect but an acront would be forced to crawl along. An excellent development.

Tungdil listened out and made markings at various junctions. He looked down into rooms and corridors, and again, scribbled marks on the walls.

Occasionally he came across a grating placed vertically in the air ducts as defence against vermin or monsters, but he was able to use his spear to lever them out. The sandstone offered little resistance.

His thirst and hunger became intolerable. When he spied a room from which the smell of food rose up, he could not resist removing the grating and letting himself down, although he was half-expecting a trap.

He landed, spear in hand, in a room that had the air of a kitchen. He knew nothing of the acronta eating habits away from the field of battle but he found loaves of bread as big as wagon wheels, sausage, cheese and tubs of salted meat. *This must be the stores for their prisoners.* He could not imagine the acronta on a diet of cheese on toast. From what he remembered about Djerůn, the maga's bodyguard used to devour defeated monsters raw.

He did not waste any time before cutting himself a hunk of bread with his spear. It tasted rough and slightly acidic but was definitely edible. He swallowed it down and helped himself to the other foodstuffs. Except for the salted meat. Not knowing its provenance, he preferred to leave that out.

Just as he was in the middle of chewing his meal, he heard a quiet rumble behind him.

Before he could act he was thumped on the back and thrust onto the floor. He felt a foot holding him down on boards that had been laid on soft sand. Nearly choking from the lump of bread in his mouth, he managed to spit it out. He had lost his spear and now he was pinned down under the boot of an acront who had crept up on him silently. 'I surrender,' he cried, in dwarf language at first and then in the common language of all Girdlegard people. He did not doubt it would be understood.

A gauntleted hand came in view, wrenching the floorboards aside to reveal the sand. The acront growled reassuringly and the steel-clad finger formed dwarf runes: 'You are the one they call Tungdil Goldhand. I can see by the mark on your hand.'

'That is so,' the dwarf replied, but he could not move under the foot pressing him down. Any more pressure and his spine would crack.

'I have heard tell of you but I thought you'd gone to the Black Abyss. And that you had died there, with the axe Keenfire in your breast,' the acronta wrote in the sand.

'Oh, it's a long story.'

The gauntleted hand wiped the runes away and formed new ones. 'You don't have much time. Convince me.'

Tungdil told him as much as he could in the circumstances, trying to keep the narration lively. 'And what you see before you is the real Tungdil.'

'Your arrival is unexpected,' was the next message. 'My young Acïjn Rhârk picked you up because they did not know what to do with you. An älf and a handful of dwarves. It seemed too odd an occurrence, so they didn't want to kill you all and march on.'

'They did well.'

'We don't know that yet.' The acronta gave a low growl.

'We are allies. I fought once with one of your kind. His name was Djerůn, and I campaigned with the ruler of Letèfora to keep out evil,' he recounted. 'A very large acront. He had wings.' Tungdil presumed the acront who had caught him eating was not just any old warrior but someone of status. 'It would have been a crime to cause harm to me and my companions.'

'I have had your friends given nursing treatment; even the half-dead one, if that's any relief for you to know,' the steel finger wrote in the sand. 'They stand every chance of recovering from their wounds and will serve to increase our young warriors' knowledge.'

'So it was really a test, when Hargorin and Beligata were made to fight?'

'A very young warrior whose future had not yet been decided. Thanks to you we realised he was not suitable for the path in question. You serve us well, you and your friends.' The finger continued to inscribe runes in the sand. 'What were you and the älf looking for in the mountains?'

Why not let me stand up? My back is giving me hell under that boot. Tungdil summarised the purpose of their mission, aware a lie would not help the situation. Maybe he could persuade the acront to come over to his side. *I know they take arms against evil. Why shouldn't they be allies in our fight against the botoicans?*

'We left on a quest to see what was happening outside our borders. Join with us. You and your race destroy evil in all its forms, don't you?' he said in conclusion.

The deep rumbling growl took on what seemed to be an amused tone. 'We fight monsters. What you've been telling me sounds like a normal sort of war. We don't take part in those. We don't take sides.'

'But a ghaist can do worse things than any monster.' Tungdil was sticking to his ground in this argument. 'If the botoicans turn on the acronta, your whole race may be wiped out.'

'We know about the botoicans. They gather lost creatures

round them to help them carry out their feuds. But they never presented any danger to us. Our scouts don't make mistakes.'

'They were mistaken when they attacked us.'

'No. They were searching for an älf and they found him,' came the written answer. 'There were älfar runes on the stones and they were following these signs.'

'Those marks were ancient,' Tungdil contradicted. 'The älf who's with us owes his life to us. We brought him because he's travelled the Outer Lands.'

'I could see he's very elderly. Not a good opponent.' The glove wrote swiftly and firmly. 'But that means the runes led you *to* us and not the other way round?'

'That's right.' A disappointed growl.

'The young ones thought they were on the tracks of fresh älfar. The two cities we had selected as targets have been utterly laid waste to. No survivors, apart from one black-eyes that got away. He had escaped from the dwarves many cycles ago and found his way to us.'

'Yes.' Then, 'Forgive the question. You mentioned two älfar cities?'

'One by the sea and one on a rock. We found both of them destroyed. Someone got there before us but we don't know who it was.' The glove smoothed the sand over. 'You won't know, either.'

'No.'

'What a shame.'

Tungdil saw no chance of wriggling out from under the heavy foot. He resented being in this position and hated being powerless to act. 'Take me to the ones who rule your people,' he tried, attempting another tack.

'Why?'

'We could make a pact against the botoicans and together spy on them to find out their intentions.'

'Pay more attention. I told you: we're not interested in other people's wars. Our aim is to eradicate the beasts and to reach Kân Thalay.' The acront appeared to have lost interest. 'Tell me what you have to offer, Tungdil Goldhand, hero as you are in the wrong place. Why should I let you live?'

Might be worth a try. 'I have knowledge.' The words groaned their way out through his lips. One of his ribs had just snapped and his breastbone was creaking ominously.

'Let's get down to business, then. Knowledge – about what, exactly?'

'A place chock-full of beasts. Exactly what you and your people have been waiting for. The älfar call the place Phondrasôn and it's full of monster scum. Enough to feed you and your friends for all eternity.'

'Sounds intriguing.' The writing sped up. 'How do we get there?'

'It's not that easy. We could do a deal. I tell you where you'll find an entrance and what to expect when you get there, and you let me and my companions go free.'

'No way.' The rumbling voice took on a threatening tone. 'But I've got another proposal: once a cycle, one of you will be selected to take the arena against one of my Acïjn Rhârk. If you win, I'll set all of you free *and* you get a handful of my young nrotai to assist in your campaign against the botoicans. They can gain some experience with you. Till then, you tell me all about the place the beasts are to be found and I'll have your story checked out.'

Did it just write 'one of my *Acïjn Rhârk*'? The choice of words confirmed that this was not an ordinary warrior who had caught him. 'And if we don't win?'

'Then you and your friends remain our prisoners. For cycles on end.'

'As long as the älf isn't harmed and he's provided with enough paper, ink and quill pens to write with, you're on.' Tungdil agreed to the deal to avoid a worse outcome. As Hargorin and Beligata were both apparently still alive, nothing should change. *We need Carmondai too.*

'Then we are in business, Tungdil Goldhand. I am only agreeing to this because your reputation precedes you,' the gauntlet scratched in the soft sand. 'I acknowledge your feats and respect you.'

There was a loud rumble. Less than four heartbeats later four armoured acronta turned up, taking Tungdil between them and marching him off with no chance to look back.

The passages they marched through were strangely-shaped corridors that he was seeing for the first time. They reminded him of Letèfora. The palace where the acront and king of the city had lived had been constructed in a similar way.

Tungdil longed to know who he had been conversing with. *I'm relying on the word of an acront I've not even seen face to face. Vraccas, please make sure I'm not going completely insane here.*

It did not take long before he found himself back in the great arena hall. He was shoved back into his cage. To his right Hargorin was snoring and smacking his lips in his sleep. On the right Beligata lay slumbering in her metal containment cell. The hidden compartment in the Thirdling's artificial leg was open and empty. Their trick had been discovered.

The acront was keeping his word. Tungdil could see Carmondai was surrounded by reams of paper, inkwells and feather quills. The älf nodded to him; he had already begun drawing.

'We have a new task,' he said, loud enough for both Gosalyn and the history-recorder to hear. He told them briefly what had happened to him. But, expecting to be overheard by the guards, he did not mention he still had a spear-tip concealed under his clothing. *It will provide the key to a second plan.*

A dwarf such as he was would not rely on being able, at some time in the future, to defeat one of the acronta in combat. He kissed the vraccasium ring. Being prepared was key. Preparation and opportunity.

Girdlegard
Black Mountains
Kingdom of the Thirdling dwarves
Eastern Gate
6493rd solar cycle, early summer

'That was quick!' Rognor stared in astonishment at the wagons with their heaps of sacks. Ropes prevented the loads slipping during the journey. The early crop of the seed variety the elves had provided had already reached the Black Mountains. The cereals had flourished and ripened under the first rays of warm sunshine and had been harvested. The Naishïon had decreed that the tent-city dwellers were to have a foretaste of life in the new homeland.

'The harvest is eighty days ahead of our oats, barley and wheat,' Rognor said to the elf who had driven the wagon.

'Sitalia blessed this variety for us. The second crop is due in late summer.' The elf reached behind and opened one of the sacks to show the dwarf the quality of the grain. 'See for yourself.'

Rognor did not know much about agriculture or grinding corn, but he was struck by the fatter grains this strain produced compared to what was normally grown in the valleys.

He bit on a stalk. At first it was mild and sweet but it had a bitter aftertaste. Rognor spat it out. 'It burns on the tongue. Are you sure it's all right?' He shook the remains out of his blue beard.

'It's elf corn. Hardly likely to appeal to a dwarf,' the coachman smiled. 'Don't worry. It's not poisoned and it's quite edible. It's just not designed for your palate. Nor for humans'. That is part of Sitalia's plan, to ensure there's enough for us and that no other race will try to grab our harvest from us.'

'It's working; I'd never want bread made of that stuff,' Rognor joked. As always when he smiled, the tattoos on his face changed their shape. Only the Lorimbur rune stayed constant. 'Ten wagons with fifty sacks each. Have I got that right?'

'That's it.'

'Not much each by the time it's distributed.' Rognor envisaged how the hungry would-be settlers would cluster round the wagons, desperate to taste what the goddess had provided. The freezing winds of winter were past and gone, but their conditions were still far from ideal. They were chronically short of food despite the generous donations the dwarves continued to make. 'I'll send some guards along with you to keep your elves from getting too eager.'

'Thank you, Chancellor.' The elf got the rest of the wagon train to move up to the front of the gate.

Rognor knew sorânïons were out and about in the camp; the interrogations had been progressing more slowly ever since the incident of the älf. Ocâstia was taking more time, too, to conduct her examinations. And because of the milder weather, more elves had turned up, so numbers had increased. All in all, the dwarf reckoned there must be close to four thousand elves now waiting for admittance. Rognor sent a hundred warriors to the gate to surround the wagons with a wall of shields and armour.

'I'll come along to speak to Phenîlas about the distribution.' Rognor climbed up next to the driver and the portcullis was pulled up. He regretted the Naishïon had not sent a replacement for Phenîlas. Indeed, no word about it had come. *Presumably there are more important things happening in Girdlegard.*

The huge dwarf face on the fortress wall looked as if it were spitting out the carts. The wagon train attracted the attention of the elf children first of all. They dropped their toys and stopped their games to run over and stare at the loads.

'Stop over there where the road is a bit wider,' Rognor instructed the coachman. 'Nobody's to get any corn until I come back here with one of the sorânïons,' he told the elf and his own guards. He jumped down.

'If people get too curious, keep them talking, friend elf, and tell them how generous the Naishïon is being.'

'I'd do that anyway.' The coachman gave a wave and stood up to blow a call on his silver bugle.

The camp started to come to life and the first inhabitants began to make their way over. The wagon train was visible from quite a distance and their ruler's emblem on the tarpaulins was distinctive.

Rognor hurried through to get to one of the tents used for interrogating the elves.

As he approached, he noticed a crowd had formed. People were talking amongst themselves but he could not hear what they were saying. Rognor pushed his way past.

An elf-woman at the entrance appeared inconsolable, her eyes red with crying. There was blood on her arm. She had already undergone the procedure and as she had been found to be a non-älf, she had received the special mark. She was holding something that looked like a toy. She pressed it to her breast in desperation.

He won't have tortured an infant? 'Is Phenîlas in there?' Rognor asked one of the sorânïons.

'He is.'

'I want to speak to him. The Naishïon has sent a delivery of grain and we have to discuss how it's to be shared out.' The bystanders started whispering to each other.

'He's currently conducting an examination.'

'And I've got ten wagons with cereal the camp inmates will be glad to see,' Rognor said, pushing the elf aside. 'Who is going to stop them helping themselves to the sacks? You?' He put his hand on the tent canvas.

A high-pitched scream came from within, full of fear and pain. The elf-woman at the entrance sobbed loudly and threw herself at one of the elves; those waiting moved closer to the tent as if they wanted to storm it.

The officer in white armour placed his hand on the hilt of his sword as a warning. 'Get back,' he ordered, but it was clear he too was affected by her suffering.

This has to stop. Rognor stormed in. *Phenîlas is off his head.*

Another sorânïon was standing guard with his back towards Rognor. He turned but let the dwarf pass unchallenged.

Phenîlas was bending over a black-haired elf-girl Rognor thought must be about three or four cycles old. The child was tied down on the interrogation table, one shirt sleeve rolled up to the shoulder to receive Sitalia's mark; the soles of her bare feet showed small cuts and stripes from being hit with a cane.

'Give her the mark and let her go,' Rognor said darkly. 'We have more important things to discuss.'

'I haven't finished,' Phenîlas said, his eyes showing a faraway glaze. 'Certainty.' He lifted the bloodied cane. 'Extreme caution.'

'Wagons with corn have arrived. The Naishïon has sent them,' the Chancellor said swiftly, to try to get the elf's attention. 'You have to tell me how you want it distributed. There might be enough for everyone if it's handled well.'

The cane whizzed through the air and landed on the soles of the girl's bare feet, hitting exactly in the cuts from previous strokes. She shrieked and sobbed.

Phenîlas kept his gaze focused on her face. 'Yes, yes. That's good,' he mumbled, giggling. 'Could there be an älf hidden inside you?' He raised his hand for the next blow. 'Show me. Show me!'

Rognor saw the officer by the entrance shaking his head and grimacing; this was obviously not to his taste. 'Is this the child of the elf-woman you've just tested?' Rognor asked Phenîlas accusingly. 'Can't you see the resemblance? Stop hurting her.'

'Weakness is our enemy.' Phenîlas gave a scornful glance over his shoulder. 'I must not be weak. I am hard. Hard as granite. Hard as the Black Mountains. Hard as stone.' His eyes shimmered with madness and there were tiny blood splashes on his face. 'Caution, Chancellor. Extreme caution. Certainty is called for.' He stretched out his arm. 'They all get ten blows of the cane and ten cuts. This candidate has only had four.'

I can't watch him do this. Rognor stood between Phenîlas and the child, who lay whimpering on the table, her whole body quivering. 'It's enough! How can the child be an älf if you've already tested her mother?'

Phenîlas widened his eyes and stared at the dwarf. 'Move aside!'

'No!'

The cane swished down, hitting Rognor in the face. His beard took some of the force out of the impact but the flexible wood still cut his skin open.

'I said: move aside.' Phenîlas drew his sword with his other hand. 'I am carrying out the Naishïon's will. Caution. Care. Certainty. Granite hard,' he said, speaking automatically. 'No one is to hold me back.' He laughed out loud. 'No one!'

'That almost touched my Lorimbur rune.' Rognor ran his fingers over the cut and looked at the blood. *He is out of his mind. His task and the pain he is inflicting have destroyed his ability to think clearly.*

'You are to stop this and you are to go with me to the wagon train,' he insisted. 'The girl is no älf.'

The dwarf had anticipated the sword-swipe and dodged it. The blade hit the table a finger's breadth away from the young girl.

Rognor pulled out his bladed morningstar, the protective covers dropping to the floor. 'Don't you dare, Phenîlas! You are in the Black Mountains. We tolerate your presence here because—'

He got no further because the elf attacked him with a wild cry, wielding his weapon in both hands with the obvious intent of killing him. The sorânïon on duty at the entrance did not intervene to help his superior officer.

Twisting his shoulder out of the path of the oncoming

blow, Rognor laid into the elf with his morningstar, striking Phenîlas in the groin and leaving a noticeable dent and a gash in the palladium armour.

The force of the bladed iron sphere hurled the elf backwards against the tent wall, where his sword slit the canvas; the sorânïon fell out of the tent into the open.

The migrant elves drew back with amazed cries at the sight of the combatants; they could hear the little girl calling for her mother.

Rognor stormed out through the tent wall to pursue his opponent, his morningstar held at the ready. 'Stop this,' he warned. 'You need a healer. Your mind is disturbed.'

'Certainty is all!' Phenîlas shrieked, saliva flying from his lips. 'Extreme caution!' He leaped to his feet and stabbed at the chancellor with his sword. The dwarf used his chain to ward off the blow and then pulled his adversary over, planning to wrench his weapon away.

But Phenîlas guessed Rognor's intention and struck out with his cane. Rognor caught it on his forearm. Retaining hold on his sword, the elf aimed the blade straight for the dwarf's head. The morningstar came into its own once more, striking the steel and deflecting its trajectory.

The sorânïon who had been on guard outside the tent tried to grab his commander's weapon hand. 'Calm down!'

'You traitor!' Phenîlas kicked him in the stomach and thrashed him across the face with the cane, splitting the cheek straight through to the jaw bone, revealing the teeth. 'You'll regret this later,' he thundered and stabbed at one of the spectators who attempted to help the wounded guard. 'Get back! You might be an älf, whispering poison into my men's ears!' Phenîlas had lost it completely. He waved the bloodied sword around, bringing its tip to a halt in front of the elf-woman whose child he had been torturing. 'Maybe I got it wrong about you? Are you one of them after all?' he muttered. 'Why is everyone so very concerned about your sprog? Even the dwarf!' He raised his weapon for a fatal blow. 'Have I discovered your secret?'

The elf-woman screamed and leaped out of range, holding out her arm with the safe mark.

'No!' Ocâstia came storming through the crowd, sword drawn, to prevent the murder her superior officer was about to commit. But just as she drew near, she tripped and fell, dropping her weapon.

No time. Rognor realised it was up to him to stop the deed. He slammed the morningstar into Phenîlas' right knee.

The elf tumbled to one side and his sword missed his intended victim by a hair's breadth. He turned on the chancellor, hobbling, his lower leg at an unnatural angle. 'You first, then her. Then all of them!' he roared. 'Caution! Certainty!'

The only thing Rognor could think of was to slam his morningstar at Phenîlas again, aiming anywhere but the head. 'If Sitalia loves you, you will survive.'

The flying metal sphere struck Phenîlas in the chest. The palladium armour could not withstand the force of the blow and the blades cut through the damaged metal. The elf fell back, groaning, blood spurting out. Rognor had released the weapon so as not to be dragged with it.

The elf dropped his sword. It clattered onto the black stone. Then Phenîlas collapsed. His mouth was still forming words but the only sounds to emerge were moans. The light in his eyes was starting to flicker; they glazed over. The dwarf's weapon had had a devastating effect and was still stuck in the blood-spattered white armour.

Sitalia made her choice. Unarmed now except for a dagger, the chancellor was now hopelessly outnumbered. He waited for the elves to turn on him.

The elf-woman whose child lay in the tent came to him – and she knelt before him, grasped his hand and kissed his fingers.

'My name is Inisëa and only you have had the grace and the courage to save my child from the clutches of that madman,' she said, sobbing with relief. 'I shall never forget what you have done and will always be grateful. All the elves shall hear about your great deed, Rognor Mortalblow. If you should ever be in need, ask for me.'

Ocâstia carried the young child out of the interrogation tent and placed her in her mother's arms. Applause broke out and the crowd started calling Rognor's name.

Some of the elves took hold of Phenîlas' corpse and began to drag it away. Ocâstia extricated the morningstar and returned it to Rognor. The dwarf gulped. He had been expecting anything but this reception.

'You have done more for the relationship between our two races than any other dwarf in history,' Ocâstia whispered to him. She raised her arms and the crowd quietened down. In her right hand she held a letter bearing the Naishïon's own seal. 'Is it not tragic that the order recalling Phenîlas has only arrived now? Our ruler has realised the commander lost competence. I pledge I shall make sure the tests are quicker, more moderate and still very thorough.' She indicated the wagon train. 'Our Naishïon has sent us this gift: elf corn. The first harvest from our new homeland. Go back to your tents, collect a bowl each and come back here so we can begin distributing the grain.'

The crowd dispersed, their relief almost palpable.

Rognor stared at the bloodstained iron morningstar that had sent the sorânïon to his endingness. He carefully replaced the protective covers.

'It was self-defence. He did not know what he was doing. He had gone insane.' Ocâstia bowed to Rognor. 'Chancellor, you are a true hero. Where my own warriors and I did not dare to act, you stepped in. Accept my gratitude.'

'That is my people's mission,' Rognor replied, though he was flattered by her words. 'It's what we are here for. We're here now and will be here in the future, too.' He took a deep breath. 'I'll leave my dwarves guarding the wagons, though I doubt that's necessary now.'

'You have removed our greatest scourge. Before autumn comes, the camp will be gone and the Black Mountains will belong to the Thirdlings once more.' Ocâstia nodded to him. 'I shall go and see to the distribution, Chancellor.'

Rognor raised a hand in acknowledgement and headed back towards the fortress.

Usually he was treated with mild indifference when he went through the camp, but now all the elves, male and female alike, bowed their heads to him as he passed.

I shall always remember this orbit. He went through the gate and climbed the steps to the walkway to watch how Ocâstia and the sorânïons shared out the grain, giving some to each resident of the tented city. Soon music was heard; songs that now had no sadness to them. The mood had changed remarkably; it was as if a shadow had been removed from the minds of those patiently awaiting admittance to Girdlegard. They were singing praise to Sitalia and to their Naishïon. He even heard his own name mentioned in their songs.

Rognor gradually came to realise the significance of what

had occurred. It had all happened too quickly for him to take it in at first. *But it really did happen.*

When his gaze swept the scene he noticed a group of elves standing at the edge of the ravine, led by the elf-woman whose daughter he had saved. They were throwing Phenîlas' armoured body over the edge without ceremony, followed by his sword. He was sent down to join the others he had killed. Neither Ocâstia nor the other officers intervened to prevent this.

Rognor knew the horrors of war well and how the cruel brutalities of the battlefield could affect one's mind. Dwarves might be less susceptible than other creatures because Vraccas had made them steadfast and resilient, but he was aware that many warriors in the elf and human armies found themselves paralysed after battle.

The pain he inflicted on others ate him up from the inside. Rognor shuddered, remembering the look on the sorânïon commander's face and how he had repeated the words 'caution' and 'certainty'. *He was a good elf when he first arrived.*

Ocâstia looked up towards the battlements. She spotted Rognor and waved her hand at the dwarf and bowed several times. Several of her entourage followed suit and his name was called again. There was no end to their gratitude. Returning their greeting, Rognor felt very proud. He knew he would have nothing to fear from the Naishïon. He had hundreds of elves to vouch for him, and Ocâstia, too, would verify that all he had done was in self-defence and to prevent an insane elf from committing murder.

But a mystery remained. Phenîlas had taken a secret to the abyss with him. What arrangement had he made with the älf? Rognor looked up at the Black Mountains whose peaks were shrouded in mist.

He was no friend of unanswered questions. But he could not come up with a solution. Not any longer.

In this way whole cycles passed. Or so I believe.

Occasionally one of the dwarves would be summoned out of his cage and sent into combat against an ashont. Often they were defeated, in spite of the heroic fight they put up. There were some minor victories but in the long run, they were not able to overcome. But we continued to observe and to hope we might find a weakness in the Towers That Walk that we could take advantage of.

I spent much time in my cage as negotiated for me by Tungdil with the emperor-mother. I was given parchment, paper, ink and nibs, so I could draw and write and sketch.

We could only guess how many cycles actually passed. It seemed to me they put the dwarves into the arena more than once every solar session, which would have been to our advantage if we had had a chance to defeat one of them.

But we made use of the time. Tungdil and I talked a great deal. He left his prison as often as he could, opening the door to his cage with the spear tip he had concealed. He would make his way clandestinely to the library and read until his eyes were sore. He would copy anything he found of value to share with us. In this way, he taught us the language and the customs of the ashont. He gave us any details about their physical makeup that he was able to glean from their healers' books.

Secretly, then, we acquired the knowledge the ashont had. Our aim was, one orbit, to be able to employ it against them. What would the Inextinguishables have given for this opportunity!

What had been happening in Girdlegard? No idea. I can only assume there was still Sha'taï in charge, manipulating the power structure. Manipulating it to her own advantage.

If I ever return alive, I'm curious about how things have turned out. Very curious indeed.

But I hardly think I will ever return there. My strength is ebbing away.

Secret notes for
The Writings of Truth
written under duress by Carmondai

XXIV

Somewhere in the Outer Lands

Tungdil hurried through the ventilation shafts bent double with copies of two documents under his arm. He got back to the arena without being spotted by the acronta guards. The writings dealt with the älfar cities and the subject of the botoicans, who were seen by the emperor-mother – as the acronta ruler was known – as an insignificant danger.

This, in the dwarf's opinion, was a considerable misjudgement.

They won't know what's hit them if they succumb to the power of the botoican magicians.

Tungdil turned a corner and jumped down, landing on the roof of his own cage and sliding down the bars. 'I've found something,' he told Carmondai, handing over the papers.

'You always do.' The älf looked at the notes and passed them to Gosalyn. The fact that they had been there for several cycles now was obvious from the state of Carmondai's hair: it was growing long and dark brown with silver strands. It covered the scar of the branded warnings on his forehead and cheeks.

In the neighbouring cages, Hargorin and Beligata were occupied with improving their knowledge of acronta script and language and their study of medical writings about their captors' physiques. Both of them had long recovered from their injuries and had been selected several times to take the arena against one of the emperor-mother's combatants. So far they had not scored a single victory, but this only motivated them further to concentrate on their studies. Beligata knew more than any of the others about how the acronta were put together. Tungdil had decoded the acronta language and taught the others; he had no problems supplying them with more information from the library.

Beligata has the makings of a scholar herself. Tungdil opened his cage and slipped back inside, pulling the lid closed over his head. *I wonder when she will tell us the truth about that scar of hers. The edges are looking inflamed again.*

He was tired. He lay down, kissed the vraccasium ring and closed his eyes to get some rest, but his head was buzzing. He had to process what he had been reading. He had never been so rich in knowledge and facts. The acronta had written records about every single race Tungdil had ever encountered. They evaluated each nation, noting how dangerous they might prove, what style of combat they preferred, what they looked like, how they spoke and how they chose to behave. There were maps of cities and settlements and details of projects and developments.

The acronta scouts had done their work thoroughly – except when it came to Girdlegard.

They had always failed to get through as long as the Children of the Smith had held the gates. This delighted Beligata and Hargorin. In the few instances when the Stone Gateway had proved permeable, spies had recorded the normal type of beast attack but noted that no intervention on their part had been necessary.

Tungdil rolled onto his back. His mind was preoccupied with all this new information. He tried to memorise everything he read; the acronta had been a totally unknown quantity until now. And here he was, held in their secret location, a place he had been unable to pinpoint despite having found several maps on the archive shelves.

They used the term Acïjn Rhârk to refer to themselves. He had learned why Andôkai's bodyguard had called himself Djerůn: it was a word derived from the concept *Daajerhůn*, a designation accorded to the prime specimens of acronta warriors. The bodyguard's name was a corrupted form of this honorary title.

From cycle to cycle the *Srai G'dàma*, or sacred emperor-mother, would decide which beasts would constitute the priority target. They would then poll the scouts for any relevant information.

The motivation did not stem purely from the wish to eradicate their enemies; it was deeply rooted in acronta mythology. Only when so-called Kân Thalay – balance – was attained in the world would the times become quiet and inner calm be established. That achieved, there would be no more need for the acronta to go into battle at all. *This was their highest aim.* Until that point, however, their whole existence was geared towards combat. Humans stood very low on their list of creatures.

Tungdil was fascinated by what he had managed to learn about the acronta way of life. They were hatched from eggs like snakes, and the young were nurtured for five cycles in the home hive. At that point they were considered fully developed; after one more cycle, they attained full size.

Tungdil had always thought they were nomadic but this proved to be wrong. The location of their home hive was kept strictly secret and was not visible as such from the outside. The ones that roamed the lands were fighting units and they could appear as if out of nowhere.

I shan't be able to sleep. He got up and stared at the

combat arena below. Very recently a troll had been torn to pieces by one of the acronta.

Their warriors were trained for three full cycles to reach the basic standard. After ten cycles they could qualify for special forces work, and fifty cycles' experience made them veterans: the elite of the fighting force.

On the march or in battle they would work in teams of five, as denoted on their armour. The decorations showed how many enemies they had despatched and what merits they had earned.

The Srai G'dàma, the sacred emperor-mother, laid particularly large eggs, which gave rise to the most dangerous specimens. They would grow to be twice as strong and twice the size of the normal acronta. These ones often grew wings. Many of them were called to higher purposes; they often ventured out at the emperor-mother's behest to found a new hive or settlement – often in the vicinity of a prolific beast population – where they would recruit further acronta to join them. However, each and every acront was under the control of the sacred emperor-mother. Tungdil knew now that she was the one who had spared him before, though the conditions she had set were proving impossible to meet.

I must not be ungrateful. We are, after all, still alive. Tungdil touched the bars of his cage. *But it's time we completed our mission. Ideally with the acronta as our allies.* Somehow or other he had to find a way to convince them of the danger the botoicans presented.

Tungdil regularly scoured the latest reports that arrived in the archives from the acronta scouts and he came across indications that a botoican had, in the course of the last two cycles, been mustering a huge army, mostly composed of large monsters. A quick study of the map told him that this was happening more than eight hundred miles away from the Stone Gateway.

His homeland was not in immediate danger.

But that can change.

Tungdil saw the access gate for the combat arena open. An armoured acront stepped in. The illuminating mirrors swung round, lighting up the floor.

A new contest.

The dwarf looked up and saw the hook dropping – heading straight for his own cage.

So it's to be me this time. 'Beligata,' he said, alarmed, getting to his feet. 'Quick, tell me about their weak points.'

'I've been investigating one thing,' she replied quickly, checking through her notes. 'What was it . . .'

But Tungdil's cage was already being lifted up and heaved down from its ledge. 'Keep looking,' he called to her. 'I'll try to keep him at arm's length until you find it.'

Carmondai pointed past them to the other end of the hall. 'Not just the one.'

Tungdil turned.

Three dozen cages were being lowered alongside his own, their inmates shaking and rattling the bars like creatures possessed. Orcs came to light, and composite beasts made up of animal and monster, as well as a troll or two and a creature that one would expect to find in the ocean. From every side of the arena came the sound of miscellaneous weaponry, shields, and bits of armour clattering down from above for the beasts to arm themselves.

Holding a super-length sword and an axe, the acront assayed a few moves, roaring from behind his visor.

One of the veterans wanting to win a new award for his armour. Tungdil kept his hidden spear-tip to hand under his garments. *He's obviously looking for a challenge.* Tungdil could see the judges assembling in the viewing box.

Tungdil's cage landed with a thump and the acront went round opening up all the lids. None of the monsters attacked. Instead they raced over to the piles of armour.

Strange. Tungdil was not attacked, either. *They have not selected the most stupid ones, then, for the contest with the warrior.*

In contrast to the others, he did not hurry to don armour. He strolled over to the heap that had already been plundered.

He watched two orcs trying to get the beasts to organise themselves and make a concerted effort, but the others did not understand their roars. This meant they all formed small groups of fighters who already knew each other, or were of the same race. *Not the sort of company I would normally seek. I'm better off on my own.*

Tungdil looked at the left-over material. On the whole they were weapons captured in battle, and unsuitable for acronta use because of their size and type. Instead of melting them down in the workshops, they supplied the prisoners with them.

Squatting down, he selected a shield that was not too much the worse for wear, a rope, a reasonably sharp hand axe and six well-balanced daggers. *That should work for me.* He kicked around at his leisure in the pile of armour, trying to find pieces that would fit together. The first death cries were already occurring behind him and the captive audience in their niches were grunting and roaring. The scum of the arena were being egged on by their caged compatriots.

In the hope the judges would not notice, Tungdil threw the daggers up to his friends. He discovered some armour-plate that would at least protect his back and chest. He put it on, then chose some forearm protectors and a helmet. He slung the rope over his shoulder. 'Beligata?'

'Still looking,' she shouted. 'He's occupied at the moment.' Tungdil straightened and fastened the leather thongs of the armour, glancing at the raging battle. *Four down already.*

Because he had previously studied numerous single-combat bouts and had read the archive instructions about sword play, Tungdil found himself able to predict what strokes the veteran would use. That would make it slightly easier to survive in combat with the Tower That Walks and to wait until a suitable opportunity occurred. But there was a big difference between successfully dodging an attack and actually landing a blow of his own skilfully enough to put the veteran out of action.

With Vraccas' help he should soon be getting tired. Tungdil waited for the next stroke, smiling when the armoured acront played exactly the one he had expected, slicing the orc attacker through from head to toe. *I want them to wear him out for me.*

The field was thinning out. There had been about forty of them but only half were still in with a chance. The survivors had now realised they were easy pickings and they were proceeding more cautiously. They formed larger groupings and were gesticulating wildly to communicate with each other. The acront grunted with delight when he saw this.

'Beligata, it would be great if you could come up with an idea now.' Tungdil leaned against a pile of armour, refusing to pay attention to what the beasts were urging him to do. *Do your best without me.*

He watched and waited.

The remaining orc led seven beasts, shouting instructions,

gesturing for them to encircle the veteran. A troll half the size of the acront was holding back, just as Tungdil was. He was waving a bludgeon in the air indecisively. He had ten monsters clustered around him; they reckoned this was their best bet.

Only the weird sea-creature, who looked a bit like a baby seal with his rolls of fat and his flippers, was isolated on his own, like Tungdil. It lay about wondering, it seemed, what on earth it could do faced with an acront on dry land.

The other captives' unrelenting cries of encouragement had not lessened at all. The stink of blood, warm meat and spilled guts made them all the more eager.

'Hey! I . . . something,' Tungdil caught a snatch of what Beligata was saying. She was on her feet and waving a piece of paper.

'Louder,' yelled the dwarf. *Curses! These wretched beasts are making so much noise.*

'You've got . . . to stab . . . where . . .' came the garbled message.

Tungdil knew he was not going to get any useful tips like this. 'Wrap the paper round a stone and chuck it down!' He tried to emphasise his meaning with mimed actions.

Beligata got the picture and threw the paper a few heartbeats later, aiming cleverly through the bars of her cage. Tungdil watched to see exactly where it would fall. Out of the corner of his eye he saw the sea-creature making its way to pick it up. Moving like a cross between a snake and a caterpillar, it slithered over, picking up a turn of speed Tungdil had not been expecting.

'Don't you dare!' he bellowed, leaping up and racing over. The combat was starting again in earnest, he realised, hearing increased clattering and shrieking. But the message from

Beligata was more important. He needed to learn about his adversary's weaknesses. The scrunched-up message landed on the arena floor, bounced a few times and rolled over to the sea-creature, which had its jaws wide open to catch it.

Oh, no, you don't! Tungdil flung his shield, intercepting the paper and stone so that the trajectory was altered. The seal-like creature caught the edge of the shield in its teeth and crunched it up as if it were a slice of toast.

I'll have to keep away from those teeth. Tungdil had reached the precious ball of paper and bent to retrieve it. Just then, a shadow lunged over him and threw him to the floor, landing a powerful blow that hurled him onto the stone a few paces away.

Where did that come from? He raised his head to take a look at his unexpected attacker.

He could not see the sea-creature anywhere. In its place was a naked humanoid form, with extremely long arms and nails like knives. It blocked his view of the message that was intended for him. He saw its black button eyes.

It's a shape-shifter. It's been fooling me by taking on the appearance of some lump of a thing to make me ignore it. He went up to it. 'What are you playing at? Give me that piece of paper.'

The clawed fingers grasped the message. The creature either perused its contents or put up a good pretence of reading. 'Good,' it said, waving the note around. 'Good, good.' It placed the message on the floor and weighed it down with a stone, but did not move out of the way. 'Read. Come. Read.' Raising a long arm it gestured with a crooked index finger.

Tungdil tried to remember what the archives had said about shape-shifters. *Surely not a trustworthy ally.* If he recalled right, this could be a shape-shifter of the type called

Fin'Sao. They were characterised by extreme cruelty. They did not merely kill their prey but also inflicted all sorts of horrors on them. Only then would the flesh be to their taste.

'Get away from the message!' Tungdil commanded. If the Fin'Sao did not cooperate, Beligata would need to send another note. *Hope she didn't throw me the original.*

The long-armed beast moved back a few paces, waving at the dwarf. Tungdil made ready to fend off an attack. *Treacherous thing.* The acront was not the adversary he had to fear, it seemed. The Fin'Sao was looking for a fight it thought it could win.

'I'll hack you to pieces if you jump me,' the dwarf threatened, picking up the damaged shield at his feet. He reached the message and pulled it to himself swiftly, ducking down behind the shield to get the gist of the lines.

But the Fin'Sao had already scratched away vital parts of the note.

You wretched creature. He lowered the paper. 'What's this in aid of?'

'The two of us' – the Fin'Sao put its head on one side – 'together. I know what to do. You do what I tell you.'

Tungdil moved away. 'You're on your own.' He signalled to Beligata that she should send another copy of the message. 'I'm not submitting to coercion.'

'My people near here. Fleeing, hiding. Want protection.' The Fin'Sao turned full circle, scratching the stone with its long nails, leaving marks. 'You and your friends. And me. Help.'

Tungdil saw no possible advantage to be gained by involvement with an untrustworthy ally. *I think we're better off sticking to the offer the emperor-mother made us.* 'No. But you know the acront's weaknesses now. So off you go.'

The Fin'Sao hissed with rage and hurled itself at the dwarf.

Tungdil ducked behind his shield and waited for the impact; he anchored his boot-clad feet fast in the sand to take the strain and grabbed hold of his hand-axe. One claw scraped his helmet but did not penetrate it. The nails of the creature's other hand dug into the shield's covering and wood.

And I had vowed never to fight again. He threw out his shield arm as far as he was able, knocking his opponent off his feet. *There's nothing for it, though.* Then he swung his axe at the Fin'Sao's vulnerable underside. The gash opened up the belly and blood gushed out of the cut. The beast hopped away, howling, only making the injury worse. Its guts started to spill out. Soon it collapsed, convulsing.

'Mind out,' screamed Beligata.

Tungdil turned to see what the acront was up to – but the giant form reared up directly in front of him. *Vraccas!*

The acront's own axe was already heading his way.

Girdlegard
Grey Mountains
Kingdom of the Fifthling dwarves
Stone Gateway
6496th solar cycle, summer

'That's by far the strangest storm I've ever seen here in the Grey Mountains.' Balyndar had known since dawn that the orbit had nothing good in store. It had started badly: his stomach was upset and he was nauseous. He had tried every remedy. He and Girgandor were in one of the portal's thick-walled defence rooms where the spear catapults were housed. He squinted out of the window slits. The wind was sharp and cut into his face.

It's not letting up, is it? Not a bit. On the contrary, an incredible thunderstorm was brewing. Black clouds piled up above the mountain peaks and swathes of heavy rain were visible in the distance. Although the sun was at its zenith, the whole area was dark as nightfall. A fresh westerly breeze had been displaced by a storm wind from the north, grabbing at the guards' beards and protective clothing. Anything not tied down was whirled along by the powerful gusts like children's toys.

Balyndar got his men to secure what they could. The increasing strength of the wind made him concerned they would lose soldiers off the battlements, so he ordered ropes to be spanned for the guards to attach themselves to.

What most worried Balyndar and his Fifthlings was that the storm was arriving *counter* to the prevailing wind direction. Who was conjuring up this elemental weather phenomenon? Samusin himself, perhaps?

Girgandor pulled his helmet strap tighter. He had no head hair to protect but his intricately coiffured beard was being tangled mercilessly. 'Magic, do you think?' he shouted above the racket. 'We don't know what ghaists are capable of. Or their masters, come to that.'

Balyndar tried to ignore this unpleasant thought. 'Let's just say the storm is unusual. At least it's keeping away any unwelcome visitors.'

'That's good.' Girgandor said out loud what his commander was saying silently. 'We can't use the catapults and throwing devices in this weather. And the kites would stand no chance. They'd break loose from their moorings or the canvas would rip to shreds.' The bald dwarf stared up at the sky. 'It'd be a miracle in this weather if we hit a single target. You couldn't even rely on a sword thrust going where you wanted it to. If you're carrying a shield, you'd be picked up and carried off.'

Something shattered near the look-out post and splinters landed on Balyndar's armour before falling to the ground.

He picked up the fragments and ran his fingers over them. *Basalt and . . . is that obsidian?*

The thing was, there was no obsidian in the Grey Mountains.

Girgandor made the same connection. 'Well, this storm is full of surprises,' he considered. 'That's not local stone.'

Balyndar slid the shutter over the arrow slit to keep the draught out. The wind hurled itself at the obstacle, shaking the wood and emitting a high-pitched screech that hurt the eardrums. The commander thought he could detect a strange smell. *Powdered stone meal? Impossible, surely. Or could it be something the wind's picked up on the way?*

Balyndar thought he heard another impact. 'I'll warn the watch. They'll have to take shelter till these stones stop raining down. We'll drag the small catapults off to safety and the throwing machines must be covered – with shields, not tarpaulins – or their mechanisms will get damaged.'

He and Girgandor left the reinforced basement section of the fortress walls and ran up the stairs to the right-hand tower above the gate itself. After giving the guards their instructions, the two of them went up to the covered look-out post; the intermittent clicking persisted but the heavy glass of the stairwell windows was still intact. When they arrived at the top of the tower, Girgandor and Balyndar listened to the rain and the stones hailing down from the clouds. The four guards on duty had retreated to the middle of the shelter for protection.

'What is Samusin up to? This is really not normal.' Girgandor grabbed a chair and thrust most of it outside, tightly hanging on to one corner as the wind buffeted it. Balyndar watched, concerned. Tiny splinters of basalt and obsidian bombarded the wood, destroying the chair in a few blinks of an eye. It was a good thing they put the small catapults away. With luck, the thick reinforced timbers of the throwing machines could withstand the barrage.

Girgandor pulled in the only chair leg still intact and handed it round.

'We can be glad our roof is tiled in granite,' said Balyndar, looking out at the empty walkways. The storm would tear the flesh from any living creature in its path and then pound the bones to powder.

'We must get our learned dwarves to check the archives to see if there's any record of a north wind carrying basalt and obsidian chips.' He turned and looked along the path that led to their fortress. He had heard something that was neither the roar of the wind nor the clicking of stones. *What's that over there? Torches?* He leaned forward and picked up the telescope.

Some kind of vehicle was on the move through the storm: perhaps a siege tower being wheeled along horizontally. It was lit from the inside but he could not make out what it contained.

Balyndar pointed it out to Girgandor. It was perhaps eighty paces in length and ten wide; its height, in this position, eleven. That would be sufficient to shelter a considerable number of attackers from the ravages of the storm. The construction was definitely coming nearer to their fortifications.

And we can't use our catapults, even though they present a simple target. Or the kites. Useless in these conditions. 'I'm afraid they're heading straight for us,' he said, lowering the seeing-tube. 'Girgandor, get the cauldrons prepared and have guards man all the corridors that are not out in the open. We'll need hot slack from the forges and heated petroleum to drop over and set fire to as soon as they get close.'

'So it's the raggle-taggle army again. They've taken their time. Them arriving now is no coincidence, I bet.' His deputy nodded. 'They knew exactly what kind of storm was brewing. That's why they brought that strange vehicle with them.'

Balyndar agreed. 'I expect they'll try to outdo their initial performance, when they set that mark on the walls.'

'They'll never do it!' Girgandor rushed down the steps and the alarm horns sounded. The fortress was on defence footing.

Here we go again. Balyndar raised the seeing-tube to his brown eye and examined the vehicle, getting as much detail as the rain and bad light allowed. There were numerous handles and indentations on the top of the carriage, some short, some long.

They want to use it as a ramp, he deduced. It could be sloped up against the gate, thus getting the enemy several paces nearer the top of the walls, and they would not have to form it with a pile of bodies. *That will be the main difference to their first attempt.* Balyndar was relying on their supply of slack, burning pitch and petroleum to seep into cracks and fissures in the aggressors' construction and burn the inmates alive.

The unusual storm with its deadly freight of sharp stone fragments was causing him a great deal of concern. As long as the wind kept up its onslaught, Balyndar could not send any of his dwarf warriors out to repel attackers who might make it on to the ramparts.

The vehicle kept coming.

Whoever it is that the Outer Lands child has made an enemy of, they're powerful. The wind is following orders. He could only hope the clouds would not be able to cross the Grey Mountains, or the sharp splintered rain would cause a bloodbath and devastate great swathes of open countryside.

The air was full of the smell of fire and boiling pitch. The cauldrons of petroleum and slack and other fiery liquids stood ready to be poured onto the enemy. The strange box-like vehicle had nearly reached the gate and was slowing its pace now. It came to a halt thirty paces away, a safe distance from the walls with their cauldrons of death.

They're waiting for something. Balyndar did not take his eyes off the vehicle for a moment. When he used the telescope, he caught sight of lights inside the contraption and shadowy figures moving to and fro, but he had no idea what they were up to.

The front part lifted up. A second metal sheet came out from under the first, lengthening the ramp.

The strong wind pushed the whole unit into the gate where it crashed to a halt, but it left the ramp at such an acute angle that no one could have used it to run up. Now the front was lifted, Balyndar could see inside. Hundreds of men and beasts were sitting waiting in the shelter of the contraption's metal sheet. At the back there were cogs and pulleys, chains and counterweights to control the angle of the ramp. *They've got nowhere near enough soldiers to trouble us.*

The dwarf started to feel relieved. The end of the ramp was below the outlets where molten pitch and hot petroleum could be poured. It was forty paces short of the balustrade. *They could hardly have placed it in a worse position.* The hail of small stones stopped abruptly, but the rain and the wind were still at full force.

Balyndar wondered why the attacking soldiers did not move. They sat side by side in silence, waiting, man and beast, large and small. *There's no ghaist in there with them.*

Girgandor returned. 'We can begin,' he reported, panting from the exertion.

'As soon as the soldiers are out on the ramp, we'll douse them with hot slack. I want to see how they respond,' said Balyndar.

'They won't do anything at all,' Girgandor commented with a confident laugh. 'Same as last time. They'll burn to death in our Vraccasfire.'

'How many do you reckon are in that box?'

'A few hundred, maybe.' He thought for a moment then added, 'Too few for an attack.'

'Yes, that's my feeling, too. They would all fit on the ramp.' Balyndar turned the telescope on the road to the north. 'Seems to me this is all far too much effort. They must know we're going to destroy that contraption.'

'A new rehearsal?' suggested Girgandor. 'Perhaps they're working on a design for a ramp that's twice as big.' Balyndar scanned the horizon. 'Still too much effort to go to, especially with this storm, just to find out how our throwing machines and catapults are deployed. Besides, they already have that information.' *There!* He froze, focusing the telescope on a point where he thought he had glimpsed a banner.

Not four heartbeats later he established there was a never-ending stream of bodies running, running, heading for the

Stone Gateway. With water splashing round their feet, raindrops sliding down their faces, some of them in armour, some not, they hurtled on, no shouts or war cries, creating with their progress a dull thunder that was louder than the storm. Neither rain nor wind was impeding their relentless march.

Now they've got more than enough! Balyndar suppressed the fear he was starting to feel. He indicated the army to Girgandor. 'Everything we've got in the way of petroleum and Vraccas fire, get it brought here,' he ordered. 'We'll need all of it.'

'At once.' His deputy was about to rush off.

'Petroleum: *now*.'

'But there are no soldiers on their ramp yet.'

'The fire will slow down the first ones and when the metal's really hot they'll all get burned feet as soon as they try to climb.' Balyndar took out his bugle and sounded the alarm tones for the guards to go out onto the balustrade. 'May Vraccas be with us!'

Once the signal was given, hot petroleum spewed down onto the ramp from the outlets; it all caught fire when a burning torch was thrown down from the ramparts. The construction's burning slope looked breathtaking in the darkness: fiery cascades dripped from the sides, splashing onto the beasts waiting below. Several of the soldiers were soon ablaze.

They're still not advancing. Or fleeing. Balyndar gave the signal for Vraccas fire to follow on the petroleum. Vraccas fire was more viscous and flowed slowly, coating the ramp with a thick, blistering layer of flame.

But the dwarf had miscalculated. The front of the endless column of soldiers sprinted through the puddles of liquid petroleum that now covered the road. Their breeches, boots and even their skin caught fire – but they did not stop. The first of them had reached the base of the ramp and they raced up as far as they could. Any that slipped and fell grabbed hold of the indentations and handles. The next wave surged on over them, trying to get to the top.

'That's . . .' Balyndar's voice faltered. *Vraccas, come to our aid. We need you.*

The monsters kept coming, catching fire and dying, falling off the slope like glowing comets. There was no end to the constant procession. Wind and rain fought with the flames. There was a smell of charred hair, burning flesh and scorched leather. But there was still not a single cry or shout to be heard from the injured and dying, though their torment must have been intolerable.

Nothing deters them. Neither pain nor the prospect of death. 'Girgandor, send for the grappling hooks. Fasten them to chains and catapult them out to catch in the machinery and pulleys. We've got to get that ramp down!'

Taking Keenfire with him, Balyndar went out onto the balustrade. *This has to work.* Otherwise it was only a question of time before the attacking army reached the high end of the ramp. 'Bring out the small catapults,' he ordered. 'Get the slings out, quick! And the spear-launchers.' He told his men to heave the heavy boulders, ammunition for the throwing machines, anything they could, over the walls onto the ramp.

Then what he had been fearing happened: the large stones hit their target but had no effect on the slope. They simply careered down the ramp, dragging some of the monsters with them and making a glowing track through the layer of Vraccas fire. Their destructive power was quite insufficient. And on the horizon the next wave of beasts was already advancing.

The monsters formed a heap of bodies, as with the first attack. They had soon attained and topped the level they had reached the first time. Balyndar glanced down. 'Another ten paces,' he yelled at the guards at his sides. 'Let's have more stones!' It was vital Girgandor destroy the ramp. 'More stones! Send them to Tion, the lot of them!'

'There's a ghaist!' The cry came through the raging wind. 'It's coming! And trolls, too!'

Trolls. That's all we need. Balyndar saw a group of ten huge beasts forcing their way through the crowd. And behind them came the ghaist.

'All catapults! Fire!' *Let's hope something gets through despite the weather.*

The arrows and bolts shot out into the wind, aiming for their targets. But Balyndar could see with the naked eye that the projectiles lost impetus only a few paces out. They would have no effect in this weather. Boulders and fire were more use against this silent army that continued to advance, ignoring all the perils of their campaign. One sacrifice after another, with the sole aim of making it to the top of the ramp and on to the walls.

The giant trolls started to climb the slope, clambering over dead bodies, pushing their way through the wall of flame, never hesitating. They had already reached the wall and were climbing over each other, forming a kind of pyramid. There was no doubt that four of them would get to the gate.

'Stand by!' Balyndar yelled, drawing Keenfire. 'Stones, now! And follow through with petroleum! Turn them into torches!'

The first troll face appeared in front of him; hairy hands

grasped the top of the wall. The beast tensed its muscles and pulled itself up.

'Never!' Balyndar sprang on to the battlements and swung the diamond-studded blade down onto the troll's head. *You shan't come through!* The gems glowed and the blade-edge went straight through the bone. *Not past me!*

The sturdy fingers opened and the troll fell backwards, making way for the next one. Balyndar watched the blood on his weapon get washed away by the rain. The cold wetness ran down his collar, too. 'Come on up!' he challenged, showing the trolls his legendary axe. 'I'll kill every single one of you!'

The dwarves on the walkway cheered.

The trolls unexpectedly grabbed some of the smaller beasts on the ramp and threw them up the last few paces to land on the ramparts.

'Mind out! Incoming!' Balyndar bellowed. 'Don't let them succeed, my warriors!'

Many of the beasts the trolls threw over broke their bones on landing but others rolled themselves into balls on impact and went straight in to the attack. Fights were breaking out on all sides, with the dwarves easily victorious. Their adversaries often had no armour, no weapons to speak of or were not in any position to wield their blades. But the trolls kept up the bombardment. The beasts continued to rain down like raindrops made flesh. The dwarves would eventually tire.

'Keep it up. That's the way. You . . .' And then Balyndar saw the trolls grasping and thrusting the ghaist upwards. His words stuck in his throat.

The boiling hot, burning petroleum gurgled out of the outlets, missing the four trolls on top. The others turned to living fire, limbs ablaze. Skin, flesh, tendons all burned so they could not climb over; the large creatures fell to the ground, killing many others as they landed.

But the ghaist and the four leading trolls had got on to the walkway.

The huge beasts represented difficult opponents for the veteran dwarf warriors, but they were well qualified to defeat them. It was up to Balyndar to take on the ghaist. He had to use Keenfire to destroy it. No conventional weapon would have the slightest effect.

Vraccas, spare me and my people if there's another explosion when I hit the ghaist. He had nearly reached it and raised his axe. 'I know you can't stand up to me,' he called into the wind.

The ghaist yanked a sand barrel that was intended to extinguish fires out of its mount on the walkway and hurled it at the dwarf with one hand. Balyndar dodged the missile and aimed a blow with Keenfire at the ghaist. But it managed to duck under his swing and pressed its outstretched hand directly into Balyndar's face. To the dwarf's astonishment, it did not try to gouge out his eyes or crush his skull.

Balyndar's features started to tingle. His scalp prickled and his throat felt warm. A strange rushing sound pervaded his mind, a curiously attractive seductive whispering.

It's magic! Balyndar snorted and tried to hit the ghaist, yanking his head away. 'I'm not falling under your master's spell!' he yelled, advancing on the being that was now retreating, trying to avoid being struck. Keenfire glowed brightly, wanting to bury itself in the adversary. The ghaist passed through the rows of fighting dwarves and beasts. Balyndar ignored these secondary figures and concentrated on eliminating the main opponent. His attacks were full of hatred.

When they had arrived at the left-hand tower, the ghaist unexpectedly jumped over the dwarf's head to get onto the battlements, where it stared down through the eye slits with their whitish shine. From there it catapulted itself back onto the Stone Gateway path. A crowd of beasts broke its fall.

That's lost me my chance. 'Get back here!' Balyndar looked down, very tense, and saw the ghaist land. At once it began to trot off, forcing its way through the river of monsters that were heading for the ramp. 'I'll get you next time. You shall die! And it'll be me and Keenfire that does it.' He ran a hand over his rain-wet face. The ghaist had left no footprints and the lingering touch of his fingers still felt odd. *He was attempting a magic spell. Probably the same spell his sovereign uses to muster his army.* 'You won't break our resolve! I . . .'

Balyndar did not notice until it was too late that he had been enticed away from the second tower. He turned quickly back to where the trolls had first appeared over the wall.

Standing tall, Balyndar felt the blood drain away from his face: the rag-tag army had reached the vital point. The army swept over the top of the wall like a torrent, forcing the dwarves aside by sheer weight of numbers. Several of the orcs, humans, gnomes and other beasts were on fire; they climbed up to the gate and took several steps before collapsing and dying.

The defending force could wreak havoc for all they were worth; that flood of bodies was never going to stop. But the rag-tag army was not interested in small skirmishes and saved them the effort: its soldiers flung themselves down, ignoring all risks, to reach the courtyard, creating a steaming carpet of bodies.

Eventually the monsters will survive the fall and scramble to their feet, inundating the dwarf kingdom. Balyndar glanced at the Stone Gateway; the river of attackers was continuous.

I think I need some divine inspiration.

On arriving somewhere for the first time, always behave as a cautious friend. And if you return there later, behave equally carefully.

Dwarf saying

XXV

Somewhere in the Outer Lands

Tungdil was aware he could not escape the axe blade.

But before it hit him, the acront cut through a heavily armoured beast whose scream ended abruptly. While the weapon sliced through iron, skin and bone, emerging in a cloud of shimmering blood, the dwarf was given two heart-beats of reprieve in which to act. With great presence of mind, Tungdil drew out two daggers that he held crosswise to protect himself.

The weapons clanged against each other. The impact pushed Tungdil sliding along the floor until his strength gave out and he fell backwards. The reddened blade appeared again in his face, spattering Tungdil with red drops. He quickly rolled to one side and avoided the acront's attempt to stamp on his head. *Only just!*

He leaped to his feet and saw four monsters where he had been standing before. In contrast to the ones that had been defeated, these four were collaborating, working together in a formation. Two of them had long spears for defence and one had a leather strap to use as a sling for shooting spiked morningstar balls. The last of them had seven throwing spears ready. And they were waiting for the acront.

Tungdil put more distance between himself and the huge warrior, who had turned away from him and, whirling his axe, headed for the four challengers. It seemed he was trying to deflect anything thrown at him.

Where is it? Where is it? He searched around until he had located the second precious note Beligata had tossed his way.

On reading it, he learned that a weak point did exist on the body of an acront, on the back where the spinal column met the pelvis. A hefty blow on that specific area, it said in the healers' manual, could induce a short-term paralysis, whereas a stab to that part could permanently destroy the nerves to the lower body.

Looking at the acront with all the heavy armour it wore, Tungdil realised he had nothing that would pierce that steel. *What use is the knowledge, then?*

'Is that all you've got for me?' he shouted to Beligata, waving the note.

'Yes, it is,' she shouted back.

He gave a hollow laugh and glanced back through the heap of discarded weaponry. Amongst the miscellaneous assortment, he detected the long handle of a blacksmith's hammer.

Should be able to deliver a hefty blow with this. When he weighed it in his hands, he calculated it was twice as heavy as an axe. It would not be suitable for quick moves. *So how do I get the berserk maniac to keep still?*

The acront pushed the spears aside as they were launched at him, and dodged the morningstar balls. Shouldering the mighty hammer, Tungdil walked around, studying the floor to see if there was anything he could use against his adversary. Any uneven surface or crack that might serve as a trap.

At the same time he kept an eye on how the fight was going. The acront had given up on avoiding the morningstars. He caught hold of one of them and hurled it back with all his might. However, he did not aim at the beast who had sent it, but at one of the spear-wielders. Tungdil frowned to see the metal spikes hit the beast's shoulder, forcing the joint out of its socket. The armour came away as well. *This veteran has stupendous strength.*

The beast fell to the ground with a scream, its green blood drenching its opponent and forming a pool on the arena floor. The giant warrior drew his sword and strode onwards, continuing to ignore the dwarf and concentrating on the group of beasts.

Word must have got round that we dwarves have lost all our fights so far, he thought with black humour. *He doesn't even see me as a threat.* Tungdil kissed the ring Balyndis had given him and made sure he kept pace with the acront. Vraccas, it seemed, would give him his chance.

The acront threw his axe flat, in a disdainful gesture; it whirled through the air at the three monsters, hitting the second spear-carrier with the blade and slicing through half the creature's chest. When the long handle spun, it struck the morningstar thrower in the belly, making him double up in pain.

Tungdil admired the beast's stamina and courage: he did not waver or give a finger's breadth. *Good lad. Keep him busy for me.*

Tungdil was about ten paces away from his adversary's back. He was close enough to the place he needed to hit with his hammer.

The beast threw the first spear. The missile was aimed at the helmet but the acront parried the blow, deflecting the dangerous tip.

Now. Tungdil kept in the acront's shadow and raised his arm to take aim. *Vraccas, make my aim true.*

But the acront made a sudden move to the side, leaping at the foe who kept throwing spears at him. The dwarf's blow missed. The towering warrior jumped up in the air to dive like a bird of prey onto his opponent, sword held vertically in both hands.

I know where you're coming down. Tungdil ran over and swung the hammer for a second time. The acront landed and split the beast from the collar blade to the foot. The noises the creature produced were unlike any Tungdil had ever heard.

Tungdil was concentrating on the weak point by the acront's pelvis. That was where he had to slam the iron head of the hammer against the armour, as if wielding a metal lightning bolt. Tensing his muscles, he put everything he had into the blow.

The hammer hit home, the head destroying the craftsmanship of the armour. Tungdil was jubilant, knowing his aim had been true.

The three-pace-tall acronta shuddered. Instead of the normal low roar, there came a high-pitched hiss like a boiling kettle giving off steam. His body went stiff and then collapsed like jelly. The warrior fell forward, burying the bodies of the injured combatants.

The creatures watching from their cages ceased their noise. This had not been expected. Surprise struck them dumb.

Tungdil could see by the steady rise and fall of the armoured breast that the acront still lived. *Paralysed. Not dead.*

'Good work, Beligata!' Tungdil kissed the vraccasium ring. Then, looking up to the judging panel in their box, he walked over to the acront and placed the hammer on its helmet. The judges would understand that a further blow would be final. 'Is that enough proof, or do I have to kill the veteran? He has fought bravely, and could yet fight again.'

'Knock him unconscious,' urged Hargorin. 'He'll be up again any moment.'

Hardly had the red-haired dwarf's words died away before the beasts in their prison cells broke into frenetic cheering. They had shaken off the shock and were celebrating Tungdil's achievement.

The sedative gas came hissing down to quell their enthusiastic response, and one row of prisoners after the next fell asleep.

'Go on! Is it enough?' Tungdil had just time to repeat his question to the judges before he succumbed to the gas and passed out.

When Tungdil came round he recognised the library where he had spent more hours of his captivity than in his wire cell. Beligata was lying at his side, as were Hargorin and Gosalyn: all still unconscious. They all had fresh linen clothing.

Carmondai, in similar garments, was seated on the black and white tiled floor. He greeted Tungdil. 'Good, you've woken up. I think they wanted to attack me.'

Four armoured acronta stood facing them, and one of them, much larger than the others, sat in the middle on a throne-like chair made of ornately-carved and decorated steel. The armour worn was not intended for combat. It was too sumptuous for that. The visor had a double image: a demon's face with one side laughing and the other side weeping. Round the brow there was a crown with long hooked points.

'I shan't be able to stop them.'

'But you defeated one of their number. They'll respect you. They have only scorn for me.' He cleared his throat. 'Scorn and the gift of hunger.'

The largest of the acronta opened a gauntleted fist, releasing a rolled parchment that dropped at Tungdil's feet. He stood and took a deep breath in and out to rid his system of the last of the gas. He picked the message up and read the dwarf runes.

> Your task is complete – one of you has defeated one of us. What is more, you spared his life.
>
> Your opponent's name is Tsatòn nar Draigònt and during his career he killed one hundred and four monsters. Tsatòn runs his own unit and was expecting an award following success in the contest.
>
> Your skilful stroke has robbed him of that hope. He will have to wait a further ten of your cycles before he is granted a second opportunity.
>
> Because I promised you: you are now free to go wherever you wish. Take the paper with my seal on it. My words shall serve as proof of my decision. Show it whenever you need to.

Underneath, the same text was written again in the acronta script.

Tungdil looked up. 'I am glad you are keeping your word.' *Is this the emperor-mother, I wonder?*

The largest of the acronta growled quietly. It was a sound denoting agreement, the dwarf thought.

The emperor-mother rose and came over to him, bending the knee to get to his level. She was handed a slate. Even crouching down, she was still two paces taller than Tungdil. She smelled of weapon oil, warm metal and fresh straw.

Using a piece of chalk, she wrote the following in the dwarf language: 'I had hoped to talk to you face to face but our languages are very different. We will stick to runes. I sent out scouts to observe the botoicans and we have learned some astounding things about them.'

Tungdil pretended he knew nothing about the acronta language. 'I am honoured by your assistance.'

'We found and followed one botoican in particular. The scouts think she is a female älf. She was accompanied by two warriors from her own race. One wears a mask over his mouth that prevents him speaking. The other one carries a spear and has armour plating incorporated directly into his skin.'

'Aiphatòn has joined the botoican?' Carmondai's expression slipped, making the Ido-mark on his face lopsided. 'Didn't you tell me he wanted to search until he had found the last of the älfar? He wanted to eliminate them all.'

'I assume it was down to him that both cities were destroyed,' Tungdil replied. 'But I've no idea why he should have wanted to join forces with the magician. A trick to get close and then bide his time before moving in for the kill?'

Carmondai wrinkled his brow. 'How would an älf-woman learn the art of a botoican? There were a few of us who could do a little magic, but it was nowhere near mass manipulation.' He thought for a while and then looked at the emperor-mother as if afraid what answer she might give. 'The älf with the gagging mask: what is his name?'

'The other älf knows him as Nodûcor. But different names have been heard.' So read the words on the slate.

Tungdil glanced at the historian's face. *He is afraid!*

'What do you suspect?' he asked carefully.

'It would be . . .' Carmondai was having trouble finding the words. 'The worst thing imaginable.'

'Worst thing for whom?'

'*All* of us.' Carmondai was looking at the giant ruler of the acronta. 'Have you noticed any instances of powerful, destructive winds in recent orbits or cycles? Unnatural winds bearing feathers, petals or pieces of gold leaf?'

'Yes,' came the written reply.

Carmondai clapped a hand over his mouth and stared in horror at the response. Tungdil did not think the älf was putting on an act. *He knows something.*

'What sort of wind?' Tungdil asked the emperor-mother.

'Four or five cycles ago. Our scouts reported large armies being mustered. They attacked each other. We were too far away to see exactly, but in the middle of the battle a storm arose with wind blowing in all directions at once. We observed feathers, pebbles and strange smells. The power of the winds tore the armies to pieces.'

'How did it end?' whispered Carmondai.

'The plain was covered in blood and powdered bones, broken armour and death.' The chalk scratched over the slate. 'No survivors.'

Tungdil grabbed the älf by the shoulder. 'What do you know?'

'It's the Voice of the Wind.' Carmondai's black eyes flickered between the dwarf and the acront ruler. 'It's a legend. It tells of Samusin granting a disgraced älf the ability to speak with the winds. That would explain the mask with the gag, the devastating storm, and the end of the armies.'

'Not long ago there was a similar storm front heading south,' the emperor-mother wrote. 'There was more damage than is usual when the winds are high. The gusts slashed the skin of living creatures.'

'That's the Wind of Transience,' Carmondai explained. 'It smells of stone and rain and carries blades of basalt and obsidian. If it rose in the west, it would have been the Wind of War. That one smells of iron and soil and carries fragments of gold leaf and splinters of glass. These winds cause utter devastation.' He ran his slender fingers through his long brown hair. 'It can only be the Voice of the Wind. By all the dark gods!'

'Too many puzzles that we can't solve from a distance.' It occurred to Tungdil that Sha'taï must have made an enemy of this group. *Aiphatòn, the Voice of the Wind and a magician who can conjure up whole armies at his behest. That's an invincible combination. This implies the elves' prophecy has in part come true. There is a threat.* 'We have to see for ourselves.'

'A large number of beasts under the command of a copper-helmet were heading south, in the shadow of the storm. Heading for where the entrance to Girdlegard is located,' the emperor-mother added. 'They had something they were taking with them. It was thought to be some kind of siege tower.'

'An attack?' Hargorin muttered sleepily as he tried to sit up. The red-bearded dwarf shook the other two sleeping figures by the shoulders. 'On the Stone Gateway?' Tungdil was annoyed with himself for not having woken his friends earlier. He had been too distracted by the conversation with the emperor-mother.

'We don't know. But it's possible,' said Carmondai slowly. 'The more I think about it, the less the whole thing hangs together. Even if an älf-woman had acquired the arts of a botoican – how did she meet Sha'taï?'

Tungdil felt confident in his decision. 'We're leaving now.' He turned to the emperor-mother. 'Your people hunt and destroy evil. I . . .'

'I know what you are going to say,' she wrote, white chalk

crumbling powder on to the tiled floor. 'But this is none of our business.' She growled. 'However, in view of your courage, I shall send a group of veterans with you. They can observe the situation and protect you at the same time. If my spies have overlooked anything which would make it necessary for us to intervene, the warriors will report back to me on that.'

'My thanks,' said Tungdil. 'That will be a great help.'

The emperor-mother got to her feet, towering over the dwarves. The many galleries of the library seemed to have shrunk in comparison. The lamps reflected on her splendidly decorated armour. 'If the älf ever crosses our path again, he will die,' she wrote in älfar language and held it out for Carmondai to read. 'On the spot.'

She threw the slate down at his feet. It shattered. She left the room.

Tungdil saw in his companions' faces that they were now wide awake and looking at him expectantly. 'Let us go and accomplish our task,' he said. *And let us pray to Vraccas that we can solve the mysteries that surround Aiphatòn.*

Girdlegard
Grey Mountains
Kingdom of the Fifthling dwarves
Stone Gateway
6496th solar cycle, summer

'The wind is dropping!' Despite his horror at the fact the beasts had gained access to the gate via the ramp, Balyndar noticed the gusts were less forceful. This meant that they could now deploy the biggest machines and catapults.

He ran over to the nearest apparatus for launching clay pots, lit their fuses in the magazine using a flint and swung the barrel round to direct fire at the attackers on the walkway.

The primed wicks gave off black smoke and the pots were immediately engulfed in flames.

Death to you all! Balyndar released the mechanism and the re-loading device sent the blazing pots off, one after the other, in an arc over the heads of his own soldiers, to hit the monsters. The enemy were knocked off their feet, enveloped in flaming liquid that spattered on those standing nearby, turning them into living torches. The heavy-duty catapults were trundled back into action. Leather bags full of petroleum and large stones were launched through the air, aimed at the monsters milling about, waiting their turn to storm the ramparts.

Then a loud metallic tearing, followed by rumbling and creaking sounds, was heard. The noise went on for several breath-lengths.

Balyndar had fired off all the missiles from the magazine. He took a look over the battlements at the gateway. A shout of utter delight escaped his lips. The dwarves had managed to throw their grappling hooks into the mechanism holding the metal ramp – which was by now thoroughly ablaze – and brought it crashing down. The enemy's path up to the battlements fell and foes in their hundreds died, involuntary missiles crushing those they plummeted onto. The last of the remaining monsters clambered up the pile of bodies, desperate to reach the walls, but it wasn't high enough.

Balyndar gave a grim smile. *They won't get a chance to form a ramp with the corpses like they did last time.*

'Send up the dragon-kites!' he commanded, raising

Keenfire in the air. 'Keep the inner gates shut. Flood the courtyard with petroleum and set fire to it!' He approached the enemies already on the walkway who were hesitating, afraid to jump down the other side. 'You will regret ever having set foot on my fortress!'

The monsters seemed suddenly to have been introduced to the concept of fear. They pushed and shoved each other in their panic to find an escape route that simply was not there. Death came to meet them. The dwarves rushed the intruders from both sides at once, swinging axes, cudgels and morningstars.

'We are the Children of the Smith!' Balyndar hurried over to the battlements, laughing, slashing troll fingers away from the stonework so that the huge creatures plunged to their deaths, burying more beasts as they fell. The last one was just about to heave itself over the ramparts when Keenfire struck and killed it with one blow straight through its ugly face. The gems and inlay on the axe shone out and the dwarves cheered their commander.

'The victory is ours!' Balyndar yelled, holding up his bloodied axe. 'To Vraccas!'

'To Vraccas!' his warriors echoed as they hurled themselves at any remaining enemies, a few hundred of whom – mostly unarmed and unprotected – were clinging to the portal doors.

Looking at their repulsive faces and wide-open eyes, Balyndar saw a kind of awakening. Their minds seemed to be coming free from the influence and indifference that had characterised their previous behaviour. Now they were reduced to a quivering mass of monsters surrounded by raging dwarves, flashing blades, a gaping void behind them and another in front of them. And there was no prospect of mercy.

'Kill them all!' Balyndar saw that the flames in the courtyard were as high as a house; the black smoke smothered the few that had jumped from the walls and survived. The rest met their deaths in the liquid fire the defenders sprayed on them. Balyndar turned his eyes towards the north. *We shall wipe them out. Once and for all.*

The retreat had begun on the Stone Gateway road. There was fire everywhere, and broken boulders were raining down on the mass of soldiers, the stones rolling destructively and crushing the enemy in large numbers.

Kites up in the sky, tethered on long ropes, dropped their burning freight in places out of range of the catapult machines. The monsters were trapped, hesitating between the pools of raging flames; they fell victim to successive waves of bolts, arrows, spears, stone and fire. For the first time since the start of their attack on the fortress, the beasts broke out in shouts, screams and roars. The spell was broken and they lost control. Suddenly they were susceptible to all the fear and pain they were experiencing.

We must have wiped out hundreds of thousands of them. Balyndar placed Keenfire down on the battlement edge and gazed out in satisfaction at the courtyard and at the road leading to the ramparts. Swathes of black smoke obscured the scene but the skilled artillery crews did not need to see their targets. There were no targets now. All the enemies had been dealt with.

The dwarves erupted in jubilant cheers, the sound echoing back from the cliffs, as if the Grey Mountains were rejoicing with them. Balyndar jumped down, grinning, clapping his men on their shoulders to congratulate them, consoling the injured and praising them for their courage. He spoke to each and every dwarf.

But he knew it was not over yet.

The ghaist had escaped.

Spreading his arms, Balyndar asked for quiet. 'Today is an orbit we shall long remember,' he announced. 'We have protected Girdlegard once more and will continue to do so.' He pointed to the defeated beasts on the walls with his weapon, then to those in the yard, and to the army outside the fortress. 'Now it is time to clear up the mess. We must treat our injured, check over the catapults, and refill our supplies so we can be ready for the next onslaught whenever it comes.' He lowered Keenfire. 'And it will come, we can be sure of that. The powers of evil want to take over Girdlegard.'

'We'll see them off. We'll give them the same send-off,' called a female dwarf, whose helmet and face were dripping with the blood of defeated foes.

Balyndar nodded to her. 'Vraccas is with us, as he is so often. We are the Children of the Smith.'

'We are the Children of the Smith!' the massed dwarves echoed enthusiastically.

Balyndar smiled. 'Let's get started. Girgandor will be in charge.' He turned back to look at the inferno raging on the roadway, where the last of the enemy were meeting their deaths. Amongst the corpses there were a few injured creatures trying desperately to escape but they were still being shot at and soon all were dead. Liquid petroleum and Vraccas fire consumed the bodies, spreading the smell of roasting flesh.

Balyndar ran his hand over his face but encountered nothing unusual. His people would have said if the ghaist's fingers had left a mark of some kind. *He was trying to force me under his master's spell. When that did not work he withdrew.* The ghaist would be returning to its master to report that the Children of the Smith could not be won over like the other creatures. *There'll be another army soon enough.*

The unknown enemy had learned much about his prospects of success at the Stone Gateway. Twice the enemy had sent thousands upon thousands of soldiers to their deaths to investigate. *They will build a new ramp. It will be stronger and likely the entire width of the roadway. That's what I'd do in their place.* If the new ramp were constructed so as to reach up to the edge of the gate and able to withstand bombardment, then the next rag-tag army could be smaller in number. Swift victory would be assured.

Balyndar hoped that building a mobile threat of this kind must present some kind of a challenge to their foe, though the Outer Lands had enough beasts to provide a third army to attack the dwarves.

But if the ramp were bigger, it would present a larger target for our artillery. No help, though, if that ferocious wind occurred again to cover the attack, because many of their devices would be put out of action and the crews handling the catapults would be badly injured when they went outside.

Balyndar looked up at the mountainsides to left and right. *We will have to install defences out on the roadway far beyond our gates if we want to deter the next assault.* He would start planning this very orbit, despite the victory celebrations; he would meet with his mother and the top engineers to discuss strategy. It would have to involve constructions that could withstand all weathers, operate round the clock and have a devastating effect.

Have we got time to think up something new? Balyndar thought the gap between attacks had been three cycles long. *I need answers.* He decided to send messages to all the dwarf realms and to the elves and Coïra, to see if they could help solve this problem. A stronger storm wind would make defence virtually impossible.

The third attack might well be successful.

Girdlegard
Black Mountains
Kingdom of the Thirdling dwarves
Eastern Gate
6496th solar cycle, summer

Rognor was touched when he saw the life-size statue hewn out of black granite. It was placed where the elves had waited to be admitted to Girdlegard – waiting far longer than originally thought, following the rigorous examinations they were subjected to.

'This is more than I deserve,' he was finally able to murmur, his throat dry.

All around him were heaps of gifts the elves had brought for the Thirdlings.

'No, it is less than you deserve,' a female elf contradicted him. Her name had slipped his mind. 'Ever since the day you dealt with the mad Phenîlas, every elf will carry your name and the story of a dwarf's brave deed into the new homeland.' She inclined her head to him. 'You have cemented the friendship between our two races.'

She turned and left with her ten companions. They would take the same route as the many hundreds of elves before them. Ocâstia and her sorânïons in their white armour kept to the background. They had completed their task and limited themselves to observation.

The tent city at the gates no longer existed. Canvas tarpaulins, stakes and heaters had been removed. The river of elves had now poured into Girdlegard.

Rognor was not surprised that not a single älf had been discovered amongst them. Älfar had only been found while Phenîlas, in his state of mental disturbance, had been in charge. His reign of terror claimed innocent figures that were only declared to have been black-eyes to prevent an uprising.

But now that Phenîlas was no more, the deaths had ceased.

And where would älfar possibly have come from? Rognor placed a hand on his stone likeness. It was so lifelike he thought he could use it to take his place – given a bit of paint here and there – if there was a tedious meeting or feast he was supposed to officiate at.

The last elves, a family of five, came to stand in front of the chancellor. Ocâstia and her sorânïons had checked them. The two youngest daughters placed at Rognor's feet a sumptuous robe embroidered with pearls and a chest of glittering emeralds of extraordinary purity.

'May Lorimbur be my witness. This is too much.' Rognor had to refuse the gift. He tugged at his blue beard in discomfort. 'We were merely doing our duty. You should take the jewels to purchase all the things you are going to need.' He handed the container back to the elves, but they did not reach out to take it.

'It belongs to you, Chancellor.' The unknown elf smiled at him in gratitude. 'You won't remember perhaps, but my loved ones and I were picked on by Phenîlas and held to be suspects. My youngest' – he placed his hand on the shoulder of the girl to his right – 'would have died at his hands if had it not been for you. For this I owe you ten times what I can give you now. So please accept this. If you have no use for the jewels yourself, then give them to a good cause.' He knelt before the dwarf and made to kiss his feet. That was a bit much for Rognor. 'Stop!' he cried, preventing the gesture. 'I accept your gratitude with pleasure – and by all means praise my name and my people – but I only let defeated enemies, preferably dead ones, kiss my feet.'

The elf gave a broad smile and strode out, his family in tow.

'May Sitalia be with you,' the girl said, waving to him. 'I shall name my first child after you.'

Rognor placed the chest on the table next to him and sighed with relief, looking at Ocâstia. 'We've done it.'

'Indeed.' The female sorânïan ordered her officers to go on ahead and get the horses saddled. 'An elf child bearing the name of a dwarf,' she said with a smile. 'That I will like to see. And I shall take to preparing my slow-cooked potted meat using the recipe you gave me. Can there be a better indicator of friendship between our peoples?'

'I would never have thought it possible.' Rognor could not take his eyes off the pile of offerings. The table had the look of a treasure house. 'If I were a Fourthling I would be keen to know where these precious emeralds are to be found. They've given me a king's ransom.'

'Because you ensured they kept the most precious thing: their lives.' Ocâstia came to sit next to him, looking at the gifts and then at him. 'Given Phenîlas' disturbed state of mind, there would have been many more victims if he had been allowed to continue. It would have led to insurrection or massacre. You, Chancellor, did something very important.' She wiped away her tears. 'What a king you would make.'

'Are you feeling a bit sentimental?' He could not stop the teasing tone in his voice.

Ocâstia laughed out loud and searched for a handkerchief. She blew her nose and dabbed away the tears. 'We have spent a good deal of time in each other's company, dwarf, and I have grown fond of you. I appreciate your wisdom and your insight and your great heart. When I depart with my officers' – she swallowed and stretched out her hand – 'it is a friend I leave behind.' Ocâstia gripped his hand. 'Thank you for the trust you gave me, Rognor Mortalblow. You have heard many of us express gratitude, but you will have to put up with me doing it as well.'

He mumbled in his beard. 'Do you have a new mission?'

'I shall be riding back to Ti Lesîndur where I'm sure the Naishïon will give us another task. There is plenty afoot at the other gates. And I think the sorânïons are doing spot inspections in the elf realms, for the security of all. Random inspections will deter black-eyes from infiltrating us. That's if there are any still in existence.'

'Hidden, perhaps,' Rognor was sorry that the elf-woman was leaving. 'They'll always keep hidden. Like evil of all kinds.' She had shown herself to be exceptionally open, keen to learn and keen to teach; they had played strategy games together and he seldom won. But she was never competitive. She also told him about the new elf settlements and the Naishïon's plans for a united elf empire, saying a new era had begun: the era of cooperation.

'Wise words, Chancellor.' Ocâstia reached into her purse and pulled out a thimble-like object wrapped in red velvet. 'Take this. It represents the blessing of my goddess. Wear it secretly. It will save your life when you are least expecting it.'

Rognor's eyes widened. 'My thanks.' He felt ashamed, having nothing to offer in return. But then his eye fell on the gaming-board on which they had played. He picked up the model chariot and scratched the rune of his own name and that of the Lorimbur sign on the piece with his dagger.

'It is nothing compared with what you have given me. I can send you away with my god's blessing but I'd feel better if I made a promise.' Rognor grasped her right hand and placed the figure in her palm. 'Whenever you are in need: send the chariot and I'll come running to help you.'

'Do you swear that?'

'I swear it.' More tears flowed down her beautiful cheeks.

'You would be a great king. Who knows if Deathbringer will ever return?' she breathed, tightening her hand round the figurine. 'Fare well, dwarf. And I hope that when we meet again it will be a happy occasion.' Ocâstia got to her feet, wiped away her tears and left the room.

Rognor watched her go. *Such a shame. I shall miss her.* He unrolled the velvet wrapped around her gift. Inside he found a little silver brooch with intricate engraving – the writing was not in the elf language nor in any other script he recognised. Several symbols had been combined to create a single ornament. He could not read it.

He was not surprised. Elves from outside had their own culture, their own dialects and their own way of writing. *So Sitalia's seal can look like this, too.* He rubbed the symbol, pouring himself some beer with the other hand. *I hope you will serve me well.* He fixed the brooch to the underside of the collar of the black leather garment he wore under his chainmail.

While he emptied his tankard he mused over recent cycles he had spent with Ocâstia.

No one had expected the rush of would-be immigrant elves to be so huge. It was good for Girdlegard, in his view, to have these new settlers. Cooperation between elf and dwarf would be the best defence against attack from outside. *The Naishïon won't hide away any longer.*

News from the various human kingdoms also made him feel optimistic.

At first he had been sceptical about Rodario's capabilities as emperor, but the actor was doing well – if you ignored his penchant for extravagant attire and overlong speeches. There were no ongoing quarrels between the rulers, and people were following the emperor's suggestions and decrees. Apart from little arguments amongst the nobility, there was a general atmosphere of peace. The gods must have sent it. As soon as Rodario turned up with the child in tow – though she was a young woman now – the hottest tempers cooled and the emperor's witticisms calmed the disputing parties.

Coïra, it was said, was exploring the power of the source and training her pupils, teaching them magic spells. Of course the famuli had to keep their distance from the magic field so as not to become prisoners like the maga herself – which did make things more complicated – but they managed.

If there was good news from the Grey Mountains, things would almost be perfect. *Everyone united.* Rognor stared at the bottom of the tankard. He stood up to get a refill. *But I don't trust that Sha'taï girl.*

The chancellor left the room and marched along to the kitchen where there was a barrel of beer. One more tankard and then he would go to bed and dream about the gifts the elves had left with him; he had to figure out what to do with it all. Rognor filled his jug with the foaming black brew. *I wonder what my master is up to right now in the Outer Lands?*

Apart from the danger threatening from the north, the

fate of Tungdil and of King Hargorin was unknown. They had set off over the Grey Mountains many cycles ago. After that there had been no word.

He remembered the lively discussion High King Boïndil had led, suggesting a search party be sent out. But the other dwarf monarchs had turned down this idea. It was madness, anyway, to travel through the mountains; they did not want to lose more valuable dwarves. There had been a charged atmosphere, but finally it was agreed that they would wait a total of five cycles. Three of those cycles were past now.

Ocâstia's words rang in his ears.

Me, a good king? He had acted as a king for all intents and purposes for a long time, whereas Hargorin had only pretended to be a vassal of the älfar.

He drained his tankard. 'Maybe it *is* time to be a king. Crown and title and everything.' He did not doubt the Thirdlings would support him. *And if Hargorin returns, then . . .*

With the confusing realisation that he had no answer, he left the kitchen.

The idea of being ruler of the Thirdlings became firmer in his mind. After all, he already had a nice statue. There could hardly be a better candidate.

Tungdil told me he had had fortress after fortress built. He had authority over those who had once been loyal to the Gålran and his like.

And when the mercenaries he had gathered around him started clamouring for the power he had, he killed their leaders and destroyed the golden towers of the Gålran Zhadar to demonstrate his dominion.

No trace of the hated former ruler should remain, he decreed.

But in private he thought: you shall have no other gods beside me.

Secret notes for
The Writings of Truth
written under duress by Carmondai

XXVI

Somewhere in the Outer Lands

You could easily forget where we are. On the tenth orbit, hilly grasslands with occasional copses formed the landscape the dwarves, the älf and the acronta were marching through. Narrow valleys alternated with plains bordered by small hills no higher than three hundred paces.

Tungdil's party had no idea of the location of the acronta hive where they had spent over two cycles. Blindfolded, they had been carried bodily by the acronta for two orbits. Apart from refreshment breaks when the scarves were lifted, they had seen nothing of their journey. On the third orbit the head coverings were removed. There had been little variation in the landscape since then.

It was warm but not so much as to make them sweat. However, the pace they set was demanding.

The grass rustled under their feet and insects buzzed round them. Luggage had been kept to a minimum, with very little in the way of provisions included. They drank from streams, gathered fruit on the way and occasionally the acronta killed animals for food.

It reminded Tungdil of his trek with Ireheart in the company of Djerůn and the maga Andôkai, when they tried to keep the homeland safe.

But this is different. In order to save Girdlegard, they had to traverse the Outer Lands, and instead of Djerůn, they now had five acronta in full armour, strangely marching more quietly than the dwarves who had little in the way of equipment. For the Towers That Walk, the urgent pace set by the dwarves merely meant they lengthened their stride.

We're covering up to fifty miles an orbit but they must think we're snails. A bead of sweat stung Tungdil's eye. They kept up a constant jog, heading for the location the scouts had reported coming across Aiphatòn and his troops.

Tsatòn nar Draigònt was in command, the veteran whose life Tungdil had spared. They communicated with him using signs or scribbles in the soil.

Tungdil regretted having to leave the four-storeyed library. *There was so much knowledge that could have helped us.*

The veteran acronta led them to a group of trees for a rest break. 'Our scouts leave messages for us here,' they were told. 'We have many places like this, dead letter boxes, if a scout can't hang around to wait for us.'

'Good trick.' Hargorin was wearing a light suit of borrowed armour he had adjusted for his needs. None of them had properly fitting armour. There had been no time to do other than take what they were offered. The dwarves were unhappy about this. They also did not like the weapons they had been landed with: badly balanced steel dumped by some beast. 'It's a good thing the Towers That Walk don't roam Girdlegard.'

'They wouldn't be your enemies. It might be no bad thing to have them there for protection.' Carmondai was dressed in reinforced leather. He liked the look and it fit his body well. He was the only one of them to have been allowed his own weapon back. The acronta had confiscated Bloodthirster when they were first captured, recognising its unique nature. Beligata had not attempted to fight for it.

They advanced into the wood, with two acronta going first and three bringing up the rear.

Tsatòn led them through to a small clearing that had some rocks at one edge. They settled there, the armed giants keeping watch as the dwarves and the älf rested and ate the fruit they had picked en route. Carmondai took out some paper and did a successful sketch of the clearing and their whole company.

A master of word and image. Tungdil was impressed.

The veteran opened up a small chamber in one of the stones to retrieve a locked metal box. Pressing symbols on the top in a particular order, he got the lid open.

Tungdil noted the code. *Just in case.*

Tsatòn took out a parchment scroll and unrolled it. The message was in acronta shorthand that Tungdil could not quite follow. Something about a village and a period of time. The frowns on the other dwarves' faces showed they were experiencing similar difficulty reading it. The acronta scratched a translation in dwarf runes on the ground. They all chose to let him believe they could not read any acronta script.

'There is a village behind the hill they can force to join their army.' Hargorin read, taking out his flask.

'Might be four thousand souls,' Tsatòn wrote.

'That's not very many.' Carmondai looked weird with his dark eyes. It was sight the others simply could not get used to.

'Four thousand is nothing. If they head for the Stone Gateway the Fifthlings will soon deal with them,' Gosalyn threw in. 'We've got catapults and spear-throwers that . . .'

'The Voice of the Wind trumps all of that,' the älf interrupted her. 'Its power is legendary. Don't forget the ashont themselves have told us about the regions laid waste by the north wind. Think about it: flying blades of basalt and obsidian that can tear through the slightest gap in someone's armour. And then the sheer force of the gusts.' Carmondai turned back to his sketchbook, chucking away the core of the apple he had been eating.

'Before we decide strategy, we need to have a good look at whatever's on the other side of the hill,' said Tungdil. 'It's vital we find out what has happened to Aiphatòn and what's brought about the change of heart.'

'That's if the black-eyes was ever being honest in the first place.' Gosalyn spat out a cherry stone and was fiddling with her belt buckle.

'He certainly was. As far as I know, he betrayed his own people and poisoned them,' Carmondai intervened in the talk again. 'Why would he make things difficult for himself and go to the trouble of attacking Girdlegard from outside when he'd had every opportunity earlier to take the whole place over with his troops after Lot-Ionan died?'

'An älf will always take an älf's part,' Hargorin muttered. He was carving a new handle for the long axe he was given; curls of shaved wood were collecting in his red beard. 'I know you lot.'

'You used to *serve* my lot,' retorted Carmondai, still sketching. 'For quite a long time, at that. And you cope with your conscience by saying that the entire time you really were on the side of the good.' He stopped drawing and glared at Hargorin, his eye sockets dark. 'Does that make it right, King of the Thirdlings? Weren't there orbits when you enjoyed the power you had when you led the Desirers and went round oppressing humans who never used to accord you any respect?'

'You have a sharp tongue and it's full of poison,' Hargorin

snapped. 'I know your kind. The Triplets were no better.' He pointed the new axe handle at the veteran. 'We should let the acronta eat you. Nobody needs you now with them showing us the way. And the stuff you know hasn't helped us one jot so far. I doubt you're of any use at all.'

Gosalyn and Beligata grinned in anticipation.

'Why don't we vote on it,' suggested the red-haired dwarf. 'What do you all say?'

Tungdil helped himself to some of the spiced dried meat from their provisions. 'Leave him be. We've got enough stuff to worry about without thinking about feeding an old älf to the acronta.'

The other dwarves laughed. It was clear they would not regret Carmondai's passing, in whatever way it occurred. The historian threw Tungdil a quick glance and went back to his pen and paper. Then he stored the page wrapped in waxed paper in his leather pouch. 'You will certainly have need of me,' he murmured. 'Treat me well and I shall help you.' His smile was cold as a winter's night.

Once an älf, always an älf. Tungdil shook out his painful legs and rubbed the talisman on his little finger. *I hope you are safe, Balyndis. You and my son.* He was looking forward to the promised shared meal with the two of them. He was not expecting more than that. But to be sitting at the same table with them was a beginning. *So is the ring she gave me.*

'Leave me in peace. I don't want to know about your precious herbs.' Hearing Beligata's rough words, Tungdil raised his head.

'I'm only trying to help,' Gosalyn said, a bandage spread with crushed leaves in her hands. 'That scar of yours is looking bad. The edges have gone black.'

'It's the ink. I told you.'

'I thought you said the ink was green?' Gosalyn laid the herbs aside.

'Green and black.' Beligata moved away from her impatiently.

'How did the tattooist manage to ruin your face like that?' Hargorin wanted to have his say on the matter. He fixed the axe head on to the new handle, hammered new horseshoe nails through the wood, then bent them round. 'There! That's good enough to smash a few skulls. It's not elegant but it's a whole lot better than the crude club it was before.' He turned to Beligata. 'Who was it that did the tattoo?'

'A friend,' she snapped back, irritated as usual by any reference to the scar. 'I wanted to do him a favour. His other tattoos had been fine.' She shook her dark-haired head. 'How often do I have to tell you?'

Carmondai laughed quietly to himself.

'I'm just concerned about you.' Gosalyn rolled the bandage up and put it away. 'The scar is getting bigger and the black is spreading.'

'What kind of ink was it?' Tungdil helped Hargorin to his feet. They were preparing to move off.

'He told me he'd mixed it himself. From essences.' Beligata pointed to the hill. 'I can cope with the scar. It won't kill me. Now, let's get on with the job in hand.'

'Leave the luggage here.' Tungdil took the lead.

The dwarves, Carmondai and Tsatòn made their way up the grass-covered mound to look down at the small valley on the far side.

The acronta scout had been telling the truth. There was a fortified village where all kinds of creatures were swarming about – creatures that normally never would have been seen in a settlement like this. Tungdil could make out the forms of humans, orcs, gnomes and other beasts he was not familiar with. They were working at improvised forges, making tools. If they were not busy with hammers they were bringing fuel and scrap metal. Others were making handles from wood scavenged from the houses.

'Spades and pickaxes?' Beligata wondered what they were for. 'Are they planning to attack a field? Or dig a mine?'

'You could be right.' Tungdil surveyed the scene. 'They could be getting ready for tunnelling.'

'To get more metal ore for making weapons,' Hargorin carried the thought on. 'There's probably not enough local iron and steel to melt down and re-use.'

'So it's not ploughshares to swords but the other way around. The monsters are useless.' Beligata shielded her eyes against the sun. 'But where's the mine?'

'There are deposits in the north, along the route to the Grey Mountains,' the acront wrote on the ground. 'An old quarry ancient peoples used. It's in the form of a funnel, going very deep down. Deep as a mountain is high. There's activity there again.'

'How far is it?'

'About four hundred miles away.' Tsatòn wrote the answer. 'Our scouts saw smoke rising. I thought it might be the local coalfields that had caught fire but it seems they have been firing up the furnaces and smithies.'

'They're getting ready to equip a new army. But the soldiers are not gathering here in this village.' Tungdil knew these monsters were no soldiers. 'These are smiths and craftsmen,' he said under his breath.

'Shall we kill them all? We'll have wiped out a supply chain the army depends on,' Hargorin suggested.

'There're four thousand of them,' Gosalyn pointed out. 'We are five acronta, four dwarves, and an älf. Nobody minds a good fight, but those are silly odds.'

'Not really. They're not trained soldiers. Without an experienced leader, they'll be easier to slaughter than a herd of sheep.' Hargorin seemed wedded to the idea of eradicating this unit of craftspeople.

'Shouldn't we assume they've been forced to do this work by the botoican?' Carmondai voiced his objection. 'I'm sure many of them would be glad to return to their families when the effect of the spell wears off.'

Beligata stared at the älf. 'You? You're appealing for clemency? I don't believe it.' She pointed in the direction of the village. 'But we're in a position to halt or delay their campaign against Girdlegard.'

'It's your decision,' Carmondai replied calmly. 'I just wanted to have mentioned it.'

'There! On the right! An älf!'

They focused on the edge of the village where a small fortified building could be seen.

Aiphatòn emerged in the company of an älf with hair like glass, wearing a mask that covered his mouth and lower jaw. A blonde female älf joined them, carrying a thick pile of papers she was trying to read through as she walked.

The former emperor of the älfar was wearing wide breeches like a divided skirt. His upper body with its tionium plates sewn in to the skin was bare. He wore his long black hair in a double braid on the back of his head.

It really is Aiphatòn. Tungdil took out the telescope and studied the three älfar.

In his opinion they were acting normally. They were communicating with the gagged älf by means of signs.

Aiphatòn and the female älf chatted and laughed – and then he kissed her passionately. Shouldering his spear he turned and went along the street, visiting each forge to inspect the workmanship.

The female älf, wearing no armour, had a close-fitting grey dress with a white pattern. She sat down on a bench in front of one of the houses and continued her reading. A monster brought her a jug and a cup, placing them on a table in front of her. The älf with the transparent hair kept her company, helping her sort through her papers and passing sheets to her. He was wearing leather armour in black, which contrasted with his own pale appearance.

He's death incarnate. Tungdil could not see any of the botoican's white runes. 'Can anyone see someone who looks like a magician?' he asked the others, passing around the telescope. No one could. *Maybe they are spells she's studying? Could she be the botoican?*

'It all looks idyllic,' said Beligata ironically. 'If we didn't know our enemies were down there working their socks off, you might think monsters and humans were dedicating themselves to peace.'

'An älf with hair like glass,' Carmondai mouthed, pulling out a sheet of paper to start a new drawing. 'It's the Voice of the Wind! It's Nodûcor!'

Tungdil had made up his mind. 'I'm going down to try to talk to Aiphatòn. He can tell us where the botoican is. If we can do away with the magician, a lot of innocent lives will be saved.' He nodded to Carmondai, who was stowing away his sketching materials. 'You're coming with me.' When the dwarves made ready to accompany them, he stopped them. 'You are needed to protect us from behind. Tsatòn, please go and fetch the other four acronta. If anything goes wrong, all of you attack. Your priority will be to kill the älfar, including the Voice of the Wind.'

Gosalyn looked at Carmondai. 'He's an älf, too.'

Hargorin and Beligata were amused. *Everyone's in the mood for a joke.* Tungdil grinned. 'No. You don't include him. We can deal with the beasts and the humans later if they attack, but I'm pretty sure they won't.'

Tsatòn slid down the incline, ran to the wood and called his warriors. Beligata, Hargorin and Gosalyn drew their weapons and held themselves in readiness.

Tungdil and Carmondai moved stealthily down the other side of the hill, bending low to avoid being seen and using the bushes as cover. They approached the little wall that surrounded the village. No guards were in sight and they were not challenged. The wall was simply rocks piled on top of each other, a dry stone wall with no mortar.

Carmondai helped Tungdil climb over, and leaped the obstacle with ease himself, which the dwarf noted. *Our elderly älf is full of surprises.* They found themselves at the rear of a squat building that had a smithy attached. Aiphatòn came along the unmade road, getting nearer to the iron works.

'Get inside,' Tungdil whispered to the history-weaver, and both of them squeezed in.

The forge had several pieces of rough metal ready for smelting. Two monsters were operating the bellows and air shot hissing into the hot coals, fanning the blaze. Two orcs and demi-creatures with human features but hairy bodies were working at the anvils. Sparks had burned holes in their fur and there was a smell of singed horn.

Tungdil and Carmondai hid as well as they could. They wanted to overhear what was being said.

'Show me what you've made so far,' came the voice of the former älfar emperor before he stepped in to the forge, a spear in his right hand. The orcs and the monsters bowed to him, holding out half-fashioned tools whose purpose was clear from their shape.

'Not bad. But you are working too slowly,' Aiphatòn complained, pointing his blade at the throat of the nearest orc.

'Then get us coal that will enable us to reach higher temperatures,' a green-skinned monster dared to protest. 'If we didn't have the bellows, the metal would hardly get warm.' He displayed his formidable muscles. 'I am strong, but if the metal isn't red-hot there's not much I can do.'

Tungdil could not read the expression in Aiphatòn's black eyes. *Is he doing this voluntarily or has he been forced to by the botoican?* Carmondai had once said that not all älfar were immune to the effects of this magic.

'Carry on with your work and stop complaining. I want you to show me the pickaxe you've made by evening. If it's no good, you will forfeit your life.' Aiphatòn examined the tool the furred creature had produced. 'Look: *he*'s managed to make one. And without a fuss.' Without any further word, Aiphatòn left the premises.

Now. Tungdil pulled Carmondai outside; they stayed by the wall of the forge for protection.

'Psst.' Tungdil hissed to get Aiphatòn's attention.

'Have you gone crazy?' the historian mouthed. 'What if –'

Aiphatòn halted and looked round. His dark eyes fixed on the dwarf and his companion standing in the shadows. He frowned and walked slowly over to them both, not seeming alarmed or even concerned.

Is he . . . angry? Tungdil raised his hand in greeting. *I wasn't expecting that.*

'Why have we got a dwarf here not working at the forge or instructing the beasts how to use a hammer properly?' Aiphatòn snapped, using the crude common language of Girdlegard. The tip of his spear swung to point at Carmondai. 'And you? Where are you from? Obviously not from one of the two cities,' he added in the älfar tongue.

'He doesn't recognise you,' the historian blurted out.

It must be the effect of the botoican's magic. Or has he lost his mind? Tungdil bowed. 'I have just arrived with my friend. We heard you're looking for good craftsmen. He's built cities, if that is something you are in need of.'

Aiphatòn stared at him, eyes narrowed. 'Who's been saying that?'

'We overheard a conversation,' Tungdil said, keeping things neutral. 'And I see it's true.'

'So you came here on your own initiative?' the älf laughed. 'That doesn't happen often, I must say. Stay as long as you want. We can talk about wages later. But I want to know what really brought you both here.' The runes on his spear took on a threatening greenish glow.

'I can hardly believe it,' whispered Carmondai. 'He's under some kind of spell.'

'We escaped from Girdlegard. Times have changed there,' Tungdil lied. 'Perhaps you recall?'

'What? Girdlegard? Of course. But that was a long time ago. We like a bit of news.' He went back to the street and motioned them both over with a gauntleted hand. 'Come with me. I've got questions. Lots of questions.'

'You shall have answers to all of them.' Carmondai was putting on a brave face as he entered into the spirit of this dangerous game. The three of them went back to the fortified house Aiphatòn had just left. The other two älfar did not look at them; they were still deep in their papers, making notes and marking passages.

'Are these your friends?' Tungdil asked, pointing at the älf-woman and the älf with the mask. *I'd love to know what they're studying.*

'Irïanora and Nodûcor. They help me with everything.' Aiphatòn looked at Carmondai. 'Beware: her beauty will catch your eye and dazzle you, and you'll be overwhelmed with love and desire. So I'm telling you now: it's only me that belongs to her.' He opened the door and let them go ahead of him. 'If you touch her I'll knock your head off, älf.'

Tungdil entered the room. He could see it was a guard-room; it must be where the officials in charge of village discipline had their quarters. There was a narrow spiral staircase to a lower floor where cells were and upstairs he could see more rooms and a look-out post. 'A bit grim.'

'It serves. Until we move on.' Aiphatòn pushed his way in after Carmondai and indicated two seats that Irïanora and Nodûcor must have been using recently. The stove was still warm and tea was simmering on the hotplate. Three mugs contained fresh dregs and a jar of honey and some crumbs were on the table. There was a faint smell of spices. 'Right. Tell me what's been happening in Girdlegard.'

'There have been many changes. It would take many orbits to tell you everything.' Tungdil selected the chair with a view of the road where he could watch the two elves talking. Carmondai took the stool and sat down with his back to the wall. 'But why should you care? And what are you doing with all these tools the smiths are making?' He laughed. 'Do you intend to tunnel your way out?'

Aiphatòn sat down opposite him. 'Nonsense. The ground is too hard here.' He was sitting upright like a monarch; the sewn-in tionium plates were scratched. On one of them, there was a hole where the edges appeared to have melted as if a red-hot bolt had pierced it. 'Talk, dwarf.'

I've got to break through the spell that's clouding his mind. Tungdil told him a few trivial facts, filling him in on the victories over evil, and he also talked about the älfar, not mentioning Aiphatòn's name. 'I'm one of the most dedicated followers of Lorimbur,' he lied. 'Not all of my tribe disliked what the black-eyes were doing.' He pointed at Carmondai. 'We jumped ship as soon as we noticed things were not going our way. And you can see how badly he's been treated.'

'I can.' Aiphatòn nodded. 'But tell me how the people reacted to the attacks.'

'I told you already.'

'You're telling me things from way back. I mean the attacks on the Stone Gateway a few orbits ago.' Aiphatòn grimaced with disappointment. 'Or have you and your companion been on the road for so long that you can't tell me anything new at all?'

'Oh, I see, you mean *those* attacks. Did you send them, then? It's said they were led by a botoican and a ghaist.' Tungdil was trying to get more information. *Did he notice how shocked I was?*

'Just tell me what they think in Girdlegard,' Aiphatòn repeated.

'Perhaps I could help.' Carmondai took over at this point, and started a lengthy, rambling speech.

A movement on the road outside caught Tungdil's eye and he stopped listening to what Carmondai was saying. A ghaist with a rune-decorated copper helmet sporting noticeable dents had come running up the street to stop where Irïanora and Nodûcor were.

Irïanora got to her feet and went to the ghaist with some sheets of paper, while the Voice of the Wind went on sorting documents. From the älf-woman's demeanour it was clear she did not regard the ghaist as an inferior being.

Look what's turned up; the botoican's lethal arm and messenger. All we need now is his master. If we wipe them all out, we'll have removed the danger threatening our homeland in one fell swoop. Quicker than the elf prophecy foretold. Tungdil looked around him carefully. *I wonder if he's anywhere nearby?*

The älf-woman handed over several pages and the ghaist approached the house. Tungdil wished he had some magic in reserve or at least Keenfire with which he could split the copper helmet open.

His glance caught Bloodthirster, hanging at Carmondai's side. He doubted the elderly älf could hold his own with a ghaist. *But maybe I could.* Since leaving Phondrasôn he had vowed never to use evil again, not even in the pursuit of good. *Was that a foolish promise to make?*

The huge giant did not knock but stood waiting at the threshold, white mist emerging from the helmet's eye holes. It seemed surprised to see the new arrivals. Irïanora had obviously not mentioned their presence. Tungdil gave a placatory signal to Carmondai, who had placed a hand on the hilt of his weapon: *not yet*.

'Now I don't need you two to tell me what's happened,' Aiphatòn said, gesturing to the ghaist to enter. 'How did it go at the Stone Gateway? Since you're here I suppose the defenders came up with some trick or other?'

The ghaist came in slowly, the floorboards creaking under its weight. Irïanora followed, ready to speak. Her expression was distant, her eyes blank. 'Yes, they did,' she intoned.

'They destroyed our ramp at the last minute. We were nearly there. They destroyed the whole army. Next time we'll succeed, I swear.'

Tungdil masked the surprise he felt. *The ghaist can't speak and he's using her to give his report.* He now knew without a doubt that the älf-woman was not the botoican. The way she stood and the way she spoke indicated her own will had been paralysed.

The ghaist came over to Carmondai.

'An älf. With a pretty tattoo message on his forehead.' The älf-woman's voice was without inflection. 'And from Girdlegard. What a nice surprise.'

For a magic being controlled by a botoican, it is acting quite independently, not at all like a slave, Tungdil thought. *Could this be the botoican in the guise of a ghaist?*

Carmondai sketched a bow. 'I left because I didn't like it there anymore.'

'And I don't like it here anymore,' Irïanora said, speaking for the ghaist. The ghaist turned to look at Tungdil. 'There is no doubt about where you are from. But dwarves don't usually leave their homeland. Certainly not in the company of an älf.'

Tungdil repeated his story and the ghaist listened acutely.

'I don't know what you mean by Thirdling, but as I see it, you and the black-eyes were allies in the past.' His words came via Irïanora's mouth. 'So if you can't stand your own people any longer, would you do a favour for me?'

'That's why I came.'

'He says that's why he came,' Irïanora's delight was feigned. 'How marvellous to hear it.'

The ghaist bent down, visor slits on a level with Tungdil's eyes. 'You all defy me. Too rebellious for me to control. I will have to kill you all. You are in my way.'

'Nothing to do with me.' Tungdil pretended to be relaxed about things. 'I couldn't care less about the others.' He raised his hand. 'But we should discuss payment. I'd like to speak to your master about it.'

Irïanora, deputising, laughed and repeated, 'To my master?'

'Whoever made you and whoever you obey like the others do.'

'Let's play a game.' The ghaist pressed the tip of his finger into Tungdil's palm. 'What do you say to that?'

The scarred surface of his hand started to tingle and a slight flash of light appeared then vanished. Nothing else happened.

'How I hate your kind,' said Irïanora, cursing without passion.

'You've just made the price go up,' said Tungdil, rubbing his palm on his breeches. *He was trying to break my will. Good thing it didn't work*. He shook himself.

'Is that so?'

He nodded. 'You just tried to take me over like the rest of the beasts and the humans. Not very polite of you. I should eliminate you on the spot, even if that means your master will have to create a new one.'

The blonde älf-woman gave another false, high-pitched laugh, her face vacant. 'You are a clever rogue. But you have not guessed right. And anyway, you can't destroy me. You haven't got the right things to do it with.' The ghaist stood up. 'What's your price for showing me the way through the Grey Mountains?'

What's all this in aid of? 'There is no way through the mountains,' Tungdil replied, realising his answer had come out too fast. *Too fast and too loud.*

'Oh, I get it. You people are known to be greedy. I think your memory will improve if more money is on offer. Is that right?'

The ghaist indicated Aiphatòn.

'My good friend – my henchman and Irïanora's lover – he followed the route once, but my scouts have failed to locate his signs,' the älf-woman explained. 'The dwarves must have removed it. But since you two have managed to get here and they didn't let you go through the gates, my suspicion is that you know exactly where the path lies.'

Quicker than Carmondai could react, the ghaist placed a hand round his neck. He froze.

'This one here,' said Irïanora dully, 'cannot resist my powers. The älfar ceased to be resistant a long time ago. No living creature can withstand my influence, apart from the wretched dwarves. They seem to have the trick of it. Plague take them.'

The ghaist turned its gleaming white gaze on the history-teller.

'I will need strength to overcome your will, but it's not impossible. Now help me out and tell me who I have here and what your intentions are. I shan't let myself be deceived.'

Vraccas, get ready to step in. Tungdil wondered how fast he could snatch at Bloodthirster. He covertly kissed his talisman ring. An attack might yet succeed. *I'll be needing . . .*

'The dwarf's name is Tungdil Goldhand,' Aiphatòn said unexpectedly, with a cold smile. 'I think they are in charge of a reconnaissance unit camped on one of the surrounding hills.'

Tungdil froze. *I got him wrong.*

'I recognised you at once but I pretended not to so you and Carmondai would follow me. I presume it's our historian I have here? There were rumours that the Triplets had imprisoned him.' He laughed, brandishing his spear. 'I wasn't sure at first, Scholar, because I thought you were dead but I must have got that wrong. You look pretty alive to me, Girdlegard's Great Hero. I wonder what your story is.' The spear tip swept around. 'Are you leading a troop of spies? Are they up there on the hill?'

We've been found out. Now everything pointed to a fight – but first he would have to give a signal to the dwarves and the acronta, telling them to attack.

Loud roars and grunts were heard outside. Looking out of the window, he saw the beasts and the humans picking up the tools they had been producing. They were storming off towards the hill. *Well, I shan't have to bother giving a signal.*

'You have lost your ally to me,' Irïanora said. 'Your life will soon be forfeit likewise.'

When Carmondai drew Bloodthirster out of its sheath and pointed the tip at him, Tungdil knew the danger had never been greater. He would have stood a better chance in an arena heaving with monsters. *If the botoican is capable of breaking Carmondai's will, then Beligata, Gosalyn and Hargorin are done for.* His instinct told him the outlook was getting grimmer. *Nothing for it, Vraccas. You'll have to send a miracle.*

Tungdil launched himself past the threat of Bloodthirster's tip and grabbed Carmondai's sword hand.

But Tungdil heard something appalling: he kept being told that he had already been somewhere when he knew he was there for the first time.

At first he treated it as a joke but then he recalled the wave of magic that had brought multiple versions of the Triplets.

And had he not caught sight of himself in that wave?

And so began the long search for himself.

Secret notes for
The Writings of Truth
written under duress by Carmondai

XXVII

Girdlegard
Grey Mountains
Kingdom of the Fifthling Dwarves
Stone Gateway
6496th solar cycle, late summer

'I'd like to ask the gods why dead flesh has to stink so when it goes off.'

Balyndar turned round at the sound of the unfamiliar voice. It was too clear in pitch to belong to a dwarf-woman. *Our visitor.*

An elf-woman in palandium armour stepped down off the lift platform and came along the recently repaired walkway past all the machines. She was dressed simply and her breastplate showed the seal of the Naishïon and the symbol denoting her a sorânïan.

She strode along determinedly. At the sides her hair was short and coloured grey and white, while the rest was black. A long braid fell on her breast. Her left hand rested on an ornate sword hilt.

'That's so the crows can locate it,' Balyndar answered. *She does look unusual.* 'If it had a pleasant smell it would confuse the bees.'

She laughed and held out her hand in greeting. 'That makes sense.'

They shook hands. 'They told me you were coming. Ocâstia, right?'

'That's correct.' She smiled warmly and took a look over

the battlements down to the road on the other side of the ramparts where there were iron tracks leading out north from the gate, going straight through the mountain of corpses. 'I can see the crows now. They are pretty fat.'

'Plenty to feed off.' Balyndar studied the slim figure of the elf-warrior. Like the other sorânïons, her task was to carry out the vetting examinations in the name of the Naishïon. 'Nothing there for you, though.'

'I wouldn't eat dead monsters.'

He grinned. 'Living ones, then?'

'Nope.' She leaned back against the wall, amused, her carnelian-coloured eyes still fixed on the mountain of dead bodies. 'You're hinting at the fact there are no more elves to test.'

Balyndar called Girgandor over. 'Not really hinting. There haven't been any at all. Not for cycles now.' He looked at her. 'Is there something I don't know?'

She clicked her tongue. 'I heard the beasts got over the gate. Judging by the state of the inner courtyard this must be true. Should I be worried?'

'Girdlegard is safe.' Balyndar's delight in the quick-wittedness and humour of the elf-woman faded. She was interfering in matters that did not concern her. *And she's casting doubt on our ability to do our job defending Girdlegard.* 'You can go any time you want, if you are afraid and don't feel safe here. I shan't stop you.'

Ocâstia realised she had spoken out of turn. 'Oh, I did not intent to imply the Children of the Smith were not up to the task of defending our homeland.' She looked distraught. 'What I meant to say was that it must have been tough. Did you have heavy losses?'

'*They* did,' he replied drily. 'For the most part what we lost was ammunition.'

Girgandor joined them and updated the commander on the progress of the clearing-up process. 'Another thirty cart-loads and we'll have cleared away the corpses.'

'What do you do with the bodies?' Ocâstia inquired. 'Hey, I like your beard; it's great.'

'We load them on tubs, roll them to the gate along the rails and heave them up by crane. Once we have them on this side of the wall, we place them on another set of rails and take them to the forges and burn them, together with any metal they have on them. Any iron we can extract in this way we use to make ammunition.' Girgandor explained it all as if Ocâstia were a child. He had not been impressed by her attempt at flattery.

Ocâstia clapped. 'Very practical.'

'It's clean,' Girgandor replied. But he did smile and run his hands over his fine beard as if stroking a cat. 'In the old days we'd have left the corpses to rot but that just attracts vermin, and anyway, dwarves don't like waste.' He nodded to his superior officer. 'After that we can start shoring up the tunnels.'

'Good.' Balyndar pointed to the walkway on the battlements. 'I want those rails up here, too. It'll be a big improvement when we're shifting the small catapults from place to place.'

Girgandor nodded and went to the lift platform. 'Thank you, elf-woman,' he called back from a distance.

'Shoring up?' Ocâstia crossed her arms and sounded interested. 'Have you got new plans for the fortifications?'

'Yes.' The way he said this made it clear to the sorânïan that he would not be more forthcoming. If she wanted more, she'd have to work for it. 'How long do you intend to stay?'

'As long as you'll put up with me.' The elf-woman held her nose as a tub full of corpses was heaved into the air. 'My sovereign said that someone should be available in case any elves turn up.'

'It is only monsters that come here.'

'That's not to say that won't change. Even in the heat of battle. And that's not quite correct, there have been elves at these gates.' Ocâstia dodged the drops of foul liquid that were escaping from the tubs. 'By Sitalia,' she said, retching. 'How do you stand it?'

'Oh, we're used to it. We tend to have more battles here than you do in your safe little groves,' he said mischievously.

'If beasts turn up again' – she tapped the hilt of her curved sword – 'you can count on me. It would be an honour for me to fight with you, side by side.' Ocâstia gestured towards the courtyard and the entrance into the mountain. 'Have you got room for me and my officers anywhere?'

'Officers? I thought you'd come on your own.'

'Never. The Naishïon sent twenty good warriors along with me. You should see it as a sign that shows elves and dwarves can work together.' She pulled out a note and handed it to Balyndar. 'And there's a gift for you.'

'From your master?'

'No. From me.'

He accepted it. 'A poem, I suppose,' he grunted. *Vraccas! It'll be stuff about sunsets and unicorns.*

'It's a recipe. For the best pickled meat I've ever tasted. A dwarf gave me the recipe and I've refined it a bit.'

Balyndar studied the lines. *Sounds delicious!* His mouth started watering. *Right, she's made up for the initial insult.*

He followed her. 'I'll have them arrange quarters for you all. I'll tell them to find somewhere the ceilings will be high enough,' he said with a grin. 'We can also take the ends off the beds for you, but you might find you get cold feet.'

Ocâstia laughed again.

Somewhere in the Outer Lands

Hargorin watched the fortified farmhouse with its tower where Tungdil and Carmondai had vanished. They had seen the ghaist and the älf-woman disappear inside.

The skinny pale älf with the mask – the one they thought must be the Voice of the Wind – was still sitting outside on the bench, sorting his papers.

It would be easy to get rid of him.

The five acronta lay nearby like metal-clad tree trunks. They also were observing the village.

'Did you see that? Nobody challenged Tungdil and the black-eyes at all.' Beligata's tone betrayed her eagerness for some action. 'I'd like to bet the beasts wouldn't notice if we marched straight down the village street and killed the älf.'

'Yeah, great idea. Except it would endanger Tungdil.' Gosalyn shook her head in disbelief. 'He's in there with Aiphatòn, the älf-woman and the ghaist. That's at least two opponents too many.'

'But he's got Carmondai to help him,' Beligata objected.

'Yeah, that one can swap sides any time he likes,' Gosalyn argued. 'We hang on here till we get the signal.'

Hargorin found the wait tortuous. 'What if they're about to kill Tungdil or they force him to say why he's there? There's nothing to be gained in those circumstances if we're just sitting here on our backsides. I don't like him being out of sight.' He came out of his hiding place and moved carefully in the direction of the wall. 'Beligata, Gosalyn, come with me. The acronta can stay here till we send them a signal. If one of us shouts,' he said, addressing Tsatòn, 'you lot need to attack. Understood? You'll figure out the best way to do that. But if I put my arm in the air twice, that means I want you to create some kind of a diversion. No attack.'

The veteran growled in response.

'I don't like the idea,' Gosalyn protested, but she followed the red-bearded dwarf nevertheless.

'I don't care. We're here to keep Girdlegard safe from harm.' Hargorin was already hobbling down the hill.

'Just as long as you're sure that's the Voice of the Wind down there.' Beligata sent Gosalyn a disapproving glance. 'Stop making that face. We've only got Carmondai's legend and the story the emperor-mother told us to go on. We don't have any proof that this älf is the one they were talking about.'

'Look, he's got a mask stopping him speaking. That's good enough for me.' Hargorin had reached the wall and was clasping his hands together to give the others a leg up. 'We'll creep up on him, kill him, and get rid of the body before anyone even notices.'

'Fantastic,' Gosalyn said scornfully, placing one foot in Hargorin's cupped hands.

'This is not the time for sophisticated long-term planning.' Hargorin chucked her bodily over the obstacle. 'We're in the Outer Lands here. Any little victory counts.' Beligata nodded in agreement but said nothing.

Once over the stone wall, they went stealthily through the village. From every corner came the sound of hammering, hot metal being plunged into water troughs, clanging and steam hissing. The orc and beast and human craftsmen were trying to demonstrate how quickly and accurately they could work. All the better for the dwarves: no one would hear them approach.

It's working. Hargorin piloted his group through the narrow alleyways, avoiding confrontations with any beasts or humans. Even when they were seen, it did not seem to cause any reaction. The villagers must have thought the dwarves were workers like themselves.

They soon arrived at the small house where the masked älf was sitting outside. They approached from behind.

Beligata spied through a window that had lost its glass. 'Sleeping quarters,' she reported. 'It's empty.'

'Excellent. We'll get him, drag him in here and finish him off.' Hargorin looked at Gosalyn. 'And if you're thinking of coming up with another objection: Voice of the Wind or not – he's still an älf. His life is therefore forfeit.' He hurried off, bent double, sneaking up behind the älf who was sitting reading.

Opportunities have to be seized when they present themselves.

'He's right.' Beligata followed him. 'Gosalyn, you open the door for us.'

The general level of noise from the smithies covered any sound Hargorin's steps might have made. When he reached the unsuspecting älf, he swung and smashed the hand-made grip of his axe into the back of the älf's neck.

Beligata grabbed the älf and dragged him off the bench and through the open door into the shed.

These are coming too. Hargorin gathered up the papers and hurried in to where the two dwarf women were. The floor was covered with straw and jute sacks. There was a smell of stale sweat.

They held their breath and listened. No alarm sounded

and there was no sound of footsteps. No one had noticed. The dwarves grinned at each other.

'As you can see, I haven't actually killed him.' Hargorin gave Gosalyn the pages he had picked up. 'Read that lot and find out what it's all about.' He nodded to Beligata. 'You and I will deal with the älf.'

'What do you intend to do?' Gosalyn asked. 'I'm curious. That's all.'

Hargorin and Beligata propped the unconscious älf against the wall and investigated his mask. It had only a tiny hole in front of the mouth. Nothing bigger than a piece of straw would have fitted. The mechanism that kept the mouthpiece shut looked fragile enough but it was covered in runes warning of the danger of triggering magic spells if it were touched.

'That's a shame. We haven't learned anything at all.' Hargorin lifted his axe. 'Let's kill him, even without learning what the Voice of the Wind sounds like.'

Beligata stepped back so as not to be splashed.

Gosalyn held the papers up in the air and spoke urgently. 'Do you know what this is?'

'If it doesn't describe the opening in the mask, you can tell me in a minute,' Hargorin mumbled.

'It's the army they're mustering. The third army. Exact lists of what provisions they'll be needing, iron ore, coal, workforce, slaves, everything for a campaign.' The dwarf girl held the papers out to Hargorin. 'They're only just starting their planning.'

Vraccas, thank you! He turned his bearded visage towards her in delight. 'Does it say where they're gathering their troops?'

Gosalyn rustled the pages. 'If I've read it correctly, it'll be in the old mine the acronta was telling us about. That's where they'll start from.'

A clicking sound attracted Hargorin's attention. When he glanced at their captive, he saw Beligata – with the älf's black mask in her left hand.

That was quick. 'How did you do that?'

'Pure chance,' she answered, but it didn't sound convincing – he made a mental note to ask her again later. The scar on her face was bleeding and the drops looked black. 'Let's wake him up!' Beligata placed the edge of her short axe against the snow-white throat, cutting through some of the glassy strands of long hair, which rustled to the floor. 'We can force him to use his power against our enemies.'

Hargorin imagined threatening the älf into using wind power against the monsters. *A victory with no losses on our part*. 'Not a bad idea.' Looking round he discovered a bucket of water with a ladle in it, which he promptly emptied on their captive's head. Hargorin did not react to Gosalyn's shout.

The älf's eyelids opened and he glared at the dwarves with his uncannily dark eyes. He quickly took in his situation and did not move.

Hargorin waved the axe blade in front of the älf's face. 'You are going to do us a favour,' he said, speaking in the älfar tongue. 'Use your strength to destroy the village. Except for this shed and the fortified building with the little tower. If even the faintest breeze tickles my red beard hairs in here, you die and no botoican or ghaist will bring you back. Understood?'

The pale-skinned älf nodded. He opened his mouth slowly, dry lips splitting and issuing drops of dark red blood from the cracks.

At first the dwarves heard nothing. Then there was a low groaning sound, perhaps the noise a dying man would make. *Is that it?*

'Gosalyn, check what's happening outside,' said Hargorin.

She went over to the window and watched the sky. 'The bushes on the slope are moving but not much. No hint of a storm. It's all quiet. And . . .'

As if from nowhere, great gusts screamed in through all the windows of the little hut, knocking the dwarves off their feet. Feathers, flower petals and specks of gold danced through the room. Splinters of glass and tiny blades of stone pelted the dwarves. The air smelled of rain and stone and fresh fruit and blossom and iron and soil.

The raging winds played with the dwarves as if they were puppets made of straw. Hargorin was hurled against the door, forcing it off its hinges. He flew back and landed on the table at which the älf had recently been sitting. *Cursed black-eyes*. He staggered up, rubbing his neck, bewildered to see his own armour in shreds and scratches and cuts all over his limbs.

He looked around the hut.

The älf was standing in the middle. The dwarf girls were being spun round, in whirling clouds of blossom, feathers, straw, and gold fragments. The papers they had been looking at were cut to ribbons by the glass splinters. The relentless gusts kept coming, pushing great volumes of air into the building, sustaining the whirlwind and rattling at the walls. Any moment now Beligata and Gosalyn would be ground to powder by the wind and the shed would collapse. In the village, none of the beasts and humans were still working. The spectacle had grabbed everyone's attention.

The winds will keep coming as long as he keeps calling

them. Hargorin lifted the axe. *We should have killed him when we had the chance. Nothing else for it*. Hargorin drew breath for a loud shout and bellowed for the acronta to attack. *I'll take the blame*.

The five huge figures appeared on top of the hill, roaring. They stormed down the hillside, weapons at the ready, heading for the terrified beasts in the village. Near-panic broke out. The villagers took hold of anything they could find in the way of weapons and prepared to face the invaders.

The storm inside the hut dropped abruptly. Beligata and Gosalyn slumped to the floor with the shredded pages fluttering down to cover them. The pale älf stepped out of the doorway, eyes fixed on the acronta. He inhaled deeply in order to summon up the gusts anew.

They can't win. No one can win in a storm like that. Hargorin twirled the axe round his head and threw it at the Voice of the Wind. But the älf had noticed the movement and stopped mid-summons, ducking under the flying weapon. Drawing a knife from his belt he turned on the dwarf, opening his lips once more. A single groan sufficed and the gusts recommenced, protecting him.

'Would you dare?' Hargorin took up another hand axe and made a challenging gesture.

But the älf came no closer. He threw the knife and the wind carried it. The Thirdling king could not parry the strike – at the last moment the tip turned sharply in the wind. The dagger sank through his armour into his right breast. It felt as if the wind was pushing the iron blade further in to his flesh.

In great pain, Hargorin grabbed hold of the hilt and stopped its progress. *If I'm going down, I'll take you with me!* With a fiery rage, he brandished his axe.

'Let's have you!' he yelled. 'I'll cut you to ribbons!'

The pale älf had other things in mind. He had a second dagger in his hand and just as he raised it to hurl, he froze in mid-movement.

A broken chair leg was sticking out of his chest and blood streamed like water down his black leather armour. Despite sinking to his knees, he kept his black eyes fixed on Hargorin. He dropped the dagger.

Gosalyn's unsteady figure appeared at his shoulder, bleeding from a number of wounds. 'You were right,' she gasped. 'He is indeed the Voice of the Wind.' She looked about her for a weapon with which to finish off the dying älf.

Distant noises announced that the acronta had clashed with and were defeating the first wave of beasts; the screams of the dying were heard.

'Take my axe,' Hargorin said, trying to get up. 'Over by the door.' The pale älf grasped the shattered chair leg and pulled it out of his body, causing a stream of blood to gush out. He drew in a lungful of air like someone about to suffocate and glared at Hargorin, black lines making wild patterns over his visage.

'By Vraccas! Break his neck!' Hargorin shouted. 'Break his neck before –'

She placed her hands on each side of the älf's head as he opened his lips for one last loud hate-filled shout.

The wind answered him, raging on all sides.

Tungdil swung Bloodthirster, which was still gripped by Carmondai. He directed it at the ghaist.

But the blade, once the sword of an Inextinguishable, left only a long cut in the armour and the form beneath. Since the ghaist was not human, the stroke did not kill him. The ghaist sprang away, snorting furiously. The eye slits shimmered white as if a silver star were rising slowly through the mists.

It's the helmet I've got to aim for. That's where the power is. Tungdil elbowed Carmondai in the face and tried to wrench the sword out of his grasp. Battle noise and the roars of the acronta came from outside. His friends must have decided to attack when he and Carmondai had not reappeared.

A stab in his hip made him grunt with pain. Tungdil turned to see the tip of the rune spear sticking out, the symbols glowing green.

'I can kill you, Tungdil Goldhand,' Aiphatòn threatened. 'A single thought. A touch with my magic and you will burst open and be spattered all over the walls.'

'That would be a shame,' said Irïanora, speaking on behalf of the ghaist. 'I could experiment on him to see when dwarf resistance finally breaks. Let me do that at my leisure. Maybe I can wear him down.'

Never. Tungdil put his hands round the spear shaft and yanked the blade free. Where he held it, the runes stopped flickering. *I'd sooner kill myself.*

Aiphatòn opened his black eyes wide – but before he could cast a spell, a piercing death scream reverberated through the village.

At the next moment a hurricane was unleashed.

The storm hurled itself howling at the thick walls, demolishing them instantly. Windows shattered, sending shards of glass everywhere. Furniture was seized by the gusts and flung aside.

The wind caught hold of Tungdil and lifted him off his feet. He shot past Aiphatòn as if he were a missile. He was swirled around with no idea where the wind was taking him, Carmondai, the ghaist or the others. The dwarf closed his eyes and protected his head between his arms against the force of the gale as he was blown hither and thither. He felt as if he were going up but he did not dare glance out from between his arms. *This is what it must be like for a leaf in autumn.*

Bits of rubble hit him, covering him in painful cuts, and yet he was surprised to register, in all the destruction, the spring-like fragrance of fresh blossom. He could hear wood fracturing in the teeth of the wind and stone being ground on stone. Sparks crackled in the confusion eddying around him.

As quickly as the hurricane had arrived, it died away.

Tungdil plummeted to the ground. Before he could spread his arms to soften his fall he landed in a prickly bush, then somersaulted out of it onto wet grass. He turned over and over as he rolled to a halt, feeling pain everywhere.

I am still alive, though. Tungdil lifted his head, still feeling giddy, to see where he had ended up.

The storm had carried him up the hillside. The entire settlement had ceased to exist; all the buildings were smashed to pieces, as if some giant had arrived to clear the place and build it anew. Fires were smouldering where there had been forges; the glowing coals had been spread abroad by the wind.

Monsters and humans lay motionless in all the destruction, many of them with broken limbs at strange angles. Bodies had been split open. Some cadavers were so deformed that it was impossible to guess what kind of creatures they might have been. Two acronta had been felled, their armour ripped open to disclose hideous gashes in their grey-skinned flesh, which oozed bright yellow blood.

Tungdil assumed the death scream had come from the Voice of the Wind and that he had instigated the vicious storm. He could not see any sign of the älf with the glass-like hair and hoped that Hargorin, Beligata and Gosalyn had killed him. *This power would be unstoppable.*

An attack of vertigo forced him to lie still in the tall, wet grass, though he was keen to jump up and search through the devastation for his friends.

He saw the ghaist get to its feet in the ruins of a house as if nothing were amiss, before going over to rummage in the rubble.

It would have been too much to ask. Tungdil's lips narrowed in disappointment. *Does this mean there is a living creature inside the ghaist? Or does it mean there isn't?*

First the ghaist pulled the limp body of Aiphatòn out from under the pile of dust and stones. It slapped his face a few times to bring him round. Then the two of them dug with their hands in the rubble to bring Irïanora out. The älf laid her carefully over his shoulder.

Is she alive as well? Inàste's power is obviously stronger here in the Outer Lands than it is in Girdlegard. Tungdil did not move. He would be easy pickings in his present state and he was not going to give his enemies that victory.

Meanwhile the three remaining Acronta began to come to their senses. Their armour was badly dented, some of it missing. However, their injuries did not seem serious.

Tungdil caught sight of Hargorin's flaming red beard on the field of devastation; Beligata and Gosalyn were lying nearby. Not one of the dwarves was moving. *Vraccas, let them still be alive. You are surely as powerful as Inàste.* There was no sign of Carmondai.

The acronta did not want the älfar to escape. The long-running feud dictated they pursue them. And they were hungry by this time, too. The veterans drew their sword-length daggers and the three of them spread out.

Aiphatòn shrunk back, either dismayed by the superior

numbers or concerned for the safety of the motionless figure of the älf-woman he was carrying over his shoulder.

The ghaist, on the other hand, did not waver. In his right hand he was holding a squashed head with glass-like hair, that of the Voice of the Wind. The ghaist's glowing eye slits were fixed on the bloodied skull and Tungdil could hear its disappointed snorts. No matter how concerned he was about his companions, Tungdil could not help experiencing a sense of triumph at this sight. *The Wind älf will no longer present any threat to the Stone Gateway.*

The ghaist tossed the head away and turned on the acronta. Dodging the first acront's attack, it rolled through its legs, touching an open wound on the warrior's grey-skinned calf where the armour had been torn off.

The acront shuddered.

No! So they are susceptible to the ghaist's influence, too. Aghast, Tungdil slipped under the shelter of a bush.

The veteran acront, now possessed by magic, turned round with a roar to attack his own kind, taking them completely by surprise.

The ghaist seemed content at this and ran off, the acront's yellow blood glistening on its hand. As it passed through the devastated village, beasts and humans got up to follow. Some collapsed back immediately due to the severity of their injuries, while others crawled along, dragging broken limbs. Aiphatòn followed as well, the lifeless form of Irïanora over his shoulder. He had located his spear and was holding it in his free hand.

The ghaist and the älfar made off along the valley towards the south, with ever more figures stumbling along in its wake. If even the slightest spark of life remained, they would follow the call of the botoican. Perhaps a hundred craftsmen were left, of whom seventy would not be able to stand at an anvil.

I should follow; it will lead me to its master. Tungdil was still feeling unsteady. *That's if it has a master. But we need to know, one way or another.*

With his head still whirling, he had only a vague idea of what was happening with the acronta. The armoured giants crossed his field of vision more than once. One of the veterans fell but the battle continued. The last two still standing were fighting each other in the ruins, using stones to bash each other with. Their struggles were so violent the ground shook.

Tungdil could not say if one of the two was Tsatòn. *It's of no consequence. I must find my friends.*

He made his way down the incline, clambered over the rubble and heard the roars of the acronta grow fainter. They were fighting some distance away and presented no immediate danger.

At last he got to where Hargorin lay.

'Can you hear me?' Tungdil whispered, noting the dagger stuck in Hargorin's armour. He pulled it out gently and saw the wound was not a deep one. *But it needs immediate attention.* 'King of the Thirdlings, awake! Or Lorimbur's fury will strike you.'

'I serve Vraccas!' Hargorin's eyes shot open and he saw Tungdil. 'Is the älf dead?'

'The Voice of the Wind? Yes. There's his skull.' He pointed to where the head had landed. 'Can you get up and give me a hand? We have to help the women.'

Hargorin unbuckled his armour to examine his injury. The bleeding was slower now. He pressed his hand against the wound to stop the blood flow. 'I'll be all right,' he grunted, then he looked down at himself in horror. 'By Vraccas!'

'What is it?' Tungdil searched for a second wound.

Hargorin lifted his stump. 'I've lost my leg!' He grinned and Tungdil had to laugh with him. 'But I can still cope if I hop. And we've already won a victory for Girdlegard.' He took his axe and used it as a crutch.

'Indeed we have.' *But we'll be needing a whole host of other victories soon, I fear.*

The climbed over to where Beligata and Gosalyn were lying half-buried and together they shifted the stones and beams and rubble. There was no sign of the last acronta. They had probably killed each other by now.

Whenever a human or a beast dug their way out, Hargorin or Tungdil would kill them with a stab to the heart to make sure they did not follow the ghaist. *Even death comes as relief.* Tungdil surveyed the corpses. This was no time to feel pity. There was no hope for any of these brainwashed victims unless the botoican were run to ground and eradicated.

At last they succeeded in freeing the two unconscious dwarf women. Tungdil examined them carefully for injuries. Gosalyn had a fractured arm, but apart from that and some scratches, the two of them seemed to have got off lightly. Beligata's scar had increased in size and the black ink made little rivers like veins.

'That old dwarf-saying is true.' Hargorin was relieved. 'The smaller you are, the harder you fall.'

'We need somewhere to rest. We can't stay here in the village, with these fires smouldering and spreading fast. Let's get back to the wood.' Tungdil thought about how best to transport the two women while they were still unconscious. *We can cobble something together out of a few broken carts.*

A large shadow fell on them.

'Get down!' Hargorin barely had time to knock Tungdil to the ground before a wooden beam swung over his head.

An acront rose up next to them, purple light flooding out of the eye-slits in his visor. Before the dwarves could take evasive action, Tsatòn flung himself against the hostile acront, hurling him to the ground and shattering his helmet and the skull within with a mighty blow from his fist.

A dagger in Tsatòn's back had gone in up to the hilt. His unusually coloured light yellow blood was already streaming down from the wound.

Tungdil got up and hurried over to the wounded veteran, who had buried his adversary under his own bulk. The dwarf knelt down. 'Accept my heartfelt thanks,' he said. 'You saved our lives.' He looked at the deep cut. 'What can we do?'

The veteran acront was dying. His gauntleted finger wrote a last message in the dirt. 'Preserve the Acïjn Rhârk. You must . . .' The writing ended.

'I shall do,' Tungdil replied, getting up. 'I promise I shall.' He pulled out the fatal knife and took it with him. The steel was of an extraordinarily high quality. Perhaps something suitable for a dwarf's hands could be formed from it.

'Let's see if we can locate the other acronta. We need good weapons.' Tungdil indicated the dwarf-women. 'Maybe they'll have woken up by the time we get back.'

Hargorin glared at his stump. 'I'd rather have a leg than a new weapon. I'm no rabbit hopping through the grass. And it's a waste of a good axe, using it as a crutch.' He searched in the rubble for a viable piece of wood. 'Let me put something together here. You go and collect up the acronta knives.'

'Watch yourself, then,' Tungdil stepped round Tsatòn and went to locate the acronta; they at least would be easy to see because of their stature. He collected quite a few daggers while listening out for any sign of danger. It seemed that Vraccas was looking after them now.

While he was there, he scratched messages on the acronta armour in their own script. The emperor-mother would be sending out search parties as soon as she realised her warriors were missing. The bodies would be found. His message would warn them about the botoican's power. *Perhaps they'll finally join us in our struggle.*

When he came back, he saw the Thirdling king had managed to carve himself a provisional limb that he could fasten to his knee with strips of leather. 'I never thought Lorimbur was much of a carpenter.'

Hargorin grinned. 'You're right. He wasn't.' He demonstrated the crude substitute prosthesis. 'Otherwise I'd have added a couple of nice swirls and a picture of a tankard. But it should serve.'

Tungdil put down the knives, which were lighter than he had expected. 'Let's see to Gosalyn's broken arm. We can re-set it and get a splint on her while she's out cold.'

While they were dealing with Gosalyn, Beligata came around, followed closely by their patient.

Tungdil gave them a potted summary of events and distributed the sword-length daggers. 'We can turn them into more suitable weapons when we've got somewhere safe to work.' He led his group up towards the copse at the brow of the hill.

'What about Carmondai?' Gosalyn shook the dirt out of her peat-coloured hair and stared at the devastation.

'He didn't get up when the other followers did,' Tungdil said. 'I assume he's dead. Neither Hargorin nor I have seen him.'

'I never trusted him.' Beligata swung the dagger and tested its edge. 'He would have betrayed us sooner or later.'

Tungdil saved himself the trouble of a reply. *She's probably right.*

They set off, leaving the ruined settlement behind them. Climbing the hill, they made for the little grove of trees and made themselves comfortable near a pile of rocks. They lit a fire.

Gosalyn explained what she had found in Nodûcor's papers: details of ore deposits, requirements for coal, slaves, workers, provisions. There were exact specifications for parts to be made for a planned, larger construction.

Tungdil considered the implications. Everything hinted at the ghaist's master mustering a third army for a new onslaught on the dwarves' homeland. And this time, the botoican was not relying on sheer numbers of soldiers bent to his will. With Aiphatòn at his side, his chances of success would increase.

Gosalyn tried to move her broken arm, with a sharp intake of breath at the discomfort. 'I looked at their calculations and worked out the numbers he was catering for. I reckoned a fighting force of five hundred thousand including slaves.'

Quite a challenge. Tungdil could see his friends were yawning. He was tired as well, despite the shocking developments. 'We'll discuss it tomorrow and decide what to do. Let's eat now and then we need to get some rest.'

Beligata, Hargorin and Gosalyn nodded in agreement. They took a few mouthfuls of the food they had brought and then, one by one, they fell asleep. Apart from Tungdil. He kept watch and attempted to sort out his thoughts, twisting the vraccasium ring on his little finger.

He wondered about the botoican's power. Neither the älf nor the acronta had been able to resist its force. Only the

Children of the Smith were immune because of their stubborn natures. *But will our immunity persist?*

The sorcerer might ramp up his magic power. In that case, no further attack would be necessary. It would suffice for the botoican (or his ghaist henchman), merely to touch one of the dwarves in the defenders' ranks. That unhappy dwarf would then turn on his own kind like the acronta had done.

Tungdil cast his thoughts to Balyndis: she would be in grave danger, along with all her Fifthlings. *Nothing must happen to her.* He kissed the ring. *I promise I shall keep you safe.*

His thoughts then drifted to Sha'taï, who was almost certainly another botoican, and only at the beginning of her vocation, at that, in Carmondai's opinion. So the threat came not only from the unknown magician with its fervent hatred for the young girl, it came from her as well. *I wonder how long it is since we left? What has happened since then?* Tungdil raked the embers and threw two logs on the fire to drive off the night's cold from the circle of stones where they were camping.

His gaze fell softly on his sleeping companions. Their dreams were not free of the horrors they had lived through. Occasionally one of them would shudder or start mumbling. *I know that feeling. I never slept properly when I was in Phondrasôn. I would wake up screaming practically every night.*

There was only one possibility for him to undertake action against the ghaist's controller and the army that was being gathered, and as soon as the others woke up, he would tell them his decision. He expected objections, but he was going to insist that Gosalyn and Hargorin go straight back to Girdlegard. The girl had a broken arm and the other was missing a serviceable artificial limb – they would be no use on his mission. He would send them back to tell Ireheart what had happened and get him to summon the Assembly.

It was clear to Tungdil that the only army that stood any chance at all in battle against the botoican's hordes had to be composed entirely of dwarves. All other races and species were susceptible to the manipulating magic spell and would be drawn into the botoican's sphere of influence. Even acronta had succumbed.

Hammer and anvil. That's what the prophecy said.

The dwarf army was to ride out under the leadership of Hargorin and Gosalyn, heading for the mine where he and Beligata would be exploring the situation. He and she would spy out every minute detail to get the information needed for a swift and decisive dwarf victory. *By the time the dwarves get here with their army, we will have found out what the botoican looks like and determined a way to win.*

In the meantime, something would have to be done about Sha'taï. He refused to entertain the idea of having her killed until there was sufficient proof that she was acting from sheer evil and depravity. *So far she had done nothing but bring peace. But we need a solution before the rest of Girdlegard falls victim to her spell.*

How long would it take for his messengers to reach Ireheart? How long would the dwarves need to muster their army? How many orbits or even cycles would it take for them to arrive? Only Vraccas could know.

But we will face the foe. Tungdil stared at the place on his hand where the ghaist had touched him and he smiled. A cold, grim smile.

Take strong, full-bodied black beer
with a powerful kick.

Heat gently in a pan
with cinnamon, honey and cloves,
aniseed and citrus fruits to taste.

Add the juice of cherries or blackberries
and even some heady dark brandy.

Enjoy your beer
whenever the wind whistles cold about your ears
and the first snowflakes start to fall.

Recipe for dwarf spiced beer (serve hot)

XXVIII

Girdlegard
United Kingdom of Gauragar-Idoslane
Freestone
6496th solar cycle, winter

'Let us debate the matter again. But this time, let's learn from our mistakes.' Ireheart surveyed the familiar round of faces. It was essential he win support for his views. *They will have to listen to the new developments with open minds.*

The dwarf leaders had assembled with little ado, as Ireheart had stipulated, in the heart of Girdlegard and with only a few dozen warriors in attendance. Without the tunnel-ways for swift communication and transport, the simplest thing was to summon everyone to the centre.

Freetown took them in without any great upheaval. The residents had got used to all the banners, regiments and heroes. The local landlord welcomed them as old friends, ushering the company into a quiet chamber where they would be undisturbed. Refreshments were ready in an anteroom.

Gosalyn and Hargorin had arrived in Freestone, travelling with Balyndis. They had brought the Scholar's message with them.

They had traversed many miles of the Outer Lands to get to the Stone Gateway, encountering no problems on the way. The botoican's army of monsters was being mustered elsewhere and so the surrounding landscape was free of threats. Hargorin referred to their journey as having been a 'boring hike' until they had come across some stray ponies. After that the trek had turned, according to Gosalyn, into 'torture by saddle'. The red-bearded dwarf had been happy enough on horseback but the dwarf-woman had hated it.

Having read the Scholar's message, Ireheart was now up to date with events, and listened attentively to Hargorin and Gosalyn while waiting for the arrival of the other tribal heads. They had told him how they had been taken prisoner, how the acronta had kept them in their home hive, how Tungdil's combat skills had won them freedom, and then how they had met with the ghaist and Aiphatòn. The High King was now convinced that the other dwarf leaders would not be able to shut their ears to the growing crisis.

Gosalyn did not look any the worse for the strenuous trek through the Outer Lands and the Thirdling king was as sturdy as ever. 'Vraccas has sent them back to us after four cycles so that we may listen to what they have to say,' Boïndil began. 'And so that we may act. We have waited around for long enough.'

'How true, High King!' Balyndis nodded in agreement. 'My son has repelled two waves of attack more dangerous than anything previously experienced,' she broke in, ignoring Gosalyn's attempt to be heard. 'We have strengthened the fortifications and are undertaking a range of further measures on the Stone Gateway in the hope of forestalling or delaying an army. But I fear a third attack may overwhelm our defences.' She related how the rag-tag army had scaled the granite gates and the use they had made of ramps, and how the mighty wind had rendered their weapons powerless. Her audience listened agog. Only when she had finished her description of the assault wave did she notice that Gosalyn had raised her hand. 'Excuse me, Gosalyn. I just had to share. Please, proceed.'

Gosalyn pulled out a map of Girdlegard and unrolled it, placing it on the table. She opened her mouth to speak but again she was interrupted.

'The Fifthlings aren't able to defend us? They can't guarantee to keep us safe from invasion?' This outburst came from Xamtor Boldface, King of the Firstlings.

'Not as things stand. The fortifications present little more than a hurdle for these beasts to overcome. We've had the ghaist actually standing on our walls, as you know. For the second time. This one tried to force my son under his master's influence. But it did not work.' Balyndis asked for a glass of water. 'They know everything about our defences that they need to put us in extreme difficulty, even if we had thousands of soldiers on our walls.'

Frandibar Gemholder, this time in a suit of polished vraccasium armour decorated with patterns picked out in rubies, malachite and agate, encouraged Gosalyn and Hargorin to enlighten them. When he talked the golden strands in his beard appeared to dance. 'We're keen to hear what you have to say.'

'I shall begin with a verse,' said Gosalyn, relieved to be given the chance to speak at last. Her skin had gone dark brown and leathery from travelling in the sun. 'It was recited to us once and then it faded away.' She took a deep breath.

With hammer and anvil.
Only those
do not let themselves be turned.

Only those
are true to form and mighty, destructive enough
and able to withstand storm and fire and steel.

Only those
are hammer and anvil.

Send the hammer and the anvil out
to the north, always to the north.

Let them find the evil
let them destroy the evil and let them shatter it.

None but those
will succeed.

Gordislan the Younger from the Freelings gave a disdainful smile. 'Those are the words of the elves' creator. Not a good beginning.'

'No, it's not, but it finally makes sense.' Hargorin, also deeply tanned, got up from his seat. 'We have been through so much. We can't tell you everything in detail here – let's save that for long winter evenings round the fire with good friends and a glass of beer when the icy wind whistles outside and we relish telling our stories – but now is the time for action.' He raised his hand and pointed north. 'Let me emphasise: if we as dwarves had not held back three cycles ago, if we had not been so sceptical about the prophecy, we might already have triumphed.'

'First, let me say how glad I am to see you both safe returned,' said Gordislan. 'Praise be to Vraccas for having kept his protective hand over you, and over Tungdil and Beligata, too, I gather. I look forward to those tales by the fireside. But I must insist you put us in the picture now.'

Xamtor chimed in his support. 'Just tell us the main events that kept you from us for three long cycles while we waited, so concerned about your safety. Tell us how you know so definitively that we need to march.'

Smooth talker. Ireheart normally liked Gordislan and Xamtor but at the moment he could do without the political rhetoric. He was impatient to get down to business.

Ireheart still had Tungdil's bottle of special essence in his pocket; it was supposed to be helpful whenever thirst and anger got out of hand, but he had never taken any of it. He could not say why not. Perhaps the fear that it was not the actual Tungdil but a counterfeit copy of his friend, and that the imposter might want to poison him.

It did not look as if Xamtor was about to give in gracefully, and Ireheart had to sit through a new recital of Hargorin and Gosalyn's exploits in the Outer Lands. He kept his temper in check with the help of a large tankard of beer and a generous application of heavy sighs.

He used the time to plan ahead.

Ireheart was sure the dwarves would eventually agree to campaign. They would gather at the mine and attack the botoican's forces mustering there. *There's nothing else for it. If we delay, they'll overrun us at the Gateway and gain entry. Or they'll find a different way through the Grey Mountains.* With the power to influence and manipulate minds, it was horribly plausible that the botoican could send out thousands of scouts to look for concealed mountain passes.

Ireheart assumed some of this had already been attempted with Aiphatòn's assistance. But he took comfort in the fact that the leaden-hued mass of rock did not welcome everyone who approached. It was not kind to beasts and humans without the correct equipment to withstand the elements. Crossing the mountains in snow and icy winds, struggling with scree and dealing with extreme altitude would put paid to most attempts within a few orbits.

They might be able to storm victoriously across a plain, but being a mighty army won't help them in the mountains. Ireheart helped himself to more tepid beer. The landlord here knew not to serve it too cold.

He was relieved to hear that the Voice of the Wind had been eliminated. So was Balyndis, who had experienced first-hand the destruction that was wrought, not only on their defences, but on their people. *Would a hurricane have sufficed to open the gates?* Ireheart was glad not to know the answer to that.

But this did not alter the fact that the botoican was building an army that, in size and scope, outnumbered anything seen before in Girdlegard, and probably in the Outer Lands as well. Gosalyn had not had time to go through the papers thoroughly, but she spoke of half a million soldiers about to gather in the quarry.

Five hundred thousand. A solid block of flesh and bone. But they had no choice – Ireheart was afraid Girdlegard would fall under the sway of the botoican if he breached their wall. The homeland would serve only to provide the magician with more battlefield-fodder. Better troops. More possibilities. Once he got rid of Sha'taï, that is. Ireheart shuddered to think what would happen if she did it as well.

He was not sure how many people lived in the human kingdoms but it must be several million, he thought. And the pointy-ears had excellently trained warriors. He imagined an army surging out in all directions while the botoican sat in the middle like an evil spider controlling them and their fate. A shiver went up and down his spine.

Our Scholar will deal the ghaist a death blow with

Keenfire and then we'll have the urgently needed time of quiet. Ireheart noticed that Hargorin and Gosalyn had finished speaking. All eyes were on him now.

Taking a swig of beer to moisten his throat, he asked, 'Do you understand now why we have to go to war?'

'We do.' Xamtor fiddled with the tips of his grey-speckled beard, looking thoughtful and ready to cooperate.

'And we need every hand that can wield a weapon,' Gosalyn urged.

'But there's still the question of whether we can trust the elves to hold our fortresses for us.' The blond-haired Frandibar played nervously with his bejewelled signet ring. The gem cutters liked to show off how good they were at their craft. 'And what if we lose too many of our best dwarves?' Then he added, after a pause, 'What if we lose *all* of them? There was nothing in the prophecy about the hammer and the anvil getting back home safely.'

The large chamber fell silent. The last of the evening winter light fell through the leaded bottle-glass windows. Lamps and torches were being lit outside.

Curses. He's got a point. 'It might be useful to look at the full version of the prediction,' Ireheart said, furious with himself for not having thought of this before. Anger boiled up inside him, stoked by his concern about his friend and the northern border. *It'll mean losing valuable time.* 'I'll ask the Naishïon . . .'

'I don't give a damn about the prophecy,' Hargorin bellowed. 'We know our people are not susceptible to the botoican's magic. We take our warriors and we march!' He crossed his arms defiantly under the impressive red beard. 'Vraccas will know what fate awaits us and that's good enough for me. I don't need Sitalia's prophecies to know what we have to do.' The Thirdling king looked at Frandibar. 'Girdlegard is relying on us yet again, on us and on our axes. If we do nothing, we go down with them.'

'You're seeing this too simplistically, Hargorin Deathbringer,' Frandibar retorted.

'I am not. I have done battle with beasts you can't even dream of. I have come through the wilderness one-legged to get here, collect a new limb and go straight back to fight,' he thundered. 'You are scared!'

'Scared?' Frandibar jumped up to answer the challenge, ignoring the fact that he was much smaller in stature. 'How dare you accuse me of cowardice!'

'You are frightened of the unknown.' Hargorin glared at him.

A clever move. Ireheart thought he knew where the red-haired dwarf was going with this. He was prepared to let the row take its course for the moment, but was ready to intervene if necessary. He mastered his own hot blood with difficulty.

'Our race marched out to battle against evil once before. And we won.' Hargorin reminded the Assembly about the battle of the Black Abyss. 'Perhaps the times have passed when our mission was to sit in our mountains and guard the gates. Perhaps we have to march out and confront the enemy in his lair, where he is gathering strength. And perhaps we have to spread the word in Girdlegard first to make sure everyone knows what we are doing for them. Humans and elves must be told what we are undertaking. We need to work together. As a community. *Only then.* No more arrogant isolation for us.'

Ireheart was impressed by what the Thirdling king had said. Hargorin's deep tones had added authority to his words.

Good thing it wasn't me talking. I'd have stammered and stuttered. 'I think I'll get you to make all my speeches from now on,' he said, raising his tankard in acknowledgement of the other's undoubted rhetoric. 'Couldn't have said it better myself.' *I'm rubbish at being High King, really. Hargorin should take over. Or Balyndar. Either one would be better.*

'I agree. We'll set out with all our forces and hand the strongholds over to the elves to guard.' Balyndis appeared thoughtful but decisive.

Frandibar sighed. 'People will suspect the elves of secretly planning to murder our children while they sleep once their fathers are away on campaign.'

'So you're against this?' Ireheart looked straight at Frandibar. This eternal feuding irritated him. *First the smooth talker, and now the gem cutter's namby-pamby views*. A red mist started to form. He grasped his beer mug quickly.

'Indeed not. He agrees with me,' Balyndis replied determinedly. 'And I'm definitely in support' – she pointed at the place on the map where the Idoslane magic source was located, Coïra's present abode – 'of tackling *this* question *afterwards*. I don't want to have to argue with every soul in Girdlegard that we have gone to the Outer Lands to do battle to protect.'

'I agree,' Xamtor faced Hargorin. 'In case you and Gosalyn are unaware: a town has been built there, quite a considerable size. It has a mighty tower in the middle. Sha'taï spends quite a bit of time there. She is now a young woman and very popular everywhere in the whole country. Emperor Rodario takes her with him wherever he goes. Word has got round that he likes to move amongst his subjects and seek their admiration. He is in good favour with the elves, too. This is all due to his adopted daughter's influence, we think.'

Hargorin and Gosalyn exchanged glances. This was the first they had heard of it.

'For now, the botoican at our northern gates has priority.' Ireheart was relieved to note the mood in the debating chamber had changed, even though this was entirely down to what Hargorin and Balyndis had said. It had nothing to do with his own authority. Sending out practically every dwarf to do battle was an incredible risk to take. *Greater than any in our entire history*. But future observers would ascribe the responsibility for any disaster to him, Boïndil, alone.

He *was* extremely concerned about Sha'taï and her influential foster parents. Ireheart had wanted to have a talk with Rodario about the dangers the young woman posed, but this plan had not come to fruition. He had not even bothered to have a word with Mallenia. She was utterly devoted to her *little one*. And there was no evidence of an ill nature or observable untoward conduct. On the contrary. *She was a sweet young thing, you'd say. If you didn't know better.*

'Are we positive now that the true Tungdil Goldhand has come back to us?' Gordislan asked. 'That, in my opinion, is the ultimate point we need to agree on.'

'Of course it's him!' Ireheart would entertain no doubts on this score. His right hand clutched the handle of his tankard and squeezed it for emphasis. 'We've been talking for too long,' he thundered, demanding a refill. *Who does this wretched idiot think he is, telling me my business?* He had a violent urge to get up and bash Gordislan on the head. He was High King, after all. *There's bound to be some law or other that gives me the right to kill him*. He kept his chestnut-coloured eyes firmly fixed on the Freeling dwarf.

'Go on, give me an excuse,' he muttered under his breath.

'Excuse?' Gordislan asked. 'Excuse for what?'

'I too am absolutely sure we have the right Tungdil Goldhand,' Gosalyn said swiftly. 'I have travelled with the dwarf for several cycles. He has saved our lives and led our band well.'

'That's what Tionium Tungdil did, too,' Gordislan objected.

Ireheart leaped up from his seat, his temper frayed to breaking point. 'I won't have –'

'I would have known if there was even a spark of evil in him.' Gosalyn made a gesture to placate the High King. 'I would trust him with my life and I would trust him with the safety of our homeland.'

'The same goes for me.' Hargorin placed his hand on the dwarf-woman's shoulder. She smiled at him.

I must give vent to my anger or I'll launch myself at him. Ireheart slammed his fist down on the tabletop with such force that it sent jugs and beakers flying. The board creaked under the impact.

'Enough talk!' he declared, aware of a certain feeling of relief. 'I will inform the Naishïon of our plans. I expect him to support them and to send his best warriors to take over our fortresses. The vital thing is to establish trust.'

'You can't command trust,' Frandibar objected, horrified by the High King's attitude. 'But I'll go along with that.'

Balyndis and the other rulers indicated agreement.

'And we won't tell the citizens about the change in guard,' Ireheart ordered, breathing heavily. 'Otherwise Sha'taï might find she wants to take advantage of the opportunity.'

'To do what exactly?' Gordislan was all attention now.

'Use your head, clev—' He bit his tongue. 'How should I know what the little botoican girl has planned?' he replied, sitting down again. 'So, no word to anyone outside this room. The elves will join us in secret. No one is to know.'

They all nodded.

'Let's get down to planning.'

Lamps and candles were lit now that night had fallen. The dwarf leaders discussed strategy, troop numbers, how units would proceed on the march to the Outer Lands, how they would be catered for, how many horses and oxen they would need, what equipment to take, which route to use, and so on. Hargorin and Balyndis took the minutes, with the High King's approval.

Ireheart was suddenly aware that it would be many orbits before this enormous undertaking was ready. Victory was not possible without meticulous planning. The dwarves knew nothing of the hundred miles of terrain leading to the mine. Their forces would not have to reckon with any beast-attack but it was essential they kept the element of surprise. That would be the only thing working in their favour if they had to face the botoican and his half a million in combat.

I hope the Scholar can get us enough information. Ireheart held back, not interfering in the planning proceedings. He kept drinking to keep his anger in check. He was bothered by the long hair on his temples. *Must get it cut.*

The candles had started to gutter and smoke and the lamps to dim before the company broke up, ready for bed, still confident that the right course of action was being taken. Only Balyndis and the High King were left.

Thousands of dwarves, male and female, would be under arms. Ireheart pulled the beer jug over to him. He was as exhausted as if he had been in single combat all day. *Every warrior we possess. Vraccas, support us in this. I don't want to be the ruler that leads your people to disaster.*

'Protection.' Balyndis had spoken under her breath.

Ireheart looked at her and took a sip. 'What?'

'Not us. The girl.' The queen of the Fifthlings stood up. 'I've been thinking about what she's attempting to achieve by making herself and the emperor more popular than any other figure in Girdlegard.'

'To protect herself.'

'She's collecting loyal supporters to defend her against any threat.' Balyndis went on: 'She ran away from her enemies and had to live in fear for a long time. That made her the way she is. If we show her that she is safe here in Girdlegard – then perhaps she will lay her powers aside.'

'Do you think it's that simple?' Ireheart put the empty jug back down.

'Could be. It's worth considering before we do anything when we return. We might regret making her frightened again. It could lead to a catastrophe.' Balyndis studied Ireheart's face. 'What was happening in here tonight?'

'I don't know what you mean.'

'Your outburst. You looked as if you first wanted to kill Xamtor, then Frandibar and finally Gordislan.' The queen gave a worried smile. 'Is it the old problem? The rage?'

'I . . . was . . .' Ireheart felt the fury well up again. 'I'm no speech-maker and they were wasting precious time, and . . .' He clenched his fists. 'I'll get rid of my rage on the battlefield and then I'll be able to calm down.'

'Will you?' She turned for the door. 'Look after yourself, old friend. I am fond of you.' Balyndis left the room before he could ask her about Tungdil.

Ireheart watched her go. He gave the jug a bad-tempered shove. It slid over the table, stopping at the edge. *They're all so bloody clever. So much bloody insight. Someone else should take over as High King.* He was totally at a loss with the responsibility of office.

This made him angrier than ever. Rage engulfed him.

I'm a warrior! I need to fight. Vraccas knows why he makes my inner forge so hot. Grabbing the table, he hurled it across the room. Chairs followed, crashing against the wall. When the landlord came in, concerned about his furniture, Ireheart slung coins his way and threw him out.

Only when the room was in ruins did he plonk himself down in despair. The raging fury subsided, but Ireheart knew it could return at any moment. He knew it was the älfar elixir that caused it.

This has got to stop or I'll kill one of my own kind. He took out the little bottle Tungdil had given him, removed the wax seal and pulled out the cork. *I trust you, my Scholar.*

He downed the contents of the phial.

Girdlegard
Grey Mountains
Kingdom of the Fifthling Dwarves
Stone Gateway
6497th solar cycle, early summer

'Are you sure you know how to operate the mobile catapults?' Balyndar looked quizzically at the elf-woman at his side. They were at the reworked constructions for the clay bottle launchers. The defensive walkway had been given an additional storey and extra fortification and the munitions engineers had ironed out the residual faults in the new system. None of the other dwarf strongholds could hold a candle to this one.

Ocâstia vaulted onto the narrow seat next to the machine and slunk down to get in the right position to view the crosshairs in the aiming viewer next to the long barrel. 'In sequence.' She pointed in turn at two locks, a bolt and the trigger. 'Then I can fire.'

'And how is the machine moved?' It was too soon to give praise. *But I would have expected nothing less from her.*

She took her foot off the rest and placed it on the rotation disc that operated the system of cogs for turning the wheels. She turned to him, a broad smile on her face. 'Satisfied?'

'Relieved. Not satisfied.' Balyndar returned the friendly smile and stuck his thumbs in his belt. 'At least I can leave knowing that you lot can be trusted with the stronghold.'

'Of course you can.' Ocâstia slipped off the operator's stool and glanced down at the courtyard where the dwarves' advance guard was mustering. The banners and pennants of the various tribes and clans fluttered in the wind, dotting the army with colour. 'It's taken nearly a full cycle for you to get this far.'

'That's because you took such a long time learning how to use all our equipment, and mastering the gate-opening mechanism,' he teased in return. He wanted her to join in the high spirits rather than worry, as other elves might have done. 'Good preparation wins over swift defeat.'

'You're right there.' The elf-woman in her white armour let her gaze sweep over the assembled mass of male and female warriors and their mounts. From up here everyone looked tiny. 'I thought the army would set out in spring.'

'Still too much snow around. It was a tough winter. The meltwater would have washed us away or barred our progress with raging torrents.' Balyndar was brought up in the mountains. The generals, under the command of the High King Boïndil, had faith in his opinion. 'It all looks more promising now.'

'How long do you think it will take you to get to the mines?' Ocâstia took her eyes off the hundred-strong unit that would be setting out to reconnoitre and warn others of potential hazards.

'Hard to say. If we managed thirty miles an orbit with all the wagons and equipment, I'd be happy. There's so much to bear in mind. We can't just storm in there.'

He signalled down to the waiting force to indicate the road was free. His mother Balyndis would now pronounce the formula that opened the ten bolts on the gates.

'But we'll be back with you by autumn, or winter at the latest,' he told the elf-woman.

'I look forward to welcoming you all back.' Ocâstia placed her hand on the launcher. 'And I wish you all the support you need on the journey.'

'Thank you.' Balyndar felt the granite shudder as the bolts were slowly activated one after the other, the runes glowing bright in response to the prescribed phrase. 'We'll need it.' He handed Ocâstia a leather-bound volume. 'This has got drawings of all the defence devices and instructions on how to deal with any faults, if a mechanism gets stuck or fractures.'

'But you've left us craftspeople,' she smiled, taking hold of the heavy book.

'Not many, and between ourselves' – he bent forward – 'some of those we're leaving behind are not the most agile, because of their age. We can only use the swiftest reactions in combat. Things can move fast in battle.'

'Or tortuously slowly.' Ocâstia placed her hand on the brown leather cover. 'Thank you.'

If only all the elves were like her. Balyndar took out a map, folded small, and handed it to her. 'This will show you the places marked on both sides of the road where the engineers have dug their traps. Don't activate them unless there's really nothing else for it. A last resort.'

'Activate how?'

'With this.' He tapped the side of the launcher. 'The traps are relatively small. Train your eye. Practise locating them so if you need to, you'll find them fast. They can be triggered by arrow if you prefer.'

Ocâstia grunted in approval. 'I knew you dwarves were inventive.' She fastened her hair back to stop the wind playing with it. 'Just take these big machines, for example. But what you've just shown me is the icing on the cake. Very clever.'

Balyndar's armour creaked and clanged as he placed his strong brown hand on the paper. 'It's *vital* no one else learns about where the traps are placed,' he said urgently.

'Why tell me? Shouldn't it be the next commander when he arrives? I think the Naishïon is sending someone competent . . .'

'I've discussed this with the queen my mother. There's been a change.' He addressed her formally. '*You* are to take charge of the stronghold if danger comes. The stronghold is in your hands.'

Ocâstia recovered quickly.

'I am only a sorânïan but I give you my solemn oath, Balyndar Steelfinger: I shall hold the fort. Come what may.' She stowed the book and the map under her left arm and held out her right hand to him. 'Take my vow with you. I swear by my own life. Nothing will get me to abandon the Stone Gateway to enemies.'

He could see that she felt honoured. *We have chosen the right one.*

The dwarf nodded. 'I know. I trust you. And that is why you are our choice. You know the place inside out. And you've been without a clear responsibility for over a cycle, with no elves turning up needing checking over. No need for boredom now.'

Ocâstia laughed. 'I shall miss your sense of humour. Come back safe, Son of the Smith. Have you taken enough of my special pickled meat?'

Balyndar gestured to one of the heavily laden wagons. 'It constitutes my entire diet.'

She grinned, placing a hand on the battlements. 'I shan't go to bed until the last of the army has ridden out.'

'It may be some time yet.'

'Oh, but I have eternal life.' The sorânïan grinned and Balyndar burst out laughing.

The gates creaked and scraped the ground as they opened. Stone dust tumbled off in clouds.

'When was the last time the gates were opened?' Ocâstia wanted to know.

Balyndar could not answer: he was so moved by the sound of drums and trumpets and the magnificent glory of the troops in their splendid armour. They were waiting for the gap to get wider and let them through as the warm breeze played on their faces.

His mother, Queen Balyndis, was at the head of the unit and she was now lowering her arms. She had held her hands in the air while speaking the solemn words that released the locking mechanism and the gates opened as if by some higher power. The portal represented the might of Vraccas. The god's strength, combined with the masterly metal-working skills of his people, had produced the ten securing bolts.

This is our kind of magic. Balyndar was overcome with

emotion and filled with energy. 'I must go,' he whispered, shuddering with excitement. 'Keenfire is desperate to be released. The axe wants to see some action.' Balyndar glanced at the elf-woman.

'I shall protect Girdlegard. I swear.' Ocâstia nodded to him. 'Ride.'

Balyndar turned and went down on the lift platform. He hurried to his quarters to collect the legendary weapon. *You will bring us victory.*

A pony, already saddled, awaited him at the gate and he mounted among cheers from his men. Looking at his mother he pulled Keenfire out and brandished it high in the air. 'We are the Children of the Smith!'

'We are the Children of the Smith!' The echo came from a hundred throats, and the soldiers clanged and clattered their weapons against their armour, the noise resounding from the walls.

Bugle blasts, drum rolls and cries of *Vraccas* accompanied the troop as the vanguard moved off.

Balyndar knew he could trust Ocâstia. She would be steadfast and she would protect the stronghold against any attack. *We could not have found anyone better.*

Ocâstia had put the map and the book of machinery plans on the ledge next to her and was watching as the last of the dwarves left the stronghold.

The granite doors closed seamlessly shut. The bolts crashed noisily back into position, definitively securing the entrance. *So off they've gone.* She wiped her tears away, her left hand playing with the game figurine Rognor had given her.

'You must be the sorânïan they're all talking about.' The elf-voice sounded spiteful. 'A proper little heroine.'

Turning her head, she saw an elf in silver-dyed leather armour, wearing a polished golden helmet with elaborate decoration and a bright red cloak. He was striding along the corridor towards her. 'And you, presumably, are the captain the Naishïon has sent that the dwarves deselected before you even reached the Grey Mountains,' she replied.

'That's fighting talk.' He came to a halt, the wind playing with the red material of his cloak. 'I am Menahîn, sent by and good friend of Ataimînas.'

'You imply that you know him personally.'

Menahîn smiled arrogantly. 'Correct.' *And a boastful one at that.*

'And that'll be why you're about to tell me that you must insist on my ceding command of the stronghold and informing the dwarves accordingly.' She was watching the last of the torches in the column fade into the dark on the road. *That means I am now in office.*

'That is indeed exactly what I was about to say. Let's stop wasting time.' Menahîn looked at her disdainfully. 'A sorânïan might be all very well when it comes to torturing men, women and children who can't defend themselves, but a female officer would be useless when it comes to combat.'

'Why do you think I had anything to do with torturing anyone?'

'I only have to look at you.' He gave a fleeting scornful glance at her map and book. 'Gifts to match your tears?'

'Instructions for using the machines' – she indicated the catapults behind him – 'and a list of the traps the dwarves have set up.' She pointed over her shoulder with her thumb. 'Very ingenious, the Children of Vraccas.'

As Menahîn tried to pick them up, she placed her hand firmly on the items.

'How dare you?' he snapped. 'I shall inform Ataimînas of your conduct.'

Ocâstia leaned back, watching how his cloak was caught by the wind. 'Terribly impracticable, you know, cloaks, when we're patrolling the walkway. Up here in the mountains, the wind comes in sudden gusts.' She grasped the corner of his cloak and tossed it up over his helmet. 'Like this. Suddenly you can't see a thing, can you, so you might miss a potential attack.'

'What do you think you are playing at?' Menahîn yanked the cloak, but the material had got stuck on his helmet.

'What was it you were saying just now?' Ocâstia delivered a kick to the back of the elf's knee, making him lose his balance. She gave him a push.

Menahîn crashed into the battlements, his hands meeting thin air.

He stumbled over the low wall and plunged down into the courtyard, his body shattering on the granite ground. His cloak was still stuck on his helmet.

She looked down. 'Oh, how terrible!' she cried, the wind pulling at her long hair. 'A sharp gust of wind! It took his cloak like a sail and over he went!' She pulled herself back, not able to suppress her laughter. It would not fit with the horrified attitude she had to portray.

She strolled along to the lift to go down, not forgetting to take book and map with her. *I made a solemn oath to Balyndar*, she thought, contentedly. *I shall keep my word.*

Somewhere in the Outer Lands

I never thought it would take this long. Tungdil sat at the entrance to their hidden shelter, observing, as usual. He refused to entertain the idea that Hargorin and Gosalyn might have met with an accident. *An army of the size we need will take some preparing, for sure. I expect Ireheart is erring on the side of caution.*

The quarry, a vast hole, was nothing like the älfar domiciles in Girdlegard or the palaces of Phondrasôn. There was a demonic vibe here, as if evil had dug itself into the heart of the earth and died, leaving a plague-ridden miasma poisoning everything within range.

Perhaps this is the birthplace of the demon that once rampaged through Girdlegard.

It had taken Tungdil and Beligata some time to locate a spot in the mine where they could watch what was happening without being spotted by the sentries. The botoican – wherever he might be – seemed to have become suspicious after the events in the settlement. He sent groups of ten or twelve monsters on patrol round the circumference of the crater at irregular intervals. Every hundred paces there were watchtowers manned by beasts.

There was no going back for Tungdil and Beligata. So they did what neither the botoican nor the älfar would have expected: they dug themselves in, using stolen tools, making a cave about ten paces below the top of the quarry. Not much imagination had gone into camouflaging the entrance, just a pile of old rags and some dirt. They increased the size of their shelter by working on it ceaselessly every day.

They took care to make as little noise as possible. One of them would stand guard, making notes on developments now that the army was here. Whatever the two of them needed in the way of food they stole from the delivery wagons as they arrived.

Tungdil could see that the original excavation of this mine must have taken place a long time ago. Many cycles previously, at least a hundred, this had been a coalmine. Now there were horizontal galleries. Perhaps people had altered their focus and started instead to search for gold or gemstones.

Where terraces had been created, there were vertical shafts from which steam and smoke welled up. Sometimes the wind would waft the fumes over to the dwarves. Sometimes there was a smell of rotten eggs, or red-hot metal or bitter vapours that stung their eyes and made them feel sick.

The beasts and humans labouring in the mine did not seem to be affected. They were subjected to the cruel will of the botoican as they worked tirelessly to extract coal from the old shafts.

Various forges had been erected in the open air, sending up flames and smoke. At night it was an impressive spectacle with fires blazing in furnaces that were seventy paces tall. They were smelting ore, the raw material for the weapons that were being manufactured in the nearby smithies. Ramps and flights of steps had been cut into the sides of the mine, and there were pulleys fastened to beams by ropes. Tents and primitive sheds served as shelters for the workers. Tungdil reckoned there were currently around a hundred thousand miscellaneous creatures at work here.

But the botoican would certainly have more subjects waiting in the vicinity. Columns of supply vehicles were constantly trundling through bringing food and meat. They also brought building materials and more slaves; these were not under direct mind-control but were disciplined by others with whips. Most of the slaves were set to work in the mine galleries and shafts.

'Anything new?' Beligata came to Tungdil's side.

'The sorcerer seems to want to be sparing with the use of

his magic powers.' He pointed south where orcs with whips were herding a hundred human slaves through into the mine-shafts, and forcing them to push empty tubs along. 'He's not hypnotising any of the new ones.'

'What can be behind it all?' She shuffled in next to him, her clothing smelling as intense as his own.

'He might be storing up his energy with the intention of tackling a very resistant opponent.' Tungdil made more notes about the most recent bunch of slaves.

Beligata brushed sand from her shoulder. 'How long have we been here in this hole?'

He smiled. 'Nearly a full cycle. Asking that every three orbits doesn't change anything.'

The gallery they were sitting in started to vibrate slightly, and stones and pebbles fell from the roof. This was something that often happened; it was as if the ground itself was protesting against the ghaist's master, and was trying to shake the invaders out. The tremors did not last longer than ten breaths and the dwarves' shelter had never suffered any damage. Nor had the terraces.

'Our troops should have got here by now.' Beligata flashed him an angry look. 'You should have sent me. I'm not a cripple like Hargorin or weak like Gosalyn.'

'That's why you're with me.' Tungdil patted her encouragingly on the back. 'They'll come. Soon.'

'How do you know?' She flicked a pebble. It rolled out of the entrance. No one would notice.

'Because it's summer now. The mountain passes are open and the rivers are no longer raging torrents and are easier to cross. There was no point in setting out in winter or the early part of the year.' He was trying to soothe her impatience before she had a chance to infect him with it. 'Tell me, how would you plan an attack on this quarry? Bear in mind they've got sentries everywhere. Of course they'd notice an army approaching. So I don't want any silly answers like *Set fire to the mine. Send an avalanche.*'

That made Beligata laugh. 'But it would work if they didn't see our warriors arriving.'

'No it wouldn't. The beasts have an excellent sense of smell.'

'So why don't they know we're here?'

'Because' – Tungdil took a piece of her clothing between his thumb and forefinger – 'we smell just as rank as they do.'

Beligata grinned, and this time the scar on her cheek did not react. 'I'd use a third of my forces to simulate an attack, making a lot of noise. That would concentrate the enemy in one place. The slopes here would be full of beasts surging up. Our soldiers would only have to prevent the beasts getting up over the rim.' She then pointed to the other side, indicating a terrace level below theirs. 'Then I'd send the rest of my army over there, with crossbows and catapults. They could take out the ones at the bottom of the crater. Further up, the sides are too wide and it'd all be out of range. Doing that would deprive them of their reinforcements and remove at least a third of them without any hand-to-hand combat at all.' She looked down at the main workshop areas at the base of the quarry where the smelting, the pouring of molten metal and the hammering was constant. 'A fire could spread nicely down there.'

Tungdil laughed. 'You can't resist it, can you?'

'I like fire. And it makes sense.'

'Carry on.' *She's good. Can't just be learned, this way of thinking.*

'My soldiers up at the top of the quarry would have killed

about a quarter of the beasts. They'd be needing back-up now. The more beasts are killed, the more furiously the rest'll fight.'

'And the botoican will be urging them on,' Tungdil pointed out.

'I suggest we have our archers move round the crater on both sides, shooting at the mass of beasts. Meanwhile our engineers can prepare the edge behind our troops. They withdraw at our signal and we demolish the edge of the quarry, sending it down as a landslide, burying the beasts and sending them straight into the fires by the furnaces.' Beligata had not hesitated at all; she had spoken calmly and with deliberation.

Let's see if I can catch you out. 'Sounds good. It reminds me of the Tenûbi manoeuvre.'

'Not really comparable. The . . .' The dark-haired dwarf-woman fell silent, embarrassed.

Tungdil continued with his note-taking as if nothing had happened. 'I'm missing quite a lot of what occurred in Girdlegard in the last two hundred and fifty cycles. There are masses I still have to read up on before I'm up to speed. But a few things stand out when it comes to the Thirdlings.' He smiled at her. 'After all, I'm one of them myself.'

'But I'm a Freeling,' Beligata protested.

'You belong to the Thirdling tribe, as I understand it.' Tungdil kept studying activity in the crater as minutely as always, even while he was speaking to her. 'I spent a great deal of time in Phondrasôn with all kinds of monsters. You can only know about the Tenûbi manoeuvre if you've played Tharc. It's a strategy game exclusive to the älfar. You are a very good tactician and you have a quick temper, and you can be cold and cruel when it is not appropriate.'

Beligata said nothing. Her breathing became faster.

'That's not intended as an insult. It's an observation. The

scar on your cheek that glows green and the skin that won't heal' – he still had his eyes fixed on the work in the mine – 'is not a tattoo that went wrong. There is poison in your body. Poison for which there is no antidote, but one that won't kill you.' He turned to face her. 'Instead it changes you.'

'No, it doesn't,' she muttered. 'Not anymore.'

'What excuse do you normally use when people ask you about the scar?'

'I tell them it was a poisoned arrow.'

Tungdil pursed his lips. 'Stick with the tattoo story, even though Thirdlings tend not to go in much for skin decoration.'

'I have tattoos in places you can't see.' Beligata sighed. 'Carmondai knew.'

'And I guessed.' Tungdil had seen enough. As there was nothing new happening in the crater today, he laid aside his paper and writing instruments. 'Don't worry, I shan't tell anyone. Your secret is safe. You have nothing to fear from me. Neither your transformation nor your training was complete. You are able to resist.'

'It's why I fled to the Freelings,' Beligata admitted, cursing, one hand pressed to the scar. 'The prospect of being an älfar tool no longer seemed desirable.'

Tungdil moved her hand aside and scrutinised the scar. It was longer now and the black vein-like marks were spreading under the skin. 'We'll think of something to make it go away.'

She gave a bitter laugh. 'As if I hadn't tried everything already.'

'It's not in your power, Beligata. But I know a bit about the black-eyes and the treatments they use.'

He removed his hand from her face. *I know their methods all too well.*

A low blast on a horn sounded. Torches were lit along all

the levels of the old mine. In the flickering light the two dwarves could see a dozen or so shadowy figures flitting between the furnaces and the ladders at the walls.

'It's slaves making a run for it,' Tungdil guessed. 'They don't stand a chance.'

'No.' Beligata went to the back of the cave. 'I'll get back to my digging.'

'How far have we got?'

'It goes back forty-eight paces from the edge.'

'Take it to fifty paces then head straight up. It'll be our only chance of getting out. These notes will be no help to Ireheart if we can't hand them over.'

'Right.' Beligata went back to work.

Tungdil saw the runaway slaves reach the third gallery, where they were caught and killed by two orcs. Their jagged blades cut the humans in pieces. Lumps of meat were chucked down for the beasts to devour in silence.

Beligata's tactical sense is excellent. The stratagem she chose was exactly what I had thought of doing. Tungdil pulled the rags back over the viewing hole before he lit the lamp. *I'll come up with an idea to deal with Aiphatòn and the ghaist.*

By the light of the little flame, he noted down the details of how Beligata had envisaged taking on the army of the botoican.

He heard the sound of bones being snapped open as the beasts sucked out the marrow. The hastily lit fires died down and work continued as normal.

Tungdil finished writing. *Who would have thought it?* He stretched his limbs as far as was possible in the constricted cave. *Our Beligata is a half-zhadár.*

Then something else occurred to him.

Then was a new development: drinks could not be brewed properly. Tungdil had lost the recipe.

Or had it been stolen?

His mind lost its evil and his spirit started to recover. A Child of the Smith has a very stubborn nature!

The old memories came flooding back and gave him cause for thought.

He thought of the love he had rejected. He lost the unscrupulousness, the cruelty and the instincts that had made him an undisputed ruler. His magic powers receded and vanished.

He tried to conceal it, for otherwise the monsters and beasts under his command would have torn him to pieces.

There was no place for weakness in Phondrasôn.

Secret notes for
The Writings of Truth
written under duress by Carmondai

XXIX

Somewhere in the Outer Lands

Once they finished the vertical part of the tunnel, Tungdil and Beligata sat well-camouflaged in their cave shelter from dawn to sunset. Tungdil observed the mine and Beligata watched out for any sign of scouts from the army that they were expecting to arrive from the south.

There had been new developments in the crater recently and Tungdil was still trying to work out their significance. He started to count the beasts and the humans, and, out of sheer curiosity, compared their numbers with the amount of food being delivered.

He came to the surprising conclusion that three times the amount necessary was being brought to the crater with each supply train. *More food implies more mouths that need feeding.* Tungdil watched the openings to the side galleries. *I think we've been fooled.*

With these new calculations, he had to re-think the situation. The botoican had mustered not one hundred thousand but *three* hundred thousand, and the troops were concealed in the mines. That could explain why the slaves' minds were not being manipulated: perhaps the botoican had run out of magic.

They needed a good plan if they were going to defeat the enemy.

The dwarf hardly noticed the ground shaking any more, even though the rumblings and the shaking occurred more frequently.

Wouldn't it be great if we were all sitting on an ancient volcano about to erupt? Tungdil grinned. *No need for a battle at all.*

Beligata's plan would have to be modified, given the new numbers. With so many extra troops, the enemy could respond to anything they had to offer and outflank them. *The best tack would be to get the mines to collapse, burying all the soldiers who are sitting and waiting for orders to go out and fight.*

Tungdil scraped at the wall to study its composition. The top layer of the quarry was made up of soft sandstone, but there was granite lower down with coal seams mixed in, and at the bottom it looked like basalt. He had never seen this combination of rock layers before, neither in Girdlegard nor in Phondrasôn. Volcanic? *Sadly, no. It's not the right sort of rock. A volcano would have basalt and more granite through it.*

On the floor of the crater he detected cracks that had formed round the furnaces. *The mountain's anger-lines.* On further study, he noted other cracks going up the side walls and spreading throughout the terraces. Perhaps the works equipment was proving too heavy. Was the subsoil giving way? *Maybe I can use that to my advantage.*

Beligata came along in high excitement, screeching to a halt to avoid colliding with Tungdil in her enthusiasm and sending him flying out into the crater. 'They've come!' she squeaked. 'I've seen their scouts!'

'Did you signal to them?'

'Yes. They're expecting us.'

'They're expecting *you*. I'm staying here, keeping my eye on what happens.'

Beligata shook her head. 'Oh no, you're not. We need heroes like you with our troops.'

'You'll have Ireheart. *He* is the greatest hero. His fame outshines my own. I was in Phondrasôn while a false Tungdil did my work for me.' He smiled at her. 'Off you go, and don't forget to take the notes with you.' He handed her the latest page.

When she perused it, her delight at the army's imminent arrival faded. '*Three* hundred thousand!'

'It changes our Tharc strategy, doesn't it?' Tungdil pointed down into the mine, indicating where he thought they were concealed. 'That's why it's vital I keep watch here and let you know what's happening. As soon as things look dicey, I'll pull out.'

'How will you get in touch with us?'

'That's easy. I'll run to and fro.' He laughed and shooed her off. 'Hurry up! They're waiting to see what we've discovered. Let the High King know exactly what's happening down in the crater. He and his planners will need a tailor-made strategy and you'll have to help them form it. But don't mention Tharc, whatever you do.'

Beligata did not look happy, but she nodded and left.

Tungdil had wanted to suggest they smuggle a small unit in via their narrow tunnel, but in view of the new circumstances, that would be suicide. And anyway, the tunnel ended too high up on the crater side for there to be any possibility of wielding Keenfire against the ghaist and Aiphatòn.

Many hundreds of paces, many terraces and thousands of beasts stand between us. On his own, with only an acronta dagger and armour that was patchy at best, he would achieve nothing at all. Everything depended on having all the dwarves work together to ensure Balyndar got a chance to use Keenfire.

My son. Tungdil felt pride surge in his breast, matched with fear for his warrior son. He wanted to get to know the lad. The way to Balyndar went via Balyndis, for whose safety he was even more concerned. Phondrasôn had opened his eyes for him. *I have been a fool. More than once in my life.* He kissed the ring. *A meal together. That'll be the start. Vraccas will decide how it goes on from there.*

Tungdil forced himself to concentrate on the task in hand. He had not told Beligata about it. It was time to entice the botoican out into the open.

In all the time Beligata and Tungdil had been at their posts, the botoican had made no move, preferring to let Aiphatòn and the ghaist represent him. And sometimes it had been the blonde-haired elf-woman who gave orders to the workforce and the troops. Tungdil was starting to feel uneasy about this mystery.

At nightfall he set off. Pulling the filthy cloth away from the entrance, he hung it round his shoulders. *Vraccas, stay with me.* The pungent smell of dirt, earth and sweat would ensure the guards did not detect the presence of a Child of Vraccas. As long as he kept his face covered, he ought to be able to get through. He was familiar with the various languages the monsters spoke; he ought to be able to pass as one of them.

He started a mini-landslide of sandstone fragments as he rolled down to the next terrace. Such incidents were frequent in the mine and rubble was only cleared away if it impeded progress directly or if it landed on the tents. Sliding down with his self-induced rock fall, he reached the terrace below and waited for a moment to see if anyone paid any attention to the pile of stones clattering down. When it was clear nobody had noticed, he made his way stealthily down to the place where the ground looked in imminent danger of cracking under the weight of the works equipment.

He managed to carry out the first part of his plan without attracting attention. He slipped through the array of ancient blast furnaces, examining them to see where they had originated. It seemed that on this particular orbit, not much was required in the way of pig iron. The fires were burning but only one of the huge pear-shaped vessels, measuring about seventy paces high and forty wide, was full. Only a few slaves were working. This aroused Tungdil's suspicions. *Have they already got wind of our dwarf army?*

The cracked, rusty signs on the furnace sides led him to believe the equipment had been left behind by the quarry's original users. The writing employed simple pictograms, easy enough for him to interpret. The acronta had detailed everything in their archives. The notices warned what to be aware of during the smelting process and stressed it was essential not to touch the molten metal, however enticing it might look. *No surprise there.* Tungdil rubbed the golden mark on his hand that he had acquired during the competition to be appointed High King.

When some beasts and slaves turned up, he moved back to the edge of the smelting area, staying in the dark and testing out the fundament. Most of the cracks in the ground were fresh and a different colour from the rest of the surface. Kneeling and placing his ear against a narrow gap, he picked up a crackling sound. The stone was constantly moving. When one of the pear-shaped containers was lowered to facilitate loading, there was an audible thump in the ground, followed by substantial vibration.

Have we got a hollow cavern under here? Could it be a part of Phondrasôn? Tungdil had to find out what was going on. He placed a hand on the basalt, looking, as he did so, at the heavy furnaces. If he were to release all of them from their fittings, one at a time, the impact of the colossal ovens crashing down on this porous ground would have the effect of mighty hammer blows. With the help of Vraccas, maybe the earth would open up and swallow the entire mine.

All of it, I hope. Then nobody would have to do battle at all and we would not lose a single dwarf in combat. And the botoican would be forced to reveal himself.

Tungdil knew the operation would have to be carefully thought through. He would need enough time to get out before it collapsed. He decided to implement his plan of action when the first battle alarm sounded in the camp. The diversion would work in his favour.

I'll have to get used to hanging around; it could be a while. He crept about, collecting tools: tongs, a heavy hammer, and a number of steel levers with which to break chains and fastenings. He took his loot to the dark niche by the heaps of coal, then crouched down to wait, finding a smooth place in the wall to rest against.

His gaze swept over the sloping sides of the quarry and the terraces in the middle, where he noticed a huge chiselled message, half-obliterated by weathering and deliberate damage. It was located higher up than the cave where he and Beligata had conducted their observations and that was why he had never seen it before.

The writing was not dissimilar to dwarf runes but much less sophisticated in form, as if aped by a simple human.

Flee!
Flee the curse of this mine
The curse of the stone
The curse of the depths.
We realised too late
the price we paid for our gems
was too high by far.

If the dome is broken
the curse will increase.
Its hunger for life
is without limit.

Flee this place!

Tungdil looked at the galleries. *Hunger without limit.* He thought of the incalculable amounts of food being brought to the quarry. *A curse that demands living beings. Are they feeding something else in there?* Phondrasôn had produced the biggest and ugliest monsters imaginable, such as the kordrion. Is there something similar living here in the mine? *A dragon, perhaps?* Tungdil got up carefully. *Curses.*

If this were a game of Tharc, he would have run out of winning strategies. His plans were in disarray and all his suppositions were dissolving in the air. The dwarf army was totally unaware of what awaited them, and would be expecting to be confronted with a force of three hundred thousand.

I need to find out for certain. Tungdil had paid attention to where the food supplies were taken. *That's where I'll start my search. The botoican won't be far away.* But as soon as he took the first step, he heard a raucous, threatening horn blast coming from one of the lookouts at the top of the crater. The Girdlegard army had been spotted.

Drums summoned the beasts out of the tents and shelters. They surged out of the galleries, climbed ladders and ramps and stairs and hastened to form units on the terraces, all of them armed with different kinds of weaponry. Tungdil was amazed. *They're well-disciplined. No panic and uproar.* Aiphatòn seemed to have trained them well. Strategy and mass hypnosis made for a dangerous combination.

The ghaist and Aiphatòn turned up, with Irïanora at their side wearing armour. It seemed she was also in a commanding role.

No botoican. What could . . .

The quarry shook again. There was a sudden glow at the top of one of the vertical shafts and a flare erupted into the sky. It was like a column of light and energy, forming a connection between the stars and the underworld.

Tungdil grasped his hammer firmly and held his breath. A sparkling worm with pincers and enormous black eyes in a snake-like head forced its way out of the tube. The body had the girth of five tree trunks, and the mouth gaped open to reveal further spikes and pincer-sharp teeth; the heat came rolling over in a wave to where Tungdil stood.

What's that sticking to it? Gold! The creature must live in the passageways of the mine. Its high temperature must have caused the metal ore to drip out of the stone onto itself, where it remained molten. Its body a good eighty paces long, the worm hissed and writhed to get nearer to the vicinity of the furnaces.

It craves heat. The scholar in Tungdil racked his brains to determine what kind of creature this might be. He had once read in the annals of his ancestors about such beings, greedy for precious metals and posing a serious threat to the dwarves' treasure hoards.

Goldfireworms, that's what they were called. They had first appeared a thousand cycles previously in the Red Mountains where there were extensive lakes of lava. Under Queen Vraccaina the worms had been exposed and driven out by dint of cooling the lava. This was affected by diverting rivers into the lakes. The creatures were thought to be relatives of the dragons, if very much less intelligent. Tungdil noticed the reptile had a long gash in the golden membrane that covered it. *It is about to slough its skin.*

The botoican would surely have appeared by now to calm the dangerous creature before it attacked his beasts and humans. Tungdil saw the ghaist leaping down with enormous strides. *So the botoican only sends his henchman? Hardly a wise move. Unless . . .*

The ghaist reached the floor of the crater and strode up to the huge beast, the eye slits on its copper helmet turned toward the snake-head that was big enough to swallow him whole. The worm dragon hissed – and took up a submissive pose.

So I was right. Tungdil was convinced now that the idea that had come to him a few nights previously was correct. *The ghaist itself was the botoican. It was not following the decree of any master, but still let others believe it was merely a lackey like the rest of its kind. It took me too long to realise that.*

The heat streaming over increased and the air shimmered with it. The goldfireworm was the ghaist's newest ally. *That's why he has been saving his skills. It has to control the worm so that it doesn't reap carnage among his own army.*

Tungdil imagined the eighty-pace-long creature creeping up the slopes of the Grey Mountains and surmounting the portal to Girdlegard, destroying the defences and allowing the ghaist and Aiphatòn to take over his whole homeland. *It will squirm its way through the ranks of the dwarves, burning anything it touches.*

He was amazed to see a lizard's foot emerging from the gash as the tear in the worm's skin widened. *It's a larva. It's hatching out a larger monster still!* There had been no word of this aspect in the ancestral tomes. The Firstlings had never given the goldfireworm time to reach its next developmental stage. *Can this one turn into a genuine dragon?* The transformation certainly entailed a great deal of pain; the ghaist was having trouble getting the beast to settle.

Tungdil took a quick glance round. The terraces and galleries were full of silent enemies, eyes fixed on what was happening in the depths of the quarry. Their terrifying faces – some adorned with war paint, some covered with masks – were highlighted by the glow from the golden creature. The fighting force was waiting for the creature to come up and start the battle against Girdlegard.

The ghaist stretched out one hand. The worm dragon hesitated but came nearer, ready to submit.

If that happens, then . . . The dwarf had an idea. *This has to work!* Tungdil took the hammer and a steel wedge and went over to the furnaces, where the fires were still smouldering. His expert eye had seen a weak point in the crumbling fixture. He climbed up the wobbly ladder to the scaffold platform twenty paces above ground where the coal and the slack were stored.

Vraccas, give me the strength I need. He secured the sharp end of the wedge under the rusty arch that anchored the vessel on the right-hand side, directly on the bolt, pushing the wedge into place as well as he could. He took careful aim. After a quick kiss on his ring he swung his hammer up above his head in both hands.

The hammer head smashed down on to the broad part of his lever. Metal clanged against metal and the sharp blade of the wedge fractured the bolt at the very first attempt. But the huge vessel only tilted forward slightly. The second bolt showed no inclination to give way.

The ghaist snorted and turned round and the goldfireworm

gave an angry hiss. If it had not been for the creature, the botoican would surely have stormed over, but he obviously did not dare to leave the worm unsupervised before submission was complete.

Come on! Drop, confound it! Tungdil let the hammer swing again, this time striking the pear-shaped vessel itself. Finally it gave way and tipped over. Molten metal surged and boiled onto the floor, splashing out towards the ghaist and the worm. As it rolled, the vessel felled two other furnaces and more liquid metal flowed in wavelets across the floor, seeping down into the cracks and dispersing. Sparks and steam shot up.

The ghaist had no trouble escaping the flood; it simply stepped up onto a rock. The dragon-worm was not adversely affected; in fact, it seemed to relish the hot bath. Tungdil's plan – to strike the ghaist with molten metal and destroy it – had failed. The long worm wriggled and disported itself in the molten metal, its black tail tip flicking to and fro with delight.

I've got one more go. Surrounded by glowing molten iron, Tungdil stepped forward on his scaffolding. *My last chance.* Scorching heat came up in a wave, making him break out in a sweat. His hair shifted in the hot air.

'I am Tungdil Goldhand,' he called out clearly, his voice loud enough to drown out the sound of the boiling metal. 'Vraccas has sent me to stop you in your tracks. Whatever you are: you will be destroyed!' He hurled the hammer – but not in the direction of the last furnace. The hammer was aimed at the goldfireworm; it dodged out of the way in fury, tensing its body to attack. A roared instruction from the ghaist held it back. But the creature's waving tail caught the last of the furnaces and pulled it out of its anchorage.

The pear-shaped vessel tipped forward. The ghaist was attempting to calm the irate creature, and this took every ounce of its concentration, preventing it noticing the new danger.

'Look out!' Aiphatòn came bounding down the terraces. But by this time a seething wave had hit the botoican on the shoulders, melting its human body away. The weight of the glowing red-hot liquid brought the ghaist down, and the molten cast iron swept it under – submerging even the copper helmet.

Out of here, now! Tungdil made a mighty leap from the high platform edge and landed on the terrace above it. He struggled to his feet. Ignoring the throng of perplexed beasts, he forced his way through and climbed the nearest ladder. He knew what was about to happen and he did not want to get caught up in it.

The monsters started to shift themselves. The expressions on their faces told him they did not know where they were or why they were there. *The hypnosis spell is fading.* Tungdil hurried on without looking back. *That means . . .*

The first explosion reverberated. After this incredible noise, the pressure wave swept along, followed by enormous heat and utter destruction. The terrified screeches of the dragon-worm were swallowed up in the general shouts of horror coming from beasts and humans on the ramps and terraces.

A searing hot wind blew past Tungdil, forcing him from the ladder and sending him hurtling further up the side of the quarry. The terraces flew by and he landed just below the top with a thump. The impact could have been greater but he landed in a heap of beasts. Instead of getting to his feet, he rolled himself into a ball and took shelter amongst them, covering his head with his hands. *It's not finished yet.* The detonation had left his ears ringing.

A wave of heat rolled up the slope, devouring whatever it came across. Tongues of fire flared up all around him, but they gorged themselves on the shrieking monsters above him. Tungdil lost a good deal of his beard and some hair but was otherwise unscathed.

Only when the temperature had dropped did he dare get to his feet to survey the devastation. The goldfireworm lay in shimmering pieces dispersed on the crater floor and on the terraces amongst the charred remains of beasts. The worm had been unable to withstand the annihilating power of the explosion.

That's one less worry. Monsters that had survived the initial blast were fleeing in all directions and struggling desperately to get out of the crater. Their mouths gaped wide, but they made no sound. The whole scene took on elements of a nightmare. The base of the crater and the bottom six layers showed nothing but black walls and smoking cadavers. On the adjoining terraces many lay dead or dying, horribly injured by the blast-wave and the hurtling rocks. Those with thin clothing had been badly burned when the surge of heat flared through. Most of the beasts and slaves had lost skin and were writhing in agony with huge blisters forming on their flesh.

It all seemed even more unreal and horrific to Tungdil because he could hear nothing at all. The explosion had damaged his hearing. His legs gave way and he collapsed. He became aware of a spear sticking out of his left thigh. He must have spiked himself when he hurtled into the crowd of enemies.

He groaned, fighting to stay conscious. *I must get to the battle, I must get to the battle.*

On the other side of the crater Aiphatòn stood brandishing his green-glowing spear. *He's leading the rest of his forces into combat.* When Tungdil tried to get up, fiery rings obscured his field of vision; he decided to remain seated. Vraccas was telling him he had already done his bit.

There will be warriors enough to cope, he said to himself, kissing the ring on his little finger. It had really stood him in good stead. The he pulled the blade out of his thigh.

He knew he yelled out with the pain: he had felt the vibration in his chest and in his throat. But he heard nothing.

'Over to the right! More orcs!' Ireheart urged his pony to a gallop and shouldered his crow's beak in glee, ready to sink it into the skull of a greenskin. *This kind of riding is fun.* 'Oink, oink, pig-faces! Are you looking forward to meeting me?'

His companions laughed.

The stars lit the way for the dwarf army as they hunted down the monsters that had survived the mine explosion. It could not be designated *combat*: they were skirmishes at best, with occasional bouts of thirty or forty enemies gathering together to fight back rather than let themselves be slaughtered.

I bet the Scholar was behind all that. Ireheart was delighted to see an orc force approaching. He circled the crow's beak above his head. *He will have caused the explosion.*

Beligata had just begun explaining her notes and suggesting strategies against the overwhelming numbers of the enemy when the first burst of light came streaming up into the night sky. A few blinks of the eye later the noise that followed was like a volcano erupting. The earth shook. Balyndar immediately realised this meant the ghaist must have been destroyed. Jubilation broke out among the troops. Instead of having to face crushing odds as they had feared, all they had to do was mow down the terrified few running for their lives away from the smoking crater.

'Huzzah!' yelled Ireheart, slamming the flat side of his crow's beak down onto an orc, shattering the skull. His troop of two hundred riders swept through the band of sixty opponents. None of the enemy was left alive.

Ireheart urged his pony forward and the unit regrouped. They were some distance from the mine and had been pursuing the strongest of the orcs. Now that they had tackled them, they had run out of adversaries. 'Curses! Is it over already?' Ireheart took off his helmet, revealing he had shaved his temples. 'Would you look at that? I'm not even sweating!'

His troops burst out laughing.

'To the southwest,' said Beligata merrily. 'There are at least four hundred orcs. I counted. Some of them are nice big ones.'

'You've got good eyes.' Ireheart grinned, cramming his helmet back on and shouldering his weapon. *This is my kind of thing. So much more fun than being king. The Scholar should take over the High King's job and let me get on with fighting.* 'Let's go for them. For Vraccas!'

The troops rode on with ecstatic battle cries, galloping at full speed in order to strike the foe with optimum force; they would smash their shields and armour.

'We've got visitors. Balyndar's coming up.' Beligata pointed to the left. 'He'll get to them before we do.'

'But I'm High King! Who does he think he is?' Ireheart pretended to be outraged, provoking more merriment. 'He'll ruin my good mood. If he carries on like that, I'll make *him* wear the crown.'

They spurred their ponies on, overtaking their own forces. But the orcs heard the drumming of their hoofbeats and halted. The merriment turned to tension.

The first rows of orcs knelt and placed their spears at the ready to stop the advancing riders. Behind them were the warriors, covered by lines of archers. Bowstrings were pulled back and arrow tips pointed skyward.

'We've picked us some beasts with a bit more sense than usual.' Ireheart spat and lifted his shield. 'Watch out. When the hail stops we'll make their blood fall like rain.'

Missiles came flying at the dwarves. Some of the ponies fell, burying their riders under them. Soldiers screamed with pain; a few took a spear through their shield or chainmail, and others fell out of the saddle without making a sound.

'We shall avenge them!' bellowed Ireheart, giving orders to swerve to the right shortly before meeting the wall of spears. His warriors were to attack the beast army's more vulnerable flanks. This manoeuvre took the orcs by surprise, particularly because Balyndar was taking a similar tack on the left.

There we have it: hammer and anvil, thought Ireheart, charging into the enemy lines with a loud battle cry of 'Oink, oink!' As it struck home, the crow's beak reduced a shield to splinters, the long spike piercing thick armour and wrenching the orc off its feet. The dwarf troop followed at Ireheart's heels, the crash of battle increasing in volume all the time. He saw Keenfire's diamonds light up as Balyndar laid about him many paces ahead. The combined smells of upturned earth, grass and blood filled the air.

'Vraccas!' Ireheart whooped, yanking out an orc's throat with the long spike. 'We are the Chi—'

Green runes lit up in front of him and he was struck in the

chest, tumbling from his pony with the impact. He landed in some short grass, the fall knocking all the air out of his lungs. A long spear held in gauntleted hands protruded from his breast. In a daze he recognised the bearer: *Aiphatòn!*

The orcs immediately formed an impenetrable defence wall of spear tips, holding the dwarves off. On the right of the shintoìt a blonde älf-warrior woman stood looking indecisive.

'I've got the High King,' Aiphatòn crowed. He was wearing a pair of blue leg-coverings but his upper body was bare. The tionium plates sewn into his skin absorbed the starlight just as his dark eyes did. 'He's survived one hit but I don't think he'll live through a second one.'

'What are you doing?' Ireheart groaned.

'Defending myself,' the älf replied coolly. 'I know what you want of me.'

'Of you?' Ireheart could taste blood and hoped it came from a split lip and not from his insides. 'We have destroyed the ghaist.' He would have been glad to be visited by his habitual rage – the super strength he needed to free himself from the spear – but since taking Tungdil's potion, his raging fury had disappeared, giving way to merriment and elation.

'You want her.' Aiphatòn gestured towards the älf-woman. 'No one lays a finger on Irïanora.'

The powerful orcs stayed silent as mice, watching their foes and holding axes and swords at the ready while lance-bearers and archers offered backup.

'What are your terms?' Balyndar's voice sounded out through the night.

'Your forces retreat and I take the High King as hostage until I can be sure that Irïanora and I are safe.' Aiphatòn turned his black eyes on his surroundings. 'You can count yourselves lucky that I have not used my magic powers. Or you would be ash by now.'

Ireheart's chest was burning. 'You said you wanted to find and kill all the älfar,' he gasped. He looked at Irïanora. 'What made you change your mind? Or are you in league with the botoican? And bound to it by its spell?'

'The botoican has ceased to be. I serve no one now. I listen only to my own heart. I am bound by love to Irïanora.'

That's all we need. Ireheart lowered his head onto the grass.

'You have injured him. He needs a healer,' Balyndar shouted back. 'What use is a dead hostage?'

'But a High King who is wounded will make you more cautious.' Aiphatòn pointed down at Ireheart. 'The longer you spend talking, the more blood he'll be losing. Withdraw your troops. Irïanora and I will go our ways.'

Could it be some kind of spell? Ireheart coughed, tasting more blood. *I forgot. Of course, love is the strongest magic there is.* He grinned. *Vraccas, what were you thinking of? Not some ugly pig-face but a lovelorn älf is to be my downfall.*

'Then be off with you, Aiphatòn. Get yourselves to safety but know we shall regard you from this moment on as our mortal foe,' Balyndar thundered. 'If anything happens to the High King, our army will hunt you down.'

He could hardly believe it when he heard the hooves of the ponies clatter off into the distance. The dwarves made off into the night.

Only some time later did Aiphatòn pull the spear out of Ireheart's chest and heave him onto the saddle of his pony, which was prancing nervously. It did not like being near the orcs.

'Keep still,' Ireheart tried to calm the animal with his voice.

He was hanging face down like a sack of wet sand and could hardly speak for the pain he was in. Blood trickled out of the corner of his mouth and he spat out more. As a veteran of many battles he knew he needed a healer's attention. *And sharpish.*

One of the orcs took the reins and dragged the terrified animal along. The rest of the group of sixty beasts started to trot.

'I'm telling the truth: I'll let you go as soon as Irïanora and I are safe.' Ireheart could distinctly hear Aiphatòn's words. 'You mustn't die, or you won't appreciate it when I release you.'

The dwarf held tight to the little horse's mane and concentrated on his breathing and his heartbeat. Occasionally he lost consciousness or dozed off, while the pony kept moving swiftly on.

Next time Ireheart opened his eyes it was morning. He was lying on the grassy bank of a stream and his pony was drinking nearby. Trees were rustling their leaves in the gentle wind and birds were singing. *Where are we?*

'Go on. Drink. There's plenty of water,' Aiphatòn encouraged him from the other side of the stream as he bit into an apple. Irïanora was nearby, tending to her armour. The orcs were ten paces away, devouring a deer they had killed. 'What do you fancy? Fruit or venison?'

Ireheart was burning up and his limbs were shaking with fever. *Or is it Tungdil's confounded potion?* With great difficulty he collected some water in his hand and rubbed his face with it, then dipped his hands again and drank as noisily as the horse. 'I am too exhausted to eat.'

The clear waters of the stream splashed along between them but did not drown out the sound of the orcs tearing raw meat with their teeth. The horse danced nervously but remained near its master.

'If you don't eat, you'll die. It's a miracle of your god that you've stayed alive so far with nothing to drink. We've been travelling for many orbits. But I couldn't wake you, stubborn dwarf that you are.' Aiphatòn went on eating his apple.

Ireheart's head was buzzing with a thousand questions he wanted the onetime älfar emperor to answer, but he was not strong enough to confront him. He dropped his head back into the cool of the damp grass. *I'd rather die in battle than in this miserable fashion.*

From the distance came the sound of a dwarf melody played on a bugle. It was meant as a sign to the High King that the others were still around. *Balyndar. Good lad.*

But it was not only Ireheart who recognised the tune.

'Go and see!' Aiphatòn ordered his orcs angrily as he chucked the apple core in the stream. 'Kill the spies and then come back here quickly. Five of you stay here.'

The beasts quickly swallowed down what they were eating and set off. The five who were staying grunted happily as they chewed at the bones, breaking them open and sucking out the marrow. There would be no meat left over.

Ireheart looked across the stream. *Vraccas, don't let me die like this.*

Rune-spear in her hand, Irïanora looked around. 'Will it take long?'

'We'll have to head further east until we get to the sea. From there we'll take a boat to the island and build our new home in the ruins.' He came over to her side and embraced the blonde älf-woman, stroking her face tenderly, as if he could never be capable of any violence toward a living creature. 'It will be just you and me. We'll have all we need. There's no better place for us.'

In Ireheart's opinion she did not seem overjoyed to hear

this. The 'being in love' thing was wearing thin, he thought. The passion seemed pretty one-sided.

Ireheart forced himself to drink and then cooled his brow once more. His whole body was on fire. *This is not the normal reaction to a wound.* The cold drops on his face brought no relief. *The Scholar has given me something that's burning me up from the inside. It's devoured my rage. Fire to combat fire. And I'm in flames.* He crawled closer to the edge of the water, shivering when the stream soaked his clothing and cooled his hot flesh. *Elria won't be watching. She wouldn't bother drowning a half-dead dwarf.*

'Good idea.' Aiphatòn looked over at the deer carcass. 'Sure you don't want anything to eat?'

There was a rustling in the bushes. Out came a slim form with an unusual sword at its side. The älfar brand on the face and scarred writing on the brow disfigured it. Long brown hair fell shoulder-length. 'You should have waited for me,' said the new arrival accusingly to Aiphatòn. 'You left me behind in the ruined village.'

'Carmondai!' Irïanora called his name in joy and surprise. 'Wonderful to see you! We thought . . .'

'You thought I was dead?' He looked at the two älfar, disgruntled. The historian had got himself some sensible clothing, green, and he wore brown- and rust-coloured leather armour over it. He would be practically invisible in the woods. 'You made no effort at all to find me.'

Yet another black-eyes. Ireheart groaned to himself. The water steamed off him. *They stick together, don't they?*

'There was no time. The ghaist and Irïanora wanted to go on,' Aiphatòn explained. He was obviously suspicious and wanting to avoid a confrontation. 'Have you come across any dwarves?'

'Yes. About a quarter of an hour from here.' He pointed. 'Why are you so keen to move on?'

'It is Irïanora's wish. Her wish is my command.' Aiphatòn beamed at her. Turning to Carmondai he said, 'What do you want?'

'To come with you. As an älf hereabouts one doesn't have much choice of travelling companion.'

'You can travel on your own. We have no use for you,' Aiphatòn snapped. 'Irïanora and I have our own plans.'

Ireheart detected the jealousy in Aiphatòn's voice. *He must be very much in love. Or infatuated.* He took another mouthful of water. It ran cold down his throat. The fever seemed to be receding. He looked at the pony where his crow's beak hung.

'But perhaps Irïanora would like me to come along.' Carmondai went nearer to the älf-woman. 'I'd be a splendid addition.'

'No, she would not.'

'I think *you're* the one who wouldn't like it,' the elderly älf smiled. 'But if she should wish it, surely you will accede to her request? You just said her wish was your command.'

'Yes,' Aiphatòn said furiously. 'But she *won't* wish it.'

Despite his fever, Ireheart could see that Carmondai was pulling a fast one. When he spotted the bugle at the älf's side, he guessed it had been Carmondai playing the dwarf tune. *So there's no Balyndar nearby. What plan is the älf hatching?*

'Oh, but I think she will.' Carmondai approached the älf-woman but Aiphatòn shoved himself in the way. 'What's your problem? Am I not allowed to greet my friend?'

'She's mine!' the älf roared.

'Oh, so she *belongs* to you, does she? I was not aware she was your slave.' The history-weaver looked past him to

Irïanora. 'And are you his slave? Times have changed if älfar are owning älfar.'

Ireheart saw the fear in the woman's eyes. It was clear she had not accompanied Aiphatòn of her own free will. Despite the fact the botoican's power had now lapsed.

'No . . . but he . . . is not right in the head,' she stuttered pathetically. 'It's not really love at all!'

'What?' Aiphatòn turned to her. 'How can you say that?'

Swift as lightning, Carmondai drew Bloodthirster from its scabbard and deployed the weapon. Aiphatòn twisted his upper body out of the way and dodged the blow. He screamed with rage, black lines zigzagging across his face. The gauntleted right hand grabbed the spear from Irïanora. 'You won't take her from me.'

Carmondai threw something. A cloud of glass splinters and gold dust spread through the air, blurring Aiphatòn's vision and spoiling his aim. He had countless tiny wounds in his face from the sharp fragments and his eyes were affected as well.

'I'm not stealing her from you.' Carmondai feigned a blow that the dazzled shintoìt tried to avoid then whirled around and rammed Bloodthirster's long blade into the hole in his armour plating. 'I'm liberating her from you.' The sword that had once belonged to Aiphatòn's father now dug its way into the son's body.

With a scream, Aiphatòn thrust Carmondai away and the sword pulled itself out of his wound. A stream of red blood came gushing out, followed by black. The anger lines increased and Aiphatòn aimed the rune-spear at his elderly adversary. The symbols glowed emerald clear as if they were filled with the same hatred. 'No one takes her from me!'

A stream of green light shot out of the spear's tip. Seizing Bloodthirster in both hands, Carmondai parried the magic attack. Ireheart saw the bloodied weapon glow. Carmondai gave a cry but the deflected beam turned one of the orcs to ashes instead. The others grunted and ran for cover. Ireheart tried to get up. The cold water of the stream helped but his head spun when he attempted it, forcing him to sink back.

Aiphatòn twirled the spear and brandished it at Carmondai. 'How often will you succeed?' he said angrily – then froze. The runes flickered and died.

Irïanora was standing behind the shintoìt, dagger in her hand. She had stabbed him in the nape of his neck. 'I do not belong to you,' she hissed, wrenching the long blade out to plunge it repeatedly into Aiphatòn's back, past the protective tionium plates on his skin. She left the dagger in him and stepped back. 'May you be released from the spell so that I can be free.'

The älf fell at Carmondai's feet without a word, black blood pulsing out. 'You must not harm her,' he struggled to tell Carmondai. 'Look after her. And . . .' Aiphatòn dropped, his eyes black and broken.

They have defeated him! Ireheart did not know how long he had left for rejoicing. The orcs attacked as soon as they had recovered from their shock. Ireheart knew they stood no chance against the two älfar.

'You should just have left.' With skilful thrusts of his blade Carmondai felled them all. Bloodthirster was scornful of their protective armour. Irïanora had picked up the rune spear but she had not had to intervene.

The victorious älf came over to Ireheart looking dangerous rather than elderly or fragile. 'And now let's see to you.'

'Don't you dare drown me! Give me a weapon, at least. I want to have the illusion of dying in battle.'

But Carmondai grabbed him by the right foot and heaved

him out of the stream as Ireheart spluttered and cursed. 'You must get away if you want to live. Get on your pony and head back along your own tracks. And pray to your Vraccas that the fever doesn't finish you off.' He got him up onto his pony using a lot more consideration than Aiphatòn had employed.

It was hard for Ireheart to hold himself in the saddle. He was expecting some trick, a shout perhaps, to alert the other orcs, who would not be far away. Only slowly did he realise he had nothing of this kind to fear. 'You are helping me?' He saw the branding marks on the älfar visage. 'You could so easily kill me!'

'What would I gain from that?' Carmondai was smiling. 'I killed Aiphatòn because he left me no alternative. His mind was irretrievably anchored in a baseless emotion.'

Pale as wax, Irïanora crouched at the edge of the stream to wash her face and to drink. She glanced at Carmondai, relief visible in her expression. She used the spear as a support. 'My thanks,' she said. 'It was a cîanoi spell that bewitched him and bound me to him. It was nothing to do with the botoican.' The blonde älf-woman got to her feet. 'I would never have escaped. He watched me all the time.'

Carmondai nodded at her in a fatherly way. 'We must be off. Orcs are not good company.' He fixed his black eyes on the High King. 'Tell Tungdil I will deliver an episode once a cycle at the Stone Gateway. As long as I have the strength to keep writing, I'll let him know everything I learn about the Outer Lands. That is all you will ever see of me from now.'

Ireheart nodded, biting his lip against the pain. Carmondai led the pony round to head south. Ireheart's inner fire had ceased but the wound was very painful.

'You're more valuable alive, Boïndil Doubleblade. You are a gift for any story-teller and the deeds you do in future will be celebrated when dwarves sing round the fire.' Carmondai indicated the body of Aiphatòn. 'A tragic death is still a death.' He slapped Boïndil's pony on the rump and it trotted off. 'Don't give in to death. You are still too young.'

Too young? Ireheart had to grin despite himself. *Look who's talking.*

He concentrated on keeping tight hold of the reins, remembering to breathe and watching that his heart kept beating – he must keep the bellows feeding his life's inner furnace.

Never provoke an unarmed orc or a drunk one – it's no fun at all.

Dwarf saying

XXX

Girdlegard
Grey Mountains
Kingdom of the Fifthling dwarves
Stone Gateway
6497th solar cycle, summer

Ireheart opened his eyes to find he was staring up at a tarpaulin wagon roof. The straw mattress he was lying on cushioned the bumps as the cart rumbled on.

'The High King has rested sufficiently.' It was Tungdil's voice. 'Excellent. Just in time for our re-entry to Girdlegard.'

Ireheart turned his head and saw his friend lying next to him. 'Are you ill, too? The battle did not spare you, my Scholar friend.' Ireheart lifted the sheet off his hairy chest and took in the bandage covering his wound. He still felt hot, but his head was clear now. *Like a newborn baby.*

'Indeed. I got a spear through the leg and I lost blood and muscle.' Tungdil beamed with delight as he stretched out his hand in welcome. 'But we've made it. We've survived, my High King.'

'So we have. By Vraccas, so we jolly have!' Ireheart could remember nothing about the journey so he asked his friend to fill him in.

'Beligata and some scouts followed the orcs' trail but they kept their distance. Just as they were about to set off to free you, you rode up, half-dead.' Tungdil laughed softly. 'They almost had to break your fingers, you were holding the pony's neck so tightly. You nearly throttled the poor creature.'

'And then?'

'They brought you back and got a healer for you. The orcs pursued them to start with but changed their minds once Balyndar showed up. They didn't like the look of Keenfire.'

'Huzzah! I'd like to have seen that.' Ireheart laughed to himself. His friend helped him drink from a ladle of water. 'Aiphatòn is dead,' he told Tungdil.

'Really?'

'Carmondai and the black-eye girl did for him,' Ireheart said, before giving a quick recap of events by the stream. 'I'm to tell you he'll deposit the next chronicle for you, a new one every cycle. Everything he knows and learns about the Outer Lands.' He drank some more. 'Couple of scholars, you two, aren't you?'

'He may be thinking that way.' Tungdil was thoughtful. 'Beligata slipped back into the wood after you'd said something in your delirium about the spear and Bloodthirster. But she couldn't find Aiphatòn 's body. The trail left by the two älfar soon faded.'

But he was definitely dead . . . wasn't he? 'The orcs must have eaten the body.'

'You're quite sure about his having been killed?'

There was no doubt in Ireheart's mind. 'He died right in front of me. Carmondai stabbed him through the hole in his armour plating and the älf-woman stuck her dagger in his neck and then again into his heart from behind. No one can survive wounds like that. He lay dead on the ground right in front of me and I saw his eyes cloud over.' He looked up at the flapping canopy. 'I felt strangely sorry for him.'

'Yes, I am sorry for him and I won't hide the fact. He was

on a campaign to eradicate his own race and then he falls foul of a spell and dies at the hands of one of his own kind, killed by his own father's weapon.' Tungdil took out a piece of blood-spattered paper. 'Carmondai secreted this message in your clothing. We found it when we took your armour off. The historian explains what happened to him after the events in that village.'

'What *did* happen?' Ireheart struggled to sit up. 'Don't keep me in suspense, Scholar.'

'I'll tell you by and by. You need rest, High King.'

'I need a beer, I think.'

'I'd fancy one, too, but they didn't bring any. Balyndis thought we should wait till we're with the Fifthlings before we start celebrating.' Tungdil checked the bandage on his own leg.

'Then at least tell me how you dealt with the ghaist.'

'Good question. But it's a long story. In brief, let me just say I used dwarf warfare on him.' He grinned. 'I meant what I said: you must take it easy. The healers say the fever could still finish you off if you're not careful.'

'What the hell do they know?' grumbled Ireheart. 'Perhaps it was something you gave me, not the injury at all.'

'You'll have to explain what you mean.'

'I took your antidote just before I rode in to battle. I thought it would suppress the rages I was going through. Maybe it burned me up.' Ireheart was breathing freely now that he had cleared this off his chest.

'It was over four cycles ago that I gave it to you. You took your time.' Tungdil's comment did not sound judgemental. 'It's possible that fever might be one of the reactions to the medication. I can't exclude the possibility. The distilled älf blood that you had previously taken is one of the most dangerous substances the Triplets ever thought up. But' – he nodded to his friend – 'it's over at last. If you want a drink now there'll be a good reason.'

'And that would be?'

'Thirst.' Tungdil grinned.

Ireheart laughed out loud. After another mouthful of water he cleared his throat. 'Scholar?'

'Yes?'

'I don't want to be High King any longer.'

Now it was Tungdil's turn to laugh. 'Everyone knows it's not to your taste. But they admire your bravery in agreeing to take it on. If you had not taken the lead as you did, none of this would have been possible.'

Ireheart clapped his hands in amusement. 'I like that. So they've just been waiting for me to call it a day?'

'Put it this way: they won't be surprised if you give the office up. But they won't mind if you carry on, either.'

'What I want is for *you* to be High King,' Ireheart said with determination.

'You sound like a stroppy child. You can't order me to be king of the kings.'

'Maybe not.' Ireheart was not pleased to hear this. *We haven't got anyone better. He's destroyed the ghaist and the whole of the rag-tag army, so his fame has only increased recently.* 'But who would you suggest? Who is qualified to take over? For goodness' sake, don't say Frandibar. I can't stand the fellow. I do think it should be you.'

Tungdil grinned. 'I'm a scholar and I have different plans. The adventures of recent cycles have been more than enough. I wanted to give my soul time to recuperate; I still need to recover from my time in Phondrasôn. I also want to get my knowledge up to date.'

'Other things. I see. And what would they be?' Ireheart

rolled his eyes. 'There can't be anything more important than being High King. That's why the title is High King.'

'Sha'taï.'

The little one. Ireheart grimaced. 'I was trying not to think about her.'

'Balyndis said something very wise . . .'

'I know, I know: the girl is frightened,' Ireheart interrupted his friend. 'She's using her powers to gain popularity, so she can get the whole of Girdlegard prepared to die for her sake if need be.'

'Exactly. It might be enough if we make sure Sha'taï understands that we don't represent any threat to her and that she is completely safe.' Tungdil wiped the sweat droplets from his face. 'We must make her remove the influence she has placed on the rulers. Without making her frightened.'

'Yes, and then?' Ireheart rubbed his temples where the hair was shaved short. *Soon I'll be a simple warrior again. Though still king of the Secondlings.* 'She is still a botoican. As soon as she feels threatened or as soon as something happens she doesn't like – what will happen then?' He did not want to be more explicit. *The best protection for Girdlegard would come with her death.*

'Exile. Imprisonment. Let's hope the worst never happens.' Tungdil was excluding the possibility of having her killed. 'We'll talk to her first and try to find out more about her.' He tapped Ireheart on the head. 'What a good thing that we dwarves are not susceptible to her influence.'

'Maybe we're the ones she's most scared of,' he joked. 'Tell me, are you sure there's only water to drink in the wagon?' He stared crossly at the small barrel.

His friend looked at him as if thunderstruck. 'There could be a lot in what you say.'

'There you have it, Scholar!' Ireheart laughed. He noticed the vraccasium ring on Tungdil's little finger. 'So you'll be bringing that back to Balyndis. Do you think you two will get back together?'

'We'll have to see.'

'Or did anything happen between you and Beligata in all that time you were alone together? Anything you want to tell me about?' He smirked.

Instead of an answer Tungdil raised his hand for silence. He listened out, then vaulted over, pulling the tub over them both. The cold bath made Ireheart curse roundly until a spike forced its way through the wood stopping a finger's width from his nose.

The wagon halted. There were loud shouts and shrieks, and ponies were whinnying. Alarm horns sounded.

'Those confounded pig-faces,' Ireheart bellowed, reaching for the crow's beak.

'No, these are bolts from our own catapults!' Tungdil pointed. 'I'm going outside to take a look. You, get yourself under the wagon.'

The tarpaulin was pulled aside. Beligata appeared, her chain mail shirt in tatters and a scratch on her shoulder. A wound like that must have come from a sharp weapon. 'I'm to collect the High King,' she said, jumping in beside them, ready to toss Ireheart over her shoulder. Tungdil assisted her and wrapped a blanket round him. 'We're to get to the back of the column until the situation becomes clear.'

'What's happening out there?' Despite the discomfort, Ireheart managed to get hold of his crow's beak.

'The Fifthling stronghold is firing at us.' Beligata panted under the weight as she carried Ireheart off the wagon. 'Balyndis and her son are trying to find out the reason.'

'I'll wager it's to do with that wretched child! We need to kill that girl, Scholar.' Ireheart looked at Tungdil, hoping for approval.

But his friend had gone.

Tungdil limped along as quickly as his injured leg would permit. *I must keep Balyndis safe!*

The Fifthling stronghold was bombarding the dwarves with missiles. The advance guard and the main body of the column were in catapult range. Burning leather pouches of petroleum were raining down, burning dwarves and ponies to death. Then the slits below the walkway opened, emitting bolts and spears as individual projectiles and waves.

Small blasts caused sections of the slopes next to the Stone Gateway to crumble and roll on to the road, covering the army with rubble and boulders. The debris formed a wall behind them that made it impossible for the troops to withdraw. There was equally no point in storming the granite portal.

We're stuck. Tungdil dived for cover under abandoned wagons each time he saw bolts coming his way. Pennants showed that Balyndis and Balyndar were less than a hundred paces from the gate surrounded by two hundred sturdy warriors.

They will be trying to get near enough to speak the secret code to open it. Tungdil grabbed himself a riderless pony and set out after them. *I've got to help them.*

The fortress truly was an extraordinary sight: a masterpiece of dwarf engineering, a stronghold flanked by impregnable towers. It spoke clearly to any invader: *Give up in despair!*

Phondrasôn had clouded my memory of the place.

Tungdil remembered hearing what enormous strength and firepower the fortress represented. Now he was struck by the fact there were so few people up on the walkway operating the machines. *They're just running hither and thither to make it look like there's more of them.* The lack of manpower on the walls aided the two hundred soldiers approaching the gate at full gallop. Not a shot was directed at them: their speed made them difficult targets.

But it was too soon to feel relief. Tungdil saw an armoured figure looking down from the battlements and shouting in rage. *They've seen my brave dwarves coming.*

A long barrel appeared on the battlements, its opening aimed diagonally downwards. The first burning clay container was released in the direction of Balyndis and her troops. The riders noticed it hurtling towards them and they sprang apart before it struck. But the aim had been true and further attempts saw the agonizing end of dozens of dwarves as the clay smashed, spreading blazing petroleum. Black smoke rose stinking to the skies.

Balyndis, Balyndar and their companions did not give up. The hail of fire ended, to be replaced by spears from the launchers. Many more dwarves were killed by the steel-tipped shafts. Tungdil was horrified to see the pony Balyndis was riding get hit. The queen fell with her horse, sliding and slithering on the stony ground all the way over to the portal. *No, Vraccas, not her!*

He urged his own mount on, keeping an eye on potential danger from above where death could pour down in liquid form from the gutters. Boiling water, pitch, red-hot slack or Vraccas fire would deter even the hardiest of attackers.

At long last he reached the group; they had all dismounted by this time. He jumped down and ran to Balyndis. It was clear she had suffered broken limbs and was unconscious. Dwarves gathered round her, forming a protective dome with their shields.

'Take her away from the gateway,' Tungdil ordered. 'She is in danger of burning pitch here.' He turned to Balyndar and told him to open the gate.

'Leave my mother where she is,' Balyndar called, countermanding the order. He glared at his father. 'I am in charge here. It is not up to you to issue orders.'

'She'd be . . .'

'The fortress catapults can hit anywhere in front of the gate. She would be no safer away from the wall. And we need her here.' He took a few deep breaths. 'Only she and Barborin Doughtyarm know the secret words that release the bolts.' He laid one hand on the black stone. 'And Barborin is on the other side. As the gate won't open for us, I can only assume he is dead.' He took a step forward and clanged Keenfire against the place where the two halves of the gate touched, leaving hardly a seam visible. But his legendary weapon left not a scratch on the stone surface. This was not going to help them gain entry.

Tungdil went cold all over. Kneeling next to the dwarf-woman whose face had featured in his every dream back in Phondrasôn, giving him the strength needed to survive that ordeal, he stroked the brown hair away from her face. The rim of her helmet had cut into her brow. 'I ask your forgiveness for everything I put you through,' he said. 'Everything . . .'

'Take cover!' came a shout.

There was a whizz and a whistling sound as a shower of bolts rained down onto the shields. Grim responses to pain and loud curses rang out; two dwarves fell.

Tungdil seized the shields they had dropped and held them

over Balyndis. 'Wake up, I implore you. I have brought you back your ring. It protected . . .' He stared in horror; four bolts had pierced the queen's body. Blood was flowing freely. The one blink of an eye when she had been left vulnerable had sufficed. The deadly shots had found their target. On impact Balyndis opened her eyes wide, tears coursing down her cheeks. The pain had torn her out of her faint.

'Here comes another bombardment!' came the warning. A new barrage of shots rained down on the steadily decreasing numbers of dwarves.

Tungdil was past caring. 'Don't do this to me,' he whispered. 'Let me suffer if you will; reject me, if you must, but do not die. There would be no hope at all if you were no more.'

Gasping, Balyndis looked at him. 'Be there for him,' she said, forcing the words out. 'Help your son be a good king. *That* is what I was going to say to you when we met for our meal together.' She lifted her arm with difficulty and placed her right hand on the nape of his neck, pulling his head closer to her blood-spattered lips. 'Hear this: you were always in my heart, Tungdil, every cycle of the two hundred and fifty you were away. Longer, though you cast me off. *That* is another thing I wanted to tell you. And for *that* I curse you.' She breathed a kiss onto his ear and her dying breath fanned his face. The light went out of her eyes and her body fell back.

'Watch out!'

Tungdil stood up and threw the shields aside. He marched through the hail of bolts, remaining untouched but for one injury that tore off the tip of his left pinkie and another shot that went through his foot. He yanked it out without missing a step. He felt neither wound.

He felt nothing at all except for boundless hatred for the archers who had stolen all hope from him. What he had dreamt of the entire duration of his long absence. Blackness spread in his soul, seeping out into every fibre of his being. He would use the strength it gave him.

You have returned to take me over. Tungdil placed his hands on the gate and shut his eyes. *I will allow it, for once.*

Closing his eyes did not make the image of his dead love disappear. He could smell her blood, could feel the sensation of her breath on his skin and could hear her words as she uttered that curse. Something broke out inside him: something dark he had long repressed and had never intended to let come to the fore again.

Cold energy streamed out of his left hand, hot energy from his right. He heard the shocked cries of the dwarves at his back. He kept his eyes shut as the energy flowed. He could feel the blood pulsing through his temples as the bolts started to pull back.

'Did she tell you the code?' Balyndar was amazed.

Open! Tungdil shoved the gates apart.

The granite – heavy as a mountain with all the extra weight it bore from the catapults and the vast stone blocks – let itself be moved by his hands as if it were no more solid than a feather, or kindling. The two doors flung inwards.

He opened his eyes and lowered his arms. 'The path is free,' he said darkly.

The gates crashed back against the rock walls, making the mountain shudder. Rubble slid down into the empty courtyard from the hillside. The impact caused the battlement constructions on the top of the gates to collapse, falling next to the dwarves. Siege machines started to roll about on the walkways, tipping over or shattering on the ground below. Panic broke out on the levels where the burning pitch was held ready to pour on the invaders.

Balyndar strode slowly past Tungdil, advancing on the inner court. 'Find the traitors!' he bellowed, his voice full of rage. 'For the queen's sake, find them!'

Tungdil was unable to move. He kept his eyes fixed on the yard, noticing it contained corpses as well as the ruins of battlement sections. Dwarves. Elves. Their bodies were for the most part decomposed or scavenged by vultures. These were not fresh deaths.

'There is no more hope,' he said under his breath, and went back to Balyndis. He closed her eyelids tenderly. *None at all.* He stayed kneeling, motionless at her side while the surviving dwarves streamed through to secure the stronghold.

The catapults were silent.

Tungdil did not move until the dwarves came with a stretcher to carry Balyndis away. He still took no notice of the injuries to his hand and foot. His body was numb. He watched in silence as they lifted her body and carried her in to the fortress. Blood left a path of droplets on the stone as they bore her along.

If a boulder had fallen on Tungdil from the walkways at that moment, he would not have moved aside.

He would have welcomed it with open arms.

Girdlegard
Grey Mountains
Kingdom of the Fifthling dwarves
Stone Gateway
6497th solar cycle, summer

Ocâstia was seated opposite the dwarf leaders in the Fifthlings' conference chamber. This was where judicial hearings normally took place. 'I could not restrain Venîlahíl. He was . . . insane!'

The elf-woman with the black and white hair looked care-worn. She had suffered significant injuries and had lost weight. The dwarves had found her in the dungeon in an even worse state; she had been cowering in the same cell where the corpse of one of the sorânïons lay.

'Venîlahíl was obsessed with the idea of our being taken over by the botoican.' Ocâstia had told her story several times: how one of her warriors had secretly started killing dwarves and elves with poison, until his madness grew so bold that he took over the walkways and used the machines and catapults to put down resistance. Only a few had survived and they had hidden in the extensive mountain tunnels. 'How did you kill him?' she asked.

Tungdil listened with the kings and the clan leaders. Occasionally there was a brief muttered discussion amongst the audience, but nobody interrupted her. *This has to be sufficient, Vraccas. We have suffered enough.* 'He was hit by crossbow bolts. Two of them. We found his corpse next to a catapult he was about to load.'

'Praise be to Vraccas and Sitalia! Here is the letter that started it all.'

A message on the stone table in front of Ocâstia was written in dwarf runes and bore the High King's signature and his personal seal. This false missive had set the scene for the tragedy that had played out in the fortress while the dwarves were campaigning in the Outer Lands.

Ireheart picked up the document. It looked genuine enough in everything, from the type of paper to the handwriting, from the phraseology to the actual signature and seal. 'And it was a dwarf who brought you the message?'

'Yes.'

'And his name was?'

'I don't know. The dwarves met with him. Then Barborin Doughtyarm came and told me the High King had written to say the botoican had unexpectedly won the battle and captured most of the dwarf army. The stronghold was immediately made ready to repel invaders.' Ocâstia wiped the tears from her cheeks; she had been deeply affected by events. 'That's when Venîlahîl went berserk. When I confronted him, he stabbed me and had me imprisoned. Together with the injured elf I was unable to save.'

Boïndil looked round at the assembled faces. Balyndis, of course, was missing. Balyndar was there in her place, his face marked with grief at her passing.

'Seven hundred and eleven dead, three hundred and seventy wounded. That's more than we lost in the battle against the beasts,' Boïndil thundered, hurling the letter to the floor. 'And we've lost Balyndis! Venîlahîl's poison also saw to a further three hundred here. Sha'taï's trick worked a treat.'

'Why do we think the botoican was behind it?' Xamtor wanted to know.

'It's devious enough. But I disagree. It must have come from an älf.' Balyndar gripped his hands together. 'I say it was Carmondai's parting gift to us.'

They're looking for the simplest reason. Tungdil frowned. 'Carmondai saved the High King's life.'

'Only because he knew he could cause more mayhem later.' Balyndar pointed to the letter. 'The forgery is perfect in every detail. Even the royal seal. For a master in word and image like him this would be no problem.'

'But he had no motive,' Tungdil insisted.

'He is an *älf,*' his son retorted. 'Why would he need a

motive? It's in his nature. Just because you had him along on your trek doesn't mean the doddery black-eyes has turned harmless. In his core' – here the dwarf laid his hand on his own heart – 'he is warped. He is Inàste's creation. Like Aiphatòn.'

'If that were the case, ' said Frandibar, 'where did the dwarf messenger come from? A gnome in disguise? Hardly.'

Gordislan cleared his throat. 'Hargorin, what do you say?'

'I don't know what I could contribute.' The King of the Thirdlings continued to scowl.

'Perhaps that you considered the dwarf feud to be over, but there still might be some of your tribe who do not share your enlightened opinion?' Gordislan was making an effort not to sound accusatory, but his tone of voice was making things worse.

This is how trust is destroyed. Tungdil expected Hargorin to fly into a rage and grab Gordislan, but the red-bearded dwarf remained admirably calm. 'It's no secret, if *you* know it.' He nodded. 'Everybody knows it. But the Thirdlings made up the majority of our army. It can hardly have been their idea to wipe themselves out in this way.'

Xamtor snorted, 'We won't get nearer the truth till we've questioned the traitor who delivered that message.'

And since Ocâstia never saw him, she can't tell us who it is, even if he is among the survivors. This realisation brought Tungdil to a conclusion the dwarf rulers were not going to like. 'Put that aside for now. We need to concentrate on Sha'taï.'

'I am *not* going to put it aside.' Balyndar was indignant. 'And I want Carmondai found and punished!'

'You know the situation. Tell me how you think you're

going to be able to find him.' Tungdil gave the faintest of smiles. 'Are you planning on sending out a hunting party to get the älf? Where? The Outer Lands? At a time the Fifthlings are reduced to eleven hundred?'

Balyndar was about to launch into a reply but thought better of it.

He's come to see sense. Good. 'Vraccas will send us an opportunity to get to the bottom of things when the time is right.' Turning to Ocâstia, Tungdil asked: 'Did the false news get out into Girdlegard, about the army being defeated?'

'Possibly.' She looked unsure. In her right hand she was clutching a figurine bearing Rognor's symbol.

'That would mean they all mistrust us, and will think we're controlled by the ghaist. As soon as Sha'taï hears, she'll hit us with everything she's got. Everyone will join in her side out of affection for her.' Tungdil helped himself to some water. *One trial after another.* 'We need to come up with an idea fast.'

'You really ought to be High King,' Boïndil found himself saying.

'Never!' snapped Balyndar. Tungdil understood his passionate response. He saw the elf-woman wanting to add something.

'Before things got out of hand, we'd heard that Coïra had retired into her tower,' said Ocâstia.

'Tower? What tower?' Boïndil was as surprised as all the others. Then he remembered there had been talk of it at their last meeting. *There's so much to take in.*

'Soon after you left, the maga used her magic to build herself an eight-sided tower, measuring around a hundred paces in diameter at the base. It's supported by buttresses that rear up over the town, it's so big.' Her words and gestures were compelling. The dwarves were able to picture the magic building. 'It reaches up to the clouds, many hundreds of paces high. If the botoican girl has taken refuge there and is amassing an army to defend herself, we'll never get her out.'

Xamtor laughed. 'No tower is stronger than its foundation.'

'Undermining it won't work. It's no doubt built on the magic source,' Tungdil told them, quashing that idea. *But what can we do?* Each of those present deliberated in silence about how the tower might be captured without a tremendous loss of life or destroying the building, and without recourse to a time-consuming siege. The gates still had to be protected. And anyway, Coïra could conjure herself anything she needed.

This is worse than fighting the ghaist.

'If we had the wind-älf it'd be easy,' muttered Boïndil. 'He could have blasted the Sha'taï girl straight out through the window.'

Wind! Now there's an idea! 'You may've come up with something, my friend. Let's send out scouts. Before taking any course of action, we need to assess the situation in the interior.'

The rulers agreed.

Ocâstia gave Tungdil a smile. 'And, you know, you *are* their king,' she said quietly, so quietly that only he could hear it. 'Of course I shall be at your side when you march out to capture the young girl.' She stood up. 'Has it been decided what to do with her?'

Nobody spoke.

The elf-woman came to her own conclusions. 'I understand. That will be the best thing.'

Girdlegard
United Kingdom of Gauragar-Idoslane
Idoslane
6497th solar cycle, autumn

A building that is only held up by magic. Tungdil observed the octagonal tower, which was larger and taller than anything Girdlegard had ever previously seen. The dwarves had halted a safe distance away and were making their preparations. The mighty tower looked impregnable. *And it's partly my fault it exists. It was me that brought Coïra to the source.*

A strong wind swept through Idoslane, driving the clouds from the west to disperse round the topmost third of the edifice.

'It's the magic source that keeps it erect.' Tungdil looked at the town that appeared insignificant under the massive flying buttresses that were one hundred paces wide. 'The supports are just for show.'

'I can see what you mean. A battering-ram would be no use at all.' Boïndil scratched the closely shaved side of his head and then readjusted his helmet. 'Looks like your plan is the only way, Scholar.'

'It may well cost us more dwarves.' Tungdil turned to look at the army that Sha'taï had mustered – it was all of Girdlegard's fighting forces. The troops surrounding the tower like living ramparts were ready to sacrifice their lives for the young woman. 'They outnumber you four to one. But it's important not to inflict too much damage on them.'

'I hope they'll see we're the good guys.' Boïndil lifted his new crow's beak. He had created the whole thing out of wood and padded it with fabric. 'This shouldn't cause too much damage.'

'It won't be as heavy as the original, but be careful who you're hitting. It could still crush a skull or tear a throat.' Tungdil bade his friend farewell. 'And before you ask again: no, I shan't be standing as High King. I have to help my son to be a good ruler. I promised Balyndis.'

Boïndil nodded. 'Did you tell him the code?'

'No. And that's the only reason he lets me stay near him. Without my say-so, the gates won't close or open.' Tungdil could not tell his friend the truth about how he did it. Not without a protracted revelation of all the events during his time in Phondrasôn.

'I get it.' Boïndil swung himself into the saddle. 'Balyndar told me something that should make your doubters quieten down.'

Tungdil frowned. *He won't be meaning the grief I feel, surely?* 'Did he?'

'Keenfire. He said the diamonds did not light up in warning when the two of you were standing together. May Vraccas and Samusin be with you.' He galloped off.

'May they be with us all, old friend,' Tungdil watched him ride off to join their army. *So my own weapon has declared me innocent.*

The remaining dwarf forces were waiting for their High King at the south of the tower. Against all normal practice, the warriors were armed only with wooden clubs and sturdy shields. Their catapult projectiles and crossbow bolts had padded tips, intended merely to knock their opponents off their feet or to stun them.

The army had been equipped specifically with the aim of causing no deaths. The injuries amongst the elves and humans would be broken limbs, bumps and bruises. The dwarves knew their opponents doing battle against them were not in possession of the full facts and therefore should be treated magnanimously. They did not, however, expect any such clemency for themselves. The troops had taken pains with their armour, expecting bolts and blades.

'A brave band.' Beligata came up to Tungdil, attaching leather straps over her shoulders and fastening them to her belt. 'We'll try to get this over with quickly.' She handed him a set of leather straps and steel rings. 'We have a favourable wind. We've been waiting a long time.'

Tungdil slipped into the harness and made sure the straps were tight. His leg still hurt but that must not be allowed to impede him. All he took to defend himself with was the slim acronta dagger. He wore no metal plate armour. It would have weighed him down too much.

He walked up to the hill where Beligata, Gosalyn and Ocâstia were waiting. They were similarly dressed. The elf-woman had insisted on accompanying them. In her capacity as sorânïan she saw this as her duty. She was light on her feet and this might be an advantage if Samusin lost interest in their cause and stopped providing the necessary wind force.

It's a mad idea. But it's the only one we've got. 'We talk to Sha'taï first of all,' he reminded them. 'We've got to persuade her that we mean her no harm. She's to be promised safety. The enemy she so fears has been eliminated. Then we'll see what happens next.'

'What if she doesn't let us talk to her?' Beligata had her short axes in her hands.

'Then we do what the gods demand of us.' Ocâstia answered for Tungdil. She bent down and hooked the chain of her reins to the equipment lying tamely on the grass.

'Different gods, different opinions,' said Gosalyn, copying her actions. 'That's what makes it exciting.'

Tungdil and Beligata attached themselves likewise. Then he signalled down to the little valley and crawled underneath the construction made of wood, wire and canvas. He pushed himself forward to where he could grab the crossbar with both hands and stood erect, heaving the frame up to meet the wind. *What's this going to feel like?*

'Now!' he yelled.

The crew yanked the ropes and the swirling up-wind gathered under the spanned fabric, filling the silken screen until it was taut. The kite rose up with Tungdil dangling underneath.

His crew paid out the rope to keep the kite in the optimum air current so that it would gain height and carry him, they hoped, over to the tower. The same was happening for Beligata and Gosalyn by his side. Ocâstia, being lighter, was already high above them. Tungdil heard her shriek with delight.

'It's amazing,' she called down to them. 'Flying! Like birds!'

'We're flying like *kites*,' Beligata corrected pedantically, but she had a broad grin on her face. The scar had not faded. 'On strings.'

'I'm praying to Samusin,' Gosalyn said, not enjoying the trip as much as the others. 'Vraccas will forgive us. This is not his jurisdiction up here.'

The earth fell away beneath their feet as the air pushed them up toward the layer of clouds.

The harness reins allowed them to turn and investigate the best place for landing, while their speed and trajectory were controlled from below. They were totally dependent on the crew holding the strings, and also on Samusin's grace. They hoped against hope that the wind the god was providing would not suddenly drop and send them plummeting to the ground. The kites had long tails that floated this way and that, stabilising their flight.

They went ever higher as the cords were played out. Loops at the end of the strings allowed the crew to fasten on extension reels. *Like a leaf in the wind. Or like a heavy sack filled with petroleum.* Tungdil's view of the sky was obscured by the spanned silk. But what he could see two hundred paces below was compensation enough. He had to force his attention back to the task at hand. The first few cloudlets sailed past him like curious onlookers, astonished to see a dwarf flying.

Beneath them the dwarf force was making its first advance. The planned tactic was to storm at full speed and then turn suddenly to one side, doing no more than alerting the opposition to their presence.

Tungdil knew his ground crews were observing them through telescopes and were awaiting his instructions. The cords were securely anchored to the ground under heavy stones to counteract the powerful drag on the ropes. He indicated he wanted to be brought closer to the building. He reached back and held tight to the crossbar to keep from rocking about.

Beligata and Gosalyn were ten paces to his left and to his right respectively. Ocâstia was higher up.

The grey and white clouds became denser and cloaked them from sight. The crews on the ground would not be able to pick them out clearly any more.

The tower wall reared up in front of Tungdil's eyes as the kite tail flapped at the stone. *It's not going to be easy.* He could see neither windows nor balconies nor anything they could grab hold of. The kites did not allow much freedom of movement since they were tethered by the ropes.

Tungdil approached the walls cautiously. The tail's flapping affected his stability and the kite started to swirl about, losing the support of the column of air. The kite dropped. *Nothing for it.* Tungdil cut through the anchoring cord and the rope fell back down to the ground. He rose again.

Before she knew it, Gosalyn had got caught up in swathes of damp, cold vapour.

This is Samusin's realm. She felt distinctly uneasy. She was familiar with not being able to see where she was, having being caught in mountain mist, but up there you merely had to wait until the clouds lifted or feel your way along the rock face. This time she was stuck two hundred paces above the ground and the wind was whistling slightly, filling the silk sheet. She could see nothing but the wet white softness of the cloud.

She could not see Beligata or Tungdil. The octagonal tower could have been a trick of her imagination.

What shall I do? Gosalyn thought about sending a message down to the ground crew: a piece of paper on a hook could be sent sliding down the cord. She wanted to be brought down until visibility improved, rather than be crushed against the walls or have the cords get tangled.

A shadow shot down, colliding with her kite.

I've been hit! Her contraption lost its equilibrium and started shaking uncontrollably. She watched in horror as the kite tail tore away and vanished in the fog.

The shadow ceased its downward flight and floated up to her level. *Ocâstia!*

'Turbulence, dammit,' explained the elf-woman, gripping the cross bar of her kite. She seemed quite adept at steering the contraption. 'Samusin is not on our side, it seems.'

'You're right.' Gosalyn made an effort to suppress a cry of fear when her kite threatened to topple over. If that happened, it would be bound to fall. *With me.*

Ocâstia realised what was happening. She stretched her arms out. 'There's no time for the ground crew to haul you back down. Hold tight to the bars and unhook yourself from the harness. I'll bring my kite over towards you and when we're close enough, you jump.'

'Never!' Gosalyn was horrified. 'If we miss . . .'

'We won't miss,' Ocâstia said firmly.

A gust took the silk and pushed the kite up. Gosalyn's faulty contraption creaked and shook and one of the bars cracked. Gosalyn felt sick with fear.

'Now!' called Ocâstia, flying her own kite close. 'Trust me!'

Vraccas, you know I have never doubted you. Gosalyn held on to the wood with one hand while unhooking herself with the other.

The gap between the two grew narrower.

Gosalyn watched Ocâstia nod to her and stretch out her arms. She used the next contortion of the kite to gather her strength and then she let go. No longer floating on the air. Just dropping. Falling. The ground where dwarves really belonged was pulling her down like a stone dropping into water. All the previous sense of adventure and excitement was lost.

I'll never, ever do that again. Gosalyn heard herself scream. A new gust forced Ocâstia's kite to the side. To her inordinate relief, Gosalyn felt the elf-woman's fingertips touch her hands. Ocâstia was smiling down in encouragement.

*

Tungdil's kite tumbled, spun and scraped along the stones as he spiralled round the building.

To his relief he saw a ledge, narrow though it was, just beneath him. *Good!* Without hesitation, he released himself from the flying contraption and grabbed the window ledge as he fell. He pulled himself inside, landing on a spiral staircase, while his kite careered into a corner, smashed and fell in pieces onto the town below. *Samusin, that was not kind!*

The stone ledge had been decorated with coloured chalk. Someone without much of an artistic gift had tried to capture the view from this lofty window. *That would probably be the work of Sha'taï.* Tungdil scanned the sky. The others' kites were in the clouds, invisible by now. He yelled out regardless: 'I'm going up the stairs. Stay where you are as long as the wind allows it.'

'Will do,' Beligata called back.

As quickly as he could with his injured leg, he limped up the staircase, which was lit by glowing stones embedded in the walls. From time to time there were ventilation ducts like arrow slits. Panting, Tungdil kept going. He thought he had long passed the level the kites were floating at outside, but there was nowhere they could make a landing. *I struck lucky, coming across that window ledge.*

He did not believe that Coïra and Sha'taï spent their days tackling this incredible number of steps. The staircase was wide but with the tower's diameter at a hundred paces, there was plenty of room in the middle for a lift.

He noticed a double set of shutters the height of a grown man in the outer wall. He opened them. They led onto a balcony where a table and chair stood. A pile of papers weighed down with a stone was next to an inkwell and a glass writing implement. Was someone about to return to the desk?

The balcony gave on to a view to the south. Tungdil was above the cloud level and blinked in the bright autumn sunlight.

A shadow flitted past, then a tall, delicate figure leaped on to the balcony, bending its knees to land elegantly.

'That was a near thing.' Ocâstia stood tall and looked over her shoulder. 'The kite was useless when the wind changed direction.'

Tungdil was overcome with concern. 'Beligata and Gosalyn?'

'The ground crews got them down safely.' She nodded to him and wiped the tears from her eyes. 'It is so cold out there when you drop. I thought my eyeballs would freeze.'

'So it's up to the two of us.' He gestured for her to join him. *Sitalia and Vraccas.* 'An elf-woman and a dwarf will save Girdlegard.'

Ocâstia nodded and grasped his arm as he was about to pound up the next flight of steps. 'Wait! Who says they're up there?'

'The girl will want to get as far away as possible from those that can harm her.' Tungdil was doing a good job of convincing himself. 'She'll feel safer up high.'

'But if she goes down, she's nearer the troops and can manipulate them. And we've got no idea how tall this tower is; we could be climbing for orbits. The battle might be over and we're gasping for breath without knowing if we're anywhere near the top.' Ocâstia pointed to the steps going down. 'I wonder which one of us is right?'

We can't waste time doing unnecessary climbing. 'Do you think we should separate?'

'It would be better.' Ocâstia lifted her left hand. 'If I find them first, I swear I won't kill Coïra or her protegée unnecessarily.'

'I'm more worried about the influence Sha'taï may have on you. What use is it to us if you find her but in the blink of an eye you're her devoted slave?' Tungdil cursed the fraught situation. 'We stay together.'

'Then it's down, rather than up,' Ocâstia demanded. 'As soon as the wind turns, Beligata and Gosalyn will make another attempt with the kites.'

They went down the steps together, Tungdil taking things slowly because of his injured leg. They reached the painted window ledge and went past the ventilation ducts, but saw no kite strings leading up to the clouds. The wind had not turned favourable yet. Samusin had only shown them his grace for a very limited time.

The steps went on and on. The air changed. Tungdil could smell food being prepared.

'Looks like we made the right choice,' Ocâstia whispered.

Ocâstia and Tungdil came across a locked door that they managed to heave off its hinges. It gave onto a large room that served as a storage chamber and passageway. There were pieces of furniture, lamps and torch holders, tables piled on top of each other, and mirrors – items that had presumably fallen out of favour with Coïra and Sha'taï. And yet more stairs.

Then they saw grating surrounding a shaft of some sort, and behind it two slender chains. It could be entered via a door.

'That will be the lift,' said Ocâstia quietly. 'We should use it to go down. It will be easier than using the steps. We would have surprise on our side.'

'Good idea.' Tungdil opened the arched door and looked up and then down. *No platform.* He took off his helmet, fastened it to his belt, then grasped the chain and slid down. Ocâstia followed his lead.

Their progress was faster now. And quieter. On other levels, the tube apparatus was closed in with movable parchment segments. This lent privacy for the rooms the lift passed; they could only be seen vaguely. Tungdil and Ocâstia slid past bedrooms, libraries, guardrooms, dressing rooms, fencing practice halls, eating areas and kitchens. They decided to come back later to investigate.

They saw nobody, only a few cats lounging on furniture or sitting on shelves.

'They must be at the top of the tower after all,' Tungdil muttered as they continued without success. He was angry. *I should have followed my instincts.* Then Ocâstia motioned him to silence and he heard it, too: from the room they were now approaching there came a heated exchange.

Tungdil recognised the voices of Mallenia, Rodario, and Coïra and also a childish treble. *Excellent. We're getting warm.* But if they were spotted in the lift shaft, the alarm would be sounded. *Slowly does it.* Tungdil came to a stop, and holding on to the chain with his feet, he turned upside down. Hanging there he could spy into the room. He ignored the pain from the fresh wounds he had on hand and feet; they were throbbing badly.

There was a large cupboard placed against the caged lift shaft, hiding him but allowing him to see through a gap. Two men in armour emblazoned with the insignia of Urgon and Idoslane stood at a map table arguing about battle tactics. He saw the pointer one of them was employing was in fact a crossbow bolt – with a padded end.

'. . . understand why they'd be attacking with dummy weapons. Wooden arrows? Is it some kind of game?'

'I think the dwarves are reluctant to hurt any of us.' This was from Rodario, seen twirling his moustache. As usual he was in flamboyant attire and had not been ashamed to put on a feather ruff. 'But if they've set their sights on Sha'taï and they've been sent by the botoican, I can't see the reasoning.'

Mallenia was wearing armour over a dark blue robe, her black hair pinned up under her helmet. She was staring at the map, her arm around the waist of a young woman Tungdil finally recognised as Sha'taï.

So they're trying to work out our motives? Then maybe they will listen if we try to explain. Signalling to the elf-woman to follow him, he reversed direction, opened the door carefully and stepped inside, keeping behind the wardrobe, which thankfully did not creak. He put his helmet back on.

'The botoican needs you alive for his army.' Sha'taï spoke forcefully. 'You're no use to him as casualties.'

'But his dwarves may lose the battle. It's risky for him. My soldiers are fully armed and their arrows are steel-tipped.' This was the Idoslane captain. 'Why didn't he send out some expendable orcs?'

'You don't know how devious and cunning he is,' howled Sha'taï. 'He knows exactly what he's doing. And so do I. You need to kill the dwarves before they defeat us. Get the troops out on the attack immediately. Believe me, I'm really sorry that we have to destroy them. You have to understand.'

'Of course, dear. We were just taken aback by the fact they're using dummy weapons,' said Mallenia softly. 'But now you've explained. Thank you.'

She didn't explain anything. She just manipulated you. Tungdil was relieved that the girl's powers did not seem to measure up to the botoican's in any way. Sha'taï had to work with trickery and deceit. She exerted her charm over people to get them to carry out her plans while convincing them they had come to their own decisions. *She is a far cry from being able to subjugate a goldfireworm. Thank the gods.*

'We have to intervene,' Ocâstia whispered. She indicated the captains. 'I'll take those two. We can't let them issue the command to attack or the gates in the mountains will have nobody manning them.' Pulling out her short axes with their original sharp blades, she saw Tungdil's hesitation. 'I know. I'll do my best not to kill them. Then I'll come over and help you.' She moved stealthily round the side of the room to where the military men were.

And me? Tungdil hesitated. Then he stepped out into full view.

'There!' Sha'taï shrieked, clung to Mallenia and grabbed Coïra's hand. This made it easier for her to influence the two women directly.

'Tungdil?' Rodario was amazed. 'I shan't ask how you got in. What could you be wanting, I wonder?' He pretended to stare at the ceiling as if thinking hard. 'Let me guess: you'd like to negotiate on behalf of the botoican?'

Ignoring him and the two women, Tungdil addressed Sha'taï. 'Listen to me. We have killed the ghaist. He was the botoican himself. He can't hurt you anymore. You are safe here with us in Girdlegard.'

'He's got you under his spell,' said the young woman fearfully. 'No one can withstand his power.'

Mallenia drew her weapon. Coïra kept her eyes on the dwarf and Rodario placed his hand on the hilt of his ornamental sword. Their faces went blank and the expression in their eyes changed.

She is afraid of me. 'No, that is not true. Vraccas created us so stubborn that we are strong enough to resist him. We can stand up to you, as well. You can't influence our will. Our friends at the gates downstairs are only making sham attacks. We don't want to kill or even harm anyone at all. All we wanted was to reach you and beg you to stop using your power to harm Girdlegard.' He raised his arm slowly and stretched his empty hand out to her. 'If you touch my hand and try to influence my mind, you will fail. This should be enough to convince you of the truth of what I have been telling you.'

Sha'taï shook her head, her dark blonde hair flying. 'I don't trust you. I trust only those in my control.'

'Then is your future life to be spent in a permanent state of fear, sharing this tower with Coïra and an army at your gates?' Tungdil sent her a friendly smile. 'That's no life, is it?'

'I am safe here. No one can hurt me,' she blurted out. 'It must not happen again. All that suffering and then running away, my family all dead . . .' Sha'taï sobbed. 'But I'm really looking after Girdlegard,' she sniffed. 'Have you noticed how well everyone is looking? And everybody gets on famously. They're all friends and there's no suspicion or feuding any more. All the kingdoms are full of harmony.'

'And it's harmony that you have brought about.' Tungdil kept his hand raised. *This is true. The peace is down to her.* 'I would let you live however you wish, if I knew you would never commit any evil deeds.'

'Me?' Sha'taï's eyes were red with crying. 'I had to go through so much. Why would I want to do evil?'

I've got through to her. 'I swear by Vraccas that we shall look after you,' he said firmly. 'But I must ask you this: please take your spell off my friends and all the humans and elves whose minds you have manipulated.'

Mallenia strode forward and thrust the tip of her sword at his throat. 'One false move and you die.'

Sha'taï pushed past the queen and touched Tungdil's outstretched index finger. The result was no more than a tickling sensation in his hand. She was startled at first, but it was followed quickly by disbelief and then curiosity. 'It's true,' she said in surprise. 'I can't make you do what I want. I suspected it, but I wasn't sure until now.'

'No dwarf ever obeys a botoican.' Tungdil was hoping he had got through to her. *She only needs to understand we are her best hope of protection.*

Sha'taï returned to her seat at the table. Her eyes narrowed as she spoke. 'That means the dwarves are my enemies.'

He had not expected this turn of events. 'No, we are not.' Tungdil was upset. *I don't want to have to kill her.*

'If I can't control you, how would I deal with you? You'll travel around making trouble and spreading lies about me. There'll be disagreements, fighting, and good soldiers will die that I need to protect me. To protect *me*!' she repeated, accusingly. 'You must all die or leave Girdlegard for ever and find yourselves somewhere else to live. There are mountains in other regions.'

Mallenia's sharp sword tip was still at his throat. 'That would be a possibility,' Tungdil said, pretending to consider the suggestion.

Ocâstia suddenly appeared on the scene and vaulted feet-first, kicking Mallenia and knocking her flying to the other side of the room where the queen crashed into a set of shelves that fell on her. Executing a forward roll, the elf-woman pulled Rodario's feet out from under him so that she could get close to Sha'taï. She whipped her drawn dagger towards the young woman.

'Don't!' Tungdil prepared to leap to the botoican girl's defence. *If only I had more time to talk to her.* 'Let her live!'

A magical protective sphere formed around Sha'taï – but it did not include Coïra, who had cast the spell. The dagger's path was deflected by the aura and plunged straight into the maga's breast, piercing through the blue robe. Coïra collapsed with a groan and her spell immediately lost its potency.

What a tragedy! Tungdil knocked into Ocâstia and brought her down. They both fell to the floor behind Sha'taï. Sha'taï screamed and touched Ocâstia on the leg.

The elf-woman immediately fell under the young botoican's spell. She turned on Tungdil, stabbing at him. He was able to dodge the blow before drawing his own weapon, the blade of acronta origin.

'You have killed the maga!' Sha'taï shrieked in horror.

'It was your power that started this all,' Tungdil called out, holding off the elf-attacker. 'See sense, child! No one wants to harm you.'

'I never wanted her hurt.' Sha'taï knelt down at Coïra's side, trying to close the wound and stop the bleeding.

Tungdil had seen the injury. *It went straight through her heart. There's no saving her.* He overcame his shock. There was a further catastrophe that had to be prevented. 'See what your powers can do. Set my friends free and release Girdlegard.'

'I didn't kill her.' White-faced, Sha'taï stared at her bloodied fingers and at the red blotches forming on her light-coloured dress. 'It was her own sphere. It deflected the knife tip.'

'Nothing will happen to you.' Tungdil saw Mallenia getting up. Rodario was already on his feet. Both of them were armed.

'That would never have happened if you hadn't charged in

here, dwarf! You and that elf-woman,' Sha'taï shouted. 'The dwarves must clear out of Girdlegard and then everything will come right. It will be peaceful.' She stood up. 'One more death and then it's enough.'

Ocâstia raised her daggers and approached Tungdil, who found himself confronting three experienced warriors.

'Then what must be must be,' he murmured. *And I was all set to spare your life.*

His attention turned to the adversaries he would have to overcome without killing them. Mallenia's long blade came near and Tungdil parried with the acronta dagger, then he ducked under Rodario's attack and leaped to one side. He did not wish to get stuck in the middle of this affray.

The blonde Ido queen struck again diagonally, wielding her blade with both hands. Tungdil had seen this coming and got ready to receive a mighty blow that would land heavily on hands and shoulders. But Ocâstia's daggers came between them and diverted the queen's murderous thrust – sending it directly in to Rodario's side. The king fell with a cry.

'I thought I'd make the fight a little more balanced. A nice duel was what I fancied.' The elf-woman laughed, stabbing at Mallenia, aiming at the vulnerable spot under her arm and kicking her so she fell on top of the actor. Their red blood combined in pools on the floorboards. 'There you are: the lovers are lying in their own blood, united in death.'

Sha'taï screamed again. 'What do you think you are doing? It's the *dwarf* you're supposed to be killing! The dwarf! Not the others!'

Tungdil held his knife in front of him and watched Ocâstia's blank features. *An even duel. Warrior versus warrior. Elves' code of honour?'*

'I'll kill him for you.' Ocâstia put one of her daggers away and picked up Mallenia's sword, trying it for weight. 'But then you'll owe me.' In the next heartbeat her expression had changed. It was no longer distant. Her face bore a cold smile. Her eyes were free of any veil. 'My mind is not so weak as theirs. Your power is not as great as you imagine, botoican child.' Without warning, she hurled the dagger and hit the young woman on the temple with the handle. Sha'taï fell down behind the table. 'When you wake up again, we'll have a chat about how you're going to make me ruler of the whole of Girdlegard. Three thrones are now vacant.'

Tungdil launched his attack, crying, 'Traitor!'

Ocâstia parried the blow with a disdainful laugh. 'I am no traitor. There is nothing wrong with staying true to oneself.'

There followed an exchange of blows. Tungdil was inexperienced with this particular weapon and struggled to defeat Ocâstia. *Didn't one of the captains have an axe hanging at his belt?* The men in question lay near the doorway with their throats cut. Imperceptibly Tungdil directed the fight towards the corpses and dropped down.

Ocâstia mocked him. 'And *you're* Girdlegard's famous hero?' She looked down. 'You've not inflicted a single scratch. This was as easy as killing Gosalyn.' She stopped to listen to something – the chains were starting to move in the lift shaft. 'Before the next uninvited guest turns up, I want to finish this. And then I'll find out how Girdlegard's throne suits me.'

Gosalyn is dead? Tungdil wrenched the captain's axe from his belt and tossed the acronta dagger aside, getting swiftly to his feet. 'That won't be happening. I had hoped the new elves would know how to abide by their own laws, but you seem to be the exception.'

Ocâstia spied the axe. 'Feel more at home with the axe, do you?'

'Let me show you.' Tungdil attacked abruptly, immediately noticing how much better this weapon lay in his hand. Ocâstia was scornful, but after the dwarf had attacked her three or four times, she fell silent and started to fight for breath. Tungdil knew exactly what he was doing and anticipated every trick she attempted. His time in Phondrasôn had served him well in that respect.

When the lift arrived it held Beligata. Seeing the fight, she brought the platform to a halt. Tungdil was able to take advantage of his opponent's slight hesitation: he feigned a high strike, but then ducked down and aimed for her ankles. Ocâstia jumped up and the axe swept harmlessly under her feet. *I'll get you.* Tungdil tucked his helmeted head between his shoulders and butted the elf-woman in the belly. She sailed through the air, the impact hurtling her backwards.

The dwarf pursued her and used his heavy weapon to attack her from above. The blade missed the tip of her nose, but cleft the chin and sliced her breast to the navel. 'That's for your treachery and the murders you committed!' Ocâstia staggered back against a wooden chest, enveloped in a cloud of blood. Her guts spilled out and splashed onto the floor. She dropped Mallenia's sword with a clang and her eyes misted over.

'Look to the wounded!' Tungdil commanded Beligata. 'The king and queen must be saved.' He hurried over to where Sha'taï lay unconscious. 'What happened to Gosalyn?'

'She fell to her death.' Beligata answered from across the room. 'I saw her body on a rooftop.' *Ocâstia arranged for her to fall.* Beligata was unaware that she would have shared the same fate, had the opportunity arisen.

The dwarf stood over the young girl, who was curled into the foetal position. There was a cut on her temple but her breathing showed she was still alive. Her eyes were open but vacant. She was in a state of deep shock. Ocâstia's dagger lay temptingly close. *It would be so easy.* There would be no more subjugation of people's minds and no more devious creatures like the elf-woman desperate to get their greedy hands on the child's power in order to take over Girdlegard.

Tungdil gritted his teeth. *Vraccas, no. There must be some other way.* He gently rolled Sha'taï onto her back. *She's a confused child, she's not evil incarnate. She can be made to see reason. Her gifts may prove useful, to preserve peace in the homeland, come what may.*

He noticed she had a splinter of glass in her right eye. It had not pierced the eyeball but had entered her skull through her eye socket. She was breathing steadily. Her gaze was fixed on the dwarf but her eyes were blank. There was no sign she recognised him.

Unconscious and with open eyes. How long her condition might persist, the healers would have to deliberate on. *But could it be that . . .* He hurried to the window to look out.

He was overjoyed to see the first unusual troop movements in the army at the foot of the tower: there were shouts and gestures as the soldiers questioned what was happening. It was as though they had just woken up; confusion reigned. The dwarf forces had withdrawn to a nearby hill, readying themselves to feign a further attack.

I've got to stop them. He glanced quickly at Sha'taï, at the dead Coïra and at the injured humans who were being treated by Beligata. Her expression indicated Mallenia and Rodario were in a bad way.

The living have priority. 'I shall end the fighting,' he called to Beligata. He limped over to the murdered captain to take the bugle at the man's belt, before hobbling to the lift.

On the way down, he was a jumble of emotions. *Gosalyn, too, was the victim of a delusional, power-crazed elf.* Grief, anger and relief – he could only give way to these feelings once the violence outside had ceased.

It occurred to him that he had guessed wrong. The tower itself was not held together merely by Coïra's spell. *It will be the power from the magic source.* Tungdil sent a prayer to Vraccas. *May the walls hold.* If it collapsed everyone in the vicinity would die.

'Wait!' The platform had reached ground level and Tungdil hurried towards the exit. He kicked the door open. 'Hold back on the attack!'

He put the horn to his lips.

Girdlegard
United Kingdom of Gauragar-Idoslane
Idoslane
6497th solar cycle, late autumn

'I hereby relinquish the title of emperor.' Rodario announced his abdication with all due ceremony in the presence of the dwarf kings, the human monarchs and the Naishïon, who had insisted on being present. The actor had retained his penchant for ostentatious clothing. Too loud. Too showy. 'I did not attain the imperial crown through rightful means. I shall in future limit myself to Urgon's throne.'

They were gathered in the glass-walled hall in Coïra's tower. Girdlegard was visible on all sides.

I don't think that is a wise move. Tungdil looked over at Boïndil before speaking. 'With respect, sire. Please remain emperor until the human kingdoms have recovered. You would be able to provide the necessary stability and support until such time as they feel able to elect one of their own. A replacement is also needed for the maga. Under your safe leadership, they will feel able to begin their search.'

Mallenia tapped the table to indicate her support. Her left arm was in a sling. According to the healers' prognosis, she would never regain its use. Ocâstia's blade had severed tendons and nothing could be done, not without magic. And that was the trouble – with the last maga gone, there was no one who could do it. This meeting was the first time the Idoslane queen had left her bed, having nearly died from extreme blood loss.

Tungdil saw from her face how near she had been to death. She had lost her normal wild and warlike posturing and had become much more thoughtful. The realisation that she had long been little more than a puppet had taken its toll. The assertive and confident ruler of the past would never have dreamt that possible.

Rodario, on the other hand, had retained his accustomed manner. The theatrical vein, as he termed it, was still fully functional, even though it, too, had bled inordinately. He had lost two ribs to the sword and his breathing was audibly impaired. 'Oh, you want me to mount the throne again?' He grinned. 'Not bad at all. And without external assistance. I shall show myself worthy of it.'

'Let us hope for some peace and quiet,' murmured Isikor.

'There has never been unrest. Apart from the army summoned by Sha'taï, Girdlegard was getting along fine. Everyone was content.' This objection came from Dirisa. 'Even in my country there was peace, once the succession was sorted.'

'The emperor will ensure that peace continues,' said Mallenia. 'I would offer the gods my leg as well if it meant another couple of decades free of the need to wage war.'

'How about for ever?' asked Balyndar. 'The strongholds are as good as empty. The dwarf folk will need time to build up strength and bring new life to the mountains. There are' – and his voice broke – 'many losses to mourn.'

Tungdil watched his son. They would be travelling to the Grey Mountains together.

No one guessed that there were other ways of opening the portal. Everyone believed Balyndis had entrusted the formula to him as she lay dying. *She did not. Instead, she gave me her curse.* What he would do when the Fifthlings asked him for the gate-code, he had yet to decide.

Ataimînas got to his feet. Dressed in robes of silver and gold silk, outdoing Rodario in elegance and taste, he said, 'I feel the need to speak. As Naishïon, and also as the commanding officer of the deceitful elf-woman who committed such heinous treason at a time when cooperation was more vital than ever.' He directed his speech to Mallenia and Rodario. 'We elves can only beg your forgiveness. Whether you are willing to pardon us is up to you. We pray to Sitalia that none of us will ever be tricked in that way again.'

Ataimînas turned to Tungdil and took out a ring. 'This is my gift to you. It bears the Naishïon seal. Show it whenever you need an elf to do something and he will obey instantly. No matter what it is you demand. You might be asking for a drink of water or requiring him to go into battle at your side. Despite all the terrible things that have recently occurred, this orbit represents the triumph of the dwarves. You managed to save our homeland twice over. No one else could have done that.'

The elves watched Tungdil slip the Naishïon's gift on to the middle finger of his own left hand. A perfect fit. *If they knew the things I got up to in Phondrasôn . . .*

'Watch it, Scholar,' mouthed Boïndil. 'They'll be appointing you High King whether you like it or not.'

'Is there any news of the dead maga's apprentices?' Tungdil asked quickly, wanting to get in before anyone started cheering. 'Do we have famuli and famulae that could eventually take her place?'

'We have two,' Boïndil replied. 'Coïra sent them to me in the Blue Mountains, equipped with teaching volumes. They are there now, acquiring basic competence. They were supposed to report back to their maga when they were finished.'

'But they mustn't return to this tower. The source would not let them go,' Mallenia pointed out, 'and we will need them mobile to defend us.'

'There is a much less powerful source in the elf realm they can investigate, as well as the one in the Blue Mountains,' said Ataimînas. 'I am happy to put ours at their disposal and we can give them accommodation. The learning they will have to do on their own, of course. We don't have any sorcerers among us.'

This offer was greeted with applause.

'What about Sha'taï? Has she succumbed to her injuries?' Hargorin asked, his voice blatantly hopeful. 'I know she is a young woman who only acted out of fear. But consider what a danger she represented for us all.'

'She won't be able to do anything like that ever again.'

Tungdil had spoken to the expert healers before coming to the Assembly and spent time in the medical archives, studying similar cases concerning damage to the faculty of the mind. One learned paper in particular had impressed him: it dealt with calming measures suitable for sedating a patient in a troubled mental state. The procedure it described was effectively what had happened to Sha'taï. Many writers credited the älfar with inventing the procedure while others argued it had been developed following an accident involving a nail.

'The shard of glass has destroyed a vital section of her brain. What happened is akin to a technique previously used to pacify dangerously obstreperous patients,' Tungdil explained. 'The process entails inserting a narrow point past the eye, through the socket and into the brain itself, where it severs the tissue. The patients so treated lose their savage behaviour and other negative attributes.'

'So that means we let her live.' Hargorin did not look happy at the thought.

'I'm not putting a young woman to death when she only acted out of fear for her own safety.' Tungdil surveyed the assembled heads of state. 'Do any of you want us to decree she be killed?' There was silence. He announced that on his own initiative he had had her taken to an unspecified location. 'It's extremely remote. And she is under constant supervision.' He looked at the Thirdling king. 'To reassure you: if she should ever try to use her powers, the guards are under orders to kill her.'

'Then that's fine by me.' The red-bearded dwarf nodded assent.

After that the elves, dwarves and humans discussed what measures were needed to ensure lasting peace in Girdlegard.

There were plans for a combined army and they talked about a fair system of food distribution to prevent want in any one section of the community. Food would still be paid for, but equitable prices would be set centrally, allowing the farmers to cover their outlay.

As the grain the elves had brought with them was doing spectacularly well in Tabaîn, Ataimînas offered to send the surplus to areas where there was currently a dearth. The elf corn could be processed to make it palatable to humans and dwarves and their cattle.

Tungdil was only half-listening. It was Balyndis that occupied his thoughts. He was not happy with the conclusions he came to. *Hope is gone. The dream that kept me alive in Phondrasôn is no more. I was not able to save the love of my life as I had vowed to do.* He looked at Balyndar. *A fine figure of a son. But he hates me. And now I must spend my life in the Grey Mountains because I am the only one who can open the gate.*

Was that the curse Balyndis had wished on him?

Tungdil pulled himself together. *I must stop feeling so sorry for myself. Others are grieving, too. It's not just me.* He looked at Rodario, who was playing down his own sadness at the loss of Coïra. *Well, that's the advantage of being an actor.* And Mallenia had lost both a friend and her own precious foster child; the pain was visible in her face. She had grown noticeably older.

And the dwarves in the Grey Mountains have lost their nearest and dearest. Tungdil forced himself to pay attention to the debate. *I owe it to every fallen comrade to act the hero now. A hero capable of supporting others through difficult times.* He glanced at Balyndar again. *I promised Balyndis.* From now on he would make every effort to see his task not as a curse but as a mission. *I have nothing else to lose. So I can surrender myself if need be.*

'Now that we have discussed the main items,' said Boïndil, 'I want to be the ruler who abdicates successfully, where the actor failed.' There was polite laughter on all sides and Rodario smirked. 'In hard times I held the throne. But reluctantly. I am not really suited to being High King.' He ran his hands over his temples where the hair was shorn short. He looked at Tungdil. 'I therefore nominate Tungdil Goldhand to be High King.'

'And I thank you and turn down your kind offer,' said Tungdil, taking up the thread. 'I am as little suited as any to be High King. Phondrasôn took all my energy. I am more attuned to books and writings than I am to warfare nowadays. If I fancy an adventure, I'll go and investigate the abandoned settlement in the Grey Mountains. That will suffice.'

'That's not the feeling we got in the Outer Lands,' objected Hargorin. 'I'd vote for you without hesitation.'

The other dwarf kings clattered their axe shafts on the floor in agreement. All of them except for Balyndar. He stared at his tankard in silence, his hands palm-down, flat on the tabletop.

'Then suggest someone you think could take it on,' Boïndil said. 'But not the Fourthling,' he whispered. 'I told you before. Frandibar is a weakling.'

Tungdil's brown eyes came to rest on Balyndar. 'The bearer of Keenfire should be the one to lead the five tribes. As I understand it, he earned respect at the battle of the Black Abyss and his leadership at the Stone Gateway is without equal. He is young and yet rich in experience.'

'I would entrust my tribe's safety to him.' Hargorin

immediately raised his short axe as a sign of approval. 'Balyndar Steelfinger of the Clan of the Steel Fingers from the tribe of the Fifthlings: the Thirdling tribe will follow you.'

One by one the dwarf leaders chose Balyndar; his features displayed at first disbelief, then pride and delight. When Boïndil asked him whether he would accept the high office, he was practically speechless with emotion. He blurted out a 'By Vraccas' through tears.

The tribal leaders slapped him on the back and Mallenia, Rodario, Dirisa, Astirma and Isikor all congratulated him; Ataimînas joined in, shaking his hand enthusiastically.

'Right! Time to celebrate,' announced Boïndil, 'then let us go down to the town. The people are waiting for us.'

Tungdil withdrew to a quiet corner. The party would not be overly rowdy: painful losses were still too fresh. The festivities in the street would honour the names of those who had given their lives and would celebrate those who had survived.

Tungdil watched his son receive his compatriots' congratulations. The young dwarf was having to raise his jug each time he was toasted and was making slow progress. There was a young brown-haired dwarf girl always nearby, accepting gifts on his behalf and passing out freshly filled tankards, making herself generally useful. At first Tungdil thought it might be Gosalyn until he remembered that she, too, was one of the fallen. Ocâstia should have received a slower and more painful death for her part in all this. A death such as Phondrasôn dealt out. Observing the dwarf girl closely, Tungdil saw she bore the crest of the Fourthlings. *She's making herself very useful. Who is she, I wonder?*

Beligata emerged from the crowd. She came over to bring

Tungdil a mug of beer and he drank to her health. 'You know they chose him because it was clear you would be standing by and instructing him?'

He nodded. 'That's what they think. But Balyndar does not need me. He has made many good decisions. He is wise, through and through.'

'Much like his father.' Beligata drank. Tungdil said nothing.

Things were calming down and the assembled company had now joined the throng that was surging merrily along in the carnival atmosphere of the streets. Tungdil and Beligata remained in the hall for a moment.

Beligata said, 'I thought I'd come with you to the Grey Mountains. You'll need warriors to defend the Stone Gateway.'

'You will be very welcome, I'm sure. And that way' – he turned to examine the state of her scar – 'I'll be able to keep my eye on you.'

'There's no need to issue threats. I was there when you killed the last zhadár.' Beligata was not discomforted by his intense stare.

'Then mind you don't forget. I shan't put up with the presence of evil. This is Girdlegard.'

'You have ensured that Girdlegard is once more secure and safe.' Beligata looked out through the glass wall at the jollifications on the streets below. 'I expect I will occasionally set off to hunt down the odd black-eyes. It's thought that there are still some in hiding. I don't like unfinished business.'

'You may as well try. But keep away from their blood.'

'May it gush out and seep away into the ground.' She leaned forward. 'I shall never be more than a half-zhadár, you know.' Beligata waved at Hargorin, who had popped his head round the door and was encouraging her to join the others. 'He'll be wanting me to join the Thirdlings. But I know my place.' She levered herself away from the wall and left.

Tungdil looked down at the Naishïon's ring on his hand; it sat on his finger near the talisman that Balyndis had given him. *Any elf I meet . . .* He grinned at the thought when he spotted Ataimînas in the crowd. *I wonder if he realises he's included in that, himself?* Tungdil had the feeling that he would be taking advantage of the ring's promise sooner or later. *I could have some fun with this. Maybe I'll ask them for something really impossible. Or I'll demand something entirely un-elf-like.*

He looked out through the glass towards the Grey Mountains in the north where Balyndis was buried. He would soon be with her but he would now never reach her. Never. An eternity of never.

You were so proud of your son. I shall not disappoint him. A tear spilled over. Tungdil was not ashamed of it as he kissed her dear ring.

Perhaps there'll be something else to write about their great hero when I find the time.
But first they are forcing me to chronicle the defeats of my own race.
What a waste.

The adventures Tungdil lived through, so far away, are of such great import, so incredible in scope, so cruel. They inspire me and my hand flies over the page.
I shall write them down as soon as I have found a way out of Girdlegard and a way to escape from my prison guards.

It could become a classic.

Secret notes for
The Writings of Truth
written under duress by Carmondai

Epilogue

Girdlegard
Black Mountains
Kingdom of the Thirdling dwarves
Eastern Gate
6497th solar cycle, late autumn

Let them celebrate if they want to. I have stuff to do. Rognor had politely turned down his king's invitation to return to the maga's abandoned tower to participate in the festivities. 'Have the elves all gone now?'

One of his female officers handed him a list of names showing who had occupied the pass to the east to protect it against attack while the Thirdlings had been away in the Outer Lands.

'They have all left, Chancellor,' she reported. 'The elves are all on their way to Ti Lesîndur.'

'Then make sure everyone gets an extra ration of beer. We'll drink the health of the new High King.' *The happy end was a relative kind of success.* Rognor was glad to have survived the Outer Lands campaign, glad to be back in post, commanding the Thirdlings' stronghold.

Friendship between the races was all well and good but Rognor was sure the mountains were secretly relieved to have the dwarves back in charge of everything. He had half-expected the mountains to rampage in their absence with avalanches, mudslides and raging torrents, in an effort to wash the elves away from the slopes. But the Black Mountains must have guessed that the elves were only there as visitors, nothing permanent.

'Thank you, Chancellor.' She saluted and strode off, calling out orders and spreading the news that the black beer barrels were to be rolled out. 'To the health of High King Balyndar!'

The cheers resounded. *They know the young king is a half-Thirdling. Father and son will be sharing the throne. They need good soldiers in the north. Balyndar is the best.* He laughed to himself. *Though generally the best ones live here, of course.*

He strolled out through the gate and observed the plain stretching out in front of the dwarf-head ramparts. His hand played with the end of his blue-dyed beard. It was still strange to see no tents out here. There were no more elves arriving; they had passed through to found settlements in Girdlegard's forests.

He would have liked to see the Idoslane tower everyone was talking about – they described it as some sort of wonder – but he was worried Hargorin would use the opportunity to appoint him king of the Thirdlings. He would not be able to turn down the title if there were witnesses present, so he chose to avoid the situation entirely. It was too soon to promote him from chancellor to higher office. There were preparations to undertake.

The orbit will come. Rognor looked at the mountain escarpment that stretched steeply away towards the east, a seemingly never-ending range. *Then I shall set about strengthening the link to our ancestor Lorimbur.* He touched the tattooed rune on his face.

The intertribal feuds were over, but Vraccas had left the Thirdlings in the lurch and Rognor was not prepared to forgive him. They had suffered appalling losses at the Stone Gateway when the mad elf had opened fire. It was important to bring Lorimbur to the fore. Hargorin tended to forget this and preferred to swan around with the kings.

'What beauty,' Rognor said, as he admired the mountains, bowing to them. 'Accept my thanks for your protection.'

Rognor returned to the interior of the stronghold and closed grating and door behind him to keep the wind from whistling round the courtyard. It was growing chillier and the snowline was nearing their ramparts. Braziers were lit, and torches in sheltered spots illuminated the walkways and rooms in the fortress. The wind picked up, playing with loose straw in the yard, spiralling it into the air and letting it drop.

Rognor thought about the kites the Fifthlings had used to get up onto the maga's tower. The plans had arrived for the Thirdlings to study and their workshops were busy producing replicas to help with the eastern defences. Excellent idea. As long as Samusin cooperated, of course.

He walked in to the accommodation quarters. *A child's plaything adapted to rain death down from the skies.* The mere idea of hanging from one of these devices and going up into the clouds sent shivers up and down his spine. *Quite a dangerous undertaking. And if we've had the idea, our enemies may have worked out the same technique.*

He would ask Hargorin to speak to the High King about these concerns. If birds had no problems crossing the mountains, it was entirely possible that a more sophisticated aerial contraption might be able to sail clear over their ramparts.

Rognor checked the rooms the elves had been allocated. They would have to be sorted out in case any travellers needed accommodation.

He heard the first round of songs from the troop quarters. Tambourines and small drums gave the rhythm, while horns and bagpipes joined in, with a barrel organ and a set of bells picking out the melody, soon drowned out by the chorus of dwarf voices.

Break out the barrels!
Good red wine
Or spiced dark beer.
If your throat is dry
Then your soul will wonder why
And will set off in despair.
But take my word for it
Drinking is the cure for it
Out with the bung! Out with it!

Pour it out! Pour it out!
Fill the glasses, mistress dwarf!
One for me and one for you
So you stay happy when I'm gone
From village or castle, that's all one
If you take my fancy, I'll take yours
Pour it out! Some more, of course!

Drain the cask, drain it dry!
Everything tastes better
In Vraccas' smithy to the letter
He has the coolest cellars
And a furnace for fire wine
Drain the cask, and drain it dry!

Rognor relished the festival atmosphere that had broken out. The dwarves had gone through hard cycles with battles, losses and triumphs. They had earned their celebration.

He arrived at the generously proportioned room where the sorânïons had had their quarters, first under Phenîlas and latterly under Ocâstia.

He stopped and mused in the clean and tidy room where the elves had been accommodated. Insanity seemed to have been common amongst the sorânïons. It was perhaps related to the type of work they did: it demanded merciless dedication to duty, irrespective of the pain and distress caused by the vetting of their fellow elves. Phenîlas was the first to fall victim to madness, then Venîlahíl, and he had heard it rumoured that the same thing had happened to Ocâstia: she had become power-hungry. *An elf-woman on Girdlegard's throne? As if we would have permitted that to happen!* Rognor entered the room, noting it needed sweeping; there was a lot of dust on the floor.

As the festivities were in full swing and he did not want to recall his men, he grabbed the broom himself. A chancellor and commander was not above lowly domestic duties. And with all that dust, his throat would be readier than ever for the beer.

Shifting the beds aside, he swept along the wainscot and saw there was a crevice in the wall. He bent down, frowning, to investigate. The opening gaped between the stones. There was no question of it having been caused by damp or burrowing insects. The mortar looked to have been deliberately scraped out.

Rognor lit a lantern to examine the cavity. Something inside the slit reflected the light. He took out his knife and ferretted around, finally retrieving a folded piece of paper. *It will be a message left by one of the sorânïons.* He opened the paper carefully, where he found not writing, but crystalline powder.

Medicine? Drugs? The chancellor now became suspicious. He undertook an intensive search of the whole room, while outside, songs, music and exuberant dwarf voices reflected the mood of the orbit.

Rognor called a sentry over and told him to take the find to one of the alchemists who could examine it in the laboratory where they normally worked on the production of inextinguishable fire.

Nearby he noticed another stone with a crack in it. *More of the same?* He scrabbled with his knife and part of the stone came away in his hand. It had been fashioned to hide another cavity. And in that cavity he found a phial.

He fished it out. The tiny vessel was empty. But when he stared at it in the lantern light, the hairs stood up on the back of his neck. It bore an älfar rune.

Elf eyes!

Rognor wanted to believe that one of the officers had discovered the empty bottle in the pocket of one of the examinees – maybe some älf they had exposed – and had wanted to hide it away for safe-keeping.

But there was another, more terrible explanation.

Lorimbur! No, No, No. Rognor raced through the fortress to get to the laboratory. It was essential he knew the truth straight away, this very night. *I don't care if they have to stay up till dawn.*

He reached the room with its high, vaulted ceiling supported on stone columns. The chamber sported an impressive selection of equipment: shelving, cupboards, tables, burners. Here he came across Furobil Sparkeater talking to one of the healers. They were looking at a glass vessel being heated over a flame.

The contents of the flask were bubbling, a greenish fluid

reacting to the heat and giving off vapour, which condensed via a glass spiral to collect in a corked jar.

'You working on a solution?' Rognor burst out, not bothering with a greeting. He was too intent on getting an answer. He kept the phial close in his hand.

'Exactly, Chancellor,' replied Furobil, who was wearing a floor-length leather apron. Unusually for a dwarf, he was bald, but dealing with chemical fumes and fire had robbed him of his hair. His scarred nose was witness to failed experiments in the past. He picked up a crumb of the crystal powder with tiny pincers. 'It looks like salt but it has to be something else. The envelope had traces of a colour that makes me think of a poison of some kind. That's why I got Lorimgon to come and join me.'

The fair-haired healer with an elaborately sculpted beard bowed to the chancellor. He was wearing a cloak over his night attire and his feet were in slippers. He had rushed over to the laboratory as soon as he had been summoned.

'Can we find out what it is?'

'It's definitely an artificial substance. A distillation of some kind.' Furobil opened a tube leading off the flask and dropped the crystal into the liquid, replacing the cork immediately. The green changed to blue and then, simmering, to yellow, all without the application of a heat source. Black vapour filled the glass spiral. The bald alchemist took a dried leaf and, loosening the cork on the tube, held it in the vapour for a time. Before their very eyes, the leaf crumbled away as if destroyed with acid.

'So inside the vial we've got . . .' Furobil attempted a description of the solution but Rognor interrupted him briskly. 'What *is* it?'

The healer furrowed his brow. 'It is mad-salt. In the past it could be found in certain circumstances in caves. If you scratched off the walls and ate it, you would die suffering from terrifying hallucinations. In minute doses, it could be used as a pain-reducing measure but too many died as a result. It is never used in treatment nowadays.'

'But this has been produced artificially,' the alchemist said. 'And in an extremely high concentration, much stronger than anything ever found on a cave wall.'

Rognor clutched the empty phial tightly. Mad-salt and eye-white had been hidden next to where Ocâstia had had her bed. *Phenîlas first, then the sorânïon at the Stone Gateway. Had she deliberately driven them mad? Perhaps it wasn't the work they were involved in?*

He remembered that Ocâstia's eyes sometimes watered and were red-rimmed, but she always had an excuse ready. Icy wind, a draught, a cold, an infection and so on.

Did anyone interrogate and examine her when she arrived, I wonder? He recalled her showing the symbol on her forearm but did it have the rune that torchlight would have revealed? With her glamorous confidence, she had made clever use of Rognor's readiness to trust her.

He remembered she had been responsible for vetting about three thousand elves once Phenîlas had been removed. *She would have been more or less on her own during those tests.* Rognor gulped.

How many älfar had Ocâstia allowed through to Girdlegard? How many had settled there with Sitalia's mark on their skin? How many of them might have broken away from the new elf settlements to hide? Were they forming their own colony? A new empire?

Ocâstia had left nothing to chance. She had ushered älfar in to Girdlegard, then she arranged her own spell of duty at the Stone Gateway, where she could weaken dwarves and elves alike and cause heavy casualties. Rognor imagined Ocâstia operating the heavy catapults, then locking herself in the prison cell so that the dwarves could eventually liberate her. Every word of her story had been believed without question, thanks to her title as sorânïan and thanks to her previous service.

The height of her treachery had been to accompany the dwarves on their outing to the maga's tower. *It's a miracle she didn't get to take over Girdlegard with Sha'taï's help. And to think I gave her that talisman.* Rognor was furious and thoroughly disgusted.

'What's wrong, Chancellor?' Furobil was concerned.

Rognor came to with a start. 'Don't tell a soul about this stuff,' he instructed them. 'Now go off and join the party.'

'What about you?' Lorimgon asked, confused.

Not me. Rognor turned on his heel and ran back to his quarters to write a letter by candlelight. It was vital the dwarf leaders and the Naishïon read it.

They have to be told that Ocâstia was an älf-woman. His hand flew over the page, describing what he had found and what he suspected. He had more than one purpose in writing: the news would also help clear the reputation of the elves and heighten awareness. The jubilation at having rid the homeland of älfar apart from a few assassins had come too soon. Now it was clear than any number of them could be roaming freely amongst the elf and dwarf populations in disguise.

Rognor re-read his lines and made copies, sealing the letters and putting them in leather pouches sealed with wax. He arranged them on his desk and stared at them. Too many thoughts, worries and fears were surging through his head.

He would send the messengers off first thing in the morning. There was no point in trying to get the letters delivered overnight. Everyone would be drunk.

How could I have been so blind? Rognor took out the phial with the eye-white, threw it on the floor and ground it with his heel.

Ocâstia had forced him to fight Phenîlas. He had killed the elf in single combat, but his opponent had not been of sound mind. He had been under the influence of the mad-salt. Ocâstia must have been chortling to herself seeing Rognor finish the sorânïon commander off with a crushing blow from a morningstar.

And they honoured me as their protector. Their defender. There was a bitter taste in his mouth. Phenîlas had been innocent.

The chancellor wished now that he had gone out to the tower with the others. He wanted to spit on the älf-woman's corpse, defile and curse it. Her black soul should never find rest. *I should have been the one to slit her open.*

He could not imagine how the elves were going to react to the new information. He had obviously been the victim of a perfidious deception. But would the fact that he had himself been duped be enough to hold back others' fury?

He got up, blew out the candle and left the room.

People were still partying. The celebrations were in full swing and there was feasting, singing, and good humour and beer a-plenty. Rognor took a tankard, too, but not because he was in the mood for rejoicing. He needed to dull his senses. As he wandered through the stronghold, his mind gloomily preoccupied, he remembered that he still had Ocâstia's memento in his possession.

He turned his collar and found the tiny brooch the false

sorânïan had given him. *It's sure to be bathed in black-eye magic.* It felt as if it were branding his skin and leaving the runes as a mark. He did not understand its meaning. *Off with you!* He hurried out, pulled the brooch off and hurled it from the battlements with all his strength. It disappeared in the abyss.

He immediately started to feel better. He rubbed his fingertips where he had felt some tingling.

Nothing must deter us. Girdlegard was in greater need of the cooperation of all its peoples than he could previously have imagined. More so now than ever. 'We will win through,' he vowed to the mountains, before going back into the warmth.

The mountains gave his words back as an echo, in which the tinkling of the brooch dancing from rock to rock mingled as it shone in the starlight.

As if it were calling to someone to come and find it and pick it up.

Acknowledgements

I made the mistake before and I promise not to make it again. Otherwise this would be where I announce the definitive end of the älfar and dwarf series. I shan't be doing that!

The älfar and the dwarves are now on an equal footing as far as the number of volumes is concerned. Some mysteries have been solved, such as Tungdil's return and the origin of the acronta. Even the historian Carmondai has survived.

How many black-eyes have inveigled their way into Girdlegard is not known and must remain a matter of speculation. Two? Twenty? Two hundred? Or perhaps none at all?

Taking the focus from the älfar and putting it back on the dwarves made me smile with disbelief as I realised that the little folk had been out and about for nearly a dozen years and had their loyal fan base waiting for them. And new devotees are joining them all the time. Well, that's about the most success any fiction writer can have.

And so I'd like to express my gratitude clearly: THANK YOU!

As always I have relied on the reactions of my test readers and here my thanks go to the following for their sharp eyes and astute examination of the text: Sonja Rüther, Yvonne Schöneck and our 'token man', Markus Michalek.

It was Hanka Jobke's task as copyeditor to call the dwarves to order, as she had previously done in disciplining the älfar. Thank you for your honing and sharpening skills.

Carsten Polzin of Piper Verlag Publishers is due a special mention. He was as glad as I was to see the return of the dwarves. (No, that's not the next title! Although . . .)

Further thanks go to Anke Koopmann and the Guterpunkt agency for their fantastic work for the book cover, giving a new twist to the familiar image.

I hereby pay my respects to Rainer Maria Rilke, from whose work *Cornet* I borrowed the phrase 'iron black as . . . night.' It is a thrilling tale I came across again prompted by a performance by Mareike Greb and Thomas Streipert from WerkEnsembL.E. Merci!

My English readers and I send a very big 'Thank you!' to Sheelagh Alabaster for her excellent translations.

My thanks to the German folk song that suits the dwarves so well – as long as you change the lyrics a bit. Artistic licence.

And if anyone wants to but doesn't yet know about Aiphatòn's adventures in the Outer Lands before he met the ghaist, try the fourth volume of the älfar series: *Raging Storm.* All will be revealed.

Oh yes. One more thing.

I am sensibly not going to tell you the publication dates for new älfar or dwarf books.

But I am sure the series will continue. It should not take seven years this time.

However, next in line are the scaly horrors and the heroes of *Powers of the Fire* and *Emperor of the Dragons*. The third volume of Silena adventures is calling and wants to be written. Absolutely insistent. The Twenties are waiting for me.

Markus Heitz, autumn 2014

Dramatis Personae

Dwarves

Firstling Kingdom

Xamtor Boldface of the clan of the Bold Faces, King of the Firstlings

Secondling Kingdom

Boïndil 'Ireheart' Doubleblade, of the clan of the Axe Swingers, King of the Secondlings and High King of the Dwarf Tribes

Thirdling Kingdom

Tungdil Goldhand, warrior and scholar
Goda Flameheart, of the clan of the Steadfast, warrior maga, wife of Ireheart
Hargorin Deathbringer, of the clan of the Stone Crushers, leader of the Black Squadron and King of the Thirdlings
Rognor Mortalblow, of the clan of the Orc Slayers, Chancellor
Bolîngor Bladecatcher, of the clan of the Iron Fists, warrior dwarf
Furobil Sparkeater, of the clan of the Fire Swallowers, alchemist
Lorimgon Healthmaker, of the clan of the Bone Setters, healer

Fourthling Kingdom

Frandibar Gemholder, of the clan of the Gold Beaters, King of the Fourthlings

Aurogar Broadhand, of the clan of the Silver Seekers

Fifthling Kingdom

Balyndis Steelfinger, of the clean of the Steel Fingers, Queen of the Fifthlings

Balyndar Steelfinger, her son

Belogar Strifehammer, of the clan of the Boulder Heavers

Gosalyn Landslip, of the clan of the Tunnel Seekers

Girgandor Summitstormer, of the clan of the Iron Pressers

Goïmbar Gemfinder, of the clan of the Opal Eyes

Barborin Doughtyarm, of the clan of the Swift Blow

Freelings

Beligata Hardblow, a former Thirdling, now a free dwarf

Gordislan 'The Younger' Starfist, King of Trovegold

Carâhnios, the last zhadár

HUMANS

Mallenia, Queen of Gauragar and Idoslane

Sha'taï, her young ward

Rodario the Incomparable, King of Urgon

Isikor, King of Rân Ribastur

Astirma, Queen of Sangpûr

Coïra Weytana, maga and Queen of Weyurn

Rodîr Bannerman, warrior

Lot-Ionan, magus and one-time foster father to Tungdil Goldhand

Natenian, King of Tabaîn

Raikan Fieldwood, nobleman, heir apparent to Tabaîn's throne
Tenkil Hoge, nobleman, Tabaîn warrior accompanying Raikan
Lilia, female warrior from Tabaîn
Irtan, warrior from Tabaîn
Ketrin, female warrior from Tabaîn
Cledenia, noblewoman from Tabaîn
Dirisa, noblewoman from Tabaîn
Heidor, tavern worker from Gauragar

Elves

Ilahín, Delegate of Ti Lesinteïl
Fiëa, his wife
Phenîlas, a sorânïon
Ocâstia, a sorânïan
Ataimînas, regent in Ti Lesinteïl and Naishïon of all elves
Nafinîas, elf-leader
Tehomín, Naishïon emissary
Menahîn, Naishïon emissary
Venîlahíl, a sorânïon
Chynêa, spokeswoman for the newcomers at the Eastern Gate
Semhîlas, elf-immigrant
Rahîlas, elf-immigrant
Inisëa, elf-immigrant
Vilêana, elf-immigrant, princess

Älfar

Carmondai, Master of Word and Image
Aiphatòn, formerly emperor of the älfar in Girdlegard and offspring of the Inextinguishables

Nodûcor, älf, the Voice of the Wind
Irïanora, älf-woman

Others

narshân beast, predatory beast found in Phondrasôn and the Outer Lands
Acïjn Rhârk, the Towers That Walk, huge creatures that hunt monsters. Called the acronta by the dwarves or Dorón Ashont in the älfar tongue
Tsatòn nar Draigònt, acront warrior
Djerůn, acront bodyguard of the maga Andôkai
Fin'Sao, shapeshifters that are only able to imitate beasts
goldfireworm, a snake-like creature related to a dragon
shintoìt, designation for offspring of the Inextinguishables
botoican, human with magic powers in the Outer Lands
Phondrasôn, subterranean place of banishment
Srai G'dàma, sacred emperor-mother, ruler over the Acïjn Rhârk
nrotai, the first wave in an Acïjn Rhârk attack; often young warriors who need to prove themselves
Kân Thalay, a mystical word describing a state of perfect inner peace
zhadár, älfar word for the Invisibles
Naishïon, supreme ruler of the elves
sorânïon (m) or **sorânïan** (f), investigator for the Naishïon
twentner, unit of weight, approximately two hundred pounds
Ido, a member of the ruling class from Idoslane
famulus/famula, human magician trainee
magus/maga: sorcerer/sorceress

The origin of the dwarves and älfar?

As a keen role-playing gamer, mainly as a game master, I've always maintained a strong interest in classical fantasy settings. In the late 1980s and early '90s we tried our hand at pretty much every role-playing game out there: *AD&D*, *D&D*, *Warhammer*, *Vampire*, *Twilight 2000*, *Justifiers*, *Star Wars*, *Traveller*, *Space 1889*, *HârnMaster*, *Rolemaster*, *Shadowrun* and anything of that ilk.

Those were the halcyon days of RPGs! And it was ultimately the best way to prepare myself for what I'm doing now. Through the various insights gained into all manner of fantasy worlds, I have been able to draw from a large amount of baseline knowledge about world-building, character development and narrative techniques (the last thanks to my having been a game master).

And, of course, one of my characters was a dwarf.

It's the species I understand the most: they share my sense of humour, as well as my straightforwardness, steadfastness and love of beer. What more could you ask for? So I decided to make them the focus of my first trilogy, which was a great deal of fun. They had all the basic features of the dwarven race, onto which I then added my own ideas to make them stand out from the rest. Or, at least, that was the plan.

However, in the second volume it became apparent to me that the älfar were just as much fun.

I consider myself an old-school gothic type, and have a strong affinity to the Dark Side of the Force, still going to those sorts of festivals as and when I can. So it soon became obvious that my älfar, as a rather sophisticated group of villains, would have to have their own series to allow them to explain their side of the story. It was either that or I'd have had to fill the blind spots in the Dwarves series until both sides converged at a single point. The älfar, of course, had to differentiate themselves from the standard dark elves tropes I remembered from my role-playing days, hence their affinity for art and stylish élan. Fantasy already has its fair share of violent meatheads in the shape of orcs, ogres and trolls, I thought.

The point at which everything comes together is the fifth instalment of the Dwarves series: *The Triumph of the Dwarves*. That's the provisional end of the series, with the emphasis firmly on 'provisional'. Dwarves and the number seven go hand-in-hand, so it's yet to be decided when I'll get around to adding more volumes. There's still plenty to tell, but I've got other ideas that take priority, so the rest will have to sit on the back-burner for now.

Who knows what is yet to come?

I know what the plan is, at least in Germany, up to 2019. My latest fantasy worlds have already been planned out and are in the process of being painstakingly put together.

I wish you all a great deal of fun with Tungdil and his friends! Read it slowly. It'll be quite some time before reinforcements arrive. ☺

Markus Heitz
Saarland, Germany

Continue the adventure in

The Dwarves
The War of the Dwarves
The Revenge of the Dwarves
The Fate of the Dwarves